D0936792

TRUE GHOST STORIES

TRUE GHOST STORIES

by
Hans Holzer

Galahad Books · New York

Published in 1994 by

Galahad Books
A division of Budget Book Service, Inc.
386 Park Avenue South
New York, NY 10016

Galahad Books is a registered trademark of Budget Book Service, Inc.

Library of Congress Catalog Card Number: 92-73078

ISBN: 0-88365-850-X

Designed by Hannah Lerner
Photographs by Leon Sokolsky

Printed in the United States of America

Table of Contents

THE WASHINGTON AREA

THE OLD SOUTH

MIDDLE AMERICA

THE WEST

TRUE GHOST STORIES

1

What Exactly is a Ghost?

WHAT EXACTLY IS a ghost? Something people dream up in their cups or on a sickbed? Something you read about in juvenile fiction? Far from it. Ghosts—apparitions of "dead" people or sounds associated with invisible human beings—are the surviving emotional memories of people. They are people who have not been able to make the transition from their physical state into the world of the spirit—or as Dr. Joseph Rhine of Duke University has called it, the world of the *mind*. Their state is one of emotional shock induced by sudden death or great suffering, and because of it the individuals involved cannot understand what is happening to them. They are unable to see beyond their own immediate environment or problem, and so they are forced to continually relive those final moments of agony until someone breaks through and explains things to them. In this respect they are like psychotics being helped by the psychoanalyst, except that the patient is not on the couch, but rather in the atmosphere of destiny. Man's electromagnetic nature makes this perfectly plausible; that is, since our individual personality is really nothing more than a personal energy field encased in a denser outer layer called the physical body, the personality can store emotional stimuli and memories indefinitely without much dimming, very much like a tape recording that can be played over and over without losing clarity or volume.

Those who die normally under conditions of adjustment need not go through this agony, and they seem to pass on rapidly into that next state of consciousness that may be a "heaven" or a "hell," according to what the individual's mental state at death might have been. Neither state is an objective place, but is a subjective state of being. The sum total of similar states of being may, however, create a quasi-objective state approaching a condition or "place" along more orthodox religious lines. My contact with the confused individuals unable to depart from the earth's sphere, those who are commonly called "ghosts" or earthbound spirits, is through a trance medium who will lend her physical body temporarily to the entities in difficulty so that they can speak through the medium and detail their problems, frustrations, or unfinished business. Here again, the parallel with psychoanalysis becomes apparent: in telling their tales of woe, the restless ones relieve themselves of their pressures and anxieties and thus may free themselves of their bonds. If fear is the absence of information, as I have always held, then knowledge is indeed the presence of understanding. Or view it the other way round, if you prefer. Because of my books, people often call on me to help them understand problems of this nature. Whenever someone has seen a ghost or heard noises of a human kind that do not seem to go with a body, and feel it might be something I ought to look into, I usually do.

To be sure, I don't always find a ghost. But I frequently do find one, and moreover, I find that many of those who have had the uncanny experiences are themselves mediumistic, and are therefore capable of being communications vehicles for the discarnates. It is more common than most people realize, and, really quite natural and harmless.

At times, it is sad and shocking, as all human suffering is, for man is his worst enemy, whether in the flesh or outside of it. But there is nothing mystical about the powers of ESP or the ability to experience ghostly phenomena.

Scoffers like to dismiss all ghostly encounters by cutting the witnesses down to size—their size. The witnesses are probably mentally unbalanced, they say, or sick people who hallucinate a lot, or they were tired that day, or it must have been the reflection from (pick your light source), or finally, in desperation, they may say yes, something probably happened to them, but in the telling they blew it all up so you can't be sure any more what really happened.

I love the way many people who cannot accept the possibility of ghosts being real toss out their views on what happened to strangers. "Probably this or that," and from "probably," for them, it is only a short step to "certainly." The human mind is as clever at inventing away as it is at hallucinating. The advantage in being a scientifically trained reporter, as I am, is the ability to dismiss people's interpretations and find the facts themselves. I talked of the *Ghosts I've Met* in a book that bore that title. Even more fascinating are the people I've met who encounter ghosts. Are they sick, unbalanced, crackpots, or other unrealistic individuals whose testimony is worthless?

Far from it.

Those who fall into that category never get to me in the first place. They don't stand up under my methods of scrutiny. Crackpots, beware! I call a spade a spade, as I proved when I exposed the fake spiritualist camp practices in print some years ago.

The people who come across ghostly manifestations are people like you.

Take the couple from Springfield, Illinois, for instance. Their names are Gertrude and Russell Meyers and they were married in 1935. He worked as a stereotyper on the local newspaper, and she was a high-school teacher. Both of them were in their late twenties and couldn't care less about such things as ghosts.

At the time of their marriage, they had rented a five-room cottage which had stood empty for some time. It had no particular distinction but a modest price, and was located in Bloomington where the Meyerses then lived.

Gertrude Meyers came from a farm background and had studied at Illinois Wesleyan as well as the University of Chicago. For a while she worked as a newspaperwoman in Detroit, later taught school, and as a sideline has written a number of children's books. Her husband Russell, also of farm background, attended Illinois State Normal University at Normal, Illinois, and later took his apprenticeship at the Bloomington Pantograph.

The house they had rented in Bloomington was exactly like the house next to it, and the current owners had converted what was formerly *one* large house into two separate units, laying a driveway between them.

In the summer, after they had moved into their house, they went about the business of settling down to a routine. Since her husband worked the night shift on the newspaper, Mrs. Meyers was often left alone in the house. At first, it did not bother her at all. Sounds from the street penetrated into the house and gave her a feeling of people nearby. But when the chill of autumn set in and the windows had to be closed to keep it out, she became aware, gradually, that she was not really alone on those lonely nights.

One particular night early in their occupancy of the house, she had gone to bed leaving her bedroom door ajar. It was ten-thirty and she was just about ready to go to sleep when she heard rapid, firm footsteps starting at the front door, inside the house, and coming through the living room, the dining room, and finally approaching her bedroom door down the hall leading to it.

She leapt out of bed and locked the bedroom door. Then she went back into bed and sat there, wondering with sheer terror what the intruder would do. But nobody came.

More to calm herself than because she really believed it, Mrs. Meyers convinced herself that she must have been mistaken about those footsteps.

It was probably someone in the street. With this reassuring thought on her mind, she managed to fall asleep.

The next morning, she did not tell her new husband about the nocturnal event. After all, she did not want him to think he had married a strange woman!

But the footsteps returned, night after night, always at the same time and always stopping abruptly at her bedroom door which, needless to say, she kept locked.

Rather than facing her husband with the allegation that they had rented a haunted house, she bravely decided to face the intruder and find out what this was all about. One night she deliberately waited for the now familiar brisk footfalls. The clock struck ten, then ten-thirty. In the quiet of the night, she could hear her heart pound in her chest.

Then the footsteps came, closer and closer, until they got to her bedroom door. At this moment, Mrs. Meyers jumped out of bed, snapped on the light, and tore the door wide open.

There was nobody there, and no retreating footsteps could be heard.

She tried it again and again, but the invisible intruder never showed himself once the door was opened.

The winter was bitterly cold, and it was Russell's habit to build up a fire in the furnace in the basement when he came home from work at three-thirty A.M. Mrs. Meyers always heard him come in, but did not get up. One night he left the basement, came into the bedroom and said, "Why are you walking around this freezing house in the middle of the night?"

Of course she had not been out of bed all night, and told him as much. Then they discovered that he, too, had heard footsteps, but had thought it was his wife walking restlessly about the house. Meyers had heard the steps whenever he was fixing the furnace in the basement, and by the time he got upstairs they had ceased.

When Mrs. Meyers had to get up early to go to her classes, her husband would stay in the house sleeping late. On many days he would hear someone walking about the house and investigate, only to find himself quite alone.

He would wake up in the middle of the night thinking his wife had gotten up, but immediately reassured himself that she was sleeping peacefully next to him. Yet there was *someone* out there in the empty house!

Since everything was locked securely, and countless attempts to trap the ghost had failed, the Meyerses shrugged and learned to live with their peculiar boarder. Gradually the steps became part of the atmosphere of the old house, and the terror began to fade into the darkness of night.

In May of the following year, they decided to work in the garden and, as they did so, they met their next-door neighbors for the first time. Since they lived in identical houses, they had something in common, and conversation between them and the neighbors—a young man of twenty-five and his grandmother—sprang up.

Eventually the discussion got around to the footsteps. They, too, kept hearing them, it seemed. After they had compared notes on their experiences, the Meyerses asked more questions. They were told that before the house was divided, it belonged to a single owner who had committed suicide in the house. No wonder he liked to walk in *both* halves of what was once his home!

You'd never think of Kokomo, Indiana as particularly haunted ground, but one of the most touching cases I know of occurred there some time ago. A young woman by the name of Mary Elizabeth Hamilton was in the habit of spending many of her summer vacations there in her grandmother's house. The house dates back to 1834 and is a handsome place, meticulously kept up by the grandmother.

Miss Hamilton had never had the slightest interest in the supernatural, and the events that transpired that summer, when she spent four weeks at the house, came as a complete surprise to her. One evening she was walking down the front staircase when she was met by a lovely young lady coming up the stairs. Miss Hamilton, being a female, noticed that she wore a particularly beautiful evening gown. There was nothing the least bit ghostly about the woman, and she passed Miss Hamilton closely, in fact so closely that she could have touched her had she wanted to.

But she did notice that the gown was of a filmy pink material, and her hair and eyes dark brown, and the latter full of tears. When the two women met, the girl in the evening gown smiled at Miss Hamilton and passed by.

Since she knew that there was no other visitor in the house, and that no one was expected at this time, Miss Hamilton was puzzled as to who the lady might be. She turned her head to follow her up the stairs, when she saw the lady in pink reach the top of the stairs and vanish—into thin air.

As soon as she could, she reported the matter to her grandmother, who shook her head and would not believe her account. She would not even discuss it, so Miss Hamilton let the matter drop out of deference to her grandmother. But the dress design had been so unusual, she decided to check it out in a library. She found, to her amazement, that the lady in pink had worn a dress of the late 1840s period.

In September of the next year, her grandmother decided to redecorate the house. In this endeavor she used many old pieces of furniture, some of which had come from the attic of the house. When Miss Hamilton arrived and saw the changes, she was suddenly stopped by a portrait hung in the hall.

It was a portrait of her lady of the stairs. She was not wearing the pink gown in this picture but, other than that, it was the same person.

Miss Hamilton's curiosity about the whole matter was again aroused and, since she could not get any cooperation from her grandmother, she turned to her great aunt for help. This was particularly fortunate since the aunt was a specialist in family genealogy.

Finally the lady of the stairs was identified. She turned out to be a distant cousin of Miss Hamilton's, and had once lived in this very house.

She had fallen in love with a ne'er-do-well, and after he died in a brawl, she threw herself down the stairs to her death.

Why had the family ghost picked on her to appear before, Miss Hamilton wondered.

Then she realized that she bore a strong facial resemblance to the ghost. Moreover, their names were almost identical—Mary Elizabeth was Miss Hamilton's, and Elizabeth Mary the pink lady's. Both women even had the same nickname, Libby.

Perhaps the ghost had looked for a little recognition from her family and, having gotten none from the grandmother, had seized upon the opportunity to manifest for a more amenable relative?

Miss Hamilton is happy that she was able to see the sad smile on the unfortunate girl's face, for to her it is proof that communication, though silent, had taken place between them across the years.

Mrs. Jane Eidson is a housewife in suburban Minneapolis. She is middle-aged and her five children range in age from nine to twenty. Her husband Bill travels four days each week. They live in a cottage-type brick house that is twenty-eight years old, and they've lived there for the past eight years.

The first time the Eidsons noticed that there was something odd about their otherwise ordinary-looking home was after they had been in the house for a short time. Mrs. Eidson was in the basement sewing, when all of a sudden she felt that she was not alone and wanted to run upstairs. She suppressed this strong urge but felt very uncomfortable. Another evening, her husband was down there practicing a speech when he had the same feeling of another presence. His self-control was not as strong as hers, and he came upstairs. In discussing their strange feelings with their next-door neighbor, they discovered that the previous tenant also had complained about the basement. Their daughter, Rita, had never wanted to go to the basement by herself and, when pressed for a reason, finally admitted that there was a man down there. She described him as dark-haired and wearing a plaid shirt.

Sometimes he would stand by her bed at night and she would become frightened, but the moment she thought of calling her mother, the image disappeared. Another spot where she felt his presence was the little playhouse at the other end of their yard.

The following spring, Mrs. Eidson noticed a bouncing light at the top of the stairs as she was about to go to bed in an upstairs room, which she occupied while convalescing from surgery.

The light followed her to her room as if it had a mind of its own!

When she entered her room the light left, but the room felt icy. She was disturbed by this, but nevertheless went to bed and soon had forgotten all about it as sleep came to her. Suddenly, in the middle of the night, she woke and sat up in bed.

Something had awakened her. At the head of her bed she saw a man who was "beige-colored," as she put it. As she stared at the apparition it went away, again leaving the room very chilly.

About that same time, the Eidsons noticed that their electric appliances were playing tricks on them. There was the time at five A.M. when their washing machine went on by itself as did the television set in the basement, which could only be turned on by plugging it into the wall socket. When they had gone to bed, the set was off and there was no one around to plug it in.

Who was so fond of electrical gadgets as to turn them on in the small hours of the morning?

Finally Mrs. Eidson found out. In May of 1949, a young man who was just out of the service had occupied the house. His hobby was electrical wiring, it seems, for he had put in a strand of heavy wires from the basement underground through the yard to the other end of the property. When he attempted to hook them up with the utility pole belonging to the electric company, he was killed instantly. It happened near the place where Mrs. Eidson's girl had seen the apparition. Since the wires are still in her garden, Mrs. Eidson is not at all surprised that the dead man likes to hang around.

And what better way for an electronics buff to manifest as a ghost than by appearing as a bright, bouncy light? As of this writing, the dead electrician is still playing tricks in the Eidson home, and Mrs. Eidson is looking for a new home—one a little less unusual than their present one.

Eileen Courtis is forty-seven years old, a native of London, and a well-balanced individual who now resides on the West coast but who lived previously in New York City. Although she has never gone to college, she has a good grasp of things, an analytical mind, and is not given to hysterics. When she arrived in New York at age thirty-four, she decided to look for a quiet hotel and then search for a job.

The job turned out to be an average office position, and the hotel she decided upon was the Martha Washington, which was a hotel for women only on Twenty-Ninth Street. Eileen was essentially shy and a loner who only made friends slowly.

She was given a room on the twelfth floor and, immediately on crossing the threshold, she was struck by a foul odor coming from the room. Her first impulse was to ask for another room, but she was in no mood to create a fuss so she stayed.

"I can stand it a night or two," she thought, but did not unpack. It turned out that she stayed in that room for six long months, and yet she never really unpacked.

Now all her life, Eileen had been having various experiences of what we now call extrasensory perception, and her first impression of her new "home" was that someone had died in it. She examined the walls inch by inch. There was a spot where a crucifix must have hung for a long time, judging by the color of the surrounding wall. Evidently it had been removed when someone moved out . . . permanently.

That night, after she had gone to bed, her sleep was interrupted by what sounded like the turning of a newspaper page. It sounded exactly as if someone were sitting in the chair at the foot of her bed reading a newspaper. Quickly she switched on the light and she was, of course, quite alone. Were her nerves playing tricks on her? It was a strange city, a strange room. She decided to go back to sleep. Immediately the rustling started up again, and then someone began walking across the floor, starting from the chair and heading toward the door of the room.

Eileen turned on every light in the room and it stopped. Exhausted, she dozed off again. The next morning she looked over the room carefully. Perhaps mice had caused the strange rustling. The strange odor remained, so she requested that the room be fumigated. The manager smiled wryly, and nobody came to fumigate her room. The rustling noise continued, night after night and Eileen slept with the lights on for the next three weeks.

Somehow her ESP told her this presence was a strong-willed, vicious old woman who resented others occupying what she still considered "her" room. Eileen decided to fight her. Night after night, she braved it out in the dark, only to find herself totally exhausted in the morning. Her appearance at the office gave rise to talk. But she was not going to give in to a ghost. Side by side, the living and the dead women now occupied the same room without sharing it.

Then one night, something prevented her from going off to sleep. She lay in bed quietly, waiting.

Suddenly she became aware of two skinny but very strong arms extended over her head, holding a large downy pillow as though to suffocate her!

It took every ounce of her strength to force the pillow off her face.

Next morning, she tried to pass it off to herself as a hallucination. But was it? She was quite sure that she had not been asleep.

But still she did not move out and, one evening when she arrived home from the office with a friend, she felt a sudden pain in her back, as if she had been stabbed. During the night, she awoke to find herself in a state of utter paralysis. She could not move her limbs or head. Finally, after a long time, she managed to work her way to the telephone receiver and call for a doctor. Nobody came. But her control seemed to start coming back and she called her friend, who rushed over only to find Eileen in a state of shock.

During the next few days she had a thorough examination by the company physician, which included the taking of X-rays to determine if there was anything physically wrong with her that could have caused this condition. She was given a clean bill of health and her strength had by then returned, so she decided to quit while she was ahead.

She went to Florida for an extended rest, but eventually came back to New York and the hotel. This time she was given another room, where she lived very happily and without incident for over a year.

One day a neighbor who knew her from the time she had occupied the room on the twelfth floor saw her in the lobby and insisted on having a visit with her. Reluctantly, for she is not fond of socializing, Eileen agreed. The conversation covered various topics until suddenly the neighbor came out with "the time you were living in that haunted room across the hall."

Since Eileen had never told anyone of her fearsome experiences there, she was puzzled. The neighbor confessed that she had meant to warn her while she was occupying that room, but somehow never had mustered enough courage. "Warn me of what?" Eileen insisted.

"The woman who had the room just before you moved in," the neighbor explained haltingly, "well, she was found dead in the chair, and the woman who had it before her also was found dead in the bathtub."

Eileen swallowed quickly and left. Suddenly she knew that the pillow had not been a hallucination.

The Buxhoeveden family is one of the oldest noble families of Europe, related to a number of royal houses and—since the eighteenth century when one of the counts married the daughter of Catherine the Great of Russia—

also to the Russian Imperial family. The family seat was Lode Castle on the island of Eesel, off the coast of Estonia. The castle, which is still standing, is a very ancient building with a round tower somewhat apart from the main building. Its Soviet occupants have since turned it into a museum.

The Buxhoevedens acquired it when Frederick William Buxhoeveden married Natalie of Russia; it was a gift from mother-in-law Catherine.

Thus it was handed down from first-born son to first-born son, until it came to be in the hands of an earlier Count Anatol Buxhoeveden. The time was the beginning of this century, and all was right with the world.

Estonia was a Russian province, so it was not out of the ordinary that Russian regiments should hold war games in the area, and on one occasion when the maneuvers were in full swing, the regimental commander requested that his officers be put up at the castle. The soldiers were located in the nearby town, but five of the staff officers came to stay at Lode Castle. Grandfather Buxhoeveden was the perfect host, but was unhappy that he could not accommodate all five in the main house. The fifth man would have to be satisfied with quarters in the tower. Since the tower had by then acquired a reputation of being haunted, he asked for a volunteer to stay in that particular room.

There was a great deal of teasing about the haunted room before the youngest of the officers volunteered and left for his quarters.

The room seemed cozy enough and the young officer congratulated himself for having chosen so quiet and pleasant a place to spend the night after a hard day's maneuvers.

And being tired, he decided to get into bed right away. But he was too tired to fall asleep quickly, so he took a book from one of the shelves lining the walls, lit the candle on his night table, and began to read for a while.

As he did so, he suddenly became aware of a greenish light toward the opposite end of the circular room. As he looked at the light with astonishment, it changed before his eyes into the shape of a woman. She seemed solid enough and, to his horror, came over to his bed, took him by the hand and demanded that he follow her. Somehow he could not resist her commands, even though not a single word was spoken. He followed her down the stairs into the library in the castle itself. There she made signs indicating that he was to remove the carpet. Without questioning her, he flipped back the rug. She then pointed at a trap door that was underneath the carpet. He opened the door and followed the figure down a flight of stairs until they came to a big iron door that barred their progress. Now the figure pointed to the right corner of the floor and he dug into it. There he found a key, perhaps ten inches long, and with it he opened the iron gate. He now found himself in a long corridor that led him to a circular room. From there another corridor led on and again he followed eagerly, wondering what this was all about.

This latter corridor suddenly opened into another circular room which seemed familiar—he was back in his own room. The apparition was gone.

What did it all mean? He sat up trying to figure it out, and when he finally dozed off it was already dawn. Consequently he overslept and came down to breakfast last. His state of excitement immediately drew the attention of the Count and his fellow officers. "You won't believe this," he began and told them what had happened to him.

He was right. Nobody believed him.

But his insistence that he was telling the truth was so convincing that the Count finally agreed, more to humor him than because he believed him, to follow the young officer to the library to look for the alleged trap door.

"But," he added, "I must tell you that on top of that carpet are some heavy bookshelves filled with books which have not been moved or touched in over a hundred years. It is quite impossible for any one man to flip back that carpet."

They went to the library, and just as the Count had said, the carpet could not be moved. But Grandfather Buxhoeveden decided to follow through anyway and called in some of his men. Together, ten men were able to move the shelves and turn the carpet back. Underneath the carpet was a dust layer an inch thick, but it did not stop the intrepid young officer from looking for the ring of the trap door. After a long search for it, he finally located it. A hush fell over the group when he pulled the trap door open. There was the secret passage and the iron gate. And there, next to it, was a rusty iron key. The key fit the lock. The gate, which had not moved for centuries perhaps, slowly and painfully swung open and the little group continued their exploration of the musty passages. With the officer leading, the men went through the corridors and came out in the tower room, just as the officer had done during the night.

But what did it mean? Everyone knew there were secret passages—lots of old castles had them as a hedge in time of war.

The matter gradually faded from memory, and life at Lode went on. The iron key, however, was preserved and remained in the Buxhoeveden family until some years ago, when it was stolen from Count Alexander's Paris apartment.

Ten years went by, until, after a small fire in the castle, Count Buxhoeveden decided to combine the necessary repairs with the useful installation of central heating, something old castles always need. The contractor doing the job brought in twenty men who worked hard to restore and improve the appointments at Lode. Then one day, the entire crew vanished to a man—like ghosts.

Count Buxhoeveden reported this to the police, who were already being besieged by the wives and families of the men who had disappeared without leaving a trace.

Newspapers of the period had a field day with the case of the vanishing workmen, but the publicity did not help to bring them back, and the puzzle remained.

Then came the revolution and the Buxhoevedens lost their ancestral home. Count Alexander and the present Count Anatol, my brother-in-law, went to live in Switzerland. The year was 1923. One day the two men were walking down a street in Lausanne when a stranger approached them, calling Count Alexander by name.

"I am the brother of the Major Domo of your castle," the man explained. "I was a plumber on that job of restoring it after the fire."

So much time had passed and so many political events had changed the map of Europe that the man was ready at last to lift the veil of secrecy from the case of the vanishing workmen.

This is the story he told: when the men were digging trenches for the central heating system, they accidentally came across an iron kettle of the kind used in the Middle Ages to pour boiling oil or water down on the enemies besieging a castle. Yet this pot was not full of water, but rather of gold. They had stumbled onto the long-missing Buxhoeveden treasure, a hoard reputed to have existed for centuries but which was never found. Now, at this stroke of good fortune, the workmen became larcenous. To a man, they opted for distributing the find among themselves, even though it meant leaving everything behind—their families, their homes, their work—and striking out fresh somewhere else. But the treasure was large enough to make this a pleasure rather than a problem, and they never missed their wives, it would seem, finding ample replacements in the gentler climes of western Europe, where most of them went to live under assumed names.

At last the apparition that had appeared to the young officer made sense: it had been an ancestor who wanted to let her descendants know where the family gold had been secreted. What a frustration for a ghost to see her efforts come to naught, and worse yet, to see the fortune squandered by thieves while the legal heirs had to go into exile. Who knows how things might have turned out for the Buxhoevedens if *they* had gotten to the treasure in time.

At any rate there is a silver lining to this account: since there is nothing further to find at Lode Castle, the ghost does not have to put in appearances under that ghastly new regime. But Russian aristocrats and English lords of the manor have no corner on uncanny phenomena. Nor are all of the haunted settings I have encountered romantic or forbidding. Certainly there are more genuine ghostly manifestations in the American Midwest and South than anywhere else in the world. This may be due to the fact that a great deal of violence occurred there during the nineteenth and early twentieth centuries. Also, the American public's attitude toward such phenomena is different from that of Europeans. In Europe, people are inclined to reserve their accounts of bona fide ghosts for those people they can trust. Being ridiculed is not a favorite pastime of most Europeans.

Americans, by contrast, are more independent. They couldn't care less what others think of them in the long run, so long as their own people believe them. I have approached individuals in many cases with an assurance of scientific inquiry and respect for their stories. I am not a skeptic. I am a searcher for the truth, regardless of what this truth looks or sounds like.

Some time ago, a well-known TV personality took issue with me concerning my conviction that ESP and ghosts are real. Since he was not well informed on the subject, he should not have ventured forth into an area I know so well. He proudly proclaimed himself a skeptic.

Irritated, I finally asked him if he knew what being a skeptic meant. He shook his head.

"The term skeptic," I lectured him patiently, "is derived from the Greek word *skepsis*, which was the name of a small town in Asia Minor in antiquity. It was known for its lack of knowledge and people from Skepsis were called skeptics."

The TV personality didn't like it at all, but the next time we met on camera, he was a lot more human and his humility finally showed.

I once received a curious letter from a Mrs. Stewart living in Chicago, Illinois, in which she explained that she was living with a ghost and didn't mind, except that she had lost two children at birth and this ghost was following not only her but also her little girl. This she didn't like, so could I please come and look into the situation?

I could and did. On July 4, I celebrated Independence Day by trying to free a hung-up lady ghost on Chicago's South Side. The house itself was an old one, built around the late 1800s, and not exactly a monument of architectural beauty. But its functional sturdiness suited its present purpose—to house a number of young couples and their children, people who found the house both convenient and economical.

In its heyday, it had been a wealthy home, complete with servants and backstairs for them to go up and down on. The three stories are even now connected by an elaborate buzzer system which, however, hasn't worked for years.

I did not wish to discuss the phenomena at the house with Mrs. Stewart until after Sybil Leek, who was with me, had had a chance to explore the situation. My good friend Carl Subak, a stamp dealer, had come along to see how I worked. He and I had known each other thirty years ago when we were both students, and because of that he had overcome his own—ah—skepticism—and come along. Immediately on arrival, Sybil ascended the stairs to the second floor as if she knew where to go! Of course she didn't; I had not discussed the matter with her at all. But despite this promising beginning, she drew a complete blank when we arrived in the apartment upstairs. "I feel absolutely nothing," she confided and looked at me doubtfully. Had I made a mistake? She seemed to ask. On a hot July day, had we come all the way to the South Side of Chicago on a wild ghost chase?

We gathered in a bedroom where there was a comfortable chair and windows on both sides that gave onto an old-fashioned garden; there was a porch on one side and a parkway on the other. The furniture, in keeping with the modest economic circumstances of the owners, was old and worn, but it was functional and they did not seem to mind.

In a moment, Sybil Leek had slipped into trance. But instead of a ghost's personality, the next voice we heard was Sybil's own, although it sounded strange. Sybil was "out" of her own body, but able to observe the place and report back to us while still in trance.

The first thing she saw were maps, in a large round building somehow connected with the house we were in.

"Is there anyone around?" I asked.

"Yes," Sybil intoned, "James Dugan."

"What does he do here?"

"Come back to live."

"When was that?"

"1912."

"Is there anyone with him?"

"There is another man. McCloud."

"Anyone else?"

"Lots of people."

"Do they live in this house?"

"Three, four people . . . McCloud . . . maps . . ."

"All men?"

"No . . . girl . . . Judith . . . maidservant . . ."

"Is there an unhappy presence here?"

"Judith . . . she had no one here, no family . . . that man went away . . . Dugan went away. . . . "

"How is she connected with this Dugan?"

"Loved him."

"Were they married?"

"No. Lovers."

"Did they have any children?"

There was a momentary silence, then Sybil continued in a drab, monotonous voice.

"The baby's dead."

"Does she know the baby's dead?"

"*She cries . . . baby cries* . . . neglected . . . by Judith . . . guilty . . ."

"Does Judith know this?"

"Yes."

"How old was the baby when it died?"

"A few weeks old."

Strange, I thought, that Mrs. Stewart had fears for her own child from this source. She, too, had lost children at a tender age.

"What happened to the baby?"

"She put it down the steps."

"What happened to the body then?"

"I don't know."

"Is Judith still here?"

"She's here."

"Where?"

"This room . . . and up and down the steps. She's sorry for her baby."

"Can you talk to her?"

"No. She cannot leave here until she finds—You see if she could get Dugan—"

"Where is Dugan?"

"With the maps."

"What is Dugan's work?"

"Has to do with roads."

"Is he dead?"

"Yes. She wants him here, but he is not here."

"How did she die?"

"She ran away to the water . . . died by the water . . . but is here where she lived . . . baby died on the steps . . . downstairs . . ."

"What is she doing here, I mean how does she let people know she is around?"

"She pulls things . . . *she cries. . . .*"

"And her Christian name?"

"Judith Vincent, I think. Twenty-one. Darkish, not white. From an island."

"And the man? Is he white?"

"Yes."

"Can you see her?"

"Yes."

"Speak to her?"

"She doesn't want to, but perhaps . . ."

"What year does she think this is?"

"1913."

"Tell her this is the year 1965."

Sybil informed the spirit in a low voice that this was 1965 and she need not stay here any longer. Dugan is dead, too.

"She has to find him," Sybil explained and I directed her to explain that she need only call out for her lover in order to be reunited with him "Over There."

"She's gone . . . ," Sybil finally said, and breathed deeply.

A moment later she woke up and looked with astonishment at the strange room, having completely forgotten how we got here, or where we were.

There was no time for explanations now, as I still wanted to check out some of this material. The first one to sit down with me was the owner of the flat, Mrs. Alexandra Stewart. A graduate of the University of Iowa, twenty-five years old, Alexandra Stewart works as a personnel director. She had witnessed the trance session and seemed visibly shaken. There was a good reason for this. Mrs. Stewart, you see, had met the ghost Sybil had described.

The Stewarts had moved into the second floor apartment in the winter of 1964. The room we were now sitting in had been hers. Shortly after they moved in, Mrs. Stewart happened to be glancing up toward the French doors, when she saw a woman looking at her. The figure was about five feet three or four, and wore a blue-gray dress with a shawl, and a hood over her head, for which reason Mrs. Stewart could not make out the woman's features. The head seemed strangely bowed to her, almost as if the woman were doing penance.

I questioned Mrs. Stewart on the woman's color in view of Sybil's description of Judith. But Mrs. Stewart could not be sure; the woman could have been white or black. At the time, Mrs. Stewart had assumed it to be a reflection from the mirror, but when she glanced at the mirror, she did not see the figure in it. When she turned her attention back to the figure, it had disappeared. It was toward evening and Mrs. Stewart was a little tired, yet the figure was very real to her. Her doubts were completely dispelled when the ghost returned about a month later. In the meantime she had had the dresser that formerly stood in the line of sight moved farther down, so that any reflection as explanation would simply not hold water. Again the figure appeared at the French doors. She looked very unhappy to Mrs. Stewart, who felt herself strangely drawn to the woman, almost as if she should help her in some way as yet unknown.

But the visual visitations were not all that disturbed the Stewarts. Soon they were hearing strange noises, too. Above all there was the crying of a baby, which seemed to come from the second-floor rear bedroom. It could also be heard in the kitchen though less loud, and it seemed to come from the walls. Several people had heard it and there was no natural cause to account for it. Then there were the footsteps. It sounded like someone walking down the backstairs, the servants' stairs, step by step, hesitatingly, and not returning, but just fading away!

They dubbed their ghostly guest "Elizabeth," for want of a better name. Mrs. Stewart did not consider herself psychic, nor did she have any interest in such matters. But occasionally things had happened to her that defied natural explanations such as the time just after she had lost a baby. She awoke from a heavy sleep with the intangible feeling of a presence in her room. She looked up and there, in the rocking chair across the room, she saw a woman, now dead, who had taken care of her when she herself was a child. Rocking gently in the chair, as if to reassure her, the Nanny held Mrs. Stewart's baby in her arms. In a moment the vision was gone, but it had left Alexandra Stewart with a sense of peace. She knew her little one was well looked after.

The phenomena continued, however, and soon they were no longer restricted to the upstairs. On the first floor in the living room, Mrs. Stewart heard the noise of someone breathing close to her. This had happened only recently, again in the presence of her husband and a friend. She asked them to hold their breath for a moment, and still she heard the strange breathing continue as before. Neither of the men could hear it or so they said. But the following day the guest came back with another man. He wanted to be sure of his observation before admitting that he too had heard the invisible person breathing close to him.

The corner of the living room where the breathing had been heard was also the focal point for strange knockings that faulty pipes could not explain. On one occasion they heard the breaking of glass, and yet there was no evidence that any glass had been broken. There was a feeling that someone other than the visible people was present at times in their living room, and it made them a little nervous even though they did not fear their "Elizabeth."

Alexandra's young husband grew up in the building trade, and now works as a photographer. He too has heard the footsteps on many occasions, and he knows the difference between them and a house settling or timbers creaking—these were definitely human noises.

Mrs. Martha Vaughn is a bookkeeper who had been living in the building for two years. Hers is the apartment in the rear portion of the second floor, and it includes the back porch. Around Christmas of 1964, she heard a baby crying on the porch. It was a particularly cold night, so she went to investigate immediately. It was a weird, unearthly sound—to her it seemed right near the porch, but there was nobody around. The yard was deserted. The sound to her was the crying of a small child, not a baby, but perhaps a child of from one to three years of age. The various families shared the downstairs living room "like a kibbutz," as Mrs. Stewart put it, so it was not out of the ordinary for several people to be in the downstairs area. On one such occasion Mrs. Vaughn also heard the breaking of the *invisible* glass.

Richard Vaughn is a laboratory technician. He too has heard the baby cry and the invisible glass break; he has heard pounding on the wall as have the others. A skeptic at first, he tried to blame these noises on the steam pipes that heat the house. But when he listened to the pipes when they were acting up, he realized at once that the noises he had heard before were completely different.

"What about a man named Dugan? Or someone having to do with maps?" I asked.

"Well," Vaughn said, and thought back, "I used to get mail here for people who once lived here, and of course I sent it all back to the post office. But I don't recall the name Dugan. What I do recall was some mail from a Washington Bureau. You see, this house belongs to the University of Chicago and a lot of professors used to live here."

"Professors?" I said with renewed interest.

Was Dugan one of them?

Several other people who lived in the house experienced strange phenomena. Barbara Madonna used to live there too. But in May of that year she moved out. She works three days a week as a secretary and moved into the house in November of the previous year. She and her husband much admired the back porch when they first moved in, and had visions of sitting out there drinking a beer on warm evenings. But soon their hopes were dashed by the uncanny feeling that they were not alone, that another presence was in their apartment, especially around the porch. Soon, instead of using the porch, they studiously avoided it, even if it meant walking downstairs to shake out a mop. Theirs was the third-floor apartment, directly above the Stewart apartment.

A girl by the name of Lolita Krol also had heard the baby crying. She lived in the building for a time and bitterly complained about the strange noises on the porch.

Douglas McConnor is a magazine editor, and he and his wife moved into the building in November of the year Barbara Madonna moved out, first to the second floor and later to the third. From the very first, when McConnor was still alone—his wife joined him in the flat after their marriage a little later—he felt extremely uncomfortable in the place. Doors and windows would fly open by themselves when there wasn't any strong wind.

When he moved upstairs to the next floor, things were much quieter, except for one thing: always on Sunday nights, noisy activities would greatly increase toward midnight. Footsteps, the sounds of people rushing about, and of doors opening and closing would disturb Mr. McConnor's rest. The stairs were particularly noisy. But when he checked, he found that everybody was accounted for, and that no living person had caused the commotion.

It got to be so bad he started to hate Sunday nights.

I recounted Sybil's trance to Mr. McConnor and the fact that a woman named Judith had been the central figure of it.

"Strange," he observed, "but the story also fits my ex-wife who deserted her children. She is of course very much alive now. Her name is Judith."

Had Sybil intermingled the impression of a dead maidservant with the imprint left behind by an unfit mother? Or were there two Judiths? At any rate the Stewarts did not complain further about uncanny noises, and the girl in the blue-gray dress never came back.

On the way to the airport, Carl Subak seemed unusually silent as he drove us out to the field. What he had witnessed seemed to have left an impression on him and his philosophy of life.

"What I find so particularly upsetting," he finally said, "is Sybil's talking about a woman and a dead baby—all of it borne out afterwards by the people in the house. But Sybil did not know this. She couldn't have."

No, she couldn't.

In September, three years later, a group consisting of a local television reporter, a would-be psychic student, and an assortment of clairvoyants descended on the building in search of psychic excitement. All they got out of it were more mechanical difficulties with their cameras. But the ghosts were long gone.

Ghosts are not just for the thrill seekers, nor are they the hallucinations of disturbed people. Nothing is as democratic as seeing or hearing a ghost, for it happens all the time to just about every conceivable type of person. Neither age nor race nor religion seem to stay these spectral people in their predetermined haunts.

Naturally I treat each case reported to me on an individual basis. Some I reject on the face of the report, and others only after I have been through a long and careful investigation. But other reports have the ring of truth about them and are worthy of belief, even though some of them are no longer capable of verification because witnesses have died or sites have been destroyed.

A good example is the case reported to me recently by a Mrs. Edward Needs, Jr., of Canton, Ohio. In a small town by the name of Homeworth, there is a stretch of land near the highway that is today nothing more than a neglected farm with a boarded-up old barn still standing. The spot is actually on a dirt road, and the nearest house is half a mile away, with wooded territory in between. This is important, you see, for the spot is isolated and a man might die before help could arrive . . . On rainy days, the dirt road is impassable. Mrs. Needs has passed the spot a number of times, and does not particularly care to go there. Somehow it always gives her an uneasy feeling. Once, the Needs's car got stuck in the mud on a rainy day, and they had to drive through open fields to get out.

It was on that adventure-filled ride that Mr. Needs confided for the first time what had happened to him at that spot on prior occasions. It was the year when Edward Needs and a friend were on a joy ride after dark. At that time Needs had not yet married his present wife, and the two men had been drinking a little, but were far from drunk. It was then that they discovered the dirt road for the first time.

On the spur of the moment, they followed it. A moment later they came to the old barn. But just as they were approaching it, a man jumped out of nowhere in front of them. What was even more sobering was the condition this man was in: engulfed in flames from head to toe!

Quickly Needs put his bright headlights on the scene, to see better. The man then ran into the woods across the road, and just disappeared.

Two men never became cold sober more quickly. They turned around and went back to the main highway fast. But the first chance they had, they returned with two carloads full of other fellows. They were equipped with strong lights, guns, and absolutely no whiskey. When the first of the cars was within twenty feet of the spot where Needs had seen the apparition, they all saw the same thing: there before them, was the horrible spectacle of a human being blazing from top to bottom, and evidently suffering terribly as he tried to run away from his doom. Needs emptied his gun at the figure: it never moved or acknowledged that it had been hit by the bullets. A few seconds later, the figure ran into the woods—exactly as it had when Needs had first encountered it.

Now the ghost posse went into the barn, which they found abandoned although not in very bad condition. The only strange thing was spots showing evidence of fire: evidently someone or something had burned inside the barn without, however, setting fire to the barn as a whole. Or had the fiery man run outside to save his barn from the fire?

Betty Ann Tylaska lives in a seaport in Connecticut. Her family is a prominent one going back to Colonial days, and they still occupy a house built by her great-great-great-grandfather for his daughter and her husband back in 1807.

Mrs. Tylaska and her husband, a Navy officer, were in the process of restoring the venerable old house to its former glory. Neither of them had the slightest interest in the supernatural, and to them such things as ghosts simply did not exist except in children's tales.

The first time Mrs. Tylaska noticed anything unusual was one night when she was washing dishes in the kitchen.

Suddenly she had the strong feeling that she was being watched. She turned around and caught a glimpse of a man standing in the doorway between the kitchen and the living room of the downstairs part of the house. She saw him only for a moment, but long enough to notice his dark blue suit and silver buttons. Her first impression was that it must be her husband, who of course wore a Navy blue uniform. But on checking she found him upstairs, wearing entirely different clothes.

She shrugged the matter off as probably a hallucination due to her tiredness, but the man in blue kept returning. On several occasions, the same uncanny feeling of being watched came over her, and when she turned around, there was the man in the dark blue suit.

It came as a relief to her when her mother confessed that she too had seen the ghostly visitor—always at the same spot, between living room and kitchen. Finally she informed her husband, and to her surprise, he did not laugh at her. But he suggested that if it were a ghost, perhaps one of her ancestors was checking up on them.

Perhaps he wanted to make sure they restored the house properly and did not make any unwanted changes. They were doing a great deal of painting in the process of restoring the house, and whatever paint residue was left they would spill against an old stone wall in the back of the house.

Gradually the old stones were covered with paint of various hues.

One day Mr. Tylaska found himself in front of these stones. For want of anything better to do at the moment, he started to study them. To his amazement, he discovered that one of the stones was different from the others: it was long and flat. He called his wife and they investigated the strange stone;

upon freeing it from the wall, they saw to their horror that it was a gravestone—her great-great-great-grandfather's tombstone, to be exact.

Inquiry at the local church cleared up the mystery of how the tombstone had gotten out of the cemetery. It seems that all the family members had been buried in a small cemetery nearby. But it filled up, and one day a larger cemetery was started. The bodies were removed to it and a larger monument had been erected over great-great-great-grandfather's tomb. Since the original stone was of no use any longer, it was left behind. Somehow the stone got used when the old wall was being built. But evidently great-great-great-grandfather did not like the idea. Was that the reason for his visits? After all, who likes having paint splashed on one's precious tombstone? I ask you.

The Tylaska family held a meeting to decide what to do about it. They could not very well put two tombstones on grandad's grave. What would the other ancestors think? Everybody would want to have two tombstones then; and while it might be good news to the stonecutter, it would not be a thing to do in practical New England.

So they stood the old tombstone upright in their own backyard. It was nice having grandad with them that way, and if he felt like a visit, why, that was all right with them too.

From the moment when they gave the tombstone a place of honor, the gentleman in the dark blue suit and the silver buttons never came back. But Mrs. Tylaska does not particularly mind. Two Navy men in the house might have been too much of a distraction anyway.

Give a ghost his due, and he'll be happy. Happy ghosts don't stay around: in fact, they turn into normal spirits, free to come and go (mostly go) at will. But until people come to recognize that the denizens of the Other World are real people like you and me, and not some benighted devils or condemned souls in a purgatory created for the benefit of a political church, people will be frightened of ghosts quite needlessly. Sometimes even highly intelligent people shudder when they have a brush with the uncanny.

Take young Mr. Bentine, for instance, the son of my dear friend Michael Bentine, the British TV star. He, like his father, is very much interested in the psychic. But young Bentine never bargained for first hand experiences.

It happened at school, Harrow, one of the finest British "public schools" (in America they are called private schools), one spring. Young Bentine lived in a dormitory known as The Knoll. One night around two A.M., he awoke from sound sleep. The silence of the night was broken by the sound of footsteps coming from the headmaster's room. The footsteps went from the room to a nearby bathroom, and then suddenly came to a halt. Bentine thought nothing of it, but why had it awakened him? Perhaps he had been studying too hard and it was merely a case of nerves. At any rate, he decided not to pay any attention to the strange footsteps. After all, if the headmaster wished to walk at that ungodly hour, that was his business and privilege.

But the following night the same thing happened. Again, at two A.M. he found himself awake, and there came the ominous footsteps. Again they stopped abruptly when they reached the bathroom. Coincidence? Cautiously young Bentine made some inquiries. Was the headmaster given to nocturnal walks, perhaps? He was not.

The third night, Bentine decided that if it happened again, he would be brave and look into it. He fortified himself with some tea and then went to bed. It was not easy falling asleep, but eventually his fatigue had the upper hand and our young man was asleep in his room.

Promptly at two, however, he was awake again. And quicker than you could say, "Ghost across the hall," there were the familiar footsteps!

Quickly our intrepid friend got up and stuck his head out of his door, facing the headmaster's room and the bathroom directly across the corridor.

The steps were now very loud and clear. Although he did not see anyone, he heard someone move along the passage.

He was petrified. As soon as the footsteps had come to the usual abrupt halt in front of the bathroom door, he crept back into his own room and bed. But sleep was out for the night. The hours were like months, until finally morning came and a very tired Bentine went down to breakfast, glad the ordeal of the night had come to an end.

He had to know what this was all about, no matter what the consequences. To go through another night like that was out of the question.

He made some cautious inquiries about that room. There had been a headmaster fourteen years ago who had died in that room. It had been suicide, and he had hanged himself in the shower. Bentine turned white as a ghost himself when he heard the story. He immediately tried to arrange to have his room changed. But that could not be done as quickly as he had hoped, so it was only after another two and a half weeks that he was able to banish the steps of the ghostly headmaster from his mind.

His father had lent him a copy of my book, *Ghost Hunter*, and he had looked forward to reading it when exams eased up a bit. But now, even though he was in another room without the slightest trace of a ghost, he could not bring himself to touch my book. Instead, he concentrated on reading humor.

Unfortunately nobody did anything about the ghostly headmaster, so it must be that he keeps coming back down that passage to his old room, only to find his body still hanging in the shower.

You might ask, "What shall I do if I think I have a ghost in the house? Shall I run? Shall I stay? Do I talk to it or ignore it? Is there a rule book for people having ghosts?" Some of the questions I get are like that. Others merely wish to report a case because they feel it is something I might be interested in. Still others want help: free them from the ghost and vice versa. Some are worried: how much will I charge them for the house-cleaning job? When I explain that there is no charge and that I will gladly do it, they are relieved. This is because ghostly manifestations often occur to people with very little money.

But so many people have ghosts—almost as many as have termites, not that there is any connection—that I cannot personally go after each and every case brought to my attention by mail, telephone, telegram, or television.

In the most urgent cases, I try to come and help the people involved. Usually I do this in connection with a TV show or lecture at the local university, for *someone* has to pay my expenses. The airlines don't accept ghost money, nor do the innkeepers. And thus far I have been on my own, financially speaking, with no Institute or Research Foundation to take up the slack. For destruction and bombs there is always money, but for research involving the psychic, hardly ever.

Granted, I can visit a number of people with haunted-house problems every year, but what do the others do when I can't see them myself? Can I send them to a local ghost hunter, the way a doctor sends patients to a colleague if he can't or does not wish to treat them?

Even if I could, I wouldn't do it. When they ask for my help, they want my approach to their peculiar problems and not someone else's. In this field every researcher sees things a little differently from the next one. I am probably the only parapsychologist who is unhesitatingly pro-ghost. Some will admit they exist, but spend a lot of time trying to find "alternate" explanations if they cannot discredit the witnesses.

I have long, and for good scientific reasons, become convinced that ghosts exist. Ghosts are ghosts. Not hallucinations, necessarily, and not mistakes of casual observers. With that sort of practical base to start from, I go after the cases by concentrating on the situation and problems, rather than, as some researchers will do, trying hard to change the basic stories reported to me. I don't work on my witnesses; I've come to help them. To try and shake them with the sophisticated apparatus of a trained parapsychologist is not only unfair, but also foolish. The original reports are straight reports of average people telling what has happened in their own environment. If you try to shake their testimony, you may get a different story—but it won't be the truth, necessarily. The more you confuse the witnesses, the less they will recall that which is firsthand information.

My job begins when the witnesses have told their story for the first time.

In the majority of cases I have handled, I have found a basis of fact for the ghostly "complaint." Once in a while, a person may have thought something was supernormal when it was not, and on rare occasions I have come across mentally unbalanced people living in a fantasy world of their own. There just aren't that many kooks who want my help: evidently my scientific method, even though I am convinced of the veracity of ghostly phenomena, is not the kind of searchlight they wish to have turned on their strange stories.

What to do until the Ghost Hunter arrives? Relax, if you can. Be a good observer, whether or not you are scared stiff. And remember, please—ghosts are also people.

There, but for the grace of God, goes someone like you.

2

Confessions of a Ghost Hunter

"ENOUGH OF THIS nonsense," the kindergarten teacher, Miss Seidler, said sternly, and a hush fell upon the assembled children. There were seven or eight boys and girls, roughly three or four years old, grouped around a boy of three who sat on a wooden chair in the middle of an imperfect circle. Imperfect was right. The teacher did not approve of our activities. I was the little boy in the middle, and I had been telling the kids some of the wildest ghost stories ever heard anywhere since Edgar Allan Poe was in knee pants.

Tales of the supernatural seemed to come to me easily, as if I had been born to tell them; where I got my raw materials is still a mystery to me. But apparently the plots hit home; parents started to complain that their offspring wouldn't sleep nights, demanding more and better ghost stories, and what the heck were they teaching their youngsters at Miss Seidler's?

It was clear that Miss Seidler did not intend to make ghost-story telling a regular—or even an irregular—part of the curriculum.

"Hans," she now demanded, "let me see that."

"That" was the book of wisdom I had been holding in my hands, pretending to read from it. It was a little futuristic, for I could neither read nor write at that point, but I had seen grownups doing it, so I copied the action. My book was no ordinary book, however. It was my father's trolley car pass, expired, in a nice black leather cover. Miss Seidler was not impressed.

After a moment of silence, she returned the *legitimation* or pass to me, and told me to stop telling ghost stories.

But you can't keep a good man down. By the time I was six, I was regaling my mothers's family in Moravia with tales told me, allegedly, by the wood sprites in the trees along the little river that flows through the city of Bruenn, where I spent every summer. My beginnings in the psychic field were humble, to say the least, and about as far from fact as you can go.

Fortunately, my uncle Henry was a dreamer and understanding. At his side, I had my first whiff of the real thing: psychic experiences really existed, I was informed, and my interest was now doubly aroused. Uncle Henry of course did not treat me like a parapsychologist: I was a boy of maybe nine or ten who liked adventure, and that was precisely what he was going to give me. In his room, furnished exclusively with eighteenth-century furniture and antiques, we held seances by candlelight. He had some early books dealing with the occult, and used to read from them the way a minister interprets the Bible. Since most of it was in distorted Latin, the sound but not the meaning penetrated my consciousness, and it was all very exciting.

Uncle Henry did not say there were ghosts and spirits; neither did he say there weren't. It was all I needed in getting my secret work cut out for me; a responsible adult approved, so I was doing the right thing!

As the years passed, my interests veered toward science and the unconquered territories of electronics and radio. A new rationalism grew in my mind and I became very cocky in my attitude toward anything I could not touch, see, hear, or feel at this point: how *could* such things as spirits exist?

There had to be a "natural" explanation, regardless of the evidence presented! I was completely unwilling to regard an unseen world around us as anything but pure fantasy, as remnants of childhood memories and totally incompatible with my brave new world of electronics.

I was about ten at the time, and such silly attitudes were perhaps normal for my age. But I know some mature, intelligent adults who have exactly the same sort of reasoning. There is that television producer, for instance, who patiently listened to all the evidence for the existence of psychic phenomena, looked carefully at the photographs taken under test conditions, and even managed to have an experience with strange pictures himself—to no avail.

"There's got to be some other explanation," he would intone regularly. He, like many others in our materialistic world today, is incapable of accepting the truth unless that truth conforms to his preconceived notions as to what that truth must look like. It is a little like the bed of Procrustes. Procrustes, you may recall, was a highwayman in ancient Greece whose particular brand of fun consisted of placing unwary travelers into his "special" bed: if they were too long, he'd cut them down, if they were too short, he'd stretch them to fit.

I did not attend the ordinary, tuition-free high school in my ancestral city of Vienna, Austria, but managed to get into a *Gymnasium*, a combination of high school and junior college, with emphasis on the humanities. My electronics spirit had somehow departed along the way, and was now replaced by a burning desire to become an archaeologist. Children often change their plans dozens of times during their school days, depending on what influences them in the world around them. But in my case, at least, the label stuck, and I did indeed become an archaeologist—at least at first.

This was in the 1930s, when Europe seethed with political unrest and the madman of Berlin had already cast a heavy shadow upon smaller countries around Germany such as the Austria I grew up in. It seemed foolish, on the fact of it, to study history and the humanities in *Gymnasium* in order to continue at the university in the hopes of eventually becoming an archaeologist, at a time when more practical pursuits might have been wiser. I also evinced a strong interest in writing, and it was clear to me that I would be a *Schriftsteller*, an author, of some kind—exactly what I have become, of course. But in the 1930s, when I was in my early teens, this was really quite outlandish to my parents and friends.

In the second half of my *Gymnasium* period, when I was sixteen years old, I was profoundly impressed by one of my teachers, Franz Spunda. This, of course, brought me into immediate disrepute with most of my classmates, since Dr. Spunda was one of the least-liked teachers and one of the most feared.

The reasons for this were in the man's character: he was a taciturn, dour man who seldom joked or said an unnecessary word, and whose scholastic behavior was stern and uncompromising. Other teachers you could soften up, but not him. What impressed me about Franz Spunda, however, was not the fact that he was disliked by my classmates, of course, for I am not a nonconformist for its own sake. Spunda was a well-known writer of historical novels who, like so many authors, even successful ones, was forced to augment his income by teaching.

Perhaps he resented this, for it interfered with his more important work, but his storehouse of knowledge was greater than called for in his teaching position. His classes dealt with literature, as was to be expected, but I soon discovered that Dr. Spunda had a deep interest in the occult, just as I used to have in the old Uncle Henry days.

I read some of Spunda's books, which led to other books on occult subjects, notably the very technical books on parapsychology by Professor Oesterreicher and by G. W. Gessmann, both published in the 1920s, which I acquired in 1935 when I was fifteen. Suddenly I realized that there was truth in these accounts, and that it was worthy of my further efforts to involve myself in the study of the occult. Whenever I had an opportunity, I let Dr. Spunda know that I shared his interests in these fields. On one occasion, I picked as the topic for a paper the rather cumbersome title of "Dr. von Schrenck-Notzing's Theory of the Telekinetic, Teleplastic Ideoplasticity," and confounded my classmates by just the title, to say nothing of the contents!

But not Dr. Spunda. After I was through reading my paper, he remarked that it was a hodgepodge of several theories and proceeded to criticize my statements with the experienced approach of an inside man. After this, it became clear to my classmates that I was something special, and many avoided me afterwards in anything but the most superficial relationships. It suited me fine, for I preferred a few close friends to general and shallow popularity.

Many years later, when I returned to Vienna as an American foreign correspondent, I met my erstwhile teacher again in the stillness of his cottage in the suburbs of Vienna. We talked freely of the past and he admitted his errors of a political nature: Spunda had welcomed the Hitler movement at first with the unrealistic emotional optimism of a Wagnerian revivalist of Pan-Germanic days, only to find the bitter truth difficult to accept. Essentially a religious man, he realized in the later war years that the German cause had been betrayed by the Third Reich, but he had a difficult time cleansing himself of his association with it for many years after. And yet, he had never done anything overt, and never denied his mistakes. Eventually his books were published again and some are still in print, especially his very profound work on the rose cross, *Jacob Boehme*, which Bauer republished recently. Spunda has since gone on in a manner worthy of his Olympian philosophy: he died of a heart attack during a trip exploring once again the beauty of ancient Greece.

At the University of Vienna, my days were occupied with the formal studies of archaeology and history, and psychic matters had to wait. In 1938, we decided that the threatening war clouds would soon erupt into rainstorms of blood and destruction, and I went to live in New York where my father had spent many years at the turn of the century as an immigrant. All this time, my interest in the world of the sixth sense lay dormant, though far from dead. In 1946, I met for the first time Eileen Garrett, whose work has influenced my thinking profoundly, even though we do not always agree on the conclusions to be drawn from it.

I was making a reasonably good living as a writer and associate editor of a magazine called *Numismatic Review*, a position utilizing my knowledge of archaeology and ancient numismatics, but none of my ESP talents.

The latter grew quietly in the dark, like mushrooms in a tunnel, until suddenly there was need to display them.

I have always maintained that people form links in chains of destiny, each of us furnishing a vital step forward in a journey someone else may be taking, without our knowledge of where it may lead him or her. This is our duty then, to serve so that someone else might prosper or succeed, and in turn be served on another occasion by someone else in the same manner. Thus it was that the British actor, writer, and comedian Michael Bentine touched off a new wave of psychic interest within me when we met backstage at the Hippodrome Theatre in London in 1950, where he was then starring.

Our friendship blossomed particularly when we discovered our common interest in psychic research. When Michael came to New York the following year, we met again.

It so happened that I had also become friendly with the late Danton Walker, the Broadway columnist of the New York *Daily News* who was, as I discovered, psychic, and very much interested in my favorite subject.

Somehow the Michael Bentine link led to the next link, Walker, when Walker asked me to arrange an interview with Bentine. Now there were three of us, meeting over a drink in Manhattan. During that afternoon, Walker started to tell us of his haunted house in the country and Michael immediately offered to go there with him. But his commitments called him back to England before this could be arranged, and it was I alone who went. Also present was the famous medium Eileen Garrett, who acted as a "telephone between worlds," using the James Crenshaw description of this gift. Dr. Robert Laidlaw came as an observer and arbiter of the investigation that followed.

I have, of course, reported this remarkable case in my earlier book, *Ghost Hunter*, and it has always stood out in my mind as one of the most interesting cases of a haunting I have ever witnessed—and I have had several thousand cases since. I don't know whether it was the stark tragedy of a Colonial runner being clubbed to death by the British soldiery and its vivid reenactment in trance by the medium, or the quality of the witnesses who had experienced the uncanny phenomena I came to know over and over again in the years that followed, but the Rockland County Ghost helped convince me that man does indeed have an immortal component. What this component was began to occupy my time more and more after my involvement with this case.

Still, I knew only that sometimes things go wrong in life and someone dies tragically, and something stays behind and becomes a "ghost" of the event. Was it the exception from the norm, and did we usually leave no residue upon expiring? That question occupied my mind a great deal. It seemed entirely consistent with my knowledge of electronics to postulate that man's emotional tensions might constitute an electromagnetic field similar to a radiation field in the atmosphere. Could it be that these ghosts were really impressions like photographs in the "ether" or atmosphere of old houses, and had no relationship to living human beings? That too seemed vaguely possible under my set of rules. After all, if an atomic explosion can make a part of the atmosphere radioactive for many years, why couldn't a miniature outburst such as sudden death have some effect?

At this point in my studies, I was still trying to find some "natural" way of explaining the phenomena I had witnessed, to correlate them with the known facts of science and nature, even though they might be new aspects or little-known facts within the customary framework of human knowledge and understanding. But the Rockland case threw me for a loop: for all intents and purposes, this was not a shallow impression of a past event, but a seemingly living human being from the past, temporarily using the body of the medium to act out his problems.

I could not reconcile what I observed with the concept of a "dead" impression left behind in the atmosphere, devoid of all further life or power to react to those making a fresh contact with it. I began to get uncomfortable as I realized what I was trying to do: that is, to select my evidence not on the basis of truth, but instead to make the facts fit the theory. Fortunately I am a very honest fellow. I can't live with half-truths and I don't fool myself about anything when I know, deep within me, that it is wrong.

Consequently, it began to dawn on me that there were psychic cases involving lifeless "impressions" in the atmosphere, and that there were also cases of authentic hauntings, where a human being was continually reliving his emotional tragedy of the past.

For me, the search was on for the proof of personal survival, that is to say, scientific evidence that man does survive physical death and continues his existence as a full individual in another dimension.

I realized that ghosts were not exactly ideal cases with which to prove or disprove the nature of that "other side" of the universe. It had become clear to me that all ghosts were either psychotic or at least psychologically disoriented minds, not balanced individuals who had passed on. Obviously, if the survival of a personality was a fact, it would be far more common than hauntings, and the evidence for it should be capable of verification on a much larger scale. More people die "normally" than under tragic conditions, and even among the latter class, those turning up as "ghosts" are again a small portion of the total thus "qualified."

Where was I to turn to find evidence for this so-called spirit world about which the spiritualists had been talking so nicely for so long, without ever convincing me of its reality?

As for so many others raised in the upper middle class, all emotional religions were alien to my way of life. I grew up considering spiritualist mediums as either outright fakes or misguided self-styled prophets at best, and the practice of seances in questionable taste. Should I now reverse myself and seek out some medium and try my hand at a seance, just so I could discover for myself what went on? This was not easy, since I hated the dark and wouldn't sit in total darkness for anything.

Torn between letting the matter rest and feeling an aroused curiosity, I attended a number of spiritualist lectures, the kind that attracts a rather motley crowd ranging from frustrated old maids of both sexes, to earnest seekers of truth, to students of the occult, to just plainly curious people more in need of a fortuneteller than a medium.

On one such occasion, I was approached by a man in the crowd just as the meeting broke up. He explained to me that he had some talents as a medium that he wished to improve upon, and was therefore trying to arrange a little group to "sit" with him. He hastened to explain that he was also a clerk in Brooklyn and that no money was involved in this project. I saw nothing wrong with it and gladly agreed to join him and some others in at least one such meeting. As it happened, they needed a quiet place in which to meet, so I suggested my offices on Fifty-Ninth Street, in New York City, after business hours.

That was agreeable, and six ladies I had never seen before came up to my office the following evening. They looked like typical New York housewives in their forties and fifties, which is what they were. I pulled down the shades, and the gentleman I had met the night before seated himself in one of the chairs and closed his eyes. For a few moments, we were all very quiet and the traffic rumbling by downstairs was all we could hear. Then his breathing became a bit labored and his head fell upon his shoulders.

Rapidly he kept calling out names and bits of information about people who evidently were recognized by one or another person in the room. Of course I immediately suspected that this was because he knew these ladies and was trying to please them by "bringing in" their favorite deceased relative. After the seance, I questioned them separately and satisfied myself that they had only met him the night before, as I had, at the lecture hall. Evidently, my observation that night had not been as good as it should have been, since I did not recall seeing these ladies there, but it had been a rather large crowd.

After the fourth or fifth person had spoken through the medium, his head turned in my direction and, in a strangely distorted voice resembling his normal speaking voice, he addressed me.

"Someone here who knows you . . . named Eric . . . says he died short time ago . . . bad accident . . . wants you to tell loved ones he's all right. . . ."

That was all.

But it was enough for me. Half a year before this seance, a friend of mine had died tragically in an accident while still quite young. His wife had been completely inconsolable since that time, taking the death of her husband of only a few months very hard. His name was Eric.

Of all the people I knew who had passed away in my family, not one of them had evidently decided to speak through this medium. But there was certainly something urgent about the message from Eric. His wife needed this bit of news.

I called her and told her, and though she did not really believe in the possibility of personal spiritual survival after death, she was not entirely sure that it didn't exist. An indication that it was possible was all that was needed to help her gradually get over the tragedy, and so she did.

In 1953, I got to know a group that met regularly at the New York headquarters of the Association for Research and Enlightenment, better known as the Edgar Cayce Foundation. This was a study group, and mediums worked with them to learn more about their own abilities. One such budding medium was Ethel Johnson Meyers, who has since become one of our more famous psychics and one of the people I frequently work with in my investigations.

At that time, however, she was just a singing teacher with mediumship who wanted to find out more about herself.

At that time, Ethel's controls—spirit personalities operating her psychic channels to regulate the flow of information and to keep out intruders—were her late husband Albert and a Tibetan named Toto Himalaya. I must confess that Toto sounded absolutely phony to me, somewhat like a vaudeville Indian making grunting noises and behaving very much like a synthetic Tibetan, or one manufactured by the unconscious of the medium herself. This, of course, is an age-old question: are these "controls" real people or are they parts of the personality of the medium that act out consciously during a trance and which the medium cannot act out when awake?

I have never been able to prove satisfactorily the reality of these controls, and some trance mediums like Sybil Leek don't have them. But I haven't any evidence to say that they are anything except what they claim to be, and am of late persuaded to accept them as indeed real human beings who have crossed the threshold into the nonphysical world. Even so great a medium and human being as Eileen Garrett has not been able to make up her own mind on this difficult question.

When I first met Toto via the entranced Ethel Meyers we had our difficulties, for I don't take kindly to generalities and bits of philosophy that seem to waste both a medium's and an investigator's time.

But if Toto was indeed an ancient Tibetan priest, he had a right to preach. I just wasn't particularly ready to listen to the sermon at that point. Instead, I decided to test Ethel's psychometry talents. Psychometry is the gift of touching an object and describing instantly its history or owners. Naturally, the medium must not know anything about the object or see its shape or outline, in order to avoid any conscious clues as to its identity.

Consequently, I took the object I had in mind, wrapped it several times in paper, then in pieces of cloth, until it became a shapeless parcel of about an arm's length and weighing perhaps three pounds. With this thing under my arm, I came down to the Association where Ethel Meyers was already in the midst of psychometrizing objects. At the first free moment, I thrust the parcel into her outstretched hands and watched for her reactions.

For a moment Mrs. Meyers sat as if stunned. Then, with a shriek, she rose from her chair, at the same time throwing the parcel onto the floor as if I had handed her a stick of dynamite with a lit fuse.

Even though it was early spring, she was sweating and I could tell she was upset.

"I see a sacrifice," she mumbled, and shuddered.

"This is some kind of ceremony . . . a dagger . . . don't like it." She looked at me sternly, almost reproachfully.

"It's all right, Ethel," I said, "I shan't ask you to touch it again."

With that, I picked up the package and started to unravel it. The others present had formed a circle around us as layer upon layer of cloth and paper disappeared. Eventually, I held in my hand a gleaming *dorje* or Tibetan sacrificial scepter, at the end of which was a dagger. I had meant to make Toto Himalaya feel at home, and all I had succeeded in doing was getting Mrs. Meyers upset!

The following year, after attending dozens upon dozens of meetings at the Association, I made a special visit because my friends had told me of a new medium who had recently joined the experimental group and seemed interesting. I was late in arriving and took a seat in the rear of the already darkened room. At the far end, a woman sat with her eyes closed, while a small red light burned next to her, casting an eerie glow over the assembled people.

This went on for about fifteen minutes—utter silence while the medium slept. Then she awoke and gave messages to some of those present. It was her brand of mediumship, this going out "alone," and then returning and talking. Most mediums go into trance and talk during, not after, the trance state. The lights came on now, and I arose to leave. I had walked down the corridor part of the way when the medium I had just observed came after me and stopped me.

"Are you Hans Holzer?"

I nodded, sure someone had told her my name. But nobody had, as I later discovered.

"Then I have a message for you. From an uncle."

Now I have lots of uncles, some dead, some living, and I was not impressed. I looked at her blankly.

The dark-haired woman shook her head impatiently.

"His initials are O. S." she said rapidly, "and he's got a wife named Alice. She's a blonde."

All at once I felt shivers down my spine.

Many years before, an uncle of mine named Otto Stransky had died tragically. I was not particularly close to him, and had not thought of him for years. There had been no reason to do so; his family lived thousands of miles away, in South America, and there was almost no contact.

Whatever it was, the medium certainly had not read my unconscious mind.

His wife's name was indeed Alice. When he had been alive, she had been a blonde, but by now, however, Alice's hair had long since turned white. Yet, to the timeless memory of her loving husband, the hair would forever be blonde!

That was the first time I had come in contact with a clearcut message from a departed relative or friend that could not be explained by fraud, coincidence, mind reading or some otherwise explainable cause. It had to be the survival of human personality. I thanked the lady, not realizing at the time that she would also play a large role in my future work. She is probably one of the finest clairvoyant mediums in America today. Her name is Betty Ritter.

Now I knew that in some instances at least, proof of survival could be shown. Then why not in all? Why not indeed. My mind was made up to turn my attention to this end: to give the average person the facts of afterlife, in terms he can both understand and accept; to be a scientist but not a negative doubter. Truth does not need interpretation, just exposure.

That's how I became a Psychic Investigator.

3

Visitors From Beyond the Grave

PEOPLE ALL OVER the world have moved into houses which seemed ordinary and pleasant, and spent years without ever encountering anything out of the ordinary. Then, one day, something happens to disturb their tranquility: a ghost appears, strange noises are heard, and a psychic presence makes itself known.

Why is it that phenomena occur at times long after someone moves into an affected house? Of course, there are just as many cases where the ominous presence is felt the very moment one steps across the threshold. But in cases where ghosts make their presence manifest long after the new tenants have moved in, certain conditions have not been right for such manifestations to take place at the beginning. For instance, it may involve the presence of youngsters in the household who furnish the energy for ghosts to appear. Or it may be that the shadowy entities remaining behind in the house are dimly aware of the new tenants, but wish to find out more about them before manifesting to them. Either way, once manifestations begin, the owner of the house has the choice of either ignoring them, fighting them—or coming to terms with them.

In the majority of cases, unfortunately, people simply think that by ignoring the phenomena or trying hard to explain them by so-called natural causes, the matter can be solved. Ignoring problems never helps, in any area of life. When it comes to psychic phenomena, the phenomena may become worse, because even the most benighted ghost, barely aware of its predicament, will become more powerful, more restless, by being ignored.

Take Mrs. A.M.B., for instance. She lives in central Illinois and is by training and profession a practical nurse, engaged in psychiatric work. If anything, she can distinguish psychosis from psychic activity. She has had ESP abilities ever since she can remember. When she was twelve years old, she was playing in front of her house when she met what to her was an old man, inquiring about a certain widow living in the next block of the village. Mrs. B. knew very well that the lady had become a widow due to her husband having been killed while working as a crossing guard during a blizzard the previous winter. She remembered the man well, but the stranger did not resemble the deceased at all, so she assumed he was a relative inquiring about the dead man.

The stranger wanted to know where the widow had moved to. Mrs. B. explained that the lady had gone to visit a sister somewhere in Missouri, due to the fact, of course, that her husband had been killed in an accident. At that, the stranger nodded; he knew of the accident, he said. "Come," Mrs. B. said to the stranger, "I'll show you where another sister of the widow lives, not more than two blocks away from here. Perhaps they can tell you what town in Missouri she is visiting." The stranger obliged her, and the two were walking along the front porch, toward the steps leading down into the street, still in conversation. At that moment, her mother appeared at the front door in back of her and demanded to know what she was talking about. The girl was surprised, and explained that the gentleman was merely asking where Mrs. C. had gone, and added, "I told him she went to Missouri." But the mother replied, in a surprised tone of voice, "What are you talking about? I don't see anyone." The little girl immediately pointed at the visitor, who by that time had had enough time to get to the steps, for the front porch was rather large.

But—to her shock—she saw no one there! Immediately the girl and her mother walked into the yard, looking about everywhere without finding any trace of the strange visitor. He had simply vanished the moment the little girl had turned around to answer her mother.

Mrs. M.R. is a housewife in her late forties, living in a medium-sized New England town. Her husband works for the United States Post Office, and Mrs. R. takes care of two of their three children, the oldest being already married and living away from home. She, too, has lived with the psychic world practically from the beginning. When she was only seven years old, she and her sister, two years her senior, were in bed, playing and whispering to each other in order not to wake up their parents, whose room was next to theirs. Suddenly, there appeared a misty figure at the door connecting the children's room with the living room. It drifted through the children's room and stopped at the door to the parents' room, facing the sleeping couple. The children both saw it: the figure seemed grayish-white and had some sort of cord around its waist. At that moment their father awoke and saw it too. Yelling out to it to go away, he awoke his wife. Even though the figure still stood in the doorway of their room, she could not see it. At that moment, the ghost just disappeared.

Although Mrs. R. has had many dreams which later came true, she did not see a ghost again until she was twenty-three years old. At that time she had already given birth to her first child, and she and her husband were staying for a week at her mother's apartment. The child was still in the hospital, having been a premature baby, and Mrs. R. lay in bed, thinking about her child. At that moment there appeared at the door to the room a very tall, dark, hooded figure. Far from being afraid, she watched the figure glide into the room, come around the foot of the bed and toward her to her side. The room seemed filled with a soft glow, not unlike moonlight, even though the shades were down; the furniture could be seen plainly as if there were lights in the room. By now the visitor stood right next to the bed and Mrs. R. was able to look up into his face; but in the emptiness of the hood, where a face should be, there was nothing, absolutely nothing. Then, very slowly, the figure bent over her from its great height, and it was only when the empty hood was almost touching her face, that Mrs. R. cried out in a kind of muffled way. Apparently, her outcry had broken the spell, for the phantom disappeared as quickly as it had come. Whether there was any connection between the ghostly visitor she had seen as a child and the monk-like phantom who came to her many years later, Mrs. R. does not know. But it may well be that both were one and the same, perhaps sent to protect her or guide her in some way, from out of the distant past.

David H. is only seventeen years old and lives in Michigan. When he was eight he had his first encounter with a ghost. The house his parents lived in was more than a hundred years old, and rather on the large side. David slept in one of two main rooms on the upper floor of the house; the room next to it was unfurnished. One night he was lying in bed when he had a sudden urge to sit up, and as he did so he looked down the hall. All of a sudden he noticed a small shadow-like man jump down from the attic and run towards him. But instead of coming into his room, he turned down the stairs. David could see that he wore a small derby hat but what was even more fascinating was the fact that the figure walked about two inches above the floor! After the figure had disappeared, David thought it was all his imagination. A particularly bright eight-year-old, he was not easily taken in by fantasies or daydreams.

But the strange figure reappeared several times more, and eventually David came to the conclusion that it was real. He asked his parents whether he could swap rooms with them and they agreed to let him sleep downstairs. It was about that time that his mother told him that she had heard the old piano playing at night downstairs. She had thought that it was the cat climbing up on the keys, but one night the piano played in plain view of herself and one of her daughters, without even a trace of the cat in the room. There was also the sound of pages in a book being turned in the same area, although nobody had a book or turned any pages.

David settled down in his room on the lower floor and finally forgot all about his ghostly experiences. Shortly after he heard a crunching noise on the stairs, as if someone were walking on them. He assumed it was his mother coming down the stairs to tell him to turn off his radio, but no one came.

As he grew older, he moved back upstairs, since the room on the ground floor had become too small for him. This proved to be somewhat of a strain for him: many times he would be lying in bed when someone would call his name. But there never was anyone there. Exasperated, the youngster spoke up, challenging the ghost to give some sign of his presence so that there could be communication between them. "If you can hear me, make a noise," David said to his ghost. At that very moment, the door to his room began to rattle without apparent cause. Still unconvinced, since the door had rattled before because of natural causes, David continued his monologue with, "If you are there, show yourself," and at that moment he heard a strange noise behind him. The door to his closet, which had been closed, was slowly opening. This wasn't very reassuring, even though it might represent some kind of dialogue with the ghost.

Shortly thereafter, and in broad daylight, just as he had gotten home from school, David heard a very loud noise in the upper portion of the house: it sounded as if all their cats were tearing each other to pieces and the sound of a lot of coat hangers falling down augmented the bedlam. Quickly, David ran up the stairs—only to find neither cats nor fallen coat hangers. And to this day, David doesn't know who the strange visitor was.

Lana T. is one of seven children from eastern Missouri, who has ESP to a considerable extent. Three of her sisters also have this ability, so perhaps it runs in the family. Today she is a housewife and she and her husband live in a big city in central Missouri. Clairvoyant dreams and other verified incidents of ESP led to an interest in the much-maligned Ouija board, and she and her three sisters, Jean, Judy, and Tony became veritable addicts of this little gadget. A close friend and her husband moved into a nearby house in the same community, without realizing that the house had become available due to the suicide of the previous owner.

Mrs. T.'s friend had come from another state, so the local facts were not too well known to her. When the new owner discovered that her neighbor, Lana T., had psychic gifts and an interest in occult matters, she confided freely in her. It appeared that one of the bathrooms was always cold, regardless of the weather outside or the temperature in the rest of the house; a certain closet door would simply not stay closed; and the heat register was bound to rattle of its own volition. Objects would move from one place to another, without anyone having touched them. Footsteps were heard going up and down the hall, as if someone were pacing up and down. Once the new owner saw a whitish mist which dissolved immediately when she spoke to it.

Her husband, who publishes a local newspaper, would not even discuss the matter, considering it foolish. But one night he woke up and informed her that he had just been touched by a cold, clammy hand. This was enough to drive the new owner to consult with her neighbor. Lana T. offered to try and find out who the disturbing ghost was. Together with one of her sisters, she sat herself down with her trusty Ouija board, and asked it to identify the disturbing entity in the house. Ouija board communication is slow and sometimes boring, but, in this instance, the instrument rapidly identified the communicator as a certain Ted. A chill went down Mrs. T.'s spine, for Ted was the man who had committed suicide in her friend's house.

From then on, a veritable conversation ensued between Mrs. T. and the ghost, in which he explained that he was angry because the new owner had burned something of his. Mrs. T. asked what the new owner could do to satisfy him, and the angry ghost replied that she should destroy something of her own to make up for his loss—something white. When Mrs. T. described her conversation with the ghost to the new owner of the house, the lady was mystified. She could not recall having burned anything belonging to the former owner. Back to the Ouija board went Mrs. T. When she demanded that the ghost describe the item in question more fully, he replied, somewhat impatiently, that it had been white with green trim and had the letters SFCC on it. Mrs. T. returned to her neighbor with this additional information. This time she struck paydirt: shortly after the couple from out of state had moved into the house, the lady of the house had discovered an old golf cap in the top drawer of one of her closets, white with green trim and the initials of the country club, SFCC, on it! The cap had somehow bothered her, so she had tossed it into the trash can and the contents of the can were later burned. The ghost had told the truth. But how could she satisfy his strange whim in return? At that time she and her husband had considered buying a small, expensive white marble statue. They decided to forego this pleasure. Perhaps their sacrifice of this "white" item would make up for the lost golf cap? Evidently it did—for the house has been quiet ever since!

Mrs. Edith F. is the wife of a law enforcement officer in the west. Her husband puts very little credence in anything "supernatural," but Mrs. F. knows otherwise. The house she and her family live in is only about twelve years old, and fifteen years before, the area was still "in the country," although people may have lived there in a previous house. In fact, rumor has it that some old houses were torn down on the land where her house now stands. The series of odd incidents which convinced Mrs. F. of the reality of another dimension began in the summer of 1972.

At that time her nine-year-old son was in the basement family room, watching television. On the north wall of this large room there was a door leading to a storeroom. A rollaway bed had been put there for possible summer company, and the boy was in this particular bed, propped up with a large pillow. He had just finished a snack, and leaned up to brush the crumbs from under him, when he happened to look up and saw an old woman standing beside the bed, staring at him. He looked away from her for a moment, then returned his eyes onto her; she was still there. Frightened, he began to yell for his mother, at which the woman moved back towards the door. The door opened about two inches, and she quickly slid through it, as if she were two-dimensional.

By that time Mrs. F. arrived downstairs and found her son so frightened he could hardly talk. He described the visitor as very old, with black and gray hair parted in the middle, wearing a long black dress and a single pair of colored beads. Mrs. F. decided not to discuss it with her husband, who would only scoff at it, but decided to return to the basement with her twenty-year-old daughter to see whether anything would occur in her presence. The two women stood on the spot where the boy had seen the ghost and asked her what she wanted of them. For a moment, nothing happened. Then, suddenly, Mrs. F. felt as though someone were lifting her right arm which turned tingly and raised up in front of her by its own volition! She broke out in goose pimples and quickly whirled around, running back upstairs.

For several days, she did not dare go back to the basement out of fear that the phenomenon might repeat itself. Still upset by it all, she telephoned the Reverend L.B., a Methodist minister, whom, she hoped, would have an open mind concerning occult phenomena. But on the fourth day, Mrs. F. could not hold back any longer; she had to know what the ghost wanted. Somehow she felt she would get it by writing. Again she went to the basement with her twenty-year-old daughter, said a prayer for protection from evil, and stood upright with a pen in her right hand—why, she didn't really know, for she is *left*-handed. She asked aloud if there was anyone present, and the pen wrote, "Yes. You must watch out to woman," and then it drew an arrow toward the northern part of the room. Mrs. F. demanded to know what the ghost wanted, and in reply, the pencil in her hand wrote, "Priest. Hear my confession." Mrs. F. demanded to know what her name was, and the ghost identified herself as Mary Arthur.

With this information Mrs. F. went to her minister friend, who decided to accompany the two women back to the house. He, too, stood in the basement and asked the ghost to give him a sign that she was present. A lamp, which they knew to be in good order, blinked on and off several times in response to their questions. Then, through automatic writing, the ghost informed them that she had died at age eighty-nine, had had nine children, and knew she had passed on in 1959. But the Methodist minister could not help her, she explained; it had to be a Catholic priest. The Reverend B. offered to talk to his Catholic colleague, but Mrs. F. suggested the ghost might find peace in nearby St. Agnes Church. On this note, the presence disappeared and was gone until the following Monday.

On that day, Mrs. F. was in the basement room, working on an ironing board. It was a very warm day, but suddenly she was startled by walking into a blast of icy air on the spot where the ghost had been originally observed by her son. Quickly she called for her daughter to join her and watch. After a moment, her daughter complained that her arm was being lifted the way her mother's had been before. She felt as if someone held it, and the arm felt tingly. Mrs. F. grabbed a pencil and paper from a nearby desk and gave it to her daughter. Her daughter then wrote "Mary" in exactly the same handwriting as Mrs. F. had originally. Then she handed the pencil and paper back to her mother, afraid to continue. So the mother continued the communication and the ghost wrote "Mary Arthur." Gradually, the reasons for her presence became clear. "Father, forgive me, for I have sinned," the ghost wrote, and demanded that the note be taken to a Roman Catholic priest. But Mrs. F. instead suggested that Mary call out to her loved ones to take her away from the place so she could find peace. "No, because of my sins," the ghost replied, and when Mrs. F. wanted to know what the sins consisted of, she simply said, "the marriage."

It was then that Mrs. F. learned that Mary had been born Catholic, had left the church and married a Lutheran and had had nine children with him. To her, this marriage was illegal, sinful. Eventually, the Roman Catholic clergy got into the act. But a special priest would have to be sent to exorcise Mary's sins. This did not sit well with Mrs. F., nor with her Methodist friend, neither of whom thought that Mary was evil.

Time passed, and things seemed to quiet down in the basement. Then, on Labor Day of the same year, 1972, with her husband and son fast asleep in bed, Mrs. F. was in the kitchen canning tomatoes from their garden. Again she felt Mary's presence upstairs, a strange feeling that was hard to describe. Again, her right arm was tingling and her fingers felt as they did when Mary first wanted to write something through her. However, since the Roman Catholic clergy had been reluctant to enter the case, Mrs. F. determined to ignore her promptings. Here she was, washing tomatoes at her kitchen sink, when all of a sudden she heard a *plop!* behind her, turned around, and saw one of the tomatoes lying split open in the middle of the floor. Since she was the only person in the kitchen, there was no rational explanation for the fall of the tomato. Had it merely fallen off the counter, it would have gone straight down instead of jumping four feet away!

Quietly, Mrs. F. turned in the direction where she assumed her ghost lady was and reprimanded her for throwing the tomato. "They are saying special prayers at the church for you," she said, and asked Mary to go there and wait for her delivery.

Everything was quiet after that. About ten days later, a lamp in Mrs. F.'s living room blinked on and off four times as if the ghost were trying to tell her she was leaving. This time Mrs. F. did not feel the tingling sensation in her arm, and somehow felt that this was a farewell message. And since that time there has been no sign of Mary's presence. With the help of her minister friend, Mrs. F. was able to check the records of various funeral homes in the area. A Mary Arthur was buried in 1959. She was black.

Mrs. E. never had any interest in the occult nor experiences along ghostly lines until after her father died. It was a great loss to her and the family, since he had been a pillar of strength and had handled all their affairs. Shortly after he died, Mrs. E. was sitting in her mother's house and suddenly, without explanation, she found herself picking up a pen with her right hand, even though she is left-handed. On the back of a used envelope she wrote the words, "Tell Mama to take that will to the lawyer." Her mother had added some postscripts to her father's will, but had not realized that these requests would not be honored unless and until they had been witnessed and notarized again by an attorney!

Jananne B. is an attractive twenty-five-year-old girl, who has had truck with the unseen since she was very small. While she was visiting her aunt in New Jersey, she remembers clearly seeing a figure in the old carriage house. There was no one in the carriage house at the time. At age seventeen, Miss B. was spending a weekend with another aunt, also in New Jersey. Both women were occupying the same bed. In the middle of the night the young girl sat up in bed, waking up her aunt. There was a tall man in a brown suit standing next to the bed, she explained, and went on to describe his brown hair and handlebar moustache in great detail. Without saying a word, her aunt got up and brought out the family album. Leafing through it, Miss B. pointed at one particular picture: it was her great-grandfather. She had never seen pictures of him, nor of course ever met him. He had died in the very room and bed in which the two women were sleeping at the time.

When she was twenty-four years old, Jananne moved into what was formerly her brother's room, her brother having moved to his own apartment. The very first night she stayed in the room, she felt a presence, and couldn't sleep. Somehow the room had always been the stuffiest room in the house, but that night it was particularly cold. This upset her greatly since she had put in a great deal of time and effort to redecorate it to her taste. Somehow she went off to sleep that night, trying to forget or ignore her feelings. A few nights later she woke up in the middle of the night, feeling extremely cold. As she sat up in bed, she saw a woman out of the corner of her eye: the woman seemed middled-aged, with brown hair pulled back in a very plain bun, wearing a long, straight skirt and a white ruffled blouse with long sleeves and high collar.

Jananne did not experience a feeling of fear, for somehow she knew the spirit was friendly. The next morning just as she was about to wake up, she saw the name "Elly" being written on the wall above her shelves. There were other lines around the name, but before she could make them out, the vision faded. Since she keeps a dream log, recording all unusual dreams, she immediately wrote this incident down, before she could forget it. She also told her mother about the incidents. Time passed, and several months later a local psychic came to the house to do a reading for the family, using her bedroom to work in.

The psychic described the entity in the room precisely the way Jananne had seen it. By now Jananne B. was not the only one to be aware of the ghost. Various friends also heard footsteps overhead while sitting in a room directly underneath hers, and had seen the lights dim of their own volition. Because of the ghostly presence, Jananne's room is unusually cold, and she frequently complains about it. Not long ago, when she remarked how cold it was, the door to the outdoor widow's walk flew wide open and her bedroom door shut of its own volition.

This has happened a number of times, making the room even colder. On several occasions, Miss B. came home to find her bedroom door tightly shut, and very hard to open. Once inside, she noticed that her bedspread was on the floor, propped up against the door from the inside. No one could have placed it there except from inside the room—and the room had been locked.

Soon enough Miss B. realized that she had to get used to sharing her room with the strange lady. Once her mind was made up to accept her as a companion, the phenomenon became less annoying. A short time ago she decided to take some random pictures of the room, to see whether anything unusual would show up on them. Only the available room light was used, no flashlight or electrical lighting. Two of the pictures came back from the laboratory with a white mist on them, one of them showing the letters Elly indistinctly, but nevertheless apparent beyond the shadow of a doubt. Miss B. showed the photographs to her brother, a professional photographer, and to some of his friends. They agreed that double exposure or light leaks were out; the white mist appears to be blotchy, almost like smoke, whereas light leaks would tend to be uniform.

Jananne realizes that Elly is able to manifest for her only because she is psychic. If she needed any further proof of her ability in this respect, it was furnished to her a month later when a friend took her to a certain lady's trailer home for dinner. Jananne's friend asked her to dress lightly because it was always warm there, he said.

But when they arrived at the trailer, it was unusually cold inside. They were having a quiet conversation after dinner, sitting on the couch, when Miss B. looked up and saw the figure of a very sad young man standing in the entrance to the hallway. His head was bowed, and he seemed very lost. Since the hostess had turned out to be rather on the nervous side, Jananne decided not to tell her about the apparition. But on the way home, she informed her friend of what she had seen, describing the man in every detail. Her friend swallowed hard, then informed her that the husband of their hostess had disappeared shortly after returning from Vietnam. Three months later his body was found in the woods; he had committed suicide.

Dorothy Mark-Moore was twelve years old when her Aunt Mary bought a house in Green Brook, New Jersey. The house was on Washington Street and the year was 1933. All the members of the family had retired for the night, and it was rather a warm night at that, so Dorothy thought she'd roll up her pajama legs, and go to sleep like that. She awoke in the early hours of the morning with a start and looked around the room. It so happened that it was a moonlit night so she could make out very clearly if there happened to be an intruder in the room.

As she looked toward the window, she saw a woman walk in, return to the window, look out of it and then turn toward her. Frightened, Dorothy pretended to be asleep for a moment, but then she opened her eyes again and to her amazement saw a nun standing there, looking at her from head to foot. Then the nun came over and moved her hand onto her legs. But when the nun touched Dorothy's legs, it felt "like an old dried-out piece of wood."

The ghostly nun was now close enough to the bed for Dorothy to make out a ring on her hand and beads around her waist, with a large cross dangling at the end of it. The woman appeared to be in her thirties, and seemed quite solid. Suddenly Dorothy realized she was looking at a ghost. She shot up and looked straight into the nun's face. For a moment, girl and ghost stared at each other. Then the nun's face softened as she walked away from Dorothy and vanished into the wall.

Four years later the ghostly nun returned. This time Dorothy was asleep in another bedroom of the same house and it was around seven o'clock in the morning. All of a sudden, Dorothy heard loud organ music and sat up in bed to find out where it came from. The music became so loud she could not stand it and fell back onto the pillows. It felt as if an invisible hand were holding her down. At that moment, the nun entered the room, with a gentleman in his forties, with dark hair and brown eyes, wearing a dark blue serge suit. Dorothy was petrified with fear, especially as the organ music increased to an almost ear-splitting level. Looking at the two apparitions, she noticed that they were reciting the Lord's Prayer, from the movement of their lips. As they did so, the music became less loud, and the two figures slowly walked towards the door. As they left the room, the music stopped abruptly. At that moment, Dorothy seemed to snap out of her trance state, sat up in bed and quickly grabbed all her clothes, running to the bathroom and locking herself in. When she had regained her composure, she made some inquiries about the house and learned that a gentleman of that description had killed himself in the very bathroom into which she had locked herself, some fifty years before.

It was a warm weekend in June of 1971, and a group of New Jersey college students decided to throw a party at a place known as "The Farmhouse," which had been rented for the occasion. Most of the young people were between nineteen and twenty-two years of age, and as the party progressed, the spirits were high. Sometime that evening, a boy named Arthur D., son of a policeman, crashed the party and a fight ensued. According to local newspapers, the fight was part of the shindig, but according to others, the boy was ejected and lay in wait to get even with those who had turned him down. But as a result of the fighting, Arthur lay dead in the street, due to wounds received from a knife. Glen F., a twenty-two-year-old youth at the party, was arrested for his murder. Another boy was in the local hospital, seriously injured, but expected to survive. . . . That was in June, 1971, and it was one graduation party long remembered in the area.

In the summer of 1972 the house was rented out to a certain Mrs. Gloria Brown. Mrs. Brown and three children were sleeping in the hayloft of the barn, which is located a certain distance from the main house. One of the girls saw a light in the house go on downstairs and the figure of a man which she thought was her father. When she investigated, the man tried to grab her. She screamed and her brothers came to her aid. By that time the "man" had run away. Later that summer, a friend was staying with the Browns one evening. There was a knock at the door of the main house about two o'clock in the morning. The friend got up and answered it, but there was no one outside. She went back to bed, only to be awakened again. This time she opened the door and looked through the screen door to see whether there might be someone outside.

There was a man standing outside all right, and she asked whether he was hurt or needed help. Then she noticed that he had neither face nor hands, only a whitish, swirly substance! Horror-stricken, she stared at him when he disappeared just as suddenly as he had come.

At this writing, the restless boy is still unable to find peace: for him, the unlucky party has never broken up.

Yellow Frame Church is an old country church at Yellow Frame, New Jersey. It stands in one of the most isolated areas of the state and is but little-known to people outside the immediate area. Even today there is only the minister's house and a graveyard across the street, but no other dwellings close by. In the early 1800s a new minister came to Yellow Frame and, after his very first sermon, dropped dead. He was duly buried in the church yard across from the church. However for unknown reasons, his body was taken some years later from the churchyard and moved to another cemetery at Johnsonburg, two miles down the road.

So much for the background of the old building. I wouldn't be writing about it if it weren't for a recent report from an alert reader, Mrs. Johanna C., who lives in a nearby town. Apparently there had been an incident involving a woman on her way home early in the morning, while it was still dark, not long ago. When the lady passed the church she heard choir music coming from it and saw that both doors were wide open. Curious as to who might be playing the organ that early in the morning, or, rather, that late at night, she stepped up and peered into the church: the inside of the building was quite dark, and when she stepped inside she noticed that there was no one in the church who could have played the organ. Frightened, she left in a hurry.

In the late 1960s, Mr. C. and a group of friends, who had heard the account of the organ music, decided to see for themselves whether there was anything unusual about the church. As so many others who think that Hallowe'en is the time to look for ghosts, Mr. C. and friends picked the night of October 31 to do their ghost hunt. Of course, there is no connection between Hallowe'en, the solemn holiday of witchcraft, the Old Religion, and ghosts; but popular superstition will always link them, since ghosts and witches *seem* to belong to the same level of reference. At any rate, Mr. C. and his friends arrived at Yellow Frame Church at exactly midnight and bravely walked up the steps of the church. At that hour, the church was of course closed. As they confronted the locked doors, the doors suddenly swung open of their own volition, startling the visitors no end. But this did not stop them; they stepped inside the church and, as they did so, each one of the group noticed a strange pressure on his ears as if the air were pushing against them!

One in the group called out, "Reverend, oh Reverend!" but there was no answer. The eerie stillness of the building was too much for them, and they left in a hurry.

A year later, again on Hallowe'en, Mrs. C. went along with the same group to see whether she could experience anything out of the ordinary. They arrived at the church shortly before midnight, driving by it at first to get a look at it. They noticed that both doors were shut. A few minutes later they returned to see that one of the doors was slightly open. They parked their car and stepped inside the church. At that moment Mrs. C. could also feel the strange pressure on her ears. She also felt as if someone were hiding in the church, watching them. There was a peaceful feeling about it, almost, she explained, as if she were being wrapped in a blanket. Mrs. C. decided to spend some time inside the church to see whether it was truly haunted, but the men would have no part of it and insisted that they all leave again. While they stood around inside, discussing whether or not they should go immediately, they clearly heard what appeared to be footsteps in the leaves. It sounded as if someone were walking around just outside the building. However, they did not stay around long enough to find out whether there was, in fact, someone walking who was not a member of their group.

But the matter did not give Mrs. C. any rest, so she returned to the church once more in the company of a girl-friend, this time during daylight hours. She managed to meet the present minister's wife, telling her of their experiences. To their relief, the minister's wife was not at all shocked: not long ago she had awakened at six in the morning, while it was still quite dark outside, and peering out the window toward the church, she became aware of lights in the church going on and off as if someone were signaling with them. Those are the facts; there is also a tradition in the area that the church is haunted by the restless spirit of the original minister, who doesn't like being buried in the wrong cemetery and comes up the Yellow Frame Road searching for his original resting place.

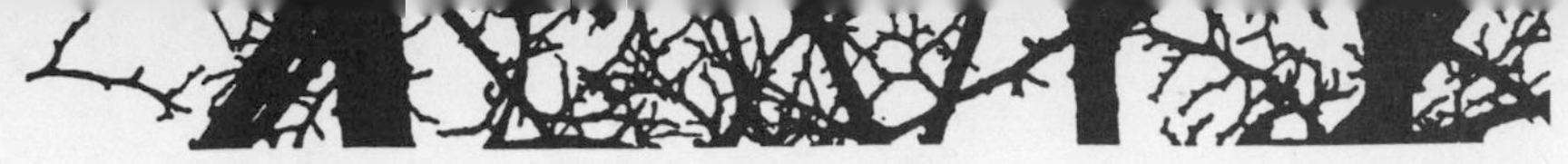

4

A Haunted House is Not a Home

A LOT OF people are particular about the privacy of their home. They like it fine when nobody bothers them, except for their own kinfolk. Some do not even mind if a relative or friend stays over or comes to visit them, because, after all, they will leave again in time. But when a ghost overstays his welcome, and stays on and on and on, the matter can become upsetting, to say the least. This becomes even more of a problem when the guest is not aware of the passage of time, or when he thinks that your home is actually his home. When that happens, the owner of the house or apartment is faced with a difficult choice: fight the intruder and do everything at one's command to get rid of him, or accept the invasion of privacy and consider it a natural component of daily living.

When the ghost comes with the house—that is, if he or she lived there before you did—there is a certain sentimentality involved; after all, the previous owner has earlier rights to the place, even if he is dead and you paid for the house, and an attempt to chase him away may create a sense of guilt in some sensitive souls. However, as often as not, the spectral personality has nothing to do with the house itself. The ghost may have lived in a previous dwelling standing on the spot prior to the building of the present one, or he may have come with the land and thus go back even further. This is entirely possible, because a ghost lives in his own environment, meaning that the past is the only world he knows. In some of these cases, telling the ghost to pack up and leave to join the regular spirits on the Other Side of Life will meet resistance: after all, to the ghost you are the invader, the usurper. He was there first. But whatever the status of the phantom in the house or place, panic will not help much.

The more the current tenant of a house or apartment becomes frightened, the more the ghost derives benefit from it, because the negative nervous energy generated by the present-day inhabitants of a house can be utilized by the ghost to create physical phenomena—the so-called poltergeist disturbances, where objects move seemingly of their own volition. The best thing to do is to consider the ghost a fellow human being, albeit in trouble, and perhaps not in his right mind. Ghosts have to be dealt with compassionately and with understanding; they have to be *persuaded* to leave, not forcefully ejected.

Mrs. Sally S. lived in what was then a nice section of Brooklyn, half an hour from Manhattan and, at the time of the happenings I am about to report, was semi-retired, working two days a week at her old trade of being a secretary. A year after the first phenomena occurred, she moved away to Long Island, not because of her ghostly experiences, but because the neighborhood had become too noisy for her: ghosts she could stand, human disturbances were too much.

Miss S. moved into her Brooklyn apartment in May of the same year. At first, it seemed nice and quiet. Then, on August 3, she had an unusual experience. It must have been around three A.M. when she awoke with an uncanny feeling that she was not alone. In the semi-darkness of her apartment, she looked around and had the distinct impression that there was an intruder in her place. She looked out into the room, and in the semi-darkness saw what appeared to be a dark figure. It was a man, and though she could not make out any features, he seemed tall and as lifelike as any human intruder might be.

Thinking that it was best for her to play possum, she lay still and waited for the intruder to leave. Picture her shock and surprise when the figure approached her and started to touch her quilt cover. About fifteen minutes prior to this experience, she had herself awakened because she was cold, and had pulled the cover over herself. Thus she was very much awake when the "intruder" appeared to her. She lay still, trembling, watching his every move. Suddenly he vanished into thin air, and it was only then that Miss S. realized she wasn't dealing with any flesh and blood person, but a ghost.

A month later, again around three A.M., Miss S. awoke to see a white figure gliding back and forth in her room. This time, however, she was somewhat sleepy, so she did not feel like doing much about it. However, when the figure came close to her bed, she stuck our her arm to touch it, and at that moment it dissolved into thin air. Wondering who the ghost might be, Miss S. had had another opportunity to observe it in November, when around six A.M. she went into her kitchen to see the dark outline of a six-foot-tall man standing in the archway between the kitchen and dinette. She looked away for a moment, and then returned her gaze to the spot. The apparition was still there. Once more Miss S. closed her eyes and looked away, and when she returned her eyes to the spot, he was gone.

She decided to speak to her landlady about the incidents. No one had died in the house, nor had there been any tragedy to the best of her knowledge, the owner of the house assured her. As for a previous owner, she wouldn't know. Miss S. realized that it was her peculiar psychic talent that made the phenomena possible. For some time now she had been able to predict the results of horse races with uncanny accuracy, getting somewhat of a reputation in this area. Even during her school days, she came up with answers she had not yet been taught. In April of the next year, Miss S. visited her sister and her husband in New Jersey. They had bought a house the year before, and knew nothing of its history. Sally was assigned a finished room in the attic. Shortly after two A.M., a ghost appeared to her in that room. But before she could make out any details, the figure vanished. By now Miss S. knew that she had a talent for such things, and preferred not to talk about them with her sister, a somewhat nervous individual. But she kept wondering who the ghost at *her* house was.

Fourteen years earlier, a close friend named John had passed away. A year before, he had given her two nice fountain pens as gifts, and Miss S. had kept one at home, and used the other at her office. A year after her friend's death, she was using one of the pens in the office when the point broke. Because she couldn't use it anymore, she put the pen into her desk drawer. Then she left the office for a few minutes. When she returned, she found a lovely, streamlined black pen on top of her desk. She immediately inquired whether any of the girls had left it there, but no one had, nor had anyone been near her desk. The pen was a rather expensive Mont Blanc, just the thing she needed. It made her wonder whether her late friend John had not presented her with it even from the Beyond.

This belief was reinforced by an experience she had had on the first anniversary of his passing, when she heard his voice loud and clear calling her "sweetheart"—the name he had always used to address her, rather than her given name, Sally.

All this ran through her head fourteen years later, when she tried to come to terms with her ghostly experiences. Was the ghost someone who came with the house, someone who had been there before, or was it someone who somehow linked up with her? Then Sally began to put two and two together. She was in the habit of leaving her feet outside her quilt cover because the room was rather warm with the heat on. However, in the course of the night, the temperature in the room fell, and frequently her feet became almost frostbitten as a result. One Saturday night in March, the same year she visited her sister, she was still awake, lying in bed around eleven P.M. Her feet were sticking out of the quilt, as the temperature was still tolerable. Suddenly she felt a terrific tug on her quilt; it was first raised from above her ankles, and then pulled down to cover her feet. Yet, she saw no one actually doing it.

Suddenly she remembered how her late friend John had been in the habit of covering her feet when she had fallen asleep after one of his visits with her. Evidently he was still concerned that Sally should not get cold feet or worse, and had decided to watch over her in this manner.

Mrs. I.B. was a recently married young wife, expecting a baby some months later. She and her husband were looking for a furnished apartment. They had picked their favorite neighborhood, and decided to just look around until they saw a sign saying "Apartment for Rent." At the time, this was still possible. They stopped into a candy store in the area and asked the owner if he knew of a vacant apartment. As they were speaking to the owner of the store, a young soldier who had been standing in the rear of the store, and had overheard the conversation, came over to them. He informed them that he had an apartment across the street from the store. When they inquired why he offered them the apartment, the soldier very quietly explained that he had come home to bury his wife. In his absence abroad, she had gone on a diet and, because of a weakened condition, had suddenly passed away. It had been the soldier's intention to live with her in the apartment after he returned from service. Under the circumstances, Mr. and Mrs. B. could have it until he returned, for he still wanted to live in it eventually.

This was agreeable to the young couple, especially as the apartment was handsomely furnished. A deal was quickly made, and that very night Mr. and Mrs. B. went to sleep in the bedroom of the apartment, with nothing special on their minds.

At four-thirty A.M., Mr. B. got up to go to work while his wife was still fast asleep. It was around five when she heard someone running around in the room, in what sounded like bare feet. The noise awoke her, and as she looked up, Mrs. B. saw at the foot of her bed the figure of a very pretty young woman wearing a nightgown.

Mrs. B. had no idea who the stranger might be, but thought that the young woman had somehow wandered into the apartment and asked her what she wanted. Instead of answering her, however, the young girl simply disappeared into thin air.

Mrs. B. flew into a panic. Dressing in haste, she left the apartment while it was still dark outside and took refuge in her mother's home. Nobody would believe her story, not her mother, not her husband, and, because Mrs. B. was pregnant at the time, her condition was blamed for the "hallucination." Reluctantly, Mrs. B. went back to the apartment the following evening. Shortly after her husband left for work, again early in the morning, Mrs. B. was awakened by the same apparition. This time Mrs. B. did not run out of the house, but instead closed her eyes; eventually the figure faded.

As soon as she was fully awake the next day, Mrs. B. determined to try and find out who the ghost might have been. Going through the various drawers in the apartment, she came across some photo albums belonging to the soldier. Leafing through them, she gave out a startled cry when her eyes fell on a photograph of the soldier, wearing plain clothes, with the very woman next to him whom she had seen early in the morning! Now Mrs. B. knew that she hadn't imagined the experiences. She showed the album to her husband, feeling that she had been visited by the soldier's dead wife. This time her husband was somewhat more impressed, and it was decided to obtain the "services" of a dog Mrs. B. had grown up with.

That night, the dog slept at the foot of her bed, as she had done many times before Mrs. B. was married. This made Mrs. B. feel a lot safer, but early in the morning she was awakened by her dog. The animal was standing on the foot of her bed, growling at the same spot where Mrs. B. had seen the apparition. The dog's fur was bristling on her back, and it was obvious that the animal was thoroughly scared.

But Mrs. B. did not see the ghost this time. It occurred to her that the ghost might resent her sleeping in what was once the bride's bed, so she and her husband exchanged beds the following night. From that moment on, the apparition did not return in the early mornings, and gradually, Mrs. B. got over her fear. A few weeks passed; then she noticed that in the kitchen some cups would fall off the shelf of their own volition whenever she tried to cook a meal. Then the clock fell off the wall by itself, and it became clear to her that objects were moved about by unseen hands. Some of this happened in the presence of her husband, who was no longer skeptical about it.

He decided it was time for them to move on. He wrote to the soldier, informing him that he was turning the apartment back to the landlord so that he could have it for himself again upon his return. Undoubtedly, that was exactly what the ghostly woman had wanted in the first place. . . .

Not all ghostly visitors are necessarily frightening or negative influences. Take the case of Mrs. M. N. One October, she signed a lease for a lovely old house on Commerce Street in New York's Greenwich Village. Legend had it that the house had been built by Washington Irving, although nothing was offered to substantiate this claim. It was a charming small white house, with three stories and a basement. It had five steps leading up from the street, and was guarded by wrought iron rails. On the first floor there was a narrow hallway, with stairs to the right; then came the living room, to the left, running the full depth of the house. The second story contained the master bedroom, with a bath and a small room, possibly used as a dressing room originally. On the third floor were three small bedrooms with dormer windows and a bathroom.

Mrs. N. loved the house like a friend; and because she was then going through a personal crisis in her life, a group of friends had gathered around her and moved into the house with her. These were people much younger than she, who had decided to share the old house with her. Before actually moving into the house, Mrs. N. made the acquaintance of a neighbor, who was astonished at her having taken this particular house.

"For goodness' sake," the neighbor said, "why are you moving in *there*? Don't you know that place is haunted?"

Mrs. N. and her friends laughed at the thought, having not the slightest belief in the supernatural. Several days before the furniture was to be moved into the house, the little group gathered in the bare living room, lit their first fire in the fireplace, and dedicated the house with prayers. It so happened that they were all followers of the Baha'i faith, and they felt that this was the best way to create a harmonious atmosphere in what was to be their home.

They had been in the empty living room for perhaps an hour, praying and discussing the future, when suddenly there was a knock on the door. Dick, one of the young people who was nearest the door, went to answer the knock. There was no one there. It was a brilliant, moonlit night, and the whole of little Commerce Street was empty. Shaking his head, Dick went back into the room, but fifteen minutes later somebody knocked again. Again, there was no one outside, and the knocking sounded once more that night. Just the same, they moved in and almost immediately heard the footsteps of an unseen person. There were six in the house at the time: Kay sleeping on the couch in the basement dining room, Dick on a huge divan in the living room, Mrs. N. in the master bedroom on the second floor, and her fifteen-year-old daughter Barbara in one of the dormer bedrooms; Evie was in the second room and Bruce in the third. The first time they heard the steps, they were all at dinner in the basement dining room. The front door, which was locked, opened and closed by itself, and footsteps went into the living room where they seemed to circle the room, pausing now and again, and then continuing.

Immediately Dick went upstairs to investigate, and found there was no one about. Despite this, they felt no sense of alarm. Somehow they knew that their ghost was benign. From that moment on, the footsteps of an unseen person became part of their lives. They were heard going upstairs and downstairs, prowling the living room, but somehow they never entered one of the bedrooms. Once in awhile they heard the opening and then a loud slamming of the front door. They checked, but there was nobody to be seen, and eventually they realized that whoever it was who was sharing the house with them preferred to remain unseen.

Since there were no other uncanny phenomena, the group accepted the presence of a ghost in their midst without undue alarm. One night, however, they had invited a group of Baha'i Youth to stay with them, and as a result, Mrs. N. had to sleep on the couch in the basement dining room. It turned into a night of sheer terror for her; she didn't see anything, but somehow the terror was all about her like a thick fog. She didn't sleep a moment that night. The following morning, Mrs. N. queried Kay, who ordinarily slept on the basement couch, as to whether she had had a similar experience. She had not. However, a few days later, Kay reported a strange dream she had had while occupying the same couch.

She had been awakened by the opening of the area-way door. Startled, she had sat up in bed and watched fascinated as a band of Indians came through the door, moved along the end of the dining room, went through the kitchen and out the back door again, where she could hear their feet softly scuffing the dead leaves! They paid no attention to her at all, but she was able to observe that they were in full war paint.

Since Kay had a lively imagination, Mrs. N. was inclined to dismiss the story. As there were no further disturbances, the matter of the ghost receded into the back of their minds. About a year after they had moved into the house, some of the little group were leaving town and the household was being broken up. It was a week before they were to part when Mrs. N. had an early morning train to catch and, not having an alarm clock herself, had asked Dick to set his for six A.M. and wake her.

Promptly at six A.M. there was a knock at her door, to which Mrs. N. responded with thanks and just as promptly went back to sleep. A few minutes later, there was a second knock on the door, and this time Mrs. N. replied that she was already getting up. Later she thanked her friend for waking her, and he looked at her somewhat sheepishly, asking her not to rub it in, for he hadn't heard the alarm at all. It appears that he had slept through the appointed hour and not awakened Mrs. N. as promised.

However, the friendly ghost had seen to it that she didn't miss her morning train. Was it the same benign spectre who had shielded them from the hostile

Indians during their occupancy? That is, if the "dream" of Indians in war paint belonged to the past of the house, and was not merely an expression of a young girl's fancy.

Adriana Victoria is a spunky, adventurous lady of Mexican ancestry, of whom I have written before. At one time she worked as a housekeeper in a Hollywood mansion that was once the property of the noted actress Carole Lombard. One night, Adriana awoke to see the blood-stained body of the actress standing by her bed, as if begging for attention. . . . By then Adriana knew that she was psychic, she knew that her mother was psychic also, and that this particular talent ran in the family. She accepted it as something perfectly natural and learned to live with it, although at times she underwent frightening experiences that were not easily forgotten.

Miss Victoria now lived in an apartment in New York City, which consisted of two-and-a-half rooms. In view of the small size of the apartment, it was something of a problem to put up her mother and her two children who were then living with her; but Adriana managed somehow, when they came for a visit to New York in the summer of that year. They were on their way from Florida to Europe, and were staying for only a few days.

Since there was little room for everybody, they put a mattress on the living room floor. One night Miss Victoria, sleeping on the mattress, was awakened by two invisible hands that she saw only in her mind's eye. At the same time, she was shaken strongly by the ankles and opened her eyes wide. She couldn't see any intruder, and didn't dare wake the others in the apartment. But nothing further happened until the end of the summer, when her mother left with her granddaughter, leaving Miss Victoria's nine-year-old son at home.

About two months later, Miss Victoria was doing the dishes after dinner, and a girlfriend from an apartment in the same building was watching television while waiting for her to finish with the dishes. Suddenly her son came running in and locked himself into the bathroom next to the kitchen, as if he were frightened by something. Before she could figure out what was happening, Miss Victoria heard heavy footsteps coming from the living room in the direction of the kitchen, and stopping right behind her. Quickly, she turned around, but her friend was still sitting on the living room couch watching TV. Obviously she hadn't heard the footsteps.

With her friend in the living room on the couch, and her nine-year-old son in the bathroom, there was no one present who could have caused the footsteps. Besides, they were heavy, like those of a man. That same night, Adriana entered her bedroom. Her bed stood against the wall with a night table on either side of it. Suddenly she saw the figure of a woman standing next to her bed, moving her hands as if she were trying to get some papers or letters in a hurry.

As Adriana watched in fascinated horror, the apparition was putting imaginary things down from the night table onto the bed. There were some real books on the night table, but they did not move. Standing at the entrance to the room, Adriana looked at the apparition: she could see right through her, but was able to make out that the woman had brown hair down to her shoulders, stood about five feet two or three, and seemed to be about thirty years old. When Adriana made a move towards the bed, the figure looked up and straight at her—then vanished before her very eyes. A little later, Adriana's little boy came to sleep with her, and of course she did not tell him about the apparition. Evidently, the child had heard the footsteps too, and there was no need to frighten him further. The following evening around nine o'clock, the boy complained about being frightened by footsteps again. It was difficult for Adriana to explain them to her son, but she tried to calm his fears. The ghost reappeared from time to time, always in the same spot, always looking for some papers or seeming so, and not necessarily at night: there were times when Adriana saw her standing by her bed in plain daylight.

In July of the following year, Adriana had to go into the hospital for a minor operation. She asked a Spanish-speaking lady, a neighbor, to stay with her son for the four days Adriana was to be in the hospital. The babysitter left the bedroom to the boy and slept on the couch herself.

When Adriana returned from the hospital on the fifth day, the babysitter grabbed her by the hand and rushed her into the bedroom, for she didn't want to talk in front of the boy. She was absolutely terrified. It seems that the previous night, she was awakened toward three in the morning by heavy footsteps right next to her. She was sure that it was a man, and heard him bump into a chair! Frightened, she screamed and called out, "Who's there?" but there was no answer. Through all this the boy had slept soundly.

She turned on the lights, and noticed that the chair had been moved a little from where it had stood before. That was enough for her! She crawled into bed with the little boy—and decided never to stay in the apartment overnight again, unless Adriana was there also.

Adriana decided to make some inquiries about the past occupants of her apartment, but all she could ascertain was that two nurses had lived there for about eight years. The building is very old and has a long history, so it may well be that one or more tragedies had taken place in what is now Adriana's apartment.

Adriana found herself invited to a Christmas party, and somehow the conversation drifted to ghosts. Her host did not believe in such things, and doubted

Adriana's experiences. When they brought her back to her apartment, Adriana invited them in. She was just bending down trying to open a bottle of soda when she suddenly heard those heavy footsteps again, coming from the bedroom and stopping right at the entrance to the living room. At the same time, the thought crossed her mind that it was like a husband, waking from sleep to greet his wife returning from a party. Somehow this terrified her, and she let out a loud scream. That night she stayed with friends.

After her son left in July of the following year, things seemed to quiet down a little. One night, shortly afterward, around six P.M., Adriana returned home from work. As soon as she opened the door, she could smell burned papers. Immediately she checked the kitchen, where everything seemed in order. Suddenly she realized that she could smell the strange smell better in her mind than with her nose. At the same time a thought crossed her mind, "My lady ghost finally found the papers and burned them." Adriana knew that they were love letters, and that all was right now with her ghost. There were no further disturbances after that.

Some ghostly invasions have a way of snowballing from seemingly quiet beginnings into veritable torrents of terror. Mrs. C. of North Dakota is a housewife with an eight-year-old daughter, a husband who does not believe in ghosts or anything of that nature. They live in an old house that would be a comfortable, roomy house if it weren't for—*them*. Mrs. C. and her family moved into the house in 1970. Whether it was because both she and her husband worked at different times, thus being absent from the house a great deal of the time, or whether the unseen forces had not yet gathered enough strength to manifest, nothing of an uncanny nature occurred until January, 1973.

One day during January, Mrs. C. was working in the basement, washing some clothes. All of a sudden she heard someone whistle; no definite tune, just one long whistle repeated several times. Immediately her dog, Pud, ran around the basement to see where the noise came from, but neither Mrs. C. nor her dog could find the origin of the whistle.

The whistling continued on several occasions during the month, and while it seemed puzzling, it did not upset her greatly. At the time she was working nights, returning home between midnight and one A.M. One night during February, she returned home, and as soon as she had entered the house, had a very strange feeling of being watched by someone. At the same time it became freezing cold, and the hair on her arms stood up. She looked all over the house but found no intruder, nothing human that could account for the strange feeling.

Mrs. C. decided to prepare for bed, and changed clothes in the kitchen as was her custom, in order not to wake her husband who was already asleep.

She then went toward the bedroom in semi-darkness, with the lights off but sufficiently illuminated to make out the details of the room. All of a sudden, about a foot and a half in front of her face and a little over her head, she noticed a smoky, whitish-gray haze. To her horror, she saw that in the middle of it there was a human face without either body or neck. It was the head of a bald man, very white, with distinctive black eyes and a very ugly face. All through it and around it was this strange white fog. Mrs. C. had never seen anything like it and became very frightened. She dashed into the bedroom, not sure whether the whole thing had been her imagination, and eventually fell asleep. The next day, the whistling returned and continued all month long. This was followed by a mumbling human voice, at first one person, then later two people speaking. Both she and her seven-year-old daughter heard it. At first the mumbling was heard only in the daytime; later it switched to nighttime as well.

At the time, Mrs. C.'s husband left for work at four o'clock in the morning, and she was in the habit of sleeping on till about eight. But now she could not; as soon as her husband had left for work the mumbling would start, always in the bedroom and seemingly coming from the foot of the bed. It then moved to the side of the bed opposite where she slept, then back to the foot of the bed again, directly in front of her feet. She tried hard not to pay any attention to it, and after listening to it for awhile, managed to fall asleep. Soon it sounded as if several women and one man were speaking, perhaps as many as four individuals. This continued every morning until April of that year. Then something new was added to the torment: something that sounded like a faint growling noise.

The growling was the last straw. Mrs. C. became very frightened and decided to do something to protect herself. She recalled a small cross her husband had given her the previous Christmas. Now she put the cross and chain around her neck, never taking it off again.

Mrs. C. loves animals. At the time of the haunting, the family owned two parakeets, six guinea pigs, two dogs and two cats. Since the uncanny events had started in her house, she had kept a day-to-day diary of strange happenings, not because she hoped to convince her husband of the reality of the phenomena, but to keep her own sanity and counsel. On May 5, 1973, Mrs. C. awoke and found her blue parakeet dead, horribly disfigured in its cage; the green parakeet next to it acted as if it were insane, running back and forth all day, screaming. The following day, May 6, Mrs. C. awoke to find the green bird dead, destroyed in exactly the same way as the first parakeet had been.

Four days later, as she was washing her hair, Mrs. C. felt the chain with the cross being lifted up from the back of her neck by an unseen hand and unclasped, then dropped to the floor. When she turned around, there was no one in back of her. Still shaken, she left her house at nine-thirty to do some errands. When she returned at eleven o'clock, she found one of her guinea pigs lying on the living room floor, flopping its head in a most pitiful fashion. A short time later the animal died. Its neck had been broken by an unseen force. No one had been in the house at the time, as her daughter and a friend who had slept over had accompanied Mrs. C. on her errands. What made the incident even more grisly was the fact that the guinea pig had been kept in a cage, that the cage was locked, and that the key rested safely in Mrs. C.'s cigarette case that she took when she went out of the house.

Two weeks passed. On May 25, while taking a bath, Mrs. C. felt the necklace with the cross being lifted up into the air from the back of her neck and pulled so hard that it snapped and fell into the tub. This was the beginning of a day of terror. During the night, the two children heard frightening noises down in the basement, which kept them from sleeping. Mrs. C., exhausted from the earlier encounters, had slept so deeply she had not heard them. The children reported that the dogs had growled all night and that they had heard the meowing of the cats as well.

Mrs. C. went downstairs to check on things. The dogs lay asleep as if exhausted; the cats were not there, but were upstairs by now; on the floor, scattered all over the basement, lay the remaining guinea pigs except for one. That one was alive and well in its cage, but two others lay dead inside their cage, which was still locked and intact. Their bodies were bloody and presented a horrible sight—fur all torn off, eyes gone and bodies torn apart. At first, Mrs. C. thought that the dogs might have attacked them, but soon realized that they could not have done so inside the animals' cages.

For a few days, things quieted down somewhat. One morning, the ominous growling started again while Mrs. C. was still in bed. Gradually, the growling noise became louder and louder, as if it were getting closer. This particular morning the growling had started quietly, but when it reached a deafening crescendo, Mrs. C. heard over it a girl's voice speak quite plainly, "No, don't hurt her! Don't hurt her!" The growling continued, nevertheless. Then, as Mrs. C. looked on in horror, someone unseen sat down in front of her feet on the bed, for the bed sank down appreciably from the weight of the unseen person.

Then the spectral visitor moved up closer and closer in the bed towards her, while the growling became louder. Accompanying it was the girl's voice, "No, no! Don't do it!" That was enough for Mrs. C. Like lightning, she jumped out of bed and ran into the kitchen and sat down trembling. But the growling followed her from the bedroom, started into the living room across from the kitchen, then went back to the bedroom—and suddenly stopped.

That was the last time Mrs. C. slept on in the morning after her husband left for work. From that moment on she got up with him, got dressed, and sat in the kitchen until the children got up, between seven-thirty and nine A.M.

About that time they heard the sound of water running, both at night and in the morning upon arising. Even her husband heard it now and asked her to find out where it was coming from. On checking the bathroom, kitchen, upstairs sink, basement bathroom and laundry room, Mr. and Mrs. C. concluded that the source of the running water was invisible.

From time to time they heard the sound of dishes being broken and crashing, and furniture being moved with accompanying loud noise. Yet when they looked for the damage, nothing had been touched, nothing broken.

At the beginning of the summer of 1973, Mrs. C. had a sudden cold feeling and suddenly felt a hand on her neck coming around from behind her, and she could actually feel fingers around her throat! She tried to swallow and felt as if she were being choked. The sensation lasted just long enough to cause her great anxiety, then it went away as quickly as it had come.

Some of the phenomena were now accompanied by rapping on the walls, with the knocks taking on an intelligent pattern, as if someone were trying to communicate with them. Doorknobs would rattle by themselves or turn themselves, even though there was no one on the other side of them. All over the house footsteps were heard. One particular day, when Mrs. C. was sitting in the kitchen with her daughter, all the doors in the house began to rattle. This was followed by doors all over the house opening and slamming shut by themselves, and the drapes in the living room opening wide and closing quickly, as if someone were pulling them back and forth. Then the window shades in the kitchen went up and down again, and windows opened by themselves, going up, down, up, down in all the rooms, crashing as they fell down without breaking.

It sounded as if all hell had broken loose in the house. At the height of this nightmare, the growling started up again in the bedroom. Mrs. C. and her little daughter sat on the bed and stared towards where they thought the growling came from. Suddenly Mrs. C. could no longer talk, no matter how she tried; not a word came from her mouth. It was clear to her that something extraordinary was taking place. Just as the phenomena reached the height of fury, everything stopped dead silent, and the house was quiet again.

Thus far only Mrs. C. and her little daughter shared the experiences, for her husband was not only a skeptic but prided himself on being an atheist.

No matter how pressing the problem was, Mrs. C. could not unburden herself to him.

One night, when the couple returned from a local stock car race and had gone to bed, the mumbling voices started up again. Mrs. C. said nothing in order not to upset her husband, but the voices became louder. All of a sudden Mr. C. asked, "What is that?" and when she informed him that those were the ghostly voices she had been hearing all along, he chided her for being so silly. But *he* had heard them *also*. A few days later Mr. C. told his wife he wanted a cross similar to the one she was wearing. Since his birthday was coming up, she bought one for him as a gift. From that moment on, Mr. C. also always wore a necklace with a cross on it.

In despair Mrs. C. turned to her brother, who had an interest in occult matters. Together with him and her young brother-in-law, Mrs. C. went downstairs one night in August to try and lay the ghosts to rest. In a halting voice, her brother spoke to the unseen entities, asking them to speak up or forever hold their peace. There was no immediate response. The request to make their presence felt was repeated several times.

All of a sudden, all hell broke loose again. Rattling and banging in the walls started up around them, and the sound of walking on the basement steps was clearly heard by the three of them. Mrs. C.'s brother started up the stairs and, as he did so, he had the chill impression of a man standing there.

Perhaps the formula of calling out the ghosts worked, because the house has been quiet since then. Sometimes Mrs. C. looks back on those terrible days and nights, and wishes it had happened to someone else, and not her. But the empty cages where her pet animals had been kept are a grim reminder that it had all been only too true.

Mrs. J.H. is a housewife living in Maryland. At the time of the incidents I am about to report, her son Richard was seven and her daughter Cheryl, six. Hers was a conventional marriage, until the tragic death of her husband Frank. On September 3, he was locking up a restaurant where he was employed near Washington, D.C. Suddenly, two men entered by the rear door and shot him while attempting a robbery. For more than a year after the murder, no clue as to the murderers' identities was found by the police.

Mrs. H. was still grieving over the sudden loss of her husband when something extraordinary took place in her home. Exactly one month to the day of his death, she happened to be in her living room when she saw a "wall of light" and something floated across the living room towards her. From it stepped the person of her late husband Frank. He seemed quite real to her, but somewhat transparent. Frightened, the widow turned on the lights and the apparition faded.

From that moment on, the house seemed to be alive with strange phenomena: knocks at the door which disclosed no one who could have caused them, the dog barking for no good reason in the middle of the night, or the cats staring as if they were looking at a definite person in the room. Then one day the two children went into the bathroom and saw their dead father taking a shower! Needless to say, Mrs. H. was at a loss to explain that to them. The widow had placed all of her late husband's clothes into an unused closet that was kept locked. She was the last one to go to bed at night and the first one to arise in the morning, and one morning she awoke to find Frank's shoes in the hallway; nobody could have placed them there.

One day Mrs. H.'s mother, Mrs. D. who lives nearby, was washing clothes in her daughter's basement. When she approached the washer, she noticed that it was spotted with what appeared to be fresh blood. Immediately she and the widow searched the basement, looking for a possible leak in the ceiling to account for the blood, but they found nothing. Shortly afterwards, a sister of the widow arrived to have lunch at the house. A fresh tablecloth was placed on the table. When the women started to clear the table after lunch, they noticed that under each dish there was a blood spot the size of a fifty-cent piece. Nothing they had eaten at lunch could possibly have accounted for such a stain.

But the widow's home was not the only place where manifestations took place. Her mother's home was close by, and one night a clock radio alarm went off by itself in a room that had not been entered by anyone for months. It was the room belonging to Mrs. H.'s grandmother, who had been in the hospital for some time before.

It became clear to Mrs. H. that her husband was trying to get in touch with her, since the phenomena continued at an unabated pace. Three years after his death, two alarm clocks in the house went off at the same time, although they had not been set, and all the kitchen cabinets flew open by themselves. The late Frank H. appeared to his widow punctually on the third of each month, the anniversary of the day he was murdered, but the widow could not bring herself to address him and ask him what he wanted. Frightened, she turned on the light, which caused him to fade away. In the middle of the night Mrs. H. would feel someone shake her shoulder, as if to wake her up. She recognized this touch as that of her late husband, for it had been his habit to wake her in just that manner.

Meanwhile the murderers were caught. Unfortunately, by one of those strange quirks of justice, they got off very lightly, one of the murderers with three years in prison, the other with ten. It seemed like a very light sentence for having taken a man's life so deliberately.

Time went on, and the children were ten and eleven years of age, respectively. Mrs. H. could no longer take the phenomena in the house and moved out. The house was rented to strangers who are still living in it. They have had no experiences of an uncanny nature since, after all, Frank wants nothing from *them.*

As for the new house where Mrs. H. and her children live now, Frank has not put in an appearance as of yet. But there are occasional tappings on the wall, as if he still wanted to communicate with his wife. Mrs. H. wishes she could sleep in peace in the new home, but then she remembers how her late husband, who had been a believer in scientology, had assured her that when he died, he would be back. . . .

Alice H. is sixty-nine years old, and lives in a five-room bungalow flat in the Middle West. She still works part-time as a saleswoman, but lives alone. Throughout her long life she never had any real interest in psychic phenomena. She even went to a spiritualist meeting with a friend and was not impressed one way or another. She was sixty-two when she had her first personal encounter with the unknown.

One night she went to bed and awoke because something was pressing against her back. Since she knew herself to be alone in the apartment, it frightened her. Nevertheless, she turned around to look—and to her horror she saw the upper part of her late husband's body. As she stared at him, he glided over the bed, turned to look at her once more with a mischievous look in his eye, and disappeared on the other side of the bed. Mrs. H. could not figure out why he had appeared to her, because she had not been thinking of him at that time. But evidently he was to instigate her further psychic experiences.

Not much later, she had another manifestation that shook her up a great deal. She had been sound asleep when she was awakened by the whimpering of her dog. The dog, a puppy, was sleeping on top of the covers of the bed. Mrs. H. was fully awake now and looked over her shoulder where stood a young girl of about ten years, in the most beautiful shade of blue tailored pajamas that had a T-pattern. She was looking at the dog. As Mrs. H. looked closer, she noticed that the child had neither face nor hands nor feet showing. Shaken, she jumped out of bed and went toward the spirit. The little girl moved back toward the wall, and Mrs. H. followed her. As the little girl in the blue pajamas neared the wall, it somehow changed into a beautiful flower garden with a wide path!

She walked down the path in a mechanical sort of way, with the wide cuffs of her pajamas showing, but still with no feet. Nevertheless, it was a happy walk, then it all disappeared.

The experience bothered Mrs. H. so she moved into another room. But her little dog stayed on in the room where the experience had taken place, sleeping on the floor under the bed. That first experience took place on a Sunday in October, at four A.M. The following Sunday, again at four o'clock, Mrs. H. heard the dog whimper, as if he were conscious of a presence. By the time she reached the other room, however, she could not see anything. These experiences continued for some time, always on Sunday at four in the morning. It then became clear to Mrs. H. that the little girl hadn't come for her in particular—but only to visit her little dog.

Mrs. S.F. works in an assembly plant, putting together electronic parts. She is a middle-aged woman of average educational background, is divorced, and is living in a house in central Pennsylvania. A native of Pittsburgh, she went to public school in that city where her father worked for a steel company, and she has several brothers and sisters.

When she was fourteen years of age, she had her first remembered psychic experience. In the old house her parents then lived in, she saw a column of white smoke in front of her, but since she didn't understand it, it didn't bother her, and she went off to sleep anyway.

Many times she would get impressions of future events and foretell things long before they happened, but she paid little attention to her special gift. It was only when she moved into her present house that the matter took on new dimensions.

The house Mrs. F. moved into is a small house, two stories high, connected to two similar houses by what is locally called a party wall, in which two houses share the same wall. Two rooms are downstairs and two rooms are upstairs. Her house has its bathroom down in the cellar, and when you first enter it, you are in the living room, then the kitchen. Upstairs there are two bedrooms, with the stairs going up from the kitchen. There is no attic; the house is small and compact, and it was just the thing Mrs. F. needed since she was going to live in it alone. The house next door was similar to hers, and it belonged to a woman whose husband had passed away some time previously. Next to that was another similar house in which some of the widowed woman's family lived at the time Mrs. F. moved in. There were four houses in all, all identical and connected by "party walls." The four houses share a common ground, and seemed rather old to her when she first saw them.

When Mrs. F. moved into the house, she decided to sleep in the bedroom in back of the upper story and she put her double bed into it. But after she had moved into the house, she discovered that the back room was too cold in the winter and too hot in the summer, so she decided to sleep in the front room, which had twin beds in it. Depending upon the temperature, she would switch from one bedroom to the other. Nothing much out of the ordinary happened to her at first, or perhaps she was too busy to notice.

Then one spring night, when she was asleep in the back bedroom, she woke from her sound sleep around four o'clock in the morning. Her eyes were open, and as she looked up, she saw a man bending over her, close to her face. She could see that he had a ruddy complexion, a high forehead, and was partly bald with white hair around his ears.

When he noticed that she was looking at him, he gave her a cold stare and then slowly drifted back away from her until he disappeared. She could not see the rest of his body, but had the vague impression of some sort of robe. Immediately Mrs. F. thought she had had a hallucination or had dreamt the whole thing, so she went back to sleep.

Not much later Mrs. F. was in bed, reading. It was around two-thirty in the morning. The reading lamp was on, as was the light in the hall, when she suddenly heard a swish-like sound followed by a thump. At the same time something punched her bed, and then hit her in the head. She clearly felt a human hand in the area of her eye, but could not see anything. Immediately, she wondered, what could have hit her? There was no one in the room but her. After a while, she dismissed the matter from her mind and went back to reading.

A few days later, when she was reading again in the late hours of the night, she noticed that the bed would go down as if someone had sat on it. It clearly showed the indentation of a human body, yet she could not see anything. This disturbed her, but she decided to pay it no attention—until one night she also heard a man's voice coming to her as if from an echo chamber. It sounded as if someone were trying to talk to her but couldn't get the words out properly, like a muffled "hello."

Mrs. F. never felt comfortable in the back bedroom, so she decided to move into the front room. One night she was in bed in that room, when her eyes apparently opened by themselves and rested on a cupboard door across from the bed. This time she clearly saw the figure of a man, but she couldn't make out legs or feet. It was a dark silhouette of a man, but she could clearly see his rather pointed ears. His most outstanding features were his burning eyes and those strangely pointed ears. When he saw her looking at him, he moved back into the door and disappeared.

Again, Mrs. F. refused to acknowledge that she had a ghost, but thought it was all a hallucination since she had been awakened from a deep sleep. Not much later, she happened to be watching television a little after midnight because her work ended at twelve. She felt like getting some potato chips from a cupboard in the corner, and as she got up to get the potato chips and rounded the bend of the hall, she happened to glance at the wall in the hallway. There was the same man again. She could clearly make out his face and the pointed ears, but again he had neither legs nor feet. As soon as the ghost realized that she had discovered him, he quickly moved back into the wall and disappeared. Now Mrs. F.'s composure was gone; clearly, the apparition was not a hallucination, since she was fully awake now and could not blame her dreams for it.

While she was still debating within herself what this all meant, she had another experience. She happened to be in bed reading when she thought she heard something move in the kitchen. It sounded like indistinct movements, so she tried to listen, but after awhile she didn't hear anything further and went back to reading. A little while later she decided to go down to get a fruit drink out of the refrigerator. The hall lights were on, so the kitchen wasn't too dark. Just the same, when she reached the kitchen, Mrs. F. turned on the fluorescent lights. As soon as the lights came on, she saw the same ghostly apparition standing there in the kitchen, only this time there was a whole view of him, with feet, legs, and even shoes with rounded toes. He wore pants and a shirt, and she could see his color; she could see that he had curly hair, a straight nose, and full lips. She particularly noticed the full lips, and, of course, the pointed ears.

At first the apparition must have been startled by her, perhaps because he had thought that it was the cat coming down the stairs into the kitchen. He turned towards her and Mrs. F. could see his profile. As soon as he noticed her, he ran into the wall and disappeared. But she noticed that his legs started to shake when the lights went on, as if he were trying to get going and didn't quite know how. Then he hunched over a little, and shot into the wall.

Mrs. F. was shocked. She shut off the light and went back to bed. For a long time she just lay there, with the eeriest, chilliest feeling. Eventually she drifted off to sleep again. The entire incident puzzled her, for she had no idea who the ghost might be. One day she was leaving her house, and as she passed her neighbor's house, there was a young man sitting on the steps looking out into the street. She saw his profile, and like a flash it went through her mind that it was the same profile as that of the man she had seen in her kitchen! She looked again, and noticed the same full lips and the same pointed ears she had seen in the face of the ghost!

Immediately she decided to discuss the matter with a neighbor, a Mrs. J.M. Mrs. M. lived at the end of the street, and she was a good person to talk to because she understood about such matters. In fact, Mrs. F. had spent a night at her house at one time when she was particularly upset by the goings-on in her *own* house. The neighbor assured her that the widow's son, the one she had seen sitting on the steps, was the spit and image of his father. The reason Mrs. F. had not seen him before was that he was married and lived somewhere else, and had just been visiting on that particular day.

Well, Mrs. F. put two and two together, and realized that the ghost she had seen was her late neighbor. On making further inquiries, she discovered that the man had suffered from rheumatic fever, and had been in the habit of lying on a couch to watch television. One day his family had awakened him so he wouldn't miss his favorite program. At that moment he had a heart attack, and died right there on the couch. He was only middle-aged.

With this information in her hands, Mrs. F. wondered what she could do about ridding herself of the unwelcome visitor from next door. In August a niece was visiting her with some friends and other relatives. One of the people in the group was an amateur medium, who suggested that they try their hand at a seance. There were about seven in the group, and they sat down and tried to make contact with the late neighbor. The seance was held in the upstairs bedroom, and they used a card table borrowed from Mrs. M. from the other end of the street.

They all put their hands on the table, and immediately felt that the table was rising up. Nothing much happened beyond that, however, and eventually the amateur medium had to leave. But Mrs. F. wanted an answer to her problem, so she continued with those who were still visiting with her. They moved the table down into the kitchen, turned out all the lights but one, and waited. Mrs. F. asked the ghost questions: who he was, what he wanted, etc. Sure enough, her questions were answered by knocks. Everybody could hear them, and after awhile they managed to get a conversation going. From this communication, Mrs. F. learned that her neighbor had been forty-three years old when he died, that his name was Bill, and that he wasn't very happy being dead! But apparently he appreciated the fact that they had tried to get through to him because he never appeared to Mrs. F. again after that.

Only a small fraction of ghosts are "fortunate" enough to be relieved of their status by an investigation in which they are freed from their surroundings and allowed to go into the greater reaches of the World Beyond. The majority have no choice but to cling to the environment in which their tragedy has occurred. But what about those who are in an environment that suddenly ceases to exist? As far as houses are concerned, tearing down one house and building another on the spot doesn't alter the situation much. Frequently, ghosts continue to exist in the new house, even more confused than they were in the old one. But if the environment is radically changed and no new dwelling is erected on the spot, what is there to occupy the ghost in his search for identity?

Mrs. Robert B. is a housewife and mother of four children, leading a busy life in Pittsburgh. Because of her interest in parapsychology, she was able to assist her parents in a most unusual case. In a small town north of Pittsburgh on the Ohio River, her parents occupied a house built approximately seventy-five years ago. They were the second owners, the house having been planned and partially built by the original owner, a certain Daniel W.

Mr. W. had lived in the house with his brother and sister for many years, and had died a bachelor at the age of ninety-four. His last illness was a long one, and his funeral was held in what later became the living room of Mrs. B.'s parents. Thus, Mr. W. not only "gave birth" to the little house, but he lived in it for such a long period that he must have become very attached to it, and formed one of those rare bonds that frequently lead to what I have called "Stay-Behinds," people who live and die in their houses and just don't feel like leaving them.

One spring, Mrs. B.'s parents decided to remodel the house somewhat. In particular, they tore through the wall connecting her mother's bedroom with that of her father, which was next to it. Each room had a cupboard in it, but instead they decided to build a new closet with sliding doors. Although they had occupied the house for fourteen years, this was the first change they had made in it.

One week after the alteration had been completed, Mrs. B.'s mother found it difficult to fall asleep. It was toward one o'clock in the morning and she had been tossing for hours. Suddenly, from the direction of the cupboard in the left-hand corner of the room, came the sound of heavy breathing. This startled her, as she could also hear her husband's breathing from the room next to hers. The mysterious breathing was husky, labored, and sounded as though it came from an echo chamber. Frightened, she lay still and listened. To her horror, the breathing sound moved across the room and stopped in front of the bureau against the far wall. Then, as she concentrated on that spot, she saw a mist starting to form above the chest. At this point, she managed to switch on the light and call out, "Who is there?" Immediately, the breathing stopped.

Mrs. B.'s mother then called Mrs. B., knowing of her interest in the occult, and reported the incident to her. Her daughter advised her not to be alarmed, but to watch out for further occurrences, which were bound to happen. Sure enough, a few days later a curtain was pulled back in full view of her mother, as if by an unseen hand, yet no window was open that would have accounted for it. Shortly thereafter, a chair in the living room sagged as if someone were sitting in it, yet no one was visible. That was enough for one day! A few days later, a window was lowered in the hall while Mrs. B.'s mother was talking to her on the telephone and there was no one else in the house. Shadowlike streaks began to appear on the dining room and living room floors; a Japanese print hanging in the living room, two-by-four feet in size and very heavy, moved of its own volition on the wall. Mrs. B.'s father began to hear the heavy breathing on his side of the dividing wall, but as soon as he had taken notice of it, it moved to the foot of his bed.

By now it was clear to both parents that they had a ghost in the house; they suspected the original owner. Evidently he was displeased with the alterations in the house, and this was his way of letting them know. Mr. W.'s continued presence in the house also shook up their dog. Frequently she would stand in the hall downstairs and bark in the direction of the stairs, with the hair on her back bristled, unable to move up those stairs. At times she would run through the house as if someone were chasing her—someone unseen, that is.

It looked as if Mrs. B.'s parents would have to get used to the continued presence of the original owner of the house, when the authorities decided to run a six-lane state highway through the area, eliminating about half of the little town in which they lived, including their house. This has since been done, and the house exists no more. But what about Mr. W.? If he couldn't stand the idea of minor alterations in his house, what about the six-lane highway eliminating it altogether?

Ghosts, as a rule, do not move around much. They may be seen in one part of the house or another, not necessarily in the room in which they died as people, but there are no cases on record in which ghosts have traveled any kind of distance to manifest.

5

Haunted Houses, Haunted People

THERE ARE TWO areas of the United States that the average person frequently connects with hauntings: New England and the South. Perhaps it is because these two regions are more likely to inspire romantic notions; perhaps it's because their physical appearance is more conducive to unusual phenomena than, let us say, the Plains States or the Rocky Mountains.

But it is not only the unusual and varied geographical appearance of New England and the South that is seemingly conducive to the occurrence of hauntings, but the people who live there as well. Both regions have one thing in common: they were settled at an early stage in American history, mainly from western European roots, and they share a fierce loyalty to basic nationalistic values. In New England, Yankeeland, the traditions of the mother country, England, are continued and the cultural backgrounds of the old country extended into the new. In the South, the traditions of Great Britain have been largely overshadowed by native-grown values inherent to the region, such as plantation life, the horse country appeal of the wide-open spaces, and the gentility of a closely-knit society going back several hundred years. While the "aristocracy" of New England is likely to be of the middle-class, perhaps even the lower-class such as fishermen and hereditary homesteaders, it is more often on the higher social scale in the South. This Southern Aristocracy is frequently an extension of European nobility concepts, to the point where land grants dating back to pre-Colonial days are still considered important documents, and where the changes of history are not quite able to wipe out firmly-rooted concepts of a feudal past.

The ghosts of an area are likely to reflect the people of that region; frequently, they *are* people who once lived in the region. Thus the appearances of spectres may differ greatly in New England and the South, but the degree of their involvement with the land, with traditions, and with strongly parochial points of view is very similar. For that reason I have grouped the following cases together, rather than trying to reconcile the erstwhile Civil War foes.

Mrs. Geraldine W. is a graduate of Boston City Hospital and works as a registered nurse; her husband is a teacher, and they have four children. Neither Mr. nor Mrs. W. ever had the slightest interest in the occult; in fact, Mrs. W. remembers hearing some chilling stories about ghosts as a child and considering them just so many fairy tales.

One July, the W.'s decided to acquire a house about twenty miles from Boston, as the conditions in the city seemed inappropriate for bringing up their four children. Their choice fell upon a Victorian home sitting on a large rock that overlooked a golf course in this little town. Actually, there are two houses built next door to each other by two brothers. The one to the left had originally been used as a winter residence, while the other, upon which their choice fell, was used as a summer home. It presented a remarkable sight, high above the other houses in the area. The house so impressed the W.'s that they immediately expressed their interest in buying it. They were told that it had once formed part of the H. estate, and had remained in the same family until nine years prior to their visit. Originally built by a certain Ephraim Hamblin, it had been sold to the H. family and remained a family property until it passed into the hands of a family initialed P. It remained in their possession until the W.'s acquired it that spring.

Prior to obtaining possession of the house, Mrs. W. had a strange dream in which she saw herself standing in the driveway, looking up at the house. In the dream she had a terrible feeling of foreboding, as if something dreadful had happened in the house. On awakening the next morning, however, she thought no more about it and later put it out of her mind.

Shortly after they moved in on July 15, Mrs. W. awoke in the middle of the night for some reason. Her eyes fell upon the ceiling and she saw what looked to her like a sparkler-type of light. It swirled about in a circular movement, then disappeared. On checking, Mrs. W. found that all the shades were drawn in the room, so it perplexed her how such a light could have occurred on her ceiling. But the matter quickly slipped from her mind.

Several days later, she happened to be sitting in the living room one evening with the television on very low since her husband was asleep on the couch. Everything was very quiet. On the arm of a wide-armed couch there were three packages of cigarettes side by side. As she looked at them, the middle package suddenly flipped over by itself and fell to the floor. Since Mrs. W. had no interest in psychic phenomena, she dismissed this as probably due to some natural cause. A short time thereafter, she happened to be sleeping in her daughter's room, facing directly alongside the front hall staircase. The large hall light was burning since the lamp near the children's rooms had burned out. As she lay in the room, she became aware of heavy, slow, plodding footsteps coming across the hallway.

Terrified, she kept her eyes closed tight because she thought there was a prowler in the house. Since everyone was accounted for, only a stranger could have made the noises. She started to pray over and over in order to calm herself, but the footsteps continued on the stairs, progressing down the staircase and around into the living room where they faded away. Mrs. W. was thankful that her prayers had been answered and that the prowler had left.

Just as she started to doze off again the footsteps returned. Although she was still scared, she decided to brave the intruder, whoever he might be. As she got up and approached the area where she heard the steps, they resounded directly in front of her—yet she could see absolutely no one. The next morning she checked all the doors and windows and found them securely locked, just as she had left them the night before. She mentioned the matter to her husband, who ascribed it to nerves. A few nights later, Mrs. W. was again awakened in the middle of the night, this time in her own bedroom. As she woke and sat up in bed, she heard a woman's voice from somewhere in the room. It tried to form words, but Mrs. W. could not make them out. The voice was of a hollow nature and resembled something from an echo chamber. It seemed to her that the voice had come from an area near the ceiling over her husband's bureau, but the matter did not prevent her from going back to sleep, perplexing though it was.

By now Mrs. W. was convinced that they had a ghost in the house. She was standing in her kitchen, contemplating where she could find a priest to have the house exorcised, when all of a sudden a trash bag, which had been resting quietly on the floor, burst and crashed with its contents spilling all over the floor. The disturbances had become so frequent that Mrs. W. took every opportunity possible to leave the house early in the morning with her children, and not go home until she had to. She did not bring in a priest to exorcise the house, but managed to obtain a bottle of blessed water from Lourdes. She went through each room, sprinkling it and praying for the soul of whoever was haunting the house.

About that time, her husband came home from work one evening around six o'clock and went upstairs to change his clothes while Mrs. W. was busy setting the table for dinner. Suddenly Mr. W. called his wife and asked her to open and close the door to the back hall stairs. Puzzled by his request, she did so five times, each time more strenuously. Finally she asked her husband the purpose of this exercise. He admitted that he wanted to test the effect of the door being opened and closed in this manner, because he had just observed the back gate to the stairs opening and closing by itself!

This was as good a time as any to have a discussion of what was going on in the house, so Mrs. W. went up the stairs to join Mr. W. in the bedroom where he was standing. As she did so, her eye caught a dim, circular light that seemed to skip across the ceiling in two strokes; at the same time, the shade at the other end of the room suddenly snapped up, flipping over vigorously a number of times. Both Mr. and Mrs. W. started to run from the room; then, catching themselves, they returned to the bedroom.

On looking over these strange incidents, Mr. W. admitted that there had been some occurrences that could not be explained by natural means. Shortly after they had moved to the house, he had started to paint the interior, at the same time thinking about making some structural changes in the house because there were certain things in it he did not like. As he did so, two cans of paint were knocked out of his hands, flipping over and covering a good portion of the living room and hall floors.

Then there was that Saturday afternoon when Mr. W. had helped his wife vacuum the hall stairs. Again he started to talk about the bad shape the house was in, in his opinion, and as he condemned the house, the vacuum cleaner suddenly left the upper landing and traveled over the staircase all by itself, finally hitting him on the head with a solid thud!

But their discussion did not solve the matter; they had to brace themselves against further incidents, even though they did not know why and who caused them.

One evening Mrs. W. was feeding her baby in the living room near the fireplace, when she heard footsteps overhead and the dragging movement of something very heavy across the floor. This was followed by a crashing sound on the staircase, as if something very heavy had fallen against the railing. Her husband was asleep, but Mrs. W. woke him up and together they investigated, only to find the children asleep and no stranger in the house.

It was now virtually impossible to spend a quiet evening in the living room without hearing some uncanny noises. There was scratching along the tops of the doors inside the house, a rubbing sound along the door tops, and once in awhile the front doorknob would turn by itself, as if an unseen hand were twisting it. No one could have done this physically, because the enclosed porch leading to the door was locked and the locks were intact when Mrs. W. examined them.

The ghost, whoever he or she was, roamed the entire house. One night, Mrs. W. was reading in her bedroom at around midnight, when she heard a knocking sound halfway up the wall of her room. It seemed to move along the wall and then stop dead beside her night table. Needless to say, it did not contribute to a peaceful night. By now the older children were also aware of the disturbances. They, too, heard knocking on doors with no one outside, and twice Mrs. W.'s little girl, then seven years old, was awakened in the middle of the night because she heard someone walking about the house. At the time, both her parents were fast asleep.

That year, coming home on Christmas night to an empty house, or what they *presumed* to be an empty house, the W.'s noticed that a Christmas light was on in the bedroom window. Under the circumstances, the family stayed outside while Mr. W. went upstairs to check the house. He found everything locked and no one inside. The rest of the family then moved into the lower hall, waiting for Mr. W. to come down from upstairs. As he reached the bottom of the stairs, coming from what he assured his family was an empty upper story, they all heard footsteps overhead from the area he had just examined.

On the eve of St. Valentine's Day, Mrs. W. was readying the house for a party the next evening. She had waxed the floors and spruced up the entire house, and it had gotten late. Just before going to bed, she decided to sit down for awhile in her rocking chair. Suddenly she perceived a moaning and groaning sound coming across the living room from left to right. It lasted perhaps ten to fifteen seconds, then ended as abruptly as it had begun.

During the party the next evening, the conversation drifted to ghosts, and somehow Mrs. W. confided in her sister-in-law about what they had been through since moving to the house. It was only then that Mrs. W. found out from her sister-in-law that her husband's mother had had an experience in the house while staying over one night during the summer. She, too, had heard loud footsteps coming up the hall stairs; she had heard voices, and a crackling sound as if there had been a fire someplace. On investigating these strange noises, she had found nothing that could have caused them. However, she had decided not to tell Mrs. W. about it, in order not to frighten her.

Because of her background and position, and since her husband had a respected position as a teacher, the W.'s were reluctant to discuss their experiences with anyone who might construe them as imaginary, or think the family silly. Eventually, however, a sympathetic neighbor gave her one of my books, and Mrs. W. contacted me for advice. She realized, of course, that her letter would not be read immediately, and that in any event, I might not be able to do anything about it for some time. Frightening though the experiences had been, she was reconciled to living with them, hoping only that her children would not be hurt or frightened.

On March 3, she had put her three young boys to bed for a nap, and decided to check if they were properly covered. As she went up over the stairway, she thought she saw movement out of the corner of her eye. Her first thought was that her little boy, then four years old, had gotten up instead of taking his nap. But, on checking, she found him fast asleep. Exactly one week later, Mrs. W. was in bed trying to go to sleep when she heard a progressively louder tapping on the wooden mantle at the foot of the bed. She turned over to see where the noise was coming from or what was causing it when immediately it stopped. She turned back to the side, trying to go back to sleep, when suddenly she felt something or someone shake her foot as though trying to get her attention. She looked down at her foot and saw absolutely nothing.

Finally, on March 26, she received my letter explaining some of the phenomena to her and advising her what to do. As she was reading my letter, she heard the sound of someone moving about upstairs, directly over her head. Since she knew that the children were sleeping soundly, Mrs. W. realized that her unseen visitor was not in the least bit put off by the advice dispensed her by the Ghost Hunter. Even a dog the W.'s had acquired around Christmas had its difficulty with the unseen forces loose in the house.

At first, he had slept upstairs on the rug beside Mrs. W.'s bed. But a short time after, he began to growl and bark at night, especially in the direction of the stairs. Eventually he took to sleeping on the enclosed porch and refused to enter the house, no matter how one would try to entice him. Mrs. W. decided to make some inquiries in the neighborhood, in order to find out who the ghost might be or what he might want.

She discovered that a paper-hanger, who had come to do some work in the house just before they had purchased it, had encountered considerable difficulties. He had been hired to do some paper-hanging in the house, changing the decor from what it had been. He had papered a room in the house as he had been told to, but on returning the next day found that some of his papers were on upside down, as if moved around by unseen hands. He, too, heard strange noises and would have nothing further to do with the house. Mrs. W. then called upon the people who had preceded them in the house, the P. family, but the daughter of the late owner said that during their stay in the house they had not experienced anything unusual. Perhaps she did not care to discuss such matters; at any rate, Mrs. W. discovered that the former owner, Mr. P., had actually died in the house three years prior to their acquisition of it. Apparently, he had been working on the house, which he loved very much, and had sustained a fracture. He recovered from it, but sustained another fracture in the same area of his leg. During the recovery, he died of a heart attack in the living room.

It is conceivable that Mr. P. did not like the rearrangements made by the new owners, and resented the need for repapering or repainting, having done so much of that himself while in the flesh. But if it is he who is walking up and down the stairs at night, turning doorknobs, and appearing as luminous balls of light—who, then, is the woman whose voice has also been heard?

So it appears that the house overlooking the golf course for the past hundred and twenty-two years has more than one spectral inhabitant in it. Perhaps Mr. P. is only a johnny-come-lately, joining the earlier shades staying on in what used to be their home. As far as the W.'s are concerned, the house is big enough for all of them; so long as they know their place!

Peter Q. comes from a devout Catholic family, part Scottish, part Irish. One June, Peter Q. was married, and his brother Tom, with whom he had always maintained a close and cordial relationship, came to the wedding. That was the last time the two brothers were happy together. Two weeks later Tom and a friend spent a weekend on Cape Cod. During that weekend, Tom lost his prize possession, his collection of record albums worth several hundred dollars. Being somewhat superstitious, he feared that his luck had turned against him and, sure enough, his car was struck by a hit-and-run driver shortly afterwards.

Then, in August of the same year, Tom and his father caught a very big fish on a fishing trip and won a prize consisting of a free trip during the season. As he was cleaning the fish to present it to the jury, the line broke and Tom lost the prize fish. But his streak of bad luck was to take on ominous proportions soon after. Two weeks later, Tom Q. and the same friend who had been with him when his record collection had been stolen were planning another trip together. Tom was very happy the night before because he was looking forward to the trip. He was joyful, and in the course of conversation said, "When I die, I want a good send-off," meaning a good traditional Irish wake. His friend, David, on the other hand, was quiet and withdrawn, not quite himself that evening.

The following morning, the two young men set out on their trip. Before the day was out, they were involved in an automobile accident. Tom Q. died instantly and David died the next day.

Even before the bad news was brought home to Peter Q. and the family, an extraordinary thing happened at their house. The clock in the bedroom stopped suddenly. When Peter checked it and wound it again, he found nothing wrong with it. By then, word of Tom's death had come, and on checking out the time, Peter found that the clock had stopped at the very instant of his brother's death.

During the following days, drawers in their bedroom would open by themselves when there was no one about. This continued for about four weeks, then it stopped again. On the anniversary of Tom's death, Peter, who was then a junior at the university, was doing some studying and using a fountain pen to highlight certain parts in the books. Just then, his mother called him and asked him to help his father with his car. Peter placed the pen inside the book to mark the page and went to help his father. On returning an hour later, he discovered that a picture of his late brother and their family had been placed where Peter had left the pen, and the pen was lying outside the book next to it. No one had been in the house at the time, since Peter's wife was out working.

Under the influence of Tom's untimely death and the phenomena taking place at his house, Peter Q. became very interested in life after death and read almost everything he could, talking with many of his friends about the subject, and becoming all the time more and more convinced that man does in some mysterious way survive death. But his wife disagreed with him and did not wish to discuss the matter.

One night, while her husband was away from the house, Peter's wife received a telepathic impression concerning continuance of life, and as she did so, a glowing object about the size of a softball appeared next to her in her bed. It was not a dream, for she could see the headlights from passing cars shining on the wall of the room, yet the shining object was still there next to her pillow, stationary and glowing. It eventually disappeared.

Many times since, Peter Q. has felt the presence of his brother, a warm, wonderful feeling; yet it gives him goose bumps all over. As for the real big send-off Tom had wanted from this life, he truly received it. The morning after his accident, a number of friends called the house without realizing that anything had happened to Tom. They had felt a strong urge to call, as if someone had communicated with them telepathically to do so.

Tom Q. was a collector of phonograph records and owned many, even though a large part of his collection had been stolen. The night before his fatal accident, he had played some of these records. When Peter later checked the record player, he discovered that the last song his brother had played was entitled, "Just One More Day." Of the many Otis Redding recordings his brother owned, why had he chosen that one?

Mr. Harold B. is a professional horse trainer who travels a good deal of the time. When he does stay at home, he lives in an old home in W., a small town in Massachusetts. Prior to moving to New England, he and his wife lived in Ohio, but he was attracted by the old world atmosphere of New England and decided to settle down in the East. They found a house that was more than two hundred years old, but unfortunately it was in dire need of repair.

There was neither electricity nor central heating, and all the rooms were dirty, neglected, and badly in need of renovating. Nevertheless, they liked the general feeling of the house and decided to take it.

The house was in a sad state, mostly because it had been lived in for fifty-five years by a somewhat eccentric couple who had shut themselves off from the world. They would hardly admit anyone to their home, and it was known in town that three of their dogs had died of starvation. Mr. and Mrs. B. moved into the house on Walnut Road in October. Shortly after their arrival, Mrs. B. fractured a leg, which kept her housebound for a considerable amount of time. This was unfortunate, since the house needed so much work. Nevertheless, they managed. With professional help, they did the house over from top to bottom, putting in a considerable amount of work and money to make it livable, until it became a truly beautiful house.

Although Mrs. B. is not particularly interested in the occult, she has had a number of psychic experiences in the past, especially of a precognitive nature, and has accepted her psychic powers as a matter of course. Shortly after the couple had moved into the house on Walnut Road, they noticed that there *was* something peculiar about their home.

One night, Mrs. B. was sleeping alone in a downstairs front room off the center entrance hall. Suddenly she was awakened by the sensation of a presence in the room, and as she looked up she saw the figure of a small woman before her bed, looking right at her. She could make out all the details of the woman's face and stature, and noticed that she was wearing a veil, as widows sometimes did in the past. When the apparition became aware of Mrs. B.'s attention, she lifted the veil and spoke to her, assuring her that she was not there to harm her, but that she came as a friend. Mrs. B. was too overcome by it all to reply, and before she could gather her wits, the apparition drifted away.

Immediately, Mrs. B made inquiries in town, and since she was able to give a detailed description of the apparition, it was not long until she knew who the ghost was. The description fit the former owner of the house, Mrs. C., to a tee. Mrs. C. died at age eighty-six, shortly before the B.'s moved into what was her former home. Armed with this information, Mrs. B. braced herself for the presence of an unwanted inhabitant in the house. A short time afterwards, she saw the shadowy outline of what appeared to be a heavy-set person moving along the hall from her bedroom. At first she thought it was her husband so she called out to him, but she soon discovered that her husband was actually upstairs. She then examined her room and discovered that the shades were drawn, so there was no possibility that light from traffic on the road outside could have cast a shadow onto the adjoining hall. The shadowy figure she had seen did not, however, look like the outline of the ghost she had earlier encountered in the front bedroom.

While she was still wondering about this, she heard the sound of a dog running across the floor. Yet there was no dog to be seen. Evidently her own dog also heard or sensed the ghostly dog's doings, because he reacted with visible terror.

Mrs. B. was still wondering about the second apparition when her small grandson came and stayed overnight. He had never been to the house before, and had not been told of the stories connected with it. As he was preparing to go to sleep, but still fully conscious, he saw a heavy-set man wearing a red shirt standing before him in his bedroom. This upset him greatly, especially when the man suddenly disappeared without benefit of a door. He described the apparition to his grandparents, who reassured him by telling him a white lie: namely, that he had been dreaming. To this the boy indignantly replied that he had not been dreaming, but in fact had been fully awake. The description given by the boy not only fitted the shadowy outline of the figure Mrs. B. had seen along the corridor, but was a faithful description of the late Mr. C., the former owner of the house.

Although the ghost of Mrs. C. had originally assured the B.'s that they meant no harm and that she had, in fact, come as a friend, Mrs. B. had her doubts. A number of small items of no particular value disappeared from time to time, and were never found again. This was at times when intruders were completely out of the question.

Then Mrs. B. heard the pages of a wallpaper sampler lying on the dining room table being turned one day. Thinking her husband was doing it, she called out to him, only to find that the room was empty. When she located him in another part of the house, he reported having heard the pages being turned also, and this reassured Mrs. B. since she now had her husband's support in the matter of ghosts. It was clear to her that the late owners did not appreciate the many changes they had made in the house. But Mrs. B. also decided that she was not about to be put out of her home by a ghost. The changes had been made for the better, she decided, and the C.'s, even in their present ghostly state, should be grateful for what they had done for the house and not resent them. Perhaps these thoughts somehow reached the two ghosts telepathically; at any rate, the atmosphere in the house became quiet after that.

Not all ghosts have selfish motives, so to speak, in reasserting their previous ownership of a home: some even help later occupants, although the limits of a ghost's rationality are very narrow. For one thing, if a ghost personality is aware of later inhabitants of a house and wants to communicate with them—

not in order to get them out but to warn them—such a ghost is still unable to realize that the warning may be entirely unnecessary because time has passed, and the present reality no longer corresponds to the reality he or she knew when his or her own tragedy occurred.

Still, there is the strange case of Rose S., now a resident of New York State, but at one time living in Fort Worth, Texas. Miss S. is a secretary by profession, and during the middle 1960s worked for a well-known social leader. That summer, Miss S. moved into an old house in Fort Worth, renting a room at one end of the house. At the time, she wanted to be near her fiancé, an army pilot who was stationed not far away.

The old house she chanced upon was located on Bryce Avenue, in one of the older sections of Fort Worth. The owner was renting out a furnished room because the house had become too large for her. Her husband, an attorney, had passed away, and their children were all grown and living away from home.

The house seemed pleasant enough, and the room large and suitable, so Miss S. was indeed happy to have found it. Moreover, her landlady did not restrict her to the rented room, but allowed her to use the kitchen and in fact have the freedom of the house, especially as there were no other tenants. The landlady seemed a pleasant enough woman in her middle or late sixties at the time, and except for an occasional habit of talking to herself, there was nothing particularly unusual about her. Miss S. looked forward to a pleasant, if uneventful stay at the house on Bryce Avenue.

Not long after moving in, it happened that the landlady went off to visit a daughter in Houston, leaving the house entirely to Miss S. That night, Rose S. decided to read and then retire early. As soon as she switched off the lights to go to sleep, she began to hear footsteps walking around the house. At the same time, the light in the bathroom, which she had intended to leave on all night, started to grow dimmer and brighter alternately, which puzzled her. Frightened because she thought she had to face an intruder, Miss S. got up to investigate, but found not a living soul anywhere in the house. She then decided that the whole thing was simply her imagination acting up because she had been left alone in the house for the first time, and went to bed. The days passed and the incident was forgotten. A few weeks later, the landlady was again off for Houston, but this time Miss S.'s fiancé was visiting her. It was evening, and the couple was spending the time after dinner relaxing.

Miss S.'s fiancé, the pilot, had fallen asleep. Suddenly, in the quiet of the night, Miss S. heard someone whistle loudly and clearly from the next room. It was a marching song, which vaguely reminded her of the well-known melody, the Colonel Bogey March. Neither TV nor radio were playing at the time, and there was no one about. When she realized that the source of the whistling was uncanny, she decided not to tell her fiancé, not wishing to upset him.

Time went on, and another periodical trip by her landlady left Miss S. alone again in the house. This time she was in the TV den, trying to read and write. It was a warm night, and the air cooler was on.

As she was sitting there, Miss S. gradually got the feeling that she was not alone. She had the distinct impression that someone was watching her, and then there came the faint whining voice of a woman above the sound of the air cooler. The voice kept talking, and though Miss S. tried to ignore it, she had to listen. Whether by voice or telepathy, she received the impression that she was not to stay in the house, and that the voice was warning her to move out immediately. After another restless night with very little sleep, Miss S. decided she could take the phenomena no longer.

As soon as the landlady returned, she informed her that she was leaving, and moved in with friends temporarily. Eventually, her experiences at the house on Bryce Avenue aroused her curiosity and she made some quiet inquiries. It was then that she discovered the reasons for the haunting. On the very corner where the house stood, a woman and a girl had been murdered by a man while waiting for a bus. As if that were not enough to upset her, something happened to her fiancé from that moment on. Following the incident with the whistling ghost, of which her fiancé knew nothing, his behavior towards her changed drastically. It was as if he was not quite himself any more, but under the influence of another personality. Shortly afterwards, Miss S. and her pilot broke off their engagement.

Mike L. lives in Tennessee, where his family has been in residence for several generations. Ever since he can remember, he has had psychic ability. At the time when a favorite uncle was in the hospital, he was awakened in the middle of the night to see his uncle standing by his bed. "Goodbye, Michael," the uncle said, and then the image faded away. At that instant, Mike knew that his uncle had passed away, so he went back to sleep. The following morning, his mother awoke him to tell him that his uncle had passed away during the night.

In April, he and his wife moved to a residential section in one of the large cities of Tennessee. They bought a house from a lady well in her seventies, who had the reputation of being somewhat cranky. She was not too well-liked in the neighborhood.

Shortly after they had settled down in the house, they noticed footsteps in the rafters over their bedroom. Regardless of the hour, these footsteps would come across the ceiling from one side of the room to the other. Whenever they checked, there was no one there who could have caused the footsteps.

While they were still puzzled about the matter, though not shocked, and since they had had psychic presences in other houses, something still more remarkable occurred. There were two floor lamps in the living room, on opposite sides of the room. In order to make them work, a switch had to be turned on. One night, Mr. L. awoke and noticed one of the floor lamps lit. Since he clearly remembered having turned it off on going to bed, he was puzzled, but got out of bed and switched it off again. As if to complement this incident, the other floor lamp came on by itself a few nights later, even though it had been turned off by hand a short time before.

This was the beginning of an entire series of lights being turned on in various parts of the house, seemingly by unseen hands. Since it was their practice not to leave any lights on except for a small night light in their daughter's room, there was no way in which this could be explained by negligence or on rational grounds. The house has a basement, including a small space below the wooden front porch. As a result of this hollow space, if anyone were walking on the porch, the steps would reverberate that much more audibly. The L's frequently heard someone come up the porch, approach the door and stop there. Whenever they looked out, they saw no one about. Not much later, they were awakened by the noise of a large number of dishes crashing to the floor of the kitchen, at least so they thought. When they checked everything was in order; no dish had been disturbed.

They were still wondering about this when they caught the movement of something—or someone—out of the corner of their eye in the living room. When they looked closer, there was no one there. Then the dresser in the bedroom *seemed* to be moving across the floor, or so it sounded. But when they got to the room, they saw that nothing had been changed.

One night, just after retiring, Mr. L. was shocked by a great deal of noise in the basement. It sounded as if someone were wrecking his shop. He jumped out of bed, grabbed a gun, opened the basement door, and turned on the light. There was an audible scurrying sound, as if someone were moving about, which was followed by silence.

Immediately Mr. L. thought he had a burglar, but realized he would be unable to go downstairs undetected. Under the circumstances, he called for his wife to telephone the police while he stood at the head of the stairs guarding the basement exit. As soon as he heard the police arrive, he locked the only door to the basement and joined them on the outside of the house. Together they investigated, only to find no one about, no evidence of foul play. Even more inexplicable, nothing in the shop had been touched. About that time, Mr. L. noticed a tendency of the basement door to unlock itself seemingly of its own volition, even though it was Mr. L.'s custom to lock it both at night and when leaving the house. During the daytime, Mrs. L. frequently heard footsteps overhead when she was in the basement, even though she was fully aware of the fact that there was no one in the house but her.

By now, Mr. and Mrs. L. realized that someone was trying to get their attention. They became aware of an unseen presence staring at them in the dining room, or bothering Mrs. L. in one of the other rooms of the house. Finally, Mike L. remembered that a Rosicrucian friend had given them a so-called Hermetic Cross when they had encountered ghostly troubles in another house. He brought the cross to the dining room and nailed it to the wall. This seemed to relieve the pressure somewhat, until they found a calendar hung in front of the cross, as if to downgrade its power.

Mr. L. made some further inquiries in the neighborhood, in order to find out who the unseen intruder might be. Eventually, he managed to piece the story together. The woman from whom they had bought the house had been a widow of about nine years when they had met her. The husband had been extremely unhappy in the house; he was not permitted to smoke, for instance, and had to hide his cigarettes in a neighbor's basement. Nothing he did in his own house met with his wife's approval, it appeared, and he died a very unhappy man. Could it not be that his restless spirit, once freed from the shackles of the body, finally enjoyed his unobstructed power to roam the house and do whatever he pleased? Or perhaps he could now even enjoy the vicarious thrill of frightening the later owners, and for the first time in his long life, become the stronger party in the house.

Finally is the strange case of Dorothy B., a young Pennsylvanian woman in her early thirties, who spent many years living with a maternal uncle and aunt in North Carolina. The house was a two-hundred-year-old farmhouse, surrounded by a medium-sized farm. Her uncle and aunt were people in their late fifties, who continued farming on a reduced scale since they lived alone; their two children had long gone to the city. Dorothy was assigned a pleasant corner room in the upper story of the house, and when she moved into it one April, she thought she had, at last, found a place where she could have peace and quiet.

This was very necessary, you see, because she had just been through a nervous breakdown due to an unhappy love affair, and had decided to withdraw from life in the city. Fortunately, she had saved up some money so she could afford to live quietly by herself for at least a year. When her uncle had heard of her predicament, he had offered the hospitality of the house in return for some light chores she could easily perform for him. The first night after her arrival at the farmhouse, Dorothy slept soundly, due probably to the long journey and the emotional release of entering a new phase of her life. But the following night, and she remembers this clearly because there was a full moon that night, Dorothy went to bed around ten P.M. feeling very relaxed and hopeful for the future. The conversation at the dinnertable had been about art and poetry, two subjects very dear to Dorothy's heart. Nothing about the house or its background had been mentioned by her uncle and aunt, nor had there been any discussion of psychic phenomena. The latter subject was not exactly alien to Dorothy, for she had had a number of ESP experiences over the years, mainly precognitive in nature and not particularly startling.

She extinguished the lights and started to drift off to sleep. Suddenly her attention was focused on a low level noise, seemingly emanating from below the ceiling. It sounded as if someone were tapping on the wall. At first, Dorothy assumed that the pipes were acting up, but then she remembered that it was the middle of spring and the heat was not on.

She decided not to pay any attention, assuming it was just one of those noises you hear in old houses when they settle. Again she tried to drift off to sleep and was almost asleep when she felt a presence close to her bed. There was an intense chill accompanying that feeling, and she sat bolt upright in bed, suddenly terrified. As she opened her eyes and looked toward the corner of her room, she saw that she was not alone. Due to the strong moonlight streaming in from the window, she could make out everything in the room. Perhaps a yard or a yard and a half away from her stood the figure of a young girl, motionless, staring at her with very large, sad eyes!

Despite her terror, Dorothy could make out that the girl was dressed in very old-fashioned clothes, unlike the kind that are worn today. She seemed like a farm girl; the clothes were simple but clean, and her long brown hair cascaded down over her shoulders. There was a terrible feeling of guilt in her eyes, as if she were desperately seeking help. "What do you want?" Dorothy said, trembling with fear as she spoke. The apparition did not reply, but continued to stare at her. At this moment, Dorothy had the clear impression that the girl wanted her to know how sorry she was. At this point Dorothy's fear got the better of her, and she turned on the light. As she did so, the apparition vanished immediately.

Still shaken, she went back to sleep and managed a somewhat restless night. The following morning she asked her aunt whether there had ever been any psychic experience in the family, in particular whether anyone had ever seen or heard anything unusual in the house. Her aunt gave her a strange look and shook her head. Either there hadn't been anything, or she didn't care to discuss it. Dorothy, as the newcomer, did not feel like pressing her point, so she changed the subject.

That night she went to bed with anticipatory fears, but nothing happened. Relieved that it might all have been her imagination due to the long trip the day before, Dorothy began to forget the incident. Three days later, however, she was again awakened by the feeling of a presence in her room. The cold was as intense as it had been the first time, and when she opened her eyes, there was the same apparition she had seen before. This time she was pleading for help even more, and since Dorothy did not feel the same gripping fear she had experienced the first time, she was able to communicate with the apparition.

"I want to help you; tell me who you are," she said to the spectre, waiting for some sort of reply. After what seemed to her an eternity, but could have been no more than a few seconds, Dorothy received the impression that the girl was in trouble because of a man she had become involved with. To be sure, the ghost did not speak to her; the thoughts came to Dorothy on a telepathic level, haltingly, in bits, picturing the apparition with a tall, good-looking man, also wearing old-fashioned farm clothes. In her mind's eye, Dorothy saw the two lovers, and then she heard what sounded like a tiny infant. At that point, the apparition vanished, leaving Dorothy very much shaken.

The following morning she broached the subject of ghosts to her aunt. But the reaction she got was so cold, she hesitated to go on, and again, she did not relate her experiences. Several weeks passed, without any incident of any kind. That is, except for some strange noises Dorothy ascribed to a settling of the house, or perhaps a squirrel or two in the rafters above her room. It sounded like furtive, light footsteps if one were so inclined to interpret the sounds. Again there was a full moon, and Dorothy realized that she had been at the house for a full month. That night, Dorothy went to bed earlier than usual, hoping to get a good start toward a night's sleep since she had been particularly active during the day helping her aunt clear out a woodshed in the back of the farmhouse.

It had not been an easy chore. Somehow the atmosphere in the woodshed was very depressing, and Dorothy wanted to leave more than once, but hesitated to do so lest her aunt accuse her of being lazy. But the feeling inside the woodshed was heavy with tragedy and unhappiness, even though Dorothy could not pinpoint the reasons for it.

Now she lay in bed, waiting for sleep to come. She had drawn the blinds, but the moonlight kept streaming in through them, bathing the room in a sort of semi-darkness, which allowed Dorothy to see everything in the room in good detail. After a few minutes she became aware of an intense chill toward the left side of her bed. She realized she was not about to drift into peaceful sleep after all, and prepared herself for what she knew would be her nocturnal visitor. In a moment, there was the pale-looking girl again, this time standing by the window as if she did not dare come near Dorothy.

"Very well," Dorothy thought, "let's get to the bottom of this. I've had about enough of it, and if this ghost is going to make my life miserable here, I might as well know why." Somehow the ghost seemed to have read her mind, because she came closer to the bed, looking at Dorothy again with her tearful, large eyes. As if someone had told her to, Dorothy now closed her own eyes, and allowed the apparition to impress her with further details of her story. Again she saw the husky young man and the ghost girl together, and this time there was an infant with them. Next she saw an old woman entering what appeared to be a very run-down shack or room, and something in Dorothy recognized the shack as the woodshed she had been in during the day!

Then something horrible happened: although she could not see it with her mind's eye, Dorothy knew that the child was being *butchered*, and that the old woman was the instigator of it! Quickly, Dorothy opened her eyes and looked at the apparition. For a moment the girl looked at Dorothy again as if to say *now you understand why I am still here*—but then the ghost faded into the woodwork. Somehow Dorothy was able to sleep peacefully that night, as if a burden had been lifted from her.

The following morning, she told her aunt everything that had happened from the very first day on. This time her aunt did not interrupt her, but listened in stony silence, as Dorothy recounted her ghostly experiences. Finally, she said, "I wish you had been left in peace; that is why I did not want to tell you anything about this ghost." She explained that a young girl named Anne, who had been working for them for a number of years prior to Dorothy's arrival, had also slept in the same room. She, too, had seen the apparition, although she was unable to understand the reasons for the ghostly encounter. A few years after taking over the farm, Dorothy's uncle had stumbled across an unmarked grave in back of the woodshed. It was clear to him that it was a grave, even though the headstone had been partially destroyed by time and weather. He had assumed that it belonged to a slave, for there were slaves in the area at the time when the farm was first built.

But the grave seemed unusually small, and Dorothy's aunt wondered whether perhaps it might not be that of a child. As she said this, Dorothy felt a distinct chill and received the clear impression that her aunt had hit on something connected with her ghost. On the spur of the moment, the two women went to the spot where the grave had been discovered. It was barely discernible amid the surrounding rocks and earth, but eventually they located it. Dorothy fetched some flowers from the house and placed them upon what must have been the headstone at one time. Then she fashioned a crude cross from two wooden sticks and placed them in the center. This done, she said a simple prayer, hoping that the soul of whoever was underneath the stones would find an easy passage into the world beyond.

When Dorothy went to bed that night, she had a sense of relief at having done something constructive about her ghost. She half-expected the ghostly girl to appear again, but nothing happened that night, or the following night, or any night thereafter, until Dorothy left the farmhouse to go back to the city about a year later.

6

The Ghostly Stay-Behinds

THE AVERAGE PERSON thinks that there is just one kind of ghost, and that spirits and ghosts are all one and the same. Nothing could be further from the truth; ghosts are not spirits, and psychic impressions are not the same as ghosts. Basically, there are three phenomena involved when a person dies under traumatic, tragic circumstances and is unable to adjust to the passing from one state of existence to the next. The most common form of passing is of course the transition from physical human being to spirit being, without difficulty and without the need to stay in the denser physical atmosphere of the Earth. The majority of tragic passings do not present any problems, because the individual accepts the change and becomes a free spirit, capable of communicating freely with those on the Earth plane, and advancing according to his abilities, likes and dislikes, and the help he or she may receive from others already on the other side of life. A small fraction of those who die tragically are unable to recognize the change in their status and become so-called ghosts: that is, parts of human personality hung up in the physical world, but no longer part of it or able to function in it. These are the only *true* ghosts in the literal sense of the term.

However a large number of sightings of so-called ghosts are not of this nature, but represent imprints left behind in the atmosphere by the individual's actual passing. Anyone possessed of psychic ability will sense the event from the past and, in his or her mind's eye, reconstruct it. The difficulty is that one frequently does not know the difference between a psychic imprint having no life of its own and a true ghost. Both seem very real, subjectively speaking. The only way one can differentiate between the two phenomena is when several sightings are compared for minute details. True ghosts move about somewhat, although not outside the immediate area of their passing. Imprints are always identical, regardless of the observers involved, and the details do not alter at any time. Psychic imprints, then, are very much like photographs or films of an actual event, while true ghosts are events themselves, which are capable of some measure of reaction to the environment. Whenever there are slight differences in detail concerning an apparition, we are dealing with a true ghost-personality; but whenever the description of an apparition or scene from the past appears to be identical from source to source, we are most likely dealing only with a lifeless imprint reflecting the event but in no way suggesting an actual presence at the time of the observation.

However, there is a subdivision of true ghosts that I have called "the Stay-Behinds." The need for such a subdivision came to me several years ago when I looked through numerous cases of reported hauntings that did not fall into the category of tragic, traumatic passings, nor cases of death involving neither violence nor great suffering—the earmarks of true ghosts. To the contrary, many of these sightings involved the peaceful passings of people who had lived in their respective homes for many years and had grown to love them. I realized, by comparing these cases one with the other, that they had certain things in common, the most outstanding of which was this: they were greatly attached to their homes, had lived in them for considerable periods prior to their death, and were strong-willed individuals who had managed to develop a life routine of their own. It appears, therefore, that the Stay-Behinds are spirits who are unable to let go of their former homes, are more or less aware of their passing into the next dimension, but are unwilling to go on. To them, their earthly home is preferable, and the fact that they no longer possess a physical body is no deterrent to their continuing to live in it.

Some of these Stay-Behinds adjust to their limitations with marvelous ingenuity. They are still capable of causing physical phenomena, especially if they can draw on people living in the house. At times, however, they become annoyed at changes undertaken by the residents in their house, and when these changes evoke anger in them they are capable of some mischievous activities, like Poltergeist phenomena, although of a somewhat different nature. Sometimes they are quite satisfied to continue living their former lives, staying out of the way of flesh-and-blood inhabitants of the house, and remaining undiscovered until someone with psychic ability notices them by accident. Sometimes, however, they *want* the flesh-and-blood people to know they are still very much in residence and, in asserting their continuing rights, may come into conflict with the living beings in the house. Some of these manifestations seem frightening or even threatening to people living in houses of this kind, but they should not be, since the Stay-Behinds are, after all, human beings like all others, who have developed a continuing and very strong attachment to their former homes. Of course, not everyone can come to terms with them.

For instance, take the case of Margaret C . A few years ago when she lived in New York State, she decided to spend Christmas with her sister and brother-in-law in Pennsylvania. The husband's mother had recently passed away, so it was going to be a sad Christmas holiday for them. Mrs. C. was given a room on the second floor of the old house, close to a passage which led to the downstairs part of the house. Being tired from her long journey, she went to bed around eleven, but found it difficult to fall asleep. Suddenly she clearly heard the sound of a piano being played in the house. It sounded like a very old piano, and the music on it reminded her of music played in church. At first Mrs. C. thought someone had left a radio on, so she checked but found that this was not the case. Somehow she managed to fall asleep, despite the tinkling sound of the piano downstairs. At breakfast, Mrs. C. mentioned her experience to her sister. Her sister gave her an odd look, then took her by the hand and led her down the stairs where she pointed to an old piano. It had been the property of the dead mother who had recently passed away, but it had not been played in many years, since no one else in the house knew how to play it. With mounting excitement, the two women pried the rusty lid open. This took some effort, but eventually they succeeded in opening the keyboard.

Picture their surprise when they found that thick dust had settled on the keys, but etched in the dust were unmistakable human fingerprints. They were thin, bony fingers, like the fingers of a very old woman. Prior to her passing, the deceased had been very thin indeed, and church music had been her favorite. Was the lady of the house still around, playing her beloved piano?

The house on South Sixth Street in Hudson, New York, is one of the many fine old town houses dotting this old town on the Hudson River. It was built between 1829 and 1849, and a succession of owners lived in it to the present day. In 1904 it passed into the hands of the Parker family, who had a daughter, first-named Mabel, a very happy person with a zest for life. In her sixties, she had contracted a tragic illness and suffered very much, until she finally passed away in a nearby hospital. She had been truly house-proud, and hated to leave for the cold and ominous surroundings of the hospital. After she died, the house passed into the hands of Mr. and Mrs. Jay Dietz, who still owned it when I visited them. Mrs. Dietz had been employed by Mabel Parker's father at one time.

The psychic did not particularly interest Mrs. Dietz, although she had had one notable experience the night her step-grandfather died, a man she had loved very much. She had been at home taking care of him throughout the daytime and finally returned to her own house to spend the night. Everybody had gone to bed, and as she lay in hers with her face to the wall, she became aware of an unusual glow in the room. She turned over and opened her eyes, and noticed that on the little nightstand at the head of the bed was a large ball of light, glowing with a soft golden color. As she was still staring at the phenomenon, the telephone rang, and she was told that her step-grandfather had passed away.

Eleven years before, the Dietzes moved into the house on South Sixth Street. At first the house seemed peaceful enough. Previous tenants included a German war bride and her mother. The old lady had refused to sleep upstairs in the room that later became Mrs. Dietz's mother's. There was something uncanny about that room, she explained. So she slept down on the ground floor on a couch instead. The Dietzes paid no attention to these stories, until they began to notice some strange things about their house. There were footsteps heard going up and down the stairs and into the hall, where they stopped. The three of them, Mr. and Mrs. Dietz and her mother, all heard them many times.

One year, just before Christmas, Mrs. Dietz was attending to some sewing in the hall downstairs while her husband was in the bathroom. Suddenly she thought he came down the hall which was odd, since she hadn't heard the toilet being flushed. But as she turned around, no one was there. A few nights later she went upstairs and had the distinct impression that she was not alone in the room. Without knowing what she was doing, she called out to the unseen presence, "Mabel?" There was no reply then, but one night not much later, she was awakened by someone yanking at her blanket from the foot of the bed. She broke out into goose pimples, because the pull was very distinct and there was no mistaking it.

She sat up in her upstairs bedroom, very frightened by now, but there was no one to be seen. As she did this, the pulling ceased abruptly. She went back to sleep with some relief, but several nights later the visitor returned. Mrs. Dietz likes to sleep on her left side with her ear covered up by the blanket. Suddenly she felt the covers bèing pulled off her ear, but being already half-asleep, she simply yanked them back. There was no further movement after that.

The upstairs bedroom occupied by Mrs. Dietz's mother seemed to be the center of activities, however. More than once after the older lady had turned out the lights to go to sleep, she became aware of someone standing beside her bed, and looking down at her.

Sometimes nothing was heard for several weeks or months, only to resume in full force without warning. In February of the year I visited the Dietzes, Mrs. Dietz happened to wake up at five o'clock one morning. It so happened that her mother was awake too, for Mrs. Dietz heard her stir. A moment later, her mother went back to bed. At that moment, Mrs. Dietz heard, starting at the foot of the stairs, the sound of heavy footsteps coming up very slowly, going down the hall and stopping, but they were different from the footsteps she had heard many times before.

It sounded as if a very sick person were dragging herself up the stairs, trying not to fall, but determined to get there nevertheless. It sounded as if someone very tired was coming home. Was her friend finding a measure of rest, after all, by returning to the house where she had been so happy? Mrs. Dietz does not believe in ghosts, however, but only in memories left behind.

Thanks to a local group of psychic researchers, a bizarre case was brought to my attention. In the small town of Lafayette, Louisiana, there stands an old bungalow that had been the property of an elderly couple for many years. They were both retired people, and of late the wife had become an invalid confined to a wheelchair. One day a short time later, she suffered a heart attack and died in that chair. Partially because of her demise, or perhaps because of his own fragile state, the husband also died a month later. Rather, he was found dead and declared to have died of a heart attack.

Under the circumstances the house remained vacant for awhile, since there were no direct heirs. After about nine months, it was rented to four female students from the nearby university. Strangely, however, they stayed only two months—and again the house was rented out. This time it was taken by two women, one a professional microbiologist and the other a medical technician. Both were extremely rational individuals and not the least bit interested in anything supernatural. They moved into the bungalow, using it as it was, furnished with the furniture of the dead couple.

Picture their dismay, however, when they found out that all wasn't as it should be with their house. Shortly after moving in, they were awakened late at night by what appeared to be mumbled conversations and footsteps about the house. At first neither woman wanted to say anything about it to the other, out of fear that they might have dreamt the whole thing or of being ridiculed. Finally, when they talked to each other about their experiences, they realized that they had shared them, detail for detail. They discovered, for instance, that the phenomena always took place between one A.M. and sunrise. A man and a woman were talking, and the subject of their conversation was the new tenants!

"She has her eyes open—I can see her eyes are open now," the invisible voice said, clearly and distinctly. The voices seemed to emanate from the attic area. The two ladies realized the ghosts were talking about *them*; but what were they to do about it? They didn't see the ghostly couple, but felt themselves being watched at all times by invisible presences. What were they to do with their ghosts, the two ladies wondered.

I advised them to talk to them, plain and simple, for a ghost who can tell whether a living person's eyes are open or not is capable of knowing the difference between living in one's own house, and trespassing on someone else's, even if it *was* their former abode.

Mrs. Carolyn K. lives in Chicago, Illinois, with her husband and four children, who are between the ages of eight and thirteen. She has for years been interested in ESP experiences, unlike her husband who held no belief of this kind. The family moved into its present home some years ago. Mrs. K. does not recall any unusual experiences for the first six years, but toward the end of April, six years after they moved in, something odd happened. She and her husband had just gone to bed and her husband, being very tired, fell asleep almost immediately. Mrs. K., however, felt ill at ease and was unable to fall asleep, since she felt a presence in the bedroom.

Within a few minutes she saw, in great detail, a female figure standing beside the bed. The woman seemed about thirty years old, had fair skin and hair, a trim figure, and was rather attractive. Her dress indicated good taste and a degree of wealth, and belonged to the 1870s or 1880s. The young woman just stood there and looked at Mrs. K. and vice versa. She seemed animated enough, but made no sound. Despite this, Mrs. K. had the distinct impression that the ghost wanted her to know something specific. The encounter lasted for ten or fifteen minutes, then the figure slowly disintegrated.

The experience left Mrs. K. frightened and worried. Immediately she reported it to her husband, but he brushed the incident aside with a good deal of skepticism. In the following two weeks, Mrs. K. felt an unseen presence all about the house, without, however, seeing her mysterious visitor again. It seemed that the woman was watching her as she did her daily chores. Mrs. K. had no idea who the ghost might be, but she knew that their house was no more than fifty years old and that there had been swamp land on the spot before that. Could the ghost have some connection with the land itself, or perhaps with some of the antiques Mrs. K. treasured?

About two weeks after the initial experience, Mr. K. was studying in the kitchen, which is located at the far eastern end of the house, while Mrs. K. was watching television in the living room at the other end of the house. Twice she felt the need to go into the kitchen and warn her husband that she felt the ghost moving about the living room, but he insisted it was merely her imagination. So she returned to the living room and curled up in an easy chair to continue watching television. Fifteen minutes later, she heard a loud noise reverberating throughout the house. It made her freeze with fright in the chair, when her husband ran into the living room to ask what the noise had been.

Upon investigation, he noticed a broken string on an antique zither hanging on the dining room wall. It was unlikely that the string could have broken by itself, and if it had, how could it have reverberated so strongly? To test such a possibility, they broke several other strings of the same zither in an effort to duplicate the sound, but without success. A few weeks went by, and the ghost's presence persisted. By now Mrs. K had the distinct impression that the ghost was annoyed at being ignored. Suddenly, a hurricane lamp which hung from a nail on the wall fell to the floor and shattered. It could not have moved of its own volition. Again some time passed, and the ghost was almost forgotten. Mrs. K.'s older daughter, then six years old, asked her mother early one morning who the company was the previous evening. Informed that there had been no guests at the house, she insisted that a lady had entered her bedroom, sat on her bed and looked at her, and then departed. In order to calm the child, Mrs. K. told her she had probably dreamt the whole thing. But the little girl insisted that she had not, and furthermore, she described the visitor in every detail including the "funny" clothes she had worn. Appalled, Mrs. K. realized that her daughter had seen the same ghostly woman. Apparently, the ghost felt greater urgency to communicate now, for a few days later, after going to bed, the apparition returned to Mrs. K.'s bedroom. This time she wore a different dress than on the first meeting, but it was still from the 1880s. She was wiping her hands on an apron, stayed only for a little while, then slowly disintegrated again. During the following year, her presence was felt only occasionally, but gradually Mrs. K. managed to snatch a few fleeting impressions about her. From this she put together the story of her ghost. She was quite unhappy about a child, and one evening the following winter, when Mrs. K. felt the ghost wandering about in their basement, she actually heard her crying pitifully for two hours. Obviously, the distraught ghost wanted attention, and was determined to get it at all costs.

One day the following summer, when Mrs. K. was alone with the children after her husband had left for work, one of the children complained that the door to the bathroom was locked. Since the door can be locked only from the inside, and since all four children were accounted for, Mrs. K. assumed that her ghost lady was at it again. When the bathroom door remained locked for half an hour and the children's needs became more urgent, Mrs. K. went to the door and demanded in a loud tone of voice that the ghost open the door. There was anger in her voice and it brought quick results. Clearly the click of a *lock being turned* was heard inside the bathroom and, after a moment, Mrs. K.

opened the bathroom door easily. There was no one inside the bathroom, of course. Who, then, had turned the lock—the only way the door could be opened?

For awhile things went smoothly. A few weeks later, Mrs. K. again felt the ghost near her. One of her daughters was sitting at the kitchen table with her, while she was cutting out a dress pattern on the counter. Mrs. K. stepped back to search for something in the refrigerator a few feet away, when all of a sudden she and her daughter saw her box of dressmaking pins rise slightly off the counter and fall to the floor. Neither one of them had been near it, and it took them almost an hour to retrieve all the pins scattered on the floor.

A little later, they clearly heard the basement door connecting the dining room and kitchen fly open and slam shut by itself, as if someone in great anger was trying to call attention to her presence. Immediately they closed the door, and made sure there was no draft from any windows.

An instant later, it flew open again by itself. Now they attached the chain to the latch—but that didn't seem to stop the ghost from fooling around with the door. With enormous force, it flew open again as far as the chain allowed, as if someone were straining at it. Quickly Mrs. K. called a neighbor to come over and watch the strange behavior of the door but the minute the neighbor arrived, the door behaved normally, just as before. The ghost was not about to perform for strangers.

One evening in the summer some years later, Mr. K. was driving some dinner guests home and Mrs. K. was alone in the house with the children. All of a sudden, she felt her ghost following her as she went through her chores of emptying ashtrays and taking empty glasses into the kitchen. Mrs. K. tried bravely to ignore her, although she was frightened by her, and she knew that her ghost knew it, which made it all the more difficult to carry on.

Not much later, the K. family had guests again. One of the arriving guests pointed out to Mrs. K. that their basement light was on. Mrs. K. explained that it was unlikely, since the bulb had burned out the day before. She even recalled being slightly annoyed with her husband for having neglected to replace the bulb. But the guest insisted, and so the K.'s opened the basement door only to find the light off. A moment later another guest arrived. He wanted to know who was working in the basement at such a late hour, since he had seen the basement light on. Moreover, he saw a figure standing at the basement window looking out. Once more, the entire party went downstairs with a flashlight, only to find the light off and no one about.

That was the last the K.'s saw or heard of their ghost. Why had she so suddenly left them? Perhaps it had to do with a Chicago newspaperwoman's call. Having heard of the disturbances, she had telephoned the K.'s to offer her services and that of celebrated psychic Irene Hughes to investigate the house. Although the K.'s did not want any attention because of the children, Mrs. K. told the reporter what had transpired at the house. To her surprise, the reporter informed her that parallel experiences had been reported at another house not more than seven miles away. In the other case, the mother and one of her children had observed a ghostly figure, and an investigation had taken place with the help of Irene Hughes and various equipment, the result of which was that a presence named Lizzy was ascertained.

From this Mrs. K. concluded that they were sharing a ghost with a neighbor seven miles away, and she, too, began to call the ghostly visitor Lizzy. Now if Lizzy had two homes and was shuttling back and forth between them, it might account for the long stretches of no activity at the K. home. On the other hand, if the ghost at the K.'s was not named Lizzy, she would naturally not want to be confused with some other unknown ghost seven miles away. Be this as it may, Mrs. K. wishes her well, wherever she is.

Mrs. J. P. lives in central Illinois, in an old three-story house with a basement. Prior to her acquiring it, it had stood empty for six months. As soon as she had moved in, she heard some neighborhood gossip that the house was presumed haunted. Although Mrs. P. is not a skeptic, she is level-headed enough not to take rumors at face value.

She looked the house over carefully. It seemed about eighty years old, and was badly in need of repair. Since they had bought it at a bargain price, they did not mind, but as time went on, they wondered how cheap the house had really been. It became obvious to her and her husband that the price had been low for other reasons. Nevertheless, the house was theirs, and together they set out to repaint and remodel it as best they could. For the first two weeks, they were too busy to notice anything out of the ordinary. About three weeks after moving in, however, Mr. and Mrs. P. began hearing things such as doors shutting by themselves, cupboards opening, and particularly, a little girl persistently calling for "Mama, Mama" with a great deal of alarm. As yet, Mr. and Mrs. P. tried to ignore the phenomena.

One evening, however, they were having a family spat over something of little consequence. All of a sudden a frying pan standing on the stove lifted off by itself, hung suspended in mid-air for a moment, and then was flung back on the stove with full force. Their twelve-year-old son who witnessed it flew into hysterics; Mr. P. turned white, and Mrs. P. was just plain angry. How dare someone invade their privacy? The following week, the ten-year-old daughter was watching television downstairs in what had been turned into Mrs. P.'s office, while Mr. P. and their son were upstairs also watching television. Suddenly, a glass of milk standing on the desk in the office rose up by itself and dashed itself to the floor with full force. The child ran screaming from the room, and it took a long time for her father to calm her down.

As a result of these happenings, the children implored their mother to move from the house, but Mrs. P. would have none of it. She liked the house fine, and was not about to let some unknown ghost displace her. The more she thought about it, the angrier she got. She decided to go from floor to floor, cursing the unknown ghost and telling him or her to get out of the house, even if they used to own it.

But that is how it is with Stay-Behinds: they don't care if you paid for the house. After all, they can't use the money where they are, and would rather stay on in a place they are familiar with.

Strange places can have Stay-Behind ghosts. Take Maryknoll College of Glen Ellyn, Illinois, a Roman Catholic seminary that closed its doors in June of 1972, due to a dwindling interest in what it had to offer. In the fall a few years before, a seminarian named Gary M. was working in the darkroom of the college. This was part of his regular assignments, and photography had been a regular activity for some years, participated in by both faculty and students.

On this particular occasion, Mr. M. felt as though he were being watched while in the darkroom. Chalking it up to an active imagination, he dismissed the matter from his mind. But in the spring a few years later, Mr. M. was going through some old chemicals belonging to a former priest, when he received the strongest impression of a psychic presence. He was loading some film at the time, and as he did so, he had the uncanny feeling that he was not alone in the room. The chemicals he had just handled were once the property of a priest who had died three years before. The following day, while developing film in an open tank, he suddenly felt as though a cold hand had gone down his back. He realized also that the chemicals felt colder than before. After he had turned the lights back on, he took the temperature of the developer. At the start it had been 70° F., while at the end it was down to 64° F. Since the room temperature was 68° F., there was a truly unaccountable decrease in temperature.

The phenomena made him wonder, and he discussed his experiences with other seminarians. It was then learned that a colleague of his had also had experiences in the same place. Someone, a man, had appeared to him, and he had felt the warm touch of a hand at his cheek. Since he was not alone at the time, but in a group of five students, he immediately reported the incident to them. The description of the apparition was detailed and definite. Mr. M.

quickly went into past files, and came up with several pictures, so that his fellow student, who had a similar experience, could pick out that of the ghostly apparition he had seen. Without the slightest hesitation, he identified the dead priest as the man he had seen. This was not too surprising; the students were using what was once the priest's own equipment and chemicals, and perhaps he still felt obliged to teach them their proper use.

Mr. and Mrs. E. live in an average home in Florida that was built about thirteen years ago. They moved into this house in August. Neither of them had any particular interest in the occult, and Mr. E. could be classified as a complete skeptic, if anything. For the first few months of their residence, they were much too busy to notice anything out of the ordinary, even if there were such occurrences.

It was just before Christmas when they got their first inkling that something was not as it should be with their house. Mrs. E. was sitting up late one night, busy with last-minute preparations for the holiday. All of a sudden the front door, which was secured and locked, flew open with a violent force, and immediately shut itself again, with the handle turning by itself and the latch falling into place. Since Mrs. E. didn't expect any visitors, she was naturally surprised. Quickly walking over to the door to find out what had happened, she discovered that the door was locked. It is the kind of lock that can only be unlocked by turning a knob. Shaking her head in disbelief, she returned to her chair, but before she could sit down again and resume her chores, the door to the utility room began to rattle as though a wind were blowing. Yet there were no open windows that could have caused it. Suddenly, as she was staring at it, the knob turned and the door opened. Somehow nonplussed, Mrs. E. thought, rather sarcastically, "While you're at it, why don't you shake the Christmas tree too?" Before she had completed the thought, the tree began to shake. For a moment, Mrs. E. stood still and thought all of this over in her mind. Then she decided that she was just overtired and had contracted a case of the holiday jitters. It was probably all due to imagination. She went to bed and didn't say anything about the incident.

Two weeks later, her fourteen-year-old daughter and Mrs. E. were up late talking, when all of a sudden every cupboard in the kitchen opened by itself, one by one. Mrs. E.'s daughter stared at the phenomena in disbelief. But Mrs. E. simply said, "Now close them." Sure enough, one by one, they shut with a hard slam by themselves, almost like a little child whose prank had not succeeded. At this point Mrs. E. thought it best to tell her daughter of her first encounter with the unseen, and implored her not to be scared of it, or tell the younger children or anyone else outside the house. She didn't want to be known as a weird individual in the neighborhood into which they had just moved. However, she decided to inform her husband about what had happened. He didn't say much, but it was clear that he was not convinced. However, as with so many cases of this kind where the man in the house takes a lot longer to be convinced than the women, Mr. E.'s time came about two weeks later.

He was watching television when one of the stereo speakers began to tilt back all of a sudden, rocking back and forth without falling over, on its own, as if held by unseen hands. Being of a practical bent, Mr. E. got up to find an explanation, but there was no wind that would have been strong enough to tilt a twenty-pound speaker. At this point, Mr. E. agreed that there was something peculiar about the house. This was the more likely as their dog, an otherwise calm and peaceful animal, went absolutely wild at the moment the speakers tilted, and ran about the house for half an hour afterwards, barking, sniffing, and generally raising Cain.

However, the ghost was out of the bag, so to speak. The two younger children, then nine and ten years old, noticed him—it was assumed to be a man all along. A house guest remarked how strange it was that the door was opening seemingly by itself. Mrs. E. explained this with a remark that the latch was not working properly. "But how did the knob turn, then?" the house guest wanted to know.

Under the circumstances, Mrs. E. owned up to their guest. The ghost doesn't scare Mrs. E., but he makes it somewhat unpleasant for her at times, such as when she is taking a shower and the doors fly open. After all, one doesn't want to be watched by a man while showering, even if he *is* a ghost. The Stay-Behind isn't noticeable all the time, to be sure, but frequently enough to count as an extra inhabitant of the house. Whenever she feels him near, there is a chill in the hall and an echo. This happens at various times of day or night, early or late. To the children he is a source of some concern, and they will not stay home alone.

But to Mrs. E. he is merely an unfortunate human being, caught up in the entanglement of his own emotions from the past, desperately trying to break through the time barrier to communicate with her, but unable to do so because conditions aren't just right. Sometimes she wishes she were more psychic than she is, but in the meantime she has settled down to share her home with someone she cannot see, but who, it appears, considers himself part of the family.

One of the most amazing stories of recent origin concerns a family of farmers in central Connecticut. Some people have a ghost in the house, a Stay-

Behind who likes the place so much he or she doesn't want to leave. But this family had entire *groups* of ghosts staying on, simply because they liked the sprawling farmhouse, and simply because it happened to be their home too. The fact that they had passed across the threshold of death did not deter them in the least. To the contrary, it seemed a natural thing to stay behind and watch what the young ones were doing with the house, to possibly help them here and there, and, at the very least, to have some fun with them by causing so-called "inexplicable" phenomena to happen.

After all, life can be pretty dull in central Connecticut, especially in the winter. It isn't any more fun being a ghost in central Connecticut, so one cannot really hold it against these Stay-Behinds if they amuse themselves as best they can in the afterlife. Today the house shows its age; it isn't in good condition, and needs lots of repairs. The family isn't as large as it was before some of the younger generation moved out to start lives of their own, but it's still a busy house and a friendly one, ghosts or no ghosts. It stands on a quiet country road off the main route, and on a clear day you can see the Massachusetts border in the distance; that is, if you are looking for it. It is hardly noticeable, for in this part of the country, all New England looks the same.

Because of the incredible nature of the many incidents, the family wants no publicity, no curious tourists, no reporters. To defer to their wishes, I changed the family name to help them retain that anonymity, and the peace and quiet of their country house. The house in question was already old when a map of the town, drawn in 1761, showed it. The present owners, the Harveys, have lived in it all their lives, with interruption. Mrs. Harvey's great-great-grandparents bought it from the original builder, and when her great-great-grandfather died in 1858, it happened at the old homestead. Likewise, her great-great-grandmother passed on in 1871, at the age of eighty, and again it happened at home. One of their children died in 1921, at age ninety-one, also at home.

This is important, you see, because it accounts for the events that transpired later in the lives of their descendants. A daughter named Julia married an outsider and moved to another state, but considers herself part of the family just the same, so much so that her second home was still the old homestead in central Connecticut. Another daughter, Martha, was Mrs. Harvey's great-grandmother. Great-grandmother Martha died at age ninety-one, also in the house. Then there was an aunt, a sister of her great-great-grandfather's by the name of Nancy, who came to live with them when she was a widow; she lived to be ninety and died in the house. They still have some of her furniture there. Mrs. Harvey's grandparents had only one child, Viola, who became her mother, but they took in boarders, mostly men working in the nearby sawmills. One of these boarders died in the house too, but his name is unknown. Possibly several others died there too.

Of course the house doesn't look today the way it originally did; additions were built onto the main part, stairs were moved, a well in the cellar was filled in because members of the family going down for cider used to fall into it, and many of the rooms that later became bedrooms originally had other purposes. For instance, daughter Marjorie's bedroom was once called the harness room because horses' harnesses were once made in it, and the room of one of the sons used to be called the cheese room for obvious reasons. What became a sewing room was originally used as a pantry, with shelves running across the south wall.

The fact that stairs were changed throughout the house is important, because in the mind of those who lived in the past, the original stairs would naturally take precedence over later additions or changes. Thus phantoms may appear out of the wall, seemingly without reason, except that they would be walking up staircases that no longer exist.

Mrs. Harvey was born in the house, but at age four her parents moved away from it, and did not return until much later. But even then, Mrs. Harvey recalls an incident which she was never to forget. When she was only four years old, she remembers very clearly an old lady she had never seen before appear at her crib. She cried, but when she told her parents about it, they assured her it was just a dream. But Mrs. Harvey knew she had not dreamt the incident; she remembered every detail of the old lady's dress.

When she was twelve years old, at a time when the family had returned to live in the house, she was in one of the upstairs bedrooms and again the old lady appeared to her. But when she talked about it with her parents, the matter was immediately dropped. As Frances Harvey grew up in the house, she couldn't help but notice some strange goings-on. A lamp moved by itself, without anyone being near it. Many times she could feel a presence walking close behind her in the upstairs part of the house, but when she turned around, she was alone. Nor was she the only one to notice the strange goings-on. Her brothers heard footsteps around their beds, and complained about someone bending over them, yet no one was to be seen. The doors to the bedrooms would open by themselves at night, so much so that the boys tied the door latches together so that they could not open by themselves. Just the same, when morning came, the doors were wide open with the knot still in place.

It was at that time that her father got into the habit of taking an after-dinner walk around the house before retiring. Many times he told the family of seeing a strange light going through the upstairs rooms, a glowing luminosity for which there was no rational explanation. Whenever Frances Harvey had to be alone upstairs she felt uncomfortable, but when she mentioned this to her parents she was told that all old houses made one feel like that and to never mind. One evening, Frances was playing a game with her grandfather when both of them clearly heard footsteps coming up the back stairs. But her grandfather didn't budge. When Frances asked him who this could possibly be, he merely shrugged and said there was plenty of room for *everyone.*

As the years passed, the Harveys would come back to the house from time to time to visit. On these occasions, Frances would wake up in the night because someone was bending over her. At other times there was a heavy depression on the bed as if someone were sitting there! Too terrified to tell anyone about it, she kept her experiences to herself for the time being.

Then, in the early 1940s, Frances married, and with her husband and two children, eventually returned to the house to live there permanently with her grandparents. No sooner had they moved in when the awful feeling came back in the night. Finally she told her husband, who of course scoffed at the idea of ghosts.

The most active area in the house seemed to be upstairs, roughly from her son Don's closet, through her daughter Lolita's room, and especially the front hall and stairs. It felt as if someone were standing on the landing of the front stairs, just watching.

This goes back a long time. Mrs. Harvey's mother frequently complained, when working in the attic, that all of a sudden she would feel someone standing next to her, someone she could not see.

One day Mrs. Harvey and her youngest daughter went grocery shopping. After putting the groceries away, Mrs. Harvey reclined on the living room couch while the girl sat in the dining room reading. Suddenly they heard a noise like thunder, even though the sky outside was clear. It came again, only this time it sounded closer, as if it were upstairs! When it happened the third time, it was accompanied by a sound as if someone were making up the bed in Mrs. Harvey's son's room upstairs.

Now, they had left the bed in disorder because they had been in a hurry to go shopping. No one else could have gone upstairs, and yet when they entered the son's room, the bed was made up as smoothly as possible. As yet, part of the family still scoffed at the idea of having ghosts in the house, and considered the mother's ideas as dreams or hallucinations. They were soon to change their minds, however, when it happened to them as well.

The oldest daughter felt very brave and called up the stairs, "Little ghosties, where are you?" Her mother told her she had better not challenge them, but the others found it amusing. That night she came downstairs a short time after she had gone to bed, complaining that she felt funny in her room, but thought it was just her imagination. The following night, she awoke to the feeling that someone was bending over her. One side of her pillow was pulled away from her head as though a hand had pushed it down. She called out and heard footsteps receding from her room, followed by heavy rumblings in the attic above. Quickly she ran into her sister's room, where both of them lay awake the rest of the night listening to the rumbling and footsteps walking around overhead. The next day she noticed a dusty black footprint on the light-colored scatter rug next to her bed. It was in the exact location where she had felt someone standing and bending over her. Nobody's footprint in the house matched the black footprint, for it was long and very narrow. At this point the girls purchased special night lights and left them on in the hope of sleeping peacefully.

One day Mrs. Harvey felt brave, and started up the stairs in response to footsteps coming from her mother's bedroom. She stopped, and as the footsteps approached the top of the stairs, a loud ticking noise came with them, like a huge pocket watch. Quickly she ran down the stairs and outside to get her son to be a witness to it. Sure enough, he too could hear the ticking noise. This was followed by doors opening and closing by themselves. Finally, they dared go upstairs, and when they entered the front bedroom, they noticed a very strong, sweet smell of perfume. When two of the daughters came home from work that evening, the family compared notes and it was discovered that they, too, had smelled the strange perfume and heard the ticking noise upstairs. They concluded that one of their ghosts, at least, was a man.

About that time, the youngest daughter reported seeing an old woman in her room, standing at a bureau with something shiny in her hand. The ghost handed it to her but she was too frightened to receive it. Since her description of the woman had been very detailed, Mrs. Harvey took out the family album and asked her daughter to look through it in the hope that she might identify the ghostly visitor. When they came to one particular picture, the girl let out a small cry: that was the woman she had seen! It turned out to be Julia, a great-great-aunt of Mrs. Harvey's, the same woman whom Mrs. Harvey herself had seen when she was twelve years old. Evidently, the lady was staying around.

Mrs. Harvey's attention was deflected from the phenomena in the house by her mother's illness. Like a dutiful daughter, she attended her to the very last, but in March of that year her mother passed away. Whether there is any connection with her mother's death or not, the phenomena started to increase greatly, both in volume and intensity, in July of that same year. To be exact, the date was July 20. Mrs. Harvey was hurrying one morning to get ready to take her daughter Lolita to the center of town so she could get a ride to work. Her mind was preoccupied with domestic chores, when a car came down the road, with brakes squealing. Out of habit, she hurried to the living room window to make sure that none of their cats had been hit by the car. This had been a habit of her mother's and hers, whenever there was the sound of sudden brakes outside.

As she did so, for just a fleeting glance, she saw her late mother looking out of her favorite window. It didn't register at first, then Mrs. Harvey realized her mother couldn't possibly have been there. However, since time was of the essence, Mrs. Harvey and her daughter Lolita left for town without saying anything to any of the others in the house. When they returned, her daughter Marjorie was standing outside waiting for them. She complained of hearing someone moving around in the living room just after they had left, and it sounded just like Grandma when she straightened out the couch and chair covers.

It frightened her, so she decided to wait in the dining room for her mother's return. But while there, she heard footsteps coming from the living room and going into the den, then the sound of clothes being folded. This was something Mrs. Harvey's mother was also in the habit of doing there. It was enough for Marjorie to run outside the house and wait there. Together with her sister and mother, she returned to the living room, only to find the chair cover straightened. The sight of the straightened chair cover made the blood freeze in Mrs. Harvey's veins; she recalled vividly how she had asked her late mother not to bother straightening the chair covers during her illness, because it hurt her back. In reply, her mother had said, "Too bad I can't come back and do it after I die."

Daughter Jane was married to a Navy man, who used to spend his leaves at the old house. Even during his courtship days, he and Mrs. Harvey's mother got along real fine, and they used to do crossword puzzles together. He was sleeping at the house some time after the old lady's death, when he awoke to see her standing by his bed with her puzzle book and pencil in hand. It was clear to Mrs. Harvey by now that her late mother had joined the circle of dead relatives to keep a watch on her and the family. Even while she was ill, Mrs. Harvey's mother wanted to help in the house. One day after her death, Mrs. Harvey was baking a custard pie and lay down on the couch for a few minutes while it was baking.

She must have fallen asleep, for she awoke to the voice of her mother saying, "Your pie won't burn, will it?" Mrs Harvey hurriedly got up and checked; the pie was just right and would have burned if it had been left in any longer. That very evening, something else happened. Mrs. Harvey wanted to watch a certain program that came on television at seven-thirty P.M., but she was tired and fell asleep on the couch in the late afternoon. Suddenly she heard her mother's voice say to her, "It's time for your program, dear." Mrs. Harvey looked at the clock, and it was exactly seventy-thirty P.M. Of course, her mother did exactly the same type of thing when she was living, so it wasn't too surprising that she should continue with her concerned habits after she passed on into the next dimension.

But if Mrs. Harvey's mother had joined the ghostly crew in the house, she was by no means furnishing the bulk of the phenomena—not by a long shot. Lolita's room upstairs seemed to be the center of many activities, with her brother Don's room next to hers also very much involved. Someone was walking from her bureau to her closet, and her brother heard the footsteps too. Lolita looked up and saw a man in a uniform with gold buttons, standing in the back of her closet. At other times she smelled perfume and heard the sound of someone dressing near her bureau. All the time she heard people going up the front stairs mumbling, then going into her closet where the sound stopped abruptly. Yet, they could not see anyone on such occasions.

Daughter Jane wasn't left out of any of this either. Many nights she would feel someone standing next to her bed, between the bed and the wall. She saw three different people, and felt hands trying to lift her out of bed. To be sure, she could not see their faces; their shapes were like dark shadows. Marjorie, sleeping in the room next to Jane's, also experienced an attempt by some unseen forces to get her out of bed. She grabbed the headboard to stop herself from falling when she noticed the apparition of the same old woman whom Mrs. Harvey had seen the time she heard several people leave her room for the front hall.

One night she awoke to catch a glimpse of someone in a long black coat hurrying through the hall. Mumbling was heard in that direction, so she put her ear against the door to see if she could hear any words, but she couldn't make out any. Marjorie, too, saw the old woman standing at the foot of her bed—the same old woman whom Mrs. Harvey had seen when she was twelve years old. Of course, that isn't too surprising; the room Marjorie slept in used to be Julia's a long time ago. Lolita also had her share of experiences: sounds coming up from the cellar bothering her, footsteps, voices, even the sound of chains. It seemed to her that they came right out of the wall by her head, where there used to be stairs. Finally, it got so bad that Lolita asked her mother to sleep with her. When Mrs. Harvey complied, the two women clearly saw a glow come in from the living room and go to where the shelves used to be. Then there was the sound of dishes, and even the smell of food.

Obviously, the ghostly presences were still keeping house in their own fashion, reliving some happy or at least busy moments from their own past. By now Mr. Harvey was firmly convinced that he shared the house with a number of dead relatives, if not friends. Several times he woke to the sound of bottles being placed on the bureau. One night he awoke because the bottom of the bed was shaking hard; as soon as he was fully awake, it stopped. This was followed by a night in which Mrs. Harvey could see a glow pass through the room at the bottom of the bed. When "they" got to the hall door, which was shut, she could hear it open, but it actually did not move. Yet the sound was that of a door opening. Next she heard several individuals walk up the stairs, mumbling as they went.

The following night a light stopped by their fireplace, and as she looked closely it resembled a figure bending down. It got so that they compared notes almost every morning to see what had happened next in their very busy home. One moonlit night Mrs. Harvey woke to see the covers of her bed folded in half, down the entire length of the bed. Her husband was fully covered, but she was totally uncovered. At the same time, she saw some dark shadows by the side of the bed. She felt someone's hand holding her own, pulling her gently. Terrified, she couldn't move, and just lay there wondering what would happen next. Then the blankets were replaced as before, she felt something cold touch her forehead, and the ghosts left. But the Stay-Behinds were benign, and meant no harm. Some nights, Mrs. Harvey would wake up because of the cold air, and notice that the blankets were standing up straight from the bed as if held by someone. Even after she pushed them back hard, they would not stay in place.

On the other hand, there were times when she accidentally uncovered herself at night and felt someone putting the covers back on her, as if to protect her from the night chills. This was more important, as the house has no central heating. Of course it wasn't always clear what the ghosts wanted from her. On the one hand, they were clearly concerned with her well-being and that of the family; on the other, they seemed to crave attention for themselves also.

Twice they tried to lift Mrs. Harvey out of her bed. She felt herself raised several inches above it by unseen hands, and tried to call out to her husband but somehow couldn't utter a single word. This was followed by a strange, dreamlike state, in which she remembered being taken to the attic and shown something. Unfortunately she could not remember it afterwards, except that she had been to the attic and how the floorboards looked there; she also recalled that the attic was covered with black dust. When morning came, she took a look at her feet: they were dusty, and the bottom of her bed was grayish as if from dust. Just as she was contemplating these undeniable facts, her husband asked her what had been the matter with her during the night. Evidently he had awakened to find her gone from the bed.

One night daughter Marjorie was out on a date. Mrs. Harvey awoke to the sound of a car pulling into the driveway, bringing Marjorie home. From her bed she could clearly see four steps of the back stairs. As she lay there, she saw the shape of a woman coming down without any sound, sort of floating down the stairs. She was dressed in a white chiffon dress. At the same moment, her daughter Marjorie entered the living room. She too saw the girl in the chiffon dress come down the stairs into the living room and disappear through a door to the other bedroom. Even though the door was open wide and there was plenty of room to go through the opening, evidently the ghostly lady preferred to walk through the door.

The miscellaneous Stay-Behinds tried hard to take part in the daily lives of the flesh-and-blood people in the house. Many times the plants in the living room would be rearranged and attended to by unseen hands. The Harveys could clearly see the plants move, yet no one was near them; no one, that is, visible to the human eye. There was a lot of mumbling about now, and eventually they could make out some words. One day daughter Marjorie heard her late grandmother say to her that "they" would be back in three weeks. Sure enough, not a single incident of a ghostly nature occurred for three weeks. To the day, after the three weeks were up, the phenomena began again. Where had the ghosts gone in the meantime? On another occasion, Marjorie heard someone say, "That is Jane on that side of the bed, but who is that on the other side? The bed looks so smooth." The remark made sense to Mrs. Harvey. Her late mother sometimes slept with Jane, when she was still in good health. On the other hand, daughter Marjorie likes to sleep perfectly flat, so her bed does look rather smooth.

Average people believe ghosts only walk at night. Nothing could be further from the truth, as Mrs. Harvey will testify. Frequently, when she was alone in the house during the daytime, she would hear doors upstairs bang shut and open again. One particular day, she heard the sound of someone putting things on Jane's bureau, so she tried to go up and see what it was. Carefully tiptoeing up the stairs to peek into her door to see if she could actually trap a ghost, she found herself halfway along the hall when she heard footsteps coming along the foot of son Don's bed, in her direction. Quickly, she hurried back down the stairs and stopped halfway down. The footsteps sounded like a woman's, and suddenly there was the rustle of a taffeta gown.

With a *whooshing* sound, the ghost passed Mrs. Harvey and went into Jane's room. Mrs. Harvey waited, rooted to the spot on the stairs.

A moment later the woman's footsteps came back, only this time someone walked with her, someone heavier. They went back through Don's room, and ended up in Lolita's closet—the place where Lolita had seen the man in the uniform with the shining gold buttons. Mrs. Harvey did not follow immediately, but that night she decided to go up to Lolita's room and have another look at the closet. As she approached the door to the room it opened, which wasn't unusual since it was in the habit of opening at the slightest vibration. But before Mrs. Harvey could close it, it shut itself tight and the latch moved into place of its own accord. Mrs. Harvey didn't wait around for anything further that night.

For awhile there was peace. But in October the phenomena resumed. One night Mrs. Harvey woke up when she saw a shadow blocking the light coming from the dining room. She looked towards the door and saw a lady dressed all in black come into her bedroom and stand close to her side of the bed. This time she clearly heard her speak.

"Are you ready? It is almost time to go."

With that, the apparition turned and started up the stairs. The stairs looked unusually light, as if moonlight were illuminating them. When the woman in black got to the top step, all was quiet and the stairs were dark again, as before. Mrs. Harvey could see her clothes plainly enough, but not her face. She noticed that the apparition had carried a pouch-style pocketbook, which she had put over her arm so that her hands would be free to lift up her skirts as she went up the stairs. The next morning, Mrs. Harvey told her husband of the visitation. He assured her she must have dreamt it all. But before she could answer, her daughter Marjorie came in and said that she had heard someone talking in the night, something about coming, and it being almost time. She saw a figure at the foot of her bed, which she described as similar to what Mrs. Harvey had seen.

The night before that Thanksgiving, Marjorie heard footsteps come down the stairs. She was in bed and tried to get up to see who it was, but somehow couldn't move at all, except to open her eyes to see five people standing at the foot of her bed! Two of them were women, the others seemed just outlines or shadows. One of the two women wore an old-fashioned shaped hat, and she looked very stern. As Marjorie was watching the group, she managed to roll over a little in her bed and felt someone next to her. She felt relieved at the thought that it was her mother, but then whoever it was got up and left with the others in the group. All the time they kept talking among themselves, but Marjorie could not understand what was being said. Still talking, the ghostly visitors went back up the stairs.

Nothing much happened until Christmastime. Again the footsteps running up and down the stairs resumed, yet no one was seen. Christmas night, Jane and her mother heard walking in the room above the living room, where Mrs. Harvey's mother used to sleep. At that time, Mr. Harvey was quite ill and was sleeping in what used to be the sewing room so as not to awaken when his wife got up early.

On two different occasions Mrs. Harvey had "visitors." The first time someone lifted her a few inches off the bed. Evidently someone else was next to her in bed, for when she extended her hand that person got up and left. Next she heard footsteps going up the stairs and someone laughing, then all was quiet again. About a week later, she woke one night to feel someone pulling hard on her elbow and ankle. She hung onto the top of her bed with her other hand. But the unseen entities pushed, forcing her to brace herself against the wall.

Suddenly it all stopped, yet there were no sounds of anyone leaving. Mrs. Harvey jumped out of bed and tried to turn the light on. It wouldn't go on. She went back to bed when she heard a voice telling her not to worry, that her husband would be all right. She felt relieved at the thought, when the voice added, "But you won't be." Then the unseen voice calmly informed her that she would die in an accident caused by a piece of bark from some sort of tree. That was all the voice chose to tell her, but it was enough to start her worrying. Under the circumstances, and in order not to upset her family, she kept quiet about it, eventually thinking that she had dreamed the whole incident. After all, if it were just a dream, there was no point in telling anyone, and if it were true, there was nothing she could do anyway, so there was no point in worrying her family. She had almost forgotten the incident when she did have an accident about a week later. She hurt her head rather badly in the woodshed, requiring medical attention. While she was still wondering whether that was the incident referred to by the ghostly voice, she had a second accident: a heavy fork fell on her and knocked her unconscious.

But the voice had said that she would die in an accident, so Mrs. Harvey wasn't at all sure that the two incidents, painful though they had been, were what the voice had referred to. Evidently, ghosts get a vicarious thrill out of making people worry, because Mrs. Harvey is alive and well, years after the unseen voice had told her she would die in an accident.

But as if it were not enough to cope with ghost people, Mrs. Harvey also had the company of a ghost dog. Their favorite pet, Lucy, passed into eternal dogdom the previous March. Having been treated as a member of the family, she had been permitted to sleep in the master bedroom, but as she became older she started wetting the rug, so eventually she had to be kept out.

After the dog's death, Marjorie offered her mother another dog, but Mrs. Harvey didn't want a replacement for Lucy; no other dog could take her place. Shortly after the offer and its refusal, Lolita heard a familiar scratch at the bathroom door. It sounded exactly as Lucy had always sounded when Lolita came home late at night. At first, Mrs. Harvey thought her daughter had just imagined it, but then the familiar wet spot reappeared on the bedroom rug. They tried to look for a possible leak in the ceiling, but could find no rational cause for the rug to be wet. The wet spot remained for about a month. During that time, several of the girls heard a noise that reminded them of Lucy walking about. Finally the rug dried out and Lucy's ghost stopped walking.

For several years the house has been quiet now. Have the ghosts gone on to their just rewards, been reincarnated, or have they simply tired of living with flesh-and-blood relatives? Stay-Behinds generally stay indefinitely; unless, of course, they feel they are really not wanted. Or perhaps they just got bored with it all.

Years ago, a tragic event took place at a major university campus in Kansas. A member of one of the smaller fraternities, TKE, was killed in a head-on automobile accident on September 21. His sudden death at so young an age—he was an undergraduate—brought home a sense of tragedy to the other members of the fraternity, and it was decided that they would attend his funeral in New York *en masse*.

Not quite a year after the tragic accident, several members of the fraternity were at their headquarters. Eventually, one of the brothers and his date were left behind alone, studying in the basement of the house. Upon completion of their schoolwork, they left. When they had reached the outside, the girl remembered she had left her purse in the basement and returned to get it. When she entered the basement, she noticed a man sitting at the poker table, playing with chips. She said something to him, explaining herself, then grabbed her purse and returned upstairs. There she asked her date who the man in the basement was, since she hadn't noticed him before. He laughed and said that no one had been down there but the two of them. At that point, one of the other brothers went into the basement and was surprised to see a man get up from his chair and walk away. That man was none other than the young man who had been killed in the automobile crash a year before.

One of the other members of the fraternity had also been in the same accident, but had only been injured, and survived. Several days after the incident in the fraternity house basement, this young man saw the dead boy walking up the steps to the second floor of the house. By now the fraternity realized that their dead brother was still very much with them, drawn back to what was to him his true home—and so they accepted him as one of the crowd, even if he was invisible at times.

On January 7, Mr. and Mrs. S. moved into an older house on South Fourth Street, a rented, fully-furnished two-bedroom house in a medium-sized city in Oklahoma. Mrs. S.'s husband was a career service man in the Army, stationed at a nearby Army camp. They have a small boy, and looked forward to a pleasant stay in which the boy could play with neighborhood kids, while Mrs. S. tried to make friends in what to her was a new environment.

She is a determined lady, not easily frightened off by anything she cannot explain, and the occult was the last thing on her mind. They had lived in the house for about two weeks, when she noticed light footsteps walking in the hall at night. When she checked on them, there was no one there. Her ten-year-old son was sleeping across the hall, and she wondered if perhaps he was walking in his sleep. But each time she heard the footsteps and would check on her son, she found him sound asleep. The footsteps continued on and off, for a period of four months.

Then, one Sunday afternoon at about two o'clock, when her husband was at his post and her son in the backyard playing, she found herself in the kitchen. Suddenly she heard a child crying very softly and mutedly, as if the child were afraid to cry aloud. At once she ran into the back yard to see if her son was hurt. There was nothing wrong with him, and she found him playing happily with a neighborhood boy. It then dawned on her that she could not hear the child crying outside the house, but immediately upon re-entering the house, the faint sobs were clearly audible again.

She traced the sound to her bedroom, and when she entered the room, it ceased to be noticeable. This puzzled her to no end, since she had no idea what could cause the sounds. Added to this were strange thumping sounds, which frequently awakened her in the middle of the night. It sounded as if someone had fallen out of bed.

On these occasions, she would get out of bed quickly and rush into her son's room, only to find him fast asleep. A thorough check of the entire house revealed no source for the strange noises. But Mrs. S. noticed that their Siamese cat, who slept at the foot of her bed when these things happened, also reacted to them: his hair would bristle, his ears would fly back, and he would growl and stare into space at something or someone she could not see.

About that time, her mother decided to visit them. Since her mother was an invalid, Mrs. S. decided not to tell her about the strange phenomena in order to avoid upsetting her. She had stayed at the house for three days, when one morning she wanted to know why Mrs. S. was up at two o'clock in the morning making coffee. Since the house had only two bedrooms, they had put a half-bed into the kitchen for her mother, especially as the kitchen was very large and she could see the television from where she was sleeping. Her mother insisted she had heard footsteps coming down the hall into the kitchen. She called out to what she assumed was her daughter, and when there was no answer, she assumed that her daughter and her son-in-law had had some sort of disagreement and she had gotten up to make some coffee.

From her bed she could not reach the light switch, but she could see the time by the illuminated clock and realized it was two o'clock in the morning. Someone came down the hall, entered the kitchen, put water into the coffee pot, plugged it in, and then walked out of the kitchen and down the hall. She could hear the sound of coffee perking and could actually smell it. However, when she didn't hear anyone coming back, she assumed that her daughter and son-in-law had made up and gone back to sleep.

She did likewise, and decided to question her daughter about it in the morning. Mrs. S. immediately checked the kitchen, but there was no trace of the coffee to be found, which did not help her state of mind. A little later she heard some commotion outside the house, and on stepping outside noticed that the dogcatcher was trying to take a neighbor's dog with him. She decided to try and talk him out of it, and the conversation led to her husband being in the service, a statement which seemed to provoke a negative reaction on the part of the dogcatcher. He informed Mrs. S. that the last GI to live in the house was a murderer. When she wanted to know more about it, he clammed up immediately. But Mrs. S. became highly agitated. She called the local newspaper and asked for any and all information concerning her house. It was then that she learned the bitter truth.

In October two years before, a soldier stationed at the same base as her husband had beaten his two-year-old daughter to death. The murder took place in what had now become Mrs. S.'s bedroom. Mrs. S., shocked by the news, sent up a silent prayer, hoping that the restless soul of the child might find peace and not have to haunt a house where she had suffered nothing but unhappiness in her short life. . . .

THE NORTH EAST

7

The Ghost at Cap'n Grey's

SOME OF THE best leads regarding a good ghost story come to me as the result of my having appeared on one of many television or radio programs, usually discussing a book dealing with the subject matter for which I am best known—psychic phenomena of one kind or another. So it happened that one of my many appearances on the Bob Kennedy television show in Boston drew unusually heavy mail from places as far away as other New England states and even New York.

Now if there is one thing ghosts don't really care much about it is time—to them everything is suspended in a timeless dimension where the intensity of their suffering or problem remains forever constant and alive. After all, they are unable to let go of what it is that ties them to a specific location, otherwise they would not be what we so commonly (and perhaps a little callously) call ghosts. I am mentioning this as a way of explaining why, sometimes, I cannot respond as quickly as I would like to when someone among the living reports a case of a haunting that needs to be looked into. Reasons were and are now mainly lack of time but more likely lack of funds to organize a team and go after the case. Still, by and large, I do manage to show up in time and usually manage to resolve the situation.

Thus it happened that I received a letter dated August 4, 1966, sent to me via station WBZ-TV in Boston, from the owner of Cap'n Grey's Smorgasbord, an inn located in Barnstable on Cape Cod. The owner, Mr. Lennart Svensson, had seen me on the show and asked me to get in touch.

"We have experienced many unusual happenings here. The building in which our restaurant and guest house is located was built in 1716 and was formerly a sea captain's residence," Svensson wrote.

I'm a sucker for sea captains haunting their old houses so I wrote back asking for details. Mr. Svensson replied a few weeks later, pleased to have aroused my interest. Both he and his wife had seen the apparition of a young woman, and their eldest son had also felt an unseen presence; guests in their rooms also mentioned unusual happenings. It appeared that when the house was first built the foundation had been meant as a fortification against Indian attacks. Rumor has it, Mr. Svensson informed me, that the late sea captain had been a slave trader and sold slaves on the premises.

Svensson and his wife, both of Swedish origin, had lived on the Cape in the early thirties, later moved back to Sweden, to return in 1947. After a stint working in various restaurants in New York, they acquired the inn on Cape Cod.

I decided a trip to the Cape was in order. I asked Sybil Leek to accompany me as the medium. Mr. Svensson explained that the inn would close in October for the winter, but he, and perhaps other witnesses to the phenomena, could be seen even after that date, should I wish to come up then. But it was not until June 1967, the following year, that I finally managed to get our act together, so to speak, and I contacted Mr. Svensson to set a date for our visit. Unfortunately, he had since sold the inn and, as he put it, the new owner was not as interested in the ghost as he was, so there was no way for him to arrange for our visit now.

But Mr. Svensson did not realize how stubborn a man I can be when I want to do something. I never gave up on this case, and decided to wait a little and then approach the new owners. Before I could do so, however, the new owner saw fit to get in touch with me instead. He referred to the correspondence between Mr. Svensson and myself, and explained that at the time I had wanted to come up, he had been in the process of redoing the inn for its opening. That having taken place several weeks ago, it would appear that "we have experienced evidence of the spirit on several occasions, and I now feel we should look into this matter as soon as possible." He invited us to come on up whenever it was convenient, preferably yesterday.

The new owner turned out to be an attorney named Jack Furman of Hyannis, and a very personable man at that. When I wrote we would indeed be pleased to meet him, and the ghost or ghosts, as the case might be, he sent us all sorts of information regarding flights and offered to pick us up at the airport. Mr. Furman was not shy in reporting his own experiences since he had taken over the house.

> There has been on one occasion an umbrella mysteriously stuck into the stairwell in an open position. This was observed by my employee, Thaddeus B. Ozimek. On another occasion when the Inn was closed in the evening early, my manager returned to find the front door bolted from *the inside* which appeared strange since no one was in the build-

ing. At another time, my chef observed that the heating plant went off at 2:30, and the serviceman, whom I called the next day, found that a fuse was removed from the fuse box. At 2:30 in the morning, obviously, no one that we know of was up and around to do this. In addition, noises during the night have been heard by occupants of the Inn.

I suggested in my reply that our little team consisting, as it would, of medium (and writer) Sybil Leek, Catherine (my wife at the time), and myself, should spend the night at the Inn as good ghost hunters do. I also requested that the former owner, Mr. Svensson, be present for further questioning, as well as any direct witnesses to phenomena. On the other hand, I delicately suggested that no one not concerned with the case should be present, keeping in mind some occasions where my investigations had been turned into entertainment by my hosts to amuse and astound neighbors and friends.

In the end it turned out to be best to come by car as we had other projects to look into en route, such as Follins Pond, where we eventually discovered the possibility of a submerged Viking ship at the bottom of the pond. The date for our visit was to be August 17, 1967—a year and two weeks after the case first came to my attention. But not much of a time lag, the way it is with ghosts.

When we arrived at the Inn, after a long and dusty journey, the sight that greeted us was well worth the trip. There, set back from a quiet country road amid tall, aged trees, sat an impeccable white colonial house, two stories high with an attic, nicely surrounded by a picket fence, and an old bronze and iron lamp at the corner. The windows all had their wooden shutters opened to the outside and the place presented such a picture of peace it was difficult to realize we had come here to confront a disturbance. The house was empty, as we soon realized, because the new owner had not yet allowed guests to return—considering what the problems were!

Quickly, we unburdened ourselves of our luggage, each taking a room upstairs, then returned to the front of the house to begin our usual inspection. Sybil Leek now let go of her conscious self the more to immerse herself in the atmosphere and potential presences of the place.

"There is something in the bedroom . . . in the attic," Sybil said immediately as we climbed the winding stairs. "I thought just now someone was pushing my hair up from the back," she then added.

Mr. Furman had, of course, come along for the investigation. At this point we all saw a flash of light in the middle of the room. None of us was frightened by it, not even the lawyer who by now had taken the presence of the supernatural in his house in his stride.

We then proceeded downstairs again, with Sybil assuring us that whatever it was that perturbed her up in the attic did not seem to be present downstairs. With that we came to a locked door, a door, Mr. Furman assured us, that had not been opened in a long time. When we managed to get it open, it led us to the downstairs office or the room now used as such. Catherine, ever the alert artist and designer that she was, noticed that a door had been barred from the inside, almost as if someone had once been kept in that little room. Where did this particular door lead to, I asked Mr. Furman. It appeared it led to a narrow corridor and finally came out into the fireplace in the large main room.

"Someone told me if I ever dug up the fireplace," Mr. Furman intoned significantly, "I might find something."

What that something would be, was left to our imagination. Mr. Furman added that his informant had hinted at some sort of valuables, but Sybil immediately added, "bodies . . . you may find bodies."

She described, psychically, many people suffering in the house, and a secret way out of the house—possibly from the captain's slave trading days?

Like a doctor examining a patient, I then examined the walls both in the little room and the main room and found many hollow spots. A bookcase turned out to be a false front. Hidden passages seemed to suggest themselves. Quite obviously, Mr. Furman was not about to tear open the walls to find them. But Sybil was right: the house was honeycombed with areas not visible to the casual observer.

Sybil insisted we seat ourselves around the fireplace, and I insisted that the ghost, if any, should contact us there rather than our trying to chase the elusive phantom from room to room. "A way out of the house is very important," Sybil said, and I couldn't help visualizing the unfortunate slaves the good (or not so good) captain had held captive in this place way back.

But when nothing much happened, we went back to the office, where I discovered that the front portion of the wall seemed to block off another room beyond it, not accounted for when measuring the outside walls. When we managed to pry it open, we found a stairwell, narrow though it was, where apparently a flight of stairs had once been. I asked for a flashlight. Catherine shone it up the shaft: we found ourselves below a toilet in an upstairs bathroom! No ghost here.

We sat down again, and I invited the presence, whomever it was, to manifest. Immediately Sybil remarked she felt a young boy around the place, a hundred and fifty years ago. As she went more and more into a trance state, Sybil mentioned the name Chet . . . someone who wanted to be safe from an enemy . . . Carson . . .

"Let him speak," I said.

"Carson . . . 1858 . . ." Sybil replied, now almost totally entranced as I listened carefully for words coming from her in halting fashion.

"I will fight . . . Charles . . . the child is missing . . ."

"Whom will you fight? Who took the child?" I asked in return.

"Chicopee . . . child is dead."

"Whose house is this?"

"Fort . . ."

"Whose is it?"

"Carson . . ."

"Are you Carson?"

"Captain Carson."

"What regiment?"

"Belvedere . . . cavalry. . . 9th . . ."

"Where is the regiment stationed?"

There was no reply.

"Who commanded the regiment?" I insisted.

"Wainwright . . . Edward Wainwright . . . commander."

"How long have you been here?"

"Four years."

"Where were you born?"

"Montgomery. . . Massachusetts."

"How old are you now?"

There was no reply.

"Are you married?"

"My son . . . Tom . . . ten . . ."

"What year was he born in?"

"Forty. . . seven . . ."

"Your wife's name?"

"Gina . . ."

"What church do you go to?"

"I don't go."

"What church do you belong to?"

"She is . . . of Scottish background . . . Scottish kirk."

"Where is the kirk located?"

"Six miles . . ."

"What is the name of this village we are in now?"

"Chicopee . . ."

Further questioning gave us this information: that "the enemy" had taken his boy, and the enemy were the Iroquois. This was his fort and he was to defend it. I then began, as I usually do, when exorcism is called for, to speak of the passage of time and the need to realize that the entity communicating through the medium was unaware of the true situation in this respect. Did Captain Carson realize that time had passed since the boy had disappeared?

"Oh yes," he replied. "Four years."

"No, a hundred and seven years," I replied.

Once again I established that he was Captain Carson, and there was a river nearby and Iroquois were the enemy. Was he aware that there were "others" here besides himself.

He did not understand this. Would he want me to help him find his son since they had both passed over and should be able to find each other there?

"I need permission . . . from Wainwright . . ."

As I often do in such cases, I pretended to speak for Wainwright and granted him the permission. A ghost, after all, is not a rational human being but an entity existing in a delusion where only emotions count.

"Are you now ready to look for your son?"

"I am ready."

"Then I will send a messenger to help you find him," I said, "but you must call out to your son . . . in a loud voice."

The need to reach out to a loved one is of cardinal importance in the release of a trapped spirit, commonly called a ghost.

"John Carson is dead . . . but not dead forever," he said in a faint voice.

"You lived here in 1858, but this is 1967," I reminded him.

"You are mad!"

"No, I'm not mad. Touch your forehead . . . you will see this is not the body you are accustomed to. We have lent you a body to communicate with us. But it is not yours."

Evidently touching a woman's head did jolt the entity from his beliefs. I decided to press on.

"Go from this house and join your loved ones who await you outside . . ."

A moment later Captain Carson had slipped away and a sleepy Sybil Leek opened her eyes.

I now turned to Mr. Furman, who had watched the proceedings with mounting fascination. Could he corroborate any of the information that had come to us through the entranced medium?

"This house was built on the foundations of an Indian fort," he confirmed, "to defend the settlers against the Indians."

"Were there any Indians here in 1858?"

"There are Indians here even now," Furman replied. "We have an Indian reservation at Mashpee, near here, and on Martha's Vineyard there is a tribal chief and quite a large Indian population."

He also confirmed having once seen a sign in the western part of Massachusetts that read "Montgomery"—the place Captain Carson had claimed as his birthplace. Also that a Wainwright family was known to have lived in an area not far from where we were now. However, Mr. Furman had no idea of any military personnel by that name.

"Sybil mentioned a river in connection with this house." Furman said, "And, yes, there is a river running through the house, it is still here."

Earlier Sybil had drawn a rough map of the house as it was in the past, from her psychic viewpoint, a house surrounded by a high fence. Mr. Furman pronounced the drawing amazingly accurate—especially as Sybil had not set foot on the property or known about it until our actual arrival.

"My former secretary, Carole E. Howes, and her family occupied this house," Mr. Furman explained when I turned my attention to the manifestations themselves. "They operated this house as an Inn twenty years ago, and often had unusual things happen here as she grew up, but it did not seem to bother them. Then the house passed into the hands of a Mrs. Nielson; then Mr. Svensson took over. But he did not speak of the phenomena until about a year and a half ago. The winter of 1965 he was shingling the roof, and hc was just coming in from the roof on the second floor balcony on a cold day—he had left the window ajar and secured—when suddenly he heard the window sash come down. He turned around on the second floor platform and he saw the young girl, her hair windswept behind her. She was wearing white. He could not see anything below the waist, and he confronted her for a short period, but could not bring himself to talk—and she went away. His wife was in the kitchen sometime later, in the afternoon, when she felt the presence of someone in the room. She turned around and saw an older man dressed in black at the other end of the kitchen. She ran out of the kitchen and never went back in again.

"The accountant John Dillon's son was working in the kitchen one evening around ten. Now some of these heavy pots were hanging there on pegs from the ceiling. Young Dillon told his father two of them lifted themselves up from the ceiling, unhooked themselves from the pegs, and came down on the floor."

Did any guests staying at the Inn during Svensson's ownership complain of any unusual happenings?

"There was this young couple staying at what Mr. Svensson called the honeymoon suite," Mr. Furman replied. "At 6:30 in the morning, the couple heard three knocks at the door, three loud, distinct knocks, and when they opened the door, there was no one there. This sort of thing had happened before."

Another case involved a lone diner who complained to Svensson that "someone" was pushing him from his chair at the table in the dining room onto another chair, but since he did not see another person, how could this be? Svensson hastily had explained that the floor was a bit rickety and that was probably the cause.

Furman then recounted the matter of the lock: he and a young man who worked with him had left the Inn to bring the chef, who had become somewhat difficult that day, home to his own place. When Mr. Furman's assistant returned to the Inn at 2:30 in the morning, the door would not open, and the key would not work. After he had climbed into the house through an upstairs window, he found to his amazement that the door had been locked *from the inside*.

The story gave me a chill: that very day, after our arrival, nearly the same thing happened to us—except that we did not have to climb to the upper floor to get in but managed to enter through a rear door! Surely, someone did not exactly want us in the house.

The chef, by the way, had an experience of his own. The heating system is normally quite noisy, but one night it suddenly stopped and the heat went off. When the repair crew came the next day they discovered that a fuse had been physically removed from the fuse box, which in turn stopped the heating system from operating. The house was securely locked at that time so no one from the outside could have done this.

The famous case of an umbrella being stuck into the ceiling of the upstairs hall was confirmed by the brother of the young man, Mr. Bookstein, living in the house. He also pointed out to us that the Chicopee Indians were indeed in this area, so Sybil's trance utterances made a lot of sense.

"There was an Indian uprising in Massachusetts as late as the middle of the nineteenth century," he confirmed, giving more credence to the date, 1858, that had come through Sybil.

Was the restless spirit of the captain satisfied with our coming? Did he and his son meet up in the Great Beyond? Whatever came of our visit, nothing further has been heard of any disturbances at Cap'n Grey's Inn in Barnstable.

8

A Plymouth Ghost

I AM NOT talking about *the* Plymouth where the Pilgrims landed but another Plymouth. This one is located in New Hampshire, in a part of the state that is rather lonely and sparsely settled even today. If you really want to get away from it all—whatever it may be—this is a pretty good bet. I am mentioning this because a person living in this rural area isn't likely to have much choice in the way of entertainment, unless of course you provide it yourself. But I am getting ahead of my story.

I was first contacted about this case in August 1966 when a young lady named Judith Elliott, who lived in Bridgeport, Connecticut, at the time, informed me of the goings-on in her cousin's country house located in New Hampshire. Judith asked if I would be interested in contacting Mrs. Chester Fuller regarding these matters? What intrigued me about the report was not the usual array of footfalls, presences, and the house cat staring at someone unseen—but the fact that Mrs. Fuller apparently had seen a ghost and identified him from a book commemorating the Plymouth town bicentennial.

When I wrote back rather enthusiastically, Miss Elliott forwarded my letter to her cousin, requesting more detailed and chronological information. But it was not until well into the following year that I finally got around to making plans for a visit. Ethel Johnson Meyers, the late medium, and my ex-wife Catherine, always interested in spooky houses since she had illustrated some of my books, accompanied me. Mrs. Fuller, true to my request, supplied me with all that she knew of the phenomena themselves, who experienced them, and such information about former owners of the house and the house itself as she could garner. Here, in her own words, is that report, which of course I kept from the medium at all times so as not to influence her or give her prior knowledge of house and circumstances. Mrs. Fuller's report is as follows:

> Location: The house is located at 38 Merrill Street in the town of Plymouth, New Hampshire. To reach the house, you leave Throughway 93 at the first exit for Plymouth. When you reach the set of lights on Main

Street, turn right and proceed until you reach the blue Sunoco service station, then take a sharp left onto Merrill Street. The house is the only one with white picket snow fence out front. It has white siding with a red front door and a red window box and is on the right hand side of the street.

1. The first time was around the middle of June—about a month after moving in. It was the time of day when lights are needed inside, but it is still light outside. This instance was in the kitchen and bathroom. The bathroom and dining room are in an addition onto the kitchen. The doors to both rooms go out of the kitchen next to each other, with just a small wall space between. At that time we had our kitchen table in that space. I was getting supper, trying to put the food on the table and keep two small children (ages 2 and 5) off the table. As I put the potatoes on the table, I swung around from the sink toward the bathroom door. I thought I saw someone in the bathroom. I looked and saw a man. He was standing about half-way down the length of the room. He was wearing a brown plaid shirt, dark trousers with suspenders, and he [wore] glasses with the round metal frames. He was of medium height, a little on the short side, not fat and not thin but a good build, a roundish face, and he was smiling. Suddenly he was gone, no disappearing act or anything fancy, just gone, as he had come.

2. Footsteps. There are footsteps in other parts of the house. If I am upstairs, the footsteps are downstairs. If I am in the kitchen, they are in the livingroom, etc. These were scattered all through the year, in all seasons, and in the daytime. It was usually around 2 or 3 and always on a sunny day, as I recall.

3. Winter—late at night. Twice we (Seth and I) heard a door shutting upstairs. (Seth is an elderly man who stays with us now. When we first moved here he was not staying with us. His wife was a distant cousin to my father. I got acquainted with them when I was in high school. I spent a lot of time at their house and his wife and I became quite close. She died 11 years ago and since then Seth has stayed at his son's house, a rooming house, and now up here. He spent a lot of time visiting us before he moved in.) Only one door in the bedrooms upstairs works right, and that is the door to my bedroom. I checked the kids that night to see if they were up or awake, but they had not moved. My husband was also sound asleep. The door was already shut, as my husband had shut it tight when he went to bed to keep out the sound of the television. The sound of the door was very distinct—the sound of when it first made contact,

then the latch clicking in place, and then the thud as it came in contact with the casing. Everything was checked out—anything that was or could be loose and have blown and banged, or anything that could have fallen down. Nothing had moved. The door only shut once during that night, but did it again later on in the winter.

4. The next appearance was in the fall. I was pregnant at the time. I lost the baby on the first of November, and this happened around the first of October. Becky Sue, my youngest daughter, was 3 at the time. She was asleep in her crib as it was around midnight or later. I was asleep in my bedroom across the hall. I woke up and heard her saying, "Mommy, what are you doing in my bedroom?" She kept saying that until I thought I had better answer her or she would begin to be frightened. I started to say "I'm not in your room," and as I did I started to turn over and I saw what seemed to be a woman in a long white nightgown in front of my bedroom door. In a flash it was gone out into the hall. All this time Becky had been saying, "Mommy, what are you doing in my room?" As the image disappeared out in the hall, Becky changed her question to, "Mommy, what were you doing in my bedroom?" Then I thought that if I told her I wasn't in her room that she would really be scared. All this time I thought that it was Kimberly, my older daughter, getting up, and I kept waiting for her to speak to me. Becky was still sounding like a broken record with her questions. Finally I heard "It" take two steps down, turn a corner, and take three steps more. Then I went into Becky's room and told her that I had forgotten what I had gone into her room for and to lie down and go to sleep, which she did. All this time Kim had not moved. The next morning I was telling Seth (who was living with us now) about it, and I remembered about the footsteps going downstairs. I wondered if Becky had heard them too, so I called her out into the kitchen and asked her where I went after I left her room. She looked at me as if I had lost my mind and said, "Downstairs!"

5. This was in the winter, around 2. Seth was helping me make the beds upstairs as they had been skipped for some reason. We heard footsteps coming in from the playroom across the kitchen and a short way into the hall. We both thought it was Becky Sue who was playing outdoors. She comes in quite frequently for little odds and ends. Still no one spoke. We waited for a while expecting her to call to me. Finally, when she did not call, I went downstairs to see what she wanted, and there was no one there. I thought that maybe she had gone back out, but there was no snow on the floor or tracks of any kind. This was also on a very sunny day.

6. This was also late at night in 1965, around 11. I was putting my husband's lunch up when there was a step right behind me. That scared me, although I do not know why; up until that time I had never had any fear. Maybe it was because it was right behind my back and the others had always been at a distance or at least in front of me.

I cannot remember anything happening since then. Lately there have been noises as if someone was in the kitchen or dining room while I was in the livingroom, but I cannot be sure of that. It sounds as if something was swishing, but I cannot *definitely* say that it is not the sounds of an old house.

History of House and Background of Previous Owners

The history of the house and its previous owners is very hard to get. We bought the house from Mrs. Ora Jacques. Her husband had bought it from their son who had moved to Florida. The husband was going to do quite a bit of remodeling and then sell it. When he died, Mrs. Jacques rented it for a year and then sold it.

Mr. Jacques' son bought it from a man who used to have a doughnut shop and did his cooking in a back room, so I have been told. There was a fire in the back that was supposedly started from the fat. They bought the house from Mrs. Emma Thompson, who, with her husband, had received the house for caring for a Mr. Woodbury Langdon, and by also giving him a small sum of money. Mrs. Thompson always gave people the impression that she was really a countess and that she had a sister in Pennsylvania who would not have anything to do with her because of her odd ways.

Mrs. Thompson moved to Rumney where she contracted pneumonia about six months later and died.

Mr. and Mrs. Thompson moved in to take care of Mr. Woodbury Langdon after he kicked out Mr. and Mrs. Dinsmore. (Mr. Cushing gave me the following information. He lives next door, and has lived there since 1914 or 1918).

He was awakened by a bright flash very early in the morning. Soon he could see that the top room (tower room) was all afire. He got dressed, called the firemen, and ran over to help. He looked in the window of what is now our dining room but was then Mr. Langdon's bedroom. (Mr. Langdon was not able to go up and down stairs because of his age.) He pounded on the window trying to wake Mr. Langdon up. Through the window he could see Mr. and Mrs. Dinsmore standing in the doorway between the kitchen and the bedroom. They were laughing and Mr. Dinsmore had an oil can in his hand. All this time Mr. Langdon was sound asleep. Mr. Cushing got angry and began pounding harder and harder. Just as he began to open the window Mr. Langdon woke up and Mr. Cushing helped him out the window. He said that no one would believe his story, even the insurance company. Evidently Mr. Langdon did because soon after he kicked the Dinsmores out and that was when Mr. and Mrs. Thompson came to take care of him. Around 1927 he came down with pneumonia. He had that for two days and then he went outdoors without putting on any jacket or sweater. Mrs. Thompson ran out and brought him back in. She put him back in bed and warmed him up with coffee and wrapped him in wool blankets. He seemed better until around midnight. Then he began moaning. He kept it up until around 3, when he died.

Mr. Langdon was married twice. His first wife and his eighteen-year-old son died [of] typhoid fever. He had the wells examined and found that it came from them. He convinced his father to invest his money in putting in the first water works for the town of Plymouth. At that time he lived across town on Russell Street.

He later married a woman by the name of Donna. He worshipped her and did everything he could to please her. He remodeled the house. That was when he added on the bathroom and bedroom (dining room). He also built the tower room so that his wife could look out over the town. He also had a big estate over to Squam Lake that he poured out money on. All this time she was running around with anyone she could find. Mr. Cushing believes that he knew it deep down but refused to let himself believe it. She died, Mr. Cushing said, from the things she got from the thing she did! He insists that it was called leprosy. In the medical encyclopedia it reads, under leprosy, "differential diag: tuberculosis and esp. syphilis are the two diseases most likely to be considered." She died either in this house or at the estate on the lake. She was buried in the family plot in Trinity Cemetery in Holderness. She has a small headstone with just one name on it, Donna. There is a large spire shaped monument in the center of the lot, with the family's names on it and their relationship. The name of Woodbury Langdon's second wife is completely eliminated from the stone. There is nothing there to tell who she was or why she is buried there. This has puzzled me up to now, because, as she died around 1911, and he did not die until around 1927, he had plenty of time to have her name and relationship added to the family stone. Mr. Cushing thinks that, after her death, Mr. Langdon began to realize more and more what she was really like. He has the impression that Mr. Langdon was quite broke at the time of his death.

I cannot trace any more of the previous owners, as I cannot trace the house back any farther than around 1860. Mr. Langdon evidently bought and sold houses like other men bought and sold horses. If this is the house I believe it to be, it was on the road to Rumney and had to be moved in a backward position to where it is now. They had something like six months later to move the barn back. Then they had to put in a street going from the house up to the main road. They also had to put a fence up around the house. This property *did* have a barn, and there was a fence here. There is a small piece of it left. The deeds from there just go around in circles.

The man who I think the ghost is, is Mr. Woodbury Langdon. I have asked people around here what Mr. Langdon looked like and they describe him VERY MUCH as the man I saw in the bathroom. The man in the bicentennial book was his father. There is something in his face that was in the face of the "ghost."

I have two children. They are: Kimberly Starr, age 9 years and Rebecca Sue, age 6 years. Kim's birthday is on April 2 and Becky's is on August 10.

I was born and brought up on a farm 4½ miles out in the country in the town of Plymouth. My father believes in spirits, sort of, but not really. My mother absolutely does not.

I carried the business course and the college preparatory course through my four years of high school. I had one year of nurses' training. I was married when I was 20, in June, and Kim was born the next April.

P.S. We have a black cat who has acted queer at times in the past.

1. He would go bounding up the stairs only to come to an abrupt halt at the head of the stairs. He would sit there staring at presumably empty space, and then take off as if he had never stopped.
2. Sometimes he stood at the bathroom door and absolutely refused to go in.
3. He had spells of sitting in the hallway and staring up the stairs, not moving a muscle. Then suddenly he would relax and go on his way.

We finally settled on August 12, a Saturday, in 1967, to have a go at Mr. Langdon or whoever it was that haunted the house, because Miss Elliott was getting married in July and Mrs. Fuller wanted very much to be present.

Eleanor Fuller greeted us as we arrived, and led us into the house. As usual Ethel began to sniff around, and I just followed her, tape recorder running and camera at the ready. We followed her up the stairs to the upper floor, where Ethel stopped at the bedroom on the right, which happened to be decorated in pink.

"I get an older woman wearing glasses," Ethel said cautiously as she was beginning to pick up psychic leads, "and a man wearing a funny hat."

I pressed Ethel to be more specific about the "funny hat" and what period hat. The man seemed to her to belong to the early 1800s. She assured me it was not this century. She then complained about a cold spot, and when I stepped into it I too felt it. Since neither doors nor windows could be held responsible for the strong cold draft we felt, we knew that its origin was of a psychic nature, as it often is when there are entities present.

I asked Ethel to describe the woman she felt present. "She is lying down . . . and I get a pain in the chest," she said, picking up the spirit's condition. "The eyes are closed!"

We left the room and went farther on. Ethel grabbed her left shoulder as if in pain.

"She is here with me, looking at me," Ethel said.

"She's been here."

"Why is she still here?" I asked.

"I got a sudden chill when you asked that," Ethel replied.

"She tells mc to go left . . . I am having difficulty walking . . . I think this woman had that difficulty."

We were walking down the stairs, when Ethel suddenly became a crone and had difficulty managing them. The real Ethel was as spry and fast as the chipmunks that used to roam around her house in Connecticut.

"I think she fell down these stairs," Ethel said and began to cough. Obviously, she was being impressed by a very sick person.

We had barely got Ethel to a chair when she slipped into full trance and the transition took place. Her face became distorted as in suffering, and a feeble voice tried to manifest through her, prodded by me to be clearer.

"Lander . . . or something . . . ," she mumbled.

What followed was an absolutely frightening realization by an alien entity inside Ethel's body that the illness she was familiar with no longer existed now. At the same time, the excitement of this discovery made it difficult for the spirit to speak clearly, and we were confronted with a series of grunts and sighs.

Finally, I managed to calm the entity down by insisting she needed to relax in order to be heard.

"Calm . . . calm . . . ," she said and cried, "good . . . he knows . . . he did that . . . for fifty years . . . the woman!"

She had seized Mr. Fuller's hand so forcefully I felt embarrassed for her, and tried to persuade the spirit within Ethel to let go, at the same time explaining her true condition to her, gently, but firmly.

After I had explained how she was able to communicate with us, and that the body of the medium was merely a temporary arrangement, the entity calmed down, asking only if he loved her, meaning the other spirit in the house. I assured her that this was so, and then called on Albert, Ethel's spirit guide, to help me ease the troubled one from Ethel's body and thus free her at the same time from the house.

And then the man came into Ethel's body, very emotionally, calling out for Sylvia.

Again I explained how he was able to communicate.

"You see me, don't you," he finally said as he calmed down. "I loved everyone . . . I'll go, I won't bother you . . ."

I called again for Albert, and in a moment his crisp voice replaced the spirit's outcries.

"The man is a Henry MacLellan . . . there stood in this vicinity another house . . . around 1810, 1812 . . . to 1820 . . . a woman connected with this house lies buried here somewhere, and he is looking for her. His daughter . . . Macy? . . . Maisie? About 1798 . . . 16 or 18 years old . . . has been done wrong . . . had to do with a feud of two families . . . McDern . . ."

Albert then suggested letting the man speak to us directly, and so he did in a little while. I offered my help.

"It is futile," he said. "My problem is my own."

"Who are you?"

"Henry. I lived right here. I was born here."

"What year? What year are we in now as I speak with you?"

"I speak to you in the year 1813."

"Are you a gentleman of some age?"

"I would have forty-seven years."

"Did you serve in any governmental force or agency?"

"My son . . . John Stuart Mc . . ."

"McDermot? Your son was John Stuart McDermot?"

"You have it from my own lips."

"Where did he serve?"

"Ticonderoga."

And then he added, "My daughter, missing, but I found the bones, buried not too far from here. I am satisfied. I have her with me."

He admitted he knew he was no longer "on the earth plane," but was drawn to the place from time to time.

"But if you ask me as a gentleman to go, I shall go," he added. Under these circumstances—rare ones, indeed, when dealing with hauntings—I suggested he not disturb those in the present house, especially the children. Also, would he not be happier in the world into which he had long passed.

"I shall consider that," he acknowledged. "You speak well, sir. I have no intention of frightening."

"Are you aware that much time has passed . . . that this is not 1813 any more?" I said.

"I am not aware of this, sir . . . it is always the same time here."

Again I asked if he served in any regiment, but he replied his leg was no good. Was it his land and house? Yes, he replied, he owned it and built the house. But when I pressed him as to where he might be buried, he balked.

"My bones are here with me . . . I am sufficient unto myself."

I then asked about his church affiliation, and he informed me his church was "northeast of here, on Beacon Road." The minister's name was Rooney, but he could not tell me the denomination. His head was not all it used to be.

"A hundred and fifty years have passed," I said, and began the ritual of exorcism. "Go from this house in peace, and with our love."

And so he did.

Albert, Ethel's guide, returned briefly to assure us that all was as it should be and Mr. McDermot was gone from the house; also, that he was being reunited with his mother, Sarah Ann McDermot. And then Albert too withdrew and Ethel returned to her own self again.

I turned to Mrs. Fuller and her cousin, Miss Elliott, for possible comments and corroboration of the information received through Mrs. Meyers in trance.

It appears the house that the Fullers were able to trace back as far as about 1860 was moved to make room for a road, and then set down again not far from that road. Unfortunately going further back proved difficult. I heard again from Mrs. Fuller in December of that year. The footsteps were continuing, it seemed, and her seven-year-old daughter Becky was being frightened by them. She had not yet been able to find any record of Mr. McDermot, but vowed to continue her search.

That was twenty years ago, and nothing further turned up, and I really do not know if the footsteps continued or Mr. McDermot finally gave up his restless quest for a world of which he no longer was a part.

As for Mr. Langdon, whom Ethel Meyers had also identified by name as a presence in the house, he must by now be reunited with his wife Donna, and I hope he has forgiven her her trespasses, as a good Christian might: over there, even her sins do not matter any longer.

9

The Ghosts of Stamford Hill

"MR. HOLZER," THE voice on the phone said pleasantly, "I've read your book and that's why I'm calling. We've got a ghost in our house."

Far from astonished, I took paper and pencil and, not unlike a grocery-store clerk taking down a telephone order, started to put down the details of the report.

Robert Cowan is a gentleman with a very balanced approach to life. He is an artist who works for one of the leading advertising agencies in New York City and his interests range widely from art to music, theater, history, and what have you. But not to ghosts, at least not until he and his actress-wife, Dorothy, moved into the 1780 House on Stamford Hill. The house is thus named for the simplest of all reasons: it was built in that year.

Mr. Cowan explained that he thought I'd be glad to have a look at his house, although the Cowans were not unduly worried about the presence of a nonrent-paying guest at their house. Although it was a bit disconcerting at times, it was curiosity as to what the ghost wanted and who the specter was that had prompted Bob Cowan to seek the help of The Ghost Hunter.

I said, "Mr. Cowan, would you mind putting your experiences in writing, so I can have them for my files?" I like to have written reports (in the first person, if possible) so that later I can refer back to them if similar cases should pop up, as they often do.

"Not at all," Bob Cowan said. "I'll be glad to write it down for you."

The next morning I received his report, along with a brief history of the 1780 House.

> Here is a brief account of the experiences my wife and I have had while living in this house during the past nine and a half years. I'll start with myself because my experiences are quite simple.
>
> From time to time (once a week or so) during most of the time we've lived here I have noticed unidentifiable movements out of the corner of

my eye . . . day or night. Most often, I've noticed this while sitting in our parlor and what I see moving seems to be in the living room. At other times, and only late at night when I am the only one awake, I hear beautiful but unidentified music seemingly played by a full orchestra, as though a radio were on in another part of the house.

The only place I recall hearing this is in an upstairs bedroom and just after I've gone to bed. Once I actually got up, opened the bedroom door to ascertain if it was perhaps music from a radio accidentally left on, but it wasn't.

Finally, quite often I've heard a variety of knocks and crashes that do not have any logical source within the structural setup of the house. A very loud smash occurred two weeks ago. You'd have thought a door had fallen off its hinges upstairs but, as usual, there was nothing out of order.

My wife, Dorothy, had two very vivid experiences about five years ago. One was in the kitchen, or rather outside of a kitchen window. She was standing at the sink in the evening and happened to glance out the window when she saw a face glaring in at her. It was a dark face but not a Negro, perhaps Indian; it was very hateful and fierce.

At first she thought it was a distorted reflection in the glass but in looking closer, it was a face glaring directly at her. All she could make out was a face only and as she recalls it, *it seemed translucent.* It didn't disappear, *she did*!

On a summer afternoon my wife was taking a nap in a back bedroom and was between being awake and being asleep when she heard the sounds of men's voices and the sound of working on the grounds—rakes, and garden tools—right outside of the window. She tried to arouse herself to see who they could be, but she couldn't get up.

At that time, and up to that time we had only hired a single man to come in and work on the lawn and flower beds. It wasn't until at least a year later that we hired a crew that came in and worked once a week, and we've often wondered if this was an experience of precognition. My wife has always had an uneasy feeling about the outside of the back of the house and still sometimes hears men's voices outside and will look out all windows without seeing anyone.

She also has shared my experiences of seeing "things" out of the corner of her eye and also hearing quite lovely music at night. She hasn't paid attention to household noises because a long time ago I told her "all old houses have odd structural noises". . . which is true enough.

Prior to our living here the house was lived in for about 25 years by the Clayton Rich family, a family of five. Mr. Rich died towards the end of their stay here. By the time we bought it, the three children were all married and had moved away.

For perhaps one year prior to that a Mrs. David Cowles lived here. She's responsible for most of the restoration along with a Mr. Frederick Kinble.

Up until 1927 or 1928 the house was in the Weed family ever since 1780. The last of the line were two sisters who hated each other and only communicated with each other through the husband of one of the sisters They had divided the house and used two different doors. One used the regular front door into the stair hall and the other used the "coffin door" into the parlor.

Mr. Cowan added that they were selling the house—not because of ghosts but because they wanted to move to the city again. I assured him that we'd be coming up as soon as possible.

Before we could make arrangements to do so, I had another note from the Cowans. On February 9, 1964, Bob Cowan wrote that they heard a singing voice quite clearly downstairs, and music again.

It wasn't until the following week, however, that my wife and I went to Stamford Hill. The Cowans offered to have supper ready for us that Sunday evening and to pick us up at the station since nobody could find the house at night who did not know the way.

It was around six o'clock in the evening when our New Haven train pulled in. Bob Cowan wore the Scottish beret he had said he would wear in order to be recognized by us at once. The house stands at the end of a winding road that runs for about ten minutes through woodland and past shady lanes. An American eagle over the door, and the date 1780, stood out quite clearly despite the dusk that had started to settle on the land. The house has three levels, and the Cowans used the large room next to the kitchen in what might be called the cellar or ground level for their dining room.

They had adorned it with eighteenth-century American antiques in a most winning manner, and the fireplace added a warmth to the room, making it seem miles removed from bustling New York.

On the next level were the living room and next to that a kind of sitting room. The fireplace in each of these rooms connected one to the other. Beyond the corridor there was the master bedroom and Bob's colorful den. Upstairs were two guest rooms, and there was a small attic accessible only through a hole in the ceiling and by ladder. Built during the American Revolution, the house stands on a wooded slope, which is responsible for its original name of Woodpecker Ridge Farm.

Many years ago, after the restoration of the house was completed, Harold Donaldson Eberlin, an English furniture and garden expert, wrote about it:

> With its rock-ribbed ridges, its boulder-strewn pastures and its sharply broken contours like the choppy surface of a wind-blown sea, the topographical conditions have inevitably affected the domestic architecture. To mention only two particulars, the dwellings of the region have had to accommodate themselves to many an abrupt hillside site and the employment of some of the omnipresent granite boulders. Part of the individuality of the house at Woodpecker Ridge Farm lies in the way it satisfies these conditions without being a type house.
>
> Before communal existence, the country all thereabouts bore the pleasantly descriptive name of Woodpecker Ridge, and Woodpecker Ridge Farm was so called in order to keep alive the memory of this early name. Tradition says that the acres now comprised within the boundaries of Woodpecker Ridge Farm once formed part of the private hunting ground of *the old Indian chief Ponus.*
>
> Old Ponus may, perhaps, appear a trifle mythical and shadowy, as such long-gone chieftains are wont to be. Very substantial and real, however, was Augustus Weed, who built the house in 1780. And the said Augustus was something of a personage.
>
> War clouds were still hanging thick over the face of the land when he had the foundation laid and the structure framed. Nevertheless, confident and forward-looking, he not only reared a staunch and tidy abode, indicative of the spirit of the countryside, but he seems to have put into it some of his own robust and independent personality as well.
>
> It is said that Augustus was such a notable farmer and took such justifiable pride in the condition of his fields that he was not afraid to make a standing offer of one dollar reward for every daisy that anyone could find in his hay.
>
> About 1825 the house experienced a measure of remodeling in accordance with the notions prevalent at the time. Nothing very extensive or ostentatious was attempted, but visible traces of the work then undertaken remain in the neo-Greek details that occur both outside and indoors.
>
> It is not at all unlikely that the "lie-on-your-stomach" windows of the attic story date from this time and point to either a raising of the origi-

nal roof or else some alteration of its pitch. These "lie-on-your-stomach" windows—so called because they were low down in the wall and had their sills very near the level of the floor so that you had almost to lie on your stomach to look out of them—were a favorite device of the *neo-Grec* era for lighting attic rooms. And it is remarkable how much light they actually do give, and what a pleasant light it is.

The recent remodeling that brought Woodpecker Farmhouse to its present state of comeliness and comfort impaired none of the individual character the place had acquired through the generations that had passed since hardy Augustus Weed first took up his abode there. It needs no searching scrutiny to discern the eighteenth-century features impressed on the structure at the beginning—the stout timbers of the framing, the sturdy beams and joists, the wide floor boards, and the generous fireplaces. Neither is close examination required to discover the marks of the 1825 rejuvenation.

The fashions of columns, pilasters, mantelpieces, and other features speak plainly and proclaim their origin.

The aspect of the garden, too, discloses the same sympathetic understanding of the environment peculiarly suitable to the sort of house for which it affords the natural setting. The ancient well cover, the lilac bushes, the sweetbriers, the August lilies, and the other denizens of an old farmhouse dooryard have been allowed to keep their long-accustomed places.

In return for this recognition of their prescriptive rights, they lend no small part to the air of self-possessed assurance and mellow contentment that pervades the whole place.

After a most pleasant dinner downstairs, Catherine and I joined the Cowans in the large living room upstairs. We sat down quietly and hoped we would hear something along musical lines.

As the quietness of the countryside slowly settled over us, I could indeed distinguish faraway, indistinct musical sounds, as if someone were playing a radio underwater or at great distance. A check revealed no nearby house or parked car whose radio could be responsible for this.

After a while we got up and looked about the room itself. We were standing about quietly admiring the furniture when both my wife and I and, of course, the Cowans, clearly heard footsteps overhead.

They were firm and strong and could not be mistaken for anything else, such as a squirrel in the attic or other innocuous noises. Nor was it an old house settling.

"Did you hear that?" I said, almost superfluously.

"We all heard it," my wife said and looked at me.

"What am I waiting for?" I replied, and faster than you can say Ghost Hunter, I was up the stairs and into the room above our heads where the steps had been heard. The room lay in total darkness. I turned the switch. There was no one about. Nobody else was in the house at the time, and all windows were closed. We decided to assemble upstairs in the smaller room next to the one in which I had heard the steps. The reason was that Mrs. Cowan had experienced a most unusual phenomenon in that particular room.

"It was like lightning," she said, "a bright light suddenly come and gone."

I looked the room over carefully. The windows were arranged in such a manner that a reflection from passing cars was out of the question. Both windows, far apart and on different walls, opened into the dark countryside away from the only road.

Catherine and I sat down on the couch, and the Cowans took chairs. We sat quietly for perhaps twenty minutes without lights, except a small amount of light filtering in from the stairwell. It was very dark, certainly dark enough for sleep, and there was not light enough to write by.

As I was gazing toward the back wall of the little room and wondering about the footsteps I had just heard so clearly, I saw a blinding flash of light, white light, in the corner facing me. It came on and disappeared very quickly, so quickly in fact that my wife, whose head had been turned in another direction at the moment, missed it. But Dorothy Cowan saw it and exclaimed, "There it is again. Exactly as I saw it."

Despite its brevity I was able to observe that the light cast a shadow on the opposite wall, so it could not very well have been a hallucination.

I decided it would be best to bring Mrs. Meyers to the house, and we went back to New York soon after. While we were preparing our return visit with Mrs. Meyers as our medium, I received an urgent call from Bob Cowan.

"Since seeing you and Cathy at our house, we've had some additional activity that you'll be interested in. Dottie and I have both heard knocking about the house but none of it in direct answer to questions that we've tried to ask. On Saturday, the twenty-ninth of February, I was taking a nap back in my studio when I was awakened by the sound of footsteps in the room above me . . . the same room we all sat in on the previous Sunday.

"The most interesting event was on the evening of Thursday, February 27. I was driving home from the railroad station alone. Dottie was still in New York. As I approached the house, I noticed that there was a light on in the main floor bedroom and also a light on up in the sewing room on the top floor, a room Dottie also uses for rehearsal. I thought Dottie had left the lights on. I drove past the house and down to the garage, put the car away and then walked back to the house and noticed that the light in the top floor was now off.

"I entered the house and noticed that the dogs were calm (wild enough at seeing me, but in no way indicating that there was anyone else in the house). I went upstairs and found that the light in the bedroom was also off. I checked the entire house and there was absolutely no sign that anyone had been there . . . and there hadn't been, I'm sure."

On Sunday, March 15, we arrived at the 1780 House, again at dusk. A delicious meal awaited us downstairs, then we repaired to the upstairs part of the house.

We seated ourselves in the large living room where the music had been heard, and where we had been standing at the time we heard the uncanny footsteps overhead.

"I sense a woman in a white dress," Ethel said suddenly. "She's got dark hair and a high forehead. Rather a small woman."

"I was looking through the attic earlier," Bob Cowan said thoughtfully, "and look what I found—a waistcoat that would fit a rather smallish woman or girl."

The piece of clothing he showed us seemed rather musty. There were a number of articles up there in the attic that must have belonged to an earlier owner of the house—much earlier.

A moment later, Ethel Meyers showed the characteristic signs of onsetting trance. We doused the lights until only one back light was on.

At first, only inarticulate sounds came from the medium's lips. "You can speak," I said, to encourage her. "You're among friends." The sounds now turned into crying.

"What is your name?" I asked, as I always do on such occasions. There was laughter—whether girlish or mad was hard to tell.

Suddenly, she started to sing in a high-pitched voice.

"You can speak, you can speak," I kept assuring the entity. Finally she seemed to have settled down somewhat in control of the medium.

"Happy to speak with you," she mumbled faintly.

"What is your name?"

I had to ask it several times before I could catch the answer clearly.

"Lucy."

"Tell me, Lucy, do you live here?"

"God be with you."

"Do you live in this house?"

"My house."

"What year is this?"

The entity hesitated a moment, then turned toward Dorothy and said, "I like you."

I continued to question her.

"How old are you?"

"Old lady."

"How old?"

"God be with you."

The conversation had been friendly until I asked her, "What is your husband's name?" The ghost drew back as if I had spoken a horrible word.

"What did you say?" she almost shouted, her voice trembling with emotion. "I have no husband—God bless you—what were you saying?" she repeated, then started to cry again. "Husband, husband," she kept saying as if it was a thought she could not bear.

"You did not have a husband, then?"

"Yes, I did."

"Your name again?"

"Lucy. . . fair day. . . where is he? The fair day. . . the pretty one, he said to me look in the pool, and you will see my face."

"Who is he?" I asked.

But the ghost paid no heed to me. She was evidently caught up in her own memories.

"I heard a voice, Lucy, Lucy. . . fair one . . . alack . . . they took him out . . . they laid him cold in the ground. . . ."

"What year was that?" I wanted to know.

"Year, year?" she repeated. "Now, *now*!"

"Who rules this country now?"

"Why, he who seized it."

"Who rules?"

"They carried him out . . . the Savior of our country. General Washington."

"When did he die?"

"Just now."

I tried to question her further, but she returned to the thoughts of her husband.

"I want to stay here . . . I wait at the pool . . . look, he is there!" She was growing excited again.

"I want to stay here now, always, forever . . . rest in peace . . . he is there always with me."

"How long ago did you die?" I asked, almost casually. The reaction was somewhat hostile.

"I have not died . . . never . . . All Saints!"

I asked her to join her loved one by calling for him and thus be set free of this house. But the ghost would have none of it.

"Gainsay what I have spoke . . ."

"How did you come to this house?" I now asked.

"Father . . . I am born here."

"Was it your father's house?"

"Yes."

"What was his name?" I asked, but the restless spirit of Lucy was slipping away now, and Albert, the medium's control, took over. His crisp, clear voice told us that the time had come to release Ethel.

"What about this woman, Lucy?" I inquired. Sometimes the control will give additional details.

"He was not her husband . . . he was killed before she married him," Albert said.

No wonder my question about a husband threw Lucy into an uproar of emotions.

In a little while, Ethel Meyers was back to her old self, and as usual, did not remember anything of what had come through her entranced lips.

Shortly after this episode my wife and I went to Europe.

As soon as we returned, I called Bob Cowan. How were things up in Stamford Hill? Quiet? Not very.

"Last June," Bob recalled, "Dottie and I were at home with a friend, a lady hair dresser, who happens to be psychic. We were playing around with the Ouija board, more in amusement than seriously. Suddenly, the Sunday afternoon quiet was disrupted by heavy footsteps coming up the steps outside the house. Quickly, we hid the Ouija board, for we did not want a potential buyer of the house to see us in this unusual pursuit. We were sure someone was coming up to see the house. But the steps stopped abruptly when they reached the front door. I opened [it], and there was no one outside."

"Hard to sell a house that way," I commented. "Anything else?"

"Yes, in July we had a house guest, a very balanced person, not given to imagining things. There was a sudden crash upstairs, and when I rushed up the stairs to the sewing room, there was this bolt of material that had been standing in a corner, lying in the middle of the room as if thrown there by unseen hands! Margaret, our house guest, also heard someone humming a tune in the bathroom, although there was no one in there at the time. Then in November, when just the two of us were in the house, someone knocked at the door downstairs. Again we looked, but there was nobody outside. One evening when I was in the 'ship' room and Dottie in the bedroom, we heard footfalls coming down the staircase.

"Since neither of us was causing them and the door was closed, only a ghost could have been walking down those stairs."

"But the most frightening experience of all," Dorothy Cowan broke in, "was when I was sleeping downstairs and, waking up, wanted to go to the bathroom without turning on the lights, so as not to wake Bob. Groping my way back to bed, I suddenly found myself up on the next floor in the blue room, which is pretty tricky walking in the dark. I had the feeling someone was forcing me to follow them into that particular room."

I had heard enough, and on December 15, we took Ethel Johnson Meyers to the house for another go at the restless ones within its confines. Soon we were all seated in the ship room on the first floor, and Ethel started to drift into a trance.

"There is a baby's coffin here," she murmured. "Like a newborn infant's."

The old grandfather clock in back of us kept ticking away loudly.

"I hear someone call Maggie," Ethel said. "Margaret."

"Do you see anyone?"

"A woman, about five foot two, in a long dress, with a big bustle in the back. Hair down, parted in the middle, and braided on both sides. There is another young woman . . . Laurie . . . very pretty face, but so sad . . . she's looking at you, Hans. . . ."

"What is it she wants?" I asked quietly.

"A youngish man with brown hair, curly, wearing a white blouse, taken in at the wrists, and over it a tan waistcoat, but no coat over it. . . ."

I asked what he wanted and why he was here. This seemed to agitate the medium somewhat.

"Bottom of the well," she mumbled, "stone at bottom of the well."

Bob Cowan changed seats, moving away from the coffin door to the opposite side of the room. He complained of feeling cold at the former spot, although neither door nor window was open to cause such a sensation.

"Somebody had a stick over his shoulder," the medium said now, "older man wearing dark trousers, heavy stockings. His hair is gray and kind of longish; he's got that stick."

I asked her to find out why.

"Take him away," Ethel replied. "He says, 'Take him away!'"

"But he was innocent, he went to the well. Who is down in the well? Him who I drove into the well, him . . . I mistook . . ."

Ethel was now fully entranced, and the old man seemed to be speaking through her.

"What is your name?" I asked.

"She was agrievin'," the voice replied, "she were grievin' I did that."

"What is your name?"

"Ain't no business to you."

"How can I help you?"

"They're all here . . . accusin' me . . . I see her always by the well."

"Did someone die in this well?" Outside, barely twenty yards away, was the well, now cold and silent in the night air.

"Him who I mistook. I find peace, I find him, I put him together again."

"What year was that?"

"No matter to you now . . . I do not forgive myself . . . I wronged, I wronged . . . I see always her face look on me."

"Are you in this house now?" I asked.

"Where else can I be and talk with thee?" the ghost shot back.

"This isn't your house anymore," I said quietly.

"Oh, yes it is," the ghost replied firmly. "The young man stays here only to look upon me and mock me. It will not be other than mine. I care only for that flesh that I could put again on the bone, and I will restore him to the bloom of life and the rich love of her who suffered through my own misdemeanor."

"Is your daughter buried here?" I asked, to change the subject. Quietly, the ghostly voice said, "Yes."

But he refused to say where he himself was laid to final—or not so final—rest.

At this point the ghost realized that he was not in his own body, and as I explained the procedure to him, he gradually became calmer. At first, he thought he was in his own body and could use it to restore to life the one he had slain. I kept asking him who he was. Finally, in a soft whisper, came the reply, "Samuel."

"And Laurie?"

"My daughter . . . oh, he is here, the man I wronged . . . Margaret, Margaret!" He seemed greatly agitated with fear now.

The big clock started to strike. The ghost somehow felt it meant him.

"The judgment, the judgment . . . Laurie . . . they smile at me. I have killed. He has taken my hand! He whom I have hurt."

But the excitement proved too much for Samuel. Suddenly, he was gone, and after a brief interval, an entirely different personality inhabited Ethel's body. It was Laurie.

"Please forgive him," she pleaded. "I have forgiven him."

The voice was sweet and girlish.

"Who is Samuel?"

"My grandfather."

"What is your family name?"

"Laurie Ho-Ho- . . . if I could only get that name."

But she couldn't.

Neither could she give me the name of her beloved, killed by her grandfather. It was a name she was not allowed to mention around the house, so she had difficulty remembering now, she explained.

"What is your mother's name?" I asked.

"Margaret."

"What year were you born?"

Hesitatingly, the voice said, "Seventeen fifty-six."

"What year is this now?"

"Seventeen seventy-four. We laid him to rest in seventeen seventy-four."

"In the church?"

"No, Grandfather could not bear it. We laid him to rest on the hill to the north. We dug with our fingers all night. Didn't tell Grandpa where we put it."

"How far from here is it?"

"No more than a straight fly of the lark."

"Is the grave marked?"

"Oh, no."

"What happened to your father?"

"No longer home, gone."

I explained to Laurie that the house would soon change hands, and that she must not interfere with this. The Cowans had the feeling that their ghosts were somehow keeping all buyers away, fantastic though this may be at first thought. But then all of psychic research is pretty unusual and who is to say what cannot be?

Laurie promised not to interfere and to accept a new owner of "their" house. She left, asking again that her grandfather be forgiven his sins.

I then asked Albert, Ethel's control, to take over the medium. That done, I queried him regarding the whole matter.

"The father is buried far from here, but most of the others are buried around here," he said. "During the year seventeen seventy-seven . . . Grandfather was not brought here until later when there was forgiveness. The body was removed and put in Christian burial."

"Where is the tombstone?" I asked.

"Lying to the west of a white structure," Albert replied in his precise slightly accented speech, "on these grounds. The tombstone is broken off, close to the earth. The top has been mishandled by vandals. The old man is gone, the young man has taken him by the hand."

"What was the young man's name?"

"She called him Benjamin."

"He was killed in the well?"

"That is right. He has no grave except on the hill."

"Is the old man the one who disturbs this house?"

"He is the main one who brings in his rabble, looking for the young man."

"Who is Lucy?" I asked, referring back to the girl who had spoken to us at the last seance in the late spring.

"That is the girl you were talking about, Laurie. Her name is really Lucy. One and the same person."

"She was not actually married to the young man?"

"In her own way, she was. But they would not recognize it. There were differences in religious ideas. . . . But we had better release the medium for now."

I nodded, and within a moment or two, Ethel was back to herself, very much bewildered as to what went on while she was in trance.

"How do you reconcile these dates with the tradition that this house was built in seventeen eighty?" I asked Bob Cowan.

He shook his head.

"It is only a tradition. We have no proof of the actual date."

We went to the upstairs sewing room where the latest manifestations had taken place, and grouped ourselves around the heavy wooden table. Ethel almost immediately fell into trance again. She rarely does twice in one sitting.

The voice reverberating in the near darkness now was clearly that of a man, and a very dominating voice it was.

"Who are you?" I demanded.

"Sergeant-major . . ." No name followed. I asked why was he here in this house.

"One has pleasant memories."

"Your name?"

"Sergeant-major Harm."

"First name?"

Instead of giving it, he explained that he once owned the house and was "friend, not foe." I looked at Bob Cowan, who knows all the owners of the property in the old records, and Bob shook his head. No Harm.

"When I please, I come. I do not disturb willingly. But I will go," the new visitor offered. "I will take him with me; you will see him no more. I am at peace with him now. He is at peace with me."

"How did you pass over?" I inquired.

"On the field of battle. On the banks of the Potomac . . . seventeen seventy-six."

"What regiment were you in?" I continued.

"York . . . Eight . . . I was foot soldier . . . eighteenth regiment . . ."

"What army?"

"Wayne . . . Wayne . . ."

"Who was your commanding general?"

"Broderick."

"Who was the colonel of your regiment?"

"Wayne, Wayne."

"You were a sergeant-major?"

"Sergeant-major, eighteenth regiment, foot infantry."

"Where were you stationed?"

"New York."

"Where in New York?"

"Champlain."

"Your regimental commander again?"

"Broderick." Then he added, not without emotion, "I died under fire, first battle of Potomac."

"Where are you buried?"

"Fort Ticonderoga, New York."

I wondered how a soldier fighting on the banks of the Potomac could be buried in upstate New York. But I must confess that the word "Potomac" had come so softly that I could have been mistaken.

"The date of your death?"

"Seventeen seventy-six."

Then he added, as the voice became more and more indistinct, "I will leave now, but I will protect you from those who . . . who are hungry to . . ." The voice trailed off into silence.

A few moments later, Ethel emerged from the trance with a slight headache, but otherwise her old self. As usual, she did not recall anything that had come through her entranced lips.

We returned to New York soon after, hoping that all would remain quiet in the Cowan house, and, more important, that there would soon be a new laird of the manor at the 1780 House.

I, too, heard the ghostly music, although I am sure it does not connect with the colonial ghosts we were able to evoke. The music I heard sounded like a far-off radio, which it wasn't since there are no houses near enough to be heard from. What I heard for a few moments in the living room sounded like a full symphony orchestra playing the music popular around the turn of this century.

Old houses impregnated with layers upon layers of people's emotions frequently also absorb music and other sounds as part of the atmosphere.

What about the sergeant-major?

I checked the regimental records. No soldier named Harm, but a number of officers (and men) named Harmon. I rechecked my tapes. The name "Harm" had been given by the ghost very quietly. He could have said Harmon. Or perhaps he was disguising his identity as they sometimes will.

But then I discovered something very interesting. In the Connecticut state papers there is mention of a certain Benjamin Harmon, Jr., Lt., who was with a local regiment in 1776. The murdered young man had been identified as "Benjamin." Suddenly we have another ghost named Harm or Harmon, evidently an older personality. Was he the father of the murdered young man?

The 1780 House is, of course, recorded as dating back to 1780 only. But could not another building have occupied the area? Was the 1780 House an adaptation of a smaller dwelling of which there is no written record?

We can neither prove nor disprove this.

It is true, however, that General "Mad" Anthony Wayne was in charge of the revolutionary troops in the New York area at the time under discussion.

At any rate, all this is knowledge not usually possessed by a lady voice teacher, which is what Ethel Meyers was when not being a medium.

Two years after our visit, the local archaeological society asked for permission to dig around the property since some interesting artifacts had been found on the grounds of the house next door. Picture their—and everyone's—surprise when they found, near a dried up well on the Cowan property, two partly damaged tombstones inscribed "Samuel" and "Benjamin." The stones and the inscriptions were of the late eighteenth century.

The house later changed hands and the Cowans moved to Georgia. I have not heard anything further about any disturbances at the 1780 House, nor do I frankly expect any: Over There Samuel and Benjamin must have made up long ago, and perhaps even have had a go at it again for another round of incarnation, somewhere, some place, some time.

10

The Ghost at Port Clyde

PORT CLYDE IS a lovely little fishing village on the coast of Maine where a small number of native Yankees, who live there all year round, try to cope with a few summer residents, usually from New York or the Midwest. Their worlds do not really mesh, but the oldtimers realize that a little—not too much—tourism is really quite good for business, especially the few small hotels in and around Port Clyde and St. George, so they don't mind them too much. But the Down Easterners do keep to themselves, and it isn't always easy to get them to open up about their private lives or such things as, let us say, ghosts.

Carol Olivieri Schulte lived in Council Bluffs, Iowa, when she first contacted me in November of 1974. The wife of a lawyer, Mrs. Schulte is an inquisitive lady, a college graduate, and the mother of what was then a young son. Somehow Carol had gotten hold of some of my books and become intrigued by them, especially where ghosts were concerned, because she, too, had had a brush with the uncanny.

"It was the summer of 1972," she explained to me, "and I was sleeping in an upstairs bedroom," in the summer cottage her parents owned in Port Clyde, Maine.

"My girlfriend Marion and her boyfriend were sleeping in a bedroom across the hall with their animals, a Siamese cat and two dogs."

The cat had been restless and crept into Carol's room, touching her pillow and waking her. Carol sat up in bed, ready to turn on the light, when she saw standing beside her bed a female figure in a very white nightgown. The figure had small shoulders and long, flowing hair . . . and Carol could see right through her!

It became apparent, as she came closer, that she wanted to get Carol's attention, trying to talk with her hands.

"Her whole body suggested she was in desperate need of something. Her fingers were slender, and there was a diamond ring on her fourth finger, on the right hand. Her hands moved more desperately as I ducked under the covers."

Shortly after this, Carol had a dream contact with the same entity. This time she was abed in another room in the house, sleeping, when she saw the same young woman. She appeared to her at first in the air, smaller than life size. Her breasts were large, and there was a maternal feeling about her. With her was a small child, a boy of perhaps three years of age, also dressed in a white gown. While the child was with Carol on her bed, in the dream, the mother hovered at some distance in the corner. Carol, in the dream, had the feeling the mother had turned the child over to her, as if to protect it, and then she vanished. Immediately there followed the appearance of another woman, a black-hooded female, seeming very old, coming toward her and the child. Carol began to realize the dark-hooded woman wanted to take the child from her, and the child was afraid and clung to her. When the woman stood close to Carol's bed, still in the dream, Carol noticed her bright green eyes and crooked, large nose, and her dark complexion. She decided to fight her off, concentrating her thoughts on the white light she knew was an expression of psychic protection, and the dark-hooded woman disappeared. Carol was left with the impression that she had been connected with a school or institution of some kind. At this, the mother in her white nightgown returned and took the child back, looking at Carol with an expression of gratitude before disappearing again along with her child.

Carol woke up, but the dream was so vivid, it stayed with her for weeks, and even when she contacted me, it was still crystal clear in her mind. One more curious event transpired at the exact time Carol had overcome the evil figure in the dream. Her grandmother, whom she described as "a very reasoning, no-nonsense lively Yankee lady," had a cottage right in back of Carol's parents'. She was tending her stove, as she had done many times before, when it blew up right into her face, singing her eyebrows. There was nothing whatever wrong with the stove.

Carol had had psychic experiences before, and even her attorney husband was familiar with the world of spirits, so her contacting me for help with the house in Maine was by no means a family problem.

I was delighted to hear from her, not because a Maine ghost was so very different from the many other ghosts I had dealt with through the years, but because of the timing of Carol's request. It so happened that at that time I was in the middle of writing, producing and appearing in the NBC series called "In Search of . . ." and the ghost house in Maine would make a fine segment.

An agreement was arranged among all concerned: Carol, her husband, her parents, the broadcasting management, and me. I then set about to arrange a schedule for our visit. We had to fly into Rockland, Maine, and then drive down to Port Clyde. If I wanted to do it before Carol and her family were in residence, that, too, would be all right though she warned me about the cold climate up there during the winter months.

In the end we decided on May, when the weather would be acceptable, and the water in the house would be turned back on.

I had requested that all witnesses of actual phenomena in the house be present to be questioned by me.

Carol then sent along pictures of the house and statements from some of the witnesses. I made arrangements to have her join us at the house for the investigation and filming for the period of May 13 to 15, 1976. The team—the crew, my psychic and me—would all stay over at a local hotel. The psychic was a young woman artist named Ingrid Beckman with whom I had been working and helping develop her gift.

And so it happened that we congregated at Port Clyde from different directions, but with one purpose in mind—to contact the lady ghost at the house. As soon as we had settled in at the local hotel, the New Ocean House, we drove over to the spanking white cottage that was to be the center of our efforts for the next three days. Carol's brother Robert had driven up from Providence, and her close friend Marion Going from her home, also in Rhode Island.

I asked Ingrid to stay at a little distance from the house and wait for me to bring her inside, while I spoke to some of the witnesses out of Ingrid's earshot. Ingrid understood and sat down on the lawn, taking in the beauty of the landscape.

Carol and I walked in the opposite direction, and once again we went over her experiences as she had reported them to me in her earlier statement. But was there anything beyond that, I wondered, and questioned Carol about it.

"Now since that encounter with the ghostly lady have you seen her again? Have you ever heard her again?"

"Well about three weeks ago before I was to come out here, I really wanted to communicate with her. I concentrated on it just before I went to sleep, you know. I was thinking about it, and I dreamed that she appeared to me the way she had in the dream that followed her apparition here in this house. And then I either dreamed that I woke up momentarily and saw her right there as I had actually seen her in this bedroom or I actually did wake up and see her. Now the sphere of consciousness I was in—I am doubtful as to where I was at that point. I mean it was nothing like the experience I experienced right here in this room. I was definitely awake, and *I definitely saw that ghost*. As to this other thing a couple of weeks ago—I wasn't quite sure."

"Was there any kind of message?"

"No, not this last time."

"Do you feel she was satisfied having made contact with you?"

"Yeah, I felt that she wanted to communicate with me in the same sense that I wanted to communicate with her. Like an old friend will want to get in touch with another old friend, and I get the feeling she was just saying, 'Yes, I'm still here.'"

I then turned to Carol's brother, Bob Olivieri, and questioned him about his own encounters with anything unusual in the house. He took me to the room he was occupying at the time of the experiences, years ago, but apparently the scene was still very fresh in his mind.

"Mr. Olivieri, what exactly happened to you in this room?"

"Well, one night I was sleeping on this bed and all of a sudden I woke up and heard footsteps—what I thought were footsteps—it sounded like slippers or baby's feet in pajamas—something like that. Well, I woke up and I came over, and I stepped in this spot, and I looked in the hallway and the sound stopped. I thought maybe I was imagining it. So I came back to the bed, got into bed again, and again I heard footsteps. Well, this time I got up and as soon as I came to the same spot again and looked into the hallway it stopped. I figured it was my nephew who was still awake. So I walked down the hallway and looked into the room where my sister and nephew were sleeping, and they were both sound asleep. I checked my parents' room, and they were also asleep. I just walked back. I didn't know what to do so I got into bed again, and I kept on hearing them. I kept on walking over, and they would still be going until I stepped in this spot where they would stop. As soon as I stepped here. And this happened for an hour. I kept getting up. Heard the footsteps, stepped in this spot and they stopped. So finally I got kind of tired of it and came over to my bed and lay down in bed and as soon as I lay down I heard the steps again, exactly what happened before—and they seemed to stop at the end of the hallway. A few minutes later I felt a pressure on my sheets, starting from my feet, and going up, up, up, going up further, further, slowly but surely. . . and finally something pulled my hair! Naturally I was just scared for the rest of the night. I couldn't get to sleep."

I thought it was time to get back to Ingrid and bring her into the house. This I did, with the camera and sound people following us every step of the way to record for NBC what might transpire in the house now. Just before we entered the house, Ingrid turned to me and said, "You know that window up there? When we first arrived, I noticed someone standing in it."

"What exactly did you see?"

"It was a woman . . . and she was looking out at us."

The house turned out to be a veritable jewel of Yankee authenticity, the kind of house a sea captain might be happy in, or perhaps only a modern antiquarian. The white exterior was matched by a spanking clean, and sometimes sparse interior, with every piece of furniture of the right period—the nineteenth and early twentieth centuries—and a feeling of being lived in by many people, for many years.

After we had entered the downstairs part where there was an ample kitchen and a nice day room, I asked Ingrid, as usual, to tell me whatever psychic impression she was gathering about the house, its people and its history. Naturally, I had made sure all along that Ingrid knew nothing of the house or the quest we had come on to Maine, and there was absolutely no way she could have had access to specifics about the area, the people in the house—past and present—nor anything at all about the case.

Immediately Ingrid set to work, she seemed agitated.

"There is a story connected here with the 1820s or the 1840s," she began, and I turned on my tape recorder to catch the impressions she received as we went along. At first, they were conscious psychic readings, later Ingrid seemed in a slight state of trance and communication with spirit entities directly. Here is what followed.

"1820s and 1840s. Do you mean both or one or the other?"

"Well, it's in that time period. And I sense a woman with a great sense of remorse."

"Do you feel this is a presence here?"

"Definitely a presence here."

"What part of the house do you feel it's strongest in?"

"Well, I'm being told to go upstairs."

"Is it a force pulling you up?"

"No, I just have a feeling to go upstairs."

"Before you go upstairs, before you came here did you have any feeling that there was something to it?"

"Yes, several weeks ago I saw a house—actually it was a much older house than this one, and it was on this site—and it was a dark house and it was shingled and it was—as I say, could have been an eighteenth century house, the house that I saw. It looked almost like a salt box, it had that particular look. And I saw that it was right on the water and I sensed a woman in it and a story concerned with a man in the sea with this house."

"A man with the sea?"

"Yes."

"Do you feel that this entity is still in the house?"

"I do, and of course I don't feel this is the *original* house. I feel it was on this property, and this is why I sense that she is throughout the house. That she comes here because this is her reenactment."

I asked her to continue.

"I can see in my mind's eye the house that was on this property before, and in my mind I sense a field back in this direction, and there was land that went with this!"

"Now we are upstairs. I want you to look into every room and give me your impressions of it," I said.

"Well, the upstairs is the most active. I sense a woman who is waiting. This is in the same time period. There are several other periods that go with this house, but I will continue with this one. I also see that she has looked out—not from this very same window, but windows in this direction of the house—*waiting for somebody to come back.*"

"What about this room?"

"Well, this room is like the room where she conducted a vigil, waiting for someone. And I just got an impression where she said that, 'She' meaning a schooner, 'was built on the Kennebec River'. . . . It seems to be a double-masted schooner, and it seems to be her husband who is on this. And I have an impression of novelties that he has brought her back. Could be from a foreign country. Perhaps the Orient or something like that."

"Now go to the corridor again and try some of the other rooms. What about this one?"

"I sense a young man in this room, but this is from a different time period. It's a young boy. It seems to be 1920s."

"Is that all you sense in this room?"

"That is basically what I sense in this room. The woman of the double-masted schooner story is throughout the house because as I have said, she doesn't really belong to this house. She is basically on the *property*—mainly she still goes through this whole house looking for the man to come home. And the front of the house is where the major activity is. She is always watching. But I have an impression now of a storm that she is very upset about. A gale of some kind. It seems to be November. I also feel she is saying something about . . . flocking sheep. There are sheep on this property."

"Where would you think is the most active room?"

"The most active room I think is upstairs and to the front, where we just were. I feel it most strongly there."

"Do you think we might be able to make contact with her?"

"Yes, I think so. Definitely I feel that she is watching *and I knew about her before I came*."

"What does she look like?"

"I see a tall woman, who is rather thin and frail with dark hair and it appears to be a white gown. It could be a nightgown I see her in—it looks like a nightgown to me with a little embroidery on the front. Hand done."

"Let us see if she cares to make contact with us?"

"All right."

"If the entity is present, and wishes to talk to us, we have come as friends; she is welcome to use this instrument, Ingrid, to manifest."

"She is very unhappy here, Hans. She says her family hailed from England. I get her name as Margaret."

"Margaret what?"

"Something like H o g e n—it begins with an H. I don't think it is Hogan, Hayden, or something like that. I'm not getting the whole name."

"What period are you in now?"

"Now she says 1843. She is very unhappy because she wanted to settle in Kennebunk; she does not like it here. She doesn't like the responsibilities of the house. Her husband liked it in this fishing village. She is very unhappy about his choice."

"Is he from England?"

"Yes, their descendants are from England."

"You mean were they born here or in England?"

"That I'm not clear on. But they have told me that their descendants are English."

"Now is she here. . . ?"

"She calls Kennebunk the city. That to her is a center."

"What does she want? Why is she still here?"

"She's left with all this responsibility. Her husband went on a ship, to come back in two years."

"Did he?"

"No, she's still waiting for him."

"The name of the ship?"

"I think it's St. Catherine."

"Is it his ship? Is he a captain?"

"He is second in command. It's not a mate, but a second something or other."

"What is she looking for?"

"She's looking to be relieved."

"Of what?"

"Of the duties and the responsibilities."

"For what?"

"This house."

"Is she aware of her passing?"

"No, she's very concerned over the flocks. She says it's now come April, and it's time for shearing. She is very unhappy over this. In this direction, Hans, I can see what appears to be a barn, and it's very old fashioned. She had two cows."

"Is she aware of the people in the house now?"

"She wants to communicate."

"What does she want them to do for her?"

"She wants for them to help her with the farm. She says it's too much, and the soil is all rocky and she can't get labor from the town. She's having a terrible time. It's too sandy here."

"Are there any children? Is she alone?"

"They have gone off, she says."

"And she's alone now?"

"Yes, she is."

"Can you see her?"

"Yes, I do see her."

"Can she see you?"

"Yes."

"Tell her that this is 1976, and that much time has passed. Does she understand this?"

"She just keeps complaining; she has nobody to write letters to."

"Does she understand that her husband has passed on and that she herself is a spirit and that there is no need to stay if she doesn't wish to?"

"She needs to get some women from the town to help with the spinning."

"Tell her that the new people in the house are taking care of everything, and she is relieved and may go on. She's free to go."

"She said, 'To Kennebunk?'"

"Any place she wishes—to the city or to join her husband on the other side of life."

"She said, 'Oh, what I would do for a town house.'"

"Ask her to call out to her husband to take her away. He's waiting for her."

"What does Johnsbury mean? A Johnsbury."

"It's a place."

"She's asking about Johnsbury."

"Does she wish to go there?"

"She feels someone may be there who could help her."

"Who?"

"It seems to be an uncle in Johnsbury."

"Then tell her to call out to her uncle in Johnsbury."

"She says he has not answered her letters."

"But if she speaks up now he will come for her. Tell her to do it now. Tell Margaret we are sending her to her uncle, with our love and compassion. That she need not stay here any longer. That she need not wait any longer for someone who cannot return. That she must go on to the greater world that awaits her outside, where she will rejoin her husband and she can see her uncle."

"She is wanting to turn on the lights. She is talking about the oil lamps. She wants them all lit."

"Tell her the people here will take good care of the house, of the lamps, and of the land."

"And she is saying, no tallow for the kitchen."

"Tell her not to worry."

"And the root cellar is empty."

"Tell her not to worry. We will take care of that for her. She is free to go—she is being awaited, she is being expected. Tell her to go on and go on from here in peace and with our love and compassion."

"She is looking for a lighthouse, or something about a lighthouse that disturbs her."

"What is the lighthouse?"

"She is very upset. She doesn't feel that it's been well kept; that this is one of the problems in this area. No one to tend things. I ought to be in Kennebunk, she says, where it is a city."

"Who lives in Kennebunk that she knows?"

"No one she knows. She wants to go there."

"What will she do there?"

"Have a town house."

"Very well, then let her go to Kennebunk."

"And go [to] the grocer, she says."

"Tell her she's free to go to Kennebunk. That we will send her there if she wishes. Does she wish to go to Kennebunk?"

"Yes, she does."

"Then tell her—tell her we are sending her now. With all our love . . ."

"In a carriage?"

"In a carriage."

"A black carriage with two horses."

"Very well. Is she ready to go?"

"Oh, I see her now in a fancy dress with a bonnet. But she's looking younger—she's looking much younger now. And I see a carriage out front with two dark horses and a man with a hat ready to take her."

"Did she get married in Kennebunk?"

"No."

"Where did she get married?"

"I don't get that."

"Is she ready to go?"

"Yes, she is."

"Tell her to get into the carriage and drive off."

"Yes, she's ready."

"Then go, Margaret—go."

"She says, many miles—three-day trip."

"All right. Go with our blessings. Do you see her in the carriage now?"

"Yes, the road goes this way. She is going down a winding road."

"Is she alone in the carriage?"

"Yes, she is, but there is a man driving."

"Who is the man who is driving?"

"A hired man."

"Is she in the carriage now?"

"Yes, she is."

"Is she on her way?"

"Yes."

"All right, then wave at her and tell her we send her away with our love."

"She looks to be about 22 now. Much younger."

"She's not to return to this house."

"She doesn't want to. She grew old in this house, she says."

"What was the house called then?"

"It was Point something."

"Did they build the house? She and her husband?"

"No, it was there."

"Who built it?"

"Samuel."

"And who was Samuel?"

"A farmer."

"They bought it from him?"

"Yes, they did. She says the deed is in the town hall."

"Of which town? Is it in this village?"

"Next town. Down the road."

"I understand. And in whose name is the deed?"

"Her husband's."

"First name."

"James."

"James what. Full name."

"It's something like Haydon."

"James Haydon from. . . ? What is Samuel's first name?"

"Samuels was the last name of the people who owned it."

"But the first name of the man who sold it. Does she remember that?"

"She never knew it."

"In what year was that?"

"1821."

"How much did they pay for the house?"

"Barter."

"What did they give them?"

"A sailing ship. A small sailing ship for fishing, and several horses. A year's supply of roots, and some paper—currency. Notes."

"But no money?"

"Just notes. Like promises, she says. Notes of promises."

"What was the full price of the house?"

"All in barter, all in exchange up here."

"But there was no sum mentioned for the house? No value?"

"She says, 'Ask my husband.'"

"Now did she and her husband live here alone?"

"Two children."

"What were their names?"

"Philip. But he went to sea."

"And the other one?"

"Francis."

"Did he go to sea too?"

"No."

"What happened to him?"

"I think Francis died."

"What did he die of?"

"Cholera. He was 17."

"Where did they get married? In what church?"

"Lutheran."

"Why Lutheran? Was she Lutheran?"

"She doesn't remember."

"Does she remember the name of the minister?"

"Thorpe."

"Thorpe?"

"Yes. Thorpe."

"What was his first name?"

"Thomas Thorpe."

"And when they were married, was that in this town?"

"No."

"What town was it in?"

"A long way away."

"What was the name of the town?"

"Something like Pickwick . . . a funny name like that . . . it's some kind of a province of a place. A Piccadilly—a province in the country she says."

"And they came right here after that? Or did they go anywhere else to live?"

"Saco. They went into Saco."

"That's the name of a place?"

"Yes."

"How long did they stay there?"

"Six months in Saco."

"And then?"

"Her husband had a commission."

"What kind of commission?"

"On a whaling ship."

"What was the name of the ship?"

"*St. Catherine*. I see *St. Catherine* or *St. Catherines*."

"And then where did they move to?"

"Port Clyde."

". . . and they stayed here for the rest of their lives?"

"Yes, until he went to sea and didn't come back one time."

"His ship didn't come back?"

"No."

"Does she feel better for having told us this?"

"Oh, yes."

"Tell her that she . . ."

"She says it's a long story."

"Tell her that she need not stay where so much unhappiness has transpired in her life. Tell her her husband is over there . . ."

"Yes."

"Does she understand?"

"Yes, she does."

"Does she want to see him again?"

"Yes."

"Then she must call out to him to come to her. Does she understand that?"

"Yes."

"Then tell her to call out to her husband James right now."

"He'll take her to Surrey or something like that, he says."

"Surrey."

"Surrey. Some funny name."

"Is it a place?"

"Yes, it is."

"Does she see him?"

"Yes."

"Are they going off together?"

"Yes, I see her leaving, slowly, but she's looking back."

"Tell her to go and not to return here. Tell her to go with love and happiness and in peace. Are they gone?"

"They are going. It's a reunion."

"We wish them well and we send them from this house, with our blessings, with our love and compassion, and in peace. Go on, go on. What do you see?"

"They are gone."

And with that, we left the house, having done enough for one day, a very full day. The camera crew packed up, so that we could continue shooting in the morning. As for me, the real work was yet to come: corroborating the material Ingrid Beckman had come up with.

I turned to Carol for verification, if possible, of some of the names and data Ingrid had come up with while in the house. Carol showed us a book containing maps of the area, and we started to check it out.

"Look," Carol said and pointed at the passage in the book, "this strip of land was owned by John Barter and it was right next to Samuel Gardner . . . and it says John Barter died in 1820 . . . the date mentioned by Ingrid! Ah, and there is also mention of the same Margaret Barter, and there is a date on the same page, November 23, 1882. . . . I guess that is when she died."

"Great," I said, pleased to get all this verification so relatively easily. "What exactly is this book?"

"It's a copy of the town's early records, the old hypothogue, of the town of St. George."

"Isn't that the town right next door?"

"Yes, it is."

"What about the name Hogden or Hayden or Samuel?"

"Samuel Hatton was a sailor and his wife was named Elmira," Carol said, pointing at the book. Ingrid had joined us now as I saw no further need to keep her in the dark regarding verifications—her part of the work was done.

"We must verify that," I said. "Also, was there ever a ship named *St. Catherine* and was it built on the Kennebec River as Ingrid claimed?"

But who would be able to do that? Happily, fate was kind; there was a great expert who knew both the area and history of the towns better than anyone around, and he agreed to receive us. That turned out to be a colorful ex-sailor by the name of Commander Albert Smalley, who received us in his house in St. George—a house, I might add, which was superbly furnished to suggest the bridge of a ship. After we had stopped admiring his mementos, and made some chitchat to establish the seriousness of our mission, I turned to the Commander and put the vital questions to him directly.

"Commander Albert Smalley, you've been a resident in this town for how long?"

"I was born in this town seventy-six years ago."

"I understand you know more about the history of Port Clyde than anybody else."

"Well, that's a moot question, but I will say, possibly, yes."

"Now, to the best of your knowledge, do the names Samuel and Hatton mean anything in connection with this area?"

"Yes, I know Hatton lived at Port Clyde prior to 1850. That I'm sure about."

"What profession did he have?"

"Sailor."

"Was there a ship named the *St. Catherine* in these parts?"

"Yes, there was."

"And would it have been built at the Kennebec River? Or connected with it in some way?"

"Well, as I recall it was, and I believe it was built in the Sewell Yard at the Kennebec River."

"Was there any farming in a small way in the Port Clyde area in the nineteenth century?"

"Oh yes, primarily that's what they came here for. But fishing, of course, was a prime industry."

"Now there's a lighthouse not far from Port Clyde which I believe was built in the early part of the nineteenth century. Could it have been there in the 1840s?"

"Yes. It was built in 1833."

"Now if somebody would have been alive in 1840, would they somehow be concerned about this comparatively new lighthouse? Would it have worried them?"

''No, it would not. The residence is comparatively new. The old stone residence was destroyed by lightning. But the tower is the same one."

"Now you know the area of Port Clyde where the Leah Davis house now stands? Prior to this house, were there any houses in the immediate area?"

"I've always been told that there was a house there. The Davis that owned it told me that he built on an old cellar."

"And how far back would that go?"

"That would go back to probably 1870. The new house was built around 1870."

"And was there one before that?"

"Yes, there was one before that."

"Could that have been a farmhouse?"

"Yes, it could have been because there is a little farm in back of it. It's small."

"Now you of course have heard all kinds of stories—some of them true, some of them legendary. Have you ever heard any story of a great tragedy concerning the owners of the farmhouse on that point?"

"Whit Thompson used to tell some weird ghost stories. But everyone called him a damned liar. Whether it's true or not, I don't know, but I've heard them."

"About that area?"

"About that area."

"Was there, sir, any story about a female ghost—a woman?"

"I have heard of a female ghost. Yes, Whit used to tell that story."

"What did he tell you?"

"That was a long time ago, and I cannot recall just what he said about it—he said many things—but she used to appear, especially on foggy nights, and it was hard to distinguish her features—that was one of the things he used to tell about—and there was something about her ringing the bell at the lighthouse, when they used to ring the old fog bell there. I don't recall what it was."

"Now the story we found involved a woman wearing a kind of white gown, looking out to sea from the window as if she were expecting her sailor to return, and she apparently was quite faceless at first."

"I don't think Whitney ever told of her face being seen."

"Do you know of anybody in your recollection who has actually had an unusual experience in that particular area?"

"No, I don't."

"Commander, if you had the choice of spending the night in the house in question, would it worry you?"

"No, why should it?"

"You are not afraid of ghosts?"

"No. Why should I be?"

"They are people after all."

"Huh?"

"They are just people after all."

"Yes."

"Have you ever seen one?"

"No, I was brought up with mediums and spiritualists and as a kid I was frightened half to death, I didn't dare go out after dark, but I got over that."

"Thank you very much."

"The lighthouse and the gale . . . the ship in a gale . . . it all seems to fit . . . ," Ingrid mumbled as we got back into our cars and left the Commander's house.

And there you have it. A girl from the big city who knows nothing about the case I am investigating, nor where she might be taken, and still comes up with names and data she could not possibly know on her own. Ingrid Beckman was (and is, I suppose) a gifted psychic. Shortly after we finished taping the Port Clyde story, I left for Europe.

While I was away, Ingrid met a former disc jockey then getting interested in the kind of work she and I had been doing so successfully for a while. Somehow he persuaded her to give a newspaper interview about this case—which, of course, upset NBC a lot since this segment would not air for six months—not to mention myself. The newspaper story was rather colorful, making it appear that Ingrid had heard of this ghost and taken care of it . . . but then newspaper stories sometimes distort things, or perhaps the verification and research of a ghost story is less interesting to them than the story itself. But to a professional like myself, the evidence only becomes evidence when it is carefully verified. I haven't worked with Ingrid since.

As for the ghostly lady of Port Clyde, nothing further has been heard about her, either, and since we gently persuaded her not to hang on any longer, chances are indeed that she has long been joined by her man, sailing an ocean where neither gales nor nosy television crews can intrude.

MID-ATLANTIC

11

A Revolutionary Spectre at Metuchen

ONE DAY, WHILE the snow was still on the ground and the chill in the air, my good friend Bernard Axelrod, with whom I have shared many a ghostly experience, called to say that he knew of a haunted house in New Jersey, and was I still interested.

I was, and Bernard disclosed that in the little town of Metuchen, there were a number of structures dating back to Colonial days. A few streets down from where he and his family live in a modern, up-to-date brick building, there stands one wooden house in particular which has the reputation of being haunted, Bernard explained. No particulars were known to him beyond that. Ever since the Rockland County Ghost in the late Danton Walker's colonial house had acquainted me with the specters from George Washington's days, I have been eager to enlarge this knowledge. So it was with great anticipation that I gathered a group of helpers to pay a visit to whoever might be haunting the house in Metuchen. Bernard, who is a very persuasive fellow, managed to get permission from the owner of the house, Mr. Kane, an advertising executive. My group included Mrs. Meyers, as medium, and two associates of hers who would operate the tape recorder and take notes, Rosemarie de Simone and Pearl Winder. Miss de Simone is a teacher and Mrs. Winder is the wife of a dentist.

It was midafternoon when we rolled into the sleepy town of Metuchen. Bernard Axelrod was expecting us, and took us across town to the colonial house we were to inspect.

Any mention of the history or background of the house was studiously avoided en route. The owners, Mr. and Mrs. Kane, had a guest, a Mr. David, and the eight of us sat down in a circle in the downstairs living room of the beautifully preserved old house. It is a jewel of a colonial country house, with an upper story, a staircase and very few structural changes. No doubt about it, the Kanes had good taste, and their house reflected it. The furniture was all in the style of the period, which I took to be about the turn of the eighteenth century, perhaps earlier. There were several cats smoothly moving about, which helped me greatly to relax, for I have always felt that no house is wholly bad where there are cats, and, where there are several cats, a house is bound to be wonderfully charming. For the occasion, however, the entire feline menagerie was put out of reach into the kitchen, and the tape recorder turned on as we took our seats in a semicircle around the fireplace. The light was the subdued light of a late winter afternoon, and the quiet was that of a country house far away from the bustling city. It was a perfect setting for a ghost to have his say.

As Mrs. Meyers eased herself into her comfortable chair, she remarked that certain clairvoyant impressions had come to her almost the instant she set foot into the house.

"I met a woman upstairs—in spirit, that is—with a long face, thick cheeks, perhaps forty years old or more, with ash-brown hair that may once have been blond. Somehow I get the name Mathilda. She wears a dress of striped material down to her knees, then wide plain material to her ankles. She puts out a hand, and I see a heavy wedding band on her finger, *but it has a cut in it*, and she insists on calling my attention to the cut. Then there is a man, with a prominent nose, tan coat and black trousers, standing in the back of the room looking as if he were sorry about something . . . he has very piercing eyes . . . I think she'd like to find something she has lost, and he blames her for it."

We were listening attentively. No one spoke, for that would perhaps give Mrs. Meyers an unconscious lead, something a good researcher will avoid.

"That sounds very interesting," I heard Bernard say, in his usual noncommittal way. "Do you see anything else?"

"Oh, yes," Mrs. Meyers nodded, "quite a bit—for one thing, there are *other* people here who don't belong to *them* at all . . . they come with the place, but in a different period . . . funny, halfway between upstairs and downstairs, I see one or two people *hanging*."

At this remark, the Kanes exchanged quick glances. Evidently my medium had hit pay dirt. Later, Mr. Kane told us a man committed suicide in the house around 1850 or 1860. He confirmed also that there was once a floor in between the two floors, but that this later addition had since been removed, when the house was restored to its original colonial condition.

Built in 1740, the house had replaced an earlier structure, for objects inscribed "1738" have been unearthed here.

"Legend has always had it that a revolutionary soldier haunts the house," Mr. Kane explained after the seance. "The previous owners told us they did hear *peculiar noises* from time to time, and that they had been told of such goings-on also by the owner who preceded *them*. Perhaps this story has been handed down from owner to owner, but we have never spoken to anyone in our generation who has heard or seen anything unusual about the place."

"What about you and your wife?" I inquired.

"Oh, we were a bit luckier—or unluckier—depending on how you look at it. One day back in 1956, the front door knocker banged away very loudly. My wife, who was all alone in the house at the time, went to see who it was. There was nobody there. It was winter, and deep snow surrounded the house. *There were no tracks in the snow*."

"How interesting," Bernard said. All this was new to him, too, despite his friendship with the family.

Mr. Kane slowly lit a pipe, blew the smoke toward the low ceiling of the room, and continued.

"The previous owners had a dog. Big, strapping fellow. Just the same, now and again he would hear some strange noises and absolutely panic. In the middle of the night he would jump into bed with them, crazed with fear. But it wasn't just the dog who heard things. They, too, heard the walking—steps of someone walking around the second floor, and in their bedroom, on the south side of the house—at times of the day when they *knew* for sure there was nobody there."

"And after you moved in, did you actually *see* anything?" I asked. Did they have any idea what the ghost looked like?

"Well, yes," Mr. Kane said. "About a year ago, Mrs. Kane was sleeping in the Green Room upstairs. *Three nights in a row, she was awakened in the middle of the night, at the same time, by the feeling of a presence*. Looking up, she noticed a white form standing beside her bed. Thinking it was me, at first, she was not frightened. But when she spoke to it, it just disappeared into air. She is sure it was a man."

Although nothing unusual had occurred since, the uncanny feeling persisted, and when Bernard Axelrod mentioned his interest in ghosts, and offered to have me come to the house with a qualified medium, the offer was gladly accepted. So there we were, with Mrs. Meyers slowly gliding into trance. Gradually, her description of what she saw or heard blended into the personalities themselves, as her own personality vanished temporarily. It was a very gradual transition, and well controlled.

"She is being blamed by him," Mrs. Meyers mumbled. "Now I see a table, she took four mugs, four large mugs, and one small one. Does she mean to say, four older people and a small one? I get a name, Jake, John, no, *Jonathan*! Then there are four Indians, and they want to make peace. *They've done something they should not have*, and they want to make peace." Her visions continued.

"Now instead of the four mugs on the table, there's a whole line of them, fifteen altogether, but I don't see the small mug now. There are many individuals standing around the table, with their backs toward me—then someone is calling and screaming, and someone says 'Off above the knees.'"

I later established through research that during the Revolutionary War the house was right in the middle of many small skirmishes; the injured may well have been brought here for treatment.

Mrs. Meyers continued her narrative with increasing excitement in her voice.

"Now there are other men, all standing there with long-tailed coats, white stockings, and talking. Someone says 'Dan Dayridge' or 'Bainbridge,' I can't make it out clearly; he's someone with one of these three-cornered hats, a white wig, tied black hair, a very thin man with a high, small nose, not particularly young, with a fluffy collar and large eyes. Something took place here in which he was a participant. He is one of the men standing there with those fifteen mugs. It is night, and there are two candles on either side of the table, food on the table—*smells like chicken*—and then there is a paper with red seals and gold ribbon. But something goes wrong with this, and now there are only four mugs on the table . . . I think it means, only four men return. *Not the small one*. This man is one of the four, and somehow the little mug is pushed aside, I see it put away on the shelf. I see now a small boy, he has disappeared, he is gone . . . but always trying to *come back*. The name *Allen* . . . he followed the man, but the Indians got him and he never came back. They're looking for him, trying to find him. . . ."

Mrs. Meyers now seemed totally entranced. Her features assumed the face of a woman in great mental anguish, and her voice quivered; the words came haltingly and with much prodding from me. For all practical purposes, the medium had now been taken over by a troubled spirit. We listened quietly, as the story unfolded.

"*Allen's* coming back one day . . . call him back . . . my son, do you hear him? They put those Indians in the tree, do you hear them as they moan?"

"Who took your boy?" I asked gently.

"They did . . . he went with them, with the men. With his father, *Jon*."

"What Indians took him?"

"Look there in the tree. They didn't do it. I know they didn't do it."

"Where did they go?"

"To the *river*. My boy, did you hear him?"

Mrs. Meyers could not have possibly known that there was a river not far from the house. I wanted to fix the period of our story, as I always do in such cases, so I interrupted the narrative and asked what day this was. There was a brief pause, as if she were collecting her thoughts. Then the faltering voice was heard again.

"December One. . . ."

December One! The old-fashioned way of saying December First.

"What year is this?" I continued.

This time the voice seemed puzzled as to why I would ask such an obvious thing, but she obliged.

"Seventeen . . . seventy. . . six."

"What does your husband do?"

"Jonathan . . . ?"

"Does he own property?"

"The field. . . ."

But then the memory of her son returned. "Allen, my son Allen. He is calling me. . . ."

"Where was he born?"

"Here."

"What is the name of this town?"

"Bayridge."

Subsequently, I found that the section of Metuchen we were in had been known in colonial times as *Woodbridge*, although it is not inconceivable that there also was a Bayridge.

The woman wanted to pour her heart out now. "Oh, look," she continued, "they didn't do it, they're in the tree . . . those Indians, dead ones. They didn't do it, I can see their souls and they were innocent of this . . . in the cherry tree."

Suddenly she interrupted herself and said—"Where am I? Why am I so sad?"

It isn't uncommon for a newly liberated or newly contacted "ghost" to be confused about his or her own status. Only an emotionally disturbed personality becomes an earthbound "ghost."

I continued the questioning.

Between sobs and cries for her son, Allen, she let the name "Mary Dugan" slip from her lips, or rather the lips of the entranced medium, who now was fully under the unhappy one's control.

"Who is Mary Dugan?" I immediately interrupted.

"He married her, Jonathan."

"Second wife?"

"Yes . . . I am under the tree."

"Where were you born? What was your maiden name?"

"Bayridge . . . Swift . . . my heart is so hurt, so cold, so cold."

"Do you have any other children?"

"Allen . . . Mary Anne . . . Georgia. They're calling me, do you hear them? Allen, he knows I am alone waiting here. He thought he was a *man* !"

"How old was your boy at the time?" I said. The disappearance of her son was the one thing foremost in her mind.

"My boy . . . eleven . . . December One, 1776, is his birthday. That was his birthday all right."

I asked her if Allen had another name, and she said, Peter. Her own maiden name? She could not remember.

"Why don't I know? They threw me out . . . it was Mary took the house."

"What did your husband do?"

"He was a *potter*. He also was paid for harness. His shop . . . the road to the south. Bayridge. In the tree orchard we took from two neighbors."

The neighborhood is known for its clay deposits and potters, but this was as unknown to the medium as it was to me until *after* the seance, when Bernard told us about it.

In *Boyhood Days in Old Metuchen*, a rare work, Dr. David Marshall says: "Just south of Metuchen there are extensive clay banks."

But our visitor had enough of the questioning. Her sorrow returned and suddenly she burst into tears, the medium's tears, to be sure, crying—"I want Allen! Why is it I look for him? I hear him calling me, I hear his step . . . I know he is here . . . why am I searching for him?"

I then explained that Allen was on "her side of the veil," too, that she would be reunited with her boy by merely "standing still" and letting him find her; it was her frantic activity that made it impossible for them to be reunited, but if she were to becalm herself, all would be well.

After a quiet moment of reflection, her sobs became weaker and her voice firmer.

"Can you see your son now?"

"Yes, I see him." And with that, she slipped away quietly.

A moment later, the medium returned to her own body, as it were, and rubbed her sleepy eyes. Fully awakened a moment later, she remembered nothing of the trance. Now *for the first time* did we talk about the house, and its ghostly visitors.

"How much of this can be proved?" I asked impatiently. Mr. Kane lit another pipe, and then answered me slowly.

"Well, there is quite a lot," he finally said. "For one thing, this house used to be a tavern during revolutionary days, known as the Allen House!"

Bernard Axelrod, a few weeks later, discovered an 1870 history of the town of Metuchen. In it, there was a remark about the house, which an early map showed at its present site in 1799:

"In the house . . . lived a Mrs. Allen, and on it was a sign 'Allentown Cake and Beer Sold Here.' Between the long Prayer Meetings which according to New England custom were held mornings and afternoons, with half hour or an hour intermission, it was not unusual for the young men to get ginger cake and a glass of beer at this famous restaurant. . . ."

"What about all those Indians she mentioned?" I asked Mr. Kane.

"There were Indians in this region all right," he confirmed.

"Indian arrowheads have been found right here, near the pond in back of the house. Many Indian battles were fought around here, and incidentally, during the War for Independence, both sides came to this house and had their ale in the evening. This was a kind of no-man's land between the Americans and the British. During the day, they would kill each other, but at night, *they ignored each other over a beer at Mrs. Allen's tavern!*"

"How did you get this information?" I asked Mr. Kane.

"There was a local historian, a Mr. Welsh, who owned this house for some thirty years. He also talked of a revolutionary soldier whose ghost was seen plainly 'walking' through the house about a foot off the ground."

Many times have I heard a ghostly apparition described in just such terms. The motion of walking is really unnecessary, it seems, for the spirit form *glides* about a place.

There are interesting accounts in the rare old books about the town of Metuchen in the local library. These stories spoke of battles between the British and Americans, and of "carts loaded with dead bodies, after a battle between British soldiers and Continentals, up around Oak Tree on June 26th, 1777."

No doubt, the Allen House saw many of them brought in along with the wounded and dying.

I was particularly interested in finding proof of Jonathan Allen's existence, and details of his life.

So far I had only ascertained that Mrs. Allen existed. Her husband was my next goal.

After much work, going through old wills and land documents, I discovered a number of Allens in the area. I found the will of his father, Henry, leaving his "son, Jonathan, the land where he lives" on April 4th, 1783.

A 1799 map shows a substantial amount of land marked "Land of Allen," and Jonathan Allen's name occurs in many a document of the period as a witness or seller of land.

The Jonathan Allen I wanted had to be from Middlesex County, in which Metuchen was located. I recalled that he was an able-bodied man, and consequently must have seen some service. Sure enough, in the *Official Register of the Officers and Men of New Jersey in the Revolutionary War*, I found my man—"Allen, Jonathan—Middlesex."

It is good to know that the troubled spirit of Mrs. Allen can now rest close to her son's; and perhaps the other restless one, her husband, will be accused of negligence in the boy's death no more.

12

The Restless Ghost of Bergenville

MRS. ETHEL MEYERS, who has frequently accompanied me on ghost-hunting expeditions, heard from friends living in Bergen County, New Jersey, about some unusual happenings at their very old house. Eventually the "safari for ghost" was organized, and Mr. B., the master of the house, picked us up in his car and drove us to Bergen County. The house turned out to be a beautifully preserved pre-Revolutionary house set within an enclosure of tall trees and lawns.

The building had been started in 1704, I later learned, and the oldest portion was the right wing; the central portion was added in the latter part of the eighteenth century, and the final, frontal portion was built from old materials about fifty years ago, carefully preserving the original style of the house. The present owners had acquired it about a year ago from a family who had been in possession for several generations. The house was then empty, and the B.'s refurbished it completely in excellent taste with antiques of the period.

After they moved into the house, they slept for a few days on a mattress on the enclosed porch, which skirted the west wing of the house. Their furniture had not yet arrived, and they didn't mind roughing it for a short while. It was summer, and not too cool.

In the middle of the night, Mrs. B. suddenly awoke with the uncanny feeling that there was *someone else* in the house, besides her husband and herself. She got up and walked toward the corridor-like extension of the enclosed porch running along the back of the house. There she clearly distinguished the figure of a man, seemingly white, with a beard, wearing what she described as "something ruffly white." She had the odd sensation that this man belonged to a much earlier period than the present. The light was good enough to see the man clearly for about five minutes, in which she was torn between fear of the intruder and curiosity. Finally, she approached him, and saw him *literally dissolve before her very eyes*! At the same time, she had the odd sensation that the stranger came to look *them* over, wondering what they were doing in *his* house! Mrs. B., a celebrated actress and choreographer, is not a scoffer, nor is she easily susceptible. Ghosts to her are something one can discuss intelligently. Since her husband shared this view, they inquired of the former owner about any possible hauntings.

"I've never heard of any or seen any," Mr. S. told them, "but my daughter-in-law has never been able to sleep in the oldest part of the house. Said there was too much going on there. Also, one of the neighbors claims he saw *something*."

Mr. S. wasn't going to endanger his recent real-estate transaction with too many ghostly tales. The B.'s thanked him and settled down to life in their colonial house.

But they soon learned that theirs was a busy place indeed. Both are artistic and very intuitive, and they soon became aware of the presence of unseen forces.

One night Mrs. B. was alone at home, spending the evening in the upper story of the house. There was nobody downstairs. Suddenly she heard the downstairs front door open and shut. There was no mistaking the very characteristic and complex sound of the opening of this ancient lock! Next, she heard footsteps, and sighed with relief. Apparently her husband had returned much earlier than expected. Quickly, she rushed down the stairs to welcome him. There was nobody there. There was no one in front of the door. All she found was the cat in a strangely excited state!

Sometime after, Mr. B. came home. For his wife these were anxious hours of waiting. He calmed her as best he could, having reservations about the whole incident. Soon these doubts were to be dispelled completely.

This time Mrs. B. was away and Mr. B. was alone in the downstairs part of the house. The maid was asleep in her room, the B.'s child fast asleep upstairs. It was a peaceful evening, and Mr. B. decided to have a snack. He found himself in the kitchen, which is located at the western end of the downstairs part of the house, *when he suddenly heard a car drive up*. Next, there were the distinct sounds of the front door opening and closing again. As he rushed to the front door, he heard the dog bark furiously. But again, there was no one either inside or outside the house!

Mr. B., a star and director, and as rational a man as could be, wondered if he had imagined these things. But he knew he had not. What he had heard were clearly the noises of an arrival. While he was still trying to sort out the meaning of all this, another strange thing happened.

A few evenings later, he found himself alone in the downstairs living room, when he heard carriage wheels outside grind to a halt. He turned his head toward the door, wondering who it might be at this hour. The light was subdued, but good enough to read by. He didn't have to wait long. A short, husky man walked into the room *through* the closed door; then, without paying attention to Mr. B., turned and walked out into the oldest part of the house, again *through a closed door*!

"What did he look like to you?" I asked.

"He seemed dotted, as if he were made of thick, solid dots, and he wore a long coat, the kind they used to wear around 1800. He probably was the same man my wife encountered."

"You think he is connected with the oldest part of the house?"

"Yes, I think so. About a year ago I played some very old lute music, the kind popular in the eighteenth century, in there—and something happened to the atmosphere in the room. As if someone were listening quietly and peacefully."

But it wasn't always as peaceful in there. A day before our arrival, Mrs. B. had lain down, trying to relax. But she could not stay in the old room. "There was someone there," she said simply.

The B.'s weren't the only ones to hear and see ghosts. Last summer, two friends of the B.'s were visiting them, and everybody was seated in the living room, when in plain view of all, the screen door to the porch opened and closed again *by its own volition*! Needless to add, the friends didn't stay long.

Only a day before our visit, another friend had tried to use the small washroom in the oldest part of the house. Suddenly, he felt chills coming on and rushed out of the room, telling Mrs. B. that "someone was looking at him."

At this point, dinner was ready, and a most delicious repast it was. Afterwards we accompanied the B.'s into the oldest part of their house, a low-ceilinged room dating back to the year 1704. Two candles provided the only light. Mrs. Meyers got into a comfortable chair, and gradually drifted into trance.

"Marie . . . Catherine . . . who calls?" she mumbled.

"Who is it?" I inquired.

"Pop . . . live peacefully . . . love . . ."

"What is your name?" I wanted to know.

"Achabrunn . . ."

I didn't realize it at the time, but a German family named Achenbach had built the house and owned it for several generations. Much later still, I found out that one of the children of the builder had been called Marian.

I continued my interrogation.

"Who rules this country?"

"The Anglish. George."

"What year is this?"

"56. 1756."

"When did you stay here?"

"Always. Pop. My house. *You* stay with *me*."

Then the ghost spoke haltingly of his family, his children, of which he had nine, three of whom had gone away.

"What can we do for you?" I said, hoping to find the reason for the many disturbances.

"Yonder over side hill, hillock, three buried . . . flowers there."

"Do you mean," I said, "that we should put flowers on these graves?"

The medium seemed excited.

"*Ach Gott, ja, machs gut*." With this the medium crossed herself.

"What is your name?" I asked again.

"Oterich . . . Oblich . . . ." The medium seemed hesitant as if the ghost were searching his memory for his own name. Later, I found that the name given was pretty close to that of another family having a homestead next door.

The ghost continued.

"She lady . . . I not good. I very stout heart, I look up to good-blood lady, I make her good . . . Kathrish, holy lady, I worship lady . . . they rest on hill too, with three . . . ."

After the seance, I found a book entitled *Pre-Revolutionary Dutch Houses in Northern New Jersey and New York*. It was here that I discovered the tradition that a poor shepherd from Saxony married a woman above his station, and built this very house. The year 1756 was correct.

But back to my interrogation. "Why don't you rest on the hillock?"

"I take care of . . . four . . . hillock . . . Petrish. Ladian, Annia, Kathrish. . . ."

Then, as if taking cognizance of us, he added—"To care for you, that's all I want."

Mrs. B. nodded and said softly, "You're always welcome here."

Afterward, I found that there were indeed some graves on the hill beyond the house. The medium now pointed toward the rear of the house, and said, "Gate . . . we put intruders there, he won't get up any more. Gray Fox made trouble, Indian man, I keep him right there."

"Are there any passages?"

"Yeah. Go dig through. When Indian come, they no find."

"Where?"

"North hillock, still stone floor there, ends here."

From Mr. B. I learned that underground passages are known to exist between this house and the so-called "Slave House," across the road.

The ghost then revealed that his wife's father, an Englishman, had built the passage, and that stores were kept in it along with Indian bones.

"Where were you born?" I inquired.

"Here. Bergenville."

Bergenville proved to be the old name of the township.

I then delicately told him that this was 1960. He seemed puzzled, to say the least.

"In 1756 I was sixty-five years old. I am not 204 years older?"

At this point, the ghost recognized the women's clothing the medium was wearing, and tore at them. I explained how we were able to "talk" to him. He seemed pacified.

"You'll accept my maize, my wine, my whiskey . . . ."

I discovered that maize and wine staples were the mainstays of the area at that period. I also found that Indian wars on a small scale were still common in this area in the middle 1700s. Moreover, the ghost referred to the "gate" as being in the *rear* of the house. This proved to be correct, for what is now the back of the house was then its front, facing the road.

Suddenly the ghost withdrew and after a moment another person, a woman, took over the medium. She complained bitterly that the Indians had taken one of her children, whose names she kept rattling off. Then she too withdrew, and Mrs. Meyers returned to her own body, none the worse for her experiences, none of which, incidentally, she remembered.

Shortly afterward, we returned to New York. It was as if we had just come from another world. Leaving the poplar-lined road behind us, we gradually reentered the world of gasoline and dirt that is the modern city.

Nothing further has been reported from the house in Bergen County, but I am sure the ghost, whom Mrs. B. had asked to stay as long as he wished, is still there. There is of course now no further need to bang doors, to call attention to his lonely self. *They know he is there with them.*

13

The Camden Ghost

NORTH FIFTH STREET in Camden, New Jersey, is in a part of town that is best avoided, especially at night. But even in the daytime it has the unmistakable imprint of a depressed—and depressing—area, downtrodden because of economic blight. The people leaning against shabby doors, idle and grim-looking, are people out of step with progress, people who don't work or can't work and who hate those who do. This is what it looks like today, with the busy factories and the smelly buildings of industrial Camden all around it, the super-modern expressway cutting a swath through it all as if those on it wouldn't want to stop even long enough to have a good look at what is on both sides of the road.

This grimy part of town wasn't always a slum area, however. Back in the 1920's, when Prohibition was king, some pretty substantial people lived here and the houses looked spic and span then.

Number 522, which has since given up its struggle against progress by becoming part of a city-wide improvement program, was then a respectable private residence. Situated in the middle of a short block, it was a gray, conservative-looking stone building with three stories and a backyard. The rooms are railroad flats, that is, they run from one to the other and if one were to go to the rear of the house one would have to enter from the front and walk through several rooms to get there. It wasn't the most inspiring way of building homes, but to the lower, or even the higher, middle classes of that time, it seemed practical and perfectly all right.

From the ground floor—with its front parlor followed by other living rooms and eventually a kitchen leading to the backyard—rose a turning staircase leading up to two more flights. This staircase was perhaps the most impressive part of the house and somehow overshadowed the simplicity of the rest of the layout. A nicely carved wooden banister framed it all the way up and though the house, in keeping with the custom of the times, was kept quite dark, the many years of handling the banister had given it a shine that sparkled even in so subdued an illumination. Heavy dust lay on stairs and floors and what there was of furniture was covered with tarpaulins that had grown black in time. Clearly, the house had seen better days but these times were over, the people were gone, and only a short time stood between the moment of rest and the sledge hammer of tomorrow.

Edna Martin is a bright young woman working for a local radio station in Camden, and spooks are as far removed from her way of thinking as anything could possibly be. When her parents moved into what was then a vacant house, she laughed a little at its forbidding appearance, but being quite young at the time, she was not at all frightened or impressed. Neither was her mother, who is a woman given to practical realities. There is a sister, Janet, and the two girls decided they were going to enjoy the big old house, and enjoy it they did.

Eventually, Edna began to notice some peculiar things about their home: the noise of rustling silk, the swish of a dress nearby when no one who could be causing these sounds was to be seen. On one occasion, she was having a quiet evening at home when she heard someone come up the stairs and enter the middle bedroom.

At that moment, she heard someone sigh as if in great sadness. Since she was quite sure that no one but herself was upstairs, she was puzzled by these things and entered the middle bedroom immediately. It was more out of curiosity than any sense of fear that she did so, not knowing for sure what she might find, if anything.

Before she entered the room, she heard the bedsprings squeak as if someone had lain down on the bed. She examined the bedspread—there was no indication of a visitor. Again, the rustling of clothes made her keenly aware of another presence in the room with her. Thoughtfully, she went back to her own room.

The parents and their married daughters, with their husbands and children, eventually shared the big house, and with so many people about, extraneous noises could very easily be overlooked or explained away.

And yet, there were ominous signs that the house was home to others besides themselves.

Janet woke up one night soon after the incident in the middle bedroom, and listened with a sharpened sense of hearing, the kind of super hearing one sometimes gets in the still of night. Something very light was walking up the stairs, and it sounded like the steps of a very light person, such as a child. The steps came gradually nearer. Now they were at the top of the stairs and then down the hall, until they entered the girl's room. She could hear every single floor board creak with the weight of an unseen person. Frozen with fright, she dared not move or speak. Even if she had wanted them to, her lips would not have moved. Then, as she thought she could stand it no longer, the steps came to a sudden halt beside her bed. She clearly felt the presence of a person near her staring at her!

Somehow, she managed to fall asleep, and nothing happened after that for a few weeks. She had almost forgotten the incident when she came home late one night from a date in town.

It was her custom to undress in the middle bedroom, and put her clothes on the bed in it, which was not occupied. She did not wish to wake the others, so she undressed hurriedly in the dark. As she threw her clothes upon the bed, *someone in the bed* let out a sigh, and turned over, as if half-awakened from deep sleep. Janet assumed her niece had come to visit and that she had been given the room. So she gathered her clothes from the bed and placed them on the chair instead, thinking nothing further about the matter.

Next morning, she went downstairs to have breakfast and at the same time have a chat with her niece, Miki. But the girl wasn't around. "Where is Miki, Mother?" she inquired. Her mother looked at her puzzled.

"I haven't the faintest idea," she shrugged. "She hasn't been here for weeks."

Janet froze in her tracks. Who had turned with a sigh in the empty bed?

The two girls had a close friend, Joanne, with whom they shared many things, including the eerie experiences in the house that somehow increased as the years went on. One evening Joanne was typing in the front bedroom on the second floor while Janet lay on the bed on her stomach.

Joanne's back was turned towards Janet at the time and the two girls were both spending the evening in their own way. Suddenly, Janet felt a strange sensation on the sole of her shoe. It felt as if someone had hit her in that spot, and hit her hard. The noise was so strong Joanne turned around and asked what had happened. Janet, who had jumped up and moved to the window, could only shrug. Was someone trying to communicate with her in this strange way?

Then there was the time the three girls were sitting on the bed and their attention was drawn to the foot of the bed, somehow. There, wriggling about five inches into the night air, was a greenish "thing" that had materialized out of nowhere. Letting out a shriek, Janet stared at it. Evidently she was the only one who could see it. As she looked through horror-stricken eyes, she could vaguely make out a small head nearby. Memories of the ghostly footsteps she had taken for a child some time ago came back to haunt her. Was there not a connection? Then the "thing" vanished.

The girls did not talk about these things if they could help it, for by now they knew there was something very peculiar about the house. But as yet they were not willing to believe in such things as ghosts of the departed. It all seemed terribly unreal to them.

When Edna was not yet married, the man she later married was an airman stationed at a base near Trenton, New Jersey. After one visit to her in Camden, he happened to miss the midnight bus back to camp, and there was nothing to be done but wait up for the next one, which was at 2:20 A.M. Since Edna had to get up early the next day, she went upstairs to get ready for bed. She left her fiance downstairs where there was a couch he could use, to rest up before going out to catch his bus. The young airman settled back with a smoke and relaxed.

Suddenly he heard the front door open. The door is a very heavy, old-fashioned one, with a lock that is hard to open unless you have the key. The airman was puzzled because he himself had seen Edna set the lock a few moments ago. Before he could try to figure this out, he heard the vestibule door open and suddenly there was an icy atmosphere in the room. True, it was winter, but until then he had not been cold. He immediately assumed a burglar had entered the house and rolled up his sleeves to receive him properly.

But then he experienced an eerie feeling quite different from anything he had ever felt before. His hair stood up as if electric current were going through it, and yet he was not the least bit frightened. Then a bell started to ring. The bell was inside a closed case, standing quietly in the corner. He suddenly realized that a bell could not clang unless someone first lifted it. When he came to that conclusion and saw no flesh-and-blood invader, he decided he'd rather wait for his bus outside. He spent the next hour or so at a drafty corner, waiting for his bus. Somehow it seemed to him a lot cozier.

That same night, Edna was awakened from light sleep by the sound of a disturbance downstairs. As her senses returned she heard someone clanging against the pipes downstairs. She immediately assumed it was her fiance playing a trick on her, for he had a talent for practical jokes. She hurriedly put on her robe and went downstairs. Immediately the noise stopped. When she reached the vestibule, her fiance was not there.

When she told him about this later and he reported the incident of the bell, she thought that he was now sufficiently impressed to accept the reality of ghosts in the house. But the young airman did not take the psychic occurrences too seriously despite his own encounter. He thought the whole thing extremely funny and one night he decided to make the ghosts work overtime. By then he and Edna were married. That night, he tied a string to the door of their bedroom, a door leading out into the hall. The other end of the string he concealed so that he could pull it and open the door, once they were in bed.

As soon as the lights were out, but sufficient light coming in through the windows remained, he started to stare at the door so as to attract his wife's attention to that spot. While she looked, he pointed at the door and said in a frightened voice, "Look, it's opening by itself!"

And so it was. He pulled off the trick so well, Edna did not notice it and in near-panic sprinkled the door with holy water all over. This made him laugh and he confessed his joke.

"Don't ever do such a thing," she warned him, when she realized she had been made a fool of. But he shrugged. She returned to bed and admonished him never to tempt the unseen forces lest they "pay him back" in their own kind.

She had hardly finished, when the door to the middle room began to open slowly, ever so slowly, by its own volition. As her husband stared in amazement, and eventually with mounting terror, the door kept swinging open until it had reached the back wall, then stopped. For a moment, neither of them moved. There was nothing else, at least not for the moment, so they jumped out of bed and the airman tried the door to see if he could explain "by natural means" what had just taken place before their eyes. But they both knew that this particular door had been taken off its hinges sometime before and had been propped into a closed position. In addition, in order to open it at all, it would have had to be lifted over two rugs on the floor. For several hours they tried to make this door swing open, one way or another. It would not move. Edna held the door by the hinges to keep it from falling forward while her husband tried to open it. It was impossible. Then they managed to get it to stay on the hinges, finally, and started to open it. It swung out about an inch before the rugs on the floor stopped it. What superior force had lifted the door over the rugs and pushed it against the back wall?

Still, he argued, there *had* to be some logical explanation. They let the matter rest and for a while nothing unusual happened in the house. Then, Edna and her husband had moved to the Middle West and were no longer aware of day to day goings-on in Camden. When they came to visit the family in Camden, after some time, they naturally wondered about the house but preferred not to bring up the subject of ghosts. Actually, Edna prayed that nothing would mar their homecoming.

Then it was time to leave again, and Edna's husband, good-naturedly, reminded her that he had neither seen nor heard any ghosts all that time. On that very day, their little son took sick, and they had to stay longer because of his condition.

They set up a cot for him in the living room, where they were then sleeping. If the boy were in need of help, they would be close by. During the night, they suddenly heard the cot collapse. They rushed over and quickly fixed it. The boy had not even awakened, luckily. As they were bent over the cot, working on it, they heard someone coming down the stairs.

Edna paid no particular attention to it, but her husband seemed strangely affected.

"Did you hear someone just come down the stairs?" he finally asked.

"Of course I did," Edna replied. "That was probably Miss Robinson."

Miss Robinson was a boarder living up on the third floor.

"No, it wasn't," her husband said, and shook his head, "I watched those stairs closely. I saw those steps bend when someone walked over them—but there was no Miss Robinson, or for that matter, anyone else."

"You mean . . .?" Edna said and for the first time her husband looked less confident. They made a complete search of the house from top to bottom. No one else was home at the time but the two of them and the sick child.

Edna, who is now a divorcee, realized that her family home held a secret, perhaps a dark secret, that somehow defied a rational explanation. Her logical mind could not accept any other and yet she could not find any answers to the eerie phenomena that had evidently never ceased.

If there was a ghostly presence, could she help it get free? What was she to do? But she knew nothing about those things. Perhaps her thoughts permeated to the ether areas where ghostly presences have a shadowy existence, or perhaps the unhappy wraith simply drew more and more power from the living in the house to manifest.

Sometime later, Joanne, Edna's close friend, came to her for help in the matter of a costume for a barn dance she had been asked to attend. Perhaps Edna had some suitable things for her? Edna had indeed.

"Go down to the basement," she directed her friend. "There are some trunks down there filled with materials. Take what you can use." Joanne, a teacher, nodded and went down into the cellar.

Without difficulty, she located the musty trunks. It was not quite so easy to open them, for they had evidently not been used for many years. Were those remnants left behind by earlier tenants of the house? After all, the present tenants had taken over a partially furnished house and so little was known about the people before them. The house was at least sixty years old, if not older.

As Joanne was pulling torn dresses, some of them clearly from an earlier era, she was completely taken up with the task at hand, that of locating a suitable costume for the dance. But she could not help noticing that something very strange was happening to her hair. It was a strange sensation, as if her hair suddenly stood on end! She passed her hand lightly over her forehead and felt that her hair was indeed stiff and raised up! At the same time she had a tingling sensation all over her body.

She dropped the dress she had been holding and waited, for she was sure someone was standing and staring at her. Any moment now, that person would speak. But as the seconds ticked away and no one spoke, she began to wonder. Finally, she could no longer contain herself and turned slowly around.

Back a few yards was a whirlpool of smoke, whirling and moving at a rapid pace. It had roughly the shape of a human figure, and as she looked at this "thing" with mounting terror, she clearly saw that where the face should be there was a gray mass of smoke, punctuated only by two large holes—where the eyes would normally be!

As she stared in utter disbelief, the figure came toward her. She felt the air being drawn from her lungs at its approach and knew that if she did not move immediately she would never get out of the cellar.

Somehow she managed to inch her way toward the stairs and literally crawled on all fours up to the ground floor. When she reached the fresh air, she managed to gather her wits sufficiently to tell Edna what she had seen.

But so terrible was the thought of what she had witnessed she preferred not to accept it, as time went by. To her, to this day, it was merely the shadow of someone passing by outside the cellar windows. . . .

Meanwhile the footsteps on the stairs continued but somehow the fury was spent. Gradually, the disturbances receded or perhaps the people in the house became used to them and paid them no further heed.

After Edna finally left the house and moved into a modern, clean flat, the house was left to its own world of ghosts until the wreckers would come to give it the *coup de grace*.

But Edna had not forgotten her years of terror, so when she heard of a famed psychic able to communicate with such creatures as she imagined her house was filled with, she tried to make contact and invite the lady to the house. She herself would not come, but the door was open.

It was a muggy day in July of 1967 that the psychic lady and a friend and co-worker paid the house a fleeting visit. Perhaps an hour at the most, then they would have to go on to other, more urgent things and places. In that hour, though, they were willing to help the unseen ones out of their plight, if they cared to be helped.

The psychic had not been inside the musty living room for more than ten seconds when she saw the woman on the stairs.

"There is a little boy, also, and the woman has fallen to her death on the stairs," she said, quietly, and slowly walked back and forth, her footsteps echoing strangely in the empty, yet tense old house.

"Go home" she pleaded with the woman. "You've passed over and you mustn't stay on here where you've suffered so much."

"Do you get any names?" asked her companion, ever the researcher. The psychic nodded and gave a name, which the gentleman quickly wrote down.

"All she wants is a little sympathy, to be one of the living," the psychic explained, then turned again to the staircase which still gleamed in the semi-darkness of the vestibule. "Go home, woman," she intoned once more and there seemed a quiet rustling of skirts, as she said it.

Time was up and the last visitors to the house on Fifth Street finally left.

The next day, the gentleman matched the name his psychic friend had given him with the name of a former owner of the house.

But as their taxi drew away in a cloud of gasoline fumes, they were glad they did not have to look back at the grimy old house.

For had they done so, they would have noticed that one of the downstairs curtains, which had been down for a long time, was now drawn back a little—just enough to let someone peek out from behind it.

14

A Very Haunted House in Pittsburgh

MRS. G. THREW a hasty look toward the third floor window of the modest wooden house on Mountview Place set back a few paces from the street. Then she shuddered and quickly hurried past, without looking back. Mrs. G. knew that was the best way to pass *that* house.

Everyone in the neighborhood knew the house was haunted and there was no point in seeing things one wasn't supposed to. Still—if the figure at the window was there, perhaps a glance would not hurt. It was a question of curiosity versus fear of the unknown, and fear won out.

The house itself looks like a typical lower-middle-class dwelling built around the turn of the century. White sides are trimmed in green, and a couple of steps lead up to the entrance door. Its three stories—you can call the third floor an attic, if you prefer—look no different than the floors in any of the smaller houses in suburban Pittsburgh. There is an appropriately sized backyard to the rear of the house, with some bushes and flowers. And there are houses to both sides of this one. The block is quiet with very little traffic running through it. By car, it is about forty minutes from downtown Pittsburgh, and most people don't go there more than maybe once in a while to shop. Life on Mountview Place is unexciting and drab and if it weren't for people like Mrs. G. worrying about the third floor window, nobody would even notice the house. But things were a little different when it was new and the neighborhood was a lot more rustic than it is now.

The early history of the house is somewhat shrouded, except that it was already in existence exactly as it looks today at the turn of the century. At that time Mr. Allshouse, the local plumber—he has his own shop and is in his late sixties now—was only a mere child. So he did not know the strange man who came to live in the house until many years later. But in 1908, a Hollander named Vander bought the house and he and his family lived in it until his wife died. In 1953 he left the house, and thereby hangs the first part of this strange tale. Although there were three children in the Vander family, he evidently had decided not to remain where his wife had died, but we can't be altogether sure as to why he left. In later years Mr. Allshouse and Vander had become friends, and even after his wife's passing Vander maintained contact with the plumber.

One day Allshouse was walking toward the house when he met Vander's niece en route. They stopped to chat and he mentioned where he was going. "Then you don't know?" the niece intoned. "My uncle has been dead for a month."

This came as a surprise to the plumber and he wondered how the otherwise hale and hearty Hollander had died so suddenly. He remembered well their initial meeting. This was several years ago, when Vander had needed some repairs done in the house. The work completed, the plumber presented his bill. Mr. Vander asked him to wait.

"Don't believe much in banks," he explained. "You don't mind taking cash, do you?"

"Not at all," the plumber assured him. The Dutchman then walked up the already shakey stairs to the attic. Allshouse could clearly hear him walk about up there as if he were moving some heavy object around, looking for something. Then the sound of a drawer closing was heard, and soon after, the Dutchman's heavy footsteps came down the stairs again.

"Here's your money," he said and smiled. He was a friendly man who didn't mind a chat with strangers. After a minute or two of discussing the state of the world and the weather in Pittsburgh in particular, the two men parted.

And now the Hollander was dead. It seemed very strange to the plumber. Why had Vander left the comfortable house just before his death and what was to happen to the house now?

Two weeks went by and other matters occupied the plumber's mind. He was walking down Trenton Avenue one afternoon, when he looked up and who should be trotting towards him but Mr. Vander!

Without thinking, the plumber called out a friendly "Hello!" The man did not react, so Allshouse shouted, "Mr. Vander! Mr. Vander!"

At this the man, who had meanwhile passed him, turned, smiled rather wanly, and said, "Hello."

But he did not stop to chat as he had always done before, and it seemed strange that this time Vander was cool and distant when normally he had been so friendly.

Long after the Dutchman had disappeared in the opposite direction, the plumber wondered why his friend had behaved so strangely. Then it suddenly hit him that the man had been dead and buried for six weeks.

Prior to his death Vander had sold the house to a couple named McBride. Apparently it was a private transaction for no one knows exactly how it happened, or even why, but the McBrides were installed in the house by the time Mr. Vander passed on or at least part of the way on.

The McBrides had no children, and Mrs. McBride was crippled, having once fallen in an alley. Consequently she dragged one leg in a rather pronounced manner when walking.

Around 1964, Mrs. McBride died, leaving the house to her husband, Franklin. Soon after, Mr. McBride's usual calm behavior changed rapidly. Where he had hardly been known for any eccentricities in the neighborhood, he seemed now a subject for discussion up and down the street. For one thing, he soon refused to go upstairs under any circumstances, and made his bed in an old Morris chair in the front parlor downstairs.

On more than one occasion, neighbors saw the man run out into the street in a state of abject fear. Not understanding his reasons, gossip blamed it on alcohol, but the fact is Mr. McBride never drank anything at all.

Ultimately, the widow's sister, a Mrs. Naugle, had him placed in the state mental institution at Torrence, where he is still living.

The power of attorney then passed into her hands, and it was she who rented the house to the Kennedy family. For about a year the house had stood empty after Mr. McBride's forced departure. In that time, dust had gathered and the house looked eerie even in the daytime. But at night people absolutely refused to walk close by it and even sensible people would rather cross the street to the other side than face walking close to its windows. Mrs. Evelyn Kennedy had not heard anything special about the house one way or the other.

It seemed like the kind of house she wanted for her brood and so she and her husband rented it in 1965. For almost a year the Kennedys lived quietly in the house on Mountview Place and kept busy with the ordinary routines of daily living. There was, first of all, Mrs. Evelyn Kennedy herself, a portly lady of mixed Irish-German ancestry, as so many are in this area, age forty-five and a lively and articulate housewife. At one time she had operated a beauty parlor downtown but now she was much too busy for that. Some of her equipment was still in the attic and on occasion she would perform her erstwhile duties for members of the family or friends there.

Mr. Wilbert Kennedy manages a nearby gas station. Five years her senior, he is a wiry, quiet-spoken man who is rarely around the house, the nature of his business being one of long hours.

Of their four children, two are married and live away from home. The other two daughters, Claudia and Penny, live with their parents. Claudia was married, but her husband had disappeared, and at twenty-four, she was kept busy with her two children, Debra, then seven, and Maria, the one year old. Penny, unmarried, was eighteen at the time they moved into the house. Except for an occasional friend, this was the entire cast of characters in the strange tale that was about to unfold.

On July 7, 1966, the landlady, Mrs. Naugle, decided she wanted to sell the house. Actually, it belonged to her brother-in-law in the institution but she had power of attorney so there was really nothing to stop her. Why she suddenly decided to sell, no one but she knows and she is hardly likely to tell us. But the very same real estate dealer, a man named McKnight, who had gotten the Kennedys into the house, was now entrusted with the disposal of the house to a new owner. Where this would leave the tenants no one knew or cared.

Actually, selling the house should not have proved too difficult. It was reasonably well kept, had an attractive exterior and a nice, large backyard, and the block was quiet and treelined. The downstairs parlor was separated from the dining room by a heavy oaken double door that could be pulled back entirely to make the downstairs into one large room, if one had many guests. To the right was the staircase which led straight up two flights. The second story contained the bedrooms and the third floor, actually the attic, was occupied by an additional bedroom in front and a large "rear room" which Mrs. Kennedy had filled with the remnants of her beauty parlor days and sundry suitcases, boxes, and the sort of things people have placed in attics ever since houses were built with them. The house was eminently suitable for any family with children.

Although the For Sale sign was up outside their home, the Kennedys continued with their daily business. Somehow they felt it would be some time before the house would be sold and then, perhaps, to an owner who did not wish to live in it. Why worry?

Penny, a determined young lady, had decided she preferred the privacy of the attic to the family presence on the second floor and moved her bed to the empty bedroom in the attic. The day after the For Sale sign had been installed outside, she came down to use the bathroom.

When she went back up to the attic, she found her way barred by a woman standing at the window. Since it was broad daylight, Penny had ample opportunity to look her over. She was an elderly woman with gray hair, wearing a somewhat unusual amount of rouge on her face. Her blue dress was like a long robe. In her hands she held some beads, and when Penny noticed her, the woman held out her arms toward her, all the while smiling at her. But Penny did not feel friendly at all. She knew there couldn't possibly be anyone of flesh-and-blood standing there. She let out a scream and rushed down the stairs, almost falling in the process.

Within hours, she was back in her old room on the second floor, and ten horses wouldn't get her up into the attic again.

But her troubles were far from over even on the second floor. The water kept turning itself on day and night. Her alarm clock was unplugged. Jewelry disappeared and could not be found despite careful and exhaustive search. The next day it would be back at the same spot it disappeared from.

Soon the phenomena spread to other members of the family. Mrs. Evelyn Kennedy, suffering from arthritis and a bad heart, would sometimes be unable to bend down because of swollen legs. One day she found herself all alone in the house. Her shoes were always kept under a chest of drawers in the bedroom. That day the shoes had somehow been pushed too far back under the chest and she could not reach them.

"Oh my," she said out loud. "I wish I could get at my shoes. What shall I do?"

With that she entered her bathroom for a shower. Afterwards, as she opened the bathroom door, the door hit something solid. She looked down. Someone had placed her shoes, which a few minutes before had been under the chest of drawers in her room, in front of the bathroom door. Yet, she was alone in the house.

Mrs. Kennedy put two and two together. Who was the woman in the blue robe that had frightened her daughter Penny?

Cautiously, she called the landlady, Mrs. Naugle and explained what had happened.

"Oh my God," the lady sighed, "that sounds just like my sister. She was laid out in a blue robe."

But she would not discuss this any further. It upset her, and she wanted no part of it.

Shortly after, Mrs. Kennedy was ironing downstairs in the parlor. All of a sudden a heavy object shot out of the door jamb and narrowly missed her. She stopped working and examined the object. It was a homemade pin of some sort. When she showed it to the landlady, the latter turned away, advising her to destroy the object. It was even harder to talk about the house after that incident.

Sobbing sounds were soon heard in the dining room when it was completely empty. Up in the attic the family would hear the sound of someone dragging legs, someone crippled, and they remembered in terror how the late Mrs. McBride had been thus afflicted. Was this her ghost, they wondered?

They had scarcely enough time to worry about what to do about all this that had suddenly burst upon them, when Mrs. Kennedy got to talking to the mailman, a Mr. Packen, who lived nearby. Somehow the talk turned to psychic phenomena and the mailman nodded gravely.

"I seen her, too," he confided, "back in '63, I seen her sweeping the pavement. Right in front of the house, I seen her."

"Who have you seen?" asked Mrs. Kennedy, as if she didn't know.

"Who but that lady, Mrs. McBride?" the mailman answered. "Big as life she was."

He in turn had been no stranger to this sort of thing. In his own house down the street he once saw a little old lady who seemed strangely familiar. As a mailman, he knows most of his "customers" well enough and the little old lady in his house rang a bell.

"What are you doing in my house?" he demanded. "You're supposed to be dead!"

Reproachfully he glanced at her and she nodded sadly and dissolved into the evening mist.

So it wasn't particularly shocking for him to hear about the goings-on at the Kennedy house.

The little old lady who had visited the mailman apparently had some business of her own, and as it is unfinished business that keeps these denizens of the netherworld from going on into the Great Beyond, he wondered what it was she had wanted.

One afternoon, ten-year-old Debra was playing in the downstairs parlor, when she felt herself not alone. In looking up she saw a little old lady standing in the room. Wearing black clothes, she seemed strangely old-fashioned and unreal to her, but there was no doubt in Debra's mind that she had a visitor. While she rose to meet the stranger, the woman disappeared. Having heard of her Aunt Penny's encounter with the lady on the stairs, she knew at once that this was not the same person. Whereas the lady on the stairs had been tall and smiling, this woman was short and bent and quizzical in her expression.

The excitement of this vision had hardly died down when Mrs. Kennedy found her work in the kitchen, washing dishes, interrupted by the feeling that she was about to have a visitor. Since she was alone in the house at the moment, she immediately proceeded to the front door to open it. Without thinking anything special, she opened the front door and standing there and waiting was a lady. She was short of stature, her dress had big, puffed sleeves, she wore gloves and carried a big black umbrella. Mrs. Kennedy also noticed a golden pin and the bustle of her dress. In particular, she was astonished to see her hat, which was large and had a big bill on it—something no woman today would wear.

As she still wondered who this strange woman might be, she motioned to her to come in, which the woman did, brushing past her. Only then did it occur to Mrs. Kennedy that she had *not* heard the doorbell ring! Turning around and going after her visitor, she found that no one had come in.

Now she, too, realized that it was someone other than the late Mrs. McBride, if indeed it was she, who kept coming to the house. It was the mailman's friend, strange as it might seem, but from the description she was sure it was the same person.

The mystery deepened even further when Debra reported seeing a man in the kitchen at a time when no man was in the house. The man had worn a blue shirt and brown pants, but they were not the sort of clothes worn by people today. He stood in a corner of the kitchen as if he belonged there and though Debra was frightened, she managed to see enough of the wraith before he faded away again.

It was a Monday night some weeks after this experience, that Claudia and Penny were on the stairs alone. Mr. Kennedy and the two grandchildren were already in bed in their rooms. All the lights were out and only the street lights cast a reflection of sorts into the house through the windows. Suddenly the two girls heard the sound of someone running from the kitchen toward the living room. They looked up and what they saw made their blood turn to ice: there in the dim light of the kitchen stood the outline of a very large man. *With a huge leap, he came after them.* Faster than lightning, they ran up the stairs, with the shadowy man in hot pursuit. As they looked back in sheer terror, they saw him coming, but he stopped at the landing. Then he was gone, just disappeared like a puff of smoke.

From that moment on, the two young women refused to stay downstairs at night.

The downstairs parlor was as "unsafe" from the incursions of the ghosts as was the attic, and before long even the backyard was no longer free from whatever it was that wanted attention. It was almost as if the unseen forces were engaged in a campaign of mounting terror to drive home the feeling that the Kennedy's were not in possession of the house: *the ghosts were.*

Lights would go on and off by themselves. Water started to gush in the bathroom and when they investigated they found someone unseen had turned the tap on. Late at night, they often heard someone cry softly in their backyard. Enough light from the windows illuminated that plot of land to assure them that it was no human agent. They huddled together, frightened, desolate, and yet unwilling to give up the house which they truly loved. The attic was particularly active during those weeks immediately following the landlady's decision to sell their house. Someone was moving heavy furniture around up there at night—or so it sounded. Nothing ever was changed in the morning. Mrs. Kennedy sought the advice of a good friend, Mrs. Lucille Hags, who had been to the house often.

One evening, when things had been particularly active, Evelyn Kennedy dialed her friend. The soothing voice at the other end of the phone momentarily calmed her. But then she clearly heard someone else dialing her phone.

"Are you dialing?" she asked her friend, but Mrs. Hags had not touched her telephone either. Perhaps there had been some kind of cross-connection. Mrs. Kennedy decided to ignore it and bravely started to tell her friend what had happened that evening at the house.

"I wonder if it has something to do with Mrs. McBride," she ventured. No sooner had she said this, when heavy breathing, the breath of someone very close by, struck her ear.

"Do you hear that?" she asked, somewhat out of breath now herself.

"Yes, I did," said Mrs. Hags. Six times the heavy breathing interfered with their telephone conversation during the following weeks. Each time it started the moment either of them mentioned the phenomena in the house. Was one of their ghostly tenants listening in? So it would seem. The telephone people assured Mrs. Kennedy there was nothing wrong with her line.

Nothing wrong? she asked herself. Everything was wrong; the house was all wrong and what were they to do?

One sunny morning she decided to fight back. After all, this had been their happy home for a while now and no phantoms were going to drive them out of it. She tried to reason it out but no matter how many of the noises she could explain by ordinary causes, too many things remained that simply could not be explained away. There were, as far as she could make out, three ghosts in the house. The two women and the heavy-set man. She wasn't quite sure who the man was, and yet it seemed to her it must be the Hollander, Vander, whose money had always been hidden up there in the attic. Had he returned for it, or was he simply staying on because he didn't like the way he left? Those were the questions racing through Mrs. Kennedy's mind often now.

To be sure, at least one of the *stay-behinds* was friendly.

There was the time Mrs. Kennedy slipped on the stairs and was about to fall headlong down the whole flight of stairs. It was a warm summer day and she was alone at home, so that she would have lain there helpless had she injured herself. But something kept her from falling! Some force stronger than gravity held on to her skirts and pulled her back onto her feet. It wasn't her imagination and it wasn't a supreme effort of her own that did it. She was already half into the air, falling, when she was yanked back, upright.

Shortly after, she managed to repair to the attic, where her hair-drying equipment was stored. As she sat there, resting, she suddenly felt something wet and cold across her legs. She reached down only to feel a soft, moist mass that dissolved rapidly at her touch! This was enough to give her the willies, and she began to fear for her life, bad heart and all.

And yet, when the prospective buyers came more frequently to look at the house, and it seemed that the house might be sold after all, she found herself turning to her ghostly protector.

"Please, Mrs. McBride," she prayed silently, "don't let her sell the house!"

As if by a miracle, the most interested buyer who had been close to a decision in favor of taking the house, went away and was never seen again. The house remained unsold. Coincidence? If there be such things, perhaps. But not to Mrs. Kennedy.

She did not particularly care to have word of their predicament get around. It was bad enough to have ghosts, but to be known as a haunted family was even worse. And yet how could it be avoided? It wasn't just she and her two daughters who experienced these strange things.

Even her husband, who wasn't exactly given to a belief in ghosts, was impressed when he saw a chair move from under a desk by its own force. He tried it several times afterwards, hoping he could duplicate the phenomena by merely stomping his feet or gently touching the chair, but it required full force to move it.

The insurance man who had been servicing them for years was just as doubtful about the whole thing, when he heard about it.

"No such thing as a ghost," he commented as he stood in the hallway. At this moment the banister started to vibrate to such an extent they thought it would explode. He grabbed his hat and took his doubts to the nearest bar.

Sandra, a friend, had been sitting with Mrs. Kennedy downstairs not long ago, when suddenly she clearly heard someone in the bedroom overhead, the footsteps of someone running across it.

"I didn't know you had other company," she remarked to Mrs. Kennedy.

"I don't," Mrs. Kennedy answered dryly, and the friend left, somewhat faster than she had planned to.

Penny, 21 years old, and single, turned out to be more psychic than any of them. Hardly had she recovered from her terrible experience on the stairs, when something even more unspeakable occurred.

One evening, as she was retiring for the night, and had the lights turned off in her room, she felt something cold lie down in bed beside her. With a scream she jumped out and switched the lights back on. There was nothing, but a chill still pervaded the entire area!

In the summer of 1967, Penny found herself alone on the stairs on one occasion, when she suddenly heard a voice speak to her.

"It's all right . . . she can come out now," some woman said somewhere in back of her. There was no one visible who could have spoken these words and no one nearby. Besides, it was not a voice she recognized. It sounded strangely hollow and yet imperious at the same time. Someone was giving an order, but who, and to whom? Clearly, this someone still considered herself mistress of this house.

Although Penny had no interest in psychic matters, she wondered about these phenomena. Who was the man she had seen on the stairs? Who was the woman whose voice she had heard?

Somewhere she read an advertisement for a pendulum as an aide to psychic perception. As soon as it had come in the mail, she retired to her room, and tried it out.

Holding the pendulum over a piece of board, she intoned, more in jest than for serious research reasons, "Mr. Vander, are you here?"

With a swift move, the pendulum was ripped from her hands and landed clear across the room. She hasn't used it since, nor does she really care if Mr. Vander is the ghost she saw. She just wants to be left alone.

Somehow, the summer passed, and it was in September, 1967, that Mrs. Kennedy realized there was more to this triangle of ghosts than just their presence. She was standing outside the house, chatting with a neighbor.

"Are the children having a party?" the neighbor asked.

"Why, no," she replied, knowing full well the children were all out of the house at the moment.

She was wondering why her neighbor had asked such a peculiar question, and was about to say so, when she heard a loud noise coming from the empty house: it sounded indeed as if a group of children were having a party upstairs, running up and down in the house. All she could do was shrug and turn away.

Maria, the three-year-old, is a precocious youngster who speaks better than her years would call for. One day she accompanied her grandmother to the attic. While Mrs. Kennedy was busy with her chores in the front room, the little girl played in the rear of the attic. Suddenly she came running out of the back room and beckoned her grandmother to follow her.

"There is a nice lady back there and she likes me," she explained.

Immediately Mrs. Kennedy went back but she saw nothing this time.

Whether this visit to the attic had stirred up some sort of psychic contact, or whether her growing years now allowed her to express herself more clearly, the little girl had something more to say about the ghosts before long. Naturally, no one discussed such matters with her. Why frighten the child?

"There is a little boy in the attic," Maria explained earnestly, "and his name is Yackie. He died up there. He plays snowball out the window because he isn't allowed out of the attic."

At first these stories were dismissed as the fantasies of a child. Mrs. Kennedy was even a bit amused about the way Maria said "Yackie" instead of Jackie. They did not wish to stop her from telling this story over and over, out of fear that repressing her might make it more interesting. But as the weeks went on the little girl developed a strange affinity for the attic, especially the rear portion.

"Why are you always running up there, Maria?" her grandmother finally asked.

"Because," the little girl said, and became agitated, "because there is a man up there. Yackie told me about him."

"What about this man?"

"He died. He was shot in the head and all of his blood came out and he's buried in the back yard under the bushes."

"Why was he shot in the head, child?" the grandmother asked, almost as if she believed the story.

"Because he was crazy and he cried, that's why," the child replied. Her grandmother was silent for a moment, trying to sort things out.

Could a three-year-old make up such a yarn? she wondered.

"Come," the little girl said, and took her by the hand, "I'll show you." She led Mrs. Kennedy to the dining room window and pointed at the bushes in their backyard.

"It's under the bushes there," Maria repeated and stared out the window.

Mrs. Kennedy shuddered. It was a spot she had wondered about many times. No matter how she tried, no matter what she planted, *nothing would grow on that spot*!

But as it turned colder, the house seemed to settle down and the disturbances faded away. True, no one came to inquire about buying it either. The Kennedys half believed their troubles might just have faded away, both their worldly and their unworldly difficulties.

They thought less and less about them and a spark of hope returned to Mrs. Kennedy about staying on at the house. She tried to make some discreet inquiries about the former owners of the house and even attempted to find the official records and deeds of sale. But her efforts were thwarted on all sides. Neighbors suddenly turned pale and would not discuss the matter. Nobody admitted knowing anything at all about the Hollander, Mr. Vander. Why, for instance, had she been told he left no children when he died? Only accidentally did she discover that there were three children. Was one of them named Jackie perhaps? She could not be sure.

The winter came and a bitterly cold winter it was. Late in January, her composure was rudely shattered when a representative of the real estate agent paid them a visit. The house was being offered for sale once again.

That day one of her married daughters was visiting Mrs. Kennedy. She had brought her baby along and needed some toys for it to play with. "Go up into the attic. There's plenty of stuff there," Mrs Kennedy suggested.

The woman, accompanied by her sister Claudia, went up into the attic. She was barefoot and casually dressed. Suddenly, Claudia pushed her to one side. "Watch out," she said and pointed to the floor boards. There, stuck between two boards, with the cutting edge pointing up, was a single-edged razor blade.

Somewhat shaken by their experience, the two women went back downstairs, after having pulled the blade out of the floor with some difficulty. It had been shoved into the crack between the boards with considerable strength. Nobody in the house used single-edged razor blades. In fact, few people do nowadays. The only man in the house uses an electric shaver.

Suddenly, the activities started all over. The front door would continually open by itself and shut by itself, and there was never anyone there when someone went to check. This happened mainly at night and in each case Mrs. Kennedy found the door securely locked. The door she and the others heard open was not a physical door, apparently, but an echo from the past!

The Kennedys were patient for several days, then they decided that something had to be done. It was a nice house all right, but sooner or later someone would buy it, and they couldn't afford to buy it themselves, unfortunately. Since they could stop neither the landlady from trying to sell it, nor the ghostly inhabitants from playing in it, it was perhaps the wisest thing to look for another home.

By April they had finally found a nice house in nearby Penn Hills, and the moment they set foot in it they knew it would do fine.

With her deeply developed psychic sense Mrs. Kennedy also knew at once that she would have no problems with unseen visitors in *that* house.

It gave them a degree of pleasure to be moving out on their landlady rather than waiting to be evicted by the new owner. Gradually their belongings were moved to their new home.

On the last day, when almost everything had already been removed, Mrs. Kennedy, her husband, and their son, who had come to help them move, stood in the now almost empty house once more. There were still a few boxes left in the cellar. The two men went back into the cellar to get them out, while Mrs. Kennedy waited for them upstairs.

"Come," Mr. Kennedy said, and shivered in the spring air, "it's late. Let's finish up."

The clock of a nearby church started to strike twelve midnight.

They loaded the boxes into the car, carefully locked the front door of the house and then the garden gate.

At this precise moment, all three clearly heard the front door open and close again, and loud steps reverberate inside the empty house.

"There must be someone in there," Mrs. Kennedy's son murmured. He did not believe in ghosts and had always poo-pooed the tales told by his mother and sisters.

Quickly he unlocked the gate and front door once more and reentered the dark house.

After a few moments, he returned, relocked house and gate and, somewhat sheepishly, shook his head.

"Nothing. It's all empty."

Not at all, Mrs. Kennedy thought, as the car pulled out into the night, not at all.

That was only the reception committee for the next tenant.

15

The Somerset Terror

SOMERSET IS ONE of those nondescript small towns that abound in rural Pennsylvania and that boast nothing more exciting than a few thousand homes, a few churches, a club or two and a lot of hardworking people whose lives pass under pretty ordinary and often drab circumstances. Those who leave may go on to better things in the big cities of the East, and those who stay have the comparative security of being among their own and living out their lives peacefully. But then there are those who leave not because they want to but because they are driven, driven by forces greater than themselves that they cannot resist.

The Manners are middle-aged people with two children, a fourteen-year-old son and a six-year-old daughter. The husband ran a television and radio shop which gave them an average income, neither below middle-class standards for a small town, nor much above it. Although Catholic, they did not consider themselves particularly religious. Mrs. Manner's people originally came from Austria, so there was enough European background in the family to give their lives a slight continental tinge, but other than that, they were and are typical Pennsylvania people without the slightest interest in, or knowledge of, such sophisticated matters as psychic research.

Of course, the occult was never unknown to Mrs. Manner. She was born with a veil over her eyes, which to many means the Second Sight. Her ability to see things before they happened was not "precognition" to her, but merely a special talent she took in her stride. One night she had a vivid dream about her son, then miles away in the army. She vividly saw him walking down a hall in a bathrobe, with blood running down his leg. Shortly after she awakened the next day, she was notified that her son had been attacked by a rattlesnake and, when found, was near death. One night she awoke to see an image of her sister standing beside her bed. There was nothing fearful about the apparition, but she was dressed all in black.

The next day that sister died.

But these instances did not frighten Mrs. Manner; they were glimpses into eternity and nothing more.

As the years went by, the Manners accumulated enough funds to look for a more comfortable home than the one they were occupying, and as luck—or fate—would have it, one day in 1966 they were offered a fine, old house in one of the better parts of town. The house seemed in excellent condition; it had the appearance of a Victorian home with all the lovely touches of that bygone era about it. It had stood empty for two years, and since it belonged to an estate, the executors seemed anxious to finally sell the house. The Manners made no special inquiries about their projected new home simply because everything seemed so right and pleasant. The former owners had been wealthy people, they were informed, and had lavished much money and love on the house.

When the price was quoted to them, the Manners looked at each other in disbelief. It was far below what they had expected for such a splendid house. "We'll take it," they said, almost in unison, and soon the house was theirs.

"Why do you suppose we got it for such a ridiculously low price?" Mr. Manner mused, but his wife could only shrug. To her, that was not at all important. She never believed one should look a gift horse in the mouth.

It was late summer when they finally moved into their newly acquired home. Hardly had they been installed when Mrs. Manner knew there was something not right with the place.

From the very first, she had felt uncomfortable in it, but being a sensible person, she had put it down to being in a new and unaccustomed place. But as this feeling persisted she realized that she was being *watched* by some unseen force all the time, day and night, and her nerves began to tense under the strain.

The very first night she spent in the house, she was aroused at exactly two o'clock in the morning, seemingly for no reason. Her hair stood up on her arms and chills shook her body. Again, she put this down to having worked so hard getting the new home into shape.

But the "witching hour" of two A.M. kept awakening her with the same uncanny feeling that something was wrong, and instinctively she knew it was not her, or someone in her family, who was in trouble, but the new house.

With doubled vigor, she put all her energies into polishing furniture and getting the rooms into proper condition. That way, she was very tired and hoped to sleep through the night. But no matter how physically exhausted she was, at two o'clock the uncanny feeling woke her.

The first week somehow passed despite this eerie feeling, and Monday rolled around again. In the bright light of the late summer day, the house somehow seemed friendlier and her fears of the night had vanished.

She was preparing breakfast in the kitchen for her children that Monday morning. As she was buttering a piece of toast for her little girl, she happened to glance up toward the doorway. There, immaculately dressed, *stood a man*. The stranger, she noticed, wore shiny black shoes, navy blue pants, and a white shirt. She even made out his tie, saw it was striped, and then went on to observe the man's face. The picture was so clear she could make out the way the man's snowy white hair was parted.

Her immediate reaction was that he had somehow entered the house and she was about to say hello, when it occurred to her that she had not heard the opening of a door or any other sound—no footfalls, no steps.

"Look," she said to her son, whose back was turned to the apparition, but by the time her children turned around, the man was gone like a puff of smoke.

Mrs. Manner was not too frightened by what she had witnessed, although she realized her visitor had not been of the flesh and blood variety. When she told her husband about it that evening, he laughed.

Ghosts, indeed!

The matter would have rested there had it not been for the fact that the very next day something else happened. Mrs. Manner was on her way into the kitchen from the backyard of the house, when she suddenly saw a woman go past her refrigerator. This time the materialization was not as perfect. Only half of the body was visible, but she noticed her shoes, dress up to the knees, and that the figure seemed in a hurry.

This still did not frighten her, but she began to wonder. All those eerie feelings seemed to add up now. What had they gotten themselves into by buying this house? No wonder it was so cheap. It was haunted!

Mrs. Manner was a practical person, the uncanny experiences notwithstanding, or perhaps because of them. They had paid good money for the house and no specters were going to dislodge them!

But the fight had just begun. A strange kind of web began to envelop her frequently, as if some unseen force were trying to wrap her into a wet, cold blanket. When she touched the "web," there was nothing to be seen or felt, and yet, the clammy, cold force was still with her. A *strange scent of flowers* manifested itself out of nowhere and followed her from room to room. Soon her husband smelled it too, and his laughing stopped. He, too, became concerned: their children must not be frightened by whatever it was that was present in the house.

It soon was impossible to keep doors locked. No matter how often they would lock a door in the house, it was found wide open soon afterwards, the locks turned by unseen hands. One center of particular activities was the old china closet, and the scent of flowers was especially strong in its vicinity.

"What are we going to do about this?" Mrs. Manner asked her husband one night. They decided to find out more about the house, as a starter. They had hesitated to mention anything about their plight out of fear of being ridiculed or thought unbalanced. In a small town, people don't like to talk about ghosts.

The first person Mrs. Manner turned to was a neighbor who had lived down the street for many years. When she noticed that the neighbor did not pull back at the mention of weird goings-on in the house, but, to the contrary, seemed genuinely interested, Mrs. Manner poured out her heart and described what she had seen.

In particular, she took great pains to describe the two apparitions. The neighbor nodded gravely.

"It's them, all right," she said, and started to fill Mrs. Manner in on the history of their house. This was the first time Mrs. Manner had heard of it and the description of the man she had seen tallied completely with the appearance of the man who had owned the house before.

"He died here," the neighbor explained. "They really loved their home, he and his wife. The old lady never wanted to leave or sell it."

"But what do you make of the strange scent of flowers?" Mrs. Manner asked.

"The old lady loved flowers, had fresh ones in the house every day."

Relieved to know what it was all about, but hardly happy at the prospect of sharing her house with ghosts, Mrs. Manner then went to see the chief of police in the hope of finding some way of getting rid of her unwanted "guests."

The chief scratched his head.

"Ghosts?" he said, not at all jokingly. "You've got me there. That's not my territory."

But he promised to send an extra patrol around in case it was just old-fashioned burglars.

Mrs. Manner thanked him and left. She knew otherwise and realized the police would not be able to help her.

She decided they had to learn to live with their ghosts, especially as the latter had been in the house before them. Perhaps it wouldn't be so bad after all, she mused, now that they knew who it was that would not leave.

Perhaps one could even become friendly, sort of one big, happy family, half people, half ghosts? But she immediately rejected the notion. What about the children? So far, they had not *seen* them, but they knew of the doors that wouldn't stay shut and the other uncanny phenomena.

Fortunately, Mrs. Manner did not understand the nature of poltergeists. Had she realized that the very presence of her teen-age son was in part responsible for the physical nature of the happenings, she would no doubt have sent him away. But the phenomena continued unabated, day and night.

One night at dinner, with everyone accounted for, an enormous crash shook the house. It felt as if a ton of glass had fallen on the kitchen floor. When they rushed into the kitchen, they found everything in order, nothing misplaced.

At this point, Mrs. Manner fell back on her early religious world.

"Maybe we should call the minister?" she suggested, and no sooner said than done. The following day, the minister came to their house. When he had heard their story, he nodded quietly and said a silent prayer for the souls of the disturbed ones.

He had a special reason to do so, it developed. They had been among his parishioners when alive. In fact, he had been to their home for dinner many times, and the house was familiar to him despite the changes the present owners had made.

If anyone could, surely their own minister should be able to send those ghosts away.

Not by a long shot.

Either the couple did not put much stock into their minister's powers, or the pull of the house was stronger, but the phenomena continued. In fact, after the minister had tried to exorcise the ghosts, things got worse.

Many a night, the Manners ran out into the street when lights kept going on and off by themselves. Fortunately, the children slept through all this, but how long would they remain unaffected?

At times, the atmosphere was so thick Mrs. Manner could not get near the breakfast nook in the kitchen to clear the table. Enveloped by the strong vibrations, she felt herself tremble and on two occasions fainted and was thus found by her family.

They were seriously considering moving now, and letting the original "owners" have the house again. They realized now that the house had never been truly "empty" for those two years the real estate man had said it was not in use.

It was 2 A.M. when they finally went up to bed.

Things felt worse than ever before. Mrs. Manner clearly sensed *three* presences with her now and started to cry.

"I'm leaving this house," she exclaimed. "You can have it back!" Her husband had gone ahead of her up the stairs to get the bedding from the linen closet. She began to follow him and slowly went up the stairs. After she had climbed about half way up, something forced her to turn around and look back.

What she saw has remained with her ever since, deeply impressed in her mind with the acid of stark fear.

Down below her on the stairway, was a big, burly man, trying to pull himself up the stairs.

His eyes were red with torture as he tried to talk to her.

Evidently he had been hurt, for his trousers and shirt were covered with mud. Or was it dried blood?

He was trying to hang onto the banister and held his hand out towards her.

"Oh, God, it can't be true," she thought and went up a few more steps. Then she dared look down again.

The man was still holding out his hand in a desperate move to get her attention. When she failed to respond, he threw it down in a gesture of impatience and frustration.

With a piercing scream, she ran up the stairs to her husband, weeping out of control.

The house had been firmly locked and no one could have gained entrance. Not that they thought the apparitions were flesh and blood people. The next morning, no trace of the nocturnal phenomenon could be found on the stairs. It was as if it had never happened.

But that morning, the Manners decided to pack and get out fast. "I want no more houses," Mrs. Manner said firmly, and so they bought a trailer. Meanwhile, they lived in an apartment.

But their furniture and all their belongings were still in the house, and it was necessary to go back a few more times to get them. They thought that since they had signed over the deed, it would be all right for them to go back. After all, it was no longer *their* house.

As Mrs. Manner cautiously ascended the stairs, she was still trembling with fear. Any moment now, the specter might confront her again. But all seemed calm. Suddenly, the scent of flowers was with her again and she knew the ghosts were still in residence.

As if to answer her doubts, the doors to the china closet flew open at that moment.

Although she wanted nothing further to do with the old house, Mrs. Manner made some more inquiries. The terrible picture of the tortured man on the stairs did not leave her mind. Who was he, and what could she have done for him?

Then she heard that the estate wasn't really settled, the children were still fighting over it. Was that the reason the parents could not leave the house in peace? Was the man on the stairs someone who needed help, someone who had been hurt in the house?

"Forget it," the husband said, and they stored most of their furniture. The new house trailer would have no bad vibrations and they could travel wherever they wanted, if necessary.

After they had moved into the trailer, they heard rumors that the new owners of their house had encountered problems also. But they did not care to hear about them and studiously stayed away from the house. That way, they felt, the ghosts would avoid them also, now that they were back in what used to be their beloved home!

But a few days later, Mrs. Manner noticed a strange scent of flowers wafting through her brand-new trailer. Since she had not bought any flowers, nor opened a perfume bottle, it puzzled her. Then, with a sudden impact that was almost crushing, she knew where and when she had smelled this scent before. It was the personal scent of the ghostly woman in the old house! Had she followed her here into the trailer?

When she discussed this new development with her husband that night, they decided to fumigate the trailer, air it and get rid of the scent, if they could. Somehow they thought they might be mistaken and it was just coincidence. But the scent remained, clear and strong, and the feeling of a presence that came with it soon convinced them that they had not yet seen the last of the Somerset ghosts.

They sold the new trailer and bought another house, a fifty-seven-year-old, nice rambling home in a nearby Pennsylvania town called Stoystown, far enough from Somerset to give them the hope that the Unseen Ones would not be able to follow them there.

Everything was fine after they had moved their furniture in and for the first time in many a month, the Manners could relax. About two months after they had moved to Stoystown, the scent of flowers returned. Now it was accompanied by another smell, that resembling burned matches.

The Manners were terrified. Was there no escape from the Uncanny? A few days later, Mrs. Manner observed a smokey form rise up in the house. Nobody had been smoking. The form roughly resembled the vague outlines of a human being.

Her husband, fortunately, experienced the smells also, so she was not alone in her plight. But the children, who had barely shaken off their terror, were now faced with renewed fears. They could not keep running, running away from what?

They tried every means at their command. Holy water, incense, a minister's prayer, their own prayers, curses and commands to the Unseen: but the scent remained.

Gradually, they learned to live with their psychic problems. For a mother possessed of definite mediumistic powers from youth and a young adult in the household are easy prey to those among the restless dead who desire a continued life of earthly activities. With the physical powers drawn from these living people, they play and continue to exist in a world of which they are no longer a part.

As the young man grew older, the available power dwindled and the scent was noticed less frequently. But the tortured man on the stairs of the house in Somerset will have to wait for a more willing medium to set him free.

16

The House of Evil

PARKER KEEGAN IS a practical man not much given to daydreaming or speculation. That is as it should be. For Parker makes his living, if you can call it that, driving a truck with high explosives, tanks containing acetylene, oxygen, nitrogen, and other flammable substances for a welding company in upstate New York.

So you see, he has to have his mind on his work all the time, if he wants to get old.

His wife Rebecca is a more emotional type. That, too, is as it should be. She is an artist, free-lancing and now and again making sales. There is some Indian blood in her and she has had an occasional bout with the supernatural. But these were mainly small things, telepathy or dream experiences and nothing that really worried her. Neither she nor her husband had any notions that such things as haunted houses really existed, except, of course, in Victorian novels.

Now the Keegans already had one child and Rebecca was expecting her second, so they decided to look for a larger place. As if by the finger of fate, an opportunity came their way just about then. Her teen-age cousin Jane telephoned Rebecca at her parents' home to tell them of a house they might possibly rent. It developed she did this not entirely out of the goodness of her heart, but also because she didn't like being alone nights in the big place she and her husband lived in. He worked most of the night in another city.

"There are two halves to this house," Jane explained, and she made it so enticing that Parker and Rebecca decided then and there to drive over and have a look at it.

Even though they arrived there after dark, they saw immediately that the house was attractive, at least from the outside. Built in pre-Civil War days, it had stood the test of time well. As is often the case with old houses, the servant quarters are in a separate unit and parallel, but do not intrude upon, the main section of the house. So it was here, and it was the former servant quarters that Jane and Harry occupied. As the visitors had not spoken to the landlord about their interest, they entered the unused portion of the building from their cousin's apartment. This was once the main house and contained eight rooms, just what they needed.

The ground floor consisted of a large front room with two windows facing the road and two facing the other way. Next to it was an old-fashioned dining room, and branching off from it, a narrow kitchen and a small laundry room. In the dim light they could make out a marvelous staircase with a lovely, oiled banister. It was at this point that the two apartments which made up the house connected, and one could be entered into from the other. Underneath the front stairway was a closet and the door leading to the other side of the house, but they found another, enclosed, stairway leading from the bedroom at the top of the front stairs into the dining room. Exactly below this enclosed staircase were the cellar stairs leading into the basement. There were three cellars, one under the servant quarters, one underneath the front room, and one below the dining room.

As Rebecca set foot into the cellar under the dining room, which had apparently served as a fruit cellar, she grew panicky for a moment. She immediately dismissed her anxiety with a proper explanation: they had seen the thriller "Psycho" the night before and this cellar reminded her of one of the gruesome incidents in that movie. But later she was to learn that the feeling of panic persisted whenever she came down into this particular part of the basement, even long after she had forgotten the plot of that movie.

For the present, they inspected the rest of the house. The upstairs portion contained two large bedrooms and two smaller ones. Only the larger rooms were heated. There was an attic but nobody ever investigated it during their entire stay in the house.

They decided the house was just what they wanted and the next morning they contacted the owner.

George Jones turned out to be a very proper, somewhat tight-lipped man. He inquired what they did for a living and then added, "Are you religious people?"

Rebecca thought this an odd question, but since she had told him she was an artist, she assumed he considered artists somewhat unreliable and wanted to make sure he had responsible and "God-fearing" tenants. Only much later did it occur to her that Jones might have had other reasons.

It was a cold, miserable day in December of 1964 when the Keegans moved into their new home. They were happy to get into a home full of atmosphere, for Rebecca was an avid amateur archaeologist who read everything on antiques she could get her hands on. At the same time they were doing a good deed for her cousin, keeping her company on those long nights when her husband was away at work. It all seemed just right and Rebecca did not even mind the difficulties the moving brought them. For one thing, they could not afford professional moving men, but had turned to friends for help. The friends in turn had borrowed a truck that had to be back in the garage by nightfall, so there was a lot of shoving and pushing and bad tempers all around. On top of that, the stinging cold and snow made things even more uncomfortable, and Rebecca could do little to help matters, being pregnant with their second child at the time.

Late that first night, they finally climbed the stairs to the large bedroom. They were both exhausted from the day's work and as soon as they fell into bed, they drifted off into deep sleep.

But even though they were very tired, Rebecca could not help noticing some strange noises, crackling sounds emanating seemingly from her cousin's side of the house. She put them down to steam pipes and turned to the wall.

When the noises returned night after night, Rebecca began to wonder about them. Parker also worked nights now and she and Jane sat up together until after the late show on television was over, around 1:30 A.M. All that time, night after night, they could hear the steam pipes banging away. Nobody slept well in the house and Jane became jumpier and jumpier as time went on. Her mood would change to a certain sullenness Rebecca had not noticed before, but she dismissed it as being due to the winter weather, and of no particular significance.

Then one night, as she was thinking about some of the events of the recent past while lying awake in bed, Rebecca heard heavy footsteps coming up the stairs. They were the steps of a heavy man, and since she had not heard the characteristic clicking of the front door lock, she knew it could not be her husband.

Alarmed, and thinking of burglars, she got out of bed and called out to her cousin. She then went to the top of the stairs and was joined by Jane coming through the connecting door, and standing at the foot of the stairs. What the two women saw from opposite ends of the staircase was far from ordinary. Someone was walking up the stairs and the stairs were bending with each step as if a heavy person were actually stepping upon them!

Only there was no one to be seen. They did not wait until the footsteps of the invisible man reached the top of the stairs. Rebecca dove back into her bedroom banging the door shut after her. Just before she did, she could still hear her young cousin downstairs screaming, before she, too, ran back into the assumed safety of her bedroom.

The experience on the stairs made Jane even moodier than before and it was not long afterwards that she took her little girl and left her husband. There had been no quarrel, no apparent reason for her sudden action. He was a handsome young man who had treated her well, and Jane loved him. Yet, there it was—she could not stand the house any longer and did what her panicky mind told her to do.

Rebecca was now left alone nights with the noisy wraith on the stairs and she scarcely welcomed it. Soon after the incident, Jane's abandoned husband sold his belongings and moved away, leaving the former servant quarters empty once again.

It was then that Rebecca kept hearing, in addition to the heavy footsteps, what seemed to be someone crying in the empty side of the house. She convinced herself that it wasn't just a case of nerves when the noises continued at frequent intervals while she was fully awake. Her time was almost at hand, and as often happens with approaching motherhood, she grew more and more apprehensive. It did not help her condition any when she heard a loud banging of the cupboards in the dining room at a time when she was all alone in the house. Someone was opening and closing the doors to the cupboard in rapid succession soon after she had retired for the night. Of course she did not run downstairs to investigate. Who would?

Fortunately, Parker came home a little earlier that night, because when he arrived he found Rebecca in a state of near hysteria. To calm her fears as much as to find out for himself, he immediately went downstairs to investigate. There was no one there and no noise. Getting into bed with the assurance of a man who does not believe in the supernatural, he was about to tell his wife that she must have dreamed it all, when he, too, clearly heard the cupboard doors open and close downstairs.

He jumped out of bed and raced down the stairs. As he took the steps two at a time, he could clearly hear the doors banging away louder and louder in the dining room. It must be stated to Parker's eternal credit, that not once did he show fear or worry about any possible dangers to himself: he merely wanted to know what this was all about.

The noise reached a crescendo of fury, it seemed to him, when he stood before the dining room door. Quickly he opened the door and stepped into the dark expanse of the chilly dining room.

Instantly, the noise stopped as if cut off with a knife.

Shaking his head and beginning to doubt his own sanity, or at least, power of observation, Parker got into bed once more and prepared to go to sleep. Rebecca looked at him anxiously, but he did not say anything. Before she could question him, the ominous noise started up again downstairs.

Once more, as if driven by the furies, Parker jumped out of bed and raced down the stairs. Again the noise stopped the moment he opened the dining room door.

He slowly went up the stairs again and crawled into bed. Pulling the covers over his ears, he cursed the ghosts downstairs, but decided that his badly needed sleep was more important than the answer to the puzzle.

Shortly after, their son was born. When they returned from the hospital, they were greeted by a new couple, the Winters, who had meanwhile moved into the other half of the house. Although friendly on the surface, they were actually stern and unbending and as they were also much older than the Keegans, the two families did not mingle much. Mrs. Winters was a tough and somewhat sassy old woman and did not look as if anything could frighten her. Her husband worked as a night watchman, and there were no children. It was not long before Mrs. Winters knocked at Rebecca's door in fear.

"Someone is trying to break in," she whispered, and asked to be let in. Rebecca knew better but did not say anything to frighten the old woman even further.

It seemed as if winter would never yield to spring, and if you have ever lived in the cold valleys of upstate New York, you know how depressing life can be under such circumstances.

To brighten things a little, the Keegans acquired a female German shepherd dog for the children, and also for use as a watchdog.

All this time Rebecca was sure she was never alone in the house. There was someone watching her, night and day. Her husband no longer scoffed at her fears, but could do little about them. The strange noises in the walls continued on and off and it got so that Rebecca no longer felt fear even when she saw the doorknob of a perfectly empty room turn slowly by its own volition. By now she knew the house was haunted, but as yet she did not realize the nature of the uncanny inhabitants.

One day she left the baby securely strapped in his seat while she ran to catch her little girl who was climbing the front stairs and was in immediate danger of falling off. Just at that precise moment, the strap broke and the baby fell to the floor, fracturing his skull.

All during their stay at the house, someone was always having accidents or becoming unaccountably ill. Their debts increased as their medical expenses grew higher, so it was decided that Rebecca should go to work and earn some money. In addition, Parker started working extra shifts. But far from helping things, this only served to incite the landlord to raise their rent, on the theory that they were earning more. To make things even more difficult for them, Rebecca could not find a proper baby-sitter to stay with the children while she was at work. Nobody would stay very long in the house, once they got to know it.

She turned to her mother for help, and her mother, after a short stay, refused to spend any more time in the house, but offered to take the children to her own home. There was no explanation, but to Rebecca it seemed ominous and obvious. Finally, her teen-age sister consented to become a baby-sitter for them. She could use the money for school, but soon her enthusiasm waned. She began to complain of a closed-in feeling she experienced in the old house and of course she, too, heard all the strange noises. Each day, Mary became more and more depressed and ill, whereas she had been a happy-go-lucky girl before.

"There are prowlers about," she kept saying, and one day she came running to Rebecca in abject fear. On a moonless night she happened to be glancing out of a living room window when she saw what appeared to be a face. Rebecca managed to calm her by suggesting she had seen some sort of shadow, but the incessant barking of the dog, for no apparent reason, made matters worse. Added to this were incidents in which objects would simply fly out of their hands in broad daylight. The end of the rope was reached one day when they were all in the front room. It was afternoon and Mary was holding a cup in her hand, about to fill it with tea. That instant it flew out of her hands and smashed itself at Parker's feet. Without saying another word, the young girl went up the stairs to her room. Shortly after, her things all packed, she came down again to say goodbye.

Once again they were without help, when Rebecca's sister-in-law Susan saved the day for them. A simple and quite unimaginative person, she had put no stock into all the tales of goings-on she had heard and was quite willing to prove her point.

Within a day after her arrival, she changed her tune.

"Someone is watching me," she complained, and refused to stay alone in the house. She, too, complained of things flying off the shelves seemingly by their own volition and of cupboard doors opening and closing as if someone were looking into the drawers for something or other.

The footsteps up the stairs continued and Susan heard them many times. She took the dog into the house with her but that was of little use: the dog was more afraid than all of the people together.

Incredible though it seemed to the Keegans, two years had passed since they had come to the House of Evil. That they still had their sanity was amazing, and that they had not moved out, even more of a miracle. But they simply could not afford to, and things were difficult enough in the physical world to allow the unseen forces to add to their problems. So they stuck it out.

It was the night before Christmas of 1966, and all through the house a feeling of ominous evil poisoned the atmosphere. They were watching television in order to relax a little. Rebecca suddenly saw a presence out of the corner of her eye, a person of some kind standing near the window in back of the sofa where her sister-in-law was sitting. Without raising her voice unduly or taking her eyes off the spot, she said, "Susan, get the rifle!" They had a rifle standing ready in the corner of the room.

Only then did Susan take a sharp look at the face peering into the window. It was a man's face, either Indian or Negro, and so unspeakably evil it took her breath away. Scowling at them with hatred, the face remained there for a moment, while Susan grabbed the gun. But when she pointed it towards the window, the face had disappeared.

Immediately, they rushed outside. The ground was frozen hard, so footprints would not have shown, had there been any. But they could not see anyone nor hear anyone running away.

The dog, chained at a spot where an intruder would be visible to her, evidently did not feel anything. She did not bark. Was she in some strange way hypnotized?

Soon after Christmas, Susan had to leave and the Keegans no longer could afford a baby-sitter. Rebecca had quit her job, and things were rough financially again.

To help matters, they invited a young couple with a small child to move in with them and help share expenses. The husband did not believe in the supernatural and the wife, on being told of their "problems," showed herself openminded, even interested, although skeptical.

What had appeared to be a sensible arrangement soon turned out a disaster and additional burden to an already overburdened family. The Farmers weren't going to contribute to the household, but spend what money they earned on liquor and racing. The tension between the Keegans and the Farmers mounted steadily. But the monetary problems were not the sole cause. The Farmers, too, noticed the noises and the unbearable, heavy atmosphere of the house and instinctively blamed the Keegans for these things. Then there was a quilt with an early American eagle and ship motif printed on it. Soon the wife had noticed that *someone* had turned the quilt around after she had put it away safely for the night. In the morning, the motif would face the opposite way. They could not blame the Keegans for that, since the quilt had been stored out of anyone's reach, and they dimly realized that the house was indeed haunted.

As the tension grew, the two couples would scarcely speak to each other even though they naturally shared the same quarters. Rebecca began to realize that no matter how gay a person might have been on the outside, once such a person moved into the House of Evil, there would be changes of personality and character. Although far from superstitious, she began to believe that the house itself was dangerous and that prolonged life in it could only destroy her and her loved ones.

Early in April Rebecca and Parker were in the bedroom upstairs one night, when they saw a form cross from where their telephone was, over their bed, and then down the stairs. As it crossed past the telephone, the phone rang. An instant later, as the form reached the bottom of the stairs, the downstairs telephone also rang.

This brought the Farmers out screaming and demanding to know what was going on?

For once, there was unison in the house as the four adults gathered together soberly downstairs to discuss what they just witnessed and compare impressions.

They agreed there was a blue-white light around the form, a light so intense it hurt the eyes. They all had felt an icy chill as the form passed them. Only Parker bravely insisted it might have been lightning. But nobody had heard any thunder.

For the Farmers, this was the ghost that broke their patience's back. They moved out immediately.

Left once again to themselves, Rebecca and her husband decided it was time for them to look elsewhere, too.

Tired from the long struggle with the uncanny, they moved soon afterwards.

As soon as they had settled in a new house, life took on a different aspect: where ominous presences had dampened their spirits, there was now gaiety and a zest for life they had not known for four years. Nobody has been sick in the family since and they have no problems getting and keeping baby-sitters.

The House of Evil still stands on lonely Route 14, and there are people living in it now. But whenever Parker has occasion to pass Route 14 in his car, he steps on the gas and drives just a little bit faster. No sense taking chances!

NEW YORK AREA

17

A Ghost in Greenwich Village, or John LaFarge's Unfinished Business

I SPENT MUCH of my time writing and editing material of a most mundane nature, always, of course, with a weather eye cocked for a good case of hunting. I picked up a copy of *Park East* and found to my amazement some very palatable grist for my psychic mills. "The Ghost of Tenth Street," by Elizabeth Archer, was a well-documented report of the hauntings on that celebrated Greenwich Village street where artists make their headquarters, and many buildings date back to the eighteenth century. Miss Archer's story was later reprinted by *Tomorrow* magazine, upon my suggestion. In *Park East*, some very good illustrations accompany the text, for which there was no room in *Tomorrow*.

Up to 1956, the ancient studio building at 51 West 10th Street was a landmark known to many connoisseurs of old New York, but it was demolished to make way for one of those nondescript, modern apartment buildings that are gradually taking away the charm of Greenwich Village, and give us doubtful comforts in its stead.

Until the very last, reports of an apparition, allegedly the ghost of artist John La Farge, who died in 1910, continued to come in. A few houses down the street is the Church of the Ascension; the altar painting, "The Ascension," is the work of John La Farge. Actually, the artist did the work on the huge painting at his studio, Number 22, in 51 West 10th Street. He finished it, however, in the church itself, "in place." Having just returned from the Orient, La Farge used a new technique involving the use of several coats of paint, thus making the painting heavier than expected. The painting was hung, but the chassis collapsed; La Farge built a stronger chassis and the painting stayed in place this time. Years went by. Oliver La Farge, the great novelist and grandson of the painter, had spent much of his youth with his celebrated grandfather. One day, while working across the street, he was told the painting had fallen again. Dashing across the street, he found that the painting had indeed fallen, and that his grandfather had died *that very instant*!

The fall of the heavy painting was no trifling matter to La Farge, who was equally as well known as an architect as he was a painter. Many buildings in New York for which he drew the plans seventy-five years ago are still standing. But the construction of the chassis of the altar painting may have been faulty. And therein lies the cause for La Farge's ghostly visitations, it would seem. The artists at No. 51 insisted always that La Farge could not find rest until he had corrected his calculations, searching for the original plans of the chassis to find out what was wrong. An obsession to redeem himself as an artist and craftsman, then, would be the underlying cause for the persistence with which La Farge's ghost returned to his old haunts.

The first such return was reported in 1944, when a painter by the name of Feodor Rimsky and his wife lived in No. 22. Late one evening, they returned from the opera. On approaching their studio, they noticed that a light was on and the door open, although they distinctly remembered having *left it shut*. Rimsky walked into the studio, pushed aside the heavy draperies at the entrance to the studio itself, and stopped in amazement. In the middle of the room, a single lamp plainly revealed a stranger behind the large chair in what Rimsky called his library corner; the man wore a tall black hat and a dark, billowing velvet coat. Rimsky quickly told his wife to wait, and rushed across the room to get a closer look at the intruder. But the man *just vanished* as the painter reached the chair.

Later, Rimsky told of his experience to a former owner of the building, who happened to be an amateur historian. He showed Rimsky some pictures of former tenants of his building. In two of them, Rimsky easily recognized his visitor, wearing exactly the same clothes Rimsky had seen him in. Having come from Europe but recently, Rimsky knew nothing of La Farge and had never seen a picture of him. The ball dress worn by the ghost had not been common at the turn of the century, but La Farge was known to affect such strange attire.

Three years later, the Rimskys were entertaining some guests at their studio, including an advertising man named William Weber, who was known to have had psychic experiences in the past. But Weber never wanted to discuss this "special talent" of his, for fear of being ridiculed. As the conversation flowed among Weber, Mrs. Weber, and two other guests, the advertising man's wife noticed her husband's sudden stare at a cabinet on the other side of the room, where paintings were stored. She saw nothing, but Weber asked her in an excited tone of voice—"Do you see that man in the cloak and top hat over there?"

Weber knew nothing of the ghostly tradition of the studio or of John La Farge; no stranger could have gotten by the door without being noticed, and none had been expected at this hour. The studio was locked from the *inside*.

After that, the ghost of John La Farge was heard many times by a variety of tenants at No. 51, opening windows or pushing draperies aside, but not until 1948 was he *seen* again.

Up a flight of stairs from Studio 22, but connected to it—artists like to visit each other—was the studio of illustrator John Alan Maxwell. Connecting stairs and a "secret rest room" used by La Farge had long been walled up in the many structural changes in the old building. Only the window of the walled-up room was still visible from the outside. It was in this area that Rimsky felt that the restless spirit of John La Farge was trapped. As Miss Archer puts it in her narrative, "walled in like the Golem, sleeping through the day and close to the premises for roaming through the night."

After many an unsuccessful search of Rimsky's studio, apparently the ghost started to look in Maxwell's studio. In the spring of 1948, the ghost of La Farge made his initial appearance in the illustrator's studio.

It was a warm night, and Maxwell had gone to bed naked, pulling the covers over himself. Suddenly he awakened. From the amount of light coming in through the skylight, he judged the time to be about one or two in the morning. *He had the uncanny feeling of not being alone in the room.* As his eyes got used to the darkness, he clearly distinguished the figure of a tall woman, bending over his bed, lifting and straightening his sheets several times over. Behind her, there was a man staring at a wooden filing cabinet at the foot of the couch. Then he opened a drawer, looked in it, and closed it again. Getting hold of himself, Maxwell noticed that the woman wore a light red dress of the kind worn in the last century, and the man a white shirt and dark cravat of the same period. It never occurred to the illustrator that they were anything but *people*; probably, he thought, models in costume working for one of the artists in the building.

The woman then turned to her companion as if to say something, but did not, and walked off toward the dark room at the other end of the studio. The man then went back to the cabinet and leaned on it, head in hand. By now Maxwell had regained his wits and thought the intruders must be burglars, although he could not figure out how they had entered his place, since he had locked it from the *inside* before going to bed! Making a fist, he struck at the stranger, yelling, "Put your hands up!"

His voice could be heard clearly along the empty corridors. *But his fist went through the man and into the filing cabinet.* Nursing his injured wrist, he realized that his visitors had dissolved into thin air. There was no one in the dark room. The door was still securely locked. The skylight, 150 feet above ground, could not very well have served as an escape route *to anyone human*. By now Maxwell knew that La Farge and his wife had paid him a social call.

Other visitors to No. 51 complained about strange winds and sudden chills when passing La Farge's walled-up room. One night, one of Maxwell's lady visitors returned, shortly after leaving his studio, in great agitation, yelling, "That man! That man!" The inner court of the building was glass-enclosed, so that one could see clearly across to the corridors on the other side of the building. Maxwell and his remaining guests saw nothing there.

But the woman insisted that she saw a strange man under one of the old gaslights in the building; he seemed to lean against the wall of the corridor, dressed in old-fashioned clothes and *possessed of a face so cadaverous and death-mask-like, that it set her ascreaming*!

This was the first time the face of the ghost had been observed clearly by anyone. The sight was enough to make her run back to Maxwell's studio. Nobody could have left without being seen through the glass-enclosed corridors and no one had seen a stranger in the building that evening. As usual, he had vanished into thin air.

So much for Miss Archer's account of the La Farge ghost. My own investigation was sparked by her narrative, and I telephoned her at her Long Island home, inviting her to come along if and when we held a seance at No. 51.

I was then working with a group of parapsychology students meeting at the rooms of the Association for Research and Enlightenment (Cayce Foundation) on West Sixteenth Street. The director of this group was a phototechnician of the *Daily News*, Bernard Axelrod, who was the only one of the group who knew the purpose of the meeting; the others, notably the medium, Mrs. Meyers, knew nothing whatever of our plans.

We met in front of Bigelow's drugstore that cold evening, February 23, and proceeded to 51 West Tenth Street, where the current occupant of the La Farge studio, an artist named Leon Smith, welcomed us. In addition, there were also present the late *News* columnist, Danton Walker, Henry Belk, the noted playwright Bernays, Marguerite Haymes, and two or three others considered students of psychic phenomena. Unfortunately, Mrs. Belk also brought along her pet chihuahua, which proved to be somewhat of a problem.

All in all, there were fifteen people present in the high-ceilinged, chilly studio. Dim light crept through the tall windows that looked onto the courtyard, and one wished that the fireplace occupying the center of the back wall had been working.

We formed a circle around it, with the medium occupying a comfortable chair directly opposite it, and the sitters filling out the circle on both sides; my own chair was next to the medium's.

The artificial light was dimmed. Mrs. Meyers started to enter the trance state almost immediately and only the loud ticking of the clock in the rear of the room was heard for a while, as her breathing became heavier. At the threshold of passing into trance, the medium suddenly said—

"Someone says very distinctly, *Take another step and I go out this window*! The body of a woman . . . close-fitting hat and a plume . . . close-fitting bodice and a thick skirt . . . lands right on face . . . I see a man, dark curly hair, *hooked nose, an odd, mean face* . . . cleft in chin . . . light tan coat, lighter britches, boots, whip in hand, cruel, mean . . . ."

There was silence as she described *what I recognized as the face of La Farge*.

A moment later she continued: "I know the face is not to be looked at anymore. It is horrible. It should have hurt but I didn't remember. Not long. I just want to scream and scream."

The power of the woman who went through the window was strong. "I have a strange feeling," Mrs. Meyers said, "*I have to go out that window* if I go into trance." With a worried look, she turned to me and asked, "If I stand up and start to move, *hold me*." I nodded assurance and the seance continued. A humming sound came from her lips, gradually assuming human-voice characteristics.

The next personality to manifest itself was apparently a woman in great fear. "They're in the courtyard . . . . He is coming . . . they'll find me and whip me again. I'll die first. Let me go. I shouldn't talk so loud. Margaret! Please don't let him come. See the child. My child. Barbara. Oh, the steps, I can't take it. Take Bobby, raise her, I can't take it. He is coming . . . *let me go*! I am free!"

With this, the medium broke out of trance and complained of facial stiffness, as well as pain in the shoulder.

Was the frantic woman someone who had been mistreated by an early inhabitant of No. 22? Was she a runaway slave, many of whom had found refuge in the old houses and alleys of the Village?

I requested of the medium's "control" that the most prominent person connected with the studio be allowed to speak to us. But Albert, the control, assured me that the woman, whom he called Elizabeth, was connected with that man. "He will come only if he is of a mind to. He entered the room a while ago."

I asked Albert to describe this man.

"Sharp features, from what I can see. You are closer to him. Clothes . . . nineties, early 1900's."

After a while, the medium's lips started to move, and a gruff man's voice was heard: "*Get out* . . . get out of my house."

Somewhat taken aback by this greeting, I started to explain to our visitor that we were his friends and here to help him. But he didn't mellow.

"I don't know who you are . . . who is everybody here. Don't have friends."

"I am here to help you," I said, and tried to calm the ghost's suspicions. But our visitor was not impressed.

"I want help, but not from you . . . *I'll find it*!"

He wouldn't tell us what he was looking for. There were additional requests for us to get out of his house. Finally, the ghost pointed the medium's arm toward the stove and intoned—"I put it there!" A sudden thought inspired me, and I said, lightly—"We found it already."

Rage took hold of the ghost in an instant. "You took it . . . you betrayed me . . . it is mine . . . I was a good man."

I tried in vain to pry his full name from him.

He moaned. "I am sick all over now. Worry, worry, worry. Give it to me."

I promised to return "it," if he would cooperate with us.

In a milder tone he said, "I wanted to make it so pretty. *It won't move*."

I remembered how concerned La Farge had been with his beautiful altar painting, and that it should not fall *again*. I wondered if he knew how much time had passed.

"Who is President of the United States now?" I asked.

Our friend was petulant. "I don't know. I am sick. William McKinley." But then he volunteered—"I knew him. Met him. In Boston. Last year. Many years ago. Who are you? I don't know any friends. *I am in my house*."

"What is your full name?"

"Why is that so hard? I know William and I don't know my *own* name."

I have seen this happen before. A disturbed spirit sometimes cannot recall his own name or address.

"Do you know you have passed over?"

"I live here," he said, quietly now. "Times changed. I know I am not what I used to be. *It is there*!"

When I asked what he was looking for, he changed the subject to Bertha, without explaining who Bertha was.

But as he insisted on finding "*it*," I finally said, "You are welcome to get up and look for it."

"I am bound in this chair and can't move."

"Then tell us where to look for it."

After a moment's hesitation, he spoke. "On the chimney, in back . . . it was over there. I will find it, but I can't move now . . . *I made a mistake* . . . I can't talk like this."

And suddenly he was gone.

As it was getting on to half past ten, the medium was awakened. The conversation among the guests then turned to any feelings they might have had during the seance. Miss Archer was asked about the building.

"It was put up in 1856," she replied, "and is a copy of a similar studio building in Paris."

"Has there ever been any record of a murder committed in this studio?" I asked.

"Yes . . . between 1870 and 1900, *a young girl went through one of these windows*. But I did not mention this in my article, as it *apparently* was unconnected with the La Farge story."

"What about Elizabeth? And Margaret?"

"That was remarkable of the medium," Miss Archer nodded. "You see, Elizabeth was La Farge's wife . . . and Margaret, well, she also fits in with his story."

For the first time, the name La Farge had been mentioned in the presence of the medium. But it meant nothing to her in her conscious state.

Unfortunately, the ghost could not be convinced that his search for the plans was unnecessary, for La Farge's genius as an architect and painter has long since belonged to time.

A few weeks after this seance, I talked to an advertising man named Douglas Baker. To my amazement, he, too, had at one time occupied Studio 22. Although aware of the stories surrounding the building, he had scoffed at the idea of a ghost. But one night he was roused from deep sleep by the noise of someone opening and closing drawers. Sitting up in bed, he saw a man in Victorian opera clothes in his room, which was dimly lit by the skylight and windows. Getting out of bed to fence off the intruder, he found himself alone, just as others had before him.

No longer a scoffer, he talked to others in the building, and was able to add one more episode to the La Farge case. It seems a lady was passing No. 51 one bleak afternoon when she noticed an odd-looking gentleman in opera clothes standing in front of the building. For no reason at all, the woman exclaimed, "My, you're a funny-looking man!"

The gentleman in the opera cloak looked at her in rage. "Madam—how dare you!"

And with that, *he went directly through the building—the wall of the building, that is*!

Passers-by revived the lady.

Now there is a modern apartment building at 51 West 10th Street. Is John La Farge still roaming its ugly modern corridors? Last night, I went into the Church of the Ascension, gazed at the marvelous alter painting, and prayed a little that he shouldn't *have to.*

Presumably, at this writing, he must be at peace. The *New York Times* reported to its readers interested in Little Old New York, on July 30, 1988, to be exact, that the parishioners of the Church of the Ascension were finally doing something about the matter. Apparently, the mural by John La Farge had gotten dirtier with time, darker, too, and desperately needed a good cleaning job. The experts hired to do the job, Holly Hotchner and Robert Sawchuck, spent the entire summer trying to clean the old painting lying on their stomachs on a rickety scaffold which continuously threatened to collapse.

Apparently the job was greatly complicated by Mr. La Farge's unusual technique of using encaustic painting, which is a method used by the ancient Romans and not too frequently since: mixing wax with pigment and fusing it to the canvas with hot irons. But it does give a sense of richness to the work, like a fresco painting, and while this makes the painting look more three-dimensional, it also represents trouble, since wax does melt sometimes.

Nonetheless, the pair did clean the painting, proud of their job, and never once interrupted by a ghostly La Farge. Nor did the scaffolding fall, nor the painting, for that matter.

As of this writing, it is still in place at the church to be admired by one and all, and the artist, is probably painting angels and cherubs by now, all things considered.

18

The Conference House Ghosts

PEACE CONFERENCES MAY go on for years and years without yielding tangible results—so it is a refreshing thought to remember that a peace conference held on Staten Island between Lord Howe, the British commander in America, and a Congressional committee consisting of Benjamin Franklin, John Adams, and Edward Rutledge lasted but a single day—September 11, 1776, to be exact.

The position was this: the British were already in command of New York, Long Island and Staten Island, and the Yankees still held New Jersey and Pennsylvania, with Philadelphia as the seat of the Continental Congress. In view of his tremendous successes in the war against the colonists, Lord Howe felt that the suppression of the independence movement was only a matter of weeks. Wanting to avoid further bloodshed and, incidentally, to save himself some trouble, he suggested that a peace conference be held to determine whether an honorable peace could be concluded at that juncture of events.

Congress received his message with mixed emotions, having but lately worked out internal differences of opinion concerning the signing of the Declaration of Independence. A committee was appointed, consisting of the aforementioned three men, and empowered to investigate the offer. The three legislators went by horse to Perth Amboy, New Jersey, and were met at the New Jersey shore by a barge manned by British soldiers under a safe-conduct pass across the bay. They landed on the Staten Island shore and walked up to Bentley Manor, the residence of Lord Howe. There they were met with politeness and courtesies but also with a display of British might, for there were soldiers in full battle dress lined up along the road.

Later, the flamboyant John Adams told of soldiers "looking as fierce as ten furies, and making all the grimaces and gestures and motions of their muskets, with bayonets fixed, which, I suppose, military etiquette requires, but which we neither understood nor regarded."

Lord Howe outlined his plan for a settlement, explaining that it was futile for the Americans to carry on the war and that the British were willing to offer peace with honor. Of course, any settlement would involve the colonies' remaining under British rule. The three envoys listened in polite silence, after which Benjamin Franklin informed Lord Howe that the Declaration of Independence had already been signed on July 4, 1776, and that they would never go back under British rule.

The conference broke up, and Lord Howe, still very polite, had the trio conveyed to Amboy in his own barge, under the safe-conduct pass he had granted them. The following day, September 12, 1776, the War of Independence entered a new round: the Yankees knew what the British government was willing to offer them in order to obtain peace, and they realized that they might very well win the war with just a little more effort. Far from discouraging them, the failure of the peace conference on Staten Island helped reinforce the Continental Congress in its determination to pursue the War of Independence to its very end.

This historical event took place in a manor house overlooking Raritan Bay, and at the time, and for many years afterward, it was considered the most outstanding building on Staten Island. The two-story white building goes back to before 1680 and is a colonial manor built along British lines. It was erected by a certain Christopher Billopp, a somewhat violent and hardheaded sea captain who had served in the British Navy for many years. Apparently, Captain Billopp had friends at court in London, and when the newly appointed Governor Andros came to America in 1674, he gave Billopp a patent as lieutenant of a company of soldiers. In the process, Billopp acquired nearly one thousand acres of choice land on Staten Island. But Billopp got into difficulties with his governor and reentered navy service for awhile, returning to Staten Island under Governor Thomas Dongan. In 1687 he received a land grant for Bentley Manor, sixteen hundred acres of very choice land, and on this tract he built the present manor house. The Billopp family were fierce Tories and stood with the Crown to the last. The Captain's grandson, also named Christopher, who was already born in the manor, lived there till the end of the Revolution, when he moved to New Brunswick, Canada, along with many other Tories who could not stay on in the newly independent colonies.

From then on, the manor house had a mixed history of owners and gradually fell into disrepair. Had it not been built so solidly, with the keen eye of a navy man's perception of carpentry, perhaps none of it would stand today. As it was, an association was formed in 1920 to restore the historical landmark to its former glory. This has now been done, and the Conference House, as it is commonly called, is a museum open to the public. It is located in what was once Bentley Manor but today is called Tottenville, and it can easily be reached from New York City via the Staten Island Ferry. The ground floor contains two large rooms and a staircase leading to the upper story, which is also divided into two rooms. In the basement is a kitchen and a vault-like enclosure. Both basement and attic are of immense proportions. The large room downstairs to the left of the entrance was originally used as a dining room and the room to the right as a parlor. Upstairs, the large room to the left is a bedroom while the one to the right is nowadays used as a Benjamin Franklin museum. In between the two large rooms is a small room, perhaps a child's room at one time. At one time there also was a tunnel from the vault in the basement to the water's edge, which was used as a means of escape during Indian attacks, a frequent occurrence in early Colonial days. Also, this secret tunnel could be used to obtain supplies by the sea route without being seen by observers on land.

As early as 1962 I was aware of the Conference House and its reputation of being haunted. My initial investigation turned up a lot of hearsay evidence, hardly of a scientific nature, but nevertheless of some historical significance inasmuch as there is usually a grain of truth in all legendary stories. According to the local legends, Captain Billopp had jilted his fiancee, and she had died of a broken heart in the house. As a result, strange noises, including murmurs, sighs, moans, and pleas of an unseen voice, were reported to have been heard in the house as far back as the mid-nineteenth century. According to the old Staten Island newspaper *The Transcript*, the phenomena were heard by a number of workmen during the restoration of the house after it had been taken over as a museum.

My first visit to the Conference House took place in 1962, in the company of Ethel Johnson Meyers and two of her friends, who had come along for the ride since they were interested in the work Mrs. Meyers and I were doing. Mrs. Meyers, of course, had no idea where we were going or why we were visiting Staten Island. Nevertheless, when we were still about a half-hour's ride away from the house, she volunteered her impressions of the place we were going to. When I encouraged her to speak freely, she said that the house she had yet to see was white, that the ground floor was divided into two rooms, and that the east room contained a brown table and eight chairs. She also stated that the room to the west of the entrance was the larger room of the two, and that some silverware was on display in that room.

When we arrived at the house, I checked these statements at once; they were entirely correct, except that the number of chairs was seven, not eight as Mrs. Meyers had stated. I questioned the resident curator about this seeming discrepancy. One of the chairs and the silverware had indeed been on display for years but had been removed from the room eight years prior to our visit.

"Butler," Mrs. Meyers mumbled as we entered the house. It turned out that the estate next to Bentley belonged to the Butlers; undoubtedly, members of that family had been in the Conference House many times. As is my custom, I allowed my medium free rein of her intuition. Mrs. Meyers decided to settle on the second-story room to the left of the staircase, where she sat down on the floor for want of a chair.

Gradually entering the vibrations of the place, she spoke of a woman named Jane whom she described as being stout, white-haired, and dressed in a dark green dress and a fringed shawl. Then the medium looked up at me and, as if she intuitively knew the importance of her statement, simply said, "Howe." This shook me up, since Mrs. Meyers had no knowledge of Lord Howe's connection with the place she was in. I also found interesting Mrs. Meyer's description of a "presence," that is to say, a ghost, whom she described as a big man in a fur hat, being rather fat and wearing a skin coat and high boots, a brass-buckled belt, and black trousers. "I feel boats around him, nets, sailing boats, and I feel a broad foreign accent," Mrs. Meyers stated, adding that she saw him in a four-masted ship of a square-rigger type. At the same time she mentioned the initial T. What better description of the Tory, Captain Billopp, could she have given!

"I feel as if I am being dragged somewhere by Indians," Mrs. Meyers suddenly exclaimed, as I reported in my original account of this case in my first book *Ghost Hunter*. "There is violence, and somebody dies on a pyre of wood. Two men, one white, one Indian; and on two sticks nearby are their scalps." It seemed to me that what Mrs. Meyers had tuned in on were remnants of emotional turmoil in the early colonial days; as I have noted, Indian attacks were quite frequent during the early and middle parts of the eighteenth century.

When we went down into the cellar, Mrs. Meyers assured us that six people had been buried near the front wall during the Revolutionary War and that they were all British soldiers. She also said that eight more were buried somewhere else on the grounds, and she had the impression that the basement had been used as a hospital during an engagement. Later investigation confirmed that members of the Billopp family had been buried on the grounds near the road and that British soldiers might very well have been buried there too, since there were frequent skirmishes around the house from July, 1776, to the end of the year. Captain Billopp was twice kidnapped from his own house by armed bands operating from the New Jersey Shore.

It was clear to me that Mrs. Meyers was entering various layers of history and giving us bits and pieces of her impressions, not necessarily in the right order but as she received them. The difficulty with trance mediumship is that you cannot direct it the way you want to, that is to say, ferret out just those entities or layers from the past you are interested in. You have to take "pot luck," as it were, hoping that sufficient material of interest will come through the medium.

Once more we returned to the upper part of the house. Suddenly, Mrs. Meyers turned white in the face and held on for dear life to the winding staircase. For a moment she seemed immobilized. Then, coming to life again, she slowly descended the stairs and pointed to a spot near the landing of the second story. "A woman was killed here with a crooked knife!" she said.

Aha, I thought, there is our legend about Captain Billopp and his jilted fiancée. But he didn't kill her; she had died of a broken heart. Mrs. Earley, the custodian, was trying to be helpful, so I questioned her about any murder that might have occurred in the house. "Why, yes," she obliged. "Captain Billopp once flew into a rage and killed a female slave on that very spot on the stairs." As she spoke, I had the impression that the custodian was shuddering just a little herself.

From time to time people had told me of their visits to the Conference House and wondered whether the "ghost in residence" was still active. Finally, I asked a young lady I had been working with for some time to try her hand at picking up whatever might be left in the atmosphere of the Conference House. Ingrid Beckman, an artist by profession, knew very little about the house but had access to the short account of my investigation given in *Ghost Hunter*.

I asked Ingrid to go to the house by herself, and on the afternoon of November 25, 1972, she paid a visit.

In order to avoid tourists, she had arrived at the house about one o'clock. The house was still closed to visitors so she sat down on a bench outside. "I walked around, and even on the outside I felt a presence," Ingrid began her report to me. "I felt as if the place were really alive. Then I went up to the front porch and peeked into the main hallway, and when I looked up the stairs I had a feeling of gloom and foreboding. I had the distinct sensation of a dangerous situation there."

Strangely enough, Ingrid seemed to have been led to that house. Two weeks prior to her visit, she had happened to find herself in Nyack, New York, browsing through some antique shops. There she met a woman who started to talk to her. The woman explained that she was from Staten Island, and when she discovered that Ingrid lived there also, she suggested that Ingrid visit a certain house, once the property of an old sea captain. The house, the lady said, had an interesting tunnel which began behind a fireplace and ran down to the water's edge. Ingrid, always interested in visiting old houses, had promised to look into the matter. This was two weeks before I mentioned a visit to the Conference House to her.

The following weekend, Ingrid was with some friends at her apartment on Staten Island. She took the opportunity of asking whether any of them had ever heard of the house as described by her acquaintance. One of the young men present affirmed that there was such a house, called the Conference House, and that it was haunted by the spirit of a slave who had been killed there. That was on Sunday. The following Monday I telephoned Ingrid with the request to go to the Conference House.

As Ingrid was sitting on the front porch of the house, waiting for the door to be opened, she had the distinct feeling that someone was watching her. "I felt as if someone knew I was there," she explained, "and I especially felt this coming from the window above the hallway. It is a crooked window, and I felt that it had some sort of significance. If anyone were looking at me or wanted to get my attention, it would be through that window. But when I went in, as soon as the door had been opened to visitors, the first place I went was the basement. As I was looking around the basement, I came upon a little archway, as if I had been *directed* to go there."

The spot made her literally jump; she felt that something terrible had occurred near the fireplace, and she experienced heavy chills at the same time; someone had been brutalized at the entrance to the tunnel. Fortunately, she had managed to go there by herself, having discouraged the tourist guide from taking her around. "The tunnel entrance is particularly terrorizing," Ingrid said. "This tunnel caused me chills all the way up to my neck."

Finally tearing herself away from the basement, she went up the stairs, again by herself. Immediately she arrived at the upper landing and went to the bedroom to the left; as she stood in the entranceway, she heard a noise like a knock.

"The hallway upstairs felt terrible," Ingrid explained. "I turned around and looked down the stairs. As I looked, I almost became dizzy. It felt as if someone had been pushed down them or hurt on them." To be sure that she wasn't imagining things or being influenced by what she had read, Ingrid decided to go up and down those stairs several times. Each time, the sensation was the same. On one of her trips up the stairs, she ascertained that the window, which had so attracted her while she was still waiting outside, was indeed just outside the haunted stairwell.

"I got the impression of a slave woman, especially in the upstairs bedroom; I also felt there was a disturbance around the table downstairs, but I don't think the two are connected. I felt the woman was associated with the upstairs bedroom and the stairway and possibly the tunnel entrance; but the feeling in the basement is another episode, I think."

"What period do you think the disturbances go back to?" I asked.

"I'd say the 1700s, going back before the Revolution."

"Do you have the feeling that there is still something there that hasn't been fully resolved?"

"Yes, definitely. I think that is why I had such strong vibrations about it, and I think that is also why I got the information two weeks beforehand."

"Do you think that it is a man or a woman who is 'hung up' in there?"

"I think it is a woman, but there may also be a man because the scene at the table had something to do with a man. He may have been shot, or he may have been abducted from that room—you know, taken through the tunnel."

I suddenly recalled that Captain Billopp was twice abducted by Yankee irregulars from the Jersey shore. Gabriel Disosway, in his 1946 account of the Manor of Bentley, reported that "Colonel Billopp, at the time a warm party man and military leader, was closely watched, and, it is said, was twice taken from his own house by armed bands from 'the Jerseys,' and thus made a prisoner. Amboy is in sight, and upon one of these occasions, he was observed by some Americans, who had stationed themselves with a spy glass in the church steeple of that town. As soon as they saw him enter his abode, they ran to their boats, rapidly crossed the river, and he was soon their captive."

On January 28, 1973, Ingrid made another, spontaneous visit to the Conference House. She had much the same impressions as before, but this time she managed to speak to the caretaker. The lady admitted hearing heavy footsteps upstairs at times, which sounded to her like those of a man wearing heavy boots with spurs attached. Also, on the anniversary of "the murder," the caretaker claims to have seen a man run up the stairs toward a girl waiting on the first landing. "Her story is that the girl was beheaded," Ingrid reported further. "She says that one afternoon last summer, as she was dusting the room on the left of the ground floor, she could put her hand 'right through' a British soldier! This past summer her daughter from South Carolina came to visit and insisted on staying upstairs in the haunted rooms. That night the daughter allegedly heard a man's laughter, followed by a woman's laughter, and then a shriek. According to the caretaker, this happens at regular intervals."

19

Valerie, Reaching Out from Beyond

SOMETIMES BEING A psychic investigator puts a heavy moral burden on one, especially where there may be a possibility of preventing someone's death. Of course, you're never sure that you can. Take the case of Valerie K., for instance. I am not using her full name because the case is far from closed. The police won't talk about it, but her friends are only too sure there is something mysterious about her death, and they *will* talk about it. They speak mainly to me, for that's about all they can do about it—now.

To start at the beginning, one April I got a phone call from Sheila M.—an English girl whom I had met through a mutual friend—inviting my wife and me to a cocktail party at her house on New York's East Side. Now if there's one thing my wife and I hate it's cocktail parties, even on the East Side, but Sheila is a nice person and we thought she was likely to have only nice friends, so I said we'd come. The party was on April 20, and when we arrived everybody was already there, drinking and chatting, while the butler passed between the guests, ever so quietly seeing after their needs.

Since I don't drink, I let my wife talk to Sheila and sauntered over to the hors d'oeuvres, hopefully searching for some cheese bits, for I am a vegetarian and don't touch meat or fish. Next to the buffet table I found not only an empty chair, unusual at a cocktail party, but also a lovely young woman in a shiny silver Oriental-style dress. In fact, the young lady was herself an Oriental, a very impressive-looking girl perhaps in her middle twenties, with brown hair, dark eyes, and a very quiet, soigné air about her. It turned out that the girl's name was Valerie K., and I had been briefly introduced to her once before on the telephone when Sheila had told her of my interest in psychic research, and she had wanted to tell me some of her experiences.

We got to talking about our mutual interest in ESP. She sounded far away, as if something was troubling her, but I had the impression she was determined to be gay and not allow it to interfere with her enjoyment of the party.

I knew she was Sheila's good friend and would not want to spoil anything for her. But I probed deeper, somehow sensing she needed help. I was right, and she asked me if she could talk to me sometime privately.

There were several eager young men at the party whose eyes were on the lovely Oriental, so I thought it best not to preempt her time, since I knew she was not married. I gave her my telephone number and asked her to call me whenever she wanted to.

About an hour later we left the party, and when we got home I suppressed a desire to telephone this girl and see if she was all right. I dismissed my feeling as undue sentimentality, for the girl had seemed radiant, and surely the reason for her wanting to see me would have to be psychic rather than personal in the usual sense.

All through the weekend I could not get her out of my mind, but I was busy with other work and decided to call her first thing the following week.

Monday night, as I read the *Daily News*, my eye fell on a brief article tucked away inside the newspaper, an article telling of the death of two women a few hours before. The paper's date was Tuesday morning. The deaths had occurred early Monday morning. One of the two women was Valerie K.

With a shudder I put down the paper and closed my eyes.

Could I have prevented her death? I will let you be the judge. But first let me show you what happened in the final hours of this girl's life on earth. Every word is the truth . . . .

Valerie K. came from a well-to-do Chinese family residing in Hawaii. She was as American as anyone else in her speech, and yet there was that undefinable quality in the way she put her words together that hinted at Eastern thought. After an unhappy and brief marriage to a Hong Kong businessman, she came to New York City to try living on her own. Never particularly close to her parents, she was now entirely self-supporting and needed a job. She found a job vaguely described as a public relations assistant, but in fact was the secretary to the man who did publicity for the company. Somehow she was not quite right for the job or the job for her, and it came to a parting of the ways.

The new girl hired to take her place was Sheila. Despite the fact that the English girl replaced her, they struck up a friendship that developed into a true attachment to each other, so much so that Valerie would confide in Sheila to a greater extent than she would in anyone else.

When Valerie left the office, there was no job waiting for her; fortunately, however, she had met the manager of a firm owned by the same company, and the manager, whose initial was G., took her on for somewhat selfish reasons. He had a sharp eye for beauty and Valerie was something special. Thus she found herself earning considerably more than she would have been paid in a similar job elsewhere. Soon the manager let her know that he liked her and she got to like him, too. Between August and October of the year before her death, they became close friends.

But in October of that year she called her friend Sheila to complain bitterly of the humiliation she had been put through. G. had found another girl to take her place. Innocently, the new girl, Lynn, became the pawn in the deadly game between the manager and the Chinese beauty.

G. found fault with her very appearance and everything she did, criticizing her and causing her to lose face—to an Oriental an important matter not easily forgotten.

Still, she cared for the man and hoped that he would resume his former attentions. He didn't, and after a miserable Christmas which she partially shared with Sheila, the axe fell. He fired her and gave her two weeks' pay, wishing her the best.

When Sheila heard about this she suggested that Valerie register at the Unemployment Office. Instead, the proud girl took sleeping pills. But she either did not take enough or changed her mind in time, for she was able to telephone Sheila and tell her what she had done. A doctor was called and she was saved. She had a session with a psychiatrist after that and seemed much more cheerful.

But the humiliation and rejection kept boiling within her. Nothing can be as daring as a person whose affections have been rejected, and one day Valerie wrote a personal letter to the owner of the companies she had once worked for, denouncing the manager and his work.

As if nourished by her hatred, her psychic abilities increased and she found she was able to influence people through telepathy, to read others' thoughts and to put herself into a state of excitement through a form of meditation.

All this of course was for the purpose of getting even, not only with the manager but with the world that had so often hurt her.

Nobody knew for sure if she ever got a reply to her letter. But she was a regular at an Oriental restaurant near her apartment and became friendly with the owners. There she talked about her plans and how she would show the world what sort of girl she was.

Meanwhile the manager found himself short of help and asked her back. Despite her deep hatred for the man, she went back, all the time scheming and hoping her fortunes would take a turn for the better. But she did confide in Sheila that she had taken a big gamble, and if it worked she'd be all right in more ways than one. The owner of the restaurant saw her on Friday, April 21—a day after the party at which I had met her for the first time—and she seemed unusually happy.

She would marry a prominent European, she told him; she had been asked and would say yes. She was almost obsessed at this point with the desire to tell the whole world she would marry him; her parents in Hawaii received a letter requesting them to have formal Chinese wedding attire made up for her in Paris because she would marry soon. Had the idea of getting even with G. robbed her of her senses? It is difficult to assess this, as the principals involved quite naturally would not talk, and even I prefer that they remain anonymous here.

That weekend—April 22 and 23—the pitch of her "wedding fever" rose higher and higher. A neighbor who had dropped in on her at her apartment found her clad only in a bikini and drinking heavily. She observed her running back and forth from her telephone, trying to reach the man overseas she said she would marry. But she couldn't get through to him. In the meantime, she started giving possessions away, saying she would not need them any longer now that she would marry so rich a man.

She also drew up a list of all those whom she would help once she had become the wife of the millionaire. The neighbor left rather perturbed by all this, and Valerie stayed alone in her apartment—or did she?

It was four A.M. when the police received a call from her telephone. It was a complaint about excessive noise. When an officer—initialed McG.—arrived on the scene at four-twenty A.M. Valerie herself opened the door in the nude.

"Go away," she said, and asked to be left alone. The officer quickly surveyed the scene. She became rude and explained she was expecting a phone call and did not wish to be disturbed. The officer reported that she had been alone and was drinking, and there the matter stood.

The minutes ticked away. It was early Monday morning, April 24.

At precisely five A.M. the building superintendent looked out his window and saw something heavy fall on his terrace.

Rushing to the scene, he discovered Valerie's broken body. She had been killed instantly. The girl had taken two roses with her—but one somehow remained behind on the window sill of the open window from which she had plunged to her death. The other sadly fluttered to earth even as she did.

The police officers found themselves back at the apartment sooner than they had expected, only this time there was a cause for action. After a routine inspection of the girl's tenth floor apartment, her death was put down to accidental death or suicide by falling or jumping from her window. Since she had been drinking heavily, they were not sure which was the actual cause of death.

Monday night Sheila called me frantically, wondering what she should do. There was no one to claim the girl's body. Neither her sister Ethel nor her parents in Hawaii could be reached. I told her to calm down and keep trying, meanwhile berating myself for not having called Valerie in time to prevent her death.

Eventually the parents were found and a proper funeral arranged.

But the puzzle remained. Had she committed suicide or not?

Did that call from Europe finally come and was it so humiliating that Valerie could no longer face the world? Was there not going to be a wedding after all—then at least there must be a funeral?

Valerie had been particularly fond of two things in life—flowers and jewelry. To her, losing a favorite piece of jewelry was bad luck.

Lynn, the girl who now worked at Valerie's office, is a rather matter-of-fact person not given to emotional scenes or superstitions.

Valerie owned a pair of jade earrings that G. had had made for her in the days when they were close. About a month before her death, Valerie gave those earrings to Lynn as a gift. There was a special stipulation, however. She must not wear them around the office, since people had seen Valerie wear them and presumably knew their history.

Lynn agreed not to wear them around the office, but when she wore them outside a most unusual phenomenon took place. Suddenly the earrings would not stay put. One and then the other would drop off her ears as if pulled by some unseen force. That was on April 13, and Valerie was still alive though she had seemed very distraught.

Word of Lynn's concern with the falling earrings got back to the former owner, and finally Valerie called to assure her the falling was a "good omen." Then a week later, on Saturday April 22, she suddenly called Lynn shortly before midnight and asked her to wear "her" earrings at the office. Lynn promised she would wear them to work Monday.

That was the day Valerie died. The following day, Lynn was still wearing the earrings, which now seemed to cling properly to her ears. She found herself in the ladies' room, when she felt her right earring forced off and thrown into the toilet. It felt as if it had been snatched from her ear by an unseen hand.

Returning to her desk, she noticed that an unusual chill pervaded the area where Valerie's desk had stood. It disappeared at 4:30, which was the time Valerie usually left for home.

All this proved too much for Lynn and she went on a week's vacation.

Sheila was still very upset when a male friend dropped in to help her in this sorry matter. The gentleman, a lawyer by profession, had taken off his jacket when he suddenly felt a cufflink leave his shirt. It was a particularly intricate piece of jewelry, and no matter how they searched it was never found.

Was the dead girl trying to show her hand? Too fantastic, and yet . . . .

There was no rational explanation for the sudden disappearance, in plain light and in the presence of two people, of so definite an object as a cufflink.

On Friday of that week, after the girl had been buried, her sister, Ethel, who had finally arrived in town, went to the apartment to find out what she could about her sister's effects.

As soon as she entered the apartment, she realized that a terrific fight had taken place in it. Nothing had been touched from the moment of death until her arrival, as the apartment had been sealed. Three knives were lying on the floor and the place was a shambles. On the table she noticed two glasses, one partially filled with Scotch and one almost empty. When she called the police to report the strange appearance of the place, she was given the cold shoulder.

Who was the person Valerie had entertained during her last hours on earth?

The superintendent reported to the sister that Valerie had received two letters since her death, but when they looked in the mailbox, it was empty.

A friend, the owner of the restaurant Valerie had frequented, notified the telephone company to cut off service and forward the final bill to her. She was told the bill could not be found.

And so it went. Was someone covering up his traces? Sheila heard these things and went to work. To her, something was terribly wrong about her friend's death and she was going to find out what. Questioning both the restaurant owner and the girl's sister again, she came upon another strange fact. The ash trays Ethel had found in the apartment had two different types of cigarettes in them—L&M and Winston. Valerie always smoked L&M, but who smoked Winston?

The police seem not particularly interested in pursuing the matter. They think it was Valerie herself who called them the first time, and that she just decided to end it all in a drunken stupor. That at least is the impression they gave Sheila.

The following day, Saturday, the window was still open. The rose Valerie had left behind was still on the sill, despite the windy weather of April.

That night when Sheila was putting on her jacket, she felt somebody helping her into it. She was alone, or so she thought.

It occurred to her then that Valerie's spirit was not at rest and that I might be able to help. The very least I could do was talk to her *now*, since fate had prevented me from getting to her in time.

I arranged with Betty Ritter to be ready for me the following weekend, without telling her where we would be going, of course. The date was May 6, the time three P.M. and Sheila was to meet us at the apartment that once belonged to Valerie, but now was cleaned out and ready for the next occupant. The superintendent agreed to let us in, perhaps sensing why we had come or not caring. At any rate he opened the tenth floor apartment and left us alone inside.

As we reached the elevator of the East Sixty-Third Street building, Betty Ritter suddenly remarked that she felt death around her. I nodded and we went upstairs.

As soon as we had stepped through the door into Valerie's place, Betty became a psychic bloodhound. Making straight for the window—now closed—she touched it and withdrew in horror, then turned around and looked at me.

"There is a man here jumping around like mad," she said, "but there is also someone else here—I am impressed with the initial E." She then took off her coat and started to walk toward the bathroom. There she stopped and looked back at me.

"I hear a woman screaming . . . I saw blood . . . now I see the initial M . . . she was harmed . . . it is like suicide . . . as if she couldn't take it any more."

Betty had difficulty holding back her emotions and was breathing heavily.

"She left *two* behind," she said. "I see the initials L. and S."

Betty Ritter, not a trance medium but essentially a clairvoyant, is very strong on initials, names, letters, and other forms of identification and she would naturally work that way even in this case.

"I heard her say, 'Mama, Mama'—she is very agitated."

"I also get a man's spirit here . . . initial J."

"How did this girl die?" I interjected at this point.

"She couldn't take it any more. She shows the initial R. This is a living person. She gulped something, I think."

I thought that Betty was picking up past impressions now and wanted to get her away from that area into the current layer of imprints.

"How exactly did she die?" I queried the medium. Betty had no idea where she was or why I had brought her here.

"I think she tried . . . pills . . . blood . . . one way or the other . . . in the past. She was a little afraid but she did plan this. She is very disturbed now and she does not know how to get out of this apartment. I get the initial G. with her."

I asked Betty to convey our sympathies to her and ask her if there was something she wished us to do.

While Betty talked to the spirit woman in a low voice, I reflected on her evidence so far. The initials given—E. was the first initial of Valerie's sister's name, Ethel, M. was Mary, her mother, and G. the manager of the company with whom she had had a relationship—it all seemed to make sense. Betty Ritter had also correctly "gotten" the attempted suicide by pills and pointed out the window as a "hot" area.

What was to follow now?

"She is crying," Betty reported. "She wants her loved ones to know that she didn't mean it. She shows me the head of an Indian and it is a symbol of a car—a brand name I think—it's red—the initial H. comes with this and then she shows me writing, something she has left unfinished. She asks her mother to forgive her because she could not help herself."

I decided to ask Valerie some important questions through the medium. Was she alone at the time of her death?

"Not alone. Initial A. A man, I feel him walking out of the door. Agitating her, agitating her."

"Was he with her when she died or did he leave before?"

"She says, 'I slammed the door on him.' And then she says, 'And then I did it.'"

"Why?"

"I had gone completely out of my mind . . . could not think straight . . . he drove me to it . . ."

"This man is a living person?"

"Yes."

"Is he aware of what happened to her?"

"Yes."

"Did she know him well?"

"Yes, definitely."

"What was his connection with her?"

Betty was herself pretty agitated now; in psychic parlance, she was really hot.

"I see a bag of money," she reported, "and the letters M. or W."

I handed her some personal belongings of Valerie's, brought to the scene in a shopping bag by Sheila and now placed on the stove for Betty to touch. She first took up a pendant—costume jewelry—and immediately felt the owner's vibrations.

"How I loved this," she mumbled. "I see D. R., Doctor . . . this was given to her and there is much love here in connection with this . . . this goes way back . . ."

Somehow the personalities of Betty Ritter and Valerie K. melted into one now and Betty, not quite herself, seemed not to listen any more to my queries, but instead kept talking as if she were Valerie, yet with Betty's own voice and intonation.

"There's so much I wanted to say and I couldn't at the time . . . ."

Now returning to herself again, she spoke of a man in spirit, who was very agitated and who had possessed the woman, not a ghost but someone who had died . . . an older man who had a link with her in the past. J.W. Dark-skinned, but not Negro—India or that part of the world.

It struck me suddenly that she might be talking of Valerie's late husband, the man she had married long ago in Hong Kong; he was much older than she at the time.

"I have a feeling of falling," Betty suddenly said, "I don't know why. May have something to do with her."

I decided to let her walk around the entire apartment and to try to pick up "hot" areas. She immediately went for the lefthand window.

"Something terrible happened here . . . this is the room . . . right here . . . stronger here . . ."

"Is there another woman involved in this story?" I asked.

"I see the initial M." Betty replied, "and she is with a man who is living, and there is also some jealousy regarding a woman's boyfriend . . . she could not take it."

I decided to start the exorcism immediately.

"It's such a short time ago that she went," Betty remarked. "She wants to greet Mary . . . or Marie . . . and an L. To tell L. she is relieved now. Just carry on as usual."

L. was the initial of Lynn, the girl at the office who had encountered the strange happenings with the earrings.

I decided to test this connection.

"Did she communicate with L. in any way?" I asked.

"Yes," Betty nodded, "I see her by L.'s bed . . . perhaps she frightened her . . . but now she knows . . . didn't mean to frighten her . . . she is leaving now, never wants to get back again . . . ."

We were quiet for a moment.

"She's throwing us kisses now," Betty added.

"She would do that," Sheila confirmed, "that was the way she would do it."

And that was that.

Betty lit a cigarette and relaxed, still visibly shaken by the communications for which she had been the carrier.

We put Valerie's pitiful belongings back into the paper bag and left the apartment, which now looked shiny and new, having been given a hasty coat of paint to make it ready for the next occupant.

No further snatching of jewelry from anyone's ears occurred after that, and even Sheila, my friend, no longer tried to reopen the case despite her belief that there was more to it than met the eyes of the police.

We decided to allow Valerie a peaceful transition and not to stir up old wounds that would occur with a reopening of the case.

But somehow I can't quite bring myself to forget a scene, a scene I only "saw" through the eyes of a laconic police detective making a routine report: the tall, lovely Oriental woman, intoxicated and nude, slamming the door on the police . . . and two liquor glasses on her table.

Who was that other glass for . . . and who smoked the second cigarette, the brand Valerie never smoked?

Who, then, was the man who left her to die?

20

Alexander Hamilton's Restless Spirit

THERE STANDS AT Number 27, Jane Street, in New York's picturesque artists' quarters, Greenwich Village, a mostly wooden house dating back to pre-Revolutionary days. In this house Alexander Hamilton was treated in his final moments. Actually, he died a few houses away, at 80 Jane Street, but No. 27 was the home of John Francis, his doctor, who attended him after the fatal duel with Aaron Burr.

However, the Hamilton house no longer exists, and the wreckers are now after the one of his doctor, now occupied by a writer and artist, Jean Karsavina, who has lived there since 1939.

The facts of Hamilton's untimely passing are well known; D. S. Alexander (in his *Political History of the State of New York*) reports that, because of political enmity, "Burr seems to have deliberately determined to kill him." A letter written by Hamilton calling Burr "despicable" and "not to be trusted with the reins of government" found its way into the press, and Burr demanded an explanation. Hamilton declined, and on June 11, 1804, at Weehawken, New Jersey, Burr took careful aim, and his first shot mortally wounded Hamilton. In the boat back to the city, Hamilton regained consciousness, but knew his end was near. He was taken to Dr. Francis' house and treated, but died within a few days at his own home, across the street.

Ever since moving into 27 Jane Street, Miss Karsavina has been aware of footsteps, creaking stairs, and the opening and closing of doors; and even the unexplained flushing of a toilet. On one occasion, she found the toilet chain still swinging, when there was no one around! "I suppose a toilet that flushes *would* be a novelty to someone from the eighteenth century," she is quoted in a brief newspaper account in June of 1957.*

* *Fate*, June, 1957.

She also has seen a blurred "shape," without being able to give details of the apparition; her upstairs tenant, however, reports that one night not so long ago, "a man in eighteenth-century clothes, with his hair in a queue" walked into her room, looked at her and walked out again.

Miss Karsavina turned out to be a well-read and charming lady who had accepted the possibility of living with a ghost under the same roof. Mrs. Meyers and I went to see her. The medium had no idea where we were going.

At first, Mrs. Meyers, still in waking condition, noticed a "shadow" of a man, old, with a broad face and bulbous nose; a woman with a black shawl whose name she thought was Deborah, and she thought "someone had a case"; she then described an altar of white lilies, a bridal couple, and a small coffin covered with flowers; then a very old woman in a coffin that was richly adorned, with relatives including a young boy and girl looking into the open coffin. She got the name of Mrs. Patterson, and the girl's as Miss Lucy. In another "impression" of the same premises, Mrs. Meyers described "an empty coffin, people weeping, talking, milling around, *and the American Flag atop the coffin*; in the coffin a man's hat, shoes with silver buckles, gold epaulettes . . ." She then got close to the man and thought his lungs were filling with liquid and he died with a pain in his side.

Lapsing into semitrance at this point, Mrs. Meyers described a party of men in a small boat on the water, then a man wearing white pants and a blue coat with blood spilled over the pants. "Two boats were involved, and it is dusk," she added.

Switching apparently to another period, Mrs. Meyers felt that "something is going on in the cellar, they try to keep attention from what happens downstairs; there is a woman here, being stopped by two men in uniforms with short jackets and round hats with wide brims, and pistols. There is the sound of shrieking, the woman is pushed back violently, men are marching, someone who had been harbored here has to be given up, an old man in a nightshirt and red socks is being dragged out of the house into the snow."

In still another impression, Mrs. Meyers felt herself drawn up toward the rear of the house where "someone died in childbirth"; in fact, this type of death occurred "several times" in this house. Police were involved, too, but this event or chain of events is of a later period than the initial impressions, she felt. The name Henry Oliver or Oliver Henry came to her mind.

After her return to full consciousness, Mrs. Meyers remarked that there was a chilly area near the center of the downstairs room. There is; I feel it too. Mrs. Meyers "sees" the figure of a slender man, well-formed, over average height, in white trousers, black boots, dark blue coat and tails, white lace in front; *he is associated with George Washington and Lafayette*, and their faces appear to her, too; she feels Washington may have been in this house. The man she "sees" is a *general*, she can see his epaulettes. The old woman and the children seen earlier are somehow connected with this, too. He died young, and there "was fighting in a boat." Now Mrs. Meyers gets the name "W. Lawrence." She has a warm feeling about the owner of the house; he took in numbers of people, like refugees.

A "General Mills" stored supplies here—shoes, coats, almost like a military post; food is being handed out. The name Bradley is given. Then Mrs. Meyers sees an old man playing a cornet; two men in white trousers are "seen" seated at a long table, bent over papers, with a crystal chandelier above.

After the séance, Miss Karsavina confirmed that the house belonged to Hamilton's physician, and as late as 1825 was owned by a doctor, who happened to be the doctor for the Metropolitan Opera House. The cornet player might have been one of his patients.

In pre-Revolutionary days, the house may have been used as headquarters of an "underground railroad," around 1730, when the police tried to pick up the alleged instigators of the so-called "Slave Plot," evidently being sheltered here.

"Lawrence" may refer to the portrait of Washington by Lawrence which *used* to hang over the fireplace in the house. On the other hand, I found a T. Lawrence, M. D., at 146 Greenwich Street, *Elliot's Improved Directory for New York* (1812); and a "Widow Patterson" is listed by Longworth (1803) at 177 William Street; a William Lawrence, druggist, at 80 John Street. According to Charles Burr Todd's *Story of New York*, two of Hamilton's pallbearers were *Oliver* Wolcott and John L. *Lawrence*. The other names mentioned could not be found. The description of the man in white trousers is of course the perfect image of Hamilton, and the goings-on at the house with its many coffins, and women dying in childbirth, are indeed understandable for a doctor's residence.

It does not seem surprising that Alexander Hamilton's shade should wish to roam about the house of the man who tried, vainly, to save his life.

Today, in 1992, the house stands no more. Ten years ago, someone in City Hall looked the other way when an eager developer asked for permission to tear down the house.

Before preservationists and historians found out, the little old house was gone.

In its place, there is an ugly ordinary apartment house, distinguished by nothing other than its location.

If anything, getting a good look at what replaced his doctor's house, the late Alexander Hamilton would finally stay away for good.

21

The Old Merchant's House Ghost

WHEN NEW YORK was still young and growing, a neighborhood that is now given over to derelicts and slums was an elegant, quiet area of homes and gardens. The world was right and peaceful in the young republic circa 1820. Gradually, however, the in people, as we call them nowadays, moved farther uptown, for such is the nature of a city confined to a small island. It can only move up, never down or out. Greenwich Village was still pretty far uptown, although the city had already spread beyond its limits, and the center of New York was somewhere around the city hall district (now considered way downtown).

Real estate developers envisioned the east side of Fifth Avenue as the place to put up elegant homes for the well-to-do. One of the more fashionable architects of that time was John McComb, who had plans for a kind of terrace of houses extending from Lafayette Street to the Bowery, with the back windows of the houses looking out on John Jacob Astor's property nearby. Now Mr. Astor was considered somewhat uncouth socially by some of his contemporaries (on one occasion he mistook a lady's voluminous sleeve for a dinner napkin), but nobody had any second thoughts about his prosperity or position in the commercial world. Thus, any house looking out upon such a desirable neighborhood would naturally attract a buyer, the builders reasoned, and they proved to be right.

Called brownstones because of the dark brick material of their facades, the houses were well-appointed and solid. Only one of them is still left in that area, while garages, factories, and ugly modern structures have replaced all the others.

The house in question was completed in 1830 and attracted the eagle eye of a merchant named Seabury Tredwell, who was looking for a proper home commensurate with his increasing financial status in the city. He bought it and moved in with his family.

Mr. Tredwell's business was hardware, and he was one of the proud partners in Kissam & Tredwell, with offices on nearby Dey Street. A portly man of fifty, Mr. Tredwell was what we would today call a conservative. One of his direct ancestors had been the first Episcopal bishop of New York, and though a merchant, Tredwell evinced all the outward signs of an emerging mercantile aristocracy. The house he acquired certainly looked the part: seven levels, consisting of three stories, an attic and two cellars, large, Federal style windows facing Fourth Street, a lovely garden around the house, and an imposing columned entrance door that one reached after ascending a flight of six marble stairs flanked by wrought-iron gate lanterns—altogether the nearest a merchant prince could come to a real nobleman in his choice of domicile.

Inside, too, the appointments are lavish and in keeping with the traditions of the times: a Duncan Phyfe banister ensconces a fine staircase leading to the three upper stories and originates in an elegant hall worthy of any caller.

As one steps into this hall, one first notices a huge, high-ceilinged parlor to the left. At the end of this parlor are mahogany double doors separating the room from the dining room, equally as large and impressive as the front room. The Duncan Phyfe table was at one time set with Haviland china and Waterford crystal, underlining the Tredwell family's European heritage. Each room has a large fireplace and long mirrors adding to the cavernous appearance of the two rooms. Large, floor-to-ceiling windows on each end shed light into the rooms, and when the mahogany doors are opened, the entire area looks like a ballroom in one of those manor houses Mr. Tredwell's forebears lived in in Europe.

The furniture—all of which is still in the house—was carefully chosen. Prominent in a corner of the parlor is a large, rectangular piano. Without a piano, no Victorian drawing room was worth its salt. A music box is on top for the delight of those unable to tinkle the ivories yet desirous of musical charms. The box plays "Home Sweet Home," and a sweet home it is indeed.

Farther back along the corridor one comes upon a small family room and a dark, ugly kitchen, almost L-shaped and utterly without charm or practical arrangements, as these things are nowadays understood. But in Victorian New York, this was a proper place to cook. Maidservants and cooks were not to be made cheerful, after all; theirs was to cook and serve, and not to enjoy.

On the first floor—or second floor, if you prefer, in today's usage—two large bedrooms are separated from each other by a kind of storage area, or perhaps a dressing room, full of drawers and cabinets. Off the front bedroom there is a small bedroom in which a four-poster bed takes up almost all the available space. The bed came over from England with one of Mrs. Tredwell's ancestors.

Leading to the third floor, the stairs narrow, and one is well advised to hold on to the banister lest he fall and break his neck. The third floor now serves as the curator's apartment. The Old Merchant's House is kept up as a private museum and is no longer at the mercy of the greedy wrecker. But when Seabury Tredwell lived in the house, the servants' rooms were on the third floor. Beyond that, a low-ceilinged attic provided additional space, and still another apartment fills part of the basement, also suitable for servants' usage.

All in all, it is the kind of house that inspires confidence in its owner. Mr. Tredwell's acquisition of the house helped establish him in New York society as a force to be reckoned with, for that, too, was good for his expanding business. He was eminently aided in this quest by the fact that his wife Eliza, whom he had married while still on his way up, had given him six daughters. Three of the girls made good marriages, left the parental homestead, and apparently made out very well, for not much was heard about them one way or another. Of the remaining three girls, however, plenty is recorded, and lots more is not, though it's undoubtedly true.

The three bachelor girls were named Phoebe, Sarah, and Gertrude. Phoebe's main interest was the Carl Fischer piano in the parlor, and she and her sister Sarah would often play together. Gertrude, the last of the Tredwell children, born in 1840, was different from the rest of them and kept herself apart. There were also two boys, but somehow they did not amount to very much, it is said, for it became necessary later, when of all the children only they and Gertrude were left, to appoint a cousin, Judge Seabury, to supervise the management of the estate. Brother Horace, in particular, was much more interested in tending the four magnolia trees that dominated the view from the tearoom.

To this day, nobody knows the real reason for a secret passage from a trap door near the bedrooms to the East River, a considerable distance. Recently, it was walled up to prevent rats from coming through it, but it is still there, holding on to its strange mystery—that is, to those who do not *know*.

Some of the things that transpired behind the thick walls of the Old Merchant's House would never have been brought to light were it not for the sensitive who walked its corridors a century later and piece for piece helped reconstruct what went on when the house was young. Only then did the various pieces of the jigsaw puzzle slowly sink into place, pieces that otherwise might never have found a common denominator.

When the house finally gave up its murky secrets, a strange calm settled over it, as if the story had wanted to be told after all those years to free it from the need of further hiding from the light.

Seabury Tredwell's stern Victorian ways did not sit well with all members of his family. The spinster girls in particular were both afraid of and respectful toward their father, and found it difficult to live up to his rigid standards. They wanted to marry but since no suitable person came along they were just as happy to wait. Underneath this resignation, however, a rebellious spirit boiled up in Sarah. Five years older than Gertrude, she could not or would not wait to find happiness in an age where the word scarcely had any personal meaning.

Tredwell ruled the family with an iron hand, demanding and getting blind submission to his orders. Thus it was with considerable misgivings that Sarah encouraged a budding friendship with a young man her father did not know, or know of, whom she had met accidentally at a tearoom. That in itself would have been sufficient reason for her father to disallow such a friendship. He was a man who considered anyone who referred to chicken *limbs* as legs, indecent. He ordered the legs of his chairs and tables covered, so they might not incite male visitors to unsavory ideas!

It took a great deal of ingenuity for Sarah to have a liaison with a strange man and not get caught. But her mother, perhaps out of rebellion against Tredwell, perhaps out of compassion for her neglected daughter, looked the other way, if not encouraged the relationship. And ingenious Sarah also found another ally in her quest for love. There was a Negro servant who had known and cared for her since her birth, and he acted as a go-between for her and the young man. For a few weeks, Sarah managed to sneak down to meet her paramour. Accidentally, she had discovered the secret passageway to the river and used it well. At the other end it led to what was then pretty rough ground and an even rougher neighborhood, but the young man was always there waiting with a carriage, and she felt far safer with him than in the cold embrace of her father's fanatical stare. Although Tredwell boasted to his friends that his house had "seven hundred locks and seven hundred keys," this was one door he had forgotten about.

Why an architect in 1830 would want to include a secret passageway is a mystery on the surface of it. But there were still riots in New York in those years, and the British invasion of 1812 was perhaps still fresh in some people's memories. A secret escape route was no more a luxury in a patrician American home than a priest hole was in a Catholic house in England. One never knew how things might turn. There had been many instances of slave rebellions, and the underground railroad, bringing the escapees up from the South, was in full swing then in New York.

One meeting with the young man, who shall remain nameless here, led to another, and before long, nature took its course. Sarah was definitely pregnant. Could she tell her father? Certainly not. Should they run off and marry? That seemed the logical thing to do, but Sarah feared the long arm of her family. Judge Seabury, her father's distinguished cousin, might very well stop them. Then too, there was the question of scandal. To bring scandal upon her family was no way to start a happy marriage.

Distraught, Sarah stopped seeing the young man. Nights she would walk the hallways of the house, sleepless from worry, fearful of discovery. Finally, she had to tell someone, and that someone was her sister Gertrude. Surprisingly, Gertrude did understand and comforted her as best she could. Now that they shared her secret, things were a little easier to bear. But unfortunately, things did not improve. It was not long before her father discovered her condition and all hell broke loose.

With the terror of the heavy he was, Tredwell got the story out of his daughter, except for the young man's name. This was especially hard to keep back, but Sarah felt that betraying her lover would not lead to a union with him. Quite rightfully, she felt her father would have him killed or jailed. When the old merchant discovered that there had been a go-between, and what was more, a man in his employ, the old Negro man was hauled over the coals. Only the fact that he had been with them for so many years and that his work was useful to the family prevented Tredwell from firing him immediately. But he abused the poor man and threatened him until the sheer shock of his master's anger changed his character: where he had been a pleasant and helpful servant, there was now only a shiftless, nervous individual, eager to avoid the light and all questions.

This went on for some weeks or months. Then the time came for the baby to be born and the master of the house had another stroke of genius. He summoned the black servant and talked with him at length. Nobody could hear what was said behind the heavy doors, but when the servant emerged his face was grim and his eyes glassy. Nevertheless, the old relationship between master and servant seemed to have been restored, for Tredwell no longer abused the man after this meeting.

What happened then we know only from the pieces of memory resurrected by the keen insight of a psychic: no court of law would ever uphold the facts as true in the sense the law requires, unfortunately, even if they are, in fact, true. One night there was a whimpering heard from the trapdoor between the two bedrooms upstairs, where there is now a chest of drawers and the walled-off passageway down to the river. Before the other servants in the house could investigate the strange noises in the night, it was all over and the house was silent again. Tredwell himself came from his room and calmed them.

"It is nothing," he said in stentorian tones, "just the wind in the chimney."

Nobody questioned the words of the master, so the house soon fell silent again.

But below stairs, in the dank, dark corridor leading to the river, a dark man carried the limp body of a newborn baby that had just taken its first, and last, breath.

Several days later, there was another confrontation. The evil doer wanted his pay. He had been promised a certain sum for the unspeakable deed. The master shrugged. The man threatened. The master turned his back. Who would believe a former slave, a runaway slave wanted down South? Truly, he didn't have to pay such a person. Evil has its own reward, too, and the dark man went back to his little room. But the imprint of the crime stuck to the small passage near the trap door and was picked up a century later by a psychic. Nobody saw the crime. Nobody may rightfully claim the arrangement between master and servant ever took place. But the house knows and its silence speaks louder than mere facts that will stand up in court.

When Sarah awoke from a stupor, days later, and found her infant gone, she went stark raving mad. For a time, she had to be restrained. Somehow, word leaked out into the streets of the city below, but no one ever dared say anything publicly. Sarah was simply indisposed to her friends. Weeks went by and her pain subsided. Gradually a certain relief filled the void inside her. She had lost everything, but at least her lover was safe from her father's clutches. Although she never knew for sure, whenever she glanced at the colored manservant, she shrank back: his eyes avoided her and her heart froze. Somehow, with the illogical knowledge of a mother, she *knew*. Then too, she avoided the passage near the trap door. Nothing could get her to walk through it. But as her health returned, her determination to leave also received new impetus. She could not go on living in this house where so much had happened. One day, she managed to get out of the door. It was a windy fall night, and she was badly dressed for it. Half-mad with fear of being followed, she roamed the streets for hours. Darkness and her mental condition took their toll. Eventually she found herself by the water. When she was found, she was still alive, but expired before she could be brought back to the house.

Her death—by her own hands—was a blow to the family. Word was given out that Sarah had died in a carriage accident. It sounded much more elegant, and though no one ever found out what carriage, as she had been in bed for so long, and just learned to walk about the house again, it was accepted because of the unspoken code among the Victorians: one man's tragedy is never another's gossip. Then, too, the question of suicide was a thorny one to resolve in an age that had not yet freed the human personality even in the flesh: it had to be an accident.

Thus Sarah was laid to rest along with the others of her family in the Christ Churchyard in Manhasset, Long Island, properly sanctified as behooves the daughter of an important citizen whose ancestor was a bishop.

What had happened to Sarah did not pass without making a deep and lasting impression on the youngest girl, Gertrude, who was called Gitty when she was young. She tried not to talk about it, of course, but it made her more serious and less frivolous in her daily contacts.

She was now of the age where love can so easily come, yet no one had held her hand with the slightest effect on her blood pressure. True, her father had introduced a number of carefully screened young men, and some not so young ones, in the hope that she might choose one from among them. But Gertrude would not marry just to please her father, yet she would not marry against his wishes. There had to be someone she could love and whom her father could also accept, she reasoned, and she was willing to wait for him.

While she was playing a game with time, spring came around again, and the air beckoned her to come out into the garden for a walk. While there, she managed to catch the eye of a young man on his way past the house. Words were exchanged despite Victorian propriety, and she felt gay and giddy.

She decided she would not make the mistake her sister had made in secretly seeing a young man. Instead, she encouraged the shy young man, whose name was Louis, to seek entry into her house openly and with her father's knowledge, if not yet blessings. This he did, not without difficulties, and Seabury Tredwell had him investigated immediately. He learned that the young man was a penniless student of medicine.

"But he'll make a fine doctor someday," Gertrude pleaded with her father.

"Someday," the old man snorted. "And what is he going to live on until then? I tell you what. *My* money."

Tredwell assumed, and perhaps not without reason, that everybody in New York knew that his daughters were heiresses and would have considerable dowries as well. This idea so established itself in his mind, he suspected every gentleman caller of being a fortune hunter. The young man was, of course, he argued, not after his daughter's love, but merely her money and that would never do.

Gertrude was no raving beauty although she possessed a certain charm and independence. She was petite, with a tiny waistline, blue eyes and dark hair, and she greatly resembled Britain's Princess Margaret when the latter was in her late twenties.

Tredwell refused to accept the young medical student as a serious suitor. Not only was the young man financially unacceptable, but worse, he was a Catholic. Tredwell did not believe in encouraging marriages out of the faith and even if Louis had offered to change religions, it is doubtful the father would have changed his mind. In all this he paid absolutely no heed to his daughter's feelings or desires, and with true Victorian rigidity, forbade her to see the young man further.

There was finally a showdown between father and daughter. Tredwell, no longer so young, and afflicted with the pains and aches of advancing age, pleaded with her not to disappoint him in his last remaining years. He wanted a good provider for her, and Louis was not the right man. Despite her feelings, Gertrude finally succumbed to her father's pleading and sent the young man away. When the doors closed on him for the last time, it was as if the gates of Gertrude's heart had also permanently closed on the outside world: hence she lived only for her father and his well-being and no young man ever got to see her again.

Seabury Tredwell proved a difficult and thankless patient as progressive illness forced him to bed permanently. When he finally passed away in 1865, the two remaining sisters, Gertrude and Phoebe, continued to live in the house. But it was Gertrude who ran it. They only went out after dark and only when absolutely necessary to buy food. The windows were always shuttered and even small leaks covered with felt or other material to keep out the light and cold.

As the two sisters cut themselves off from the outside world, all kinds of legends sprang up about them. But after Phoebe died and left Gertrude all alone in the big house, even the legends stopped and gradually the house and its owner sank into the oblivion afforded yesterday's sensation by a relentless, everchanging humanity.

Finally, at age ninety-three, Gertrude passed on. The year was 1933, and America had bigger headaches than what to do about New York's last authentic brownstone. The two servants who had shared the house with Gertrude to her death, and who had found her peacefully asleep, soon left, leaving the house to either wreckers or new owners, or just neglect. There was neither electricity nor telephone in it, but the original furniture and all the fine works of art Seabury Tredwell had put into the house were still there. The only heat came from fireplaces with which the house was filled. The garden had long gone, and only the house remained, wedged in between a garage and nondescript modern building. Whatever elegance there had been was now present only inside the house or perhaps in the aura of its former glories.

The neighborhood was no longer safe, and the house itself was in urgent need of repairs. Eventually, responsible city officials realized the place should be made into a museum, for it presented one of the few houses in America with everything—from furniture to personal belongings and clothes—still intact as it was when people lived in it in the middle of the nineteenth century. There were legal problems of clearing title, but eventually this was done and the Old Merchant's House became a museum.

When the first caretaker arrived to live in the house, it was discovered that thieves had already broken in and made off with a pair of Sheffield candelabra, a first edition of Charlotte Bronte, and the Tredwell family Bible. But the remainder was still intact, and a lot of cleaning up had to be done immediately.

One of the women helping in this work found herself alone in the house one afternoon. She had been busy carrying some of Miss Gertrude's clothing downstairs so that it could be properly displayed in special glass cases. When she rested from her work for a moment, she looked up and saw herself being watched intently by a woman on the stairs. At first glance, she looked just like Princess Margaret of England, but then she noticed the strange old-fashioned clothes the woman wore and realized she belonged to another age. The tight fitting bodice had a row of small buttons and the long, straight skirt reached to the floor. As the volunteer stared in amazement at the stranger, wondering who it could be, the girl on the stairs vanished.

At first the lady did not want to talk about her experience, but when it happened several times, and always when she was alone in the house, she began to wonder whether she wasn't taking leave of her senses. But soon another volunteer moved into the picture, a lady writer who had passed the house on her way to the library to do some research. Intrigued by the stately appearance of the house, she looked into it further and before long was in love with the house.

There was a certain restlessness that permeated the building after dark, but she blamed it on her imagination and the strange neighborhood. She did not believe in ghosts nor was she given to fancies, and the noises didn't really disturb her.

She decided that there was a lot of work to be done if the museum were to take its proper place among other showplaces, and she decided to give the tourists and other visitors a good run for their money—all fifty cents' worth of it.

The next few weeks were spent in trying to make sense out of the masses of personal effects, dresses, gowns, shoes, hats. The Tredwells had left everything behind them intact—as if they had intended to return to their earthly possessions one of these days and to resume life as it was.

Nothing had been given away or destroyed and Mrs. R., writer that she was, immediately realized how important it was that the residence be kept intact for future research of that period. She went to work at once and as she applied herself to the job at hand, she began to get the *feel* of the house as if she had herself lived in it for many years.

She started her job by taking an inventory of the late Gertrude Tredwell's wardrobe once again. This time the job had to be done properly, for the visitors to the museum were entitled to see a good display of period costumes. As she picked through Gertrude's vast wardrobe one article at a time, she had the uncanny feeling of being followed step for step. The house was surrounded by slums and the danger of real break-ins very great, but this was different: no flesh and blood intruders followed her around on her rounds from the third floor down to the basement and back again for more clothes.

Often a chilly feeling touched her as she walked through the halls, but she attributed that to the moist atmosphere in the old house.

One day when she entered the front bedroom that used to be Gertrude's, from the hall bedroom, she had the distinct impression of another presence close to her. Something was brushing by her to reach the other door that opened into the front bedroom before she did!

When this happened again sometime later, she began to wonder if the stories about the house being haunted, which circulated freely in the neighborhood, did not have some basis in fact. Certainly there was a presence, and the sound of another person brushing past her was quite unmistakable.

While she was still deliberating whether or not to discuss this with any of her friends, an event took place that brought home the suspicion that she was never quite alone in the house.

It was on a morning several months after her arrival, that she walked into the kitchen carrying some things to be put into the display cases ranged along the wall opposite the fireplace. Out of the corner of her eye she caught sight of what looked like the figure of a small, elegant woman standing in front of this huge fireplace. While Mrs. R. was able to observe the brown taffeta gown she was wearing, her head was turned away, so she could not see her features. But there were masses of brown hair. The whole thing was in very soft focus, rather misty without being insubstantial. Her hands, however, holding a cup and saucer, were very beautiful and quite sharply defined against her dark gown.

Mrs. R. was paralyzed, afraid to turn her head to look directly at her. Suddenly, however, without any conscious volition, she spun around and quickly walked out of the room into the hall. By the time she got to the stairs she was covered with cold perspiration, and her hands were shaking so violently she had to put down the things she was carrying.

Now she knew that Gertrude Tredwell was still around, but not the way she looked when she died. Rather, she had turned back her memory clock to that period of her life when she was gayest and her young man had not yet been sent away by a cruel and unyielding father.

When the realization came to Mrs. R. as to who her ghostly friend was, her fears went away. After all, who would have a better right to be in this house than the one who had sacrificed her love and youth to it and what it stood for in her father's view. This change of her attitude must have somehow gotten through to the ghostly lady as well, by some as yet undefinable telegraph connecting all things, living and dead.

Sometime thereafter, Mrs. R. was arranging flowers for the table in the front parlor. The door was open to the hallway and she was quite alone in the house. She was so preoccupied with the flower arrangement, she failed to notice that she was no longer alone.

Finally, a strange sound caught her attention, and she looked up from the table. The sound was that of a taffeta gown swishing by in rapid movement. As her eyes followed the sound, she saw a woman going up the stairs. It was the same, petite figure she had originally seen at the fireplace sometime before. Again she wore the brown taffeta gown. As she rounded the stairs and disappeared from view, the sound of the gown persisted for a moment or two after the figure herself had gotten out of sight.

This time Mrs. R. did not experience any paralysis or fear. Instead, a warm feeling of friendship between her and the ghost sprang up within her, and contentedly, as if nothing had happened, she continued with her flower arrangement.

During this time, the curator of the Old Merchant's House was a professional antiquarian named Janet Hutchinson who shared the appointments with her friend Emeline Paige, editor of *The Villager*, a neighborhood newspaper, and Mrs. Hutchinson's son, Jefferson, aged fourteen. In addition, there was a cat named Eloise who turned out to be a real fraidicat for probably good and valid reasons.

Although Mrs. Hutchinson did not encounter anything ghostly during her tenure, the lady editor did feel very uneasy in the back bedroom, where much of the tragedy had taken place.

Another person who felt the oppressive atmosphere of the place, without being able to rationalize it away for any good reasons, was Elizabeth Byrd, the novelist, and her friend, whom I must call Mrs. B., for she shies away from the uncanny in public. Mrs. B. visited the house one evening in 1964. As she stood in what had once been Gertrude's bedroom, she noticed that the bedspread of Gertrude's bed was indented *as if someone had just gotten up from it.* Clearly, the rough outline of a body could be made out.

As she stared in disbelief at the bed, she noticed a strange perfume, in the air. Those with her remarked on the scent, but before anyone could look for its sources, it had evaporated. None of the ladies with Mrs. B. had on any such perfume, and the house had been sterile and quiet for days.

Since that time, no further reports of any unusual experiences have come to mind. On one occasion in 1965, photographs of the fireplace near which Mrs. R. had seen the ghost of Gertrude Tredwell were taken simultaneously by two noted photographers with equipment previously tested for proper functioning. This was done to look into the popular legend that this fireplace could not be photographed and that whenever anyone attempted it, that person would have blank film as a result. Perhaps the legend was started by a bad photographer, or it was just that, a legend, for both gentlemen produced almost identical images of the renowned fireplace with their cameras. However, Gertrude Tredwell was not standing in front of it.

This is as it should be. Mrs. R., the untiring spirit behind the Historical Landmarks Society that keeps the building going and out of the wreckers' hands, feels certain that Gertrude need not make another appearance now that everything is secure. And to a Victorian lady, that matters a great deal.

The Old Merchant's House, forever threatened by the wrecker's ball, receives visitors Sundays from 1 to 4. I saw it last some years ago, with a psychic lady named Kathleen Roach. Directly she stepped inside Gertrude's parlor, she turned around and asked me to get her out of the house; the jealousy and anger of the old girl evidently never left the house. So if you happen to run into her, be kind.

22

The Ghosts at the Morris-Jumel Mansion

MY FRIEND ELIZABETH Byrd telephoned to inquire if I had gotten that grave opened yet. I hadn't, but I should really let you in at the beginning.

You see, it all started with an article in the *New York Journal-American* on January 11, 1964, by Joan Hanauer, in which the ghostly goings-on at Jumel Mansion in New York City were brought to public attention. Youngsters on a field trip from P.S. 164, Edgecombe Avenue and 164th Street, said a tall, gray-haired, elderly woman stepped out onto the balcony and told them to be quiet.

The description fit Mme. Jumel.

Could it have happened?

Mrs. Emma Bingay Campbell, curator of the Mansion at 160th Street and Edgecombe, said no.

"I don't believe in ghosts," she said, "but it was very strange. The house was locked and empty. We know that. There could not have been a woman there. But several of the children insist they saw and heard her.

"It was shortly before 11, opening time for the house, which dates back to 1765.

"When I came over to the children to explain they must wait for John Duffy, the second gardener, to unlock the doors at 11," Mrs. Campbell said, "one of the girls wanted to know why the tall woman who had come out on the balcony to reprimand them for boisterousness couldn't let them in. There couldn't have been any such woman—or anyone else—in the house.

"The woman the children described resembled Mme. Jumel, who some thought murdered her husband in the house in 1832, then married Aaron Burr the following year.

"But the children couldn't know that, or what she looked like.

"They also couldn't know that the balcony on which the apparition appeared separated Mme. Jumel's and Burr's bedrooms."

Elizabeth Byrd was then working on a story about Manhattan ghosts for a magazine, so we decided to follow up this case together. First we contacted the public school authorities and obtained permission to talk to the children. The teacher assembled the entire group she had originally taken to the Jumel Mansion, and we questioned them, separately and together. Their story was unchanged. The woman appeared on the balcony, suddenly, and she told them to be quiet.

"How did she disappear?" I wanted to know.

One youngster thought for a moment, then said hesitantly, "She sort of glided back into the house."

"Did you see the balcony doors open?" I asked the girl.

"No, sir," she replied firmly.

"Then did she glide through the door?"

"She did."

The dress they described the ghost as wearing does exist—but it is put away carefully upstairs in the mansion and was not on display, nor is this common knowledge, especially among eleven-year-old schoolgirls.

There was a cooking class in progress when we arrived, and the girls cheerfully offered us samples of their art. We declined for the moment and went on to see the curator of the mansion, Mrs. Campbell. This energetic lady takes care of the mansion for the Daughters of the American Revolution in whose charge the City of New York had placed the museum.

"Is this the first report of a haunting here?" I wanted to know.

Mrs. Campbell shook her head. "Here," she said, and took down from one of the shelves in her office a heavy book. "William Henry Shelton's work, *The Jumel Mansion*, pages two hundred and seven and two hundred and eight report earlier ghosts observed here."

"Have you ever seen or heard anything?"

"No, not yet, but others have. There was that German nurse who lived here in eighteen sixty-five—she heard strange noises even then. Footsteps have been heard by many visitors here when there was no one about. The ghost of Mme. Jumel appeared to a retired guard at the door of this room."

"How would you like me to investigate the matter?" I offered. A date was set immediately.

First, I thought it wise to familiarize myself with the physical layout of the historic house. I was immediately struck by its imposing appearance. Historian John Kent Tilton wrote:

> Located on the highest elevation of Manhattan is one of the most famous old historic houses in the nation, the Morris-Jumel Mansion. The locality

was originally called Harlem Heights by the Dutch in the days of New Amsterdam and was then changed to Mount Morris during the English ownership, before receiving the present name of Washington Heights.

The plot of land upon which the old mansion is situated was originally deeded in 1700 to a Dutch farmer named Jan Kiersen, from part of the "half morgen of land of the common woods" of New Haarlem.

Lieutenant Colonel Roger Morris purchased the estate in 1765. The new owner was born in England in 1728 and came to America at the age of eighteen with a commission of captaincy in the British army.

It was here that the Morris family, with their four children, spent their summers, living the domestic life typical of a British squire and family until the outbreak of the Revolution.

Colonel Morris fled to England at the beginning of hostilities, where he remained for two and one-half years.

As early in the war as August 1776, Mount Morris was taken over by the American troops and General Heath and staff were quartered there. After the disastrous Battle of Long Island, General Washington retreated to Haarlem Heights and made the place his headquarters. After Washington decided to abandon this location, the British moved in and the Morris Mansion housed General Sir Henry Clinton and his officers and, at intervals, the Hessians, during the seven years the British occupied New York.

During the following quarter of a century it was sold and resold several times and witnessed many changes in its varied career. Renamed Calumet Hall, it served for a time as a Tavern and was a stopping place for the stage coaches en route to Albany. It was the home of an unknown farmer when President Washington paid a visit to his old headquarters and entertained at dinner, among others, his cabinet members, John Adams, Alexander Hamilton, Henry Knox, and their wives.

The locality was one that Stephen Jumel with his sprightly and ambitious wife delighted driving out to on a summer's day from their home on Whitehall Street. Mme. Jumel became entranced with the nearby old Morris Mansion and persuaded her husband to purchase it for their home in 1810, for the sum of $10,000 which included 35 acres of land still remaining of the original tract.

The old house was fast falling into decay when Mme. Jumel energetically went about renovating and refurnishing it, and when completed, it was one of the most beautiful homes in the country. The Jumels restored the mansion in the style of the early nineteenth century, when the Federal influence was in fashion.

Mme. Jumel first married, some say by trickery, the rich Frenchman, Stephen Jumel. He had at one time owned a large plantation in Santo Domingo from whence he was obliged to flee at the time of the insurrection. Arriving in the United States, a comparatively poor man, he soon amassed a new fortune as a wine merchant, and at his death in 1832, his wife became one of the richest women in America. A year later she married Aaron Burr, former vice president of the United States. This second marriage, however, was of short duration and ended in divorce. Mme. Jumel died at the age of 93 in 1865.

The Morris-Jumel Mansion is of the mid-Georgian period of architecture. The front facade has four columns, two stories in height, with a pediment at the top.

The exterior is painted white. One of the post-Colonial features added by the Jumels is the imposing front entrance doorway, with flanking sidelights and elliptical fanlight.

In the interior, the wide central hall with arches is furnished with late eighteenth and early nineteenth century pieces. At the left of the entrance is the small parlor or tearoom where the marriage ceremony of the Widow Jumel and Aaron Burr was performed in 1833 when the bride was fifty-eight and the groom twenty years her senior.

Across the hall is the stately Georgian dining room where many persons of fame assembled for elaborate dinner parties.

At the rear of the hall is the large octagonal drawing room.

The broad stairway leads to the spacious hall on the upper floor, which is furnished with personal belongings of the Jumels. There is a group portrait of Mme. Jumel and the young son and daughter of her adopted daughter, Mary Eliza, who married Nelson Chase.

The northwest bedroom contains furniture owned by the Jumels, including a carved four-poster bed.

In the old days the rooms on the third floor were probably used as extra guest chambers since the servants' quarters were then located in the basement with the kitchen.

On January 19, 1964, a small group of people assembled in Betsy Jumel's old sitting room upstairs. Present were a few members of the New York Historical Society and the Daughters of the American Revolution, *Journal- American* writer Nat Adams, and a late-comer, Harry Altschuler of the *World-Telegram*. I was accompanied by Ethel Meyers, who had not been told where we were going that winter afternoon, and Jessyca Russell Gaver, who was serving as my secretary and doing a magazine article on our work at the same time.

We had barely arrived when Ethel went in and out of the Jumel bedroom as if someone were forcing her to do so. As she approached the room across the hall, her shoulder sagged and one arm hung loose as if her side had been injured!

"I feel funny on my left side," Ethel finally said, and her voice had already taken on some of the coloring of someone else's voice.

We went back to the bedroom, which is normally closed to the public. One side is occupied by a huge carved four-poster, once the property of Napoleon I, and there are small chairs of the period in various spots throughout the room. In one corner, there is a large mirror.

"The issue is confused," Ethel said, and sounded confused herself. "There is more than one disturbed person here. I almost feel as though three people were involved. There has been sickness and a change of heart. Someone got a raw deal."

Suddenly, Ethel turned to one of the men who had sat down on Napoleon's bed. "Someone wants you to get up from that bed," she said, and evinced difficulty in speaking. As if bitten by a tarantula, the young man shot up from the bed. No ghost was going to goose *him*.

Ethel again struggled to her feet, despite my restraining touch on her arm. "I've got to go back to that other room again," she mumbled, and off she went, with me trailing after her. She walked almost as if she were being taken over by an outside force. In front of the picture of Mme. Jumel, she suddenly fell to her knees.

"I never can go forward here . . . I fall whenever I'm near there." She pointed at the large picture above her, and almost shouted, "My name isn't on that picture. I want my name there!"

Mrs. Campbell, the curator, took me aside in agitation. "That's very strange she should say that," she remarked. "You see, her name really used to be on that picture a long time ago. But that picture wasn't in this spot when Betsy Jumel was alive."

I thanked her and led Ethel Meyers back to her chair in the other room.

"Henry . . . and a Johann . . . around her . . . ," she mumbled as she started to go into a deep trance. Hoarse sounds emanated from her lips. At first they were unintelligible. Gradually I was able to make them out. Halfway into a trance, she moved over to the bed and lay down on it. I placed my chair next to her head. The others strained to hear. There was an eerie silence about the room, interrupted only by the soft words of the entranced medium.

"You think me dead . . ." a harsh, male voice now said.

"No, I've come to talk to you, to help you," I replied.

"Go away," the ghostly voice said. "Go away!"

"Are you a man or a woman?" I asked.

A bitter laugh was the reply.

"Man . . . ha!" the voice finally said.

"What is your name?"

"Everybody knows who I am."

"I don't. What is your name?" I repeated.

"Let me sleep."

"Is anything troubling you?"

There was a moment of silence, then the voice was a bit softer. "Who are *you*?"

"I'm a friend come to help you."

"Nobody talks to me. They think I'm dead."

"What exactly happened to you?"

"They took me away," the voice said in plaintive tones. "I am not dead yet. Why did they take me away?"

Now the body of the medium shook as if in great agitation, while I spoke soothing words to calm the atmosphere. Suddenly, the ghost speaking through the medium was gone, and in his place was the crisp, matter-of-fact voice of Albert, Ethel's control. I asked Albert to tell us through the entranced medium who the ghost was.

"I don't hear a name, but I see a sturdy body and round face. He complains he was pronounced dead when he in fact wasn't. I believe he is the owner of the house and it bears his name. There are many jealousies in this house. There is an artist who is also under suspicion."

"Is there a woman here?"

"One thwarted of what she desired and who wants to throw herself out the window."

"Why?" I asked.

"Thwarted in love and under suspicion."

Later, I asked Mrs. Campbell about this. She thought for a moment, then confirmed the following facts: A young servant girl involved with one of the family tried to commit suicide by jumping out the window.

I questioned Albert further. "Is there a restless woman in this house?"

"That is right. The one in the picture. Her conscience disturbs her."

"About what?"

The medium now grabbed her side, as if in pain. "I am being threatened," Albert said now, "I feel the revelation would disturb."

"But how can I release her unless I know what is holding her here?"

"It has to do with the death of her husband. That he was strangled in his coffin."

I tried to question him further, but he cut us short. The medium had to be released now.

Soon, Ethel Meyers was back to her own self. She remembered very little of the trance, but her impressions of a clairvoyant nature continued for a while. I queried her about the person on the bed.

"I get the initial J," she replied and rubbed her side.

I turned to Mrs. Campbell. "What about the story of Mme. Jumel's guilty conscience?"

"Well," the curator replied, "after her husband's death, she refused to live in this house for some time. She always felt guilty about it."

We were standing in a corner where the medium could not hear us. "Stephen Jumel bled to death from a wound he had gotten in a carriage accident. Mme. Jumel allegedly tore off his bandage and let him die. That much we know."

Mrs. Campbell naturally is a specialist on Betsy Jumel and her life, and she knows many intimate details unknown to the general public or even to researchers.

It was five-thirty in the afternoon when we left the house, which must be closed for the night after that hour.

The next morning two newspaper accounts appeared: One, fairly accurate, in the *Journal*, and a silly one in the *Telegram*, by a man who stood outside the room of the investigation and heard very little, if anything.

Several weeks went by and my ghost-hunting activities took me all over the country. Then I received a telephone call from Mrs. Campbell.

"Did you know that May twenty-second is the anniversary of Stephen Jumel's death?" I didn't and I wagered her nobody else did, except herself and the late Mr. Jumel. She allowed as to that and suggested we have another go at the case on that date. I have always felt that anniversaries are good times to solve murder cases so I readily agreed.

This time, the *Journal* and *Telegram* reporters weren't invited, but the *New York Times*, in the person of reporter Grace Glueck, was, and I am indebted to her for the notes she took of the proceedings that warm May afternoon.

Present also were the general manager of King Features, Frank McLearn; Clark Kinnaird, literary critic of the *Journal*; John Allen and Bob O'Brien of *Reader's Digest*; Emeline Paige, the editor of *The Villager*; writers Elizabeth Byrd and Beverly Balin; Ed Joyce of CBS; and several members of the New York Historical Society, presumably there as observers ready to rewrite history as needed since the famous Aaron Burr might be involved.

Ethel Meyers was told nothing about the significance of the date, nor had I discussed with her the results of the first seance.

Again we assembled in the upstairs bedroom and Ed Joyce set up his tape recorder in front of Napoleon's bed, while Ethel sat on the bed itself and I next to her on a chair. To my left, the young lady from the *Times* took her seat. All in all there must have been twenty-five anxious people in the room, straining to hear all that was said and keeping a respectful silence when asked to. Within a few minutes, Ethel was in a deep trance, and a male voice spoke through her vocal chords.

"Who are you?" I asked as I usually do when an unknown person comes through a medium.

"*Je suis Stephen*," the voice said.

"Do you speak English?"

In answer the medium clutched at her body and groaned, "Doctor! Doctor! Where is the doctor?"

"What is hurting you?" I asked.

The voice was firm and defiant now. "I'm alive, I'm alive . . . don't take me away."

"Did you have an accident? What happened to you?"

"She tricked me."

"Who tricked you?"

"I can't breathe . . . where is she? She tricked me. Look at her!"

"Don't worry about her," I said. "She's dead."

"But I'm alive!" the entranced voice continued.

"In a sense, you are. But you have also passed over."

"No—they put me in the grave when I was not yet dead."

"How did you get hurt?" I wanted to know.

The ghost gave a bitter snort. "What matter—I'm dead. You said so."

"I didn't say you were dead," I replied.

The voice became furious again. "She took it, she took it—that woman. She took my life. Go away."

"I'm your friend."

"I haven't any friends . . . that Aaron . . ."

"Aaron? Was he involved in your death?"

"That strumpet . . . hold him! They buried me alive, I tell you."

"When did this happen?"

"It was cold. She made me a fool, a fool!"

"How did she do that?"

"All the time I loved her, she tricked me."

"I want to help you."

"I'm bleeding."

"How did this happen?"

"Pitchfork . . . wagon . . . hay. . ."

"Was it an accident, yes or no?"

"I fell on it."

"You fell on the pitchfork?"

"Look at the blood bath . . . on Napoleon's bed."

"What about that pitchfork?" I insisted.

"There was a boy in the hay, and he pushed me off."

"Did you know this boy?"

"Yes . . . give me *her*. She wanted to be a lady. I saw it. I wasn't so foolish I didn't see it."

"What happened when you got home?"

"She told me I was going to die."

"Did you have a doctor?"

"Yes."

"Wasn't the wound bandaged?"

"They took me out alive. I was a live man he put in the grave. I want to be free from that grave!"

"Do you want me to set you free?"

"God bless you!"

"It is your hatred that keeps you here. You must forgive."

"She did it to me."

I then pleaded with the ghost to join his own family and let go of his memories. "Do you realize how much time has gone on since? A hundred years!"

"Hundred years!"

The medium, still entranced, buried her head in her hands: "I'm mad!"

"Go from this house and don't return."

"Mary, Mary!"

Mary was the name of Jumel's daughter, a fact not known to the medium at the time.

"Go and join Mary!" I commanded, and asked that Albert, the control, help the unhappy one find the way.

Just as soon as Jumel's ghost had left us, someone else slipped into the medium's body, or so it seemed, for she sat up and peered at us with a suspicious expression: "Who are you?"

"I'm a friend, come to help," I replied.

"I didn't ask for you."

"My name is Holzer, and I have come to seek you out. If you have a name worth mentioning, please tell us."

"Get out or I'll call the police! This is my house."

There was real anger now on the medium's entranced face.

I kept asking for identification. Finally, the disdainful lips opened and in cold tones, the voice said, "I am the wife of the vice president of the United States! Leave my house!"

I checked with Mrs. Campbell and found that Betsy Jumel did so identify herself frequently. On one occasion, driving through crowded New York streets long after her divorce from Aaron Burr, she shouted, "Make way for the wife of the vice president of the United States!"

"Didn't you marry someone else before that?" I asked. "How did your husband die?"

"Bastard!"

"You've been dead a hundred years, Madam," I said pleasantly.

"You are made like the billow in the captain's cabin," she replied, somewhat cryptically. Later I checked this out. A sea captain was one of her favorite lovers while married to Jumel.

"Did you murder your husband?" I inquired and drew back a little just in case.

"You belong in the scullery with my maids," she replied disdainfully, but I repeated the accusation, adding that her husband had claimed she had killed him.

"I will call for help," she countered.

"There is no help. The police are on your trail!" I suggested.

"I am the wife of the vice president of the United States!"

"I will help you if you tell me what you did. Did you cause his death?"

"The rats that crawl . . . they bit me. Where am I?"

"You're between two worlds. Do you wish to be helped?"

"Where is Joseph?"

"You must leave this house. Your husband has forgiven you."

"I adored him!"

"Go away, and you will see Stephen Jumel again."

"Only the crest on the carriage! That's all I did. He was a great man."

I had the feeling she wasn't at all keen on Monsieur Jumel. But that happens, even to ghosts.

I finally gave up trying to get her to go and join Jumel and tried another way.

"Go and join the vice president of the United States. He awaits you." To my surprise, this didn't work either.

"He is evil, evil," she said.

Perplexed, I asked, "Whom do you wish to join?"

"Mary."

"Then call out her name, and she'll join you and take you with her."

"No crime, no crime."

"You've been forgiven. Mary will take you away from here."

I asked Albert, the control, to come and help us get things moving, but evidently Madame had a change of heart: "This is my house. I'll stay here."

"This is no longer your house. You must go!"

The struggle continued. She called for Christopher, but wouldn't tell me who Christopher was.

"He's the only one I ever trusted," she volunteered, finally.

"It's not too late," I repeated. "You can join your loved ones."

"Good-bye."

I called for Albert, who quickly took control. "She's no longer in the right mind," he said, as soon as he had firm control of the medium's vocal chords. "You may have to talk with her again."

"Is she guilty of Jumel's death?"

"Yes. It was arranged."

"Who was the boy who pushed him?"

"A trusty in the house. She told him to."

"What about Stephen Jumel?"

"He is in a better frame of mind."

"Is there anything else we did not bring out? Who is this Christopher she mentioned?"

"A sea captain. She buried him in Providence."

Mrs. Campbell later confirmed the important role the sea captain played in Betsy's life. There was also another man named Brown.

"Did Aaron Burr help bury Jumel?"

"That is true. Burr believed Mme. Jumel had more finances than she actually had."

"What about the doctor who buried him alive? Is his name known?"

"Couldn't stop the bleeding."

"Was Aaron Burr in on the crime?"

"He is very much aware that he is guilty. He still possesses his full mental faculties."

I then asked the control to help keep the peace in the house and to bring the medium back to her own body.

A few minutes later, Ethel Meyers was herself again, remembering nothing of the ordeal she had gone through the past hour, and none the worse for it.

Jumel died in 1832 and, as far as I could find, the first ghostly reports date back to 1865. The question was: Could his remains disclose any clues as to the manner in which he died? If he suffocated in his coffin, would not the position of his bones so indicate?

I queried two physicians who disagreed in the matter. One thought that nothing would be left by now; the other thought it was worth looking into.

I thought so, too. However, my application to reopen the grave of Stephen Jumel, down in the old Catholic cemetery on Mott Street, got the official runaround. The District Attorney's office sent me to Dr. Halpern, the chief medical examiner, who told me it would be of no use to check. When I insisted, I was referred to the church offices of old St. Patrick's, which has nominal jurisdiction over the plot.

Have you ever tried to reopen a grave in the City of New York? It's easier to dig a new one, believe me!

As the years passed, I often returned to the mansion. I made several television documentaries there with the helpful support of the curator, who now is the affable and knowledgeable Patrick Broom. The famous blue gown is no longer on display, alas, having disintegrated shortly after I first published the story. But the legend persists, and the footfalls are still heard on lonely nights when the security guard locks up. Whether the Jumels, the remorseful Betsy and the victimized Stephen, have since made up on the Other Side, is a moot question, and I doubt that Aaron Burr will want anything further to do with the, ah, lady, either.

23

Uninvited House Ghosts

"MY FRIEND SAYS this skeleton tried to get into bed with her," my friend Elizabeth Byrd said with conviction and looked at me straight, to see how I would react. I did not disappoint her. I shook my head with determination and informed her somewhat haughtily that skeletons do not get into people's beds, in fact, skeletons don't do much really except maybe on Hallowe'en when there are kids inside them.

But Elizabeth is as good a researcher as she is an author—*Immortal Queen* and *Flowers of the Forest* are among her historical novels—and she insisted that this was not some sort of Hallowe'en prank.

More to please her than out of curiosity, I decided to look into this weird tale. I never take stock in anything that I don't hear firsthand, so I called on Elizabeth's friend to hear all about this skeleton myself. I was prepared for a charming, talky, and garrulous spinster whose imagination was running away with her.

The name on the door read Dianne Nicholson, and it was one of those grimy walk-ups on New York's East Side that are slowly but surely turning into slums. Downstairs there was a gun shop and the house was squeezed in between a row of other nondescript houses. Children, none of them particularly tidy-looking, were playing in the street, and trucks lumbered by me on Second Avenue creating a steady din that must have been unnerving to any resident of this building. There were perhaps a dozen names on the board downstairs and an Italian grocery across the street. All in all, it was what New Yorkers call a "neighborhood" without distinction, without much hope for improvement, and without many attractive people.

I pressed the bell and when the buzzer responded, I walked up a flight of stairs, where I found the entrance door to the apartment in the front part of the building slightly ajar.

I stepped inside and closed the door behind me.

"Miss Nicholson?" I said tentatively.

"Coming," a bell-like young voice came from the back of the dimly lit apartment.

As my eyes got used to the place I distinguished that it consisted of a longish foyer, from which doors led to a kitchen, another room, and a small room, reading right to left. It was jumble-full of furniture and things and a glance into the small room on my left showed stacks of papers, a drawing board, and other graphic art paraphernalia strewn about.

My investigation was interrupted by the arrival of Miss Nicholson. It was clear immediately that my image of her had been wrong. An ash blonde of perhaps twenty-two or three, she was slight and erect and looked very determined as she greeted me from the other room in the center.

"I'm so glad you came," she began and led me to the couch along the wall of the foyer. "This thing has been getting out of hand lately."

I held up my hand—for I did not want to lose a word of her account. Within a minute, my tape recorder was purring away and the story unfolded.

Dianne Nicholson came to New York from her native Atlanta in the middle of 1964. By training she was a writer, or more specifically, a writer of publicity, advertising, and promotional material, and she was presently working with an advertising agency in Manhattan. She was much too busy with the task, first, of looking for a job, and then of maintaining it, to pay much attention to the house and the little apartment in it that she had rented.

It was inexpensive and within her budget, she did not have to share it with a roommate, and that was what she had wanted. If it was no luxury building, well, it was also convenient to her place of work and she had no complaints.

In addition, she did a lot of extra work at home, free-lance accounts, to better her income, so she was rather absorbed in her professional activities most of the time, seldom allowing herself the luxury of aimless dreaming. Her social life was pleasant, but underneath it all ran a very practical streak, for Dianne had come to New York to make good as a career girl, and work was her way of getting there.

She knew few if any of her neighbors, most of whom were not in her social or professional strata to begin with. But she did manage to strike up a friendship with the girl who had an apartment a few stories above hers. This was a rather buxom German girl in her early thirties who went by the single name of Karina. An artist specializing in small drawings, cards, and other objects on the borderline between art and craft, Karina went around her place most of the time wearing miniskirts when miniskirts had not yet been invented. Her life was lived mainly on the inside of herself and she was happy to pursue this kind of career. Evidently she had left behind her in Germany a far different life, but there were no regrets. The two girls visited each other frequently, and it made both of them feel safe to know neither one of them was entirely alone in this dank building.

It was in the middle of 1965, after living in the building for about a year, that Dianne became alarmed by a sequence of events she could not cope with.

At the time, she slept in the smaller room, off the foyer, which later became her workroom.

She awoke there one night and saw a figure standing at her door. It was a rather tall woman, wearing what to Dianne looked like a long nightgown. The figure also wore a kind of Mother Hubbard cap, like a granny would—and yet, Dianne quickly realized that this was not an old figure at all.

As Dianne, with curiosity at first, and increasing terror later, sat up in bed and studied the apparition, she noticed that the figure was luminescent and emitted a soft, white glow. The face, or rather the area where the facial characteristics should be, was also aglow, but she could not make out any features. As yet unsure as to what the figure was, Dianne noticed she could not distinguish any hands either.

At this moment the figure left the spot at the door and got into bed with her.

Dianne's first impression, when the figure got close, was that of a skeleton, but when it got into bed with her she realized that it was more of a waxen figure, very cold but as hard as flesh would be.

Her thoughts racing through her mind while practically paralyzed by the whole thing, Dianne tried to reason it out. Then she said to herself, why, it must be my mother. What in the world would come into bed with her?

Later, she realized that it wasn't her mother, of course. But at the moment she preferred to think so, recalling how her mother had often crawled into bed with her when she was a child. And yet she knew at this moment, crystal clear, that the white figure next to her was that of a young woman.

Touching the figure, she felt hard substance underneath the gown.

"I must see your face," she mumbled and tried to see the stranger's face. But the figure acted as if she were asleep and did not wish to be disturbed.

Dianne reached out and pulled the covers off the bed. She found herself staring into a mirror. Now she realized why she had not been able to see the creature's hands before. They weren't really hands at all, but were more like a skeleton's bony fingers, holding up a mirror in front of the figure's face.

Then the mirror moved and disclosed what took the place of a face: a glowing white round in which neither eyes, nose, nor teeth could be distinguished and yet the whole figure was more than a mere anatomical skeleton—it was a roughly covered skeleton figure—more than mere bones and not quite flesh and skin, but somewhere in between.

Dianne's normal reactions finally caught up with her: she found herself sinking into a slow state of shock at what she had discovered. At this moment, the figure disappeared. Not by retreating to the doorway from where it had come, but just by dissolving from the bed itself.

Dianne leaped out of bed, threw on a robe and raced upstairs to her friend's apartment. For days after, she trembled at the thought of the unspeakable one returning, and she tried hard to convince herself that she had dreamed the whole incident. But in her heart she knew she had not.

From that day on, however, she became increasingly aware of a human presence other than her own in the apartment. More from self-preservation through knowledge than from idle curiosity she bought some books dealing with psychic phenomena

Early in December this oppressive feeling became suddenly very strong. She had moved her bed into the other bedroom, with a wall separating the two areas. One night she *knew* that an attack had been made upon her and that the evil personality involved was male. She slept with all the lights on from that moment. With mounting terror she would not go off to sleep until daylight reassured her that no further dangers were about.

Then in early January, just before I came to see her, Dianne had another visit from a white, luminous figure. It was evening, and Dianne had just gotten to sleep. Suddenly she awoke, prodded by some inborn warning system, and there in the entrance to her present bedroom stood a vague, smoke-like figure of some luminescence. After a moment it was gone, only to return again later that same night. Dianne was not alone that night, but it did not help her fears. What did the figure want of her? This was not the skeletal visitor from before but a definitely masculine personality. Dianne knew this entity was after her, and wanted to take her over. On one occasion in December she had felt him take over her nervous system, as she sat helplessly on her bed. Her muscles went into spasm as if they were no longer under her conscious control. Desperately she fought the invader, trying to keep her thoughts on an even keel, and ultimately she won out. The strange feeling left her body and she was able to relax at last.

Extrasensory experiences had plagued Dianne since childhood. When she was fourteen and going to high school, a close friend and sorority sister wrote to her with a strange request. Would she sing at her funeral? Now Dianne had been singing in choir and her friend knew this. But there was no logical reason for so strange a request from a fifteen-year-old girl. Three days after receiving the letter Dianne had a strange dream, in which she saw her friend in front of a large crowd, with her arms wide open, and calling out to Dianne, "Please help me!"

At this point, the dream faded out. She woke up after the dream and noticed that the clock showed 12:45 A.M., Friday. Sunday night, the identical dream returned, only this time it ended abruptly rather than gently fading out. She discussed the dreams with her classmates in school but could not puzzle out the meaning. On Tuesday she received a phone call from her mother, informing her that her friend had been in an automobile accident on Friday, and at the time of Dianne's first dream the friend had just gone under the anaesthetic at the hospital. At the time of the second dream, which ended abruptly, the girl died.

There were other instances of premonitions come true, of feelings about events that later transpired—making Dianne aware of the fact that she had something special, yet in no way intruding on her practical approach to life.

When she first moved into her present apartment, she found that most of the buildings in the area were occupied by people on welfare relief. But the house she moved into had recently been renovated, making it suitable for higher-rent tenants, as had two others nearby, giving hope that the entire neighborhood might eventually adopt a different image.

Although one of Dianne's boy friends, a photographer, felt nothing special about the apartment, two of her female friends did. There was Karina, the artist upstairs, for instance. She would not stay long, complaining the place gave her the creeps. Elizabeth Byrd also felt an oppressiveness not borne out by the decor or furniture of the place, for Dianne had managed to make the place comfortable and pleasant as far as the purely physical aspects were concerned.

After a while she quit her Madison Avenue job and became a free-lance. This necessitated her spending much more time at home. In the daytime, she found the place peaceful and quiet and she managed to get her work done without trouble.

But as soon as the shadows of night crept over the horizon, fear began to return to her heart. The fear was not borne from darkness or from the presence of the unknown; it was almost a physical thing with her, something very tangible that seemed to fill a space within the walls of her apartment.

Dianne thought herself safe from the specter in the daytime until one morning she was awakened by a strange noise. She had gone to bed late after putting in long hours of work, and slept until 10 A.M. The noise, she soon realized, was caused by a wooden coat hanger banging heavily against the bedroom door. Still half-asleep, Dianne assured herself that the draft was causing it. She got out of bed, fully awake now, and walked toward the door. The noise stopped abruptly. She checked the door and windows and found everything closed. There could not have been a draft. Still unconvinced, she huffed and puffed to see if her breath would move the hanger. It didn't.

She began to have some strange dreams, several similar ones in succession. In these dreams the skeleton-faced white woman appeared to her and wanted to take her with her.

As the weeks rolled by, more and more strange incidents tried her patience sorely. There was the time she had gone to sleep with all lights burning, when she saw an explosion of light in the living room. It was not hallucinatory, for she saw it reflected in the dark tube of her television set. Another time she was in the bedroom when she heard the sound of glass breaking in the living room. The lights in the living room and the kitchen went out at the same moment. She entered the living room, expecting to see the remnants of a bulb that might have blown up, but there was nothing on the floor. The light switches, however, in both living room and kitchen had been switched off by unseen hands . . . At this moment her friend Karina came down from upstairs and Dianne was never so glad in her life to see a friendly human face.

Since Dianne Nicholson had gotten to be quite frantic about all this I decided to arrange for a seance to get to the bottom of the disturbances with the help of a good medium. We agreed on June 17, 1966, as the date, Sybil Leek was to be my medium, and Theo Wilson, a reporter from the *Daily News* would come along to witness and report on the investigation.

Meanwhile, Karina, the girl upstairs, had also had her share of run-ins with the Uninvited. Her apartment is on the fifth floor. One day Karina was standing in front of her mirror when she noticed a ghostly figure—or rather a glowing outline. At the same time she felt a strong urge to cut her hair short and be like the apparition. She felt the ghostly presence wanted to possess her or express itself through her and she became frightened. A little later she was down on the second floor with Dianne, when both girls heard a sharp banging noise, as if someone had dumped a heavy object on the floor next to the entrance of the apartment. Their first impression was that a package had been delivered and they rushed to see what it was. But there was nothing there.

When the seventeenth of June arrived it turned out to be one of those oppressive, prematurely hot nights New York is famous for, or rather infamous for, but the date had been set and everyone was in readiness. I also brought along a motion picture camera and on arrival had deposited Sybil with Karina so that I might discuss the events leading up to the investigation once more for the benefit of Theo Wilson of the *News*. Naturally Sybil was not to hear any of this nor was Karina allowed to discuss anything with her temporary guest but the weather—at the moment a most timely subject.

Half an hour later I brought Sybil inside the second floor apartment. Did she feel anything here clairvoyantly?

"You'll probably laugh at this," Sybil said, "but I have a tremendous feeling about horses."

I didn't laugh, and even though I knew of Sybil's love for and interest in domestic animals, I noted the statement for later verification.

"What about people, though?" I pressed. A heavy oak chair had been placed near the entrance to the smaller room where Dianne had experienced the skeletal intruder originally. The chair was meant for Sybil to sit in and faced away from the small room.

"Behind this chair," Sybil now said, "there is a touch of coldness . . . some nonphysical being, definitely."

The feeling was only fleeting, her main sensation being of a country place with horses, and then that touch of "someone."

I decided to place Sybil into trance now and we—meaning our hostess Dianne Nicholson, a gentleman friend of hers, Karina, Theo Wilson, and myself—grouped ourselves around her. Sybil took the chair facing away from the little room.

After a few moments, heavy, labored breathing replaced the measured breath of Sybil's normal personality. Words came across her lips that I could not yet make out, gradually becoming louder and firmer. I kept asking for a name—asking that the presence identify itself. Eventually the name was clear.

"Jeremy Waters," Sybil had said.

"Speak louder," I commanded.

"Go away," the voice countered, and added, "Jeremy."

"Why should Jeremy go away?"

"Why did he do it . . . nice stock . . . I'm hurt . . . Jeremy, Jeremy Waters . . ."

"Who are you?"

"Waters."

"Who is Jeremy?"

"Jeremy Waters, my son . . . I'll find him . . . ran away . . . left me . . . what'd he leave me for? . . . Mary Collins . . ."

It dawned on me now that Jeremy Waters, Sr., was complaining about Jeremy Waters, Jr.

"Is this your house?" I asked.

"House? There is not a house," the voice came back, somewhat astonished.

"Store place . . . I work here . . . waiting for Jeremy . . . where did they go, Jeremy and Marie . . . his woman? . . ."

"How long ago was this?"

"Strange . . . fifty-four . . . where's everyone?"

"Tell me about yourself so I can help you."

"I don't trust you. What have you done with him?"

"What sort of work does he do?"

"A boat. He brings things here."

"When were you born?"

"Twenty-two."

"Where?"

"Hudson village. . . ."

"What is your wife's name?"

"Margie."

"Where was she born?"

"Far . . . in Holland."

"Any children?"

"Jeremy. . . three."

When I asked what church he belonged to I got a disdainful snort in reply.

"Churches . . . churches . . . I do not go."

"What sort of place is this?"

"What do you come here for? Fall on your knees . . . ," he said, instead, and added, "Find Jeremy . . . he should repent his sins . . . honor thy father and thy mother . . . where am I? There are too many people. . . ." The voice sounded confused and worried now.

"And where's his clothes?" he demanded to know.

I started to explain the passage of time.

"Repent, repent," he mumbled, instead, barely listening.

"Why did they do it? Hurt me?"

"Who is this woman you mentioned?"

"Maria Goulando." It had sounded like Mary Collins to me at first, but now there was no mistaking the odd name. "She is Jeremy's woman."

"Is he married to her?"

"It is wrong to marry a Catholic," the voice said sternly.

"Is the girl a Catholic?"

"Yes."

"Did he marry her?"

"Over my dead body."

"He didn't marry her then?"

"No . . . the church won."

"Where is the woman now?"

"With Jeremy."

"If you find them, what will you do?"

"Make him repent."

This was said with so much bitterness I decided to take another tack with my questioning. "Have you hurt anyone, Jeremy?" I said.

"Why are you asking me . . . I'm not going to talk," he shot back, defiant again.

"Do you know where you are?"

"Outside the church."

"What church?"

"Lutheran church."

"Are you a Lutheran then?"

"Was . . ."

"What are you now?"

"*Nothing . . .*"

"What street is the church on?"

"Vall Street."

If he meant to say Wall Street he said it with a strange inflection.

I asked him to spell it.

Puzzled and haltingly he said, "Veh—ah—el—el," spelling the W the way a European might spell it, especially a Dutchman or German.

"Wall Street," the voice said more clearly now, this time pronouncing it correctly.

"Name of the church?" I inquired.

"Why—can't—I—find—him?" it came back haltingly.

"What is this place used for?"

"Store things in the back . . ."

"Where do you live?"

"Hudson . . . up the Hudson."

Again I asked for the year he thought we were in.

"Fifty-four . . ."

This is where I made a mistake, perhaps.

"Eighteen fifty-four?" I said. I never like to lead.

"Yes," the voice acknowledged and added, "February . . . today the fifteenth . . ."

"How old are you?" I asked.

"Today is my birthday."

"And your son is not with you?"

"Yes . . . ingratitude shall be his ruin."

"Did you kill anyone?"

"Go away, go away. . . ." The voice sounded angry now as if I had hit on a sensitive topic. I reasoned with him, explaining about the passage of time.

"Your son has long died," I explained.

He would not accept this.

"You're a foreigner," he suddenly said, "what do you want? *She's* a foreigner."

"You don't like foreigners?"

"No."

"Did you kill Maria?"

"She was a foreigner," he said with contempt in his voice.

I asked him to make a clean breast of his guilt feelings so that he might free himself from the place we had found him at. There was a long, long pause. Finally he understood and listened quietly as I sent him away to rejoin his dead son. Soon after, I recalled Sybil to her own body. None the worse for her experience, she remembered absolutely nothing that had transpired during the seance.

So there were two ghosts, Jeremy Waters and the girl Maria.

My next step was to check out the names given and see how they connected with the place we were in.

Naturally I assumed that 1854 was the period I should check, since the ghost had acknowledged that date. But there was nothing in the records indicating a Jeremy Waters at that date living on 21st Street.

The only clue of some interest was the name of one James Waters, a "carman" who lived on East 22nd Street between Second and Third Avenues as of 1847, according to Doggett's *New York Directory* for that year. But the thought did not leave me that the "18" was added to the ghost's "54" by my suggestion. Could he have meant 1754?

I decided to check that earlier date. Suddenly things became more interesting.

The entire piece of land on which this and other houses in the block were standing had originally belonged to the Watts family. The Watts city residence stood at 59 East Twenty-first Street and John Watts, Sr., owned the land in 1754, together with his son, John Watts, Jr. I was struck by the similarity of names of father and son, a parallel to Jeremy, Sr., and Jeremy, Jr. They had acquired the land in 1747 from James De Lancey, the elder Watts' brother-in-law. It was then a farm of 130 acres and extended from Twenty-first Street to the East River. Spooner's *Historical Families in America*, which gives these and other details of the prominent Watts family, also states briefly that a third John Watts was born to the young John in 1775, but died unmarried.

I was still struggling with the research on this case, when Theo Wilson's piece of our seance appeared in the *New York Daily News*. Theo was impressed by the sincerity of both approach and method and reported the investigation factually.

Because of her article a gentleman named Charles Burhaus contacted me with additional information on the Watts family; his father's sister had been married to the last of the Wattses. The Wattses did indeed come from the Hudson Valley and most of them are buried at Tivoli, New York.

The Watts were very religious and fervent Protestants. "Old John" Watts, Mr. Burhaus reports, "disapproved of his son's way of living."

When Mr Burhaus' grandmother invited his Aunt Minnie to stay at the ancestral Watts house in Tivoli—Mr. Burhaus was then but a child—the lady refused to stay, explaining that the house was haunted by a ghost who liked women.

If there was a storehouse with boats nearby, as the ghost had claimed, on what is now East Twenty-first Street, 1854 would not fit, but 1754 would.

Jeremy Waters and John Watts are not identical names but I have encountered ghost personalities who, for reasons of honor, have disguised their true identities until the skill of the investigator was able to uncover their cover.

So much of the Waters father-and-son relationship seems to fit the Watts father-and-son relationship, the place is correct, and the first names are identical for father and son in both instances, that I cannot help feeling that we have this kind of situation here. If the son ran away with an unacceptable woman, the father would naturally not wish to divulge to a stranger, like me, his true identity, yet he might talk about the events themselves, being emotionally bound to them still.

Miss Nicholson had no further troubles in the apartment after that. She also moved a few weeks later and the new occupants, if they know of my investigation at all, have not seen fit to complain about any disturbances.

So I can only assume that both Jeremy Waters, Sr., and the hapless girl he hurt have found their way across the boundary of the spirit world, which in any event is much nicer than a rooming house on East Twenty-first Street.

One more item gave me food for thought. I had taken a number of still photographs during the two visits to the apartment. When they were developed, several of them showed white shadows and streaks of light that could not be accounted for by natural explanations.

I mailed a set to Dianne Nicholson via first-class mail. It never reached her. A letter, containing some data on the apartment and its past, which she had mailed to me about the same time, never reached me. When I brought the negatives of my pictures to have another set of enlargements made, the lab lost the negatives or rather could not account for them, no reason given.

Finally we had to rephotograph the only existing set of prints to make duplicates.

Coincidence? Perhaps.

If there is such a thing.

THE WASHINGTON AREA

24

Abraham Lincoln's Restless Spirit

ALL THESE YEARS after the assassination of President John F. Kennedy we are still not sure of his murderer or murderers, even though the deed was done in the cold glare of a public parade, under the watchful eyes of numerous police and security guards, not to mention admirers in the streets.

While we are still arguing the merits of various theories concerning President Kennedy's assassination, we sometimes forget that an earlier crime of a similar nature is equally unresolved. In fact, there are so many startling parallels between the two events that one cannot help but marvel.

One of the people who marveled at them in a particularly impressive way recently is a New York psychiatrist named Stanley Krippner, attached to Maimonides Medical Center, Brooklyn, who has set down his findings in the learned *Journal of Parapsychology*. Among the facts unearthed by Dr. Krippner is the remarkable "death circle" of presidential deaths: Harrison, elected in 1840, died in 1841; Lincoln, elected twenty years later, in 1860, died in 1865; Garfield, elected in 1880, was assassinated in 1881; McKinley, elected in 1900, died by a murderer's hand in 1901; Harding, elected just twenty years after him, died in office in 1923; Roosevelt, re-elected in 1940, did likewise in 1945; and finally, Kennedy, elected to office in 1960, was murdered in 1963. Since 1840, every President voted into office in a year ending with a zero has died in office.

Dr. Krippner speculates that this cycle is so far out of the realm of coincidence that some other reason might be found. Applying the principle of synchronicity of meaningful coincidence established first by the late Professor Carl G. Jung, Dr. Krippner wonders if perhaps this principle might not hold an answer to these astounding facts. But the most obvious and simplest explanation of all should not be expected from a medical doctor: fate. Is there an overriding destiny at work that makes these tragedies occur at certain times, whether or not those involved in them try to avoid them? And if so, who directs this destiny—who, in short, is *in charge of the store*?

Dr. Krippner also calls attention to some amazing parallels between the two most noted deaths among U.S. Presidents, Kennedy's and Lincoln's. Both names have seven letters each, the wives of both lost a son while their husbands were in office, and both Presidents were shot in the head from behind on a Friday and in the presence of their wives. Moreover, Lincoln's killer was John Wilkes Booth, the letters of whose name, all told, add up to fifteen; Lee Harvey Oswald's name, likewise, had fifteen letters. Booth's birth year was 1829; Oswald's, 1939. Both murderers were shot down deliberately in full view of their captors, and both died two hours after being shot. Lincoln was elected to Congress in 1847 and Kennedy in 1947; Lincoln became President in 1860 and Kennedy in 1960. Both were involved in the question of civil rights for Negroes. Finally, Lincoln's secretary, named Kennedy, advised him not to go to the theater on the fateful day he was shot, and Kennedy's secretary, named Lincoln, urged him not to go to Dallas. Lincoln had a premonitory dream seeing himself killed and Kennedy's assassination was predicted by Jeane Dixon as early as 1952, by Al Morrison in 1957, and several other seers in 1957 and 1960, not to forget President Kennedy's own expressed feelings of imminent doom.

But far be it from me to suggest that the two Presidents might be personally linked, perhaps through reincarnation, if such could be proved. Their similar fates must be the result of a higher order of which we know as yet very little except that it exists and operates as clearly and deliberately as any other law of nature.

But there is ample reason to reject any notion of Lincoln's rebirth in another body, if anyone were to make such a claim. Mr. Lincoln's *ghost* has been observed in the White House by competent witnesses.

According to Arthur Krock of the *New York Times*, the earliest specter at the White House was not Lincoln but Dolly Madison. During President Wilson's administration, she appeared to a group of workers who were about to move her precious rose garden. Evidently they changed their minds about the removal, for the garden was not touched.

It is natural to assume that in so emotion-laden a building as the White House there might be remnants of people whose lives were very closely tied to the structure. I have defined ghosts as the surviving emotional memories of people who are not aware of the transition called death and continue to function in a thought world as they did at the time of their passing, or before it. In a way, then, they are psychotics unable or unwilling to accept the realities of the nonphysical world into which they properly belong, but which is denied them by their unnatural state of "hanging on" in the denser, physical world of flesh and blood. I am sure we don't know all the unhappy or disturbed individuals who are bound up with the White House, and some of them may not necessarily be from the distant past, either. But Abigail Adams was seen and identified during the administration of President Taft. Her shade was seen to pass through the doors of the East Room, which was later to play a prominent role in the White House's most famous ghost story.

That Abraham Lincoln would have excellent cause to hang around his former center of activity, even though he died across town, is obvious: He had so much unfinished business of great importance.

Furthermore, Lincoln himself, during his lifetime, had on the record shown an unusual interest in the psychic. The Lincoln family later vehemently denied that seances took place in the White House during his administration. Robert Lincoln may have burned some important papers of his father's bearing on these sittings, along with those concerning the political plot to assassinate his father. According to the record, he most certainly destroyed many documents before being halted in this foolish enterprise by a Mr. Young. This happened shortly before Robert Lincoln's death and is attested to by Lincoln authority Emanuel Hertz in *The Hidden Lincoln*.

The spiritualists even go so far as to claim the President as one of their own. This may be extending the facts, but Abraham Lincoln was certainly psychic, and even during his term in the White House his interest in the occult was well known. The *Cleveland Plain Dealer*, about to write of Lincoln's interest in this subject, asked the president's permission to do so, or, if he preferred, that he deny the statements made in the article linking him to these activities. Far from denying it, Lincoln replied, "The only falsehood in the statement is that half of it has not been told. The article does not begin to tell the things I have witnessed."

The seances held in the White House may well have started when Lincoln's little boy Willie followed another son, Eddie, into premature death, and Mrs. Lincoln's mind gave way to a state of temporary insanity. Perhaps to soothe her feelings, Lincoln decided to hold seances in the White House. It is not known whether the results were positive or not, but Willie's ghost has also been seen in the White House. During Grant's administration, according to Arthur Krock, a boy whom they recognized as the apparition of little Willie "materialized" before the eyes of some of his household.

The medium Lincoln most frequently used was one Nettie Colburn Maynard, and allegedly the spirit of Daniel Webster communicated with him through her. On that occasion, it is said, he was urged to proclaim the emancipation of the slaves. That proclamation, as everybody knows, became

Lincoln's greatest political achievement. What is less known is the fact that it also laid the foundation for later dissension among his Cabinet members and that, as we shall see, it may indirectly have caused his premature death. Before going into this, however, let us make clear that on the whole Lincoln apparently did not need any mediums, for he himself had the gift of clairvoyance, and this talent stayed with him all his life. One of the more remarkable premonitory experiences is reported by Philip Van Doren Sterm in *The Man Who Killed Lincoln*, and also in most other sources dealing with Lincoln.

It happened in Springfield in 1860, just after Lincoln had been elected. As he was looking at himself in a mirror, he suddenly saw a double image of himself. One, real and life-like, and an etheric double, pale and shadowy. He was convinced that it meant he would get through his first term safely, but would die before the end of the second. Today, psychic researchers would explain Lincoln's mirror experience in less fanciful terms. What the President saw was a brief "out-of-the-body experience," or astral projection, which is not an uncommon psychic experience. It merely means that the bonds between conscious mind and the unconscious are temporarily loosened and that the inner or true self has quickly slipped out. Usually, these experiences take place in the dream state, but there are cases on record where the phenomenon occurs while awake.

The President's *interpretation* of the experience is of course another matter; here we have a second phenomenon come into play, that of divination; in his peculiar interpretation of his experience, he showed a degree of precognition, and future events, unfortunately, proved him to be correct.

This was not, by far, the only recorded dream experienced in Lincoln's life. He put serious stock in dreams and often liked to interpret them. William Herndon, Lincoln's onetime law partner and biographer, said of him that he always contended he was doomed to a sad fate, and quotes the President as saying many times, "I am sure I shall meet with some terrible end."

It is interesting to note also that Lincoln's fatalism made him often refer to Brutus and Caesar, explaining the events of Caesar's assassination as caused by laws over which neither had any control; years later, Lincoln's murderer, John Wilkes Booth, also thought of himself as the new Brutus slaying the American Caesar because destiny had singled him out for the deed!

Certainly the most widely quoted psychic experience of Abraham Lincoln was a strange dream he had a few days before his death. When his strangely thoughtful mien gave Mrs. Lincoln cause to worry, he finally admitted that he had been disturbed by an unusually detailed dream. Urged, over dinner, to confide his dream, he did so in the presence of Ward Hill Lamon, close friend and social secretary as well as a kind of bodyguard. Lamon wrote it down immediately afterward, and it is contained in his biography of Lincoln: "About ten days ago," the President began, "I retired very late. I had been up waiting for important dispatches from the front. I could not have been long in bed when I fell into a slumber, for I was weary. I soon began to dream. There seemed to be a death-like stillness about me. Then I heard subdued sobs, as if a number of people were weeping. I thought I left my bed and wandered downstairs. There the silence was broken by the same pitiful sobbing, but the mourners were invisible. I went from room to room; no living person was in sight, but the same mournful sounds of distress met me as I passed along. It was light in all the rooms; every object was familiar to me; but where were all the people who were grieving as if their hearts would break? I was puzzled and alarmed. What could be the meaning of all this? Determined to find the cause of a state of things so mysterious and so shocking, I kept on until I arrived at the East Room, which I entered.

"There I met with a sickening surprise. Before me was a catafalque, on which rested a corpse wrapped in funeral vestments. Around it were stationed soldiers who were acting as guards; and there was a throng of people, some gazing mournfully upon the corpse, whose face was covered, others weeping pitifully.

"Who is dead in the White House?" I demanded of one of the soldiers. 'The President,' was his answer; 'he was killed by an assassin!' Then there came a loud burst of grief from the crowd, which awoke me from my dream. I slept no more that night. . . ."

Lincoln always knew he was a marked man, not only because of his own psychic hunches, but objectively, for he kept a sizable envelope in his desk containing all the threatening letters he had received. That envelope was simply marked "Assassination," and the matter did not frighten him. A man in his position is always in danger, he would argue, although the Civil War and the larger question of what to do with the South after victory had split the country into two factions, making the President's position even more vulnerable. Lincoln therefore did not take his elaborate dream warning seriously, or at any rate, he pretended not to. When his friends remonstrated with him, asking him to take extra precautions, he shrugged off their warnings with the lighthearted remark, "Why, it wasn't me on that catafalque. It was some other fellow!"

But the face of the corpse had been covered in his dream and he really was whistling in the dark.

Had Fate wanted to prevent the tragedy and give him warning to avoid it?

Had an even higher order of things decided that he was to ignore that warning?

Lincoln had often had a certain recurrent dream in which he saw himself on a strange ship, moving with great speed toward an indefinite shore. The dream had always preceded some unusual event. In effect, he had dreamed it precisely in the same way preceding the events at Fort Sumter, the Battles of Bull Run, Antietam, Gettysburg, Stone River, Vicksburg, and Wilmington. Now he had just dreamed it again on the eve of his death. This was the thirteenth of April 1865, and Lincoln spoke of his recurrent dream in unusually optimistic tones. To him it was an indication of impending good news. That news, he felt, would be word from General Sherman that hostilities had ceased. There was a Cabinet meeting scheduled for April 14 and Lincoln hoped the news would come in time for it. It never occurred to him that the important news hinted at by this dream was his own demise that very evening, and that the strange vessel carrying him to a distant shore was Charon's boat ferrying him across the Styx into the nonphysical world.

But had he really crossed over?

Rumors of a ghostly President in the White House kept circulating. They were promptly denied by the government, as would be expected. President Theodore Roosevelt, according to Bess Furman in *White House Profile*, often fancied that he felt Lincoln's spirit, and during the administration of Franklin D. Roosevelt, in the 1930s, a girl secretary saw the figure of Abraham Lincoln in his onetime bedroom. The ghost was seated on the bed, pulling on his boots, as if he were in a hurry to go somewhere. This happened in mid-afternoon. Eleanor Roosevelt had often felt Lincoln's presence and freely admitted it.

Now it had been the habit of the administration to put important visitors into what was formerly Lincoln's bedroom. This was not done out of mischief, but merely because the Lincoln room was among the most impressive rooms the White House contained. We have no record of all those who slept there and had eerie experiences, for people, especially politically highly placed people, don't talk about such things as ghosts.

Yet, the late Queen Wilhelmina did mention the constant knockings at her door followed by footsteps—only to find the corridor outside deserted. And Margaret Truman, who also slept in that area of the White House often heard knocking at her bedroom door at 3 A.M. Whenever she checked, there was nobody there. Her father, President Truman, a skeptic, decided that the noises had to be due to "natural" causes, such as the dangerous settling of the floors. He ordered the White House completely rebuilt, and perhaps this was a good thing: It would surely have collapsed soon after, according to the architect, General Edgerton. Thus, if nothing else, the ghostly knockings had led to a survey of the structure and subsequent rebuilding. Or was that the reason for the knocks? Had Lincoln tried to warn the later occupants that the house was about to fall down around their ears?

Not only Lincoln's bedroom, but other old areas of the White House are evidently haunted. There is, first of all, the famous East Room, where the lying in state took place. By a strange quirk of fate, President Kennedy also was placed there after his assassination. Lynda Bird Johnson's room happened to be the room in which Willie Lincoln died, and later on, Truman's mother. It was also the room used by the doctors to perform the autopsy on Abraham Lincoln. It is therefore not too surprising that President Johnson's daughter did not sleep too well in the room. She heard footsteps at night, and the phone would ring and no one would be on the other end. An exasperated White House telephone operator would come on again and again, explaining she did not ring her!

But if Abraham Lincoln's ghost roams the White House because of unfinished business, it is apparently a ghost free to do other things as well, something the average specter can't do, since it is tied only to the place of its untimely demise.

Mrs. Lincoln lived on for many more years, but ultimately turned senile and died not in her right mind at the home of her sister. Long before she became unbalanced, however, she journeyed to Boston in a continuing search for some proof of her late husband's survival of bodily death. This was in the 1880s, and word had reached her that a certain photographer named William Mumler had been able to obtain the likenesses of dead people on his photographic plates under strict test conditions. She decided to try this man, fully aware that fraud might be attempted if she were recognized. Heavily veiled in mourning clothes, she sat down along with other visitors in Mumler's experimental study. She gave the name of Mrs. Tyndall; all Mumler could see was a widow in heavy veils. Mumler then proceeded to take pictures of all those present in the room. When they were developed, there was one of "Mrs. Tyndall." In back of her appears a semi-solid figure of Abraham Lincoln, with his hands resting upon the shoulders of his widow, and an expression of great compassion on his face. Next to Lincoln was the figure of their son Willie, who had died so young in the White House. Mumler showed his prints to the assembled group, and before Mrs. Lincoln could claim her print, another woman in the group exclaimed, "Why, that looks like President Lincoln!" Then Mrs. Lincoln identified herself for the first time.

There is, by the way, no photograph in existence showing Lincoln with his son in the manner in which they appeared on the psychic photograph.

Another photographic likeness of Lincoln was obtained in 1937 in an experiment commemorating the President's one-hundredth birthday. This took place at Cassadaga, Florida, with Horace Hambling as the psychic intermediary, whose mere *presence* would make such a phenomenon possible.

Ralph Pressing, editor of the *Psychic Observer*, was to supply and guard the roll of film to be used, and the exposures were made in dim light inside a seance room. The roll of film was then handed to a local photographer for developing, without telling him anything. Imagine the man's surprise when he found a clearly defined portrait of Abraham Lincoln, along with four other, smaller faces, superimposed on the otherwise black negative.

I myself was present at an experiment in San Francisco, when a reputable physician by the name of Andrew von Salza demonstrated his amazing gift of psychic photography, using a Polaroid camera. This was in the fall of 1966, and several other people witnessed the proceedings, which I have reported in my book *Psychic Photography—Threshold of a New Science*?

After I examined the camera, lens, film, and premises carefully, Dr. von Salza took a number of pictures with the Polaroid camera. On many of them there appeared various "extras," or faces of people superimposed in a manner excluding fraud or double exposure completely. The most interesting of these psychic impressions was a picture showing the face of President Lincoln, with President Kennedy next to him!

Had the two men, who had suffered in so many similar ways, found a bond between them in the non-physical world? The amazing picture followed one on which President Kennedy's face appeared alone, accompanied by the word "War" written in white ectoplasm. Was this their way to warn us to "mend our ways"?

Whatever the meaning, I am sure of one thing: The phenomenon itself, the experiment, was genuine and in no way the result of deceit, accident, self-delusion, or hallucination. I have published both pictures for all to see.

There are dozens of good books dealing with the tragedy of Abraham Lincoln's reign and untimely death. And yet I had always felt that the story had not been told fully. This conviction was not only due to the reported appearances of Lincoln's ghost, indicating restlessness and unfinished business, but also to my objective historical training that somehow led me to reject the solutions given of the plot in very much the same way many serious people today refuse to accept the findings of the Warren Commission as final in the case of President Kennedy's death. But where to begin?

Surely, if Lincoln had been seen at the White House in recent years, that would be the place to start. True, he was shot at Ford's Theatre and actually died in the Parker House across the street. But the White House was his home. Ghosts often occur where the "emotional center" of the person was, while in the body, even though actual death might have occurred elsewhere. A case in point is Alexander Hamilton, whose shade has been observed in what was once his personal physician's house; it was there that he spent his final day on earth, and his unsuccessful struggle to cling to life made it his "emotional center" rather than the spot in New Jersey where he received the fatal wound.

Even though there might be imprints of the great tragedy at both Ford's Theatre and the Parker House, Lincoln himself would not, in my estimation, "hang around" there!

My request for a quiet investigation in the White House went back to 1963 when Pierre Salinger was still in charge and John F. Kennedy was President. I never got an answer, and in March 1965 I tried again. This time, Bess Abell, social secretary to Mrs. Johnson, turned me down "for security reasons." Patiently, I wrote back explaining I merely wanted to spend a half hour or so with a psychic, probably Mrs. Leek, in two rarely used areas: Lincoln's bedroom and the East Room. Bess Abell had referred to White House policy of not allowing visitors to the President's "private living quarters." I pointed out that the President, to my knowledge, did not spend his nights in Lincoln's bedroom, nor was the East Room anything but part of the ceremonial or official government rooms and hardly "private living quarters," especially as tourists are taken through it every hour or so. As for security, why, I would gladly submit anything I wrote about my studies for their approval.

Back came another pensive missive from Bess Abell. The President and Mrs. Johnson's "restrictive schedules" would not permit my visit.

I offered, in return, to come at any time, day or night, when the Johnsons were out of town.

The answer was still no, and I began to wonder if it was merely a question of not wanting anything to do with ESP?

But a good researcher never gives up hope. I subsequently asked Senator Jacob Javits to help me get into the White House, but even he couldn't get me in. Through a local friend I met James Ketchum, the curator of the State rooms. Would he give me a privately conducted tour exactly like the regular tourist tour, except minus tourists to distract us?

The answer remained negative.

On March 6, 1967, Bess Abell again informed me that the only individuals eligible for admission to the two rooms I wanted to see were people invited for State visits and close personal friends. On either count, that left us out.

I asked Elizabeth Carpenter, whom I knew to be favorably inclined toward ESP, to intervene. As press secretary to Mrs. Johnson, I thought she might be able to give me a less contrived excuse, at the very least. "An impossible precedent," she explained, if I were to be allowed in. I refused to take the tourist tour, of course, as it would be a waste of my time, and dropped the matter for the time being.

But I never lost interest in the case. To me, finding the missing link between what is officially known about Lincoln's murderer and the true extent of the plot was an important contribution to American history.

The events themselves immediately preceding and following that dark day in American history are known to most readers, but there are, perhaps, some details which only the specialist would be familiar with and which will be found to have significance later in my investigation. I think it therefore useful to mention these events here, although they were not known to me at the time I undertook my psychic investigation. I try to keep my unconscious mind free of all knowledge so that no one may accuse my psychics of "reading my mind," or suggest similar explanations for what transpires. Only at the end of this amazing case did I go through the contemporary record of the assassination.

The War between the States had been going on for four years, and the South was finally losing. This was obvious even to diehard Confederates, and everybody wanted only one thing: to get it over with as quickly as possible and resume a normal life once again.

While the South was, by and large, displaying apathy, there were still some fanatics who thought they could change the course of events by some miracle. In the North, it was a question of freeing the slaves and restoring the Union. In the South, it was not only a question of maintaining the economic system they had come to consider the only feasible one, but also one of maintaining the feudal, largely rural system their ancestors had known in Europe and which was being endangered by the industrialized North with its intellectuals, labor forces, and new values. To save the South from such a fate seemed a noble cause to a handful of fanatics, among them also John Wilkes Booth, the man who was to play so fateful a role. Ironically, he was not even a true Southerner, but a man born on the fringe of the South, in Maryland, and his family, without exception, considered itself to be of the North.

John Wilkes Booth was, of course, the lesser known of the Booth brothers and scions of a family celebrated in the theater of their age, and when Edwin Booth, "the Prince of Players," learned of the terrible crime his younger brother had committed, he was genuinely shocked, and immediately made clear his position as a longtime supporter of Abraham Lincoln.

But John Wilkes Booth did not care whether his people were with him or not. Still in his early twenties, he was not only politically immature but also romantically inspired. He could not understand the economic changes that were sure to take place and which no bullet could stop.

And so, while the War between the States was drawing to a close, Booth decided to become the savior of his adopted Dixie, and surrounded himself with a small and motley band of helpers who had their secret meetings at Mrs. Mary Surratt's boarding house in Washington.

At first, they were discussing a plot to abduct President Lincoln and to deliver him to his foes at the Confederate capitol in Richmond, but the plot never came into being. Richmond fell to the Yankees, and time ran out for the cause of the Confederacy. As the days crept by and Booth's fervor to "do something drastic" for his cause increased, the young actor started thinking in terms of killing the man whom he blamed for his country's defeat. To Booth, Lincoln was the center of all he hated, and he believed that once the man was removed all would be well.

Such reasoning, of course, is the reasoning of a demented mind. Had Booth really been an astute politician, he would have realized that Lincoln was a moderate compared to some members of his Cabinet, that the President was indeed, as some Southern leaders put it when news of the murder reached them, "the best friend the South ever had."

Had he appraised the situation in Washington correctly, he would have realized that any man taking the place of Abraham Lincoln was bound to be far worse for Southern aspirations than Lincoln, who had deeply regretted the war and its hardships and who was eager to receive the seceded states back into the Union fold with as little punishment as possible.

Not so the war party, principally Stanton, the Secretary of War, and Seward, the Secretary of State. Theirs was a harsher outlook, and history later proved them to be the winners—but also the cause for long years of continuing conflict between North and South, conflict and resentment that could have been avoided had Lincoln's conciliatory policies been allowed to prevail.

The principal fellow conspirators against Lincoln were an ex-Confederate soldier named Lewis Paine; David Herold, a druggist's clerk who could not hold a job; George Atzerodt, a German-born carriage maker; Samuel Arnold, a clerk; Mrs. Mary Surratt, the Washington boarding house keeper at whose house they met; and finally, and importantly, John Harrison Surratt, her son, by profession a Confederate spy and courier. At the time of the final conspiracy Booth was only twenty-six, Surratt twenty-one, and Herold twenty-three, which perhaps accounts for the utter folly of their actions.

The only one, besides Booth, who had any qualities of leadership was young Surratt. His main job at the time was traveling between Washington and Montreal as a secret courier for the Washington agents of the Confederacy and the Montreal, Canada headquarters of the rebels. Originally a clerk with the Adams Express Company, young Surratt had excellent connections in communications and was well-known in Washington government circles, although his undercover activities were not.

When Booth had convinced Surratt that the only way to help the Confederacy was to murder the President, they joined forces. Surratt had reservations about this course, and Mrs. Surratt certainly wanted no part of violence or murder. But they were both swept up in the course of events that followed.

Unfortunately, they had not paid enough attention to the presence in the Surratt boarding house on H Street of a young War Department clerk named Louis Weichmann. Originally intending to become a priest, young Weichmann was a witness to much of the coming and going of the conspirators, and despite his friendship with John Surratt, which had originally brought him to the Surratt boarding house, he eventually turned against the Surratts. It was his testimony at Mrs. Surratt's trial that ultimately led to her hanging.

Originally, Mrs. Surratt had owned a tavern in a small town thirteen miles south of Washington then called Surrattsville and later, for obvious reasons, renamed Clinton, Maryland. When business at the tavern fell off, she leased it to an innkeeper named John Lloyd, and moved to Washington, where she opened a boarding house on H Street, between Sixth and Seventh Streets, where the house still stands.

Booth himself was to shoot the President. And when he discovered that the Lincolns would be in the State box at Ford's Theatre, Washington, on the evening of April 14, 1865, it was decided to do it there. Surratt was to try to "fix the wires" so that the telegraph would not work during the time following the assassination. He had the right connections, and he knew he could do it. In addition, he was to follow General Grant on a train that was to take the general and his wife to New Jersey. Lewis Paine was to kill Secretary Seward at the same time.

Booth had carefully surveyed the theater beforehand, making excellent use of the fact that as an actor he was known and respected there. This also made it quite easy to get inside at the strategic moment. The play on stage was "Our American Cousin" starring Laura Keene. Booth's plans were furthermore helped by a stroke of luck—or fate, if you prefer, namely, one of the men who was supposed to guard the President's box was momentarily absent from his post.

Lincoln lived through the night but never regained consciousness. He expired in the Parker House across the street, where he had been brought. Booth caught his heel on an American flag that adorned the stage box, and fell, breaking his leg in the process. Despite intense pain, he managed to escape in the confusion and jump on the horse he had prepared outside.

When he got to the Navy Yard bridge crossing the Anacostia River, the sentry on this road leading to the South stopped him. What was he doing out on the road that late? In wartime Washington, all important exits from the city were controlled. But Booth merely told the man his name and that he lived in Charles County. He was let through, despite the fact that a nine o'clock curfew was being rigidly enforced at that moment. Many later historians have found this incident odd, and have darkly pointed to a conspiracy: It may well be that Surratt did arrange for the easy passage, as they had all along planned to use the road over the Anacostia River bridge to make good their escape.

A little later, Booth was joined on the road by David Herold. Together they rode out to the Surratt tavern, where they arrived around midnight. The purpose of their visit there at that moment became clear to me only much later. The tavern had of course been a meeting place for Booth and Surratt and the others before Mrs. Surratt moved her establishment to Washington. Shortly after, the two men rode onward and entered the last leg of their journey. After a harrowing escape interrupted by temporary stays at Dr. Mudd's office at Bryantown—where Booth had his leg looked after—and various attempts to cross the Potomac, the two men holed up at Garrett's farm near Port Royal, Virginia. It was there that they were hunted down like mad dogs by the Federal forces. Twelve days after Lincoln's murder, on April 26, 1865, Booth was shot down. Even that latter fact is not certain: Had he committed suicide when he saw no way out of Garrett's burning barn, with soldiers all around it? Or had the avenger's bullet of Sergeant Boston Corbett found its mark, as the soldier had claimed?

It is not my intent here to go into the details of the flight and capture, as these events are amply told elsewhere. The mystery is not so much Booth's crime and punishment, about which there is no doubt, but the question of who *really* plotted Lincoln's death. The State funeral was hardly over when all sorts of rumors and legends concerning the plot started to spring up.

Mrs. Surratt was arrested immediately, and she, Paine, Atzerodt, and Herold were hanged after a trial marked by prejudice and the withholding of vital information, such as Booth's own diary, which the Secretary of War had ordered confiscated and which was never entered as an exhibit at the trial. This, along with the fact that Stanton was at odds politically with Lincoln, gave rise to various speculations, concerning Stanton's involvement in the plot. Then, too, there was the question of the role John Surratt had played, so much of it covered by secrecy, like an iceberg with only a small portion showing above the surface!

After he had escaped from the United States and gone to Europe and then to Egypt, he was ultimately captured and extradited to stand trial in 1867. But a jury of four Northerners and eight Southerners allowed him to go free, when they could not agree on a verdict of guilty. Surratt moved to Baltimore, where he went into business and died in 1916. Very little is known of his activities beyond these bare facts. The lesser conspirators, those who merely helped the murderer escape, were convicted and sentenced to heavy prison terms.

There was some to-do about Booth's body also. After it had been identified by a number of people who knew him in life, it was buried under the stone floor of the Arsenal Prison in Washington, the same prison where the four other conspirators had been executed. But in 1867, the prison was torn down and the five bodies exhumed. One of them, presumed to be Booth's, was interred in the family plot in Greenmount Cemetery, Baltimore. Yet a rumor arose, and never ceased, that actually someone else lay in Booth's grave and, though most historians refuse to take this seriously, according to Philip Van Doren Stern, "the question of whether or not the man who died at Garrett's Farm was John Wilkes Booth is one that doubtless will never be settled."

No accounts of any psychic nature concerning Booth have been reported to date, and Booth's ghost does not walk the corridors of Ford's Theatre the way Lincoln's does in the White House. The spot where Garrett's farm used to stand is no longer as it was, and a new building has long replaced the old barn.

If I were to shed new light or uncover fresh evidence concerning the plot to kill Lincoln, I would have to go to a place having emotional ties to the event itself. But the constant refusal of the White House to permit me a short visit made it impossible for me to do so properly.

The questions that, to me, seemed in need of clarification concerned, first of all, the strange role John H. Surratt had played in the plot; secondly, was Booth really the one who initiated the murder, and was he really the leader of the plot? One notices the close parallel between this case and the assassination of President Kennedy.

As I began this investigation, my own feelings were that an involvement of War Secretary Stanton could be shown and that there probably was a northern plot to kill Lincoln as well as a southern desire to get rid of him. But that was pure speculation on my part, and I had as yet nothing to back up my contention. Then fate played a letter into my hands, out of left field, so to speak, that gave me new hope for a solution to this exciting case.

A young girl by the name of Phyllis Amos, of Washington, Pennsylvania, had seen me on a television show in the fall of 1967. She contacted me by letter, and as a consequence I organized an expedition to the Surratt tavern, the same tavern that had served as home to Mrs. Mary Surratt and as a focal point of the Lincoln conspiracy prior to the move to H Street in Washington.

Phyllis's connection with the old tavern goes back to 1955. It was then occupied by a Mrs. Ella Curtain and by Phyllis's family, who shared the house with this elderly lady. Mrs. Curtain's brother, B. K. Miller, a prosperous supermarket owner nearby, was the actual owner of the house, but he let his sister live there. Since it was a large house, they subleased to the Amos family, which then consisted of Mr. and Mrs. Amos and their two girls, about two years apart in age.

Phyllis, who is now in her twenties, occupied a room on the upper floor; across the narrow hall from her room was Ella Curtain's room—once the room where John Wilkes Booth had hidden his guns. To the right of Phyllis's bedroom and a few steps down was a large room where the conspirators met regularly. It was shielded from the curious by a small anteroom through which one would have to go to reach the meeting room. Downstairs were the parents' room and a large reception room. The house stood almost directly on the road, surrounded by dark green trees. A forlorn metal sign farther back was the sole indication that this was considered a historical landmark: If you didn't know the sign was there, you wouldn't find it unless you were driving by at a very slow speed.

Mrs. Amos never felt comfortable in the house from the moment they moved in, and after eight months of occupancy the Amos family left. But during those eight months they experienced some pretty strange things. One day she was alone in the house when it suddenly struck her that someone was watching her intently. Terrified, she ran to her bedroom and locked the door, not coming out until her husband returned. The smaller of the two girls kept asking her mother who the strange men were she saw sitting on the back stairs. She would hear them talk in whispers up there.

The other occupant of the house, Mrs. Curtain, was certainly not a steadying influence on them. On one occasion she saw the figure of a woman "float" down the front steps. That woman, she felt sure, was Mary Surratt. The house had of course been Mary Surratt's true home, her only safe harbor. The one she later owned in Washington was merely a temporary and unsafe abode. Mightn't she have been drawn back here after her unjust execution to seek justice, or at the very least be among surroundings she was familiar with?

The floating woman returned several times more, and ultimately young Phyllis was to have an experience herself. It was in April of 1955 and she was in bed in her room, wide awake. Her bed stood parallel to the room where the conspirators used to meet, separated from it only by a thin wall, so that she might have heard them talk had she been present at the time. Suddenly, she received several blows on the side of her face. They were so heavy that they brought tears to her eyes. Were the ghosts of the conspirators trying to discourage her from eavesdropping on their plans?

Both Phyllis and her mother have had ESP experiences all their lives, ranging from premonitions to true dreams and other forms of precognition.

I decided to contact the present owner and ask for permission to visit with a good medium. Thomas Miller, whose parents had owned the Surratt tavern and who now managed it prior to having it restored, at great cost, to the condition it was in a hundred years ago, readily assented. So it was that on a very chilly day in November of 1967, Sybil Leek and I flew down to Washington for a look at the ghosts around John Wilkes Booth: If I couldn't interview the victim, Lincoln, perhaps I could have a go at the murderer?

A friend, Countess Gertrude d'Amecourt, volunteered to drive us to Clinton. The directions the Millers had given us were not too clear, so it took us twice as long as it should have to get there. I think we must have taken the wrong turn off the highway at least six times and in the end got to know them all well, but got no nearer to Clinton. Finally we were stopped by a little old Negro woman who wanted to hitch a ride with us. Since she was going in the same direction, we let her come with us, and thanks to her we eventually found Miller's supermarket, about two hours later than planned. But ghosts are not in a hurry, even though Gertrude had to get back to her real estate office, and within minutes we set out on foot to the old Surratt tavern, located only a few blocks away from the supermarket. Phyllis Amos had come down from Pennsylvania to join us, and as the wind blew harder and harder and our teeth began to chatter louder and louder in the unseasonable chill of the late afternoon, we pushed open the dusty, padlocked door of the tavern, and our adventure into the past began.

Before I had a chance to ask Sybil Leek to wait until I could put my tape recording equipment into operating condition, she had dashed past us and was up the stairs as if she knew where she was headed. She didn't, of course, for she had no idea why she had been brought here or indeed where she was. All of us—the Millers, Phyllis, Gertrude d'Amecourt, and myself—ran up the stairs after Sybil. We found her staring at the floor in what used to be the John Wilkes Booth bedroom. Staring at the hole in the floor where the guns had been hidden, she mumbled something about things being hidden there . . . not budging from the spot. Thomas Miller, who had maintained a smug, skeptical attitude about the whole investigation until now, shook his head and mumbled, "But how would she know?"

It was getting pretty dark now and there was no electric light in the house. The smells were pretty horrible, too, as the house had been empty for years, with neighborhood hoodlums and drunks using it for "parties" or to sleep off drunken sprees. There is always a broken back window in those old houses, and they manage to get in.

We were surrounding Sybil now and shivering in unison. "This place is different from the rest of the house," Sybil explained, "cold, dismal atmosphere . . . this is where something happened."

"What sort of thing do you think happened here?"

"A chase."

How right she was! The two hunted men were indeed on a chase from Washington, trying to escape to the South. But again, Sybil would not know this consciously.

"This is where someone was a fugitive," she continued now, "for several days, but he left this house and went to the woodland."

Booth hiding out in the woods for several days after passing the tavern!

"Who is the man?" I asked, for I was not at all sure who she was referring to. There were several men connected with "the chase," and for all we knew, it could have been a total stranger somehow tied up with the tavern. Lots of dramatic happenings attach themselves to old taverns, which were far cries from Hilton hotels. People got killed or waylaid in those days, and taverns, on the whole, had sordid reputations. The good people stayed at each other's homes when traveling.

"Foreign . . . can't get the name . . . hiding for several days here . . . then there is . . . a brother . . . it is very confusing."

The foreigner might well have been Atzerodt, who was indeed hiding at the tavern at various times. And the brother?

"A man died suddenly, violently," Sybil took up the impressions she seemed to be getting now with more depth. We were still standing around in the upstairs room, near the window, with the gaping hole in the floor.

"How did he die?" I inquired.

"Trapped in the woods . . . hiding from soldiers, I think."

That would only fit Booth. He was trapped in the woods and killed by soldiers.

"Why?"

"They were chasing him . . . he killed someone."

"Whom did he kill?"

"I don't know . . . birthday . . . ran away to hide . . . I see a paper . . . invitation . . . there is another place we have to go to, a big place . . . a big building with a gallery. . . ."

Was she perhaps describing Ford's Theatre now?

"Whose place is it?" I asked.

Sybil was falling more and more under the spell of the place, and her consciousness bordered now on the trance state.

"No one's place . . . to see people . . . I'm confused . . . lot of people to go there . . . watching . . . a gathering . . . with music . . . I'm not going there!"

"Who is there?" I interjected. She must be referring to the theater, all right. Evidently what Sybil was getting here was the entire story, but jumbled as psychic impressions often are, they do not obey the ordinary laws of time and space.

"My brother and I," she said now. I had gently led her toward another corner of the large room where a small chair stood, in the hope of having her sit in it. But she was already too deeply entranced to do it, so I let her lean toward the chair, keeping careful watch so she would not topple over.

"My brother is mad . . . ," she said now, and her voice was no longer the same, but had taken on a harder, metallic sound. I later wondered about this remark: Was this Edwin Booth, talking about his renegade brother John, who was indeed considered mad by many of his contemporaries? Edwin Booth frequently appeared at Ford's Theatre, and so did John Wilkes Booth.

"Why is he mad?" I said. I decided to continue the questioning as if I were agreeing with all she—or he—was saying, in order to elicit more information.

"Madman in the family . . . ," Sybil said now, "killed—a—friend. . . ."

"Whom did he kill?"

"No names . . . he was mad. . . ."

"Would I know the person he killed?"

"Everybody—knows. . . ."

"What is your brother's name?"

"John."

"What is *your* name?"

"Rory."

At first it occurred to me this might be the name of a character Edwin Booth had played on the stage and he was hiding behind it, if indeed it *was* Edwin Booth who was giving Sybil this information. But I have not found such a character in the biographies of Edwin Booth. I decided to press further by reiterating my original question.

"Who did John kill?"

An impatient, almost impertinent voice replied, "I won't tell you. You can read!"

"What are you doing in this house?"

"Helping John . . . escape . . . ."

"Are you alone?"

"No . . . Trevor. . . ."

"How many of you are there here?"

"Four."

"Who are the others?"

"Traitors. . . ."

"But what are their names?"

"Trevor . . . Michael . . . John. . . ."

These names caused me some concern afterward: I could identify Michael readily enough as Michael O'Laughlin, school chum of Booth, who worked as a livery stable worker in Baltimore before he joined forces with his friend. Michael O'Laughlin was one of the conspirators who was eventually sentenced to life imprisonment. But on Stanton's orders he and the other three "lesser" conspirators were sent to the Dry Tortugas, America's own version of Devil's Island, off Florida, and it was there that Michael O'Laughlin died of yellow fever in 1868.

John? Since the communicator had referred to his brother's name as John, I could only surmise this to mean John Wilkes Booth. But Trevor I could not identify. The only conspirator whose middle name we did not know was Samuel Arnold, also an ex-classmate of Booth. Was Trevor perhaps the familiar name by which the conspirators referred to this Maryland farmhand and Confederate deserter?

I pressed the point further with Sybil.

"Who is in the house?"

"Go away. . . ."

I explained my mission: To help them all find peace of mind, freedom, deliverance.

"I'm going to the city. . . ," the communicator said.

"Which city?"

"The big city."

"Why?"

"To stop him . . . he's mad . . . take him away . . . to the country to rest . . . help him . . . give him rest. . . ."

"Has he done anything wrong?"

"He . . . he's my brother!"

"Did he kill anyone?"

"Killed that man. . . ."

"Why did he kill him?"

Shouting at me, the entranced medium said, "He was unjust!"

"He was unjust toward the Irish people."

Strange words, I thought. Only Michael O'Laughlin could be considered a "professional" Irishman among the conspirators, and one could scarcely accuse Lincoln of having mistreated the Irish.

"What did he do?" I demanded to know.

"He did nothing. . . ."

"Why did he kill him then?"

"He was mad."

"Do you approve of it?"

"Yes! He did not like him because he was unjust . . . the law was wrong . . . his laws were wrong . . . free people . . . he was confused. . . ."

Now if this were indeed Edwin Booth's spirit talking, he would most certainly not have approved of the murder. The resentment for the sake of the Irish minority could only have come from Michael O'Laughlin. But the entity kept referring to his brother, and only Edwin Booth had a brother named John connected with this house and story! The trance session grew more and more confusing.

"Who else was in this?" I started again. Perhaps we could get more information on the people *behind* the plot. After all, we already knew the actual murderer and his accomplices.

"Trevor . . . four. . . ."

"Did you get an order from someone to do this?"

There was a long pause as the fully entranced psychic kept swaying a little, with eyes closed, in front of the rickety old chair.

I explained again why I had come, but it did not help. "I don't believe you," the entity said in great agitation, "traitors. . . ."

"You've long been forgiven," I said. "But you must speak freely about it now. What happened to the man he killed?"

This was followed by bitter laughter.

"What sort of work did your brother do?"

"Writing . . . acting. . . ."

"Where did he act?"

"Go away . . . don't search for me. . . ."

"I want to help you."

"Traitor . . . shot like a dog . . . the madman. . . ."

Sybil's face trembled now as tears streamed freely from her eyes. Evidently she was reliving the final moments of Booth's agony. I tried to calm the communicator.

"Go away . . . ," the answer came, "go away!"

But I continued the questioning. "Did anyone put him up to the deed?"

"He was mad," the entity explained, a little calmer now.

"But who is guilty?"

"The Army."

"Who in the Army?"

"He was wild . . . met people . . . they said they were Army people . . . Major General . . . Gee . . . I ought to go now!!"

Several things struck me when I went over this conversation afterward. To begin with, the communicator felt he had said too much as soon as he had mentioned the person of Major General Gee, or G., and wanted to leave. Why? Was this something he should have kept secret?

Major General G.? Could this refer to Grant? Up to March 1864 Grant was indeed a major general; after that time Lincoln raised him to the rank of lieutenant general. The thought seemed monstrous on the face of it, that Grant could in any way be involved with a plot against Lincoln. Politically, this seemed unlikely, because both Grant and Lincoln favored the moderate treatment of the conquered South as against the radicals, who demanded stern measures. Stanton was a leading radical, and if anyone he would have had a reason to plot against Lincoln. And yet, by all appearances, he served him loyally and well. But Grant had political aspirations of a personal nature, and he succeeded Lincoln after Johnson's unhappy administration.

I decided to pursue my line of questioning further to see where it might lead.

I asked Sybil's controlling entity to repeat the name of this Army general. Faintly but clear enough it came from her entranced lips

"Gee . . . G-E-E . . . Major General Robert Gee."

Then it wasn't Grant, I thought. But who in blazes was it? If there existed such a person I could find a record, but what if it was merely a cover name?

"Did you see this man yourself?"

"No."

"Then did your brother tell you about him?"

"Yes."

"Where did they meet?"

Hesitatingly, the reply came.

"In the city. This city. In a club. . . ."

I decided to change my approach.

"What year is this?" I shot at him.

"Forty-nine."

"What does forty-nine mean to you?"

"Forty-nine means something important. . . ."

"How old are you now?"

"Thirty-four."

He then claimed to have been born in Lowell, Virginia, and I found myself as puzzled as ever: It did not fit Edwin, who was born in 1833 on the Booth homestead at Belair, Maryland. Confusion over confusion!

"Did anyone else but the four of you come here?" I finally asked.

"Yes . . . Major . . . Robert Gee. . . ."

"What did he want?"

"Bribery."

"What did he pay?"

"I don't know."

"Did he give him any money?"

"Yes."

"What was he supposed to do?"

"Cause a disturbance. In the gallery. Then plans would be put into operation. To hold up the law."

"Did your brother do what he was supposed to do?"

"He was mad . . . he killed him."

"Then who was guilty?"

"Gee . . ."

"Who sent Gee? For whom did he speak?"

We were getting close to the heart of the matter and the others were grouping themselves closely around us, the better to hear. It was quite dark outside and the chill of the late November afternoon crept into our bones with the result that we started to tremble with the wet cold. But nobody moved or showed impatience. American history was being relived, and what did a little chill matter in comparison?

"He surveyed . . ."

"Who worked with him?"

"The government."

"Who specifically?"

"I don't know."

It did not sound convincing. Was he still holding out on us?

"Were there others involved? Other men? Other women?"

A derisive laughter broke the stillness. "Jealous . . . jealousy . . . his wife. . . ."

"Whose wife?"

"The one who was killed . . . shot."

It is a historical fact that Mrs. Lincoln was extremely jealous and, according to Carl Sandburg, perhaps the most famous Lincoln biographer, never permitted her husband to see a woman alone—for any reason whatever. The Lincolns had frequent spats for that reason, and jealousy was a key characteristic of the President's wife.

"Why are we in this room?" I demanded.

"Waiting for . . . what am I waiting for?" the communicator said, in a voice filled with despair.

"I'd like to know that myself," I nodded. "Is there anything of interest for you here?"

"Yes . . . I have to stay here until John comes back."

"Where's John?"

"And what will you do when he comes back?"

"Take him to Lowell . . . my home."

"Whom do you live with there?"

"Julia . . . my girl . . . take him to rest there."

"Where is John now?"

"In the woods . . . hiding."

"Is anyone with him?"

"Two . . . they should be back soon."

Again the entity demanded to know why I was asking all those questions and again I reassured him that I was a friend. But I'd have to know everything in order to help him. Who then was this Mayor or Major General Gee?

"Wants control," the voice said. "I don't understand the Army . . . politics . . . he's altering the government. . . ."

"Altering the government?" I repeated. "On whose side is he?"

"Insurgent side."

"Is he in the U.S. Government?"

"My brother knows them . . . they hate the government."

"But who are they? What are their names?"

"They had numbers. Forty-nine. It means the area. The area they look after.

"Is anyone in the government involved with these insurgents?"

"John knows . . . John's dead . . . knew to much . . . the names . . . he wasn't all . . . he's mad!"

"Who killed him?"

"Soldier."

"Why did he kill him?" I was now referring to John Wilkes Booth and the killing of the presidential assassin by Sergeant Boston Corbett, allegedly because "God told him to," as the record states.

"Hunted him."

"But who gave the order to kill him?"

"The government."

"You say, he knew too much. What did he know?"

"I don't know the names, I know only I wait for John. John knows the names. He was clever."

"Was anyone in this government involved?"

"Traitors . . . in the *head of the Army* . . . Sher . . . must not tell you, John said not to speak. . . ."

"You must speak!" I commanded, almost shouting.

"Sherman . . . Colonel . . . he knows Sherman . . . Johns says to say nothing. . . ."

"Does Sherman know about it?"

"I don't know . . . I am not telling you any more . . ." he said, trembling again with tears. "Everybody asks questions . . . You are not helping me."

"I will try to help you if you don't hold back," I promised. "Who paid your brother?"

"Nothing . . . promised to escape . . . look after him . . . promised a ticket. . . ."

"How often did your brother see this officer?"

"Not too often. Here. John told me . . . some things. John said not to talk. He is not always mad."

"Who is the woman with him?" I tried to see if it would trick him into talking about others.

"She's a friend," the communicator said without hesitation.

"What is her name?"

"Harriett."

"Where does she live?"

"In the city."

"How does he know her?"

"He went to play there . . . he liked her. . . ."

Evidently this was some minor figure of no importance to the plot. I changed directions again. "You are free to leave here now. John wants you to go," I said slowly. After all, I could not let this poor soul whoever he was, hang on here for all eternity!

"Where are we?" he asked, sounding as confused as ever.

"A house. . . ."

"My house? . . . No, Melville's house. . . ."

"Who is Melville?"

"Friend of Gee. Told me to come here, wait for John."

"You are free to go, free!" I intoned.

"Free?" he said slowly, "Free country?"

"A hundred years have gone by. Do you understand me?"

"No."

The voice became weaker as if the entity were drifting away. Gradually Sybil's body seemed to collapse and I was ready to catch her, should she fall. But in time she "came back" to herself. Awakening, as if she had slept a long time, she looked around herself, as completely confused as the entity had been. She remembered absolutely nothing of the conversation between the ghost and myself.

For a moment none of us said anything. The silence was finally broken by Thomas Miller, who seemed visibly impressed with the entire investigation. He knew very well that the hole in the floor was a matter he was apt to point out to visitors to the house, and that no visitors had come here in a long time, as the house had been in disrepair for several years. How could this strange woman with the English accent whom he had never met before in his life, or for that matter, how could I, a man whom he only knew by correspondence, know about it? And how could she head straight for the spot in the semi-darkness of an unlit house? That was the wedge that opened the door to his acceptance of what he had witnessed just now.

"It's cold," Sybil murmured, and wrapped herself deeper into her black shawl. But she has always been a good sport, and did not complain. Patiently, she awaited further instructions from me. I decided it was time to introduce everybody formally now, as I had of course not done so on arrival in order to avoid Sybil's picking up any information or clues.

Phyllis Amos then showed us the spot where she had been hit by unseen hands, and pointed out the area where her younger sister Lynn, seven at the time and now nineteen, had heard the voices of a group of men whom she had also seen huddled together on the back stairs.

"I too thought I heard voices here," Phyllis Amos commented. "It sounded like the din of several voices but I couldn't make it out clearly."

I turned to Thomas Miller, who was bending down now toward the hole in the floor.

"This is where John Wilkes Booth hid his guns," he said, anticlimactically. "The innkeeper, Lloyd, also gave him some brandy, and then he rode on to where Dr. Mudd had his house, in Bryantown."

"You heard the conversation that came through my psychic friend, Mr. Miller," I said. "Do you care to comment on some of the names? For instance, did John Wilkes Booth have a brother along those lines?"

"My father bought this property from John Wilkes' brother," Miller said, "the brother who went to live in Baltimore after John Wilkes was killed; later he went to England."

That, of course, would be Edwin Booth, the "Prince of Players," who followed his sister Asia's advice to try his luck in the English theater.

I found this rather interesting. So Surratt's tavern had once belonged to Edwin Booth—finger of fate!

Mr. Miller pointed out something else of interest to me. While I had been changing tapes, during the interrogation of the communicator speaking through Sybil, I had missed a sentence or two. My question had been about the ones behind the killing.

"S-T- . . ." the communicator had whispered. Did it mean Stanton?

"John Wilkes Booth was very familiar with this place, of course," Miller said in his Maryland drawl. "This is where the conspirators used to meet many times. Mary Surratt ran this place as a tavern. Nothing has been changed in this house since then."

From Thomas Miller I also learned that plans were afoot to restore the house at considerable cost, and to make it into a museum.

We thanked our host and piled into the car. Suddenly I remembered that I had forgotten my briefcase inside the house, so I raced back and recovered it. The house was now even colder and emptier, and I wondered if I might hear anything unusual—but I didn't. Rather than hang around any longer, I joined the others in the car and we drove back to Washington.

I asked Countess d'Amecourt to stop once more at a house I felt might have some relationship with the case. Sybil, of course, had no idea why we got out to look at an old house on H Street. It is now a Chinese restaurant and offers no visible clues to its past.

"I feel military uniforms, blue colors here," Sybil said as we all shuddered in the cold wind outside. The house was locked and looked empty. My request to visit it had never been answered.

"What period?"

"Perhaps a hundred years . . . nothing very strong here . . . the initial S . . . a man . . . rather confusing . . . a meeting place more than a residence . . . not too respectable . . . meeting house for soldiers . . . Army . . ."

"Is there a link between this house and where we went earlier this afternoon?"

"The Army is the link somehow. . . ."

After I had thanked the Countess d'Amecourt for her help, Sybil and I flew back to New York.

For days afterward I pondered the questions arising from this expedition. Was the "S" linking the house on H Street—which was Mary Surratt's Washington boarding house—the same man as the "S-T-. . ." Sybil had whispered to me at Mary Surratt's former country house? Were both initials referring to Secretary Stanton and were the rumors true after all?"

The facts of history, in this respect, are significant. Lincoln's second term was actively opposed by the forces of the radical Republicans. They thought Lincoln too soft on the rebels and feared that he would make an easy peace with the Confederacy. They were quite right in this assumption, of course, and all through Lincoln's second term of office, his intent was clear. That is why, in murdering Abraham Lincoln, Booth actually did the South a great disservice.

In the spring of 1864, when the South seemed to be on its last legs, the situation in Washington also came to a point where decisions would have to be made soon. The "hawks," to use a contemporary term, could count on the services of Stanton, the War Secretary, and of Seward, Secretary of State, plus many lesser officials and officers, of course. The "doves" were those in actual command, however—Lincoln himself, Grant, and Vice President Johnson, a Southerner himself. Logically, the time of crisis would be at hand the moment Grant had won victory in his command and Sherman, the other great commander, on his end of the front. By a strange set of circumstances the assassination took place precisely at that moment: Both Grant and Sherman had eminently succeeded and peace was at hand.

Whenever Booth's motive in killing Lincoln has been described by biographers, a point is made that it was both Booth's madness and his attempt to avenge the South that caused him to commit the crime. Quite so, but the assassination made a lot more sense in terms of a *northern* plot by conveniently removing the chief advocate of a soft peace treaty just at the right moment!

This was not a trifling matter. Lincoln had proposed to go beyond freeing the slaves: to franchise the more intelligent ones among them to vote. But he had never envisioned general and immediate equality of newly freed blacks and their former masters. To the radicals, however, this was an absolute must as was the total takeover of southern assets. While Lincoln was only too ready to accept any southern state back into the Union fold that was willing to take the oath of loyalty, the radicals would hear of no such thing. They foresaw a long period of military government and rigid punishment for the secessionist states.

Lincoln often expressed the hope that Jefferson Davis and his chief aids might just leave the country to save him the embarrassment of having to try them. Stanton and his group, on the other hand, were pining for blood, and it was on Stanton's direct orders that the southern conspirators who killed Lincoln were shown no mercy; it was Stanton who refused to give in to popular sentiment against the hanging of a woman and who insisted that Mrs. Surratt share the fate of the other principal conspirators.

Stanton's stance at Lincoln's death—his remark that "now he belongs to the ages" and his vigorous pursuit of the murderers in no way mitigates against a possible secret involvement in a plot to kill the President. According to Stefan Lorant, he once referred to his commander-in-chief Lincoln as "the original gorilla." He frequently refused to carry out Lincoln's orders when he thought them "too soft." On April 11, three days prior to the assassination, Lincoln had incurred not only Stanton's anger but that of the entire Cabinet by arranging to allow the rebel Virginia legislature to function as a state government. "Stanton and the others were in a fury," Carl Sandburg reports, and the uproar was so loud Lincoln did not go through with his intent. But it shows the deep cleavage that existed between the liberal President and his radical government on the very eve of his last day!

Then, too, there was the trial held in a hurry and under circumstances no modern lawyer would call proper or even constitutional. Evidence was presented in part, important documents—such as Booth's own diary—were arbitrarily suppressed and kept out of the trial by order of Secretary Stanton, who had also impounded Booth's personal belongings and any and all documents seized at the Surratt house on H Street, giving defense attorneys for the accused, especially Mrs. Mary Surratt, not the slightest opportunity to build a reasonable defense for their clients.

That was as it should be, from Stanton's point of view: fanning the popular hatred by letting the conspirators appear in as unfavorable a light as possible, a quick conviction and execution of the judgment, so that no sympathy could rise among the public for the accused. There was considerable opposition to the hanging of Mrs. Surratt, and committees demanding her pardon were indeed formed. But by the time these committees were able to function properly, the lady was dead, convicted on purely circumstantial evidence: Her house had been the meeting place for the conspirators, but it was never proven that she was part of the conspiracy. In fact, she disapproved of the murder plot, according to the condemned, but the government would not accept this view. Her own son John H. Surratt, sitting the trial out in Canada, never lifted a hand to save his mother—perhaps he thought Stanton would not dare execute her.

Setting aside for the moment the identity of the spirit communicator at the Surratt tavern, I examined certain aspects of this new material: Certainly Sherman himself could not have been part of an anti-Lincoln plot, for he was a "dove", strictly a Lincoln man. But a member of his staff—perhaps the mysterious colonel—might well have been involved. Sybil's communicator had stated that Booth knew all about the Army officers who were either using him or were in league with him, making, in fact, the assassination a dual plot of southern avengers and northern hawks. If Booth knew these names, he might have put the information into his personal diary. This diary was written during his flight, while he was hiding from his pursuers in the wooded swamplands of Maryland and Virginia.

At the conspiracy trial, the diary was not even mentioned, but at the subsequent trial of John H. Surratt, two years later, it did come to light. That is, Lafayette Baker, head of the Secret Service at the time of the murder, mentioned its existence, and it was promptly impounded for the trial. But when it was produced as evidence in court, only two pages were left in it—the rest had been torn out by an unknown hand! Eighteen pages were missing. The diary had been in Stanton's possession from the moment of its seizure until now, and it was highly unlikely that Booth himself had so mutilated his own diary the moment he had finished writing it! To the contrary, the diary was his attempt to justify himself before his contemporaries, and before history. The onus of guilt here falls heavily upon Secretary Stanton again.

It is significant that whoever mutilated the diary had somehow spared an entry dated April 21,1865:

"Tonight I will once more try the river, with the intention to cross; though I have a greater desire and almost a mind to return to Washington, and in a measure clear my name, which I feel I can do."

Philip Van Doren Stern, author of *The Man Who Killed Lincoln*, quite rightfully asks, how could a self-confessed murderer clear his name unless he knew something that would involve other people than himself and his associates? Stern also refers to David Herold's confession in which the young man quotes Booth as telling him that there was a group of *thirty-five men in Washington* involved in the plot.

Sybil's confused communicator kept saying certain numbers, "forty-nine and "thirty-four." Could this be the code for Stanton and a committee of thirty-four men?

Whoever they were, not one of the northern conspirators ever confessed their part in the crime, so great was the popular indignation at the deed.

John H. Surratt, after going free as a consequence of the inability of his trial jury to agree on a verdict, tried his hand at lecturing on the subject of the assassination. He only gave a single lecture, which turned out a total failure. Nobody was interested. But a statement Surratt made at that lecture fortunately has come down to us. He admitted that another group of conspirators had been working independently and simultaneously to strike a blow at Lincoln.

That Surratt would make such a statement fits right in with the facts. He was a courier and undercover man for the Confederacy, with excellent contacts in Washington. It was he who managed to have the telegraph go out of order during the murder and to allow Booth to pass the sentry at the Navy Yard bridge without difficulty. But was the communicator speaking through Mrs. Leek not holding back information at first, only to admit finally that John Wilkes *knew* the names of those others, after all?

This differs from Philip Van Doren Stern's account, in which Booth was puzzled about the identities of his "unknown" allies. But then, Stern didn't hold a trance session at the Surratt tavern, either. Until our visit in November of 1967, the question seemed up in the air.

Surratt had assured Booth that "his sources" would make sure that they all got away safely. In other words, Booth and his associates were doing the dirty work for the brain trust in Washington, with John Surratt serving both sides and in a way linking them together in an identical purpose—though for totally opposite reasons.

Interestingly enough, the entranced Sybil spoke of a colonel who knew Sherman, and who would look after him . . . he would supply a ticket . . . ! That ticket might have been a steamer ticket for some foreign ship going from Mexico to Europe, where Booth could be safe. But who was the mysterious Major General Gee? Since Booth's group was planning to kill Grant as well, would he be likely to be involved in the plot on the northern end?

Lincoln had asked Grant and Mrs. Grant to join him at Ford's Theatre the fateful evening; Grant had declined, explaining that he wished to join his family in New Jersey instead. Perhaps this was a natural enough excuse to turn down the President's invitation, but one might also construe it differently: did he *know* about the plot and did he not wish to see his President shot?

Booth's choice of the man to do away with Grant had fallen on John Surratt, as soon as he learned of the change in plans. Surratt was to get on the train that took Grant to New Jersey. But Grant was not attacked; there is no evidence whatever that Surratt ever took the train, and he himself said he didn't. Surratt, then, the go-between of the two groups of conspirators, could easily have warned Grant himself: The Booth group wanted to kill Lincoln and his chief aides, to make the North powerless; but the northern conspirators would have only wanted to have Lincoln removed and certainly none of their own men. Even though Grant was likely to carry out the President's "soft" peace plans, while Lincoln was his commander-in-chief, he was a soldier accustomed to taking orders and would carry out with equal loyalty the hard-line policies of Lincoln's successor! Everything here points to Surratt as having been, in effect, a double agent.

But was the idea of an involvement of General Grant really so incredible?

Wilson Sullivan, author of a critical review of a recently published volume of *The Papers of Andrew Johnson*, has this to say of Grant, according to the *Saturday Review of Literature*, March 16, 1968:

"Despite General Grant's professed acceptance of Lincoln's policy of reconciliation with the Southern whites, President Grant strongly supported and implemented the notorious Ku Klux Klan Act in 1871."

This was a law practically disenfranchising Southerners and placing them directly under federal courts rather than local and state authorities.

It was Grant who executed the repressive policies of the radical Republican Congress and who reverted to the hardline policies of the Stanton clique after he took political office, undoing completely whatever lenient measures President Johnson had instituted following the assassination of his predecessor.

But even before Grant became President, he was the man in power. Since the end of the Civil War, civil administrations had governed the conquered South. In March 1867, these were replaced by military governments in five military districts. The commanders of these districts were directly responsible to General Grant and disregarded any orders from President Johnson. Civil rights and state laws were broadly ignored. The reasons for this perversion of Lincoln's policies were not only vengeance on the Confederacy, but political considerations as well: By delaying the voting rights of Southerners, a Republican Congress could keep itself in office that much longer. Wilson Sullivan feels that this attitude was largely responsible for the emergence of the Ku Klux Klan and other racist organizations in the South.

Had Lincoln lived out his term, he would no doubt have implemented a policy of rapid reconciliation, the South would have regained its political privileges quickly, and the radical Republican party might have lost the next election.

That party was led by Secretary Stanton and General Grant!

What a convenient thing it was to have a southern conspiracy at the proper time! All one had to do is get abroad and ride the conspiracy to the successful culmination—then blame it all on the South, thereby doing a double job, heaping more guilt upon the defeated Confederacy and ridding the country of the *one* man who could forestall the continuance in power of the Stanton-Grant group!

That Stanton might have been the real leader in the northern plot is not at all unlikely. The man was given to rebellion when the situation demanded it. President Andrew Johnson had tried to continue the Lincoln line in the face of a hostile Congress and even a Cabinet dominated by radicals. In early 1868,

Johnson tried to oust Secretary Stanton from his Cabinet because he realized that Stanton was betraying his policies. But Stanton defied his chief and barricaded himself in the War Department. This intolerable situation led to Johnson's impeachment proceedings, which failed by a single vote.

There was one more tragic figure connected with the events that seemed to hold unresolved mysteries: Mrs. Mary Surratt, widow of a Confederate spy and mother of another. On April 14,1865, she invited her son's friend, and one of her boarders, Louis Weichmann, to accompany her on an errand to her old country home, now a tavern, at Surrattsville. Weichmann gladly obliged Mrs. Surratt and went down to hire a buggy. At the tavern, Mrs. Surratt got out carrying a package which she described to Weichmann as belonging to Booth. This package she handed to tavernkeeper John Lloyd inside the house to safekeep for Booth. It contained the guns the fugitives took with them later, after the assassination had taken place.

Weichmann's testimony of his errand, and his description of the meetings at the H Street house, were largely responsible for Mrs. Surratt's execution, even though it was never shown that she had anything to do with the murder plot itself. Weichmann's testimony haunted him all his life for Mrs. Surratt's "ghost," as Lloyd Lewis puts it in *Myths after Lincoln*, "got up and walked" in 1868 when her "avengers" made political capital of her execution, charging Andrew Johnson with having railroaded her to death.

Mrs. Surratt's arrest at 11:15 p.m., April 17, 1865, came as a surprise to her despite the misgivings she had long harbored about her son's involvement with Booth and the other plotters. Lewis Paine's untimely arrival at the house after it had already been raided also helped seal her fate. At the trial that followed, none of the accused was ever allowed to speak, and their judges were doing everything in their power to link the conspiracy with the Confederate government, even to the extent of producing false witnesses, who later recanted their testimonies.

If anyone among the condemned had the makings of a ghost, it was Mary Surratt.

Soon after her execution and burial, reports of her haunting the house on H Street started. The four bodies of the executed had been placed inside the prison walls and the families were denied the right to bury them.

When Annie Surratt could not obtain her mother's body, she sold the lodging house and moved away from the home that had seen so much tragedy. The first buyer of the house had little luck with it, however. Six weeks later he sold it again, even though he had bought it very cheaply. Other tenants came and went quickly, and according to the *Boston Post*, which chronicled the fate of the house, it was because they saw the ghost of Mrs. Surratt clad in her execution robe walking the corridors of her home! That was back in the 1860s and 1870s. Had Mary Surratt found peace since then? Her body now lies buried underneath a simple gravestone at Mount Olivet Cemetery.

The house at 604 H Street, N.W. still stands. In the early 1900s, a Washington lady dined at the house. During dinner, she noticed the figure of a young girl appear and walk up the stairs. She recognized the distraught girl as the spirit of Annie Surratt, reported John McKelway in the *Washington Star.* The Chinese establishment now occupying the house does not mind the ghosts, either mother or daughter. And Ford's Theatre has just been restored as a legitimate theater, to break the ancient jinx.

Both Stern and Emanuel Hertz quote an incident in the life of Robert Lincoln, whom a Mr. Young discovered destroying many of his father's private papers. When he remonstrated with Lincoln, the son replied that "the papers he was destroying contained the documentary evidence of the treason of a member of Lincoln's Cabinet, and he thought it best for all that such evidence be destroyed."

Mr. Young enlisted the help of Nicholas Murray Butler, later head of Columbia University, New York, to stop Robert Lincoln from continuing this destruction. The remainder of the papers were then deposited in the Library of Congress, but we don't know how many documents Robert Lincoln had already destroyed when he was halted.

There remains only the curious question as to the identity of our communicator at the Surratt tavern in November 1967.

"Shot down like a dog," the voice had complained through the psychic.

"Hunted like a dog," Booth himself wrote in his diary. Why would Edwin Booth, who had done everything in his power to publicly repudiate his brother's deed, and who claimed that he had little direct contact with John Wilkes in the years before the assassination—why would he want to own this house that was so closely connected with the tragedy and John Wilkes Booth? Who would think that the "Prince of Players," who certainly had no record of any involvement in the plot to kill Lincoln, should be drawn back by feelings of guilt to the house so intimately connected with his brother John Wilkes?

But he did own it, and sell it to B. K. Miller, Thomas Miller's father!

I couldn't find any Lowell, Virginia on my maps, but there is a Laurel, Maryland not far from Surrattsville, or today's Clinton.

Much of the dialogue fits Edwin Booth, owner of the house. Some of it doesn't, and some of it might be a deliberate coverup.

Mark you, this is not a "ghost" in the usual sense, for nobody reported Edwin Booth appearing to them at this house. Mrs. Surratt might have done so, both here and at her town house, but the principal character in this fascinating story has evidently lacked the inner torment that is the basis for ghostly manifestations beyond time and space. Quite so, for to John Wilkes Booth the deed was the work of a national hero, not to be ashamed of at all. If anything, the ungrateful Confederacy owed him a debt of thanks.

No, I decided, John Wilkes Booth would not make a convincing ghost. But Edwin? Was there more to his relationship with John Wilkes than the current published record shows? "Ah, there's the rub . . ." the Prince of Players would say in one of his greatest roles.

Then, to, there is the peculiar mystery of John Surratt's position. He had broken with John Wilkes Booth weeks before the murder, he categorically stated at his trial in 1867. Yes, he had been part of the earlier plot to abduct Lincoln, but murder, no. That was not his game.

It was my contention, therefore, that John Surratt's role as a dual agent seemed highly likely from the evidence available to me, both through objective research and psychic contacts. We may never find the mysterious colonel on Sherman's staff, nor be able to identify with *certainty* Major General "Gee." But War Secretary Stanton's role looms ominously and in sinister fashion behind the generally accepted story of the plot.

If Edwin Booth came through Sybil Leek to tell us what he knew of his brother's involvement in Lincoln's death, perhaps he did so because John Wilkes never got around to clearing his name himself. Stanton may have seen to that, and the disappearing diary and unseeming haste of the trial all fall into their proper places.

It is now over a hundred years after the event. Will we have to wait that long before we know the complete truth about another President's murder?

25

The Kennedys—Ghosts, Legends, and Visions

"WHEN ARE YOU going to go down to Dallas and find out about President Kennedy?" the pleasant visitor inquired. He was a schoolteacher who had come to me to seek advice on how to start a course in parapsychology in his part of the country.

The question about President Kennedy was hardly new. I had been asked the same question in various forms ever since the assassination of John F. Kennedy, as if I and my psychic helpers had the duty to use our combined talents to find out what really happened at the School Book Depository in Dallas. I suppose similar conditions prevailed after the death of Abraham Lincoln. People's curiosity had been aroused, and with so many unconfirmed rumors making the rounds the matter of a President's sudden death does become a major topic of conversation and inquiry.

I wasn't there when Lincoln was shot; I was around when President Kennedy was murdered. Thus I am in a fairly good position to trace the public interest with the assassination from the very start.

I assured my visitor that so far I had no plans to go down to Dallas with a medium and find out what "really" happened. I have said so on television many times. When I was reminded that the Abraham Lincoln murder also left some unanswered questions and that I had indeed investigated it and come up with startlingly new results, I rejoined that there was one basic difference between the Kennedy death and the assassination of President Lincoln: Lincoln's ghost had been seen repeatedly by reliable witnesses in the White House; so far I have not received any reliable reports of ghostly sightings concerning the late President Kennedy. In my opinion, this meant that the restlessness that caused Lincoln to remain in what used to be his working world has not caused John F. Kennedy to do likewise.

But I am not a hundred per cent sure any longer. Having learned how difficult it is to get information about such matters in Washington, or to gain admission to the White House as anything but a casual tourist—or, of course, on official business—I am also convinced that much may be suppressed or simply disregarded by those to whom experiences have happened simply because we live in a time when psychic phenomena can still embarrass those to whom they occur, especially if they have a position of importance.

But even if John Fitzgerald Kennedy is not walking the corridors of the White House at night, bemoaning his untimely demise or trying to right the many wrongs that have happened in this country since he left us, he is apparently doing something far better. He communicates, under special conditions and with special people. He is far from "dead and gone," if I am to believe those to whom these experiences have come. Naturally, one must sift the fantasy from the real thing—even more so when we are dealing with a famous person. I have done so, and I have looked very closely at the record of people who have reported to me psychic experiences dealing with the Kennedy family. I have eliminated a number of such reports simply because I could not find myself wholly convinced that the one who reported it was entirely balanced. I have also eliminated many other reports, not because I had doubts about the emotional stability of those who had made the reports, but because the reports were far too general and vague to be evidential even in the broadest sense. Material that was unsupported by witnesses, or material that was presented after the fact, was of course disregarded.

With all that in mind, I have come to the conclusion that the Kennedy destiny was something that could not have been avoided whether or not one accepts the old Irish Kennedy curse as factual.

Even the ghostly Kennedys are part and parcel of American life at the present. Why they must pay so high a price in suffering, I cannot guess. But it is true that the Irish forebears of the American Kennedys have also suffered an unusually high percentage of violent deaths over the years, mainly on the male side of the family. There is, of course, the tradition that way back in the Middle Ages a Kennedy was cursed for having incurred the wrath of some private local enemy. As a result of the curse, he and all his male descendants were to die violently one by one. To dismiss curses as fantasies, or at the very best workable only because of fear symptoms, would not be accurate. I had great doubts about the effectiveness of curses until I came across several cases that allowed for no other explanation. In particular, I refer back to the case of the Wurmbrand curse reported by me in *Ghosts of the Golden West*. In that case the last male descendant of an illustrious family died under mysterious circumstances quite unexpectedly even while under the care of doctors in a hospital. Thus, if the Kennedy curse is operative, nothing much can be done about it.

Perhaps I should briefly explain the distinction between ghosts and spirits here, since so much of the Kennedy material is of the latter kind rather than the former. Ghosts are generally tied to houses or definite places where their physical bodies died tragically, or at least in a state of unhappiness. They are unable to leave the premises, so to speak, and can only repeat the pattern of their final moments, and are for all practical purposes not fully cognizant of their true state. They can be compared with psychotics in the physical state, and must first be freed from their own self-imposed delusions to be able to answer, if possible through a trance medium, or to leave and become free spirits out in what Dr. Joseph Rhine of Duke University has called "the world of the mind," and which I generally refer to as the non-physical world.

Spirits, on the other hand, are really people, like you and me, who have left the physical body but are very much alive in a thinner, etheric body, with which they are able to function pretty much the same as they did in the physical body, except that they are now no longer weighted down by physical objects, distances, time, and space. The majority of those who die become free spirits, and only a tiny fraction are unable to proceed into the next stage but must remain behind because of emotional difficulties. Those who have gone on are not necessarily gone forever, but to the contrary they are able and frequently anxious to keep a hand in situations they have left unfinished on the earth plane. Death by violence or under tragic conditions does not necessarily create a ghost. Some such conditions may indeed create the ghost syndrome, but many others do not. I should think that President Kennedy is in the latter group—that is to say, a free spirit capable of continuing an interest in the world he left behind. Why this is so, I will show in the next pages.

The R. Lumber Company is a prosperous firm specializing in the manufacture and wholesale of lumber. It is located in Georgia and the owners, Mr. and Mrs. Bernard R., are respected citizens in their community. It was in April of 1970 that Mrs. R. contacted me. "I have just finished reading your book, *Life After Death*, and could not resist your invitation to share a strange experience with you," she explained, "hoping that you can give me some opinion regarding its authenticity.

"I have not had an opportunity to discuss what happened with anyone who is in any way psychic or clairvoyant. I have never tried to contact anyone else close to the Kennedys about this, as of course I know they must have received thousands of letters. Many times I feel a little guilty about not ever trying to contact Mrs. Kennedy and the children, if indeed it could have been a genuine last message from the President. It strikes me as odd that we might have received it or imagined we received it. We were never fans of the

Kennedys, and although we were certainly sympathetic to the loss of our President, we were not as emotionally upset as many of our friends who were ardent admirers.

"I am in no way psychic, nor have I ever had any supernatural experience before. I am a young homemaker and businesswoman, and cannot offer any possible explanation for what happened.

"On Sunday night, November 24, 1963, following John F. Kennedy's assassination, my family and I were at home watching on television the procession going through the Capital paying their last respects. I was feeling very depressed, especially since that afternoon Lee Oswald had also been killed and I felt we would never know the full story of the assassination. For some strange reason, I suddenly thought of the Ouija board, although I have never taken the answers seriously and certainly have never before consulted it about anything of importance. I asked my teen-age daughter to work the board with me, and we went into another room. I had never tried to 'communicate with the dead.' I don't know why I had the courage to ask the questions I did on that night, but somehow, I felt compelled to go on:

Question: Will our country be in danger without Kennedy?

Answer: Strong with, weak without Kennedy, plot—stop.

Question: Will Ruby tell why President was killed?

Answer: Ruby does not know, only Oswald and I know. Sorry.

Question: Will we ever know why Kennedy was killed?

Answer: Underground and Oswald know, Ruby does not know, gangland leader caught in plot.

Question: Who is gangland leader?

Answer: Can't tell now.

Question: Why did Oswald hate President?

Answer: Negroes, civil rights bill.

Question: Have Oswald's and Kennedy's spirits met?

Answer: Yes. No hard feelings in Heaven.

Question: Are you in contact with Kennedy?

Answer: Yes.

Question: Does Kennedy have a message he would send through us?

Answer: Yes, yes, yes, tell J. C., and J.J. about this. Thanks, JFK.

Question: Can Kennedy give us some nickname to authenticate this?

Answer: Only nickname 'John John.'

Question: Do you really want us to contact someone?

Answer: Yes, but wait 'til after my funeral.

Question: How can we be sure Jackie will see our letter?

Answer: Write personal, not sympathy business.

Question: Is there something personal you can tell us to confirm this message?

Answer: Prying public knows all.

Question: Just one nickname you could give us?

Answer: J.J. (John John) likes to swim lots, called 'Daddy's little swimmer boy.' Does that help? JFK.

Question: Anything else?

Answer: J.J. likes to play secret game and bunny.

Question: What was your Navy Serial number?

Answer: 109 P.T. (jg) Skipper— —5905. [seemed confused]

Question: Can we contact you again?

Answer: You, JFK, not JFK you.

Question: Give you address of your new home.

Answer: Snake Mountain Road.

Question: Will Mrs. Kennedy believe this, does she believe in the supernatural?

Answer: Some—tired—that's all tonight.

"At this point the planchette slid off the bottom of the board marked 'Goodby' and we attempted no further questions that night.

"The board at all times answered our questions swiftly and deliberately, without hesitation. I moved so rapidly, in fact, that my daughter and I *could not keep up with the message as it came*. We called out the letters to my eleven-year-old daughter who wrote them down, and we had to unscramble the words after we had received the entire message. We had no intention of trying to communicate *directly* with President Kennedy. I cannot tell you how frightened I was when I asked if there was a message he would send and the message came signed 'JFK.'

"For several days after, I could not believe the message was genuine. I have written Mrs. Kennedy several letters trying to explain what happened, but have never had the courage to mail them.

"None of the answers obtained are sensational, most are things we could have known or guessed. The answers given about 'John John' and 'secret game' and 'bunny' were in a magazine which my children had read and I had not. However, the answer about John John being called 'Daddy's little swimmer boy' is something none of us have ever heard or read. I have researched numerous articles written about the Kennedys during the last two years and have not found any reference to this. I could not persuade my daughter to touch the board again for days. We tried several times in December 1963, but were unsuccessful. One night, just before Christmas, a friend of mine persuaded my daughter to work the board with her. Perhaps the most surprising message came at this time, and it was also the last one we ever received. We are all Protestant and the message was inconsistent with our religious beliefs. When they asked if there was a message from President Kennedy, the planchette spelled out immediately 'Thanks for your prayers while I was in Purgatory, JFK.'"

I have said many times in print and on television that I take a dim view of Ouija boards in general. Most of the material obtained from the use of this instrument merely reflects the unconscious of one or both sitters. Occasionally, however, Ouija boards have been able to tap the psychic levels of a person and come up with the same kind of material a clairvoyant person might come up with. Thus, to dismiss the experiences of Mrs. R. merely because the material was obtained through a Ouija board would not be fair. Taking into account the circumstances, the background of the operators, and their seeming reluctance to seek out such channels of communication, I must discuss ulterior motives such as publicity-seeking reasons or idle curiosity as being the causative factor in the event. On the other hand, having just watched a television program dealing with the demise of President Kennedy, the power of suggestion might have come into play. Had the material obtained through the Ouija board been more specific to a greater extent, perhaps I would not have to hesitate to label this a genuine experience. While there is nothing in the report that indicates fraud—either conscious or unconscious—there is nothing startling in the information given. Surely, if the message had come from Kennedy, or if Kennedy himself had been on the other end of the psychic line, there would have been certain pieces of information that would have been known only to him and that could yet be checked out in a way that was accessible. Surely, Kennedy would have realized how difficult it might have been for an ordinary homemaker to contact his wife. Thus, it seems to me that some other form of proof of identity would have been furnished. This, however, is really only speculation. Despite the sincerity of those reporting the incident, I feel that there is reasonable doubt as to the genuineness of the communication.

By far the majority of communications regarding President Kennedy relate to his death and are in the nature of premonitions, dreams, visions, and other warnings prior to or simultaneous with the event itself. The number of such experiences indicates that the event itself must have been felt ahead of its realization, indicating that some sort of law was in operation that could not be altered, even if President Kennedy could have been warned. As a matter of fact, I am sure that he was given a number of warnings, and that he chose to disregard them. I don't see how he could have done otherwise—both because he was the President and out of a fine sense of destiny that is part and parcel of the Kennedy make-up. Certainly Jeane Dixon was in a position to warn the President several times prior to the assassination. Others, less well connected in Washington, might have written letters that had never gotten through to the President. Certainly one cannot explain these things away merely by saying a public figure is always in danger of assassination, or that Kennedy had incurred the wrath of many people in this country and abroad. This simply doesn't conform to the facts. Premonitions have frequently been very precise, indicating in more or less great detail the manner, time, and nature of the assassination. If it were merely a matter of vaguely foretelling the sudden death of the President, then of course one could say that this comes from a study of the situation or from a general feeling about the times in which we live. But this is not so. Many of the startling predictions couldn't have been made by anyone, unless they themselves were in on the planning of the assassination.

Mrs. Rose LaPorta lives in suburban Cleveland, Ohio. Over the years she has developed her ESP faculties—partially in the dream state and partially when awake. Some of her premonitory experiences are so detailed that they cannot be explained on the basis of coincidence, if there is such a thing, or in any other rational terms. For instance, on May 10, 1963, she dreamed she had eaten something with glass in it. She could even feel it in her mouth, so vividly that she began to spit it out and woke up. On October 4 of that same year, after she had forgotten the peculiar dream, she happened to be eating a cookie. There was some glass in it, and her dream became reality in every detail. Fortunately, she had told several witnesses of her original dream, so she was able to prove this to herself on the record.

At her place of work there is a superintendent named Smith, who has offices in another city. There never was any close contact with that man, so it was rather startling to Mrs. LaPorta to hear a voice in her sleep telling her, "Mr. Smith died at home on Monday." Shocked by this message, she discussed it with her coworkers. This was on May 18, 1968. On October 8 of the same year, an announcement was made at the company to the effect that "Mr. Smith died at home on Monday, October 7."

Mrs. LaPorta's ability to tune in on future events reached a national subject on November 17, 1963. She dreamed she was at the White House in Washington on a dark, rainy day. There were beds set up in each of the porticoes. She found herself in the dream, moving from one bed to another, because she wanted to shelter herself from the rain. There was much confusion going on and many men were running around in all directions. They seemed to have guns in their hands and pockets. Finally, Mrs. LaPorta, in the dream, asked someone what was happening, and they told her they were Secret Service men. She was impressed with the terrible confusion and atmosphere of tragedy when she awoke from her dream. That was five days before the assassination happened on November 22, 1963. The dream is somewhat reminiscent of the famed Abraham Lincoln dream, in which he himself saw his own body on the catafalque in the East Room, and asked who was dead in the White House.

Marie Howe is a Maryland housewife, fifty-two years old, and only slightly psychic. The night before the assassination she had a dream in which she saw two brides with the features of men. Upon awakening she spoke of her dream to her husband and children, and interpreted it that someone was going to die very soon. She thought that two persons would die close together. The next day, Kennedy and Oswald turned into the "brides of death" she had seen in her dream.

Bertha Zelkin lives in Los Angeles. The morning of the assassination she suddenly found herself saying, "What would we do if President Kennedy were to die?" That afternoon the event took place.

Marion Confalonieri is a forty-one-year-old housewife, a native of Chicago, has worked as a secretary, and lives with her husband, a draftsman, and two daughters in a comfortable home in California. Over the years she has had many psychic experiences, ranging from *deja vu* feelings to psychic dreams. On Friday, November 22, the assassination took place and Oswald was captured the same day. The following night, Saturday, November 23, Mrs. Confalonieri went to bed exhausted and in tears from all the commotion. Some time during the night she dreamed that she saw a group of men, perhaps a dozen, dressed in suits and some with hats. She seemed to be floating a little above them, looking down on the scene, and she noticed that they were standing very close in a group. Then she heard a voice say, "Ruby did it." The next morning she gave the dream no particular thought. The name Ruby meant absolutely nothing to her nor, for that matter, to anyone else in the country at that point. It wasn't until she turned her radio on and heard the announcement that Oswald had been shot by a man named Ruby that she realized she had had a preview of things to come several hours before the event itself had taken place.

Another one who tuned in on the future a little ahead of reality was the famed British author, Pendragon, whose real name was L. T. Ackerman. In

October 1963, he wrote, "I wouldn't rule out the possibility of attempted assassination or worse if caught off guard." He wrote to President Kennedy urging him that his guard be strengthened, especially when appearing in public.

Dr. Robert G. is a dentist who makes his home in Rhode Island. He has had psychic experiences all his life, some of which I have described elsewhere. At the time when Oswald was caught by the authorities, the doctor's wife wondered out loud what would happen to the man. Without thinking what he was saying, Dr. G. replied, "He will be shot in the police station." The words just popped out of his mouth. There was nothing to indicate even a remote possibility of such a course of action.

He also had a premonition that Robert Kennedy would be shot, but he thought that the Senator would live on with impaired faculties. We know, of course, that Senator Kennedy died. Nevertheless, as most of us will remember, for a time after the announcement of the shooting there was hope that the Senator would indeed continue to live, although with impaired faculties. Not only did the doctors think that might be possible, but announcements were made to that effect. Thus, it is entirely feasible that Dr. G. tuned in not only on the event itself but also on the thoughts and developments that were part of the event.

As yet we know very little about the mechanics of premonitions, and it is entirely possible that some psychics cannot fine-tune their inner instruments beyond a general pickup of future material. This seems to relate to the inability of most mediums to pinpoint exact time in their predictions.

Cecilia Fawn Nichols is a writer who lives in Twenty-nine Palms, California. All her life she has had premonitions that have come true and has accepted the psychic in her life as a perfectly natural element. She had been rooting for John F. Kennedy to be elected President because she felt that his Catholic religion had made him a kind of underdog. When he finally did get the nod, Miss Nichols found herself far from jubilant. As if something foreboding were preying heavily on her mind, she received the news of his election glumly and with a feeling of disaster. At the time she could not explain to herself why, but the thought that the young man who had just been elected was condemned to death entered her mind. "When the unexpected passes through my mind, I know I can expect it," she explained. "I generally do not know just how or when or what. In this case I felt some idiot was going to kill him because of his religion. I expected the assassination much sooner. Possibly because of domestic problems, I wasn't expecting it when it did happen."

On Sunday morning, November 24, she was starting breakfast. Her television set was tuned to Channel 2, and she decided to switch to Channel 7 because that station had been broadcasting the scene directly from Dallas. The announcer was saying that any moment now Oswald would be brought out of jail to be taken away from Dallas. The camera showed the grim faces of the crowd. Miss Nichols took one look at the scene and turned to her mother. "Mama, come in the living room. Oswald is going to be killed in a few minutes, and I don't want to miss seeing it."

There was nothing to indicate such a course of action, of course, but the words just came out of her mouth as if motivated by some outside force. A moment later, the feared event materialized. Along with the gunshot, however, she distinctly heard words said that she was never again to hear on any rerun of the televised action. The words were spoken just as Ruby lifted his arm to shoot. As he began pressing the trigger, the words and the gunshot came close together. Afterwards Miss Nichols listened carefully to many of the reruns but never managed to hear the words again. None of the commentators mentioned them. No account of the killing mentions them. And yet Miss Nichols clearly heard Ruby make a statement even as he was shooting Oswald down.

The fact that she alone heard the words spoken by Ruby bothered Miss Nichols. In 1968 she was with a group of friends discussing the Oswald killing, and again she reported what she had heard that time on television. There was a woman in that group who nodded her head. She too had heard the same words. It came as a great relief to Miss Nichols to know that she was not alone in her perceptions. The words Ruby spoke as he was shooting Oswald were words of anger: "Take this, you son of a bitch!"

This kind of psychic experience is far closer to truthful tuning in on events as they transpire, or just as they are formulating themselves, than some of the more complicated interpretations of events after they have happened.

Two Cincinnati amateur mediums by the names of Dorothy Barrett and Virginia Hill, who have given out predictions of things to come to the newspapers from time to time, also made some announcements concerning the Kennedy assassination. I have met the two ladies at the home of the John Straders in Cincinnati, at which time they seemed to be imitating the Edgar Cayce readings in that they pinpointed certain areas of the body subject to illness. Again, I met Virginia Hill recently and was confronted with what she believes is the personality of Edgar Cayce, the famous Seer of Virginia Beach. Speaking through her, I questioned the alleged Edgar Cayce entity and took notes, which I then asked Cayce's son, Hugh Lynn Cayce, to examine for veridity. Regrettably, most of the answers proved to be incorrect, thus making the identity of Edgar Cayce highly improbable. Nevertheless, Virginia Hill is psychic and some of her predictions have come true.

On December 4, 1967, the *Cincinnati Inquirer* published many of her predictions for the following year. One of the more startling statements is that there were sixteen people involved in the Kennedy assassination, according to Virginia's spirit guide, and that the leader was a woman. Oswald, it is claimed, did not kill the President, but a policeman (now dead) did.

In this connection it is interesting to note that Sherman Skolnick, a researcher, filed suit in April of 1970 against the National Archives and Records Services to release certain documents concerning the Kennedy assassination—in particular, Skolnick claimed that there had been a prior Chicago assassination plot in which Oswald and an accomplice by the name of Thomas Arthur Vallee and three or four other men had been involved. Their plan to kill the President at a ball game had to be abandoned when Vallee was picked up on a minor traffic violation the day before the game. Skolnick, according to *Time* magazine of April 20, 1970, firmly believes that Oswald and Vallee and several others were linked together in the assassination plot.

When it comes to the assassination of Senator Robert Kennedy, the picture is somewhat different. To begin with, very few people thought that Robert Kennedy was in mortal danger, while John F. Kennedy, as President, was always exposed to political anger—as are all Presidents. The Senator did not seem to be in quite so powerful a position. True, he had his enemies, as have all politicians. But the murder by Sirhan Sirhan came as much more of a surprise than the assassination of his brother. It is thus surprising that so much premonitory material exists concerning Robert Kennedy as well. In a way, of course, this material is even more evidential because of the lesser likelihood of such an event transpiring.

Mrs. Elaine Jones lives in San Francisco. Her husband is a retired businessman; her brother-in-law headed the publishing firm of Harper & Row; and she is not given to hallucinations. I have reported some of her psychic experiences elsewhere. Shortly before the assassination of Robert Kennedy she had a vision of the White House front. At first she saw it as it was and is, and then suddenly the entire front seemed to crumble before her eyes. To her this meant death of someone connected with the White House. A short time later, the assassination of the Senator took place.

Months before the event, famed Washington seeress Jeane Dixon was speaking at the Hotel Ambassador in Los Angeles. She said that Robert Kennedy would be the victim of a "tragedy right here in this hotel." The Senator was assassinated there eight months later.

A young Californian by the name of Lorraine Caswell had a dream the night before the assassination of Senator Kennedy. In her dream she saw the actual assassination as it later happened. The next morning, she reported her nightmare to her roommate, who had served as witness on previous occasions of psychic premonition.

Ellen Roberts works as a secretary, telephonist, and part-time volunteer for political causes she supports. During the campaign of Senator Robert Kennedy she spent some time at headquarters volunteering her services. Miss Roberts is a member of the Reverend Zenor's Hollywood Spiritualist Temple. Reverend Zenor, while in trance, speaks with the voice of Agasha, a higher teacher, who is also able to foretell events in the future. On one such occasion, long before the assassination of John F. Kennedy, Agasha—through Reverend Zenor—had said, "There will be not one assassination, but two. He will also be quite young. Victory will be almost within his grasp, but he will die just before he assumes the office, if it cannot be prevented."

The night of the murder, Ellen Roberts fell asleep early. She awakened with a sense of Robert Kennedy and President Kennedy talking. John F. Kennedy was putting his arm around his brother's shoulders and she heard him say, "Well, Bobby, you made it—the hard way." With a rueful smile they walked away. Miss Roberts took this to mean the discomfort that candidate Robert Kennedy had endured during the campaign—the rock-throwing, the insults, name-callings, and his hands had actually become swollen as he was being pulled. Never once did she accept it as anything more sinister. The following day she realized what her vision had meant.

A curious thing happened to Mrs. Lewis H. MacKibbel. She and her ten-year-old granddaughter were watching television the evening of June 4,1968. Suddenly the little girl jumped up, clasped her hands to her chest, and in a shocked state announced, "Robert Kennedy has been shot. Shot down, Mama." Her sisters and mother teased her about it, saying that such an event would have been mentioned on the news if it were true. After a while the subject was dropped. The following morning, June 5, when the family radio was turned on, word of the shooting came. Startled, the family turned to the little girl, who could only nod and say, "Yes I know. I knew it last night."

Mrs. Dawn Chorley lives in central Ohio. A native of England, she spent many years with her husband in South Africa, and has had psychic experiences at various times in her life. During the 1968 election campaign she and her husband, Colin Chorley, had been working for Eugene McCarthy, but when Robert Kennedy won the primary in New Hampshire she was very pleased with that too. The night of the election, she stayed up late. She was very keyed up and thought she would not be able to sleep because of the excitement, but contrary to her expectations she fell immediately into a very deep sleep around midnight. That night she had a curious dream.

"I was standing in the central downstairs room of my house. I was aware of a strange atmosphere around me and felt very lonely. Suddenly I felt a pain in the left side of my head, toward the back. The inside of my mouth started to crumble and blood started gushing out of my mouth. I tried to get to the telephone, but my arms and legs would not respond to my will; everything was disoriented. Somehow I managed to get to the telephone and pick up the receiver. With tremendous difficulty I dialed for the operator, and I could hear a voice asking whether I needed help. I tried to say, 'Get a doctor,' but the words came out horribly slurred. Then came the realization I was dying and I said, 'Oh my God, I am dying,' and sank into oblivion. I was shouting so loud I awoke my husband, who is a heavy sleeper. Shaking off the dream, I still felt terribly depressed. My husband, Colin, noticed the time. Allowing for time changes, it was the exact minute Robert Kennedy was shot."

Jill Taggart of North Hollywood, California, has been working with me as a developing medium for several years now. By profession a writer and model, she has been her own worst critic, and in her report avoids anything that cannot be substantiated. On May 14, 1968, she had meant to go to a rally in honor of Senator Robert Kennedy in Van Nuys, California. Since the parade was only three blocks from her house, it was an easy thing to walk over. But early in the evening she had resolved not to go. To begin with, she was not fond of the Senator, and she hated large crowds, but more than anything she had a bad feeling that something would happen to the Senator while he was in the car. On the news that evening she heard that the Senator had been struck in the temple by a flying object and had fallen to his knees in the car. The news also reported that he was all right. Jill, however, felt that the injury was more serious than announced and that the Senator's reasoning faculties would be impaired henceforth. "It's possible that it could threaten his life," she reported. "I know that temples are tricky things." When I spoke to her further, pressing for details, she indicated that she had then felt disaster for Robert Kennedy, but her logical mind refused to enlarge upon the comparatively small injury the candidate had suffered. A short time later, of course, the Senator was dead—not from a stone thrown at him but from a murderer's bullet. Jill Taggart had somehow tuned in on both events simultaneously.

Seventeen-year old Debbie Gaurlay, a high school student who also works at training horses, has had ESP experiences for several years. Two days prior to the assassination of Robert Kennedy she remarked to a friend by the name of Debbie Corso that the Senator would be shot very shortly. At that time there was no logical reason to assume an attempt upon the Senator's life.

John Londren is a machine fitter, twenty-eight years old, who lives with his family in Hartford, Connecticut. Frequently he has had dreams of events that have later transpired. In March 1968 he had a vivid dream in which he saw Senator Robert Kennedy shot while giving his Inaugural Address. Immediately he told his wife and father about the dream, and even wrote a letter to the Senator in April but decided not to send it until after the election. Even the correct names of the assassin and of two people present occurred in his dream. But Mr. Londren dismissed the dream since he knew that Roosevelt Grier and Rafe Johnson were sports figures. He felt they would be out of place in a drama involving the assassination of a political candidate. Nevertheless, those were the two men who actually subdued the killer.

In a subsequent dream he saw St. Patrick's Cathedral in New York during Senator Kennedy's funeral. People were running about in a state of panic, and he had the feeling that a bombing or shooting had taken place. So upset was Mr. Londren by his second dream that he asked his father, who had a friend in Washington, to make some inquiries. Eventually the information was given to a Secret Service man who respected extrasensory perception. The New York City bomb squad was called in and the security around the Cathedral was doubled. A man with an unloaded gun was caught fifteen minutes before the President arrived for the funeral at the Cathedral. Mr. Londren's second dream thus proved to be not only evidential but of value in preventing what might have been another crime.

Another amateur prophet is Elaine Morganelli, a Los Angeles housewife. In May 1967 she predicted in writing that President Johnson would be assassinated on June 4, and sent this prediction along with others to her brother, Lewis Olson. What she actually had heard was "President assassination June 4." Well, President Johnson was not assassinated, but on June 5, 1968, Robert Kennedy, a presidential candidate, was shot to death.

A sixteen-year-old teenager from Tennessee named John Humphreys experienced a vision late in 1963. This happened while he was in bed but not yet fully asleep. As he looked at the floor of his room he saw several disembodied heads. One of the heads was that of President Kennedy, who had just been assassinated. The others, he did not recognize at the time. Later, he realized who they had been. One was the head of Robert Kennedy; the other of Martin Luther King. He had the feeling at the time of the vision that all three men would be shot in the head. He also remembered two other heads—that of a Frenchman and of a very large Englishman—but no names.

On April 16, 1968, a Canadian by the name of Mrs. Joan Holt wrote to the *Evening Standard* premonition bureau conducted by Peter Fairley, their science editor, "Robert Kennedy to follow in his brother's footsteps and face similar danger."

"There is going to be a tragic passing in the Kennedy family very soon," said British medium Minie Bridges at a public sitting the last week of May 1968.

It seems clear to me that even the death of Senator Kennedy was part of a predestined master plan, whether we like it or not. Frequently, those who are already on the other side of life know what will happen on earth, and if they are not able to prevent it, they are at least ready to help thosc who are coming across make the transition as painlessly as possible under the circumstances.

To the people of Ireland, the Kennedys can do no wrong. Both Kennedys are great heroes to almost all Irishmen—far more so than they are to Americans. Both these thoughts should be kept in mind as I report still another psychic experience concerning the death of Robert Kennedy.

A fifty-three-year-old secretary by the name of Margaret M. Smith of Chicago, Illinois, was watching the Robert Kennedy funeral on television. As his casket was being carried out of the church to the hearse, she noticed a row of men standing at either side of the casket with their backs to it. They were dressed in gray business suits, very plain, and wore gray hats. These men looked very solemn and kept their eyes cast down. To her they looked like natives of Ireland. In fact, the suits looked homespun. As the casket went past, one of the men in the line turned his head and looked at the casket. Miss Smith thought that a person in a guard of honor should not do that, for she had taken the man in the gray suit as part of an honor guard. Then it occurred to her that the two lines of men were a little hazy, in a lighter gray. But she took this to be due to the television set, although other figures were quite clear. Later she discussed the funeral with a friend of hers in another city who had also seen the same broadcast. She asked her friend if she knew who the men in gray had been. Her friend had not seen the men in gray, nor had any of the others she then asked about them. Soon it became clear to Mrs. Smith that she alone had seen the spirit forms of what she takes to be the Kennedy's Irish ancestors, who had come to pay their last respects in a fitting manner.

The rumors and questions surrounding the deaths of both John and Robert Kennedy have never disappeared; in fact, there are more doubts and conspiracy theories than ever before. The possibility of a direct pipeline being established with one of the Kennedys on the other side of life is appealing to anyone searching for the definitive truth about past events. But to make such an attempt at communication requires two very definite things: one, a channel of communication—that is to say, a medium of the highest professional and ethical reputation—and two, the kind of questions that could establish, at least to the point of reasonable doubt, that communication really did occur between the investigator and the deceased.

26

The Ghostly Goings-on at the Octagon

COLONEL JOHN TAYLOE, in 1800, built his mansion, the magnificent building now known as the Octagon because of its shape. It stood and still stands in a fashionable part of Washington, but now houses the offices and exhibit of the American Institute of Architects.

In the early 1800s the Colonel's daughter ran away with a stranger and later returned home, asking forgiveness. This she did not get from her stern father and in despair she threw herself from the third-floor landing of the winding staircase that still graces the mansion. She landed on a spot near the base of the stairs, and this started a series of eerie events recorded in the mansion over the years.

Life magazine reported in an article in 1962 on haunted mansions that some visitors claim to have seen a shadow on the spot where the girl fell, while others refuse to cross the spot for reasons unknown; still others have heard the shriek of the falling girl.

The July, 1959, issue of the *American Institute of Architects Journal* contains a brief account of the long service record of employee James Cypress. Although he himself never saw any ghosts, he reports that at one time when his wife was ill, the doctor saw a man dressed in the clothes of 150 years ago coming down the spiral staircase. As the doctor looked at the strange man in puzzlement, the man just disappeared *into thin air*.

After some correspondence with J. W. Rankin, Director of the Institute, my wife and I finally started out for Washington on May 17, 1963. It was a warm day and the beautiful Georgian mansion set back from one of the capital's busier streets promised an adventure into a more relaxed past.

Mr. Rankin received us with interest and showed us around the house which was at that time fortunately empty of tourists and other visitors. It was he who supplied some of the background information on the Octagon, from which I quote:

The White House and the Octagon are relations, in a way. Both date from the beginning of government in the national capital; the White House was started first but the Octagon was first completed. Both have served as the official residence of the President.

It was early in 1797 that Colonel John Tayloe of Mount Airy, Virginia, felt the need for a town house. Mount Airy was a magnificent plantation of some three thousand acres, on which the Colonel, among many activities, bred and raced horses, but the call of the city was beginning to be felt, even in that early day; Philadelphia was the Colonel's choice, but his friend General Washington painted a glowing picture of what the new national capital might become and persuaded him to build the Octagon in surroundings that were then far removed from urbanity.

Dr. William Thornton, winner of the competition for the Capitol, was Colonel Tayloe's natural selection of architect.

On April 19, 1797, Colonel Tayloe purchased for $1,000 from Gustavus W. Scott—one of the original purchasers from the Government on November 21, 1796—Lot 8 in Square 170 in the new plot of Washington. Although, as the sketch of 1813 shows, the site was apparently out in a lonely countryside, the city streets had been definitely plotted, and the corner of New York Avenue and Eighteenth Street was then where it is today.

Obviously, from a glance at the plot plan, Colonel Tayloe's house derived its unique shape from the angle formed at the junction of these two streets. In spite of the name by which the mansion has always been known, Dr. Thornton could have had no intention of making the plan octagonal; the house planned itself from the street frontages.

Work on the building started in 1798 and progressed under the occasional inspection of General Washington, who did not live to see its completion in 1800. The mansion immediately took its place as a center of official and nonofficial social activities. Through its hospitable front door passed Madison, Jefferson, Monroe, Adams, Jackson, Decatur, Porter, Webster, Clay, Lafayette, Von Steuben, Calhoun, Randolph, Van Renssalaer and their ladies.

Social activities were forgotten, however, when the War of 1812 threatened and finally engulfed the new nation's capital. On August 24, 1814, the British left the White House a fire-gutted ruin. Mrs. Tayloe's foresight in establishing the French Minister—with his country's flag—as a house guest may have saved the Octagon from a like fate.

Colonel Tayloe is said to have dispatched a courier from Mount Airy, offering President Madison the use of the mansion, and the Madisons moved in on September 8, 1814.

For more than a year Dolly Madison reigned as hostess of the Octagon. In the tower room just over the entrance President Madison established his study, and here signed the Treaty of Ghent on February 17, 1815, establishing a peace with Great Britain which endures to this day.

After the death of Mrs. John Tayloe in 1855, the Octagon no longer served as the family's town house. That part of Washington lost for a time its residential character and the grand old mansion began to deteriorate.

In 1865 it was used as a school for girls. From 1866 to 1879 the Government rented it for the use of the Hydrographic Office. As an office and later as a studio dwelling, the Octagon served until about 1885, when it was entrusted by the Tayloe heirs to a caretaker.

Glenn Brown, longtime secretary of the American Institute of Architects, suggested in 1889 that the house would make an appropriate headquarters for the Institute.

When the architects started to rehabilitate the building, it was occupied by ten Negro families. The fine old drawing room was found to be piled four feet deep with rubbish. The whole interior was covered with grime, the fireplaces closed up, windows broken, but the structure, built a century before, had been denied no effort or expense to make it worthy of the Tayloes, and it still stood staunch and sound against time and neglect.

Miraculously the slender balusters of the famous stairway continued to serve, undoubtedly helped by the fact that every fifth baluster is of iron, firmly jointed to the handrail and carriage. Even the Coade Stone mantels in drawing room and dining room, with their deeply undercut sculpture, show not a chip nor scar. They had been brought from London in 1799 and bear that date with the maker's name.

On January 1, 1899, the Institute took formal possession of the rehabilitated mansion, its stable, smokehouse and garden.

So much for the house itself. I was given free rein to interview the staff, and proceeded to do so. Some of them are white, some colored; all displayed a high degree of intelligence and dignity of the kind one often finds among the staff in old Southern mansions.

I carefully tabulated the testimony given me by the employees individually, and checked the records of each of them for reliability and possible dark spots. There were none.

In view of the fact that nobody was exactly eager to be put down as having heard or seen ghosts, far from seeking publicity or public attention, I can only regard these accounts as respectable experiences of well-balanced individuals.

The building itself was then and still is in the care of Alric H. Clay, a man who is an executive with the title of superintendent. The museum part of the Octagon, as different from the large complex of offices of the American Institute of Architects, is under the supervision of Mrs. Belma May, who is its curator. She is assisted by a staff of porters and maids, since on occasion formal dinners or parties take place in the oldest part of the Octagon.

Mrs. May is not given to hallucinations or ghost stories, and in a matter-of-fact voice reported to me what she had experienced in the building. Most of her accounts are of very recent date.

Mrs. May saw the big chandelier swing of its own volition while all windows in the foyer were tightly shut; she mentioned the strange occurrence to a fellow worker. She also hears strange noises, not accounted for, and mostly on Saturdays. On one occasion, Mrs. May, accompanied by porters Allen and Bradley, found tracks of human feet in the otherwise undisturbed dust on the top floor, which had long been closed to the public. The tracks looked to her as "if someone were standing on toes, tiptoeing across the floor." It was from there that the daughter of Colonel Tayloe had jumped.

Mrs. May often smells cooking in the building when there is no party. She also feels "chills" on the first-floor landing.

Caretaker Mathew reports that when he walks up the stairs, he often feels as if someone is walking behind him, especially on the second floor. This is still happening to him now.

Ethel Wilson, who helps with parties, reports "chills" in the cloakroom.

Porter Allen was setting up for a meeting on the ground floor in the spring of 1962, when he heard noises "like someone dragging heavy furniture across the floor upstairs." In March, 1963, he and his colleague saw the steps "move as if someone was walking on them, but there was no one there." This happened at 9 :30 A.M.

Porter Bradley has heard groaning, but the sound is hard to pin down as to direction. Several times he has also heard footsteps.

Alric H. Clay, in charge of buildings, was driving by with his wife and two children one evening in the spring of 1962, when he noticed that the lights in the building were on. Leaving his family in the car, he entered the closed building by the back door and found everything locked as it should be. However, in addition to the lights being on, he also noticed that the *carpet edge was flipped* up at the spot where the girl had fallen to her death in the 1800s.

Clay, not believing in ghosts, went upstairs; there was nobody around, so he turned the lights off, put the carpet back as it should be, and went downstairs into the basement where the light controls are.

At that moment, *on the main floor above* (which he had just left) *he clearly heard someone* walk from the drawing room to the door and back. Since he had just checked all doors and knew them to be bolted firmly, he was so upset he almost electrocuted himself at the switches. The steps were heavy and definitely those of a man.

In February of 1963 there was a late party in the building. After everybody had left, Clay went home secure in the knowledge that he alone possessed the key to the back door. The layout of the Octagon is such that nobody can hide from an inspection, so a guest playing a prank by staying on is out of the question.

At 3:00 A.M. the police called Clay to advise him that all lights at the Octagon were blazing and that the building was wide open. Mr. Woverton, the controller, checked and together with the police went through the building, turning off all lights once more. Everything was locked up again, in the presence of police officers.

At 7:00 A.M., however, they returned to the Octagon once more, only to find the door unlocked, the lights again burning. Yet, Clay was the only one with the key!

"Mr. Clay," I said, "after all these weird experiences, do you believe in ghosts?"

"No, I don't," Clay said, and laughed somewhat uneasily. He is a man of excellent educational background and the idea of accepting the Uncanny was not at all welcome to him. But there it was.

"Then how do you explain the events of the past couple of years?"

"I don't," he said and shrugged. "I just don't have a rational explanation for them. But they certainly happened."

From the testimony heard, I am convinced that there are two ghosts in the Octagon, restlessly pacing the creaking old floors, vying with each other for the attention of the flesh-and-blood world outside.

There are the dainty footsteps of Colonel Tayloe's suicide daughter, retracing the walks she enjoyed but too briefly; and the heavy, guilt-laden steps of the father, who cannot cut himself loose from the ties that bind him to his house and the tragedy that darkened both the house and his life.

27

Phantoms of the American Revolution

NATHAN HALE, AS every schoolboy knows, was the American spy hanged by the British. He was captured at Huntington Beach and taken to Brooklyn for trial. How he was captured is a matter of some concern to the people of Huntington, Long Island. The town was originally settled by colonists from Connecticut who were unhappy with the situation in that colony. There were five principal families who accounted for the early settlement of Huntington, and to this day their descendants are the most prominent families in the area. They were the Sammes, the Downings, the Busches, the Pauldings, and the Cooks. During the Revolutionary War, feelings were about equally divided among the town people: some were Revolutionaries and some remained Tories. The consensus of historians is that members of these five prominent families, all of whom were Tories, were responsible for the betrayal of Nathan Hale to the British.

All this was brought to my attention by Mrs. Geraldine P. of Huntington. Mrs. P. grew up in what she considers the oldest house in Huntington, although the Huntington Historical Society claims that theirs is even older. Be that as it may, it was there when the Revolutionary War started. Local legend has it that an act of violence took place on the corner of the street, which was then a crossroads in the middle of a rural area. The house in which Mrs. P. grew up stands on that street. Mrs. P. suspects that the capture—or, at any rate, the betrayal—of the Revolutionary agent took place on that crossroads. When she tried to investigate the history of her house, she found little cooperation on the part of the local historical society. It was a conspiracy of silence, according to her, as if some people wanted to cover up a certain situation from the past.

The house had had a "strange depressing effect on all its past residents," according to Mrs. P. Her own father, who studied astrology and white magic for many years, has related an incident that occurred several years ago in the house. He awoke in the middle of the night in the master bedroom because he felt unusually cold. He became aware of "something" rushing about the room in wild, frantic circles. Because of his outlook and training, he spoke up, saying, "Can I help you?" But the rushing about became even more frantic. He then asked what was wrong and what could be done. But no communication was possible. When he saw that he could not communicate with the entity, Mrs. P.'s father finally said, "If I can't help you, then go away." There was a snapping sound, and the room suddenly became quiet and warm again, and he went back to sleep. There have been no other recorded incidents at the house in question. But Mrs. P. wonders if some guilty entity wants to manifest, not necessarily Nathan Hale, but perhaps someone connected with his betrayal.

At the corner of 43rd Street and Vanderbilt Avenue, Manhattan, one of the busiest and noisiest spots in all of New York City, there is a small commemorative plaque explaining that Nathan Hale, the Revolutionary spy, was executed on that spot by the British. I doubt that too many New Yorkers are aware of this, or can accurately pinpoint the location of the tragedy. It is even less likely that a foreigner would know about it. When I suggested to my good friend Sybil Leek that she accompany me to a psychically important spot for an experiment, she readily agreed. Despite the noises and the heavy traffic, the spot being across from Grand Central Station, Sybil bravely stood with me on the street corner and tried to get some sort of psychic impression.

"I get the impression of food and drink," Sybil said. I pointed out that there were restaurants all over the area, but Sybil shook her head. "No, I was thinking more of a place for food and drink, and I don't mean in the present. It is more like an inn, a transit place, and it has some connection with the river. A meeting place, perhaps, some sort of inn. Of course, it is very difficult in this noise and with all these new buildings here."

"If we took down these buildings, what would we see?"

"I think we would see a field and water. I have a strong feeling that there is a connection with water and with the inn. There are people coming and going—I sense a woman, but I don't think she's important. I am not sure . . . unless it would mean foreign. I hear a foreign language. Something like *Verchenen**. I can't quite get it. It is not German."

"Is there anything you feel about this spot?"

"This spot, yes. I think I want to go back two hundred years at least, it is not very clear, 1769 or 1796. That is the period. The connection with the water puzzles me."

*Verplanck's Point, on the Hudson River, was a Revolutionary strongpoint at the time.

"Do you feel an event of significance here at any time?"

"Yes. It is not strong enough to come through to me completely, but sufficiently *drastic* to make me feel a little nervous."

"In what way is it drastic?"

"Hurtful, violent. There are several people involved in this violence. Something connected with water, papers connected with water, that is part of the trouble."

Sybil then suggested that we go to the right to see if the impressions might be stronger at some distance. We went around the corner and I stopped. Was the impression any stronger?

"No, the impression is the same. Papers, violence. For a name, I have the impression of the letters P.T. Peter. It would be helpful to come here in the middle of the night, I think. I wish I could understand the connection with water, here in the middle of the city."

"Did someone die here?"

Sybil closed her eyes and thought it over for a moment. "Yes, but the death of this person was important at that time and indeed necessary. But there is more to it than just the death of the person. The disturbance involves lots of other things, lots of other people. In fact, two distinct races were involved, because I sense a lack of understanding. I think that this was a political thing, and the papers were important."

"Can you get anything further on the nature of this violence you feel here?"

"Just a disturbed feeling, an upheaval, a general disturbance. I am sorry I can't get much else. Perhaps if we came here at night, when things are quieter."

I suggested we get some tea in one of the nearby restaurants. Over tea, we discussed our little experiment and Sybil suddenly remembered an odd experience she had had when visiting the Hotel Biltmore before. (The plaque in question is mounted on the wall of the hotel.) "I receive many invitations to go to this particular area of New York," Sybil explained, "and when I go I always get the feeling of repulsion to the extent where I may be on my way down and get into a telephone booth and call the people involved and say, 'No, I'll meet you somewhere else.' I don't like this particular area we just left; I find it very depressing. I *feel trapped.*"

I am indebted to R. M. Sandwich of Richmond, Virginia, for an intriguing account of an E.S.P. experience he has connected to Patrick Henry. Mr. Sandwich stated that he has had only one E.S.P. experience and that it took place in one of the early estate-homes of Patrick Henry. He admitted that the experience altered his previously dim view of E.S.P. The present owner of the estate has said that Mr. Sandwich has not been the only one to experience strange things in that house.

The estate-home where the incident took place is called Pine Flash and is presently owned by E. E. Verdon, a personal friend of Mr. Sandwich. It is located in Hanover County, about fifteen miles outside of Richmond. The house was given to Patrick Henry by his father-in-law. After Henry had lived in it for a number of years, it burned to the ground and was not rebuilt until fifteen years later. During that time Henry resided in the old cottage, which is directly behind the house, and stayed there until the main house had been rebuilt. This cottage is frequently referred to in the area as the honeymoon cottage of young Patrick Henry. The new house was rebuilt exactly as it had been before the fire. As for the cottage, which is still in excellent condition, it is thought to be the oldest wood frame dwelling in Virginia. It may have been there even before Patrick Henry lived in it.

On the Fourth of July, 1968, the Sandwiches had been invited to try their luck at fishing in a pond on Mr. Verdon's land. Since they would be arriving quite early in the morning, they were told that the oars to the rowboat, which they were to use at the pond, would be found inside the old cottage. They arrived at Pine Flash sometime around six A.M. Mrs. Sandwich started unpacking their fishing gear and food supplies, while Mr. Sandwich decided to inspect the cottage. Although he had been to the place several times before, he had never actually been inside the cottage itself.

Here then is Mr. Sandwich's report.

"I opened the door, walked in, and shut the door tight behind me. Barely a second had passed after I shut the door when a strange feeling sprang over me. It was the kind of feeling you would experience if you were to walk into an extremely cold, damp room. I remember how still everything was, and then I distinctly heard footsteps overhead in the attic. I called out, thinking perhaps there was someone upstairs. No one answered, nothing. At that time I was standing directly in front of an old fireplace. I admit I was scared half to death. The footsteps were louder now and seemed to be coming down the thin staircase toward me. As they passed me, I felt a cold, crisp, odd feeling. I started looking around for something, anything that could have caused all this. It was during this time that I noticed the closed door open very, very slowly. The door stopped when it was half opened, almost beckoning me to take my leave, which I did at great speed! As I went through that open door, I felt the same cold mass of air I had experienced before. Standing outside, I watched the door slam itself, almost in my face! My wife was still unpacking the car and claims she neither saw nor heard anything."

Revolutionary figures have a way of hanging on to places they liked in life. Candy Bosselmann of Indiana has had a long history of psychic experiences. She is a budding trance medium and not at all ashamed of her talents. In 1964 she happened to be visiting Ashland, the home of Henry Clay, in Lexington, Kentucky. She had never been to Ashland, so she decided to take a look at it. She and other visitors were shown through the house by an older man, a professional guide, and Candy became somewhat restless listening to his historical ramblings. As the group entered the library and the guide explained the beautiful ash paneling taken from surrounding trees (for which the home is named), she became even more restless. She knew very well that it was the kind of feeling that forewarned her of some sort of psychic event. As she was looking over toward the fireplace, framed by two candelabra, she suddenly saw a very tall, white-haired man in a long black frock coat standing next to it. One elbow rested on the mantel, and his head was in his hand, as if he were pondering something very important.

Miss Bosselmann was not at all emotionally involved with the house. In fact, the guided tour bored her, and she would have preferred to be outside in the stables, since she has a great interest in horses. Her imagination did not conjure up what she saw: she knew in an instant that she was looking at the spirit imprint of Henry Clay.

In 1969 she visited Ashland again, and this time she went into the library deliberately. With her was a friend who wasn't at all psychic. Again, the same restless feeling came over her. But when she was about to go into trance, she decided to get out of the room in a hurry.

Rock Ford, the home of General Edward Hand, is located four miles south of Lancaster, Pennsylvania, and commands a fine view of the Conestoga River. The house is not a restoration but a well-preserved eighteenth-century mansion, with its original floors, railings, shutters, doors, cupboards, panelings, and window glass. Even the original wall painting can be seen. It is a four-story brick mansion in the Georgian style, with the rooms grouped around a center hall in the design popular during the latter part of the eighteenth century. The rooms are furnished with antiquities of the period, thanks to the discovery of an inventory of General Hand's estate which permitted the local historical society to supply authentic articles of daily usage wherever the originals had disappeared from the house.

Perhaps General Edward Hand is not as well known as a hero of the American Revolution as others are, but to the people of the Pennsylvania Dutch country he is an important figure, even though he was of Irish origin rather than German. Trained as a medical doctor at Trinity College, Dublin, he came to America in 1767 with the Eighteenth Royal Irish Regiment of Foote. However, he resigned British service in 1774 and came to Lancaster to practice medicine and surgery. With the fierce love of liberty so many of the Irish possess, Dr. Hand joined the Revolutionaries in July of 1775, becoming a lieutenant colonel in the Pennsylvania Rifle Battalion. He served in the army until 1800, when he was discharged as a major general. Dr. Hand was present at the Battle of Trenton, the Battle of Long Island, the Battle of White Plains, the Battle of Princeton, the campaign against the Iroquois, and the surrender of Cornwallis at Yorktown. He also served on the tribunal which convicted Major John Andre, the British spy, and later became the army's adjutant general. He was highly regarded by George Washington, who visited him in his home toward the end of the war. When peace came, Hand became a member of the Continental Congress and served in the Assembly of Pennsylvania as representative of his area. He moved into Rock Ford when it was completed in 1793 and died there in September 1802.

Today, hostesses from a local historical society serve as guides for the tourists who come to Rock Ford in increasing numbers. Visitors are taken about the lower floor and basement and are told of General Hand's agricultural experiments, his medical studies, and his association with George Washington. But unless you ask specifically, you are not likely to hear about what happened to the house after General Hand died. To begin with, the General's son committed suicide in the house. Before long the family died out, and eventually the house became a museum since no one wanted to live in it for very long. At one time, immigrants were contacted at the docks and offered free housing if they would live in the mansion. None stayed. There was something about the house that was not as it should be, something that made people fear it and leave it just as quickly as they could.

Mrs. Ruth S. lives in upstate New York. In 1967 a friend showed her a brochure concerning Rock Ford, and the house intrigued her. Since she was traveling in that direction, she decided to pay Rock Ford a visit. With her family, she drove up to the house and parked her car in the rear. At that moment she had an eerie feeling that something wasn't right. Mind you, Mrs. S. had not been to the house before, had no knowledge about it nor any indication that anything unusual had occurred in it. The group of visitors was quite small. In addition to herself and her family, there were two young college boys and one other couple. Even though it was a sunny day, Mrs. S. felt icy cold.

"I felt a presence before we entered the house and before we heard the story from the guide," she explained. "If I were a hostess there, I wouldn't stay there alone for two consecutive minutes." Mrs. S. had been to many old houses and restorations before but had never felt as she did at Rock Ford.

It is not surprising that George Washington should be the subject of a number of psychic accounts. Probably the best known (and most frequently misinterpreted) story concerns General Washington's vision which came to him during the encampment at Valley Forge, when the fortunes of war had gone heavily in favor of the British, and the American army, tattered and badly fed, was just about falling to pieces. If there ever was need for divine guidance, it was at Valley Forge. Washington was in the habit of meditating in the woods at times and saying his prayers when he was quite alone. On one of those occasions he returned to his quarters more worried than usual. As he busied himself with his papers, he had the feeling of a presence in the room. Looking up, he saw opposite him a singularly beautiful woman. Since he had given orders not to be disturbed, he couldn't understand how she had gotten into the room. Although he questioned her several times, the visitor would not reply. As he looked at the apparition, for that is what it was, the General became more and more entranced with her, unable to make any move. For a while he thought he was dying, for he imagined that the apparition of such unworldly creatures as he was seeing at that moment must accompany the moment of transition.

Finally, he heard a voice, saying, "Son of the Republic, look and learn." At the same time, the visitor extended her arm toward the east, and Washington saw what to him appeared like white vapor at some distance. As the vapor dissipated, he saw the various countries of the world and the oceans that separated them. He then noticed a dark, shadowy angel standing between Europe and America, taking water out of the ocean and sprinkling it over America with one hand and over Europe with the other. When he did this, a cloud rose from the countries thus sprinkled, and the cloud then moved westward until it enveloped America. Sharp flashes of lightning became visible at intervals in the cloud. At the same time, Washington thought he heard the anguished cries of the American people underneath the cloud. Next, the strange visitor showed him a vision of what America would look like in the future, and he saw villages and towns springing up from one coast to the other until the entire land was covered by them.

"Son of the Republic, the end of the century cometh, look and learn," the visitor said. Again Washington was shown a dark cloud approaching America, and he saw the American people fighting one another. A bright angel then appeared wearing a crown on which was written the word Union. This angel bore the American Flag, which he placed between the divided nation, saying, "Remember, you are brethren." At that instant, the inhabitants threw away their weapons and became friends again.

Once more the mysterious voice spoke. "Son of the Republic, look and learn." Now the dark angel put a trumpet to his mouth and sounded three distinct blasts. Then he took water from the ocean and sprinkled it on Europe, Asia, and Africa. As he did so, Washington saw black clouds rise from the countries he had sprinkled. Through the black clouds, Washington could see red lights and hordes of armed men, marching by land and sailing by sea to America, and he saw these armies devastate the entire country, burn the villages, towns, and cities, and as he listened to the thundering of the cannon, Washington heard the mysterious voice saying again, "Son of the Republic, look and learn."

Once more the dark angel put the trumpet to his mouth and sounded a long and fearful blast. As he did so, a light as of a thousand suns shone down from above him and pierced the dark cloud which had enveloped America. At the same time the angel wearing the word Union on his head descended from the heavens, followed by legions of white spirits. Together with the inhabitants of America, Washington saw them renew the battle and heard the mysterious voice telling him once again, "Son of the Republic, look and learn."

For the last time, the dark angel dipped water from the ocean and sprinkled it on America; the dark cloud rolled back and left the inhabitants of America victorious. But the vision continued. Once again Washington saw villages, towns, and cities spring up, and he heard the bright angel exclaim, "While the stars remain and the heavens send down dew upon the earth, so long shall the Union last." With that, the scene faded, and Washington beheld once again the mysterious visitor before him. As if she had guessed his question, the apparition then said:

"Son of the Republic, what you have seen is thus interpreted: Three great perils will come upon the Republic. The most fearful is the third, during which the whole world united shall not prevail against her. Let every child of the Republic learn to live for his God, his land, and his Union." With that, the vision disappeared, and Washington was left pondering over his experience.

One can interpret this story in many ways, of course. If it really occurred, and there are a number of accounts of it in existence which lead me to believe that there is a basis of fact to this, then we are dealing with a case of prophecy on the part of General Washington. It is a moot question whether the third peril has already come upon us, in the shape of World War II, or whether it is yet to befall us. The light that is stronger than many suns may have ominous meaning in this age of nuclear warfare.

Washington himself is said to have appeared to Senator Calhoun of South Carolina at the beginning of the War between the States. At that time, the question of secession had not been fully decided, and Calhoun, one of the most powerful politicians in the government, was not sure whether he could support the withdrawal of his state from the Union. The question lay heavily on his mind when he went to bed one hot night in Charleston, South Carolina. During the night, he thought he awoke to see the apparition of General George Washington standing by his bedside. The General wore his presidential attire and seemed surrounded by a bright outline, as if some powerful source of light shone behind him. On the senator's desk lay the declaration of secession, which he had not yet signed. With Calhoun's and South Carolina's support, the Confederacy would be well on its way, having closed ranks. Earnestly, the spirit of George Washington pleaded with Senator Calhoun not to sign the declaration. He warned him against the impending perils coming to America as a divided nation; he asked him to reconsider his decision and to work for the preservation of the Union. But Calhoun insisted that the South had to go its own way. When the spirit of Washington saw that nothing could sway Senator Calhoun, he warned him that the very act of his signature would be a black spot upon the Constitution of the United States. With that, the vision is said to have vanished.

One can easily explain the experience as a dream, coming as it did at a time when Senator Calhoun was particularly upset over the implications of his actions. On the other hand, there is this to consider: Shortly after Calhoun had signed the document taking South Carolina into the Confederacy, a dark spot appeared on his hand, a spot that would not vanish and for which medical authorities had no adequate explanation.

Mrs. Margaret Smith of Orlando, Florida, has had a long history of psychic experiences. She has personally seen the ghostly monks of Beaulieu, England; she has seen the actual lantern of Joe Baldwin, the famous headless ghost of Wilmington, North Carolina; and she takes her "supernatural" experiences in her stride the way other people feel about their musical talents or hobbies. When she was only a young girl, her grandmother took her to visit the von Steuben house in Hackensack, New Jersey. (General F. W. A. von Steuben was a German supporter of the American Revolution who aided General Washington with volunteers who had come over from Europe because of repressions, hoping to find greater freedom in the New World). The house was old and dusty, the floorboards were creaking, and there was an eerie atmosphere about it. The house had been turned into a historical museum, and there were hostesses to take visitors through.

While her grandmother was chatting with the guide downstairs, the young girl walked up the stairs by herself. In one of the upstairs parlors she saw a man sitting in a chair in the corner. She assumed he was another guide. When she turned around to ask him a question about the room, he was gone. Since she hadn't heard him leave, that seemed rather odd to her, especially as the floorboards would creak with every step. But being young she didn't pay too much attention to this peculiarity. A moment later, however, he reappeared. As soon as she saw him, she asked the question she had on her mind. This time he did not disappear but answered her in a slow, painstaking voice that seemed to come from far away. When he had satisfied her curiosity about the room, he asked her some questions about herself, and finally asked the one which stuck in her mind for many years afterward—"What is General Washington doing now about the British?"

Margaret was taken aback at this question. She was young, but she knew very well that Washington had been dead for many years. Tactfully, she told him this and added that Harry Truman was now president and that the year was 1951. At this information, the man looked stunned and sat down again in the chair. As Margaret watched him in fascinated horror, he faded away.

"Major John Andre's fateful excursion from General Sir Henry Clinton's headquarters at Number 1 Broadway to the gallows on the hill at Tappan took less than a week of the eighteenth century, exactly one hundred seventy years ago at this writing. It seems incredible that this journey should make memorable the roads he followed, the houses he entered, the roadside wells where he stopped to quench his thirst, the words he spoke. But it did." This eloquent statement by Harry Hansen goes a long way in describing the relative importance of so temporary a matter as the fate and capture of a British agent during the Revolutionary War.

In the Tarrytowns, up in Westchester County, places associated with Andre are considered prime tourist attractions. More research effort has been expended on the exploration of even the most minute detail of the ill-fated Andre's last voyage than on some far worthier (but less romantic) historical projects elsewhere. A number of good books have been written about the incident, every schoolboy knows about it, and John Andre has gone into history as a gentlemanly but losing hero of the American Revolutionary War. But in presenting history to schoolchildren as well as to the average adult, most American texts ignore the basic situation as it then existed.

To begin with, the American Revolutionary War was more of a civil war than a war between two nations. Independence was by no means desired by all Americans; in fact, the Declaration of Independence had difficulty passing the Continental Congress and did so only after much negotiating behind the scenes and the elimination of a number of passages, such as those relating to the issue of slavery, considered unacceptable by Southerners. When the Declaration of Independence did become the law of the land—at least as far as its advocates were concerned—there were still those who had not supported it originally and who felt themselves put in the peculiar position of being disloyal to their new country or becoming disloyal to the country they felt they ought to be loyal to. Those who preferred continued ties with Great Britain were called Tories, and numbered among them generally were the more influential and wealthier elements in the colonies. There were exceptions, of course, but on the whole the conservatives did not support the cause of the Revolution by any means. Any notion that the country arose *as a man* to fight the terrible British is pure political make-believe. The issues were deep and manifold, but they might have been resolved eventually through negotiations. There is no telling what might have happened if both England and the United Colonies had continued to negotiate for a better relationship. The recent civil war in Spain was far more a war between two distinct groups than was the American Revolutionary War. In the latter friends and enemies lived side by side in many areas, the lines were indistinctly drawn, and members of the same family might support one side or the other. The issue was not between Britain, the invading enemy, and America, the attacked; on the contrary, it was between the renunciation of all ties with the motherland and continued adherence to some form of relationship. Thus, it had become a political issue far more than a purely patriotic or national issue. After all, there were people of the same national background on both sides, and nearly everyone had relatives in England.

Under the circumstances, the question of what constituted loyalty was a tricky one. To the British, the colonies were in rebellion and thus disloyal to the king. To the Americans, anyone supporting the British government after the Declaration of Independence was considered disloyal. But the percentage of those who could not support independence was very large all through the war, far more than a few scattered individuals. While some of these Tories continued to support Britain for personal or commercial reasons, others did so out of honest political conviction. To them, helping a British soldier did not constitute high treason but, to the contrary, was their normal duty. Added to this dilemma was the fact that there were numerous cases of individuals crossing the lines on both sides, for local business reasons, to remove women and children caught behind the lines, or to parley about military matters, such as the surrender of small detachments incapable of rejoining their regiments, or the obtaining of help for wounded soldiers. The Revolutionary War was not savagely fought; it was, after all, a war between gentlemen. There were no atrocities, no concentration camps, and no slaughter of the innocent.

In the fall of 1780 the situation had deteriorated to a standstill of sorts, albeit to the detriment of the American forces. The British were in control of the entire South, and they held New York firmly in their grip. The British sloop *Vulture* was anchored in the middle of the Hudson River opposite Croton Point. In this position, it was not too far from that formidable bastion of the American defense system, West Point. Only West Point and its multiple fortifications stood in the way of total defeat for the American forces.

Picture, if you will, the situation in and around New York. The British Army was in full control of the city, that is to say, Manhattan, with the British lines going right through Westchester County. The Americans were entrenched on the New Jersey shore and on both sides of the Hudson River from Westchester County upward. On the American side were first of all, the regular Continental Army, commanded by George Washington, and also various units of local militia. Uniforms for the militia men ran the gamut of paramilitary to civilian, and their training and backgrounds were also extremely spotty. It would have been difficult at times to distinguish a soldier of the Revolutionary forces from a civilian.

The British didn't call on the citizens of the area they occupied for special services, but it lay in the nature of this peculiar war that many volunteered to help either side. The same situation which existed among the civilian population in the occupied areas also prevailed where the Revolution was successful. Tory families kept on giving support to the British, and when they were found out they were charged with high treason. Nevertheless, they continued right on supplying aid. Moreover, the lines between British and American forces were not always clearly drawn. They shifted from day to day, and if anyone wanted to cross from north of Westchester into New Jersey, for instance, he might very well find himself in the wrong part of the country if he didn't know his way around or if he hadn't checked the latest information. To make matters even more confusing, Sir Henry Clinton was in charge of the British troops in New York City, while Governor Clinton ruled the state of New York, one of the thirteen colonies, from Albany.

In the spring of 1779 Sir Henry Clinton received letters from an unknown correspondent who signed himself only "Gustavus." From the content of these letters, the British commander knew instantly that he was dealing with a high-ranking American officer. Someone on the American side wished to make contact in order to serve the British cause. Clinton turned the matter over to his capable adjutant general, Major John Andre. Andre, whose specialty was what we call intelligence today, replied to the letters, using the pseudonym John Anderson.

Andre had originally been active in the business world but purchased a commission as a second lieutenant in the British Army in 1771. He arrived in America in 1774 and served in the Philadelphia area. Eventually he served in a number of campaigns and by 1777 had been promoted to captain. Among the wealthy Tory families he became friendly with during the British occupation of Philadelphia was the Shippen family. One of the daughters of that family later married General Benedict Arnold.

Andre's first major intelligence job was to make contact with a secret body of Royalists living near Chesapeake Bay. This group of Royalists had agreed to rise against the Americans if military protection were sent to them. Essentially, Andre was a staff officer, not too familiar with field work and therefore apt to get into difficulties once faced with the realities of rugged terrain. As the correspondence continued, both Clinton and Andre suspected that the Loyalist writing the letters was none other than General Benedict Arnold, and eventually Arnold conceded this.

After many false starts, a meeting took place between Major General Benedict Arnold, the commander of West Point, and Major John Andre on the night of September 21, 1780, at Haverstraw on the Hudson. At the time, Arnold made his headquarters at the house of Colonel Beverley Robinson, which was near West Point.

The trip had been undertaken on Andre's insistence, very much against the wishes of his immediate superior, Sir Henry Clinton. As Andre was leaving, Clinton reminded him that under no circumstances was he to change his uniform or to take papers with him. It was quite sufficient to exchange views with General Arnold and then to return to the safety of the British lines.

Unfortunately, Andre disobeyed these commands. General Arnold had with him six papers which he persuaded Andre to place between his stockings and his feet. The six papers contained vital information about the fortifications at West Point, sufficient to allow the British to capture the strongpoint with Arnold's help. "The six papers which Arnold persuaded Andre to place between his stockings and his feet did not contain anything of value that could not have been entrusted to Andre's memory or at most contained in a few lines in cipher that would not have been intelligible to anyone else," states Otto Hufeland in his book *Westchester County during the American Revolution*. But it is thought that Andre still distrusted General Arnold and wanted something in the latter's handwriting that would incriminate him if there was any deception.

It was already morning when the two men parted. General Arnold returned to his headquarters by barge, leaving Andre with Joshua Smith, who was to see to his safe return. Andre's original plan was to get to the sloop *Vulture* and return to New York by that route. But somehow Joshua Smith convinced him that he should go by land. He also persuaded Andre to put on a civilian coat, which he supplied. General Arnold had given them passes to get through the lines, so toward sunset Andre, Smith, and a servant rode down to King's Ferry, crossing the river from Stony Point to Verplanck's Point and on into Westchester County.

Taking various back roads and little-used paths which made the journey much longer, Andre eventually arrived at a spot not far from Philipse Castle. There he ran into three militia men: John Paulding, Isaac Van Wart, and David Williams. They were uneducated men in their early twenties, and far from experienced in such matters as how to question a suspected spy. The three fellows weren't looking for spies, however, but for cattle thieves which were then plaguing the area. They were on the lookout near the Albany Post Road when Van Wart saw Andre pass on his horse. They stopped him, and that is where Andre made his first mistake. Misinterpreting the Hessian coat Paulding wore (he had obtained it four days before when escaping from a New York prison) and thinking that he was among British Loyalists, he immediately identified himself as a British officer and asked them not to detain him. But the three militia men made him dismount and undress, and then the documents were discovered. It has been said that they weren't suspicious of him at all, but that the elegant boots, something very valuable in those days, tempted them, and that they were more interested in Andre's clothing than in what he might have on him. Whatever the motivation, Andre was brought to Colonel Jameson's headquarters at Sand's Mill, which is called Armonk today.

Jameson sent the prisoner to General Arnold, a strange decision which indicates some sort of private motive. The papers, however, he sent directly to General Washington, who was then at Hartford. Only upon the return of his next-in-command, Major Tallmadge, did the real state of affairs come to light. On Tallmadge's insistence, the party escorting Andre to General Arnold was recalled and brought back to Sand's Mills. But a letter telling General Arnold of Andre's capture was permitted to continue on its way to West Point!

Benedict Arnold received the letter the next morning at breakfast. The General rose from the table, announced that he had to go across the river to West Point immediately, and went to his room in great agitation. His wife followed him, and he informed her that he must leave at once, perhaps forever. Then he mounted his horse and dashed down to the riverside. Jumping into his barge, he ordered his men to row him to the *Vulture*, some seventeen miles below. He explained to his men that he came on a flag of truce and promised them an extra ration of rum if they made it particularly quickly. When the barge arrived at the British vessel, he jumped aboard and even tried to force the bargemen to enter the King's service on the threat of making them prisoners. The men refused, and the *Vulture* sailed on to New York City. On arrival, General Clinton freed the bargemen, a most unusual act of gallantry in those days.

Meanwhile Andre was being tried as a spy. Found guilty by a court-martial at Tappan, he was executed by hanging on October 2,1780. The three militia men who had thus saved the very existence of the new republic were voted special medals by Congress.

The entire area around Tappan and the Tarrytowns is "Andre" country. At Philipse Castle there is a special exhibit of Andre memorabilia in a tiny closet under the stairs. There is a persistent rumor that Andre was trying to escape from his captors. According to Mrs. Cornelia Beekman, who then lived at the van Cortlandt House in Peekskill, there was in her house a suitcase containing an American army uniform and a lot of cash. That suitcase was to be turned over to anyone bringing a written note from Andre. Joshua Hett Smith, who helped Andre escape after his meeting with Arnold, later asked for the suitcase; however, as Smith had nothing in writing, Beekman refused to give it to him. However, this story came to light only many years after the Revolution, perhaps because Mrs. Beekman feared to be drawn into a treason trial or because she had some feelings of her own in the matter.

Our next stop was to be the van Cortlandt mansion, not more than fifteen minutes away by car. Obviously, Pat Smith was in a good mood this morning. In her little foreign car she preceded us at such a pace that we had great difficulty keeping up with her. It was a sight to behold how this lady eased her way in and out of traffic with an almost serpentine agility that made us wonder how long she could keep it up. Bravely following her, we passed Sleepy Hollow Cemetery and gave it some thought. No, we were not too much concerned with all the illustrious Dutch Americans buried there, nor with Washington Irving and nearby Sunnyside; we were frankly concerned with ourselves. Would we also wind up at Sleepy Hollow Cemetery, or would we make it to the van Cortlandt mansion in one piece. . . ?

The mansion itself is a handsome two-story building, meticulously restored and furnished with furniture and artworks of the eighteenth century, some of it from the original house. Turned into a tourist attraction by the same foundation which looked after Philipsburg Manor, the house, situated on a bluff, is a perfect example of how to run an outdoor museum. Prior to climbing the hill to the mansion itself, however, we visited the ferryboat house at the foot of the hill. In the eighteenth century and the early part of the nineteenth century, the river came close to the house, and it was possible for the ships bringing goods to the van Cortlandts to come a considerable distance inland to discharge their merchandise. The Ferryboat Inn seemed a natural outgrowth of having a ferry at that spot: the ferry itself crossed an arm of the Hudson River, not very wide, but wide enough not to be forded on foot or by a small boat. Since so much of these buildings had been restored, I wondered whether Ingrid would pick up anything from the past.

The inn turned out to be a charming little house. Downstairs we found what must have been the public room, a kitchen, and another room, with a winding staircase leading to the upper story. Frankly, I expected very little from this but did not want to offend Pat Smith, who had suggested the visit.

"Funny," Ingrid said, "when I walked into the door, I had the feeling that I had to force my way *through a crowd*."

The curator seemed surprised at this, for she hadn't expected anything from this particular visit either. "I can't understand this," she said plaintively. "This is one of the friendliest buildings we have."

"Well," I said, "ferryboat inns in the old days weren't exactly like the Hilton."

"I feel a lot of activity here," Ingrid said. "Something happened here, not a hanging, but connected with one."

We went upstairs, where I stopped Ingrid in front of a niche that contained a contemporary print of Andre's execution. As yet we had not discussed Major Andre or his connection with the area, and I doubt very much whether Ingrid realized there was a connection. "As you look at this, do you have any idea who it is?" I asked.

Ingrid, who is very nearsighted, looked at the picture from a distance and said, "I feel that he may have come through this place at one time." And so he might have.

As we walked up the hill to the van Cortlandt mansion, the time being just right for a visit as the tourists would be leaving, I questioned Pat Smith about the mansion.

"My mother used to know the family who owns the house," Pat Smith began. "Among the last descendants of the van Cortlandts were Mrs. Jean Brown and a Mrs. Mason. This was in the late thirties or the forties, when I lived in New Canaan. Apparently there were such manifestations at the house that the two ladies called the Archbishop of New York for help. They complained that a spirit was 'acting up,' that there was the sound of a coach that no one else could see and other inexplicable noises of the usual poltergeist nature."

"What did they do about it?"

"Despite his reluctance to get involved, the Archbishop did go up to the manor, partly because of the prominence of the family. He put on his full regalia and went through a ritual of exorcism. Whether or not it did any good, I don't know, but a little later a psychic sensitive went through the house also and recorded some of these noises. As far as I know, none of it was ever published, and for all I know, it may still be there—the specter, that is."

We had now arrived at the mansion, and we entered the downstairs portion of the house. Two young ladies dressed in colonial costumes received us and offered us some cornmeal tidbits baked in the colonial manner. We went over the house from top to bottom, from bottom to top, but Ingrid felt absolutely nothing out of the ordinary. True, she felt the vibrations of people having lived in the house, having come and gone, but no tragedy, no deep imprint, and, above all, no presence. Pat Smith seemed a little disappointed. She didn't really *believe* in ghosts as such, but having had some E.S.P. experiences at Sunnyside, she wasn't altogether sure. At that instant she remembered having left her shopping bag at the Ferryboat Inn. The bag contained much literature on the various colonial houses in the area, and she wanted to give it to us. Excusing herself, she dashed madly back down the hill to the Ferryboat Inn. She was back in no time, a little out of breath, which made me wonder whether she had wanted to make her solo visit to the Ferryboat Inn at dusk just as *brief* as humanly possible.

In a splendid Victorian mansion surmounted by a central tower, the Historical Society of the Tarrytowns functions as an extremely well organized local museum as well as a research center. Too prudent to display items of general interest that might be found elsewhere in greater quantity and better quality, the Historical Society concentrates on items and information pertaining to the immediate area. It is particularly strong on pamphlets, papers, maps, and other literature of the area from 1786 onward. One of the principal rooms in the Society's museum is the so-called Captors' Room. In it are displays of a sizable collection of material dealing with the capture of Major Andre. These include lithographs, engravings, documentary material, letters, and, among other things, a chair. It is the chair Andre sat in when he was still a free man at the Underhill home, south of Yorktown Heights. Mrs. Adelaide Smith, the curator, was exceptionally helpful to us when we stated the purpose of our visit. Again, as I always do, I prevented Ingrid from hearing my conversation with Mrs. Smith, or with Miss Smith, who had come along now that she had recovered her shopping bag full of literature. As soon as I could get a moment alone with Ingrid, I asked her to touch the chair in question.

"I get just a slight impression," she said, seating herself in the chair, then getting up again. "There may have been a meeting in here of some kind, or he may have been sentenced while near or sitting in this chair. I think there was a meeting in this room to determine what would happen."

But she could not get anything very strong about the chair. Looking at the memorabilia, she then commented, "I feel he was chased for quite a while before he was captured. I do feel that the chair in this room has something to do with his sentence."

"Is the chair authentic?"

"Yes, I think so."

"Now concerning this room, the Captors' Room, do you feel anything special about it?"

"Yes, I think this is where it was decided, and I feel there were a lot of men here, men from town and from the government."

Had Ingrid wanted to manufacture a likely story to please me, she could not have done worse. Everything about the room and the building would have told her that it was of the nineteenth century, and that the impression she had just described seemed out of place, historically speaking. But those were her feelings, and as a good sensitive she felt obliged to say whatever came into her mind or whatever she was impressed with, not to examine it as to whether it fit in with the situation she found herself in. I turned to the curator and asked, "Mrs. Smith, what was this room used for, and how old is the building itself?"

"The building is about one hundred twenty-five years old; our records show it was built between 1848 and 1850 by Captain Jacob Odell, the first mayor of Tarrytown. It was built as one house, and since its erection two families have lived here. First, there were the Odells, and later Mr. and Mrs. Aussie Case. Mrs. Case is eighty-seven now and retired. This house was purchased for the Society to become their headquarters. It has been used as our headquarters for over twenty years."

"Was there anything on this spot before this house was built?"

"I don't know."

"Has anyone ever been tried or judged in this room?"

"I don't know."

Realizing that a piece of furniture might bring with itself part of the atmosphere in which it stood when some particularly emotional event took place, I questioned Mrs. Smith about the history of the chair.

"This chair, dated 1725, was presented to us from Yorktown. It was the chair in which Major Andre sat the morning of his capture, when he and Joshua Smith stopped at the house of Isaac Underhill for breakfast."

The thoughts going through Andre's head that morning, when he was almost sure of a successful mission, must have been fairly happy ones. He had succeeded in obtaining the papers from General Arnold; he had slept reasonably well, been fed a good breakfast, and was now, presumably, on his way to

Manhattan and a reunion with his commanding general, Sir Henry Clinton. If Ingrid felt any meetings around that chair, she might be reaching back beyond Andre's short use of the chair, perhaps into the history of the Underhill home itself. Why, then, did she speak of sentence and capture, facts she would know from the well-known historical account of Major Andre's mission? I think that the many documents and memorabilia stored in the comparatively small room might have created a common atmosphere in which bits and snatches of past happenings had been reproduced in some fashion. Perhaps Ingrid was able to tune in on this shallow but nevertheless still extant psychic layer.

Major Andre became a sort of celebrity in his own time. His stature as a British master spy was exaggerated far out of proportion even during the Revolutionary War. This is understandable when one realizes how close the cause of American independence had come to total defeat. If Andre had delivered the documents entrusted to him by Major General Arnold to the British, West Point could not have been held. With the fall of the complicated fortifications at the point, the entire North could have soon been occupied by the British. Unquestionably, the capture of Major Andre was a turning point in the war, which had then reached a stalemate, albeit one in favor of the British. They could afford to wait and sit it out while the Continental troops were starving to death, unable to last another winter.

General Arnold's betrayal was by no means a sudden decision; his feelings about the war had changed some time prior to the actual act. The reasons may be seen in his background, his strong Tory leanings, and a certain resentment against the command of the Revolutionary Army. He felt he had not advanced quickly enough; the command at West Point was given him only three months prior to Andre's capture. Rather than being grateful for the belated recognition of his talents by the Continental command, Arnold saw it as a godsend to fulfill his own nefarious task. For several months he had been in correspondence with Sir Henry Clinton in New York, and his decision to betray the cause of independence was made long before he became commander of West Point.

But Andre wasn't the master spy later accounts try to make him out: his bumbling response when captured by the three militiamen shows that he was far from experienced in such matters. Since he had carried on his person a *laissez-passer* signed by General Arnold, he needed only to produce this document and the men would have let him go. Instead, he *volunteered* the information that he was a British officer. All this because one of the militia men wore a Hessian coat. It never occurred to Andre that the coat might have been stolen or picked up on the battlefield! But there was a certain weakness in Andre's character, a certain conceit, and the opportunity of presenting himself as a British officer on important business was too much to pass up when he met the three nondescript militia men. Perhaps his personal vanity played a part in this fateful decision; perhaps he really believed himself to be among troops on his own side. Whatever the cause of his strange behavior, he paid with his life for it. Within weeks after the hanging of Major Andre, the entire Continental Army knew of the event, the British command was made aware of it, and in a detailed document Sir Henry Clinton explained what he had had in mind in case Arnold would have been able to deliver West Point and its garrison to the British. Thus, the name Andre became a household word among the troops of both sides.

After his execution on October 2,1780, at Tappan, Andre was buried at the foot of the gallows. In 1821 his body was exhumed and taken to England and reburied at Westminster Abbey. By 1880 tempers had sufficiently cooled and British-American friendship was firmly enough established to permit the erection of a monument to the event on the spot where the three militia men had come across Major Andre. Actually, the monument itself was built in 1853, but on the occasion of the centennial of Andre's capture, a statue and bronze plaque were added and the monument surrounded with a protective metal fence. It stands near a major road and can easily be observed when passing by car. It is a beautiful monument, worthy of the occasion. There is only one thing wrong with it, be it ever so slight: *It stands at the wrong spot*. My good friend, Elliott Schryver, the eminent editor and scholar, pointed out the actual spot at some distance to the east.

In studying Harry Hansen's book on the area, I have the impression that he shares this view. In order to make a test of my own, we stopped by the present monument, and I asked Ingrid to tell me what she felt. I had purposely told her that the spot had no direct connection with anything else we were doing that day, so she could not consciously sense what the meaning of our brief stop was. Walking around the monument two or three times, touching it, and "taking in" the atmosphere psychically, she finally came up to me, shook her head, and said, "I am sorry, Hans, there is absolutely nothing here. Nothing at all."

But why not? If the Revolutionary taverns can be moved a considerable distance to make them more accessible to tourists, why shouldn't a monument be erected where everyone can see it instead of in some thicket where a prospective visitor might break a leg trying to find it? Nobody cares, least of all Major Andre.

THE OLD SOUTH

28

Haunted Alabama

NOT UNLIKE THE roll call at the national conventions I will call upon the shades of various southern states to come forward with the accounts of their psychic activities. I am speaking to you not only of haunted houses and ghosts seen or heard by living people but also of people who are themselves gifted with the ability to experience communications from the other world. This is as it should be, for where would the phantoms of Dixie be if it were not for flesh and blood people to acknowledge them, to help them understand themselves at times, or at least to relate their unhappy past?

Mrs. Nancy Anglin originally contacted me when I collected material on reincarnation cases for a previous book called *Born Again*. Although she now lives in California, she was then and had been for a long time a resident of Alabama. In her late twenties, she is married to a professional musician and is herself a licensed practical nurse. The Anglins have one son and are a happy, well-adjusted couple. What led me to accept Mrs. Anglin's amazing experiences for inclusion in *Born Again* was the way in which she described her very first memories of coming back into this physical world. These descriptions were not only precise and detailed but matched pretty closely similar descriptions obtained by me from widely scattered sources. It is a scientific axiom that parallel reports from people who have no contact with each other and who cannot draw upon a joint source of information should be accepted at face value. Her reincarnation memories go back to the very moment of her most recent birth. She recounted her earliest experiences in this lifetime to her mother at a time when the little girl could not possibly have had this knowledge. We have her mother's testimony of the validity of this statement. As Nancy Anglin grew up, her talents in the field of extrasensory perception grew with her. All through the years she had visions, clairvoyance, and other forms of extrasensory perception.

Soon after she moved to Montgomery in September of 1965 she noticed a vacant old house standing on South Court Street. Every time she passed the house she felt herself drawn to it for some unknown reason, but she did not give in to this urge until the summer of 1968. Finally she mustered enough courage to enter the dilapidated old house. It was on a Friday afternoon in May of 1968. Her husband and she were with a group of friends at the Maxwell Air Force Base Noncommissioned Officers Club. As is often the case, the conversation turned to haunted houses, and Mrs. Anglin mentioned the one she knew on Court Street. No sooner was this mentioned than the little group decided they all wanted to visit a haunted house. Mr. Anglin, however, decided to stay behind. The rest of the group piled into their convertible and drove to the house. The group included Sergeant and Mrs. Eugene Sylvester, both in their late thirties; Sergeant and Mrs. Bob Dannly, in their mid-thirties; and a Mrs. Harvey Ethridge, age thirty-five, the wife of another member of the 604th Band Squadron. The whole thing seemed like a lark to the group. But when they arrived behind the house Mrs. Dannly changed her mind and decided to wait in the car. The rest of them walked up along the shaded back drive around the left side of the house and entered it through the front door. Since the house was vacant it was also unlocked. They walked through the hall into the sitting room to their right. As soon as the group had entered that particular room Nancy Anglin became extremely alert and the hair on her arms stood up. Sergeant Dannly noticed her strange state and immediately asked her if there was anything wrong. While the others went on, she and Sergeant Dannly remained behind in this room for a few minutes. Both noticed that the temperature suddenly dropped and that there was an undefinable feeling of another presence about. They knew at once that they were not alone.

Since the others had gone on to other rooms they decided to join them in the rear of the house. Near the back stairs by the kitchen door they discovered, scattered on the floor, old Veterans of Foreign War records that seemed to have been there for a long time. Eagerly they picked up some of the papers and started to read them aloud to each other. As they did so they clearly heard the sound of a small bell. They perked their ears and the sound was heard once again. Immediately they started to look all over the first floor of the house. Nowhere was there a bell. Since both of them had clearly heard the bell they knew that they had not hallucinated it. But as their search for the bell had proven fruitless, they decided to leave by the front door. They had gone only a few steps when Sergeant Sylvester cried out in excitement. At his feet lay an old magazine illustrated with a figure pointing a finger and a caption reading "Saved by the Bell." This seemed too much of a coincidence for them, so they picked up the magazine and went back into the house. Both sergeants and Nancy Anglin went back into the area where they had heard the mysterious bell. After a moment of quiet they heard it again. As they questioned the origin of the bell and spoke about it the sound became louder and louder. Needless to say, they could not find any source for the ringing and eventually they left the house.

Now Nancy Anglin's curiosity about the house was aroused. The following Sunday she returned to the vacant house, this time armed with a camera and flash bulbs. Again she searched the house from top to bottom for any possible source for the sound of a small bell. Again there was nothing that could have made such a sound. At that point she felt a psychic urge to photograph the staircase where the bell had first been heard. Using a good camera and a setting of infinity and exposing 1/60th of a second at 5.6 on Ektachrome-X color film rated at ASA 64, she managed to produce a number of slides. It was late evening, so she used blue flash bulbs to support the natural light. However, there were no reflective surfaces or odd markings on the wall. Nevertheless, upon examining the developed slides she found that two faces appeared on one of the slides. One seems to be the outline of the head and shoulders of a man and the second one seems to be the face of a woman with her hair piled high on her head and a scarf loosely tied around her shoulders. Nancy Anglin went back to the haunted house many times and heard the bell on several occasions. Others had heard it too. Marion Foster, at the time the Montgomery County Job Corps Director, and Charles Ford, a graduate student in psychology at Auburn University, are among those who heard the bell.

The house in question was known as the Ray-Branch Home. According to Milo Howard, Director of the Alabama State Archives, the house was built in 1856 by a Scottish gentleman by the name of Ray. After the turn of the century the house was sold to the Branch family, who altered the appearance by adding six stately Corinthian columns in front. A member of the Branch family confirmed that their family had lived there for twenty years, after which time the home had been sold to the Veterans of Foreign Wars to be used as state headquarters. Despite diligent search by Nancy Anglin and her librarian friends, nothing unusual could be turned up pertaining to any tragic event in the house. But the records of the middle nineteenth century are not complete and it is entirely possible that some tragic event did take place of which we have no knowledge. Unfortunately the house has recently been demolished and replaced by a motel on the new Interstate Highway 65.

But Nancy had other psychic experiences in Alabama. Prior to her marriage she lived at 710 Cloverdale Road in Montgomery in an old house divided into four apartments, two downstairs and two upstairs. She occupied the upstairs east apartment alone for six months prior to her marriage. When she first moved in, she became immediately aware of an extraordinary presence. After her new husband moved in with her this became even stronger. Her first definite experience took place in August of 1966 around three o'clock in the morning. At the time she was sitting alone in her living room when she heard the sound of a flute playing a wandering mystical pattern of notes. Surprised at this, she looked up and saw a pink mist approaching from the bedroom where her husband was then sleeping. The mist crossed the living room and entered the den. As the cloud floated out, the music also died off. Since her husband is a professional musician and she herself is very interested in singing, this manifestation was of particular importance to her, although she could not understand its meaning.

Soon enough she had another experience. This time she was entirely alone in the big old house when the living-room door began to vibrate with the sound of footsteps. Quivering with fear, she sat while the feet walked up and down in an almost impatient manner. Finally mustering up enough courage she commanded the noise to stop. Whatever was causing the footsteps obeyed her command, because for a few minutes all was quiet. Then it started up again. Paralyzed with fear, she was just sitting there when she heard her downstairs neighbor return home. It seemed to her as if an eternity had passed. Quickly she ran downstairs and rang his bell and asked him to come up and see what he could find about the mysterious footsteps. The neighbor's arrival did not interfere with the ghost's determination to walk up and down, it soon appeared. "Someone's walking around in here," explained the somewhat perplexed neighbor. As if to demonstrate her earlier success, Nancy commanded the unseen walker to stop. Sure enough, the footsteps stopped. Shaking his head, the neighbor left, and the footsteps resumed. Finally coming to terms with the unseen visitor, Nancy tried to keep occupied until her husband returned at two o'clock in the morning. As soon as her husband returned they ceased abruptly. Evidently the ghost didn't mind the neighbor but did not want any trouble with a husband. The Anglins never did find out who the ghostly visitor was, but it seemed strange to them to have come to live in an old house where a musician had lived before them since both of them were so much involved with music themselves. Quite possibly the unseen gentleman himself had manipulated things so that they could get the apartment.

For some unknown reason a certain spot in Alabama has become a psychic focal point for Nancy Anglin. That spot is where the O'Neil Bridge crosses from the city of Sheffield to Florence, Alabama. Many years ago she had astral journeys that took her in flight across that bridge during its construction. She remembers the sensational feeling and wondering whether she would make it across or fall to her death. In that dream she clearly saw planks in a crosswalk high above the water and had the feeling of being pursued by some menacing individual. In the dream she looked down upon the water, became dizzy, and then saw nothing further. The O'Neil Bridge was built before her birth. Every time she has had to cross it in reality, Nancy Anglin has had to suppress a great fear about it. In her childhood she had a firm belief that the bridge would eventually collapse and pull her to her death. This despite the fact that it is a sturdy bridge constructed of concrete and steel.

In the fall of 1968 she began having a recurrent dream in which she drove across the O'Neil Bridge from Sheffield to Florence, then took a left turn and traveled down along the river and rode a long distance until she reached a massive stone house that stood four stories tall. In her vision she spent the night on the third floor of that house. She was visited by a rather fierce female spirit possessed of a resounding voice. With that she awoke.

On December 27, 1968, Nancy Anglin visited some friends on the far side of Florence, Alabama. The conversation turned to haunted houses, stately mansions and such, and the friends offered to show her an old house they had recently discovered. The group traveled over a series of back roads until they reached a large gray sandstone house standing four stories tall and overlooking the Tennessee River. The house was vacant and the interior had been destroyed long ago by treasure seekers. The stairs leading up to the third floor were torn down. Nancy was fascinated by the house and decided to visit it again on New Year's Day. This time, however, she traveled in the same direction as she had done in her dream, but she had not yet realized that it was the same house. Somehow the house seemed familiar, but she did not connect this particular house with the one in her recurrent dream. Finally in another dream on the 21st of March of that year she realized that the house was one and the same as the one in her dream vision. Now she found herself on the third floor of the house in a large room containing a chaise longue of an earlier period. She had lain down to rest when she heard a booming angry voice on the floor above her. Then as if blown by a strong wind came an apparition from the fourth floor. She could see a face, that of a white woman with narrow features, angry as she said something in a vibrating, commanding voice. The noise of this voice awoke her. A few weeks later the dream repeated itself. By now Nancy Anglin knew the name of the house, Smithsonia. Then in early March of 1969 she dreamed a variation in which she saw herself on the third floor. Again the forceful female spirit appeared and screamed at her. This time she could make out the words, "Get out, get out!" Subsequently Nancy found herself standing on the grounds with a group of people watching the house go up in flames while a deafening voice raged from within the burning structure. At that she awoke suddenly. Only later in the day did she realize that the house in her dream had been the Smithsonia. On the night of March 29th she awoke to hear a ringing in her ears. Her body was tingling all over as if her circulation had stopped. She felt herself weighted down by some tremendous force and could neither move nor breathe. While her conscious mind seemed to be ascending above herself all she could do was think how to get back into her body and a state of normalcy. After what seemed like an eternity she felt herself catch a deep gulping breath and her senses returned.

In late April she returned home for a visit and was informed that Smithsonia had burned down about three weeks before. The day of the fire matched her last terrifying experience. Was there any connection between the fierce spirit in the burning house and herself and was Nancy Anglin reliving something from her own past, or was she merely acting as the medium for some other tortured soul? At any rate, Smithsonia stands no more.

I am indebted to Mrs. H. L. Stevens of Foley, Alabama, for two interesting psychic cases. Mrs. Stevens is a retired schoolteacher in her sixties and a careful observer of facts. Since she has had an interest in ESP since childhood and has had various minor experiences with psychic occurrences herself, she had been an unofficial counselor to those who come to seek her advice and who cannot cope with their own psychic experiences. A fellow teacher whose initials are M. B. had just lost her husband. Reluctantly she sold her house and most of the furnishings. The following night, very tired and unhappy, she went to bed early. As a mathematics instructor, she was not given to hallucinations or idle dreams. As she lay in bed unable to fall asleep, she thought over the plans for the delivery of the furniture that had been sold and the disposition of some of the articles that no one had purchased. At the foot of her bed was a dresser on which stood a musical powder box. This was a special gift from her late husband. Suddenly as she lay there the music box began to play of its own volition. Mrs. B. was terrified, believing that someone had gotten into the room and had knocked the lid of the music box aside. That was the only way in which the box could be activated. The music box played the entire turn and Mrs. B. lay there stiff with fear, expecting someone at any moment to approach the bed. Then there was an interval, perhaps a minute or two, and the music box began again, playing the entire tune as if it had been rewound, although no one approached the bed. After what seemed like an eternity to her, she arose and turned on the light. There was no one in the room. The lid was in its proper place on the box. All the doors in the house were locked. There was no way in which the music box could have played of its own accord. Mrs. B. knew then that her late husband wanted her to know he still cared. Somehow this last greeting made things a lot easier for her the next morning.

Warren F. Godfrey is an educated man who works for the NASA Center in Houston. He and his wife Gwen had no particular interest in the occult and were always careful not to let their imagination run away with them. They lived in a house in Huntsville, Alabama, which was, at the time they moved into it, only three years old. At first they had only a feeling that *the house didn't want them*. There was nothing definite about this, but as time went on they would look over their shoulders to see if they were being followed, and felt silly doing so. Then, gradually, peculiar noises started. Ordinarily such noises would not disturb them, and they tried very hard to blame the settling of the house. There were cracks in the ceiling, the popping and cracking of corners, then the walls would join in, and after a while there would be silence again. Faucets would start to drip for no apparent reason. Doors would swing open and/or shut by themselves, and a dish would shift in the cupboard. All these things could perhaps have been caused by a house's settling, but the noises seemed to become organized. Warren noticed that the house had a definite atmosphere. There seemed to be a feeling that the house objected to the young couple's happiness. It seemed to want to disturb their togetherness in whatever way it could, and it managed to depress them.

Then there were knockings. At first these were regularly spaced single sharp raps proceeding from one part of the house to another. Warren ran out and checked the outside of the house, under it, and everywhere and could discover no reason for the knocks. As all this continued, they became even more depressed and neither liked to stay alone in the house. About Thanksgiving of 1968 they went to visit Warren's mother in Illinois for a few days. After they returned to the empty house it seemed quieter, even happier. Shortly before Christmas, Warren had to go to Houston on business. While he was gone Gwen took a photograph of their daughter Leah. When the picture was developed there was an additional head on the film, with the face in profile and wearing some sort of hat. Warren, a scientist, made sure that there was no natural reason for this extra face on the film. Using a Kodak Instamatic camera with a mechanism that excludes any double exposure, he duplicated the picture and also made sure that a reflection could not have caused the second image. Satisfied that he had obtained sufficient proof to preclude a natural origin for the second face on the film, he accepted the psychic origin of the picture.

About that time they began hearing voices. One night Warren woke up to hear two men arguing in a nearby room. At first he dismissed it as a bad dream and went back to sleep, but several nights later the same thing happened. After listening to them for a while he shrugged his shoulders and went back to sleep. He could not understand a word they were saying but was sure that there were two men arguing. After several weeks of this his wife also heard the voices. To Warren this was gratifying, since he was no longer alone in hearing them. The time when both of them heard the voices was generally around 1 A.M. In addition to the two men arguing, Gwen has also heard a woman crying and Warren has heard people laughing. The noises are not particularly directed toward them, nor do they feel that there is anything evil about them. Gradually they have learned to ignore them. As a trained scientist, Warren tried a rational approach to explain the phenomena but could not find any cause. Turning on the lights did not help either. The phenomena occurred only in the master bedroom. There are no television stations on the air at that time of the morning, and there is no house close enough for human voices to carry that far. In trying to reach for a natural explanation, Warren considered the fact that caves extended underneath the area, but what they were hearing was not the noise of rushing waters. Those were human voices and they were right there in the room with them. They decided to learn to live with their unseen boarders and perhaps the ghosts might eventually let them in on their "problem." Not that Warren and Gwen could do much about them, but it is always nice to know what your friends are talking about, especially when you share your bedroom with them.

Mary Carol Henry is in her early thirties, lives in Montgomery and is married to a medical technician in the USAF. She is the mother of seven children and has had psychic experiences from early childhood. When Mary was twelve years old one of her older brothers moved to Pittsburgh. She lent a helping hand with the furniture and other belongings and decided to stay overnight so she could help them finish up the work early in the morning. The house was an old four-story one in the Hazelwood section of Pittsburgh. Mary and the children slept up on the third floor, but she felt very uneasy about staying. Somehow the house bothered her. Since she had promised to stay overnight, however, she went to bed around 10 P.M. and lay in bed for a while thinking about why the house had troubled her. Her brother's baby slept in the same room with her and after a while her brother came up to check on the child. She then heard him go back downstairs. Mary wasn't sure how much time had elapsed when she thought she heard him come up again. There was the rustling of newspapers or something that sounded like it, and she assumed it was her brother, since he was in the habit of taking a newspaper with him when he went to the bathroom. She turned over, and instead of her brother, to her amazement she saw a young girl come out of a closet. Immediately she recognized her as her little sister Patsy who had been killed in a gas explosion in August of 1945 at the age of five. The ghost wore the same gown she had been buried in and she looked exactly as she had when she was alive but somehow larger in build. Her apparition was enveloped by a green light. As Mary stared in disbelief the ghost came over to the bed and sat on the side of it. Mary saw the bed actually sink in where Patsy sat on it. Her sister then put her hands on Mary's and kissed her on the cheek. Mary felt the kiss as if it were the kiss of a living person. Then the apparition vanished. Still dazed with fear, Mary sprang out of bed and spent the rest of the night on the stairs. When she told her experience to her mother later, her mother assured her that her late sister had only come back to comfort her in what must have been unfamiliar surroundings, for if Mary was to see a ghost that night it might just as well be someone in the family, not a stranger.

29

The Summer Cottage Ghosts

TONI S. IS a young woman of good educational background, a psychologist by profession, who works for a large business concern. She is not given to daydreaming or fantasizing. She is the daughter of Mrs. Elizabeth K., or rather the daughter of Mrs. K.'s second marriage. The thrice-married Mrs. K. is a North Carolina lady of upper middle-class background, a socially prominent woman who has traveled extensively.

Neither was the kind of person who pulls out a Ouija board to while away the time, or to imagine that every shadow cast upon the wall is necessarily a ghost. Far from it; but both ladies were taken aback by what transpired in their old house at the town of East La Porte, built on very old ground.

Originally built about fifty years ago, it was to be a home for Mrs. K.'s father who then owned a large lumber company, and the tract of timber surrounding the house extended all the way across the Blue Ridge Parkway. Undoubtedly an older dwelling had stood on the same spot, for Mrs. K. has unearthed what appears to be the remains of a much older structure. The house was renovated and a second story was built on about thirty-five years ago. At that time, her father had lost one leg as the result of an automobile accident, and retired from his lumber mill activities to East La Porte, where he intended to spend his remaining years in peace and quiet. He had liked the climate to begin with, and there was a sawmill nearby, which he could oversee. The house is a doubleboxed frame house, perhaps fifty-by-fifty square, containing around fifteen rooms.

Mrs. K.'s family refer to it as the summer cottage, even though it was a full-sized house; but they had other houses that they visited from time to time, and the house in East La Porte was merely one of their lesser properties. Downstairs there is a thirty-by-fifteen-foot reception room, richly carpeted with chestnut from Furnace Creek, one of the sawmills owned by the family. It was in this room that Mrs. K.'s father eventually passed on.

The house itself is built entirely from lumber originating in one of the family's sawmills. There was a center hall downstairs and two thirty-foot rooms, then there were three smaller rooms, a bath, a card room, and what the family referred to as a sleeping porch. On the other side of the center hall was a lounge, a kitchen, and a laundry porch. Running alongside the south and east walls of the house is a veranda. Upstairs is reached by a very gentle climb up the stairs in the middle of the floor, and as one climbs the steps, there is a bedroom at the head of the stairs. In back of the stairs, there are two more bedrooms, then a bathroom, and finally a storage room; to the left of the stairs are three bedrooms.

The attic is merely a structure to hold up the roof, and does not contain any rooms. There is a cellar, but it contains only a furnace. Although the acreage surrounding the house runs to about sixty acres, only three acres belong to the house proper. All around the house, even today, there is nothing but wilderness, and to get to the nearest town, East La Porte, one needs a car.

Mrs. K. enjoyed traveling, and didn't mind living in so many residences; in fact, she considered the house at East La Porte merely a way-station in her life. She was born in Alaska, where the family also had a sawmill. Her early years were spent traveling from one sawmill to another, accompanying her parents on business trips.

Under the circumstances, they were never very long in residence at the house in East La Porte. Any attempt to find out about the background of the land on which the house stood proved fruitless. This was Cherokee territory, but there is little written history concerning the time before the Cherokees. Anything remotely connected with psychic phenomena was simply not discussed in the circles in which Mrs. K. grew up.

The first time Mrs. K. noticed anything peculiar about the house was after her father had passed away. She and her father had been particularly close, since her mother had died when she was still a small child. That particular day, she was sitting at her late father's desk in the part of the house where her father had died. The furniture had been rearranged in the room, and the desk stood where her father's bed had previously been. Her father was on her mind, and so she thought it was all her imagination when she became aware of a distinctive sound like someone walking on crutches down the hall.

Since Mrs. K. knew for a fact that she was the only person in the house at the time, she realized that something out of the ordinary was happening. As the footsteps came closer, she recognized her father's tread. Then she heard her father's familiar voice say, "Baby:" it came from the direction of the door. This gave her a feeling of great peace, for she had been troubled by emotional turmoil in her life. She felt that her late father was trying to console her, and give her spiritual strength.

Nothing happened until about a year later. It was August, and she had been in New York for awhile. As she was coming down the stairs of the house, she found herself completely enveloped with the fragrance of lilacs. She had not put any perfume on, and there were no lilacs blooming in August. No one was seen, and yet Mrs. K. felt a presence, although she was sure it was benign and loving.

A short time later, she was sitting at a desk in what used to be her father's study upstairs, thinking about nothing in particular. Again she was startled by the sound of footsteps, but this time they were light steps, and certainly not her father's. Without thinking, she called out to her daughter, "Oh, Toni, is that you?" telling her daughter that she was upstairs.

But then the steps stopped, and no one came. Puzzled, Mrs. K. went to the head of the stairs, called out again, but when she saw no one, she realized that it was not a person of flesh and blood who had walked upon the stairs.

During the same month, Mrs. K.'s daughter Toni was also at the house. Her first experience with the unseen happened that month, in an upstairs bedroom.

She was asleep one night when someone shook her hard and said, "Hey, you!" Frightened, she did not open her eyes, yet with her inner eyes, she "saw" a man of about fifty years of age. She was much too frightened to actually look, so instead she dove underneath the covers and lay there with her eyes shut. There was nothing further that night.

In the fall of the same year, Toni decided to have a pajama party and spent the night with a group of friends. Her mother had gone to bed because of a cold. Toni and her friends returned to the house from bowling at around eleven-thirty. They were downstairs, talking about various things, when all of a sudden one of Toni's girlfriends said,

"Your mother is calling you."

Toni went out into the hallway, turning on the lights as she approached the stairs. Footsteps were coming down the stairs, audible not only to her but to her two girlfriends who had followed her into the house. And then they heard a voice out of nowhere calling out, "Toni, it is time to go to bed." It was a voice Toni had never heard before.

She went up the stairs and into her mother's room, but her mother was fast asleep, and had not been out of bed. The voice had been a woman's, but it had sounded strangely empty, as if someone were speaking to her from far away.

The following year, Toni was married and left the house. Under the circumstances, Mrs. K. decided to sublease part of the house to a tenant. This turned out to be a pleasant woman by the name of Alice H. and her husband. The lady had been injured and was unable to go far up the mountain where she and her husband were building a summer home at the time. Although Mrs. K. and her new tenants were not associated in any way except that they were sharing the same house, she and Alice H. became friendly after a while. One afternoon, Alice H. came to Mrs. K.'s apartment in order to invite her to have supper with her and her husband that night. She knew that Mrs. K. was in her apartment at the time because she heard her light footsteps inside the apartment. When there was no reply from inside the apartment Alice was puzzled, so she descended to the ground floor, thinking that perhaps Mrs. K. was downstairs.

Sure enough, as she arrived downstairs, she saw a shadow of what she assumed to be Mrs. K.'s figure walking along the hallway. She followed this shadowy woman all the way from the ground floor guest room, through the bath into Mrs. K.'s bedroom, and then through another hallway and back to the bedroom. All the time she saw the shadowy figure, she also heard light footsteps. But when she came to the bedroom again, it suddenly got very cold and she felt all the blood rush to her head. She ran back to her husband in their own apartment, and informed him that there was a stranger in Mrs. K.'s rooms.

But there was no one in the house at the time except themselves, for Mrs. K. had gone off to Asheville for the day. The experience shook Alice H. to the point where she could no longer stand the house, and shortly afterward she and her husband left for another cottage.

In August of the same year, Toni S. returned to her mother's house. By now she was a married lady, and she was coming for a visit only. Her husband was a car dealer, in business with his father. At the time of the incident, he was not in the house. It was raining outside, and Toni was cleaning the woodwork in the house.

Suddenly her Pekinese dog came running down the stairs, nearly out of her mind with terror, and barking at the top of her lungs. Toni thought the dog had been frightened by a mouse, so she picked her up and proceeded up the stairs. But the dog broke away from her and ran behind the door. All of a sudden, Toni felt very cold. She kept walking down the hall and into the room, where there was a desk standing near the window. Someone was going through papers on her desk as if looking for a certain piece of paper, putting papers aside and continuing to move them! But there was no one there. No one, that is, who could be seen. Yet the papers were moving as if someone were actually shuffling them. It was two o'clock in the afternoon, and the light was fairly good.

Suddenly, one letter was pulled out of the piles of papers on the desk, as if to catch her attention. Toni picked it up and read it. It was a letter her father had sent her in February, at the time she got married, warning her that the marriage would not work out after all, and to make sure to call him if anything went wrong. Things *had* gone wrong since, and Toni understood the significance of what she had just witnessed.

At that very moment, the room got warm again, and everything returned to normal. But who was it standing at her desk, pulling out her father's letter? The one person who had been close to her while he was in the flesh was her grandfather.

During Toni's visit at the house, her husband, now her ex-husband, also had some uncanny experiences. Somebody would wake him in the middle of the night by calling out, "Wake up!" or "Hey you!" This went on night after night, until both Toni and her husband awoke around two in the morning because of the sound of loud laughing, as if a big party were going on downstairs.

Toni thought that the neighbors were having a party, and decided to go down and tell them to shut up. She looked out the window, and realized that the neighbors were also fast asleep. So she picked up her dog and went downstairs, and as she arrived at the bottom of the stairs, she saw a strange light, and the laughing kept going on and on. There were voices, as if many people were talking all at once, having a social. In anger, Toni called out to them to shut up, she wanted to sleep, and all of a sudden the house was quiet, quiet as the grave. Evidently, Southern ghosts have good manners!

After her daughter left, Mrs. K. decided to sublease part of the house to a group of young men from a national fraternity who were students at a nearby university. One of the students, Mitchell, was sleeping in a double bed, and he was all alone in the house. Because the heat wasn't turned up, it being rather costly, he decided to sleep in a sleeping bag, keeping warm in this manner. He went to sleep with his pillow at the head of the bed, which meant due east, and his feet going due west. When he awoke, he found himself facing in the opposite direction, with his head where his feet should have been, and vice versa. It didn't surprise the young man though, because from the very first day his fraternity brothers had moved into the house, they had heard the sounds of an unseen person walking up and down the stairs.

One of their teachers, a pilot who had been a colonel in the Korean War, also had an experience at the house. One day while he was staying there, he was walking up the stairs, and when he reached about the halfway mark, someone picked him up by the scruff of his neck and pushed him up the rest of the way to the landing.

But the night to remember was Hallowe'en Eve. Mrs. K. was in the house, and the night was living up to its reputation: it sounded as if someone wearing manacles were moving about. Mrs. K. was downstairs, sleeping in one of the bunk beds, and a noise came from an upstairs hall. This went on for about two hours straight. It sounded as if someone with a limp were pulling himself along, dragging a heavy chain. Mrs. K. was puzzled about this, since the noise did not sound anything like her father. She looked into the background of the area, and discovered that in the pre-colonial period, there had been some Spanish settlers in the area, most of whom kept slaves.

Toni S. takes her involvement with hauntings in stride. She has had psychic experiences ever since she can remember; nothing frightening, you understand, only such things as events before they actually happen—if someone is going to be sick in the family, for instance, or who might be calling. Entering old houses is always a risky business for her; she picks up vibrations from the past, and sometimes she simply can't stand what she feels and must leave at once.

But she thought she had left the more uncanny aspects of the hauntings behind when she came to New York to work. Somehow she wound up residing in a house that is 110 years old.

After a while, she became aware of an old man who liked sitting down on her bed. She couldn't actually see him, but he appeared to her more like a shadow. So she asked some questions, but nobody ever died in the apartment and it was difficult for Toni to accept the reality of the phenomena under the circumstances. As a trained psychologist, she had to approach all this on a skeptical level, and yet there did not seem to be any logical answers.

Soon afterward, she became aware of footsteps where no one was walking, and of doors closing by themselves, which were accompanied by the definite feeling of another personality present in the rooms.

On checking with former upstairs neighbors, who had lived in the house for seventeen years, Toni discovered that they too had heard the steps and doors closing by themselves. However, they had put no faith in ghosts, and dismissed the matter as simply an old structure settling. Toni tried her innate psychic powers, and hoped that the resident ghost would communicate with her. She began to sense that it was a woman with a very strong personality. By a process of elimination, Toni came to the conclusion that the last of the original owners of the house, a Mrs. A., who had been a student of the occult, was the only person who could be the presence she was feeling in the rooms.

Toni doesn't mind sharing her rooms with a ghost, except for the fact that appliances in the house have a way of breaking down without reason. Then, too, she has a problem with some of her friends; they complain of feeling extremely uncomfortable and cold, and of being watched by someone they cannot see. What was she to do? But then Toni recalled how she had lived through the frightening experiences at East La Porte, North Carolina, and somehow come to terms with the haunts there. No ordinary Long Island ghost was going to dispossess her!

With that resolve, Toni decided to ignore the presence as much as she could, and go about her business—the business of the living.

30

Joe Baldwin's Ghost

SINCE I PUBLISHED my findings regarding the famous Maco Light near Wilmington, North Carolina, people have come to me with new information and others have asked me to shed additional light on the very mysterious light that has puzzled people for many, many years. There are other mysterious lights all over the world, to be sure, such as the Brown Mountain Lights in Tennessee and similar mysterious luminous bodies frequently observed in Washington state. Some of these lights are unquestionably of natural origin and have nothing whatsoever to do with the psychic. Others may be of a parallel nature to the famous Maco Light. I investigated this railroad crossing back in 1964 and in 1965 published my findings and the testimony of all witnesses I had met in a book called *Ghosts I've Met*. Under the title "The Case of the Lost Head," I described what had happened to lure me down South to look for an elusive light along a railroad track.

One of the most famous ghosts of the South is railroad conductor Joe Baldwin. The story of Joe and his lantern was known to me, of course, and a few years ago *Life* magazine even dignified it with a photograph of the railroad track near Wilmington, North Carolina, very atmospherically adorned by a greenish lantern, presumably swinging in ghostly hands.

Then one day in early 1964, the legend became reality when a letter arrived from Bill Mitcham, Executive Secretary of the South Eastern North Carolina Beach Association, a public relations office set up by the leading resort hotels in the area centering around Wilmington. Mr. Mitcham proposed that I have a look at the ghost of Joe Baldwin and try to explain once and for all—scientifically—what the famous Maco Light was or is.

In addition, Mr. Mitcham arranged for a lecture on the subject to be held at the end of my investigation and sponsored jointly by the Beach Association and Wilmington College. He promised to roll out the red carpet for Catherine and me, and roll it out he did.

Seldom in the history of ghost hunting has a parapsychologist been received so royally and fully covered by press, television, and radio, and if the ghost of Joe Baldwin is basking in the reflected glory of all this attention directed toward his personal Ghost Hunter, he is most welcome to it.

If it were not for Joe Baldwin, the bend in the railroad track which is known as Maco Station (a few miles outside of Wilmington) would be a most unattractive and ordinary trestle. By the time I had investigated it and left, in May of 1964, the spot had almost risen to the prominence of a national shrine, and sightseeing groups arrived at all times, especially at night, to look for Joe Baldwin's ghostly light.

Bill Mitcham had seen to it that the world knew about Joe Baldwin's headless ghost and Hans Holzer seeking same, and no fewer than seventy-eight separate news stories of one kind or another appeared in print during the week we spent in Wilmington.

Before I even started to make plans for the Wilmington expedition, I received a friendly letter from a local student of psychic phenomena, William Edward Cox, Jr., and a manuscript entitled *The Maco Light*. Mr. Cox had spent considerable time observing the strange light, and I quote:

> A favorite "ghost story" in the vicinity of Wilmington, N.C., is that of "Joe Baldwin's Ghost Light," which is alleged to appear at night near Maco, N.C., 12 miles west of Wilmington on the Atlantic Coast Line Railroad.
>
> On June 30-July 1, 1949, this writer spent considerable time investigating the phenomenon. The purpose was to make an accurate check on the behavior of the light under test conditions, with the view toward ascertaining its exact nature.
>
> This light has been observed since shortly after the legend of the Joe Baldwin ghost light "was born in 1867." It is officially reported in a pamphlet entitled "The Story of the Coast Line, 1830-1948." In its general description it resembles a 25-watt electric light slowly moving along the tracks toward the observer, whose best point of observation is on the track itself at the point where the tracks, double at that point, are crossed by a branch of a connecting roadway between U.S. Highway 74-76 and U.S. Highway 19.
>
> The popular explanation is that Conductor Baldwin, decapitated in an accident, is taking the nocturnal walks in search of his head. . . .

After testing the various "natural" theories put forward for the origin of the nocturnal light, Mr. Cox admits:

> Although the general consensus of opinion is that the lights stem from some relatively rare cause, such as the paranormal, "ignis fatuus," etc.,

the opinions of residents of the Maco vicinity were found by this observer to be more detailed. The proprietor of the Mobilgas Service Station was noncommittal, and a local customer said he had "never seen the light." A farmer in the area was quite certain that it is caused by automobile headlights, but would not express an opinion upon such lights as were customarily seen there before the advent of the automobile.

The proprietress of the Willet Service Station, Mrs. C. L. Benton, was firmly convinced that it was of "supernatural origin," and that the peculiar visibility of automobile headlights to observers at Maco must be more or less a subsequent coincidence.

She said that her father "often saw it as he loaded the wood burners near there over 60 years ago."

The basic question of the origin and nature of the "Maco Light," or the original light, remains incompletely answered. The findings here reported, due as they are to entirely normal causes, cannot accurately be construed as disproving the existence of a light of paranormal origin at any time in the distant past (or, for that matter, at the present time).

The unquestionable singularity of the phenomenon's being in a locale where it is so easily possible for automobiles to produce an identical phenomenon seems but to relegate it to the enigmatic "realm of forgotten mysteries."

So much for Mr. Cox's painstaking experiment conducted at the site in 1949.

The coming of the Ghost Hunter (and Mrs. Ghost Hunter) was amply heralded in the newspapers of the area. Typical of the veritable avalanche of features was the story in the *Charlotte Observer*:

Can the Spook Hunter De-Ghost Old Joe? The South Eastern N.C. Beach Association invited a leading parapsychologist Saturday to study the ghost of Old Joe Baldwin.

Bill Mitcham, executive director of the association, said he has arranged for Hans Holzer of New York to either prove or disprove the ghostly tales relating to Old Joe.

Holzer will begin his study May 1.

Tales of Joe Baldwin flagging down trains with false signals, waving his lantern on dark summer nights have been repeated since his death in 1867.

Baldwin, a conductor on the Wilmington, Manchester and Augusta Railroad, was riding the rear coach of a train the night of his death. The coach became uncoupled and Baldwin seized a lantern in an effort to signal a passenger train following.

But the engineer failed to see the signal. In the resulting crash, Baldwin was decapitated.

A witness to the wreck later recalled that the signal lantern was flung some distance from the tracks, but that it burned brightly thereafter for some time.

Soon after the accident, there were reports of a mysterious light along the railroad tracks at Maco Station in Brunswick County.

Two lanterns, one green and one red, have been used by trainmen at Maco Station so that engineers would not be confused or deceived by Joe Baldwin's light.

Most helpful in a more serious vein was the Women's Editor of the *Wilmington Star-News*, Theresa Thomas, who had for years taken an interest in the psychic and probably is somewhat sensitive herself. On April 8,1964, she asked her readers:

Have you ever seen the Maco Light? Have you ever seen Old Joe Baldwin? Or his light, that is? As far as we know, nobody has actually seen Joe himself.

But if you have seen his lantern swinging along the railroad track at Maco, you can be of great help to Hans Holzer, Ghost Hunter, who will be in Wilmington April 29th.

Either write out your experience and send it to us, or call and tell us about it.

Then the feminine point of view crashed the scientific barrier a little as Miss Thomas added:

His [Mr. Holzer's] wife is just as fascinating as he. She is a painter and great-great-great-granddaughter of Catherine the Great of Russia. Mrs. Holzer was born Countess Catherine Buxhoeveden in a haunted castle in Meran, the Tyrol, in the Italian Alps. And she paints—haven't you guessed?—haunted houses.

My visit was still three weeks away, but the wheels of publicity were already spinning fast and furiously in Wilmington.

Theresa Thomas's appeal for actual witnesses to the ghostly phenomenon brought immediate results. For the first time people of standing took the matter seriously, and those who had seen the light, opened up. Miss Thomas did not disguise her enthusiasm. On April 12 she wrote:

It seems a great many people have seen old Joe Baldwin's light at Maco and most of them are willing—even eager—to talk about it.

Among the first to call was Mrs. Larry Moore, 211 Orange Street, who said she had seen the light three or four times at different seasons of the year.

The first time it was a cloudy, misty winter night and again in the summer, misty again. Her description of the light was "like a bluish yellow flame." She and her companions walked down the track and the light came closer as they approached the trestle. When they reached the center of the trestle with the light apparently about 10 feet away, it disappeared.

Mrs. Thelma Daughty, 6 Shearwater Drive, Wrightsville Beach, says she saw it on a misty spring night. It was about 7 or 8 o'clock in the evening and the reddish light appeared to swing along at about knee height.

Mrs. Margaret Jackson, 172 Colonial Circle, a native of Vienna, Austria, saw it about seven years ago on a hazy night, a "glary shine" steady and far away but always the same distance ahead of them.

Dixie Rambeau, 220 Pfeiffer Avenue, saw it about 1 A.M. Friday morning. She says it was "real dark" and the light appeared as a red pinpoint at a distance up the track, as it neared it became yellowish white, then closer still it was a mixed red and white.

She recalls that she and her companions watched it come closer to the left side of the track and that as it came close the reflection on the rail almost reached them. At about 10 feet away it reversed its process and as they walked toward it, it disappeared. Once it appeared to cross over. They watched it five or six times, she said.

Mrs. Marvin Clark, 406 Grace Street, a practical nurse, states that she and her husband saw the light 15 years ago. It was about midnight on a cloudy, rainy night. They were standing in the middle of the tracks and "it looked like a light on a train coming at full speed."

Mrs. Clark described the light as "the color of a train light."

"We picked up our little girl and ran. All of us have always seen reflections of automobiles but beyond a doubt it was the Maco Light."

Mrs. Lase V. Dail of Carolina Beach also has a story to tell. It seems she and her husband came home late one night from Fayetteville.

She writes, "As we left the cutoff and headed into 74-76 Highway, I shall never forget the experience we had. . . ." She goes on, "All at once a bright light came down the road towards us, first I figured it was a car. But decided if so it had only one light. On it came steadily toward us.

"Then I figured it was a train, yet I heard nothing, and as suddenly as it appeared it vanished. I can say it was quite a weird feeling. I have often thought of it. I have heard many versions, but never one like this."

Three days later, Miss Thomas devoted still another full column to people who had witnessed the ghost light.

Mrs. Marjorie H. Rizer of Sneads Ferry writes: "I have seen the light three times. The last and most significant time was about a year and a half ago. My husband, three young sons and a companion from the United States Naval Hospital at Camp Lejeune were with me and we saw the same thing. It was about 10:30 P.M. and we were returning from a ball game. We decided to go to Maco since we were so near and the young man with us didn't believe there was anything to our story.

"The sky was cloudy and a light mist was falling. We parked the car beside the track and sure enough, there was the light down the track. I stayed in the car with my sons, and my husband and the corpsman walked down the track toward the light.

"The light would alternately dim and then become very bright. The two men walked perhaps a quarter of a mile down the track before they returned. They said the light stayed ahead of them, but my sons and I saw the light between them and us.

"It looked as if the light would come almost to where we were parked and then it would wobble off down the track and disappear. In a moment it would reappear and do the same time after time.

"When we had been there for about an hour and started to leave, a train approached going toward Wilmington. The light was a short distance away from us. As the train passed the light, it rose and hovered over the train. We could clearly see the top of the train as the light became very bright.

"It stayed over the train until it had passed then disappeared back down the track and finally it looked as if someone had thrown it off into the woods.

"As we pulled away from the track the light came back on the track and weaved backward and forward down the track as it had been doing."

And still the letters poured in. On April 22, after half a column devoted to my imminent arrival in the area, Miss Thomas printed a letter from a young man who had taken some interesting pictures:

He is J. Everett Huggins, home address 412 Market Street, Wilmington. The letter is addressed to Bill Mitcham and reads in part: "I read with interest the articles on your 'ghost survey,' especially since I saw the Maco light less than two weeks ago and was actually able to catch Old Joe on film.

"On the nights of April 1 and 2 a schoolmate of mine and I went to Maco Station in the hopes of seeing the light. We saw nothing on Friday, April 1, but we had more success on Saturday, when it was a little darker. Around 10:30 we saw a yellow light about 100 yards down the track from us (this distance is only a guess). It seemed to be about 10 feet above the tracks and looked as if it were moving slowly toward us for a while, then it went back and died out.

"The light appeared maybe three times in succession for periods up to what I would estimate to be about thirty seconds.

"I attempted to take two time exposures with my camera. Unfortunately I did not have a tripod, and so I had to hold the camera in my hands, which made clear results impossible. The pictures are not spectacular—just a small spot on each of the color transparencies—but they are pictures. If you are interested I will have some copies made.

"My friends had kidded me about the light, so I noted some details to try to end their skepticism. The headlights of cars traveling west on Highway 74 could be seen in the distance, and no doubt many who think they see Old Joe only see these lights. Old Joe could be distinguished in several ways, however. First, the light had a yellower tone than did the auto headlights.

"Secondly, unlike the headlights which grow brighter and brighter and then suddenly disappear, the Maco light would gradually grow brighter and then gradually fade out. Thirdly, the Maco light produced a reflection on the rails that was not characteristic of the headlights.

"More interesting was the fact that the reflection on the rails was seen only on a relatively short stretch of track. By observing the reflection, we could tell that the light moved backward and forward on the rails. It always remained directly above the tracks.

"I had seen the light once before, in 1956. It was on a cold winter night, and the light was brighter."

As the day of our arrival grew nearer, the tempo of the press became more hectic. On April 26, Arnold Kirk wrote in the *Wilmington Star News*:

> This tiny Brunswick County village, nestled in a small clearing a few miles west of Wilmington off U.S. Highway 74, is rapidly gaining acclaim as the "Ghost Capital" of North Carolina.
>
> Its few dozen inhabitants, mostly farmers of moderate means, have suddenly found their once-peaceful nights disturbed by scores of vehicles sparring for vantage points from which to view the famous "Maco Light."
>
> While the legend of the light and Old Joe Baldwin, the "Ghost" of Maco, has long been known, its popularity has become intense only in recent months.
>
> Elaborate plans have already been made to welcome Holzer to the Port City. The mayors of all the towns in New Hanover and Brunswick counties, in addition to county commissioners from both counties, have agreed to be at New Hanover County Airport Wednesday at 7:43 P.M. when the "ghost hunter's" plane arrives.
>
> Also on hand to greet the noted parapsychologist will be 1,000 high-school students, carrying, appropriately enough, lighted lanterns! The lanterns were purchased by the city years ago to offer warmth to trees and plants during blustery winter months.
>
> Adding to the fanfare of the event will be the first public offering of "The Ballad of Old Joe Baldwin," written by the senior English class of New Hanover High School.

The reception was a bash that would have made Old Joe Baldwin feel honored. A little later, we tried to sneak out to Maco and have a first glance at the haunted spot. The results were disappointing.

It was not so much that the ghost did not show, but what did show up was most disturbing. The *Wilmington Star-News* summed it up like this:

> An unwilling Old Joe Baldwin exercised his ghostly prerogative Wednesday night by refusing to perform before what may have been his largest audience.
>
> Huddled in small clusters along the railroad tracks near the center of this tiny Brunswick County village, an estimated 250 persons stared into the gloomy darkness in hopes of catching a glimpse of the famous "Maco Light."
>
> But the light would not offer the slightest flicker.

Holzer's announced visit to the scene of Baldwin's ghastly demise gave no comfort to the few dozen residents of Maco. By 10 o'clock, dozens of cars lined both sides of the narrow Maco road and scores of thrill-seeking teenagers had spilled onto the railroad track.

If Joe Baldwin had decided to make an appearance, his performance no doubt would have been engulfed in the dozens of flashlights and battery-powered lanterns searching through the darkness for at least a mile down the track.

Several times, the flashlights and lanterns were mistaken for the "Maco Light," giving hope that the mysterious glow would soon appear.

A large portion of the track was illuminated by the headlights of a jeep and small foreign car scurrying back and forth along both sides of the track. A young girl created an anxious moment when she mistook a firefly for the "Maco Light" and released a penetrating scream that sliced through the pitch-darkness.

Holzer's visit to Maco on Wednesday night was mostly for the benefit of photographers and reporters who met the noted parapsychologist at the New Hanover County airport earlier that night.

His second visit to the crossing will be kept a closely guarded secret in hopes the "ghost hunter" will be able to conduct his investigation of the light without being interrupted by pranksters and playful teenagers.

Soon I realized that it would be impossible for us to go out to the tracks alone. Crowds followed us around and crowds were ever present at the spot, giving rise to a suspicion in my mind that these people were not in a working mood while we were visiting their area. Evidently we were the most exciting thing that had happened to them for some time.

Finally, the day of a scheduled press conference arrived, and at ten o'clock in the morning, before a battery of klieg lights and microphones set up at the magnificent Blockade Runner Hotel on the beach, I started to talk in person to those who had come to tell me about their encounters with Joe Baldwin's ghost.

In addition to those who had written to Miss Thomas and reaffirmed their original stories, others came forward who had not done so previously. There was William McGirt, an insurance executive, who called the light "buoyant," flicking itself on and off, as it were, and fully reflected on the iron rails. But you cannot see it looking east, he told me, only when you look toward Maco Station.

Margaret Bremer added to her previously told story by saying the light looked to her "like a kerosene lantern swaying back and forth."

Her husband, Mr. Bremer, had not planned on saying anything, but I coaxed him. He admitted finally that twelve years ago, when his car was standing straddled across the tracks, he had seen a light coming toward him. It flickered like a lamp, and when it came closer it flared up. As an afterthought he added, "Something strange—suddenly there seemed to be a rush of air, as if a train were coming from Wilmington."

"Was there?" I inquired cautiously.

"No, of course not. We wouldn't have had the car across the track if a train were expected."

Mrs. Laura Collins stepped forward and told me of the time she was at the trestle with a boy who did not believe in ghosts, not even Joe Baldwin's. When the light appeared, he sneered at it and tried to explain it as a reflection. Six feet away from the boy, the light suddenly disappeared and reappeared in back of him—as if to show him up! Mrs. Collins, along with others, observed that misty weather made the light appear clearer.

Next in the parade of witnesses came Mrs. Elizabeth Finch of Wilmington, who had offered her original testimony only the day before.

"It appeared to me many times," she said of the light; "looked like a lantern to me. Two years ago, we were parked across the tracks in our car—we were watching for a train of course, too—when I saw two dazzling lights from both sides. It was a winter evening, but I suddenly felt very hot. There was a red streak in front of the car, *and then I saw what was a dim outline of a man walking with a lantern and swinging it*. Mind you, it was a bare outline," Mrs. Finch added in emphasis, "and it did have a head . . . just kept going, then suddenly he disappeared inside the tracks."

"Did you ever have psychic experiences before, Mrs. Finch?" I wanted to know.

"Yes, when we lived in a house in Masonborough, I used to hear noises, steps, even voices out of nowhere—later, I was told it was haunted."

I thanked Mrs. Finch, wondering if the local legend had impressed her unconscious to the point where she did see what everyone had said was there—or whether she really saw the outline of a man.

I really have no reason to doubt her story. She struck me as a calm, intelligent person who would not easily make up a story just to be sensational. No, I decided, Mrs. Finch might very well have been one of the very few who saw more than just the light.

"I tell you why it can't be anything ordinary," Mr. Trussle, my next informant, said. "Seven years ago, when I saw the light on a damp night about a mile away from where I was standing, I noticed its very rapid approach. It disappeared fast, went back and forth as if to attract attention to something.

It was three feet above the track about the height of where a man's arm might be.

"At first, it seemed yellowish white; when I came closer, it looked like kind of pinkish. Now an ordinary car headlight wouldn't go back and forth like that, would it?"

I agreed it was most unlikely for an automobile headlight to behave in such an unusual manner.

Mrs. Miriam Moore saw it three times, always on misty, humid nights. "I had a funny ringing in my ears when I reached the spot," she said. She was sure what she saw was a lamp swinging in a slow motion. Suddenly, she broke into a cold sweat for no reason at all. I established that she was a psychic person and had on occasion foretold the deaths of various members of her family.

E. S. Skipper is a dapper little man in the golden years of life, but peppery and very much alert. He used to be a freight skipper on the Atlantic Coast Line and grew up with the Maco Light the way Niagara kids grow up with the sight of the Falls.

"I've seen it hundreds of times," he volunteered. "I've seen it flag trains down—it moved just like a railroad lantern would. On one occasion I took my shot gun and walked toward it. As I got nearer, the light became so bright I could hardly look. Suddenly, it disappeared into the old Catholic cemetery on the right side of the tracks."

"Cemetery?" I asked, for I had not heard of a cemetery in this area.

Mr. Skipper was quite certain that there was one. I promised to look into this immediately. "Since you came so close to the light, Mr. Skipper," I said, "perhaps you can tell me what it looked like close up."

"Oh, I got even closer than that—back in 1929. I remember it well. It was two o'clock in the morning. I got to within six foot of it."

"What did you see?"

"I saw a flame. I mean, in the middle of the light, there was, unmistakably, a flame burning."

"Like a lantern?"

"Like a lantern."

I thanked Mr. Skipper and was ready to turn to my last witness, none other than Editor Thomas herself, when Mrs. E. R. Rich, who had already given her account in the newspaper, asked for another minute, which I gladly gave her.

"Ten years ago," Mrs. Rich said, "we were at the track one evening. My son Robert was in the car with me, and my older son went down to the track to watch for the light. Suddenly not one but two lights appeared at the car.

They were round and seemed to radiate and sparkle—for a moment they hung around, then one left, the other stayed. My feet went ice cold at this moment and I felt very strange."

"Miss Thomas," I said, "will you add your own experiences to this plethora of information?"

"Gladly," the Women's Editor of the *Star-News* replied. "There were three of us, all newspaper women, who decided a few weeks ago to go down to the trestle and not see anything."

"I beg your pardon?"

"We'd made up our minds not to be influenced by all the publicity Joe Baldwin's ghost was getting."

"What happened?"

"When we got to the track, dogs were baying as if disturbed by something in the atmosphere. We parked on the dirt road that runs parallel to the track and waited. After a while, the light appeared. It had a yellow glow. Then, suddenly, there were two lights, one larger than the other, swaying in the night sky.

"The lights turned reddish after a while. There was no correlation with car lights at all. I thought at first it was a train bearing down on us, that's how big the lights appeared. Just as suddenly the lights disappeared. One light described an arc to the left of the track, landing on the grass."

"Just as those old tales say Joe's lantern did, eh?"

"It seems so, although it is hard to believe."

"What else did you notice?"

"I had the feeling I was not alone."

And there you have it. Mass hysteria? Self-hypnosis? Suggestion? Could all these people make up similar stories?

Although the Maco Light is unique in its specific aspects, there are other lights that have been observed at spots where tragedies have occurred. There are reports of apparitions in Colorado taking the form of concentrated energy, or light globes. I don't doubt that the human personality is a form of energy that cannot be destroyed, only transmuted. The man who heard the sound of a train, the psychic chill several people experienced, the flame within the light, the two lights clearly distinguished by the newspaper women—possibly Joe's lantern and the headlight of the onrushing train—all these add up to a case.

That evening, at Bogden Hall, before an audience of some five hundred people of all ages, I stated my conviction that the track at Maco Station was, indeed, haunted. I explained that the shock of sudden death might have caused

Joe Baldwin's etheric self to become glued to the spot of the tragedy, reenacting the final moments over and over again.

I don't think we are dealing here with an "etheric impression" registered in the atmosphere and not possessing a life of its own. The phantom reacts differently with various people and seems to me a true ghost, capable of attempting communication with the living, but not fully aware of his own status or of the futility of his efforts.

I was, and am, convinced of the veracity of the phenomenon and, by comparing it to other "weaving lights" in other areas, can only conclude that the basic folklore is on the right track, except that Joe isn't likely to be looking for his head—he is rather trying to keep an imaginary train from running into his uncoupled car, which of course exists now only in his thought world.

And until someone tells Joe all's well on the line now, he will continue to wave his light. I tried to say the right words for such occasions, but I was somewhat hampered by the fact that I did not have Mrs. Ethel Meyers, my favorite medium, with me; then, too, the Wilmington people did not like the idea of having their town ghost go to his reward and leave the trestle just another second-rate railroad track.

The folks living alongside it, though, wouldn't have minded one bit. They can do without Joe Baldwin and his somewhat motley admirers.

Suddenly the thought struck me that we had no proof that a Joe Baldwin had ever really existed in this area. The next morning I went to the Wilmington Public Library and started to dig into the files and historical sources dealing with the area a hundred years ago. Bill Mitcham and I started to read all the newspapers from 1866 onward, but after a while we gave up. Instead, I had a hunch which, eventually, paid off. If Joe Baldwin was physically fit to work on the railroad in so hazardous a job as that of a train man, he must have been well enough to be in the Armed Forces at one time or another.

I started to search the Regimental Records from 1867 on backward. Finally I found in volume V, page 602, of a work called *North Carolina Regiments*, published in 1901, the following entry:

"Joseph Baldwin, Company F, 26th N. C. T., badly wounded in the thigh. Battle of Gettysburg. July 1, 1863."

It was the only Joseph Baldwin listed in the area, or, for that matter, the state.

I also inquired about the old Catholic cemetery. It was, indeed, near the railroad track, but had been out of use for many years. Only oldsters still remembered its existence. Baldwin may have been Catholic, as are many residents of the area. Time did not permit me to look among the dilapidated tombstones for a grave bearing the name of Joe Baldwin.

But it would be interesting to find it and see if all of Joe Baldwin lies buried in sacred ground!

On November 17,1964, the *Wilmington Morning Star* in their Letter to the Editor column published a communication from one Curtis Matthews in which Mr. Matthews stated he knew all about the Maco Light and what it really was. He assured the readers of the *Wilmington Morning Star* that, when he was going to New Hanover High School back in 1928 through 1933, they would make a sport out of fooling their dates so they would be real scared and cling to their arms. This was accomplished by getting out of the car and walking along the tracks and watching the mysterious Maco Light come toward them. "The light would startle you as it came down the tracks and the reflection off the tracks made it more eerie. Afterward we checked on it and determined it to be cars coming toward Wilmington at that point and encountering hills before passing Maco itself. This caused the lights to flicker off and come back on again. We thought the reflection of the lights off the tracks made it look as scary as it did. If no automobiles came by some of the fellows went up ahead and waved lights or lanterns. No one was disappointed then. We never told our dates of our findings. It would have ruined everything." Mr. Matthews, of course, makes it all sound just too easy. He was, of course, unaware of the extensive work done along those lines by Mr. Cox and other scientists with or without dates clinging to their arms.

I had thought no more about Wilmington and the Maco Light when a communication reached me on October 28, 1968. An alert young man by the name of Mack Etheridge, then age fifteen, wanted me to hear of his experiences with the Maco Light. He had been interested in the occult for many years prior to his contacting me but had never had any actual psychic experiences even though other members of his family had. Mack's family, including himself, was traveling from Maryland to South Carolina to visit his grandmother that summer. They decided to route their trip through Wilmington to have a look at the fabled Maco Light.

The family arrived in Wilmington on August 7, 1968, around 2:30 in the morning. They didn't intend to stay but only ride through. They had difficulty finding the bend in the railroad track where the Maco trestle is located, due to the darkness and the lack of signs. Nevertheless, disregarding the late hour, they continued to look for it. They knocked on doors, but no one answered. Finally they were riding back toward Wilmington on Route 74-76 when they noticed a new road parallel to it under construction. They decided to stop at a dimly lit trailer as a last try to obtain some information. A young woman directed them back down the highway from where they had just come and told them how to continue toward the track. There was a dirt road parallel to it which they assumed was the road to take. With their eyes wide open and directed toward the track, they followed the dirt road slowly till it came to a small house and ended. They realized they had gone down the wrong road. Retracing their steps they suddenly noticed a small sign reading *Maco, two miles*. They followed the sign and exactly two miles later arrived at the proper spot. The moment they arrived Mr. Etheridge, Sr., parked the car across the track and shut off the lights, and the family stayed in the car quietly and expectantly, hopefully awaiting some sort of glimpse of the light.

It was an exceptionally clear night with a full moon. Nevertheless, a moment later Mr. Etheridge, Sr., noticed a very bright light and pointed it out to his family. The light was not moving up the track toward them. At first it did not appear to be very bright and Mack immediately dismissed it as being a train and not the Maco Light because it seemed to him to be far too bright. But several minutes later the light approached and remained constant. Mack was no longer sure that the light belonged to an approaching train since there was absolutely no sound. Now the light would alternately dim and become bright again. He could observe it with the naked eye and noted that it was a yellowish light one foot in diameter and extremely bright. It would flare up to its brightest intensity for two seconds and then slowly fade out. Sometimes when it faded out it would appear to be farther up the track. There were times when the light would pulsate and he also noticed that there was a hazy luminosity around it when it faded out. At its closest point the light seemed about two hundred feet away. He noticed with mounting excitement that when it was very close the light would slowly swing at knee level as a lantern would in the hands of a man. When the light was closest it appeared to him that it shone on a relatively short stretch of track.

At this point Mr. Etheridge, Sr., reminded his family that they had brought binoculars, and immediately they put them to good use observing the phenomenon for several minutes through them. The binoculars had a seven by thirty-five power and were in excellent condition. "The following," Mack Etheridge explained, "was seen wholly by me and will be totally new to you and to your writings."

As he was gazing at the light through the binoculars about a quarter mile up the track it faded out again and he quite naturally expected it to reappear as the same, but instead it reappeared accompanied by two other lights. These additional lights appeared instantly to the side of the track. There was a red light to the far left; a few feet to the right of that was a small green light, and several feet to the right of that was the usual yellow light, the largest of them.

Mack could clearly see the center green light float into the red one and become part of it, which was then all red. Then the red moved into the yellow by way of a yellow cord. This connecting link first appeared in the yellow light, then shot forward to the red one, connecting the two. Gradually it drew the red light into itself to form the usual bright light observed as the Maco Light.

Mack was amazed at what he had just seen. He followed the light as it moved up the track to perform various maneuvers, only to move back down to repeat the previous procedure. He saw it happen twice and described what he observed to his family. They, however, could only see two of the lights due to the distance and faintness. But as seen through the binoculars the single light seemed to rise up in the air above the track, possibly to the height of a telephone pole. After the three lights had formed Mack also noticed the colors visible together a few times. At this point a train was approaching from the opposite direction and it became necessary to move the car off the track. When the train went by, the light faded out, only to return after the train had passed. At that time of night Highway 74 and 76, the crucial point in the observation of the Maco Light, was virtually desolate. They had passed only a few cars in the hours they spent searching for the station. I had surmised that the lights represented Joe Baldwin's lantern and the headlights of an onrushing train, but Mack Etheridge took issue with that explanation. He assured me that in his estimation no train could have been in sight of the track a quarter of a mile away. The two lights to him were completely separate, and as one would fade out another would continue its strange behavior.

Assuming that the Etheridges were sober and sane people, and their observation correct, it would bear out some of the previous testimony reported by me. What is fascinating in this additional report is the fact that some sort of human agency seems behind the movements of the lights.

This was by no means the end of Joe Baldwin and his lost head. In 1970 I received another communication from a certain Daniel Harrington of Flushing, Long Island. Mr. Harrington had visited the Maco Light, inspired by my account of it. He had brought along a camera, since he was somewhat of a camera fan, in the hopes of capturing the elusive light on film. His black and white pictures were taken with time exposure, 5 or 6 seconds, but unfortunately without tripods. Thus the results would, of necessity, be somewhat blurred. He had clearly seen a large light on the track circling, bobbing and weaving about. In one of the two photographs submitted to me the light seems extremely large in relation to the track. That, however, as Mr. Harrington pointed out, is due to the angle of the camera. In the first photograph there is a single light. In the second shot there are clearly three separate lights: round, brightly lit orbs of luminosity—two large ones and a small one. Mr. Harrington assured me there were no cars passing by when these pictures were taken.

So it would appear that today, seven years after my original visit to the spot, Joe Baldwin is still merrily walking along the track and holding up the lantern to stop an imaginary train. No one has yet come up with a better explanation.

MIDDLE AMERICA

31

Reba and Her Ghosts

REBA B. IS a sensitive, fragile-looking lady with two grown children. She was born in Kentucky, and hails from an old family in which the name Reba has occurred several times before. She works as a medical secretary and doctor's assistant, and nowadays shares her home with three cats, her children having moved away. Mrs. B., who is divorced, wondered whether perhaps she had a particular affinity for ghosts, seeing that she has encountered denizens of the Other World so many times, in so many houses. It wasn't that it bothered her to any extent, but she had gotten used to living by herself except for her cats, and the idea of having to share her home with individuals who could pop in and out at will, and who might hang around her at times when she could not see them, did not contribute to her comfort.

Her psychic ability goes back to age three, when she was living with her grandparents in Kentucky. Even then she had a vivid feeling of presences all around her, not that she actually saw them with her eyes. It was more a sensitivity to unseen forces surrounding her—an awareness that she was never quite alone. As soon as she would go to bed as a child, she would see the figure of a man bending over her, a man she did not know. After a long period of this she wondered if she was dreaming, but in her heart she knew she was not. However, she was much too young to worry about such things, and as she grew up, her ability became part of her character, and she began to accept it as "normal."

This incident begins when she happened to be living in Cincinnati, already divorced. Her mother shared an old house with her, a house that was built around 1900; it had all the earmarks of the post-Victorian era: brass door knobs, little doorbells that were to be turned by hand, and the various trimmings of that age. The house consisted of three floors; the ground floor contained an apartment, and the two ladies took the second and third floor of the house. Reba had her bedroom on the third floor; it was the only bedroom up there situated in the middle of the floor.

One day she was coming up those stairs, and was approaching the window when she saw a man standing by it. He vanished as she came closer, and she gave this no more thought until a few days later. At that time she happened to be lying in bed, propped up and reading a book.

She happened to look up and saw a man who had apparently come up the stairs. She noticed his features fully: his eyes were brown, and he also had brown hair. Immediately she could sense that he was very unhappy, even angry. It wasn't that she heard his voice, but somehow his thoughts communicated themselves to her, mind to mind.

From her bed she could see him approach, walking out to a small landing and standing in front of her door. Next to her room was a storage room. He looked straight at Reba, and at that moment she received the impression that he was very angry because she and her mother were in the house, because they had moved into *his* house.

Although Reba B. was fully conscious and aware of what was going on, she rejected the notion that she was hearing the thoughts of a ghost. But it did her no good; over and over she heard him say or think, "Out, out, I want you out, I don't want you here." At that moment he raised his arm and pointed outward, as if to emphasize his point. The next moment he was gone. Reba thought for a moment, whether she should tell her mother whose bedroom was downstairs. She decided against it, since her mother had a heart condition and because she herself wasn't too sure the incident had been quite real. Also, she was a little frightened and did not want to recall the incident any more than she had to. After a while, she went off to sleep.

Not too long after that her daughter, who was then fourteen, and her eleven-year-old son were home with her from school. It was a weekend, and she wanted the children to enjoy it. Consequently, she did not tell them anything about her ghostly experience. She had gone into the front storage room, when she thought she saw someone sitting on the boxes stacked in the storage area.

At first she refused to acknowledge it, and tried to look away, but when her gaze returned to the area, the man was still sitting there, quietly staring at her. Again she turned her head, and when she looked back, he was gone. The following weekend, her children were with her again. They had hardly arrived when her daughter returned from the same storage room and asked, "Mother, is there someone sitting in there?" and all Reba could do was nod, and acknowledge that there was. Her daughter then described the stranger and the description matched what her mother had seen. Under the circumstances, Reba B. freely discussed the matter with her children. But nothing further was done concerning the matter, and no inquiries were made as to the background of the house.

Summer came, and another spring and another summer, and they got into the habit of using the entrance at the side of the house. There were some shrubs in that area, and in order to enter the apartment in which they lived, they had to come up the stairs where they would have a choice of either walking into the living room on the second floor, or continuing on to the third floor where Reba's bedroom was. The tenant who had the ground floor apartment also had his own entrance.

One warm summer evening, she suddenly felt the stranger come into the downstairs door and walk up the stairs. When she went to check, she saw nothing. Still, she *knew* he was in the house. A few days passed, and again she sensed the ghost nearby. She looked, and as her eyes peered down into the hall, she saw him walking down the hall towards her. While she was thinking, "I am imagining this, there is no such thing as a ghost," she slowly walked toward him. As he kept approaching her, she walked right through him! It was an eerie sensation: for a moment she could not see, and then he was gone. The encounter did not help Reba to keep her composure, but there was little she could do about it.

Many times she sensed his presence in the house without seeing him, but early one evening, on a Sunday, just as it got dark, she found herself in the living room on the second floor of the house. She had turned on the television set, which was facing her, and she kept the volume down so as not to disturb her mother, whose room was on the same floor. She had altered the furniture in the room somewhat, in order to be closer to the television set, and there were two lounge chairs, one of which she used, and the other one close by, near the television set, so that another person could sit in it and also view the screen. She was just watching television, when she sensed the stranger come up the stairs again and walk into the living room. Next he sat down in the empty chair close to Reba, but this time the atmosphere was different from that first encounter near the door of her room. He seemed more relaxed and comfortable, and Reba was almost glad that he was there keeping her company. Somehow she felt that he was glad to be in the room with her, and that he was less lonely because of her. He was no longer angry; he just wanted to visit.

Reba looked at the stranger's face and noticed his rather high-bridged nose. She also had a chance to study his clothes; also he was wearing a brown suit, rather modern in style. Even though the house was quite old, this man was not from the early years, but his clothes seemed to indicate a comparatively recent period. As she sat there, quietly studying the ghost, she got the feeling that he had owned the house at one time, and that their living room had been the sitting room where the ghost and his wife had received people.

Reba somehow knew that his wife had been very pretty—a fair complexioned blonde, and she was shown a fire-place in the living room with a small love seat of the French Provincial type next to it, drawn up quite close to the fireplace. She saw this in her mind's eye, as if the man were showing her something from his past. At the same time, Reba knew that some tragedy had occurred between the ghost and his wife.

Suddenly, panic rose in Reba, as she realized she was sharing the evening with a ghost. Somehow her fears communicated themselves to her phantom visitor, for as she looked close, he had vanished.

As much as she had tried to keep these things from her mother, she could not. Her mother owned an antique covered casserole made of silver, which she kept at the head of her bed. The bed was a bookcase bed, and she used to lift the cover and put in receipts, tickets, and papers whenever she wanted.

One day, Reba and her mother found themselves at the far end of her bedroom on the second floor. Her bed was up against the wall, without any space between it and the wall. As the two ladies were looking in the direction of the bed, they suddenly saw the silver casserole being picked up, put down on the bed, turned upside down and everything spilled out of it. It didn't fly through the air, but moved rather slowly, as if some unseen force were holding it. Although her mother had seen it, she did not say anything because she felt it would be unwise to alarm her daughter; but later on she admitted having seen the whole thing. It was ironic how the two women were trying to spare each other's feelings—yet both knew that what they had witnessed was real.

The ghost did not put in any further appearances after the dramatic encounter in the living room. About a year later, the two ladies moved away into another old house far from this one. But shortly before they did, Reba's mother was accosted on the street by a strange middle-aged lady, who asked her whether she was living in the house just up the street. When Reba's mother acknowledged it, the lady informed her the house had once belonged to her parents. Were they happy in it, Reba's mother wanted to know. "Very happy," the stranger assured her, "Especially my father." It occurred to Reba that it might have been he who she had encountered in the house; someone so attached to his home that he did not want to share it with anyone else, especially flesh and blood people like her mother and herself.

The new home the ladies moved into proved "alive" with unseen vibrations also, but by now they didn't care. Reba realized that she had a special gift. If ghosts wanted her company, there was little she could do about it.

She had a friend who worked as a motorcycle patrolman, by the name of John H. He was a young man and well-liked on the force. One day he chased a speeder—and was killed in the process. At the time, Reba was still married, but she had known John for quite a few years before. They were friends, although not really close ones, and she had been out of touch with him for some time. One morning, she suddenly sensed his presence in the room with her; it made no sense, yet she was positive it was John H. After a while, the presence left her. She remarked on this to her mother and got a blank stare in return. The young man had been killed on the previous night, but Reba could not have known this. The news had come on the radio just that morning, but apparently Reba had had advance news of a more direct kind.

Reba B. shared her interest in the occult with an acquaintance, newscaster Bill G. In his position as a journalist, he had to be particularly careful in expressing an opinion on so touchy a subject as extrasensory perception. They had met at a local restaurant one evening, and somehow the conversation had gotten around to ghosts.

When Mr. G. noticed her apprehension at being one of the "selected" ones who could see ghosts, he told her about another friend, a young medium who had an apartment not far away. One evening she walked out onto her patio, and saw a man in old-fashioned clothes approach her. The man tried to talk to her, but she could not hear anything. Suddenly he disappeared before her eyes. The young lady thought she was having a nervous breakdown, and consulted a psychiatrist; she even went into a hospital to have herself examined, but there was nothing wrong with her. When she returned to her home and went out onto the patio again, she saw the same ghostly apparition once more. This time she did not panic, but instead studied him closely. When he disappeared she went back into her apartment, and decided to make some inquiries about the place. It was then that she discovered that a long time ago, a man of that description had been hanged from a tree in her garden.

"These things *do* happen," Bill G. assured Reba, and asked her not to be ashamed or afraid of them. After all, ghosts are people too. Since then, Reba has come to terms with her ghostly encounters. She has even had an experience with a ghost cat—but that is another story.

32

The Music Studio Ghost

BELLEVILLE, ILLINOIS IS a sleepy town about an hour's drive from St. Louis and has nothing particular to offer in the way of commerce or beauty except for a few charming old houses still standing. The people who live in Belleville are seldom troubled by the controversies of the day and the industrial strife of nearby East St. Louis.

On Main Street near 17th there is an old brick house which has stood the test of time well: built 125 years ago by a coal miner named Meyer, it has since been remodeled and also been added to, but the original structure is still sound and no one thinks of tearing it down or replacing it with something more up to date.

The house consists of two stories, with the front parlor well lit by large windows looking onto Main Street. There are four rooms downstairs, a kitchen, and a hallway leading to the second section of the house which in turn leads to a small backyard. The house stands near the corner and is accessible from downtown in a matter of minutes. Eventually, it had passed out of the Meyer family into other hands, and its history is obscure until it became the property of a certain Mr. and Mrs. Joseph Stricker. Little else is known about them but their names. After they passed on, the house was acquired by two young sisters, Dollie and Judy Walta, who bought it not as living quarters, but in order to turn the place into studios for their music business. The Walta girls are music teachers. Dollie, born in 1929 and Judy, born in 1939, were two of ten children of Fred and Julia Walta, who had come to America from Czechoslovakia while still young. They gave their family a good education, but Judy rebelled against the strict discipline of school and quit after two years of high school. This despite an IQ of 134.

At sixteen, she was already an accomplished musician and decided to devote her life to the teaching of music. To this day she is a teacher of piano. Dollie, the elder sister, teaches guitar and jointly they have operated a music studio in the house for the past eleven years. They come here every day except on weekends, and generally leave by 9 P.M. or earlier, depending on how many pupils they have that day. Once in a while, they have also come in on Saturday mornings.

At other times and at night, the house is deserted and well locked up, and the chance of burglars breaking in is small due to its solid construction and the fact that it is on Main Street, usually well guarded by the local police department.

For the first six years of their tenancy, the sisters noticed nothing out of the ordinary in the old house. True, there were the usual squeaking floorboards and the aching sounds of an old house settling on its foundations. But that was to be expected and no one paid any heed to such things. In 1962 they decided to make some alterations in the house to make the layout more suitable to their needs. Shortly after, Judy Walta had to come in late one night, because she had forgotten to leave one of the inner doors unlocked so the cleaning woman could get in there in the morning.

She entered from the rear door, which leads to 17th Street, and did not bother to turn on any lights since the door she wanted to unlock was only a few steps beyond the back door. Swiftly, she unlocked it and then turned around to leave again. As she did so, she passed a white, misty figure in the hall. There was no mistaking it for anything else, and the whole incident took her so by surprise, she just backed away from it and out the rear door.

The next morning, she discussed the matter with her sister and as nothing further happened out of the ordinary, they dropped the subject.

One of their students, a young man by the name of Jim Bawling, had been unhappy at his home and gotten into the habit of spending a great amount of time in their studio. In fact, it had gotten to be a kind of "home away from home" to him and he became genuinely attached to the place and the sisters. Almost every afternoon he would come in and chat with them, whenever they were free to do so.

Eventually, he joined the Navy, and on his first leave, he returned to Belleville for a visit. On August 26, 1962, the young man drowned in an accident. On August 30, the day after his funeral, the sisters were in the room used for lessons, when a pencil, which had been his, and which he had left on his desk on his very last visit, started to roll off the desk, bounced on the eraser and dropped—pointing to the chair which had been his last seat!

There was no one close to the desk at the time, nor was there any movement or vibration outside the house. Moreover, the room is built on a slant and the pencil rolled *against* the slant.

Shortly after this incident, the sisters and many of their students began hearing the back door open by itself and close again. This was immediately followed by footsteps of someone walking through the hall. At first, they would get up to see who it was, but there was never anyone to be seen. Gradually, they realized that these were not the footsteps of a living person. The visitor would come at various times of the day or evening, and then stay away for several months. Then it would all resume. The sisters became used to these sounds, and hardly looked up when they became audible. One day the steps continued and then they could clearly hear someone sit down in the sailor's old chair!

It was clear to them that Jim was trying to make himself felt and wanted to continue his old friendship with them from where he now was. This did not bother them, but it bothered some of their pupils who held less broadminded views of ghosts.

The sisters were sure it was Jim, for this was his chair, and he always came in through the rear door rather than the front entrance.

The footsteps continued and the door would still open and close by itself and Judy would just nod and Dollie would say "Hello, Jim" and go on with her work.

But it soon became apparent to Dollie that the footsteps were not always the same: sometimes they were soft and light, as if made by a young person, while at other times they were the heavy, almost clumsy steps of a big man.

On March 25, 1966 the two girls were in different parts of the studio busy with their chores. Judy was in the middle room, while Dollie was in the bathroom, with the door open. The time was 1:20 in the afternoon. Independently of each other, the two girls saw the same figure of a man suddenly appear out of nowhere. At first, Judy saw him. He was a big man, about 5 feet, 11 inches tall, and heavy-set, dressed in gray, and where his face should have been there was just a gray mass. But unmistakably this was a human figure. Thirty seconds later, he appeared to Dollie. She looked at him, and could see right through him into the other room!

The girls both had the impression that the man was looking *at them*. As he disappeared toward the rear of the house, they realized they had not heard a single sound. Naturally, they knew this was not Jim, their erstwhile pupil. But who was it?

After the appearance of the man in gray, the footsteps were not heard again, but the door kept opening and closing as before. Word of their strange house got around and though they did not exactly cherish the notion, their pupils began to discuss the phenomena with them.

One young man whose work in the Air police had trained him to be a particularly competent observer of details, came forward to tell of a strange encounter on May 26 of that year. He was in the downstairs studio room at about 8 P.M. when he suddenly came face to face with a man in gray. He took him to be about thirty years of age and, just like the sisters, he could not make out any facial characteristics. It was almost as if the man did not want his face to be recognized and was hiding it in a blur.

One Saturday, Judy had come to make sure the building was properly locked. This was August 27, 1966 and between 3 and 3:30 P.M. she observed in the empty building the snapping of door locks, and a footstep—just one footstep—near the door leading from the hall into the basement of the house. This was immediately followed by the sound of several objects falling to the floor, although nothing was moving. One sound in particular reminded her of the noise made by dropping a small package to the floor, *or the muffled sound of a silencer on a gun*, she thought, with a shudder. What was she thinking? This seemed like a bad melodrama by now.

All this activity began to get on her nerves. The following Tuesday, August 30, the two girls had their friends Rita Schulte and Mike Tolan in the house. It was after teaching hours and the foursome was just sitting around relaxing. Rita had been taking piano lessons for the past year and was familiar with the "problems" of the house, but Mike laughed at it all, especially the man in gray. "You and your ghosts," he chortled. "It's all in your minds."

At that moment, the toilet was being flushed violently. They looked at each other. Everybody was accounted for and the toilet could not flush by itself. Mike tried and tried to see whether it might accidentally have done so. But it couldn't have. His face took on a more thoughtful mien as he sat down again.

A drum teacher named Dick P., working out of the studio, often told of the same noises—the back door opening and closing and the footsteps of an unseen visitor coming up and stopping inside the house. One night in early 1966, he was driving by the house. He knew from the sisters that there had never been anything unusual observed upstairs. He also knew the house was locked up tight and empty. But to his surprise, the upper story was lit up as if someone were up there. No reflection from passing cars could account for this. He drove on.

Jack McCormick is a clerk for the Internal Revenue Service, an outfit with little use for ghosts, since they don't pay taxes. His son has been studying with the Walta sisters for the past year and a half, and it was and is his custom to wait for him in the downstairs waiting room. He, too, has been constantly unnerved by the sound of the door opening and closing and footsteps of someone not appearing.

Joe Bauer, a freight handler for the railroad, has heard the heavy footfalls of a man coming in the rear door, only to find no one there. Mrs. Bauer takes two lessons a week, and he often stays with her until about eight or nine in the evening. Everyone gets hungry by that time, so one of them would run out for hamburgers. One night while they—the two sisters and the Bauers—were eating and watching TV, Mrs. Bauer felt an icy hand on her back. She felt each and every finger, but when she shook herself and turned around, she saw that no one was near her. Needless to say, it did not help her appetite.

A little while after, all four saw the umbrella, which had been standing idly and quietly in its stand, move by its own volition. One of the sisters got up and stopped it. But the umbrella would not obey. A few moments later, it started swinging again. At the same time, the back door opened and closed with a bang. That evening everyone was out of the house faster than you can say "ghost".

The sisters decided something had to be done about the power frightening them in the house. First, the house itself deserved to be carefully scrutinized. It was then they discovered that it actually consisted of three separate units, with the front section, where today's main entrance is, constructed at a later date than the rear. The original entrance had been to the rear, and what was the entrance at the time the house had been built, back in the 1840s, was now situated *inside* the house, in the middle of the hallway. It so happened this was the exact spot where the ghostly footsteps had always stopped dead.

The soft footsteps they took to be the sailor's were never heard again nor was anything happening that they could consciously connect with him. They assumed the phenomena he might have caused were merely his way of saying goodby and that he had long since found a better place to hang around.

But the heavy footsteps and the man in gray remained. So did the mystery of who he was and why he was disturbing the peace of the house. Judy started to talk to various neighbors and take frequent trips to the local library. Under the guise of doing research into the background of their house for reasons of historical curiosity, the girl managed to dredge up quite a bit of information, not necessarily all of it reliable or even true.

The trouble was that in the 19th century, Main Street had not yet been named and the town was quite different. It was difficult to trace individual addresses. There was, for instance, the rumor that eighty years ago a grocer named Jack Meyer had been murdered in their house. She tried to get proof of this and found that a certain George Meyer, occupation unknown, had indeed been murdered in 1888 in Belleville, Illinois. But there was nothing to show that he had resided at this address.

She continued to search and finally hit paydirt. The local paper of Tuesday, June 26, 1923, carried a one-column notice that immediately excited her.

"Jacob Meyer, aged 77, shot himself today. Aged west side coal miner was despondent because of ill health. Was found dead in chair by wife, bullet through his brain."

Apparently Meyer had been brooding over his bad health the night before. At 10:15 he had lunch—miners rise early for breakfast—and then took a rest in his usual chair. When his wife called out to him and got no reply, she checked to see what was the matter and found blood trickling down his face. Horrified, she called on her brother Alex White to come and help. The brother, who resided next door, came and found life ebbing from the aged man. An instant later, Meyer was dead. At his feet was the .32 caliber revolver he had used to blow his brains out. The bullet had passed through his head and lay nearby on the floor. What was strange was that *nobody had heard the shot*, even though several members of the family had been within a few feet of the man all that time. How was it possible? Evidently he had held the gun to his temple and fired at close range and the sound had somehow been muffled.

There had been no threat of suicide beforehand, but Meyer had told his wife on arising, "Mary, I am feeling very bad today."

Meyer had retired six months before due to failing health. Prior to that he had still worked at a nearby mine despite his advanced age. A native of Germany, where he had been born in 1845, Meyer had come to America to seek his fortune.

Judy Walta put the clipping down and suddenly many things began to fall in place for her.

Why hadn't the ghost shown his face? Was he ashamed of having committed suicide, considered an act of cowardice in those days? Or was it because the bullet had literally torn his face to shreds?

The footsteps were those of a heavy man. Meyer was a heavy man. But the man in gray did not look 77 years of age. This at first threw the sisters for a loop until they understood, from psychic literature, that the dead usually return in their mental imagines to that which they consider the prime of life—usually around age thirty, or thereabouts.

They had noticed that the phenomena occurred towards the end of the month, usually after the twentieth and at no other times.

Meyer had killed himself June 26, 1923. The suicide, according to the newspaper, took place at their address, in their house, which was Meyer's at the time.

The sound, heard by Judy, of a package dropping sharply to the floor could very well have been a reenactment of the fatal shot that killed him.

In Jacob Meyer's day, the entrance was to the rear of the house and he would have come home that way, every day, from the mine. Was he simply continuing to go through his daily routine, refusing to accept the reality of his suicide?

Somehow the understanding of the problem changed the atmosphere in the house. Not that the phenomena ceased, far from it, but it appeared that the ghostly resident had finally found a kind of relationship with the flesh-and-blood inhabitants of what was once his home.

Cigar smoke now could be smelled on several occasions, although there was no cigar smoker in the house and all doors and windows were shut airtight. The smoke did not originate outside the house. This smell was soon followed or rather augmented by the smell of freshly brewed coffee at times when no one was brewing any coffee. The sound of papers rattling, someone sitting down in the chair as if to read his newspaper over his morning coffee and perhaps smoke a cigar, and scraping noises of a chair being half-dragged across the floor in plain view of the sisters contributed to their conviction that their ghostly visitor, far from being ready to leave upon being recognized, was getting ready for a long—to him—comfortable stay.

If the girls had any doubts as to the identity of the unbidden guest, these were soon dispelled. On the night of April 27, 1967, Dollie and Judy were about to leave the studio for the night, when they both distinctly heard the sound of a shot coming from inside the building. They had just locked the back door and knew the house was quite empty. They debated whether to run or go back in and check. Curiosity won out, they unlocked the door again and went back inside. They checked the studio and nothing was out of place. They had just gotten ready to leave again, when they heard another shot. The second shot sounded quite *muffled*, whereas the first one had been loud and clear. It came from the area of the furnace room in the middle of the house.

In November, Dollie was walking under the doorway between the front and back rooms, an area hitherto free from psychic phenomena. She was stopped cold by something that resisted her advance although she could not see anything unusual. She felt that she was walking through heavy water, halfway up to her knees. This was a physical thing, she realized, and in sudden horror it occurred to her that she was trying to penetrate the etheric body of Mr. Meyer. Hastily retreating she left the house in a hurry.

That same month a hat disappeared without a trace. Judy had bought it for a friend for Christmas and had kept it in a box along with other Christmas gifts. None of the other items were disturbed but the hat was gone. The puzzle was made worse by her discovery, several days later, of three dollar bills in the receipt book. Since neither of the girls, nor anyone else had placed them there, this was strange indeed. On checking their receipts and figures they found they were exactly three dollars over. It so happened that the hat, which was never seen again, had cost three dollars.

The reputation of the house as a haunted abode seeped out despite the sisters' reluctance to discuss it except with their friends and pupils, when necessary. One day a woman walked by the house to see if she could have a look at the "ghost." As she looked at thc front windows, she found herself tripped by an unseen force. Neighbors picked her up, but word got back to Judy and she interviewed the lady afterwards. Shaking her head, the woman insisted nothing had happened, she had not fallen. Judy was happy to let it go at that. Who wants to admit being tripped by the ghost of a man dead for forty years?

About that time Judy discovered that the ghostly miner's wedding to Mary White had taken place on September 9, 1867. When a man celebrates his one hundredth wedding anniversary he should not have time for such foolishness as tripping people outside haunted houses. Quite possibly Mrs. Meyer has since taken him in hand and made a better home for him beyond the veil. At any rate, the door in the rear no longer opens and closes as it used to, and perhaps Jacob Meyer is now retired for good.

33

The Ghostly Usher of Minneapolis

FOR THIS ACCOUNT, I am indebted to a twenty-two-year-old creative production assistant in a Minneapolis advertising agency, by the name of Deborah Turner. Miss Turner got hooked on some of my books, and started to look around in the Twin Cities for cases that might whet my appetite for ghost hunting. Being also musically inclined with an interest in theater, it was natural that she should gravitate toward the famed Guthrie Theater, named after the famous director, which is justly known as the pride of Minneapolis. At the theater she met some other young people, also in their early twenties, and shared her interest in psychic phenomena with them. Imagine her surprise when she discovered that she had stumbled upon a most interesting case.

Richard Miller was born in Manhattan, Kansas in 1951. Until age ten, he lived there with his father, a chemist in government service. Then his father was transferred to England, and Richard spent several years going to school in that country. After that, he and his family returned to the United States and moved to Edina. This left Richard not only with a vivid recollection of England, but also somewhat of an accent which, together with his childhood in Kansas, gave him a somewhat unusual personality.

His strange accent became the subject of ridicule by other students at Edina Morningside High School where he went to school, and it did not go down well with the shy, introspective young man. In the tenth grade at this school, he made friends with another young man, Fred Koivumaki, and a good and close relationship sprang up between the two boys. It gave Fred a chance to get to know Richard better than most of the other fellows in school.

As if the strange accent were not enough to make him stand out from the other boys in the area, Richard was given to sudden, jerky movements, which made him a good target for sly remarks and jokes of his fellow students. The Millers did not have much of a social life, since they also did not quite fit into the pattern of life in the small town of Edina.

During the years spent in an English school, Richard had known corporal punishment, since it is still part of the system in some English schools. This terrified him, and perhaps contributed towards his inability to express himself fully and freely. Somehow he never acquired a girlfriend as the other students did, and this, too, bothered him a lot. He couldn't for the world understand why people didn't like him more, and often talked about it to his friend Fred.

When both young men reached the age of sixteen, they went to the Guthrie Theater where they got jobs as ushers. They worked at it for two years. Richard Miller got along well with the other ushers, but developed a close friendship only with Fred Koivumaki and another fellow, Barry Peterson. It is perhaps a strange quirk of fate that both Richard Miller and Barry Peterson never reached manhood, but died violently long before their time.

However, Richard's parents decided he should go to the university, and quit his job. In order to oblige his parents, Richard Miller gave up the job as usher and moved into Territorial Hall for his first year at the university.

However, the change did not increase his ability to express himself or to have a good social life. Also, he seemed to have felt that he was catering to his parents' wishes, and became more antagonistic toward them. Then, too, it appears that these students also made him the butt of their jokes. Coincidentally, he developed a vision problem, with cells breaking off his retinas and floating in the inner humor of the eye. This causing him to see spots before his eyes, a condition for which there is no cure. However, he enjoyed skiing because he knew how to do it well, and joined the university ski club.

But Richard's bad luck somehow was still with him. On a trip to Colorado, he ran into a tree, luckily breaking only his skis. When summer came to the area, Richard rode his bike down a large dirt hill into rough ground and tall weeds at the bottom, injuring himself in the process. Fortunately, a motorcyclist came by just then, and got Richard to the emergency ward of a nearby hospital. All this may have contributed towards an ultimate breakdown; or, as the students would say, Richard just "flipped out."

He was hospitalized at the university hospital and was allowed home only on weekends. During that time he was on strong medication, but when the medication did not improve his condition, the doctor took him off it and sent him home.

The following February 4, he decided to try skiing again, and asked his father to take him out to Buck Hill, one of the skiing areas not far from town. But to his dismay Richard discovered that he couldn't ski anymore, and this really depressed him. When he got home, there was a form letter waiting for him from the university, advising him that because he had skipped all the final exams due to his emotional problems at the time, he had received F's in all his classes and was on probation.

All this seemed too much for him. He asked his mother for forty dollars, ostensibly to buy himself new ski boots. Then he drove down to Sears on Lake Street, where he bought a high-powered pistol and shells. That was on Saturday, and he killed himself in the car. He wasn't found until Monday morning, when the lot clearing crew found him with most of his head shot off.

Richard Miller was given a quiet burial in Fort Snelling National Cemetery. His parents, Dr. and Mrs. Byron S. Miller, requested that memorials to the Minnesota Association for Mental Health be sent instead of flowers. Richard's mother had always felt that her son's best years had been spent as an usher at the Guthrie Theater; consequently he was cremated wearing his Guthrie Theater blazer. The date was February 7, and soon enough the shock of the young man's untimely death wore off, and only his immediate family and the few friends he had made remembered Richard Miller.

A few weeks after the death of the young usher, a woman seated in the theater in an aisle seat came up to the usher in charge of this aisle and asked him to stop the other usher from walking up and down during the play. The usher in charge was shocked, since he had been at the top of the aisle and had seen no one walk up and down. All the other ushers were busy in their respective aisles. However, the lady insisted that she had seen this young man walk up and down the aisle during the play. The usher in charge asked her to describe what she had seen. She described Richard Miller, even to the mole on his cheek. The incident is on record with the Guthrie Theater. *Minneapolis Tribune* columnist Robert T. Smith interviewed Craig Scherfenberg, director of audience development at the theater, concerning the incident. "There was no one in our employ at the time who fit the description," the director said, "but it fit the dead young man perfectly."

In the summer several years later, two ushers were asked to spend the night in the theater to make sure some troublesome air conditioning equipment was fully repaired. The Guthrie Theater has a thrust stage with openings onto the stage on all three sides; these openings lead to an actors' waiting area, which in turn has a door opening onto an area used as a lounge during intermissions.

The two young men were sitting in this waiting area with both doors open, and they were the only people in the building. At one o'clock in the morning, they suddenly heard the piano onstage begin to play. Stunned by this, they watched in silence when they saw a cloud-like form floating through the lounge door and hovering in the center of the room. One of the ushers thought the form was staring at him. As quickly as they could gather their wits they left the room.

One of Deborah Turner's friends had worked late one evening shortly after this incident, repairing costumes needed for the next day's performance. She and a friend were relaxing in the stage area while waiting for a ride home. As she glanced into the house, she noticed that the lights on the aisle that had been the dead usher's were going on and off, as if someone were walking slowly up and down. She went to the Ladies' Room a little later, and suddenly she heard pounding on one wall, eventually circling the room and causing her great anxiety, since she knew that she and her friend were the only people in the house.

When the Guthrie Theater put on a performance of *Julius Caesar*, one of the extras was an older woman by the name of Mary Parez. She freely admitted that she was psychic and had been able to communicate with her dead sister. She told her fellow actors that she could sense Richard Miller's presence in the auditorium. Somehow she thought that the ghost would make himself known during Mark Antony's famous speech to the Romans after Caesar's death.

The scene was lit primarily by torches when the body of Julius Caesar was brought upon the stage. Jason Harlen, a young usher, and one of his colleagues, were watching the performance from different vantage points in the theater. One boy was in one of the tunnels leading to the stage, the other in the audience. Both had been told of Mary Parez's prediction, but were disappointed when nothing happened at that time. In boredom, they began to look around the theater. Independently of each other, they saw smoke rising to the ceiling, and shaping itself into a human form. Both young men said that the form had human eyes.

The aisle that the late Richard Miller worked was number eighteen. Two women in the acting company of *Julius Caesar*, named Terry and Gigi, complained that they had much trouble with the door at the top of aisle eighteen for no apparent reason. Bruce Benson, who now worked aisle eighteen, told that people complained of an usher walking up and down the aisle during performances. Bruce Margolis, who works the stage door, leaves the building after everyone else. When he was there one night all alone, the elevator began running on its own.

All this talk about a ghost induced some of the young ushers to try and make contact with him via the Ouija board. Dan Burg, head usher, took a board with him to the stage, and along with colleagues Bruce Benson and Scott Hurner, tried to communicate with the ghost. For awhile nothing happened. Then, all of a sudden the board spelled, "Tiptoe to the tech room."

When they asked why, the board spelled the word ghost. They wanted to know which tech room the ghost was referring to: downstairs? "No," the communicator informed them, "upstairs." Then the board signed off with the initials MIL. At that, one of the men tipped over the board and wanted nothing further to do with it.

In November of the next year, an usher working at the theater told columnist Robert Smith, "It was after a night performance. Everyone had left the theater but me. I had forgotten my gloves and returned to retrieve them. I glanced into the theater and saw an usher standing in one of the aisles. It was him. He saw me and left. I went around to that aisle and couldn't find anything."

There is also an opera company connected with the Guthrie Theater. One night not long ago, one of the ladies working for the opera company was driving home from the Guthrie Theater. Suddenly she felt a presence beside her in the car. Terrified, she looked around, and became aware of a young man with dark curly hair, glasses, and a mole on his face. He wore a blue coat with something red on the pocket—the Guthrie Theater blazer. With a sinking feeling, she realized that she was looking at the ghost of Richard Miller.

For the past two years, however, no new reports have come in concerning the unfortunate young man. Could it be that he has finally realized that there await him greater opportunities in the next dimension, and though his life on earth was not very successful, his passing into the spiritual life might give him most of the opportunities his life on earth had denied him? At any rate, things have now quieted down in aisle eighteen at the Guthrie Theater, in Minneapolis, Minnesota.

THE WEST

34

The Strange Case of the Santa Ana Ghost

LITTLE DID I know when I had successfully investigated the haunted apartment of Mrs. Verna Kunze in San Bernardino, that Mrs. Kunze would lead me to another case equally as interesting as her own, which I reported on in my book, *Ghosts of the Golden West*.

Mrs. Kunze is a very well-organized person, and a former employee in the passport division of the State Department. She is used to sifting facts from fancy. Her interest in psycho-cybernetics had led her to a group of like-minded individuals meeting regularly in Orange County. There she met a gentleman formerly with the FBI by the name of Walter Tipton.

One day, Mr. Tipton asked her help in contacting me concerning a most unusual case that had been brought to his attention. Having checked out some of the more obvious details, he had found the people involved truthful and worthy of my time.

So it was that I first heard of Mrs. Carole Trausch of Santa Ana.

What happened to the Trausch family and their neighbors is not just a ghost story. Far more than that, they found themselves in the middle of an old tragedy that had not yet been played out fully when they moved into their spanking new home.

Carole Trausch was born in Los Angeles of Scottish parentage and went to school in Los Angeles. Her father is a retired policeman and her mother was born in Scotland. Carole married quite young and moved with her husband, a businessman, to live first in Huntington Beach and later in Westminster, near Santa Ana.

Now in her early twenties, she is a glamorous-looking blonde who belies the fact that she has three children aged eight, six, and two, all girls.

Early the previous year, they moved into one of two hundred two-story bungalows in a new development in Westminster. They were just an ordinary family, without any particular interest in the occult. About their only link with the world of the psychic were some peculiar dreams Carole had had.

The first time was when she was still a little girl. She dreamed there were some pennies hidden in the rose bed in the garden. On awakening, she laughed at herself, but out of curiosity she did go to the rose bed and looked. Sure enough, there were some pennies in the soil below the roses. Many times since then she has dreamed of future events that later came true.

One night she dreamed that her husband's father was being rolled on a stretcher, down a hospital corridor by a nurse, on his way to an operation. The next morning there was a phone call informing them that such an emergency had indeed taken place about the time she dreamed it. On several occasions she sensed impending accidents or other unpleasant things, but she is not always sure what kind. One day she felt sure she or her husband would be in a car accident. Instead it was one of her little girls, who was hit by a passing car.

When they moved into their present house, Mrs. Trausch took an immediate dislike to it. This upset her practical-minded husband. They had hardly been installed when she begged him to move again. He refused.

The house is a white-painted two-story bungalow, which was built about five years before their arrival. Downstairs is a large, oblong living room, a kitchen, and a dining area. On the right, the staircase leads to the upper story. The landing is covered with linoleum, and there are two square bedrooms on each side of the landing, with wall-to-wall carpeting and windows looking onto the yard in the rear bedroom and onto the street in the front room.

There is a large closet along the south wall of the rear bedroom. Nothing about the house is unusual, and there was neither legend nor story nor rumor attached to the house when they rented it from the local bank that owned it.

And yet there was something queer about the house. Mrs. Trausch's nerves were on edge right from the very first when they moved in. But she accepted her husband's decision to stay put and swept her own fears under the carpet of everyday reason as the first weeks in their new home rolled by.

At first the children would come to her with strange tales. The six-year-old girl would complain of being touched by someone she could not see whenever she dropped off for her afternoon nap in the bedroom upstairs. Sometimes this presence would shake the bed, and then there was a shrill noise, somewhat like a beep, coming from the clothes closet. The oldest girl, eight years old, confirmed the story and reported similar experiences in the room.

Carole dismissed these reports as typical imaginary tales of the kind children will tell.

But one day she was resting on the same bed upstairs and found herself being tapped on the leg by some unseen person.

This was not her imagination; she was fully awake, and it made her wonder if perhaps her intuition about this house had not been right all along.

She kept experiencing the sensation of touch in the upstairs bedrooms only, and it got to be a habit with her to make the beds as quickly as possible and then rush downstairs where she felt nothing unusual. Then she also began to hear the shrill, beeplike sounds from the closet. She took out all the children's clothes and found nothing that could have caused the noise. Finally she told her husband about it, and he promptly checked the pipes and other structural details of the house, only to shake his head. Nothing could have made such noises.

For several months she had kept her secret, but now that her husband also knew, she had Diane, the oldest, tell her father about it as well.

It was about this time that she became increasingly aware of a continuing presence upstairs. Several times she would hear footsteps walking upstairs, and on investigation found the children fast asleep. Soon the shuffling steps became regular features of the house. It would always start near the closet in the rear bedroom, then go toward the stair landing.

Carole began to wonder if her nerves weren't getting the better of her. She was much relieved one day when her sister Kathleen Bachelor, who had come to visit her, remarked about the strange footsteps upstairs. Both women knew the children were out. Only the baby was upstairs, and on rushing up the stairs, they found her safely asleep in her crib. It had sounded to them like a small person wearing slippers.

Soon she discovered, however, that there were two kinds of footsteps: the furtive pitter-patter of a child, and the heavy, deliberate footfalls of a grownup.

Had they fallen heir to two ghosts? The thought seemed farfetched even to ESP-prone Carole, but it could not be dismissed entirely. What was going on, she wondered. Evidently she was not losing her mind, for others had also heard these things.

Once she had gone out for the evening and when she returned around ten P.M., she dismissed the babysitter. After the girl had left, she was alone with the baby. Suddenly she heard the water running in the bathroom upstairs. She raced up the stairs and found the bathroom door shut tight. Opening it, she noticed that the water was on and there was some water in the sink.

On January 27 of the next year, Carole had guests for lunch, two neighbors named Pauline J. and Joyce S., both young women about the same age as Carole. The children were all sleeping in the same upstairs front bedroom, the two older girls sharing the bed while the baby girl occupied the crib. The baby had her nap between eleven and two P.M. At noon, however, the baby woke up crying, and, being barely able to talk at age two, kept saying "Baby scared, Mommy!"

The three ladies had earlier been upstairs together, preparing the baby for her crib. At that time, they had also put the entire room carefully in order, paying particular attention to making the covers and spread on the large bed very smooth, and setting up the dolls and toys on the chest in the corner.

When the baby cried at noon, all three women went upstairs and found the bed had wrinkles and an imprint as though someone had been sitting on it. The baby, of course, was still in her crib.

They picked up the child and went downstairs with her. Just as they got to the stairway, all three heard an invisible child falling down the stairs about three steps ahead of where they were standing.

It was after this experience that Mrs. Trausch wondered why the ghost child never touched any of the dolls. You see, the footsteps they kept hearing upstairs always went from the closet to the toy chest where the dolls are kept. But none of the dolls was ever disturbed. It occurred to her that the invisible child was a boy, and there were no boy's toys around.

The sounds of a child running around in the room upstairs became more and more frequent; she knew it was not one of her children, having accounted for her own in other ways. The whole situation began to press on her nerves, and even her husband—who had until now tended to shrug off what he could not understand—became concerned. Feelers were put out to have me come to the house as soon as possible, but I could not make it right away and they would have to cope with their unseen visitors for the time being, or until I arrived on the scene.

All during February the phenomena continued, so much so that Mrs. Trausch began to take them as part of her routine. But she kept as much to the downstairs portion of the house as she could. For some unknown reason, the phenomena never intruded on that part of the house.

She called in the lady who managed the development for the owners and cautiously told her of their problem. But the manager knew nothing whatever about the place, except that it was new and to her knowledge no great tragedies had occurred there in her time.

When the pitter-patter of the little feet continued, Carole Trausch decided she just had to know. On March 16, she decided to place some white flour on the linoleum-covered portion of the upstairs floor to trap the unseen child. This was the spot where the footsteps were most often heard, and for the past two days the ghost child had indeed "come out" there to run and play.

In addition, she took a glass of water with some measuring spoons of graduated sizes in it, and set it all down in a small pan and put it into her baby's crib with a cracker in the pan beside the glass. This was the sort of thing a little child might want—that is, a living child.

She then retired to the downstairs portion of the house and called in a neighbor. Together the two women kept watch, waiting for the early afternoon hours when the ghost child usually became active upstairs.

As the minutes ticked off, Carole began to wonder how she would look if nothing happened. The neighbor probably would consider her neurotic, and accuse her of making up the whole story as an attention getter in this rather quiet community.

But she did not have to worry long. Sure enough, there were the footsteps again upstairs. The two women waited a few moments to give the ghost a chance to leave an impression, then they rushed upstairs.

They saw no child, but the white flour had indeed been touched. There were footmarks in the flour, little feet that seemed unusually small and slender. Next to the prints there was the picture of a flower, as if the child had bent down and finger-painted the flower as a sign of continuing presence. From the footprints, they took the child to be between three and four years of age. The water and pan in the crib had not been touched, and as they stood next to the footprints, there was utter silence around them.

Mrs. Trausch now addressed the unseen child gently and softly, promising the child they would not hurt it. Then she placed some boys' toys, which she had obtained for this occasion, around the children's room and withdrew.

There was no immediate reaction to all this, but two days later the eight-year-old daughter came running down the stairs to report that she had seen the shadow of a little boy in front of the linen closet in the hall. He wore a striped shirt and pants, and was shorter than she.

When I heard of the footprints by telephone, I set the week of June 2 aside for a visit to the house. Meanwhile I instructed the Trausches to continue observing whatever they could.

But the Trausches had already resolved to leave the house, even if I should be able to resolve their "problem." No matter what, they could never be quite sure. And living with a ghost—or perhaps two ghosts—was not what they wanted to do, what with three living children to keep them on their toes.

Across from the Trausch apartment, and separated from it by a narrow lane, is another house just like it and built about the same time, on what was before only open farmland—as far as everyone there knows. A few years before, the area was flooded and was condemned, but it dried out later. There is and always has been plenty of water in the area, a lowland studded with ponds and fishing holes.

The neighbor's name was Bonnie Swanson and she too was plagued by footsteps that had no human causing them. The curious thing is that these phenomena were heard only in the upstairs portion of her house, where the bedrooms are, just as in the Trausch house.

Twice the Swansons called in police, only to be told that there was no one about causing the footsteps. In April, the Swansons had gone away for a weekend, taking their child with them. When they returned, the husband opened the door and was first to step into the house. At this moment he distinctly heard footsteps running very fast from front to rear of the rooms, as if someone had been surprised by their return. Mrs. Swanson, who had also heard this, joined her husband in looking the house over, but there was no stranger about and no one could have left.

Suddenly they became aware of the fact that a light upstairs was burning. They knew they had turned it off when they left. Moreover, in the kitchen they almost fell over a child's tricycle. Last time they saw this tricycle, it had been standing in the corner of their living room. It could not have gotten to the kitchen by itself, and there was no sign of anyone breaking and entering in their absence. Nothing was missing.

It seemed as if my approaching visit was somehow getting through to the ghost or ghosts, for as the month of June came closer, the phenomena seemed to mount in intensity and frequency.

On the morning of May 10, at nine-thirty, Mrs. Trausch was at her front bedroom window, opening it to let in the air. From her window she could see directly into the Swanson house, since both houses were on the same level with the windows parallel to each other. As she reached her window and casually looked out across to the Swanson's rooms, which she knew to be empty at this time of day (Mr. Swanson was at work, and Mrs. Swanson and a houseguest were out for the morning) she saw to her horror the arm of a woman pushing back the curtain of Mrs. Swanson's window.

There was a curiously stiff quality about this arm and the way it moved the curtain back. Then she saw clearly a woman with a deathlike white mask of a face staring at her. The woman's eyes were particularly odd. Despite her excitement, Mrs. Trausch noticed that the woman had wet hair and was dressed in something filmy, like a white nylon negligee with pink flowers on it.

For the moment, Mrs. Trausch assumed that the houseguest must somehow have stayed behind, and so she smiled at the woman across from her. Then the curtain dropped and the woman disappeared. Carole Trausch could barely wait to question her neighbor about the incident, and found that there hadn't been anyone at the house when she saw the woman with the wet hair.

Now Mrs. Trausch was sure that there were two unseen visitors, a child and a woman, which would account for the different quality of the footsteps they had been hearing.

She decided to try and find out more about the land on which the house stood.

A neighbor living a few blocks away on Chestnut Street, who had been in her house for over twenty years, managed to supply some additional information. Long before the development had been built, there had been a farm there.

In the exact place where the Trausches now lived there had been a barn. When the house was built, a large trench was dug and the barn was pushed into it and burned. The people who lived there at the time were a Mexican family named Felix. They had a house nearby but sold the area of the farm to the builders.

But because of the flooded condition of the area, the houses stood vacant for a few years. Only after extensive drainage had taken place did the houses become inhabitable. At this time the Trausches were able to move into theirs.

The area was predominantly Mexican and the development was a kind of Anglo-Saxon island in their midst.

All this information was brought out only after our visit, incidentally, and neither Sybil Leek, who acted as my medium, nor I had any knowledge of it at the time.

Mrs. Trausch was not the only adult member of the family to witness the phenomena. Her husband finally confessed that on several occasions he had been puzzled by footsteps upstairs when he came home late at night. That was around one A.M., and when he checked to see if any of the children had gotten out of bed, he found them fast asleep. Mr. Trausch is a very realistic man. His business is manufacturing industrial tools, and he does not believe in ghosts. But he heard the footsteps too.

The Trausches also realized that the shuffling footsteps of what appeared to be a small child always started up as soon as the two older girls had left for school. It was as if the invisible boy wanted to play with their toys when they weren't watching.

Also, the ghost evidently liked the bathroom and water, for the steps resounded most often in that area. On one occasion Mrs. Trausch was actually using the bathroom when the steps resounded next to her. Needless to say, she left the bathroom in a hurry.

Finally the big day had arrived. Mr. Trausch drove his Volkswagen all the way to Hollywood to pick up Mrs. Leek and myself, and while he did not believe in ghosts, he didn't scoff at them either.

After a pleasant ride of about two hours, we arrived at Westminster. It was a hot day in June, and the Santa Ana area is known for its warm climate. Mr. Trausch parked the car, and we went into the house where the rest of the family was already awaiting our visit.

I asked Sybil to scout around for any clairvoyant impressions she might get of the situation, and as she did so, I followed her around the house with my faithful tape recorder so that not a word might be lost.

As soon as Sybil had set foot in the house, she pointed to the staircase and intoned ominously, "It's upstairs."

Then, with me trailing, she walked up the stairs as gingerly as a trapeze artist while I puffed after her.

"Gooseflesh," she announced and held out her arm. Now whenever we are in a haunted area Sybil does get gooseflesh—not because she is scared but because it is a natural, instant reaction to whatever presence might be there.

We were in the parents' room now, and Sybil looked around with the expectant smile of a well-trained bird dog casing the moors.

"Two conflicting types," she then announced. "There's anger and resentfulness toward someone. There's something here. Has to do with the land. Two people."

She felt it centered in the children's room, and that there was a vicious element surrounding it, an element of destruction. We walked into the children's room and immediately she made for the big closet in the rear. Behind that wall there was another apartment, but the Trausches did not know anything about it except that the people in it had just recently moved in.

"It's that side," Sybil announced and waved toward the backyard of the house where numerous children of various ages were playing with the customary racket.

"Vincent," Sybil added, out of the blue. "Maybe I don't have the accent right, but it is Vincent. But it is connected with all this. Incidentally, it is the land that's causing the trouble, not the house itself."

The area Sybil had pointed out just a moment before as being the center of the activities was the exact spot where the old barn had once stood.

"It's nothing against this house," Sybil said to Mrs. Trausch, "but something out of the past. I'd say 1925. The name Vincent is important. There's fire involved. I don't feel a person here but an influence . . . a thing. This is different from our usual work. It's the upper part of the building where the evil was."

I then eased Sybil into a chair in the children's room and we grouped ourselves silently around her, waiting for some form of manifestation to take place.

Mrs. Trausch was nervously biting her lips, but otherwise bearing up under what must have been the culmination of a long and great strain for her. Sybil was relaxing now, but she was still awake.

"There's some connection with a child," she said now, "a lost child . . . 1925 . . . the child was found here, dead."

"Whose child is it?" I pressed.

"Connected with Vincent . . . dark child . . . nine years old . . . a boy . . . the children here have to be careful . . ."

"Does this child have any connection with the house?"

"He is lost."

"Can you see him; can he see you?"

"I see him. Corner . . . the barn. He broke his neck. Two men . . . hit the child, they didn't like children, you see . . . they left him . . . until he was found . . . woman . . . Fairley . . . name . . . Pete Fairley . . ."

By now Sybil had glided into a semi-trance and I kept up the barrage of questions to reconstruct the drama in the barn.

"Do they live here?" I inquired.

"Nobody lives here. Woman walked from the water to find the boy. He's dead. She has connection with the two men who killed him. Maniacs, against children."

"What is her connection with the boy?"

"She had him, then she lost him. She looked after him."

"Who were the boy's parents then?"

"Fairley. Peter Fairley. 1925."

Sybil sounded almost like a robot now, giving the requested information.

"What happened to the woman?" I wanted to know.

"Mad . . . she found the boy dead, went to the men . . . there was a fight . . . she fell in the water . . . men are here . . . there's a fire . . ."

"Who were these men?"

"Vincent . . . brothers . . . nobody is very healthy in this farm . . . don't like women . . ."

"Where did the child come from?"

"Lost . . . from the riverside . . ."

"Can you see the woman?"

"A little . . . the boy I can see clearly."

It occurred to me how remarkable it was for Sybil to speak of a woman who had fallen into the water when the apparition Mrs. Trausch had seen had had wet hair. No one had discussed anything about the house in front of Sybil, of course. So she had no way of knowing that the area had once been a farm, or that a barn had stood there where she felt the disturbances centered. No one had told her that it was a child the people in the house kept hearing upstairs.

"The woman is out of tempo," Sybil explained. "That makes it difficult to see her. The boy is frightened."

Sybil turned her attention to the little one now and, with my prodding, started to send him away from there.

"Peter go out and play with the children . . . outside," she pleaded.

"And his parents . . . they are looking for him," I added.

"He wants the children here to go with him," Sybil came back.

Mrs. Trausch started to swallow nervously.

"Tell him he is to go first," I instructed.

"He wants to have the fair woman come with him," Sybil explained and I suggested that the two of them go.

"She understands," Sybil explained, "and is willing, but he is difficult. He wants the children."

I kept pleading with the ghost boy. Nothing is harder than dealing with a lost one so young.

"Join the other children. They are already outside," I said.

There was a moment of silence, interrupted only by the muffled sounds of living children playing outside.

"Are they still here?" I cautiously inquired a little later.

"Can't see them now, but I can see the building. Two floors. Nobody there now."

I decided it was time to break the trance which had gradually deepened and at this point was a full trance. A moment later Sybil Leek "was back."

Now we discussed the matter freely and I researched the information just obtained.

As I understood it, there had been this boy, age nine, Peter Fairley by name, who had somehow gotten away from his nanny, a fair woman. He had run into a farm and gone up to the upper story of a barn where two brothers named Vincent had killed him. When the woman found him, she went mad. Then she looked for the men whom she knew, and there was a fight during which she was drowned. The two of them are ghosts because they are lost; the boy lost in a strange place and the woman lost in guilt for having lost the boy.

Mrs. Kunze and Mrs. Trausch volunteered to go through the local register to check out the names and to see if anything bearing on this tragedy could be found in print.

Unfortunately the death records for the year 1925 were incomplete, as Mrs. Trausch discovered at the *Santa Ana Register*; and this was true even at the local Hall of Records in the Court House. The County Sheriff's Office was of no help either. But they found an interesting item in the *Register* of January 1, 1925:

> Deputies probe tale of "burial" in orange grove. Several Deputy Sheriffs, in a hurried call to Stanton late last night, failed to find any trace of several men who were reported to be "burying something" in an isolated orange grove near that town, as reported to them at the Sheriff's office here.
>
> Officers rushing to the scene were working under the impression that a murder had been committed and that the body was being interred, but a thorough search in that vicinity failed to reveal anything unusual, according to a report made by Chief Criminal Deputy Ed McClellan, on their return. Deputy Sheriffs Joe Scott and Joe Ryan accompanied McClellan.

Mrs. Kunze, a long-time resident of the area and quite familiar with its peculiarities, commented that such a burial in an isolated orange grove could easily have been covered up by men familiar with the irrigating system, who could have flooded that section, thus erasing all evidence of a newly made grave.

I wondered about the name Peter Fairley. Of course I did not expect to find the boy listed somewhere, but was there a Fairley family in these parts in 1925?

There was.

In the Santa Ana County Directories, S.W. Section, for the year 1925, there is a listing for a Frank Fairley, carpenter, at 930 W. Bishop, Santa Ana. The listing continues at the same address the following year also. It was not in the 1924 edition of the directory, however, so perhaps the Fairleys were new to the area then.

At the outset of the visit Mrs. Leek had mentioned a Felix connected with the area. Again consulting the County Directories for 1925, we found several members of the Felix family listed. Andres Felix, rancher, at Golden West Avenue and Bolsa Chica Road, post office Westminster, Adolph and Miguel Felix, laborers, at the same address—perhaps brothers—and Florentino Felix, also a rancher, at a short distance from the farm of Andres Felix. The listing also appears in 1926.

No Vincent or Vincente, however. But of course not all members of the family need to have been listed. The directories generally list only principals, i.e., those gainfully employed or owners of business or property. Then again, there may have been two hired hands by that name, if Vincente was a given name rather than a Christian name.

The 1911 *History of Orange County*, by Samuel Armor, described the area as consisting of a store, church, school, and a few residences only. It was then called Bolsa, and the main area was used as ranch and stock land. The area abounds in fish hatcheries also, which were started around 1921 by a Japanese named Akiyama. Thus was explained the existence of water holes in the area along with fish tanks, as well as natural lakes.

With the help of Mrs. Kunze, I came across still another interesting record.

According to the *Los Angeles Times* of January 22, 1956, "an ancient residence at 14611 Golden West Street, Westminster, built 85 years ago, was razed for subdivision."

This was undoubtedly the farm residence and land on which the development we had been investigating was later built.

And there we have the evidence. Three names were given by our psychic friend: Felix, Vincent, and Peter Fairley. Two of them are found in the printed record, with some difficulty, and with the help of local researchers familiar with the source material. Neither Mrs. Leek nor I knew this information prior to the visit to the haunted house. The body of the woman could easily have been disposed of without leaving a trace by dumping it into one of the fish tanks or other water holes in the area, or perhaps in the nearby Santa Ana River.

About a month after our investigation, the Trausch family moved back to Huntington Beach, leaving the Westminster house to someone else who might some day appear on the scene.

But Carole Trausch informed me that from the moment of our investigation onward, not a single incident had marred the peace of their house.

So I can only assume that Sybil and I were able to help the two unfortunate ghosts out into the open, the boy to find his parents, no doubt also on his side of the veil, and the woman to find peace and forgiveness for her negligence in allowing the boy to be killed.

It is not always possible for the psychic investigator to leave a haunted house free of its unseen inhabitants, and when it does happen, then the success is its own reward.

35

The Ghostly Monks of Aetna Springs

IF YOU LIKE golf, you'll enjoy our nine-hole golf course, says the brochure put out by the Aetna Springs, California, resort people. They have a really fine self-contained vacationland going there. People live in comfortable cabins, children have their own playground, adults can play whatever games *they* please, there are tennis, swimming, fishing, riding, dancing, horseshoe pitching, hunting, shuffleboarding, mineral bathing—the springs—and last, but certainly not least, there is that lovely golf course stretching for several miles on the other side of the only road leading up to the place. With all the facilities on one side of the road, the golf course looks like a million miles from nowhere. I don't know if it pleases the guests, but it is fine with the *ghosts*. For I did not come up eighty-five miles north of San Francisco to admire the scenery, of which there is plenty to admire.

As the road from Napa gradually enters the hills, you get the feeling of being in a world that really knows little of what goes on outside. The fertile Napa Valley and its colorful vineyards soon give way to a winding road and before you know it you're deep in the woods. Winding higher and higher, the road leads past scattered human habitation into the Pope Valley. Here I found out that there was a mineral spring with health properties at the far end of the golf course.

In the old days, such a well would naturally be the center of any settlement, but today the water is no longer commercially bottled. You can get as much as you want for free at the resort, though.

Incidentally there are practically no other houses or people within miles of Aetna Springs. The nearest village is a good twenty minutes' ride away over rough roads. This is the real back country, and it is a good thing California knows no snow, for I wouldn't want to tackle those roads when they are slushy.

As I said before, we had not come up all that way for the mineral water. Bill Wynn, a young engineer from San Francisco, was driving us in my friend

Lori Clerf's car. Lori is a social worker and by "us" I mean, of course, my wife Catherine and Sybil Leek. Sybil did not have the faintest idea why we were here. She honestly thought it was an excursion for the sheer joy of it, but then she knows me well and suspected an ulterior motive, which indeed was not long in coming.

My interest in this far-off spot started in 1965 when I met Dr. Andrew von Salza for the first time. He is a famous rejuvenation specialist and about as down to earth a man as you can find. Being a physician of course made him even more skeptical about anything smacking of the occult. It was therefore with considerable disbelief, even disdain, that he discovered a talent he had not bargained for: he was a photographic medium with rare abilities.

It began in 1963, when a friend, the widow of another doctor by the name of Benjamin Sweetland, asked him to photograph her. She knew von Salza was a camera bug and she wanted to have a portrait. Imagine their surprise when the face of the late Dr. Sweetland appeared on a lampshade in the room! There was no double exposure or accidental second picture. Dr. von Salza had used ordinary black and white film in his Leica.

The doctor's curiosity was aroused and his naturally inquiring mind was now stimulated by something he did not understand and, furthermore, did not really believe. But he came back with a color camera, also a Leica, and took some more pictures of Mrs. Sweetland. One out of twenty produced an image of her late husband against the sky.

The experience with Mrs. Sweetland was soon followed by another event.

A patient and friend of the doctor's, Mrs. Pierson, had been discussing her daughter with Andrew in her San Francisco apartment. The girl had recently committed suicide.

Suddenly Andrew felt impelled to reach for his camera. There was little light in the room but he felt he wanted to finish the roll of film he had. For no logical reason, he photographed the bare wall of the room. On it, when the film was developed, there appeared the likeness of the dead girl von Salza had never met!

While he was still debating with himself what this strange talent of his might be, he started to take an interest in spiritualism. This was more out of curiosity than for any partisan reasons.

He met some of the professional mediums in the Bay area, and some who were not making their living from this pursuit but who were nevertheless of a standard the doctor could accept as respectable.

Among them was Evelyn Nielsen, with whom von Salza later shared a number of séance experiences and who apparently became a "battery" for his psychic picture taking, for a lot of so-called "extras," pictures of people known to be dead, have appeared on von Salza's pictures, especially when Miss Nielsen was with him.

I have examined these photographs and am satisfied that fraud is out of the question for a number of reasons, chiefly technical, since most of them were taken with Polaroid cameras and developed on the spot before competent witnesses, including myself.

One day in New York City, Mrs. Pierson, who had been intrigued by the psychic world for a number of years, took Andrew with her when she visited the famed clairvoyant Carolyn Chapman.

Andrew had never heard of the lady, since he had never been interested in mediums. Mrs. Pierson had with her a Polaroid color camera. Andrew offered to take some snapshots of Mrs. Chapman, the medium, as souvenirs.

Imagine everybody's surprise when Mrs. Chapman's grandfather appeared on one of the pictures. Needless to say, Dr. von Salza had no knowledge of what the old man looked like nor had he access to any of his photographs, since he did not know where he was going that afternoon in New York.

A friend of Andrew's by the name of Dr. Logan accompanied him, Mrs. Pierson, and Evelyn Nielsen to Mount Rushmore, where the group photographed the famous monument of America's greatest Presidents. To their utter amazement, there was another face in the picture—Kennedy's!

Dr. Logan remained skeptical, so it was arranged that he should come to Andrew's house in San Francisco for an experiment in which he was to bring his own film.

First, he took some pictures with von Salza's camera and nothing special happened. Then von Salza tried Logan's camera and still there were no results. But when Dr. Logan took a picture of a corner in von Salza's apartment, using Andrew's camera, the result was different: on the Polaroid photograph there appeared in front of an "empty" wall a woman with a hand stretched out toward him. As Andrew von Salza reports it, the other doctor turned white—that woman had died only that very morning on his operating table!

But the reason for our somewhat strenuous trip to Aetna Springs had its origin in another visit paid the place in 1963 by Andrew von Salza. At that time, he took two pictures with the stereo camera owned by a Mr. Heibel, manager of the resort.

As soon as the pictures were developed, they were in for a big surprise. His friend's exposures showed the magnificent golf course and nothing more. But Andrew's pictures, taken at the same time, clearly had *two rows of monks* on them. There were perhaps eight or ten monks wearing white robes, with shaven heads, carrying lighted candles in their outstretched hands. Around them, especially around their heads, were flame-like emanations.

There was no doubt about it, for I have the pictures before me—these are the photographs, in color, of monks who died in flames—unless the fiery areas represent life energy. They were brightest around the upper parts of the bodies. On one of thc pictures, the monks walk to the right, on the other, to the left, but in both exposures one can clearly distinguish their ascetic hollow-eyed faces—as if they had suffered terribly.

The pictures were not only fascinating, they were upsetting, even to me, and I have often been successful in psychic photography. Here we had a scientific document of the first order.

I wanted to know more about these monks, and the only way to find out was to go up to Napa County. That is why we were winding our way through the Pope Valley that warm October afternoon.

We were still many miles away from Aetna Springs when Sybil took my hand and said:

"The place you're taking me is a place where a small group of people must have gone for sanctuary, for survival, and there is some *religious element present.*"

"What happened there?"

"They were completely wiped out."

"What sort of people were they, and who wiped them out?"

"I don't know why, but the word 'Anti-Popery' comes to me. Also a name, Hi. . . ."

A little later, she felt the influence more strongly.

"I have a feeling of people crossing water, not native to California. A Huguenot influence?"

We were passing a sign on the road reading "Red Silver Mines" and Sybil remarked she had been impressed with treasures of precious metals and the troubles that come with them.

We had now arrived at the resort. For fifteen minutes we walked around it until finally we encountered a surly caretaker, who directed us to the golf course. We drove as far onto it as we could, then we left the car behind and walked out onto the lawn. It was a wide open area, yet Sybil instantly took on a harrowed look as if she felt closed in.

"Torture . . . crucifixion and fire . . ." she mumbled, somewhat shaken. "Why do we have to go through it?"

I insisted. There was no other way to find out if there was anything ghostly there.

"There is a French Protestant Huguenot influence here . . ." she added, "but it does not seem to make sense. Religion and anti-religion. The bench over there by the trees is the center of activity . . . some wiping out took place there, I should think . . . crosses . . . square crosses, red, blood crosses. . . ."

"What nationality are they, these people?"

"Conquistadores . . ."

"Who were the victims?"

"I'm trying to get just one word fixed . . . H-I . . . I can't get the rest . . . it has meaning to this spot . . . many presences here. . . ."

"How many?"

"Nine."

"How are they dressed?"

"Like a woman's dress on a man . . . skirted dress."

"Color?"

"Brown."

"Do they have anything in their hands or doing anything, any action?"

"They have a thing around their head . . . like the Ku Klux Klan . . . can't see their faces . . . light . . . firelight . . . fire is very important . . ."

When I asked her to look closer, she broke into tears.

"No, no," she begged off, her fists clenched, tears streaming down her cheeks. I had never seen her emotionally involved that much in a haunting.

"What do you feel?" I asked softly. She was almost in trance now.

"Hate . . . ," she answered with a shaky voice choked with tears, "to be found here, secretly, *no escape* . . . from the Popish people . . . no faces. . . ."

"Did they perish in this spot?" I asked.

Almost inaudibly Sybil's voice replied:

"Yes. . . ."

"Are the people, these nine, still here?"

"Have to be . . . Justice for their lives. . . ."

"Who has hurt them?"

"Hieronymus." There was the "Hi" she had tried to bring out before.

"Who's Hieronymus?"

"The leader of the Popish people."

"What did he do to them?"

"He burned them . . . useless."

"Who were they?"

"They took the silver . . ."

I intoned some words of compassion and asked the nine ghosts to join their brothers since the ancient wrong done them no longer mattered.

"Pray for us," Sybil muttered. "Passed through the fire, crosses in hand . . . their prayers. . . ."

Sybil spoke the words of a prayer in which I joined. Her breath came heavily as if she were deeply moved. A moment later the spell broke and she came out of it. She seemed bewildered and at first had no recollection where she was.

"Must go . . . ," she said and headed for the car without looking back.

It was some time before we could get her to talk again, a long way from the lonely golf course gradually sinking into the October night.

Sybil was herself again and she remembered nothing of the previous hour. But for us, who had stood by her when the ghostly monks told their story, as far as they were able to, not a word was forgotten. If recollection should ever dim, I had only to look at the photographs again that had captured the agony in which these monks had been frozen on the spot of their fiery deaths.

I took a motion picture film of the area but it showed nothing unusual, and my camera, which sometimes does yield ghost pictures, was unfortunately empty when I took some exposures. I thought I had film in it but later discovered I had forgotten to load it . . . or had the hand of fate stayed my efforts?

Nobody at Aetna Springs had ever heard of ghosts or monks on the spot. So the search for corroboration had to be started back home.

At the Hispanic Society in New York, books about California are available only for the period during which that land was Spanish, although they do have some general histories as well.

In one of these, Irving Richman's *California under Spain and Mexico*, I was referred to a passage about the relationship between native Indian populations and their Spanish conquerors that seemed to hold a clue to our puzzle.

The specific passage referred to conditions in Santo Domingo, but it was part of the overall struggle then going on between two factions among the Spanish-American clergy. The conquistadors, as we all know, treated the native population only slightly less cruelly than Hitler's Nazis treated subjugated people during World War II.

Their methods of torture had not yet reached such infernal effectiveness in the 16th century, but their intentions were just as evil. We read of Indians being put to death at the whim of the colonists, of children thrown to the dogs, of rigid suppression of all opposition, both political and spiritual, to the ruling powers.

Northern California, especially the area above San Francisco, must have been the most remote part of the Spanish world imaginable, and yet outposts existed beyond the well-known missions and their sub-posts.

One of these might have occupied the site of that golf course near the springs. Thus, whatever transpired in the colonial empire of Spain would eventually have found its way, albeit belatedly, to the backwoods also, perhaps finding conditions there that could not be tolerated from the point of view of the government.

The main bone of contention at that time, the first half of the 16th century, was the treatment and status of the native Indians. Although without political voice or even the slightest power, the Indians had some friends at court. Strangely enough, the protectors of the hapless natives turned out to be the Dominican friars—the very same Dominicans who were most efficient and active in the Spanish Inquisition at home!

Whether because of this, or for political expediency, the white-robed Dominicans opposed the brown-robed Franciscans in the matter of the Indians: to the Dominicans, the Indians were fellow human beings deserving every consideration and humane treatment. To the Franciscans, they were clearly none of these, even after they had been given the sacraments of Christianity!

And to the Spanish land owners, the Indians were cheap labor, slaves that could not possibly be allowed any human rights. Thus we had, circa 1530, a condition in some ways paralleling the conditions leading up to the War Between the States in 1861.

Here then is the passage referred to, from Sir A. Helps' *The Spanish Conquests in America*, London 1900, volume I, page 179 *et seq*.

> The Fathers (*Jeronimite*) asked the opinions of the official persons and also of the Franciscans and Dominicans, touching the liberty of the Indians. It was very clear beforehand what the answers would be. The official persons and the Franciscans pronounced against the Indians, and the Dominicans in their favor.

The *Jeronimite Fathers* . . . and Sybil had insisted on a name, so important to this haunting: Hieronymus . . . Latin for Jerome!

How could any of us have known of such an obscure ecclesiastical term? It took me several days of research, and plain luck, to find it at all.

36

The Last Good-bye

CORONADO BEACH IS a pleasant seaside resort in southern California not far from San Diego. You get there by ferry from the mainland and the ride itself is worth the trip. It takes about fifteen minutes, then you continue by car or on foot into a town of small homes, none grand, none ugly—pleasantly bathed by the warm California sunshine, vigorously battered on the oceanside by the Pacific, and becalmed on the inside of the lagoon by a narrow body of water.

The big thing in Coronado Beach is the U.S. Navy; either you're in it and are stationed here, or you work for them in one way or another: directly, as a civilian, or indirectly by making a living through the people who are in the Navy and who make their homes here.

Mrs. Francis Jones is the wife of an advertising manager for a Sidney, Ohio, newspaper, who had returned to Coronado after many years in the Midwest. She is a young woman with a college background and above-average intelligence, and has mixed Anglo-Saxon and Austrian background. Her father died a Navy hero while testing a dive bomber, making her mother an early widow.

Gloria Jones married fairly young, and when her husband took a job as advertising manager in Sidney, Ohio, she went right along with him. After some years, the job became less attractive, and the Joneses moved right back to Coronado where Jones took up work for the Navy.

They have a thirteen-year-old daughter, Vicki, and live a happy, well-adjusted life; Mr. Jones collects coins and Mrs. Jones likes to decorate their brick house surrounded by a garden filled with colorful flowers.

One January, Mrs. Jones sought me out to help her understand a series of most unusual events that had taken place in her otherwise placid life. Except for an occasional true dream, she had not had any contact with the psychic and evinced no interest whatever in it until the events that so disturbed her tranquility had come to pass. Even the time she saw her late father in a white misty cloud might have been a dream. She was only ten years old at the time, and preferred later to think it was a dream. But the experiences she came to see me about were not in that category. Moreover, her husband and a friend were present when some of the extraordinary happenings took place.

Kathleen Duffy was the daughter of a man working for the Convair company. He was a widower and Kathleen was the apple of his eye. Unfortunately the apple was a bit rotten in spots; Kathleen was a most difficult child. Her father had sent her away to a Catholic school for girls in Oceanside, but she ran away twice; after the second time she had to be sent to a home for "difficult" children.

Gloria Jones met Kathleen when both were in their teens. Her mother was a widow and Mr. Duffy was a widower, so the parents had certain things in common. The two girls struck up a close friendship and they both hoped they might become sisters through the marriage of their parents, but it did not happen.

When Kathleen was sent away to the Anthony Home, a reform school at San Diego, Gloria was genuinely sorry. That was when Kathleen was about sixteen years of age. Although they never met again, Kathleen phoned Gloria a few times. She wasn't happy in her new environment, of course, but there was little that either girl could do about it.

In mounting despair, Kathleen tried to get away again but did not succeed. Then one day, she and her roommate, June Robeson, decided to do something drastic to call attention to their dissatisfied state. They set fire to their room in the hope that they might escape in the confusion of the fire.

As the smoke of the burning beds started to billow heavier and heavier, they became frightened. Their room was kept locked at all times, and now they started to bang at the door, demanding to be let out.

The matron came and surveyed the scene. The girls had been trouble for her all along. She decided to teach them what she thought would be an unforgettable "lesson." It was. When Kathleen collapsed from smoke inhalation, the matron finally opened the door. The Robeson girl was saved, but Kathleen Duffy died the next day in the hospital.

When the matter became public, the local newspapers demanded an investigation of the Anthony Home. The matron and the manager of the Home didn't wait for it. They fled to Mexico and have never been heard from since.

Gradually, Gloria began to forget the tragedy. Two years went by and the image of the girlfriend receded into her memory.

One day she and another friend, a girl named Jackie Sudduth, were standing near the waterfront at Coronado, a sunny, wind-swept road from which you can look out onto the Pacific or back toward the orderly rows of houses that make up Coronado Beach.

The cars were whizzing by as the two girls stood idly gazing across the road. One of the cars coming into view was driven by a young man with a young girl next to him who seemed familiar to Gloria. She only saw her from the shoulders up, but as the car passed close by she knew it was Kathleen. Flabbergasted, she watched the car disappear.

"Did you know that girl?" her friend Jackie inquired.

"No, why?"

"She said your name," her friend reported.

Gloria nodded in silence. She had seen it too. Without uttering a sound, the girl in the passing car had spelled the syllables "Glo-ri-a" with her lips.

For weeks afterward, Gloria could not get the incident out of her mind. There wasn't any rational explanation, and yet how could it be? Kathleen had been dead for two years.

The years went by, then a strange incident brought the whole matter back into her consciousness. It was New Year's Eve, twelve years later. She was now a married woman with a daughter. As she entered her kitchen, she froze in her tracks: a bowl was spinning counterclockwise while moving through the kitchen of its own volition.

She called out to her husband and daughter to come quickly. Her daughter's girlfriend, Sheryl Konz, age thirteen, was first to arrive in the kitchen. She also saw the bowl spinning. By the time Mr. Jones arrived, it had stopped its most unusual behavior.

Over dinner, topic A was the self-propelled bowl. More to tease her family than out of conviction, Mrs. Jones found herself saying, "If there is anyone here, let the candle go out." Promptly the candle went out.

There was silence after that, for no current of air was present that could have accounted for the sudden extinguishing of the candle.

The following summer, Mrs. Jones was making chocolate pudding in her kitchen. When she poured it into one of three bowls, the bowl began to turn—by itself. This time her husband saw it too. He explained it as vibrations from a train or a washing machine next door. But why did the other two bowls not move also?

Finally wondering if her late friend Kathleen, who had always been a prankster, might not be the cause of this, she waited for the next blow.

On New Year's Day that following year, she took a Coke bottle out of her refrigerator, and set it down on the counter. Then she turned her back on it and went back to the refrigerator for some ice. This took only a few moments. When she got back to the counter, the Coke bottle had disappeared.

Chiding herself for being absent-minded, she assumed she had taken the bottle with her to the refrigerator and had left it inside. She checked and there was no Coke.

"Am I going out of my mind?" she wondered, and picked up the Coke carton. It contained five bottles. The sixth bottle was never found.

Since these latter incidents took place during the three years when they lived in Sidney, Ohio, it was evident that the frisky spirit of Kathleen Duffy could visit them anywhere they went—if that is who it was.

In late May of that year, back again in Coronado, both Mr. and Mrs. Jones saw the bread jump out of the breadbox before their very eyes. They had locked the breadbox after placing a loaf of bread inside. A moment later, they returned to the breadbox and found it open. While they were still wondering how this could be, the bread jumped out.

A practical man, Mr. Jones immediately wondered if they were having an earthquake. They weren't. Moreover, it appeared that their neighbors' breadboxes behaved normally.

They shook their heads once more. But this time Mrs. Jones dropped me a letter.

On June 3, I went to San Diego to see the Joneses. Sybil Leek and I braved the bus ride from Santa Ana on a hot day, but the Joneses picked us up at the bus terminal and drove us to the Anthony Home where Kathleen had died so tragically.

Naturally Sybil was mystified about all this, unless her ESP told her why we had come. Consciously, she knew nothing.

When we stopped at the Home, we found it boarded up and not a soul in sight. The day was sunny and warm, and the peaceful atmosphere belied the past that was probably filled with unhappy memories. After the unpleasant events that had occurred earlier, the place had been turned into a school for retarded children and run as such for a number of years. At present, however, it stood abandoned.

Sybil walked around the grounds quietly and soaked up the mood of the place.

"I heard something, maybe a name," she suddenly said. "It sounds like Low Mass."

Beyond that, she felt nothing on the spot of Kathleen's unhappy memories. Was it Kathleen who asked for a Low Mass to be said for her? Raised a strict Catholic, such a thought would not be alien to her.

"The place we just left," Sybil said as we drove off, "has a feeling, of sickness to it—like a place for sick people, but not a hospital."

Finally we arrived at the corner of Ocean Avenue and Lomar Drive in Coronado, where Gloria Jones had seen the car with Kathleen in it. All through the trip, on the ferry, and down again into Coronado Island, we avoided the subject at hand.

But now we had arrived and it was time to find out if Sybil felt anything still hanging on in this spot.

"I feel a sense of death," she said slowly, uncertainly. "Despite the sunshine, this is a place of death." It wasn't that there was a presence here, she explained, but rather that someone had come here to wait for another person. The noise around us—it was Sunday—did not help her concentration.

"It's a foreign face I see," Sybil continued. "Someone—a man, with very little hair—who is alien to this place. I see an iris next to his face."

Was the man using the symbol to convey the word Irish perhaps? Was he an ancestor of Kathleen's from over there?

I turned to Mrs. Jones.

"I think what you witnessed here was the superimposition on a pair of motorists of the spirit image of your late friend. These things are called transfigurations. I am sure if the car had stopped, you would have found a stranger in it. Kathleen used her so that you could see her familiar face, I think."

Perhaps Kathleen Duffy wanted to take one more ride, a joy ride in freedom, and, proud of her accomplishment, had wanted her best friend to see her taking it.

There have been no further disturbances or prankish happenings at the Jones house since.

37

The Phantom Sailor of Alameda

ONE NIGHT IN the early spring of 1965, the telephone rang and a pleasant voice said, "I think I've got a case for you, Mr. Holzer. I'm calling from Alameda, California."

Before the young lady could run up an impressive telephone bill, I stopped her and asked her to jot down the main points of her story for my records. She promised this, but it took several months to comply. Evidently the ghost was not so unpleasant as she thought it was the night she had to call me long distance, or perhaps she had learned to live with the unseen visitor.

It had all started four years before when Gertrude Frost's grandmother bought a house in Alameda, an island in San Francisco Bay connected with the mainland by a causeway and mainly covered by small homes—many of which belong to people connected with the nearby naval installations. The house itself was built around 1917.

After the old lady died, Miss Frost's mother had the house. Noises in the night when no one was about kept Miss Frost and her mother and aunt, who shared the house with her, from ever getting a good night's sleep. It did not sound like a very exciting case and I was frankly skeptical since there are many instances where people *think* they hear unnatural noises when in fact they merely ascribe supernormal character to what is actually natural in origin. But I was going to be in the area, and decided to drop in.

I asked Claude Mann, a news reporter from Oakland's Channel 2, to accompany us—my wife Catherine and my good friend Sybil Leek, who did not have the faintest idea where Alameda was or that we were going there. Not that Sybil cared—it was merely another assignment and she was willing. The date was July 1, 1965, and it was pleasantly warm—in fact, a most unghostly type of day.

As soon as we approached the little house, we quickly unloaded the camera equipment and went inside where two of the ladies were already expecting us. I promptly put Sybil into one of the easy chairs and began my work—or rather Sybil began hers.

Although the house was in the middle of the island and no indication of the ocean could be seen anywhere near it, Sybil at once remarked that she felt the sea was connected with the house in some way; she felt a presence in the house but not associated with it directly.

As soon as Sybil was in deep trance, someone took over her vocal chords.

"What is your name?" I asked.

"Dominic . . ."

"Do you live in this house?"

"No house . . . water . . . fort . . . tower . . ."

"What are you doing here?"

"Have to wait . . . Tiana . . ."

"What does Tiana mean?"

"*Tiana* . . . boat. . . ."

"Where does the boat go?"

"Hokeite . . . Hokeite . . ."

"What year is this?"

"1902."

"What is your rank?"

"Mid-ship-man." He had difficulty in enunciating. The voice had a strangely unreal quality, not at all like Sybil's normal speaking voice but more like the thin voice of a young man.

I continued to question the ghostly visitor.

"Are you serving on this boat?"

"Left here," he replied. "I'm going to break . . . everything up."

"Why do you want to do that?"

"Those things . . . got to go . . . because they're untidy . . . I shall break them up . . . they say I'm mad . . . I'm not mad . . ."

"How old are you?"

"Thirty-one . . ."

"Where were you born?"

"I was born . . . Hakeipe. . . ."

I was not sure whether he said "Hakeipe" or "Hakeite," but it sounded something like that.

"What state?" I had never heard of such a place.

"No state," the ghost said, somewhat indignant because I did not know better.

"Then where is it?" I demanded.

"In Japan," the ghost informed me. I began to wonder if he didn't mean Hakodate, a harbor of some importance. It had a fair number of foreign people at all times, being one of the principal seaports for the trade with America and Europe. It would be pronounced "Hak-o-deit," not too different from what I had heard through Sybil's mediumship.

"Break them up, break them up," the ghost continued to mumble menacingly, "throw those little things . . . into . . . faces . . . I don't like faces . . . people . . ."

"Do you realize time has gone on?"

"Time goes on," the voice said sadly.

"What are you doing here?" I asked.

"What are *they* doing here?" the ghost shot back angrily.

It was his land, he asserted. I asked if he had built anything on it.

"The tower is here," he said cryptically, "to watch the ships. I stay here."

"Are you American?"

"No, I'm Italian."

"Are you a merchant sailor or Navy?"

"Navy . . why don't you go away?"

"What do you want here?"

"Nothing . . ."

I explained about his death and this evoked cold anger.

"Smash everything . . ."

I decided to change the subject before the snarling became completely unintelligible.

Claude Mann's cameras were busily humming meanwhile.

"Did you serve in the American Navy?"

"Yes."

"Give me your serial number!"

"Serial . . . one . . . eight . . . eight . . . four . . . three."

"Where did you enlist?"

"Hakkaite."

It did not make sense to me, so I repeated the question. This time the answer was different. Perhaps he had not understood the first time.

"In 'meda," he said.

Sailors call Alameda by this abbreviation. How could Sybil, newly arrived here, have known this? She could not, and I did not.

"Who's your commanding officer?"

"Oswald Gregory."

"What rank?"

"Captain."

"The name of your ship."

"*Triana*."

"How large a ship?"

"I don't know. . . ."

I asked about his family. Did he have a wife, was he well? He became more and more reluctant. Finally he said:

"I'm not answering questions. . . ."

"Your father's name?" I continued.

"Guiseppe."

"Mother?"

"Matilone. . . ."

"Sister or brothers?"

"Four. . . ."

"They live in 'Hokkaipe,'" he added.

"Where did you go to school?"

"Hokkeipe Mission. . . ."

He came to this place in 1902, he asserted, and was left behind because he was sick.

"I wait for next trip . . . but they never came back. I had bad headache. I was lying here. Not a house. Water."

I then asked what he was doing to let people know about his presence.

"I can walk—as well as anyone," he boasted. "I play with water, I drop things. . . ."

I reasoned with him. His father and mother were waiting for him to join them. Didn't he want to be with them? I received a flat "no." He wasn't interested in a family reunion. I tried to explain about real estate. I explained that the house was fully paid for and he was trespassing. He could not have cared less.

I questioned his honesty and he did not like that. It made him waver in his determination to break everything up.

I spoke to him of the "other side" of life. He asked that I take him there.

He now recalled his sisters' names, Matilda and Alissi, or something that sounded like it.

"We've come to fetch you, Dominic," I said, suggesting he "go across."

"You're late," he snarled.

"Better late than never," I intoned. Who said I didn't have as much of a sense of humor as a ghost?

"I was never late," he complained. "I can walk . . . without you!"

Gratitude was not his forte.

I requested that Sybil return to her own body now, but to remain in trance so as to answer my questions on what she could observe in that state.

Soon Sybil's own voice, feeble at first, was heard again from her lips.

I asked her to describe the scene she saw.

"I see a short, dark man," she replied, "who can't walk very well; he was insane. I think he had fits. Fell down. Violent man."

"Do you see a house?"

"No, I see water, and a gray ship. Big ship, not for people. Not for travelling. Low ship."

"Do you see a name on the ship?"

". . . *ana* . . . can't see it properly."

"What is this man doing here?"

"He had a fit here, and fell down and died, and somebody left him here. Somebody picked the body up . . . into the water . . ."

Sybil showed signs of strain and I decided to take her out of trance to avoid later fatigue. As soon as she was "back" to her own self, not remembering anything, of course, that had come through her the past hour, I turned to Miss Frost to find out what it was exactly that had occurred here of an unusual nature.

"Always this uneasy feeling . . . causing nervousness . . . more at night . . . ," she explained, "and noises like small firecrackers."

Miss Frost is a woman in her thirties, pleasant and soft spoken, and she holds a responsible position in San Francisco business life.

"If you pay no attention to it," she added, "then it becomes more intense, louder."

"Doesn't want to be ignored, eh?" I said.

"Occasionally at night you hear footsteps in the living room."

"When it is empty?"

"Of course."

"What does it sound like?"

"As if there were no carpets . . . like walking on boards . . . a man's footsteps."

"How often?"

"Maybe three times . . . last time was about three months ago. We've been here four years, but we only heard it about half a year after we moved in. On one occasion there was a noise inside the buffet as if there were a motor in it, which of course there isn't."

"Has anyone else had any experiences of an unusual nature in this house?"

"A painter who was painting a small room in the rear of the house suddenly asked me for a glass of water because he didn't feel well. Because of the noises."

I turned to Miss Frost's aunt, who had sat by quietly, listening to our conversation.

"Have you heard these footsteps?"

"Yes," she said. "I checked up and there was nobody there who could have caused them. That was around two in the morning. Sometimes around five or six also. They went around the bed. We had the light on, but it continued."

With the help of Miss Frost, I was able to trace the history of the area. Before the house was built here, the ground was part of the Cohen estate. The water is not far from the house although one cannot actually see it from the house.

Originally Alameda was inhabited by Indians and much of it was used as burial ground. Even today bones are dug up now and again.

Prior to Miss Frost, a Mr. Bequette owned the house, but what interested me far more than Mr. Bequette was the fact that many years ago a hospital occupied the land at this spot. Nothing is left of the old hospital.

In 1941, allegedly, a family lived at this house whose son was killed in action during the war. A mysterious letter reached Miss Frost in February of 1961 addressed to a B. Biehm at her address, but she could not locate this man.

None of this takes us back to 1902 when Dominic said he lived. A Japanese-born Italian sailor serving in the U.S. Navy is a pretty unusual combination. Was Dominic his family name?

I decided to query the Navy Department in the hope that they might have some records about such a man, although I had learned on previous occasions that Naval records that far back are not always complete.

On December 29th, 1966, I received this reply from the office of the Chief of Naval Operations:

> Dear Mr. Holzer:
>
> In reply to your letter of 8 December, we have been unable to find either DOMINIC or Oswald GREGORY in the lists of U.S. Navy officers during this century. The Navy Registers for the period around 1902 list no U.S. Naval ship named TRIANA.
>
> We have very little information on Alameda Island during the early 1900's. The attached extract from the Naval Air Station history, however, may be of some use.
>
> Sincerely yours,
> F. KENT LOOMIS
> Captain, USN (Ret.)
> Asst. Director of Naval History

Captain Loomis enclosed a history of the Alameda installations which seems to confirm the picture painted of the area (prior to that installation) by the ghostly sailor.

> The real story of the U.S. Naval Air Station, Alameda, is how it has "arisen from the waters." How it was thrown up from the bottom of San Francisco Bay; how it was anchored to the earth with grass roots; how it was, by accident, the scene of some of the earliest flights in America. This is the romance of Alameda.
>
> The Navy Department first began to consider the site now occupied by the air station toward the end of the First World War. The intention was to utilize the site as a destroyer base, but the war was over before the plans could be perfected. The land then lapsed into oblivion. *It was a rather barren land.* When the tide was out it was odious and disagreeable looking. Since people who boil soap are not fastidious concerning olfactory matters, the Twenty Mule Team Borax Company located the site of their first efforts near the "Mole" which went to San Francisco's ferries.
>
> The main part of Alameda was very pretty, covered with good rich "bottom land" and shade trees, from which it had derived its name during the Spanish occupation days. "Alameda" means "shade" or "shady lane."
>
> In 1776 the land had been granted to Don Luis Peralta, a grizzled old man who immigrated from Tabac in Sonora. His life as a soldier had been crowded with 40 years of service to His Majesty, the King of Spain, and ten children. It was only a small part of the 43,000 acres granted him by a grateful Spain.
>
> He distributed his lands among his children when he felt his time had come. Although the peninsula of Alameda was in the most part fertile, the western tip of it was nothing but barren sands and tidal flats.
>
> In 1876, engineers cut a channel through the peninsula's tip which linked San Leandro Bay with the main bay, and Alameda became an island. Deep water was on the way and dredging was begun to effect this end.

The inability of the U.S. Navy librarian to identify a ship named the *Triana* did not stop me from looking further, of course. Was there ever such a ship? A Captain Treeana commanded one of the three ships of Christopher Columbus and consequently there are towns named for him in the land he and his shipmates helped discover. Spelled nowadays Triana, one of them is in Alabama, and in the city of Huntsville there is a Triana Boulevard. It seems highly likely that so famous a captain's name should at one time or other have been chosen as the name of a ship.

Meanwhile, back at the house, things remained quiet and peaceful for 48 hours. Miss Frost was happy for the first time in years.

And then the footsteps and other noises resumed. Dominic wasn't going to ship out, after all.

That was in July 1965. I made certain suggestions. Close the door mentally; gently tell the ghost he must go, over and over again. He was free now to do so—proof of which was the fact that his footsteps, once confined to the living room area, were now heard all over the house.

A year has gone by and I have had no news from Alameda. Perhaps no news is good news and the ghostly sailor roams no more.

38

The Most Haunted House in America

I FIRST HEARD about the ghosts at San Diego's Whaley House through an article in *Cosmic Star,* Merle Gould's psychic newspaper, back in 1963. The account was not too specific about the people who had experienced something unusual at the house, but it did mention mysterious footsteps, cold drafts, unseen presences staring over one's shoulder and the scent of perfume where no such odor could logically be—the gamut of uncanny phenomena, in short. My appetite was whetted. Evidently the curators, Mr. and Mrs. James Redding, were making some alterations in the building when the haunting began.

I marked the case as a possibility when in the area, and turned to other matters. Then fate took a hand in bringing me closer to San Diego.

I had appeared on Regis Philbin's network television show and a close friendship had developed between us. When Regis moved to San Diego and started his own program there, he asked me to be his guest.

We had already talked of a house he knew in San Diego that he wanted me to investigate with him; it turned out to be the same Whaley House. Finally we agreed on June 25th as the night we would go to the haunted house and film a trance session with Sybil Leek, then talk about it the following day on Regis' show.

Sybil Leek came over from England a few years ago, after a successful career as a producer and writer of television documentaries and author of a number of books on animal life and antiques. At one time she ran an antique shop in her beloved New Forest area of southern England, but her name came to the attention of Americans primarily because of her religious convictions: she happened to be a witch. Not a Hallowe'en type witch, to be sure, but a follower of "the Old Religion," the pre-Christian Druidic cult which is still being practiced in many parts of the world. Her personal involvement with witchcraft was of less interest to me than her great abilities as a trance medium. I tested her and found her capable of total "dissociation of personality," which is the necessary requirement for good trance work. She can get "out of her own body" under my prodding, and lend it to whatever personality might be present in the atmosphere of our quest. Afterwards, she will remember nothing and merely continue pleasantly where we left off in conversation prior to trance—even if it is two hours later! Sybil Leek lends her ESP powers exclusively to my research and confines her "normal" activities to a career in writing and business.

We arrived in sunny San Diego ahead of Regis Philbin, and spent the day loafing at the Half Moon Inn, a romantic luxury motel on a peninsula stretching out into San Diego harbor. Regis could not have picked a better place for us—it was almost like being in Hawaii. We dined with Kay Sterner, president and chief sensitive of the local California Parapsychology Foundation, a charming and knowledgeable woman who had been to the haunted Whaley House, but of course she did not talk about it in Sybil's presence. In deference to my policy, she waited until Sybil left us. Then she told me of her forays into Whaley House, where she had felt several presences. I thanked her and decided to do my own investigating from scratch.

My first step was to contact June Reading, who was not only the director of the house but also its historian. She asked me to treat confidentially whatever I might find in the house through psychic means. This I could not promise, but I offered to treat the material with respect and without undue sensationalism, and I trust I have not disappointed Mrs. Reading too much. My readers are entitled to all the facts as I find them.

Mrs. Reading herself is the author of a booklet about the historic house, and a brief summary of its development also appears in a brochure given to visitors, who keep coming all week long from every part of the country. I quote from the brochure.

> "The Whaley House, in the heart of Old Town, San Diego—restored, refurnished and opened for public viewing—represents one of the finest examples extant of early California buildings.
>
> "Original construction of the two-story mansion was begun on May 6, 1856, by Thomas Whaley, San Diego pioneer. The building was completed on May 10, 1857. Bricks used in the structure came from a clay-bed and kiln—the first brick-yard in San Diego—which Thomas Whaley established 300 yards to the southwest of his projected home.
>
> "Much of 'Old San Diego's' social life centered around this impressive home. Later the house was used as a theater for a traveling company, 'The Tanner Troupe,' and at one time served as the San Diego County Court House.

"The Whaley House was erected on what is now the corner of San Diego Avenue and Harney Street, on a 150-by-217-foot lot, which was part of an 8½-acre parcel purchased by Whaley on September 25, 1855. The North room originally was a granary without flooring, but was remodeled when it became the County Court House on August 12, 1869.

"Downstairs rooms include a tastefully furnished parlor, a music room, a library and the annex, which served as the County Court House. There are four bedrooms upstairs, two of which were leased to 'The Tanner Troupe' for theatricals.

"Perhaps the most significant historical event involving the Whaley House was the surreptitious transfer of the county court records from it to 'New Town,' present site of downtown San Diego, on the night of March 31, 1871.

"Despite threats to forcibly prevent even legal transfer of the court house to 'New Town,' Col. Chalmers Scott, then county clerk and recorder, and his henchmen removed the county records under cover of darkness and transported them to a 'New Town' building at 6th and G Streets.

"The Whaley House would be gone today but for a group of San Diegans who prevented its demolition in 1956 by forming the Historical Shrine Foundation of San Diego County and buying the land and the building.

"Later, the group convinced the County of San Diego that the house should be preserved as an historical museum, and restored to its early-day splendor. This was done under the supervision and guidance of an advisory committee including members of the Foundation, which today maintains the Whaley House as an historical museum.

"Most of the furnishings, authenticated as in use in Whaley's time, are from other early-day San Diego County homes and were donated by interested citizens.

"The last Whaley to live in the house was Corinne Lillian Whaley, youngest of Whaley's six children. She died at the age of 89 in 1953. Whaley himself died December 14,1890, at the age of 67. He is buried in San Diego in Mount Hope Cemetery, as is his wife, Anna, who lived until February 24, 1913."

When it became apparent that a thorough investigation of the haunting would be made, and that all of San Diego would be able to learn of it through television and newspapers, excitement mounted to a high pitch.

Mrs. Reading kept in close touch with Regis Philbin and me, because ghosts have a way of "sensing" an impending attempt to oust them—and this was not long in coming. On May 24th the "activities" inside the house had already increased to a marked degree; they were of the same general nature as previously noticed sounds.

Was the ghost getting restless?

I had asked Mrs. Reading to prepare an exact account of all occurrences within the house, from the very first moment on, and to assemble as many of the witnesses as possible for further interrogation.

Most of these people had worked part time as guides in the house during the five years since its restoration. The phenomena thus far had occurred, or at any rate been observed, mainly between 10 A.M. and 5 :30 P.M., when the house is open to visitors. There is no one there at night, but an effective burglar alarm system is in operation to prevent flesh-and-blood intruders from breaking in unnoticed. Ineffective with the ghostly kind, as we were soon to learn!

I shall now quote the director's own report. It vouches for the accuracy and caliber of witnesses.

Phenomena Observed at Whaley House By Visitors

Oct. 9, 1960—Dr. & Mrs. Kirbey, of New Westminster, B.C., Canada. 1:30-2:30 P.M. (He was then Director of the Medical Association of New Westminster.)

While Dr. Kirbey and his wife were in the house, he became interested in an exhibit in one of the display cases and she asked if she might go through by herself, because she was familiar with the Victorian era, and felt very much at home in these surroundings. Accordingly, I remained downstairs with the Doctor, discussing early physicians and medical practices.

When Mrs. Kirbey returned to the display room, she asked me in hesitating fashion if I had ever noticed anything unusual about the upstairs. I asked her what she had noticed. She reported that when she started upstairs, she felt a breeze over her head, and though she saw nothing, realized a pressure against her seemed to make it hard to go up. When she looked into the rooms, had the feeling that someone was standing behind her, in fact so close to her that she turned around several times to look. Said she expected someone would tap her on the shoulder. When she joined us downstairs, we all walked toward the courtroom. As we entered, again Mrs. Kirbey turned to me and asked if I knew that someone inhabited the courtroom.

She pointed to the bailiff's table, saying as she did, "Right over there." I asked her if the person was clear enough for her to describe, and she said:

"I see a small figure of a woman who has a swarthy complexion. She is wearing a long full skirt, reaching to the floor. The skirt appears to be a calico or gingham, small print. She has a kind of cap on her head, dark hair and eyes and she is wearing gold hoops in her pierced ears. She seems to stay in this room, lives here, I gather, and I get the impression we are sort of invading her privacy."

Mrs. Kirbey finished her description by asking me if any of the Whaley family were swarthy, to which I replied, "No."

This was, to my knowledge, the only description given of an apparition by a visitor, and Mrs. Kirbey the only person who brought up the fact in connection with the courtroom. Many of the visitors have commented upon the atmosphere in this room, however, and some people attempting to work in the room comment upon the difficulty they have in trying to concentrate here.

By Persons Employed at Whaley House

April, 1960
10:00 A.M. By myself, June A. Reading, 3447 Kite St.
Sound of Footsteps—in the Upstairs

This sound of someone walking across the floor, I first heard in the morning, a week before the museum opened to the public. County workmen were still painting some shelving in the hall, and during this week often arrived before I did, so it was not unusual to find them already at work when I arrived.

This morning, however, I was planning to furnish the downstairs rooms, and so hurried in and down the hall to open the back door awaiting the arrival of the trucks with the furnishings. Two men followed me down the hall; they were going to help with the furniture arrangement. As I reached up to unbolt the back door, I heard the sound of what seemed to be someone walking across the bedroom floor. I paid no attention, thinking it was one of the workmen. But the men, who heard the sounds at the time I did, insisted I go upstairs and find out who was in the house. So, calling out, I started to mount the stairs. Halfway up, I could see no lights, and that the outside shutters to the windows were still closed. I made some comment to the men who had followed me, and turned around to descend the stairs.

One of the men joked with me about the spirits coming in to look things over, and we promptly forgot the matter.

However, the sound of walking continued. And for the next six months I found myself going upstairs to see if someone was actually upstairs. This would happen during the day, sometimes when visitors were in other parts of the house, other times when I was busy at my desk trying to catch up on correspondence or bookwork. At times it would sound as though someone were descending the stairs, but would fade away before reaching the first floor. In September, 1962, the house was the subject of a news article in the *San Diego Evening Tribune,* and this same story was reprinted in the September 1962 issue of *Fate* magazine.

Oct. & Nov. 1962. We began to have windows in the upper part of the house open unaccountably. We installed horizontal bolts on three windows in the front bedroom, thinking this would end the matter. However, the really disturbing part of this came when it set off our burglar alarm in the night, and we were called by the Police and San Diego Burglar Alarm Co. to come down and see if the house had been broken into. Usually, we would find nothing disturbed. (One exception to this was when the house was broken into by vandals, about 1963, and items from the kitchen display stolen.)

In the fall of 1962, early October, while engaged in giving a talk to some school children, class of 25 pupils, I heard a sound of someone walking, which seemed to come from the roof. One of the children interrupted me, asking what that noise was, and excusing myself from them, I went outside the building, down on the street to see if workmen from the County were repairing the roof. Satisfied that there was no one on the roof of the building, I went in and resumed the tour.

Residents of Old Town are familiar with this sound, and tell me that it has been evident for years. Miss Whaley, who lived in the house for 85 years, was aware of it. She passed away in 1953.

Mrs. Grace Bourquin, 2938 Beech St.

Sat. Dec. 14, 1963, noon—Was seated in the hall downstairs having lunch, when she heard walking sound in upstairs.

Sat. Jan. 10, 1964, 1:30 P.M. Walked down the hall and looked up the staircase. On the upper landing she saw an apparition—the figure of a man, clad in frock coat and pantaloons, the face turned away from her, so she could not make it out. Suddenly it faded away.

Lawrence Riveroll, resides on Jefferson St., Old Town.

Jan. 5, 1963, 12:30 noon

Was alone in the house. No visitors present at the time. While seated at the desk in the front hall, heard sounds of music and singing, described as a woman's voice. Song "Home Again." Lasted about 30 seconds.

Jan. 7, 1963, 1:30 P.M.

Visitors in upstairs. Downstairs, he heard organ music, which seemed to come from the courtroom, where there is an organ. Walked into the room to see if someone was attempting to play it. Cover on organ was closed. He saw no one in the room.

Jan. 19, 1963, 5:15 P.M.

Museum was closed for the day. Engaged in closing shutters downstairs. Heard footsteps in upper part of house in the same area as described. Went up to check, saw nothing.

Sept. 10-12, 1964—at dusk, about 5:15 P.M.

Engaged in closing house, together with another worker. Finally went into the music room, began playing the piano. Suddenly felt a distinct pressure on his hands, as though someone had their hands on his. He turned to look toward the front hall, in the direction of the desk, hoping to get the attention of the person seated there, when he saw the apparition of a slight woman dressed in a hoop skirt. In the dim light was unable to see clearly the face. Suddenly the figure vanished.

J. Milton Keller, 4114 Middlesex Dr.

Sept. 22, 1964, 2:00 P.M.

Engaged in tour with visitors at the parlor, when suddenly he, together with people assembled at balustrade, noticed crystal drops hanging from lamp on parlor table begin to swing back and forth. This occurred only on one side of the lamp. The other drops did not move. This continued about two minutes.

Dec. 15, 1964, 5:15 P.M.

Engaged in closing house along with others. Returned from securing restrooms, walked down hall, turned to me with the key, while I stepped into the hall closet to reach for the master switch which turns off all lights. I pulled the switch, started to turn around to step out, when he said, "Stop, don't move, you'll step on the dog!" He put his hands out, in a gesture for me to stay still. Meantime, I turned just in time to see what resembled a flash of light between us, and what appeared to be the back of a dog, scurry down the hall and turn into the dining room. I decided to resume a normal attitude, so I kidded him a little about trying to scare me. Other people were present in the front hall at the time, waiting for us at the door, so he turned to them and said in a rather hurt voice that I did not believe him. I realized then that he had witnessed an apparition, so I asked him to see if he could describe it. *He said he saw a spotted dog, like a fox terrier, that ran with his ears flapping, down the hall and into the dining room.*

May 29, 1965, 2:30 P.M.

Escorting visitors through house, upstairs. Called to me, asking me to come up. Upon going up, he, I and visitors all witnessed a black rocking chair, moving back and forth as if occupied by a person. It had started moving unaccountably, went on about three minutes. Caused quite a stir among visitors.

Dec. 27, 1964, 5:00 P.M.

Late afternoon, prior to closing, *saw the apparition of a woman dressed in a green plaid gingham dress.* She had long dark hair, coiled up in a bun at neck, was seated on a settee in bedroom.

Feb. 1965, 2:00 P.M.

Engaged in giving a tour with visitors, when two elderly ladies called and asked him to come upstairs, and step over to the door of the nursery. These ladies, visitors, called his attention to a sound that was like the cry of a baby, about 16 months old. All three reported the sound.

March 24, 1965, 1:00 P.M.

He, together with Mrs. Bourquin and his parents, Mr. & Mrs. Keller, engaged in touring the visitors, when for some reason his attention was directed to the foot of the staircase. He walked back to it, and heard the sound of someone in the upper part of the house whistling. No one was in the upstairs at the time.

Mrs. Suzanne Pere, 106 Albatross, El Cajon.

April 8, 1963, 4:30 P.M.

Was engaged in typing in courtroom, working on manuscript. Suddenly she called to me, calling my attention to a noise in the upstairs. We both stopped work, walked up the stairs together, to see if anyone could possibly be there. As it was near closing time, we decided to secure the windows. Mrs. Pere kept noticing a chilly breeze at the back of her head, had the distinct feeling that someone, though invisible, was present and kept following her from one window to another.

Oct. 14, 21; Nov. 18, 1964

During the morning and afternoon on these days, called my attention to the smell of cigar smoke, and the fragrance of perfume or cologne. This occurred in the parlor, hall, upstairs bedroom. In another bedroom she called my attention to something resembling dusting powder.

Nov. 28, 1968, 2:30 P.M.

Reported seeing an apparition in the study. A group of men there, dressed in frock coats, some with plain vests, others figured material. One of this group had a large gold watch chain across vest. Seemed to be a kind of meeting; all figures were animated, some pacing the floor, others conversing; all serious and agitated, but oblivious to everything else. One figure in this group seemed to be an official, and stood off by himself. This person was of medium stocky build, light brown hair, and mustache which was quite full and long. He had very piercing light blue eyes, penetrating gaze. Mrs. Pere sensed that he was some kind of official, a person of importance. He seemed about to speak. Mrs. Pere seemed quite exhausted by her experience witnessing this scene, yet was quite curious about the man with the penetrating gaze. I remember her asking me if I knew of anyone answering this description, because it remained with her for some time.

Oct. 7, 1963, 10:30 A.M.

Reported unaccountable sounds issuing from kitchen, as though someone were at work there. Same day, she reported smelling the odor of something baking.

Nov. 27, 1964, 10:15 A.M.

Heard a distinct noise from kitchen area, as though something had dropped to the floor. I was present when this occurred. She called to me and asked what I was doing there, thinking I had been rearranging exhibit. At this time I was at work in courtroom, laying out work. Both of us reached the kitchen, to find one of the utensils on the shelf rack had disengaged itself, fallen to the floor, and had struck a copper boiler directly below. No one else was in the house at the time, and we were at a loss to explain this.

Mrs. T. R. Allen, 3447 Kite Street

Was present *Jan. 7, 1963, 1:30 P.M.* Heard organ music issue from courtroom, when Lawrence Riveroll heard the same (see his statement).

Was present *Sept. 10–12, 1964*, at dusk, with Lawrence Riveroll, when he witnessed apparition. Mrs. Allen went upstairs to close shutters, and as she ascended them, described a chill breeze that seemed to come over her head. Upstairs, she walked into the bedroom and toward the windows. Suddenly she heard a sound behind her, as though something had dropped to the floor. She turned to look, saw nothing, but again experienced the feeling of having someone, invisible, hovering near her. She had a feeling of fear. Completed her task as quickly as possible, and left the upstairs hastily. Upon my return, both persons seemed anxious to leave the house.

May, 1965 (the last Friday), 1:30 P.M.

Was seated in downstairs front hall, when she heard the sound of footsteps.

Regis Philbin himself had been to the house before. With him on that occasion was Mrs. Philbin, who is highly sensitive to psychic emanations, and a teacher-friend of theirs considered an amateur medium.

They observed, during their vigil, what appeared to be a white figure of a person, but when Regis challenged it, unfortunately with his flashlight, it disappeared immediately. Mrs. Philbin felt extremely uncomfortable on that occasion and had no desire to return to the house.

By now I knew that the house had three ghosts, a man, a woman and a baby—and a spotted dog. The scene observed in one of the rooms sounded more like a psychic impression of a past event to me than a bona fide ghost.

I later discovered that still another part-time guide at the house, William H. Richardson, of 470 Silvery Lane, El Cajon, had not only experienced something out of the ordinary at the house, but had taken part in a kind of séance with interesting results. Here is his statement, given to me in September of 1965, several months *after* our own trance session had taken place.

In the summer of 1963 I worked in Whaley House as a guide.

One morning before the house was open to the public, several of us employees were seated in the music room downstairs, and the sound of someone in heavy boots walking across the upstairs was heard by us all. When we went to investigate the noise, we found all the windows locked and shuttered, and the only door to the outside from upstairs was locked. This experience first sparked my interest in ghosts.

I asked June Reading, the director, to allow several of my friends from Starlight Opera, a local summer musical theatre, to spend the night in the house.

At midnight, on Friday, August 13, we met at the house. Carolyn Whyte, a member of the parapsychology group in San Diego and a member of the Starlight Chorus, gave an introductory talk on what to expect, and we all went into the parlor to wait for something to happen.

The first experience was that of a cool breeze blowing through the room, which was felt by several of us despite the fact that all doors and windows were locked and shuttered.

The next thing that happened was that a light appeared over a boy's head. This traveled from his head across the wall, where it disappeared. Upon later investigation it was found to have disappeared at the portrait of Thomas Whaley, the original owner of the house. Footsteps were also heard several times in the room upstairs.

At this point we broke into groups and dispersed to different parts of the house. One group went into the study which is adjacent to the parlor, and there witnessed a shadow on the wall surrounded by a pale light which moved up and down the wall and changed shape as it did so. There was no source of light into the room and one could pass in front of the shadow without disturbing it.

Another group was upstairs when their attention was directed simultaneously to the chandelier which began to swing around as if someone were holding the bottom and twisting the sides. One boy was tapped on the leg several times by some unseen force while seated there.

Meanwhile, downstairs in the parlor, an old-fashioned lamp with prisms hanging on the edges began to act strangely. As we watched, several prisms began to swing by themselves. These would stop and others would start, but they never swung simultaneously. There was no breeze in the room.

At this time we all met in the courtroom. Carolyn then suggested that we try to lift the large table in the room.

We sat around the table and placed our fingertips on it. A short while later it began to creak and then slid across the floor approximately eight inches, and finally lifted completely off the floor on the corner where I was seated.

Later on we brought a small table from the music room into the courtroom and tried to get it to tip, which it did. With just our fingertips on it, it tilted until it was approximately one inch from the floor, then fell. We righted the table and put our fingertips back on it, and almost immediately it began to rock. Since we knew the code for yes, no, and doubtful, we began to converse with the table. Incidentally, while this was going on, a chain across the doorway in the courtroom was almost continually swinging back and forth and then up and down.

Through the system of knocking, we discovered that the ghost was that of a little girl, seven years old. She did not tell us her name, but she did tell us that she had red hair, freckles, and hazel eyes. She also related that there were four other ghosts in the house besides herself, including that of a baby boy. We conversed with her spirit for nearly an hour.

At one time the table stopped rocking and started moving across the floor of the courtroom, into the dining room, through the pantry, and into the kitchen. This led us to believe that the kitchen was her usual abode. The table then stopped and several antique kitchen utensils on the wall began to swing violently. Incidentally, the kitchen utensils swung for the rest of the evening at different intervals.

The table then retraced its path back to the courtroom and answered more questions.

At 5:00 A.M. we decided to call it a night—a most interesting night. When we arrived our group of 15 had had in it a couple of real believers, several who half believed, and quite a few who didn't believe at all. After the phenomena we had experienced, there was not one among us who was even very doubtful in the belief of some form of existence after life.

It was Friday evening, and time to meet the ghosts. Sybil Leek knew nothing whatever about the house, and when Regis Philbin picked us up the conversation remained polite and non-ghostly.

When we arrived at the house, word of mouth had preceded us despite the fact that our plans had not been announced publicly; certainly it had not been advertised that we would attempt a séance that evening. Nevertheless, a sizable crowd had assembled at the house and only Regis' polite insistence that their presence might harm whatever results we could obtain made them move on.

It was quite dark now, and I followed Sybil into the house, allowing her to get her clairvoyant bearings first, prior to the trance session we were to do with the cameras rolling. My wife Catherine trailed right behind me carrying the tape equipment. Mrs. Reading received us cordially. The witnesses had assembled but were temporarily out of reach, so that Sybil could not gather any sensory impressions from them. They patiently waited through our clairvoyant tour. All in all, about a dozen people awaited us. The house was lit throughout and the excitement in the atmosphere was bound to stir up any ghost present!

And so it was that on June 25, 1965, the Ghost Hunter came to close quarters with the specters at Whaley House, San Diego. While Sybil meandered about the house by herself, I quickly went over to the Court House part of the house and went over their experiences with the witnesses. Although I already had their statements, I wanted to make sure no detail had escaped me.

From June Reading I learned, for instance, that the Court House section of the building, erected around 1855, had originally served as a granary, later becoming a town hall and Court House in turn. It was the only two-story brick house in the entire area at the time.

Not only did Mrs. Reading hear what sounded to her like human voices, but on one occasion, when she was tape recording some music in this room, the tape also contained some human voices—sounds she had not herself heard while playing the music!

"When was the last time you yourself heard anything unusual?" I asked Mrs. Reading.

"As recently as a week ago," the pert curator replied, "during the day I heard the definite sound of someone opening the front door. Because we have had many visitors here recently, we are very much alerted to this. I happened to be in the Court Room with one of the people from the Historical Society engaged in research in the Whaley papers, and we both heard it. I went to check to see who had come in, and there was no one there, nor was there any sound of footsteps on the porch outside. The woman who works here also heard it and was just as puzzled about it as I was."

I discovered that the Mrs. Allen in the curator's report to me of uncanny experiences at the house was Lillian Allen, her own mother, a lively lady who remembered her brush with the uncanny only too vividly.

"I've heard the noises overhead," she recalled. "Someone in heavy boots seemed to be walking across, turning to come down the stairway—and when I first came out here they would tell me these things and I would not believe them—but I was sitting at the desk one night, downstairs, waiting for my daughter to lock up in the back. I heard this noise overhead and I was rushing to see if we were locking someone in the house, and as I got to almost the top, a big rush of wind blew over my head and made my hair stand up. I thought the windows had blown open but I looked all around and everything was secured."

"Just how did this wind feel?" I asked. Tales of cold winds are standard with traditional hauntings, but here we had a precise witness to testify.

"It was cold and I was chilly all over. And another thing, when I lock the shutters upstairs at night, I feel like someone is breathing down the back of my neck, like they're going to touch me—at the shoulder—that happened often. Why, only a month ago."

A Mrs. Frederick Bear now stepped forward. I could not find her name in Mrs. Reading's brief report. Evidently she was an additional witness to the uncanny goings-on at this house.

"One evening I came here—it was after five o'clock; another lady was here also—and June Reading was coming down the stairs, and we were talking. I distinctly heard something move upstairs, as if someone were moving a table. There was no one there—we checked. That only happened a month ago."

Grace Bourquin, another volunteer worker at the house, had been touched upon in Mrs. Reading's report. She emphasized that the sounds were those of a heavy man wearing boots—no mistake about it. When I questioned her about the apparition of a man she had seen, about six weeks ago, wearing a frock coat, she insisted that he had looked like a real person to her, standing at the top of the stairs one moment, and completely gone the next.

"He did not move. I saw him clearly, then turned my head for a second to call out to Mrs. Reading, and when I looked again, he had disappeared."

I had been fascinated by Mrs. Suzanne Pere's account of her experiences, which seemed to indicate a large degree of mediumship in her makeup. I questioned her about anything she had not yet told us.

"On one occasion June Reading and I were in the back study and working with the table. We had our hands on the table to see if we could get any reaction."

"You mean you were trying to do some table-tipping."

"Yes. At this point I had only had some feelings in the house, and smelled some cologne. This was about a year ago, and we were working with some papers concerning the Indian uprising in San Diego, and all of a sudden the table started to rock violently! All of the pulses in my body became throbbing, and in my mind's eye the room was filled with men, all of them extremely excited, and though I could not hear any sound, I knew they were talking, and one gentleman was striding up and down the center of the room, puffing on his cigar, and from my description of him June Reading later identified him as Sheriff McCoy, who was here in the 1850s. When it was finished I could not talk for a few minutes. I was completely disturbed for a moment."

McCoy, I found, was the leader of one of the factions during the "battle" between Old Town and New Town San Diego for the county seat.

Evidently, Mrs. Pere had psychically relived that emotion-laden event which did indeed transpire in the very room she saw it in!

"Was the Court House ever used to execute anyone?" I interjected.

Mrs. Reading was not sure; the records were all there but the Historical Society had not gone over them as yet for lack of staff. The Court functioned in this house for two years, however, and sentences certainly were meted out in it. The prison itself was a bit farther up the street.

A lady in a red coat caught my attention. She identified herself as Bernice Kennedy.

"I'm a guide here Sundays," the lady began, "and one Sunday recently, I was alone in the house and sitting in the dining room reading, and I heard the front door open and close. There was no one there. I went back to continue my reading. Then I heard it the second time. Again I checked, and there was absolutely no one there. I heard it a third time and this time I took my book and sat outside at the desk. From then onward, people started to come in and I had no further unusual experience. But one other Sunday, there was a young woman upstairs who came down suddenly very pale, and she said the little rocking chair upstairs was rocking. I followed the visitor up and I could not see the chair move, but there was a clicking sound, very rhythmic, and I haven't heard it before or since."

The chair, it came out, once belonged to a family related to the Whaleys.

"I'm Charles Keller, father of Milton Keller," a booming voice said behind me, and an imposing gentleman in his middle years stepped forward.

"I once conducted a tour through the Whaley House. I noticed a lady who had never been here act as if she were being pushed out of one of the bedrooms!"

"Did you see it?" I said, somewhat taken aback.

"Yes," Mr. Keller nodded, "I saw her move, as if someone were pushing her out of the room."

"Did you interrogate her about it?"

"Yes, I did. It was only in the first bedroom, where we started the tour, that it happened. Not in any of the other rooms. We went back to that room and again I saw her being pushed out of it!"

Mrs. Keller then spoke to me about the ice-cold draft she felt, and just before that, three knocks at the back door! Her son, whose testimony Mrs. Reading had already obtained for me, then went to the back door and found no one there who could have knocked. This had happened only six months before our visit.

I then turned to James Reading, the head of the Association responsible for the upkeep of the museum and house, and asked for his own encounters with the ghosts. Mr. Reading, in a cautious tone, explained that he did not really cotton to ghosts, but—

"The house was opened to the public in April 1960. In the fall of that year, October or November, the police called me at two o'clock in the morning, and asked me to please go down and shut off the burglar alarm, because they were being flooded with complaints, it was waking up everybody in the neighborhood. I came down and found two officers waiting for me. I shut off the alarm. They had meantime checked the house and every door and shutter was tight."

"How could the alarm have gone off by itself then?"

"I don't know. I unlocked the door, and we searched the entire house. When we finally got upstairs, we found one of the upstairs front bedroom windows open. We closed and bolted the window, and came down and tested the alarm. It was in order again. No one could have gotten in or out. The shutters outside that window were closed and hooked on the inside. The opening of the window had set off the alarm, but it would have been impossible for anyone to open that window and get either into or out of the house. Impossible. This happened *four times.* The second time, about four months later, again at two in the morning, again that same window was standing open. The other two times it was always that same window."

"What did you finally do about it?"

"After the fourth incident we added a second bolt at right angles to the first one, and that seemed to help. There were no further calls."

Was the ghost getting tired of pushing *two* bolts out of the way?

I had been so fascinated with all this additional testimony that I had let my attention wander away from my favorite medium, Sybil Leek. But now I started to look for her and found to my amazement that she had seated herself in one of the old chairs in what used to be the kitchen, downstairs in back of the living room. When I entered the room she seemed deep in thought, although not in trance by any means, and yet it took me a while to make her realize where we were.

Had anything unusual transpired while I was in the Court Room interviewing?

"I was standing in the entrance hall, looking at the postcards," Sybil recollected, "when I felt I just had to go to the kitchen, but I didn't go there at first, but went halfway up the stairs, and a child came down the stairs and into the kitchen and I followed her."

"A child?" I asked. I was quite sure there were no children among our party.

"I thought it was Regis' little girl and the next thing I recall I was in the rocking chair and you were saying something to me."

Needless to say, Regis Philbin's daughter had *not* been on the stairs. I asked for a detailed description of the child.

"It was a long-haired girl," Sybil said. "She was very quick, you know, in a longish dress. She went to the table in this room and I went to the chair. That's all I remember."

I decided to continue to question Sybil about any psychic impressions she might now gather in the house.

"There is a great deal of confusion in this house," she began. "Some of it is associated with another room upstairs, which has been structurally altered. There are two centers of activity."

Sybil, of course, could not have known that the house consisted of two separate units.

"Any ghosts in the house?"

"Several," Sybil assured me. "At least four!"

Had not William Richardson's group made contact with a little girl ghost who had claimed that she knew of four other ghosts in the house? The report of that séance did not reach me until September, several months after our visit, so Sybil could not possibly have "read our minds" about it, since our minds had no such knowledge at that time.

"This room where you found me sitting," Sybil continued, "I found myself drawn to it; the impressions are very strong here. Especially that child—she died young."

We went about the house now, seeking further contacts.

"I have a date now," Sybil suddenly said, "1872."

The Readings exchanged significant glances. It was just after the greatest bitterness of the struggle between Old Town and New Town, when the removal of the Court records from Whaley House by force occurred.

"There are two sides to the house," Sybil continued. "One side I like, but not the other."

Rather than have Sybil use up her energies in clairvoyance, I felt it best to try for a trance in the Court Room itself. This was arranged for quickly, with candles taking the place of electric lights except for what light was necessary for the motion picture cameras in the rear of the large room.

Regis Philbin and I sat at Sybil's sides as she slumped forward in a chair that may well have held a merciless judge in bygone years.

But the first communicator was neither the little girl nor the man in the frock coat. A feeble, plaintive voice was suddenly heard from Sybil's lips, quite unlike her own, a voice evidently parched with thirst.

"Bad . . . fever . . . everybody had the fever . . ."

"What year is this?"

"Forty-six."

I suggested that the fever had passed, and generally calmed the personality who did not respond to my request for identification.

"Send me . . . some water. . . ." Sybil was still in trance, but herself now. Immediately she complained about there being a lot of confusion.

"This isn't the room where we're needed . . . the child . . . she is the one. . . ."

"What is her name?"

"Anna . . . Bell . . . she died very suddenly with something, when she was thirteen . . . chest. . . ."

"Are her parents here too?"

"They come . . . the lady comes."

"What is this house used for?"

"Trade . . . selling things, buying and selling."

"Is there anyone other than the child in this house?"

"Child is the main one, because she doesn't understand anything at all. But there is something more vicious. Child would not hurt anyone. There's someone else. A man. He knows something about this house . . . about thirty-two, unusual name, C . . . Calstrop . . . five feet ten, wearing a green coat, darkish, mustache and side whiskers, he goes up to the bedroom on the left. He has business here. His business is with things that come from the sea. But it is the papers that worry him."

"What papers?" I demanded.

"The papers . . . 1872. About the house. Dividing the house was wrong. Two owners, he says."

"What is the house being used for, now, in 1872?"

"To live in. Two places . . . I get confused for I go one place and then I have to go to another."

"Did this man you see die here?"

"He died here. Unhappy because of the place . . . about the other place. Two buildings. Some people quarreled about the spot. He is laughing. He wants all this house for himself."

"Does he know he is dead?" I asked the question that often brings forth much resistance to my quest for facts from those who cannot conceive of their status as "ghosts."

Sybil listened for a moment.

"He does as he wants in this house because he is going to live here," she finally said. "*It's his house.*"

"Why is he laughing?"

A laughing ghost, indeed!

"He laughs because of people coming here thinking it's *their* house! When he knows the truth."

"What is his name?" I asked again.

"Cal . . . Caltrop . . . very difficult as he does not speak very clearly . . . he writes and writes . . . he makes a noise . . . he says he will make even more noise unless you go away."

"Let him," I said, cheerfully hoping I could tape-record the ghost's outbursts.

"Tell him he has passed over and the matter is no longer important," I told Sybil.

"He is upstairs."

I asked that he walk upstairs so we could all hear him. There was nobody upstairs at this moment—everybody was watching the proceedings in the Court Room downstairs.

We kept our breath, waiting for the manifestations, but our ghost wouldn't play the game. I continued with my questions.

"What does he want?"

"He is just walking around, he can do as he likes," Sybil said. "He does not like new things . . . he does not like any noise . . . except when he makes it. . . ."

"Who plays the organ in this house?"

"He says his mother plays."

"What is her name?"

"Ann Lassay . . . that's wrong, it's Lann—he speaks so badly . . . Lannay . . . his throat is bad or something. . . ."

I later was able to check on this unusual name. Anna Lannay was Thomas Whaley's wife!

At the moment, however, I was not aware of this fact and pressed on with my interrogation. How did the ghost die? How long ago?

"'89 . . . he does not want to speak; he only wants to roam around. . . ."

Actually, Whaley died in 1890. Had the long interval confused his sense of time? So many ghosts cannot recall exact dates but will remember circumstances and emotional experiences well.

"He worries about the house . . . he wants the whole house . . . for himself . . . he says he will leave them . . . papers . . . hide the papers . . . he wants the other papers about the house . . . they're four miles from here . . . several people have these papers and you'll have to get them back or he'll never settle . . . never . . . and if he doesn't get the whole house back, he will be much worse . . . and then, the police will come . . . he will make the lights come and the noise . . . and the bell . . . make the police come and see him, the master . . . of the house, he hears bells upstairs . . . he doesn't know what it is . . . he goes upstairs and opens the windows, wooden windows . . . and looks out . . . and then he pulls the . . . no, it's not a bell . . . he'll do it again . . . when he wants someone to know that he really is the master of the house . . . people today come and say he is not, but he is!"

I was surprised. Sybil had no knowledge of the disturbances, the alarm bell, the footsteps, the open window . . . and yet it was all perfectly true. Surely, her communicator was our man!

"When did he do this the last time?" I inquired.

"This year . . . not long. . . ."

"Has he done anything else in this house?"

"He said he moved the lights. In the parlor."

Later I thought of the Richardson séance and the lights they had observed, but of course I had no idea of this when we were at the house ourselves.

"What about the front door?"

"If people come, he goes into the garden . . . walks around . . . because he meets mother there."

"What is in the kitchen?"

"Child goes to the kitchen. I have to leave him, and he doesn't want to be left . . . it was an injustice, anyway, don't like it . . . the child is twelve . . . chest trouble . . . something from the kitchen . . . bad affair. . . ."

"Anyone's fault?"

"Yes. Not chest . . . from the cupboard, took something . . . it was an acid like salt, and she ate it . . . she did not know . . . there is something strange about this child, someone had control of her, you see, she was in the way . . . family . . . one girl . . . those boys were not too good . . . the other boys who came down . . . she is like two people . . . someone controlled her . . . made her do strange things and then . . . could she do that. . . ."

"Was she the daughter of the man?"

"Strange man, he doesn't care so much about the girl as he does about the house. He is disturbed."

"Is there a woman in this house?"

"Of course. There is a woman in the garden."

"Who is she?"

"Mother. Grandmother of the girl."

"Is he aware of the fact he has no physical body?"

"No."

"Doesn't he see all the people who come here?"

"They have to be fought off, sent away."

"Tell him it is now seventy years later."

"He says seventy years when the house was built."

"Another seventy years have gone by," I insisted.

"Only part of you is in the house."

"No, part of the house . . . you're making the mistake," he replied.

I tried hard to convince him of the real circumstances. Finally, I assured him that the entire house was, in effect, his.

Would this help?

"He is vicious," Sybil explains. "He will have his revenge on the house."

I explained that his enemies were all dead.

"He says it was an injustice, and the Court was wrong and you have to tell everyone this is his house and land and home."

I promised to do so and intoned the usual formula for the release of earthbound people who have passed over and don't realize it. Then I recalled Sybil to her own self, and within a few moments she was indeed in full control.

I then turned to the director of the museum, Mrs. Reading, and asked for her comments on the truth of the material just heard.

"There was a litigation," she said. "The injustice could perhaps refer to the County's occupancy of this portion of the house from 1869 to 1871. Whaley's contract, which we have, shows that this portion of the house was leased to the County, and he was to supply the furniture and set it up as a Court Room. He also put in the two windows to provide light. It was a valid agreement. They adhered to the contract as long as the Court continued to function here, but when Alonzo Horton came and developed New Town, a hot contest began between the two communities for the possession of the county seat. When the records were forcefully removed from here, Whaley felt it was quite an injustice, and we have letters he addressed to the Board of Supervisors, referring to the fact that his lease had been broken. The Clerk notified him that they were no longer responsible for the use of this house—after all the work he had put in to remodel it for their use. He would bring the matter up periodically with the Board of Supervisors, but it was tabled by them each time it came up."

"In other words, this is the injustice referred to by the ghost?"

"In 1872 he was bitterly engaged in asking redress from the County over this matter, which troubled him some since he did not believe a government official would act in this manner. It was never settled, however, and Whaley was left holding the bag."

"Was there a child in the room upstairs?"

"In the nursery? There were several children there. One child died here. But this was a boy."

Again, later, I saw that the Richardson séance spoke of a boy ghost in the house.

At the very beginning of trance, before I began taping the utterances from Sybil's lips, I took some handwritten notes. The personality, I now saw, who had died of a bad fever had given the faintly pronounced name of Fedor and spoke of a mill where he worked. Was there any sense to this?

"Yes," Mrs. Reading confirmed, "this room we are in now served as a granary at one time. About 1865 to 1867."

"Were there ever any Russians in this area?"

"There was a considerable otter trade here prior to the American occupation of the area. We have found evidence that the Russians established wells in this area. They came into these waters then to trade otters."

"Amazing," I conceded. How could Sybil, even if she wanted to, have known of such an obscure fact?

"This would have been in the 1800s," Mrs. Reading continued. "Before then there were Spaniards here, of course."

"Anything else you wish to comment upon in the trance session you have just witnessed?" I asked.

Mrs. Reading expressed what we all felt.

"The references to the windows opening upstairs, and the ringing of these bells. . . ."

How could Sybil have known all that? Nobody told her and she had not had a chance to acquaint herself with the details of the disturbances.

What remained were the puzzling statements about "the other house." They, too, were soon to be explained. We were walking through the garden now and inspected the rear portion of the Whaley house. In back of it, we discovered to our surprise still another wooden house standing in the garden. I questioned Mrs. Reading about this second house.

"The Pendington House, in order to save it, had to be moved out of the path of the freeway . . . it never belonged to the Whaleys although Thomas Whaley once tried to rent it. But it was always rented to someone else."

No wonder the ghost was angry about "the other house." It had been moved and put on *his* land . . . without his consent!

The name *Cal . . . trop* still did not fall into place. It was too far removed from Whaley and yet everything else that had come through Sybil clearly fitted Thomas Whaley. Then the light began to dawn, thanks to Mrs. Reading's detailed knowledge of the house.

"It was interesting to hear Mrs. Leek say there was a store here once . . . ," she explained. "This is correct, there was a store here at one time, but it was not Mr. Whaley's."

"Whose was it?"

"It belonged to a man named Wallack . . . Hal Wallack . . . that was in the seventies."

Close enough to Sybil's tentative pronunciation of a name she caught connected with the house.

"He rented it to Wallack for six months, then Wallack sold out," Mrs. Reading explained.

I also discovered, in discussing the case with Mrs. Reading, that the disturbances really began after the second house had been placed on the grounds. Was that the straw that broke the ghost's patience?

Later, we followed Sybil to a wall adjoining the garden; a wall, I should add, where there was no visible door. But Sybil insisted there had been a French window there, and indeed there was at one time. In a straight line from this spot, we wound up at a huge tree. It was here, Sybil explained, that Whaley and his mother often met—or are meeting, as the case may be.

I was not sure that Mr. Whaley had taken my advice to heart and moved out of what was, after all, his house. Why should he? The County had not seen fit to undo an old wrong.

We left the next morning, hoping that at the very least we had let the restless one know someone cared.

A week later Regis Philbin checked with the folks at Whaley House. Everything was lively—chandelier swinging, rocker rocking; and June Reading herself brought me up to date on July 27th, 1965, with a brief report on activities other than flesh-and-blood—at the house.

Evidently the child ghost was also still around, for utensils in the kitchen had moved that week, especially a cleaver which swings back and forth on its own. Surely that must be the playful little girl, for what would so important a man as Thomas Whaley have to do in the kitchen? Surely he was much too preoccupied with the larger aspects of his realm, the ancient wrong done him, and the many intrusions from the world of reality. For the Whaley House is a busy place, ghosts or not.

On replaying my tapes, I noticed a curious confusion between the initial appearance of a ghost who called himself Fedor in my notes, and a man who said he had a bad fever. It was just that the man with the fever did not have a foreign accent, but I distinctly recalled "fedor" as sounding odd.

Were they perhaps two separate entities?

My suspicions were confirmed when a letter written May 23, 1966—almost a year later—reached me. A Mrs. Carol DeJuhasz wanted me to know about a ghost at Whaley House . . . no, not Thomas Whaley or a twelve-year-old girl with long hair. Mrs. DeJuhasz was concerned with an historical play written by a friend of hers, dealing with the unjust execution of a man who tried to steal a harbor boat in the 1800s and was caught. Make no mistake about it, nobody had observed this ghost at Whaley House. Mrs. DeJuhasz merely thought he ought to be there, having been hanged in the backyard of the house.

Many people tell me of tragic spots where men have died unhappily but rarely do I discover ghosts on such spots just because of it. I was therefore not too interested in Mrs. DeJuhasz' account of a possible ghost. But she thought that there ought to be present at Whaley House the ghost of this man, called Yankee Jim Robinson. When captured, he fought a saber duel and received a critical wound in the head. Although alive, he became delirious and was tried without representation, *sick of the fever*. Sentenced to death, he was subsequently hanged in the yard behind the Court House.

Was his the ghostly voice that spoke through Sybil, complaining of the fever and then quickly fading away? Again it was William Richardson who was able to provide a further clue or set of clues to this puzzle. In December of 1966 he contacted me again to report some further experiences at the Whaley House.

"This series of events began in March of this year. Our group was helping to restore an historic old house which had been moved onto the Whaley property to save it from destruction. During our lunch break one Saturday, several of us were in Whaley House. I was downstairs when Jim Stein, one of the group, rushed down the stairs to tell me that the cradle in the nursery was rocking by itself. I hurried upstairs but it wasn't rocking. I was just about to chide Jim for having an overactive imagination when it began again and rocked a little longer before it stopped. The cradle is at least ten feet from the doorway, and a metal barricade is across it to prevent tourists from entering the room. No amount of walking or jumping had any effect on the cradle. While it rocked, I remembered that it had made no sound. Going into the room, I rocked the cradle. I was surprised that it made quite a bit of noise. The old floorboards are somewhat uneven and this in combination with the wooden rockers on the cradle made a very audible sound.

"As a matter of fact, when the Whaleys were furnishing carpeting for the house, the entire upstairs portion was carpeted. This might explain the absence of the noise.

"In June, Whaley House became the setting for an historical play. The play concerned the trial and hanging of a local bad man named Yankee Jim Robinson. It was presented in the Court Room and on the grounds of the mansion. The actual trial and execution had taken place in August of 1852. This was five years before Whaley House was built, but the execution took place on the grounds.

"Yankee Jim was hanged from a scaffold which stood approximately between the present music room and front parlor.

"Soon after the play went into rehearsal, things began to happen. I was involved with the production as an actor and therefore had the opportunity to spend many hours in the house between June and August. The usual footsteps kept up and they were heard by most of the members of the cast at one time or another. There was a group of us within the cast who were especially interested in the phenomenon: myself, Barry Bunker, George Carroll, and his fiancée, Toni Manista. As we were all dressed in period costumes most of the time, the ghosts should have felt right at home. Toni was playing the part of Anna, Thomas Whaley's wife. She said she often felt as if she were being followed around the house (as did we all).

"I was sitting in the kitchen with my back to the wall one night, when I felt a hand run through my hair. I quickly turned around but there was nothing to be seen. I have always felt that it was Anna Whaley who touched me. It was my first such experience and I felt honored that she had chosen me to touch. There is a chair in the kitchen which is made of rawhide and wood. The seat is made of thin strips of rawhide crisscrossed on the wooden frame. When someone sits on it, it sounds like the leather in a saddle. On the same night I was touched, the chair made sounds as if someone were sitting in it, not once but several times. There always seems to be a change in the temperature of a room when a presence enters. The kitchen is no exception. It really got cold in there!

"Later in the run of the show, the apparitions began to appear. The cast had purchased a chair which had belonged to Thomas Whaley and placed it in the front parlor. Soon after, a mist was occasionally seen in the chair or near it. In other parts of the house, especially upstairs, inexplicable shadows and mists began to appear. George Carroll swears that he saw a man standing at the top of the stairs. He walked up the stairs and through the man. The man was still there when George turned around but faded and disappeared almost immediately.

"During the summer, we often smelled cigar smoke when we opened the house in the morning or at times when no one was around. Whaley was very fond of cigars and was seldom without them.

"The footsteps became varied. The heavy steps of the man continued as usual, but the click-click of high heels was heard on occasion. Once, the sound of a small child running in the upstairs hall was heard. Another time, I was alone with the woman who took ticket reservations for *Yankee Jim*. We had locked the doors and decided to check the upstairs before we left. We had no sooner gotten up the stairs than we both heard footfalls in the hall below. We listened for a moment and then went back down the stairs and looked. No one. We searched the entire house, not really expecting to find anyone. We didn't. Not a living soul.

"Well, this just about brings you up to date. I've been back a number of times since September but there's nothing to report except the usual footfalls, creaks, etc.

"I think that the play had much to do with the summer's phenomena. Costumes, characters, and situations which were known to the Whaleys were reenacted nightly. Yankee Jim Robinson certainly has reason enough to haunt. Many people, myself included, think that he got a bad deal. He was wounded during his capture and was unconscious during most of the trial. To top it off, the judge was a drunk and the jury and townspeople wanted blood. Jim was just unlucky enough to bear their combined wrath.

"His crime? He had borrowed (?) a boat. Hardly a hanging offense. He was found guilty and condemned. He was unprepared to die and thought it was a joke up to the minute they pulled the wagon out from under him. The scaffold wasn't high enough and the fall didn't break his neck. Instead, he slowly strangled for more than fifteen minutes before he died. I think I'd haunt under the same circumstances myself.

"Two other points: another of the guides heard a voice directly in front of her as she walked down the hall. It said, 'Hello, hello.' There was no one else in the house at the time. A dog fitting the description of one of the Whaley dogs has been seen to run into the house, but it can never be found."

Usually, ghosts of different periods do not "run into" one another, unless they are tied together by a mutual problem or common tragedy. The executed man, the proud owner, the little girl, the lady of the house—they form a lively ghost population even for so roomy a house as the Whaley House is.

Mrs. Reading doesn't mind. Except that it does get confusing now and again when you see someone walking about the house and aren't sure if he has bought an admission ticket.

Surely, Thomas Whaley wouldn't dream of buying one. And he is not likely to leave unless and until some action is taken publicly to rectify the ancient wrong. If the County were to reopen the matter and acknowledge the mistake made way back, I am sure the ghostly Mr. Whaley would be pleased and let matters rest. The little girl ghost has been told by Sybil Leek what has happened to her, and the lady goes where Mr. Whaley goes. Which brings us down to Jim, who would have to be tried again and found innocent of stealing the boat.

There is that splendid courtroom there at the house to do it in. Maybe some ghost-conscious county administration will see fit to do just that.

I'll be glad to serve as counsel for the accused, at no charge.

EPILOGUE

THE WORK OF the Psychic Investigator is never done. Nor is it dull. My files keep expanding, my correspondence gets heavier and heavier, just as the limbs of my hypnotized subjects when I do psychotherapy with them.

The tools of my trade are mainly in my head—to appraise the reports and facts as they present themselves, to draw certain conclusions from them and to do something about it—or not—as the case may be.

Not every case coming in is genuine in psychic terms. The world harbors a goodly number of unbalanced people as well as a very large number of healthy individuals with strange experiences in their lives. Only long years of work in this field coupled with a certain native intelligence and a keen, open-minded judgment can give one the ability to tell the true from the false. But so much authentic material has turned up and is continuously coming into view, that only the uninformed or grossly prejudiced individual would deny the validity of this field of inquiry. Final conclusions may not be possible in certain areas of this work, but strong views may nevertheless be held by those at the epicenter of the evidence, and it is not only their privilege, but their duty to make these views known to others and to carefully report on their findings. Facts are not subject to dismissal by those who did not find the facts or were not present when someone else found them. They are subject to different personal interpretation, of course, but the validity of conclusions drawn by outsiders with hindsight seems to me a lot weaker than the fresh and carefully weighed impressions and views of the researcher on the spot.

It amazes me that psychic research, which deals with man's true nature and is certainly a vitally important endeavor, should have to continually defend itself from accusations by the unqualified and biased, while equally recent sciences, such as space research or advanced electronics, are highly honored occupations at liberty to promulgate the unproven, the hoped for, the tentative, at will—and be praised for being so progressive.

Is it perhaps because man's soul is involved when we deal with the evidence presenting proof of individual survival of death? Do we shy away from coming to grips with ultimate truth concerning our true nature, because somehow deep within us we fear that truth? Because knowledge of this great truth does not make us free—on the contrary, it makes us bound, bound to the intangible ties of morality and self-esteem. How many among us are truly satisfied with their lives? How many are proud of all they have done, thought, believed, and said through the years of their lives?

Now a science, a hard-core method of proof, comes along and tells them that the grave is not the end. That all their thoughts, actions, and feelings continue on into the next state of being.

This requires a complete overhauling of their customary philosophy of life, for if the essential part of man's personality survives physical death, any existence ignoring this future life is, at the very best, partial, at the worst, clouded with misconceptions and errors.

Few people are prepared to chuck their comfortable materialistic point of view in favor of a wider spiritual frontier. Those who do have found that their lives suddenly take on dramatic new meaning, and they are no longer part of a senseless patchwork, but links in a great, orderly universe, playing their roles properly, and finding life always rewarding, no matter what their circumstances might be.

Knowledge does not make you free, but it makes you free to choose.

Prof. Hans Holzer, Ph.D.

About the Author

Hans Holzer is the author of 104 books, including GHOSTLY LOVERS, ESP AND YOU, THE ALCHEMIST, YANKEE GHOSTS, LIFE BEYOND LIFE, AMERICA'S MYSTERIOUS PLACES, LONG BEFORE COLUMBUS, and GHOST HUNTER. Prof. Holzer taught parapsychology for eight years at the New York Institute of Technology, and lectures widely. He has been writer/producer and on-camera person or host on a number of television documentaries, such as the NBC series "In Search of . . .", the Metromedia special "Ghost in the House" and "Bishop Pike and His World" and is currently preparing his own syndicated series. Dr. Holzer is considered a leading authority on the paranormal and unusual.

Educated at the University of Vienna, Austria and at Columbia University, New York, Prof. Holzer received a Ph.D. from the London College of Applied Science. He is a member of the Authors Guild, Dramatists Guild and Writers Guild of America, East, as well as many scientific societies. He lives in New York City, and has for many years been listed in Who's Who in America.